MW01630960

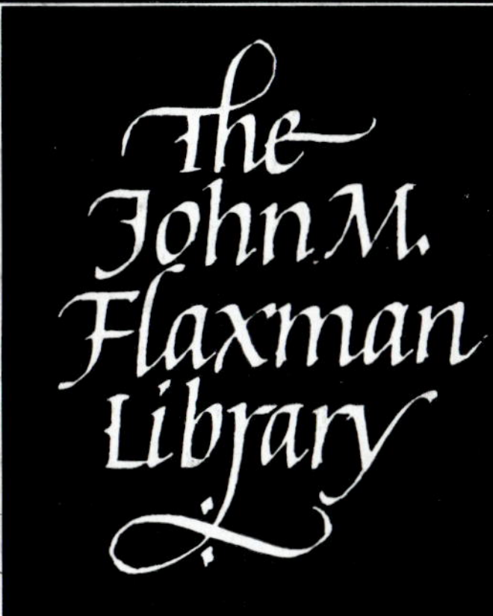
The John M. Flaxman Library

strange friends

bojan brecelj **strange friends**

EDITION STEMMLE
Zurich New York

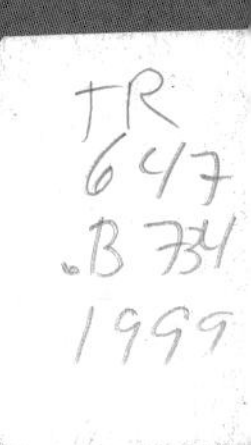

STRANGE FRIENDS

Robert Pledge

Strange Friends reminds me of one of those long solo improvisations by John Coltrane, the genius jazz musician. Wild, powerful and whose sounds unleash multiple and conflicting emotions within, forcing the body to move and the mind to swing, leaving you both somewhat exhausted and elated. This Bojan "solo" is perhaps a little louder, his mind seems less tortured than that of the great jazzman, but the effect is the same.

This is neither a book on photography nor about photography, but on how it can be used. It is a book of many colors that tells as many stories – occasionally with just a single snapshot. Yet it is a work that hinges less on single notes that really matter than on face-to-face or back-to-back pairing of images, which sometimes seem to blend and at others seem to leap at each other like two greased Turkish wrestlers. Taken one by one, many of the photographs might appear to lack deep or definite meaning. However, as a sequenced whole, Bojan's Strange Friends transport us, generating subtle and personal visions of the world, whether our own or that of the artist. It's like watching TV, a soccer game played by night, the ball bouncing back and forth from one end of the pitch to the other, the garish brilliance of the floodlights, the acrobatics of the players kitted out in their multicolored shirts, shorts and socks and all – dancing around, the crowd chanting and booing, waving and swaying, to the fortunes of one side or the other ...

The juxtaposed twinning of images is undeniably a difficult exercise to pull off. Bojan avoids lapsing into simplistic propaganda or graphic effects for the sake of mere surprise and amazement. Via a chain of images, the mirror of his experience – 204 photos on almost as many pages – he recounts his ten-year-long trek across the five continents, a vision imbued with an insatiable, often amused, curiosity and a knowing sense of humor. Although he tries to avoid overly facile effects, when he cannot do otherwise, he opts for tongue-in-cheek. The people he meets, the gestures he captures, the situations he observes, appear simple, with no particular relief. They are simply signs. The value of the work derives from how they are put together.

Hailing from that old-world Eastern Europe turned to the outside, after a childhood in Latin America – he spent his first six years in Brazil and Argentina – Bojan took to traveling and, like many before him, kept a travelogue. His took the form of photographs: so as not to forget that vultures perched on that corpse floating down the Ganges; so as to note that for some the ceremony of marriage must at all cost preserve an element of ritual (so much so that weddings in Shanghai or Jerusalem resemble those of Eastern Europe); so as to note that in Zanzibar fish-farming protects the environment, but in the Rostov region of Russia, the abandoned mines are rusting away. Like the photographer, as viewers we surprise ourselves in our search for links between the images.

Historically, culturally at a remove – an observer, rather than active player or redemptive moralizer – the author could in his own way be termed a “witness.” Unlike the concerned photojournalists in the vein of W. Eugene Smith, he’s a witness who does not denounce, a kind of narrator who brings sensations and instants within our reach and shares them with us.

Was he surprised, amused, depressed or horrified by the successive scenes that he sets in opposition or complementarily side by side? His pictures do not tell us, and it’s of no importance. The color is often grating. The world in which we live unfolds before our eyes. Tough and tender, odd and cruel, laughable and essential, with its raw lights, both artificial and real, and its endless sunsets. Bojan hints that the Pyramid of Giza may be seen from the moon. And what if it were he, Bojan, who had come from another planet to show us our own?

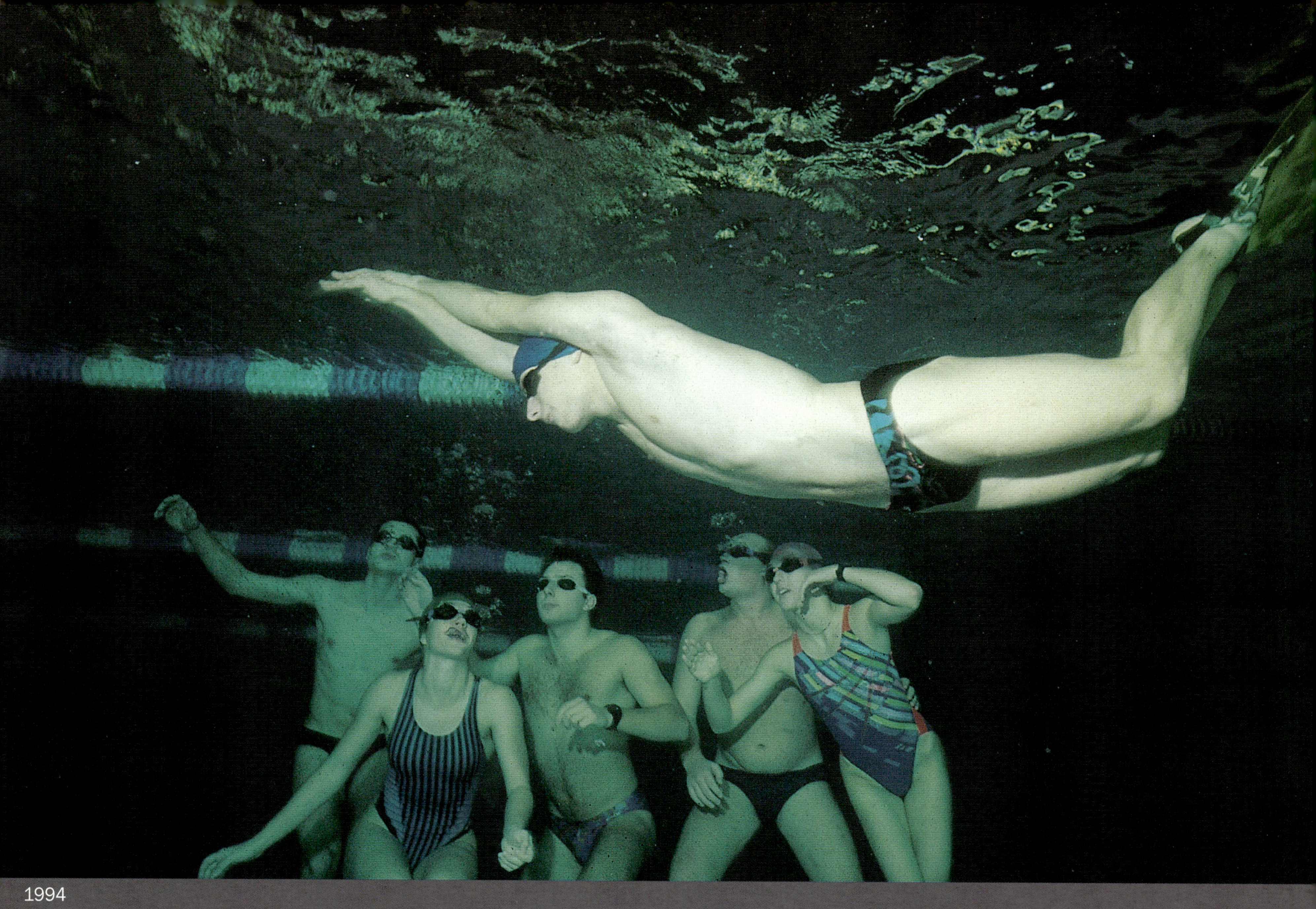

1994

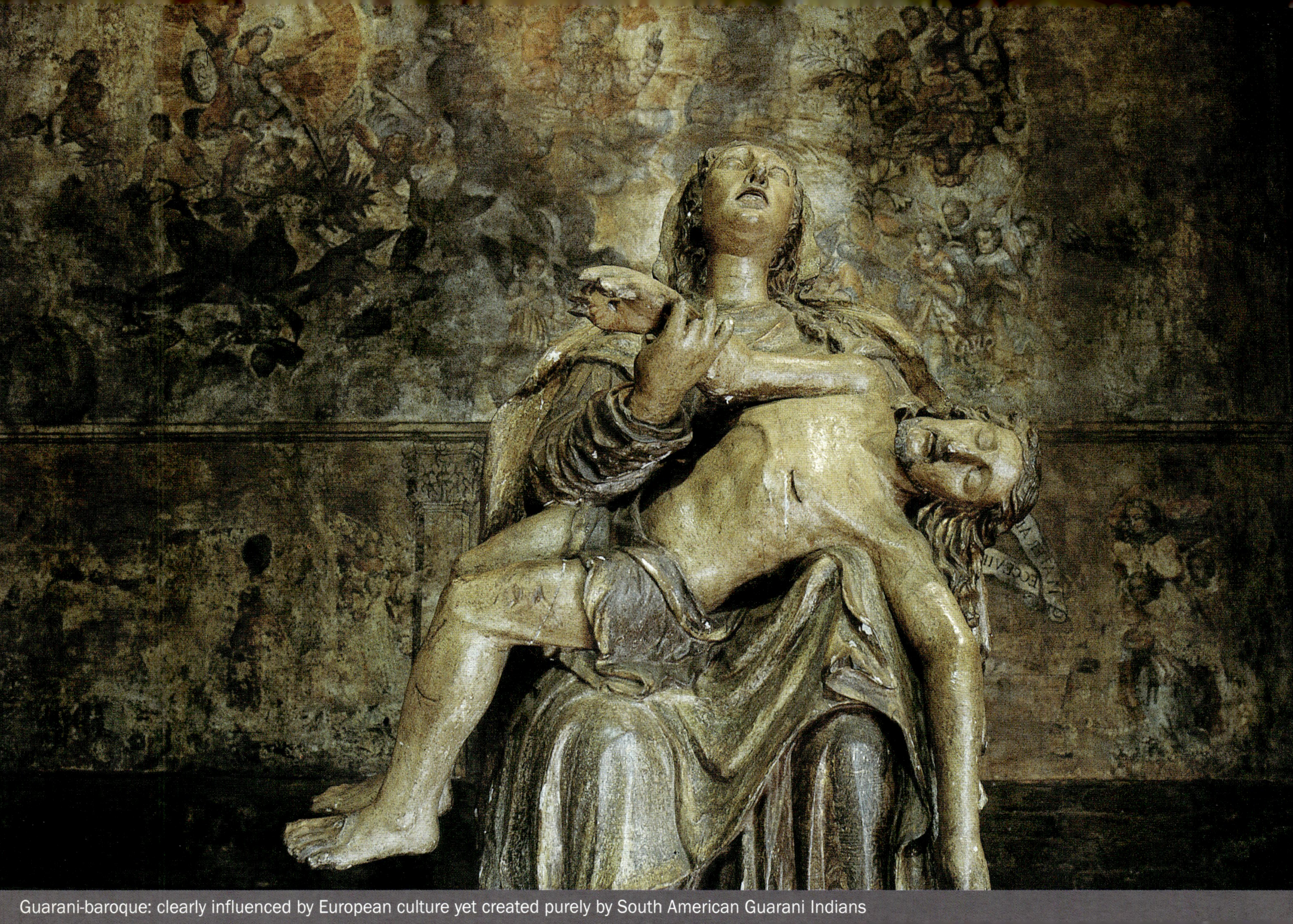

Guarani-baroque: clearly influenced by European culture yet created purely by South American Guarani Indians

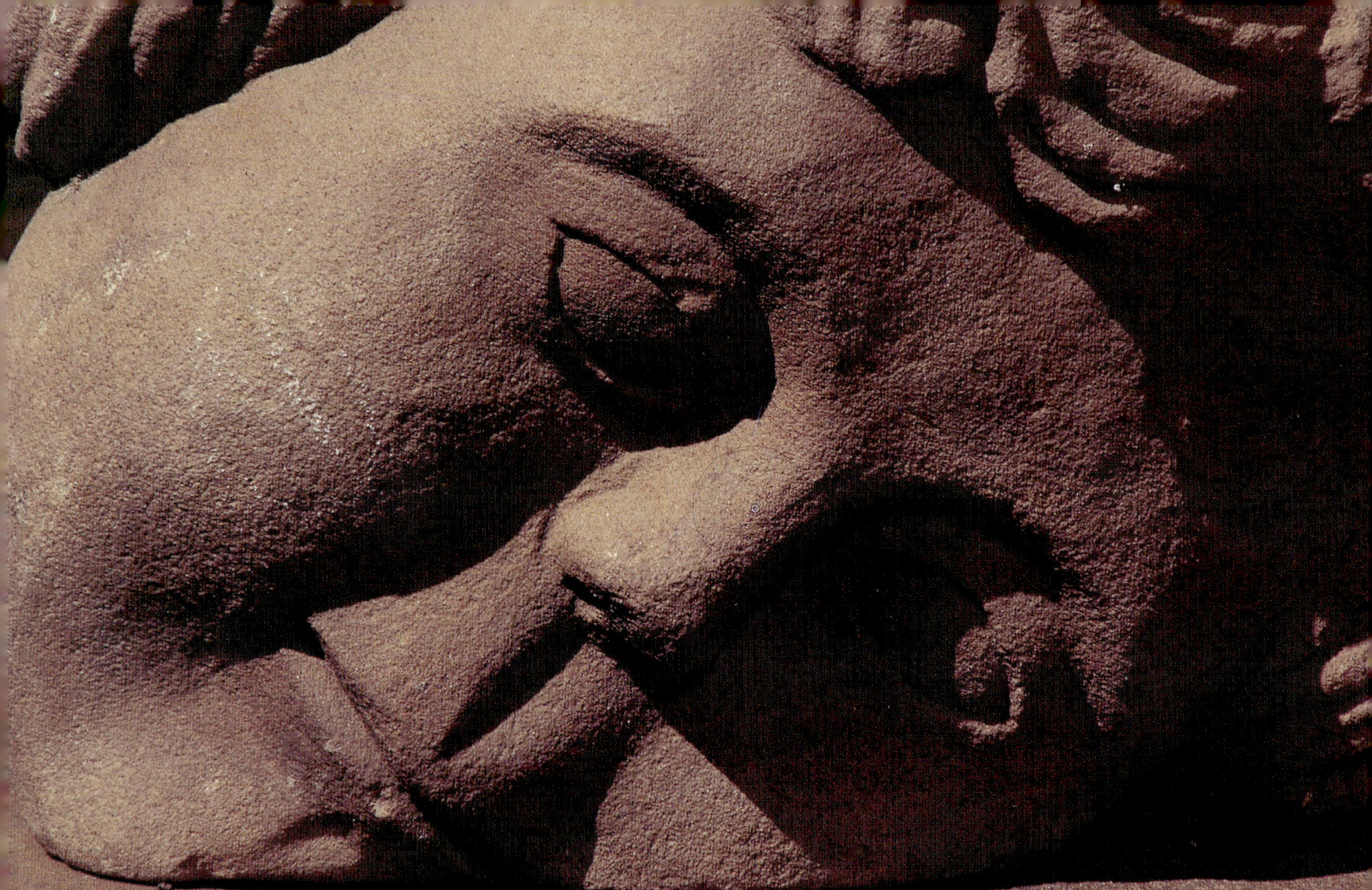
In the midst of the ruins of the Trinidad Mission, today in the territory of Argentina

Entering"the biggest tent on earth," Carson & Barns Circus on tour, USA

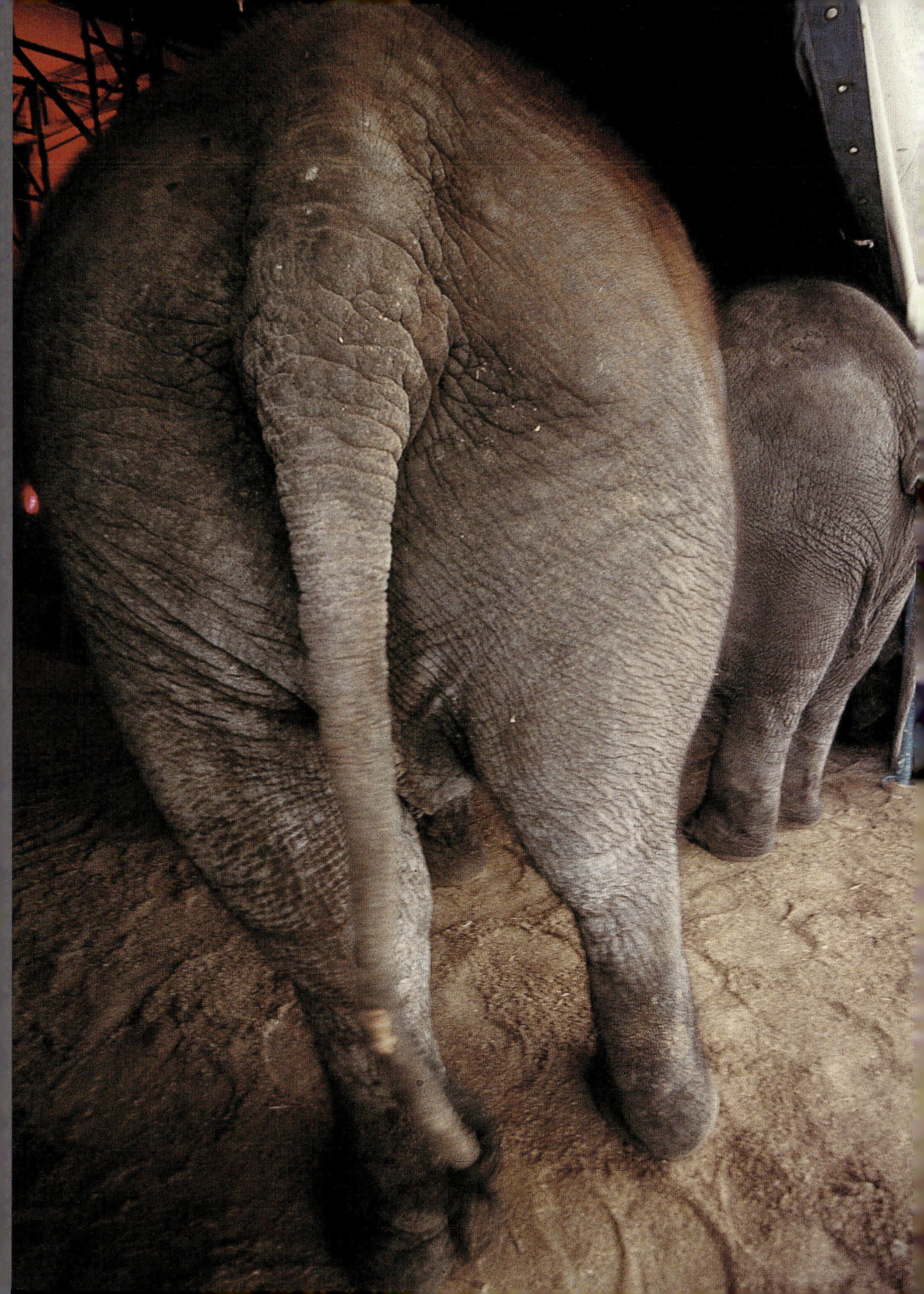

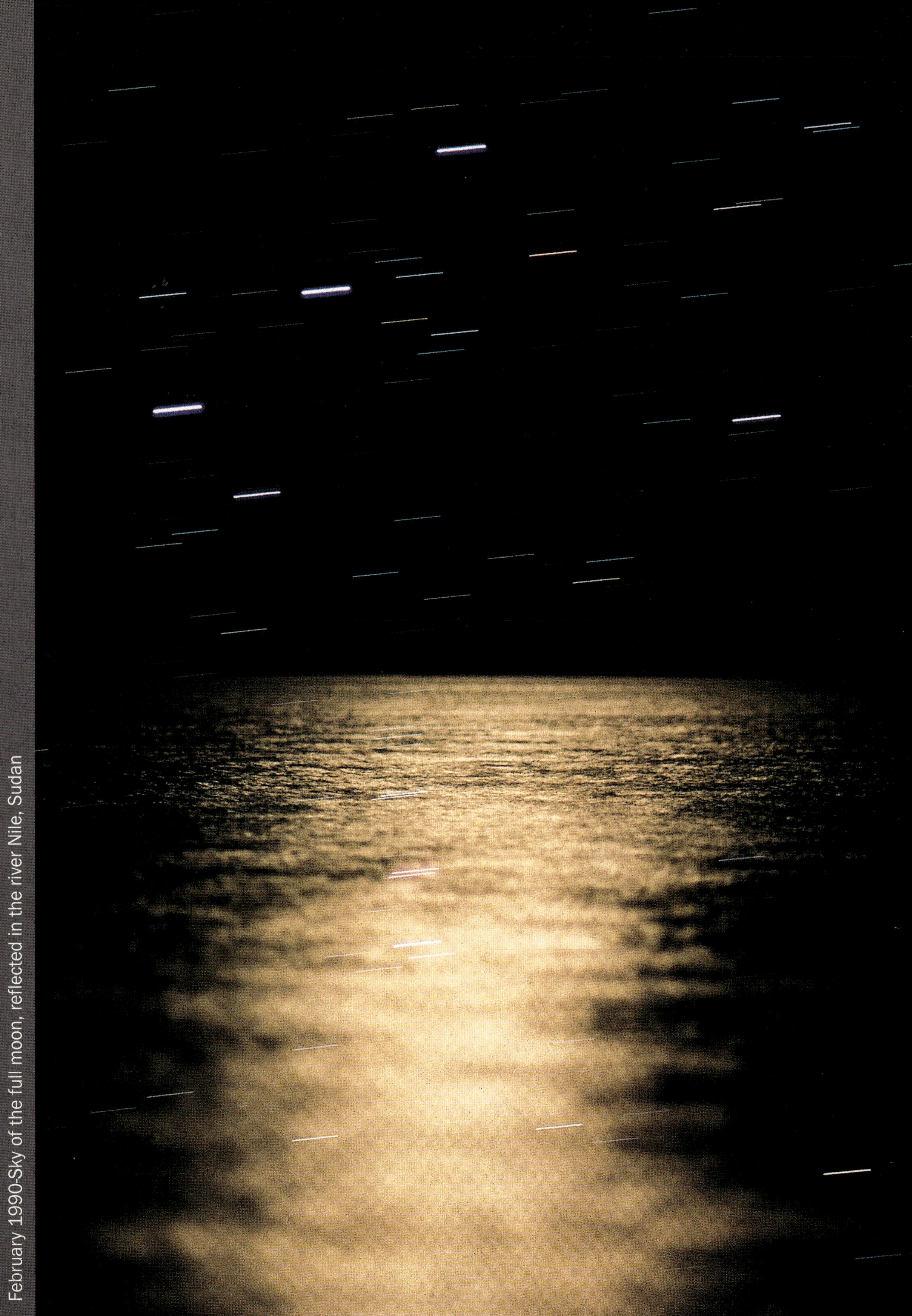

February 1990-Sky of the full moon, reflected in the river Nile, Sudan

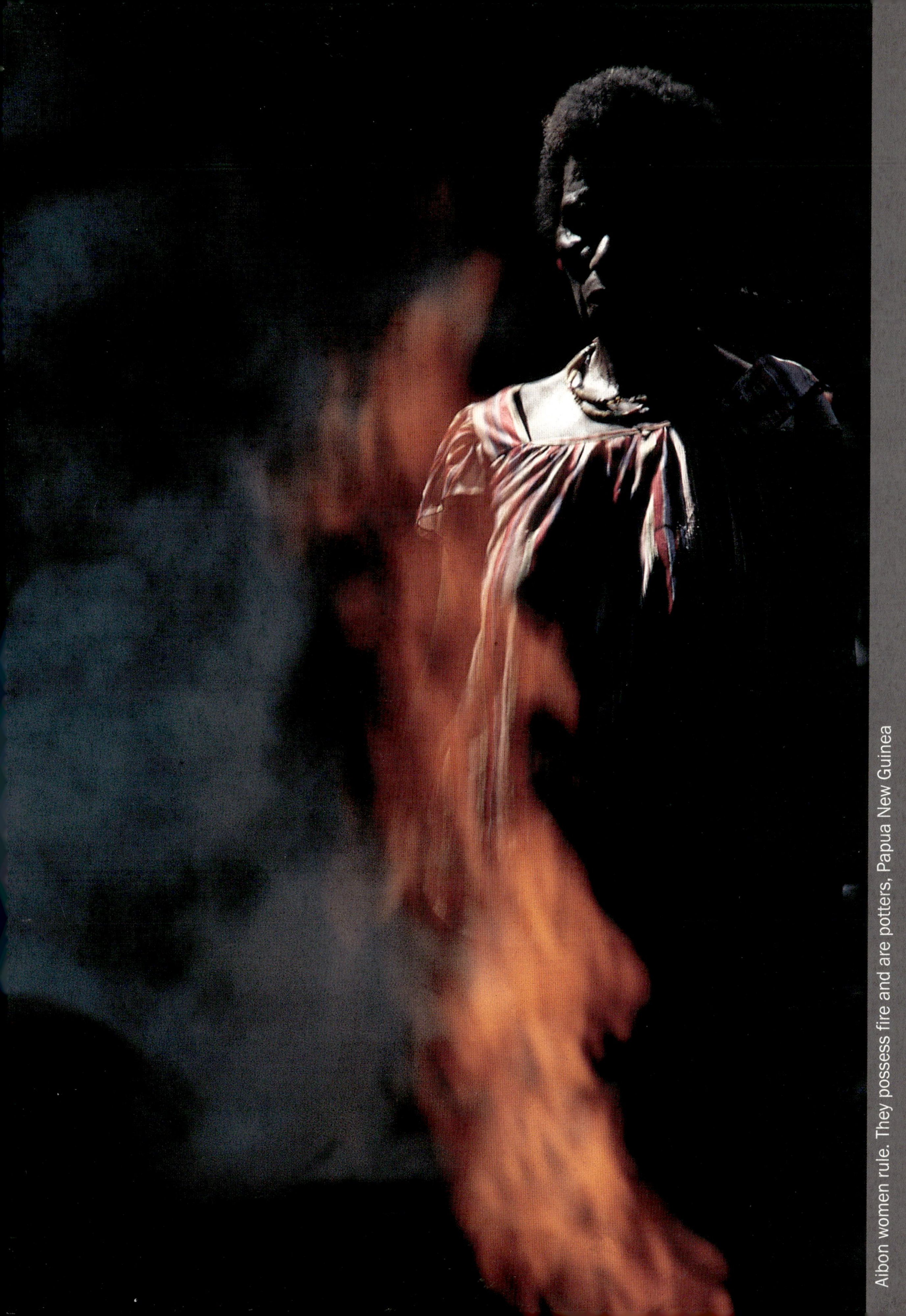

Aibon women rule. They possess fire and are potters, Papua New Guinea

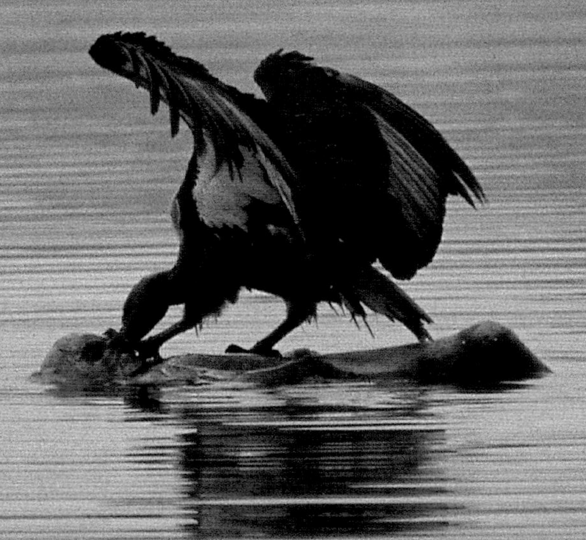

Ganges, the holiest place for Hindus to leave their body behind, India

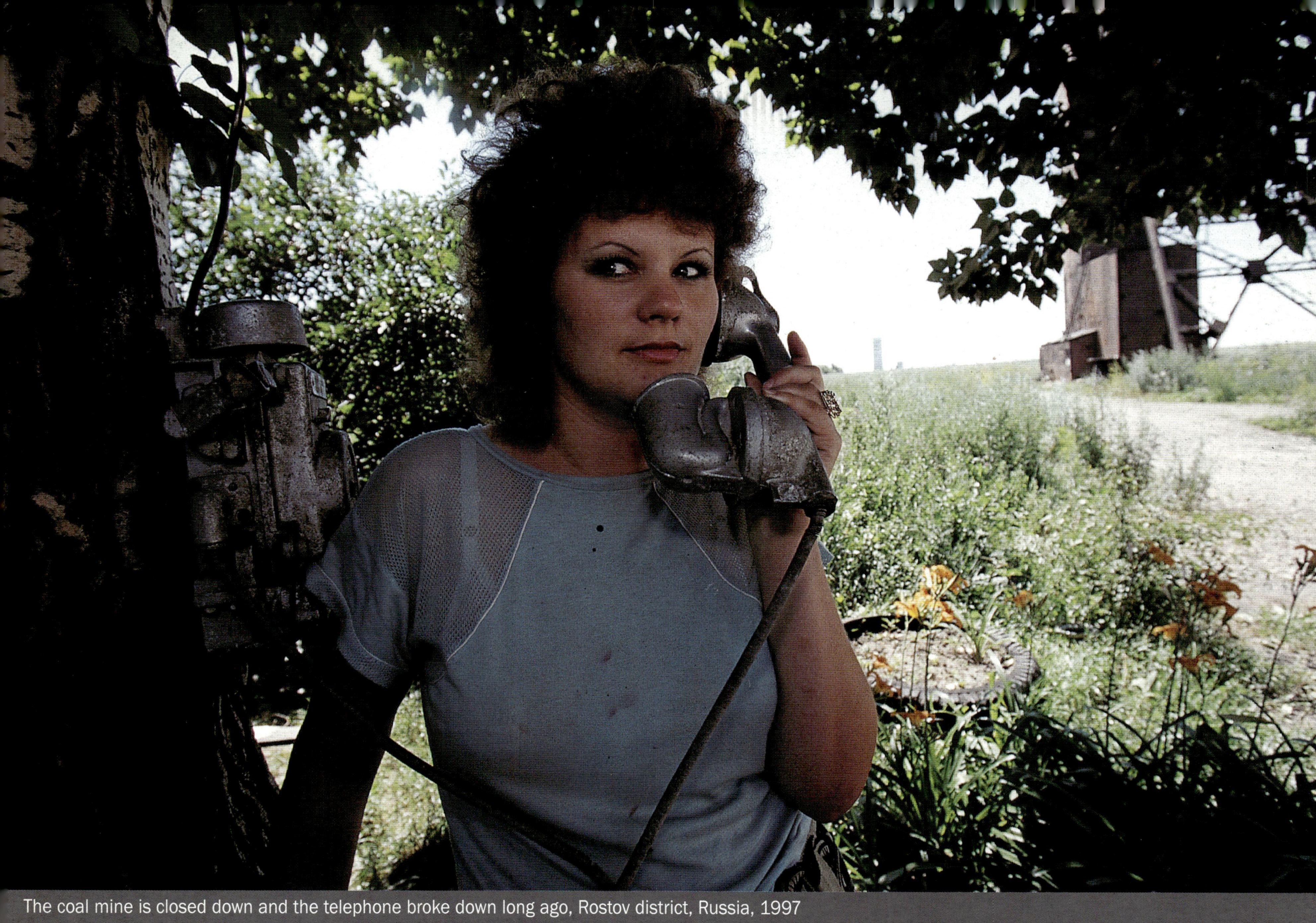

The coal mine is closed down and the telephone broke down long ago, Rostov district, Russia, 1997

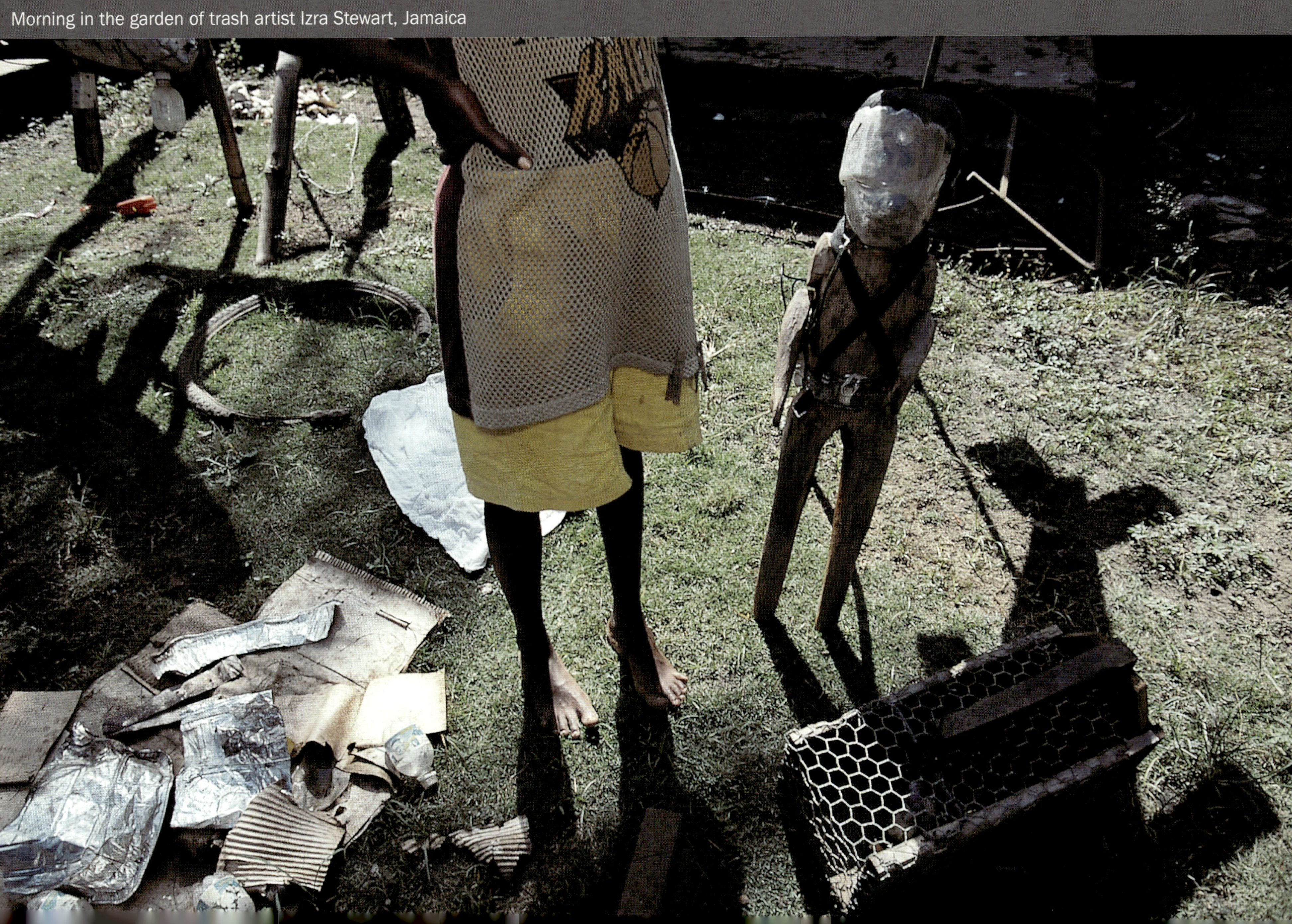

Morning in the garden of trash artist Izra Stewart, Jamaica

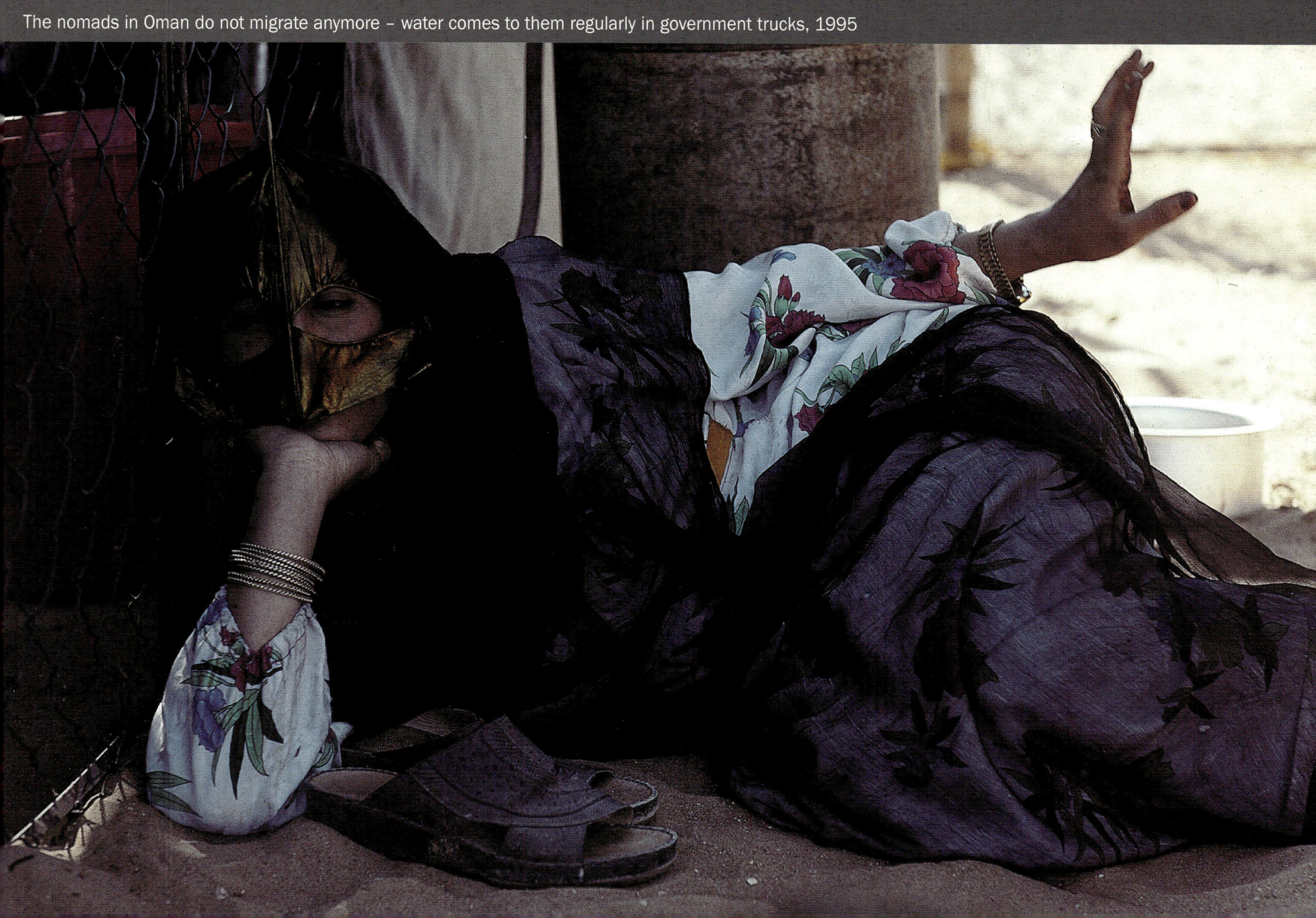

The nomads in Oman do not migrate anymore – water comes to them regularly in government trucks, 1995

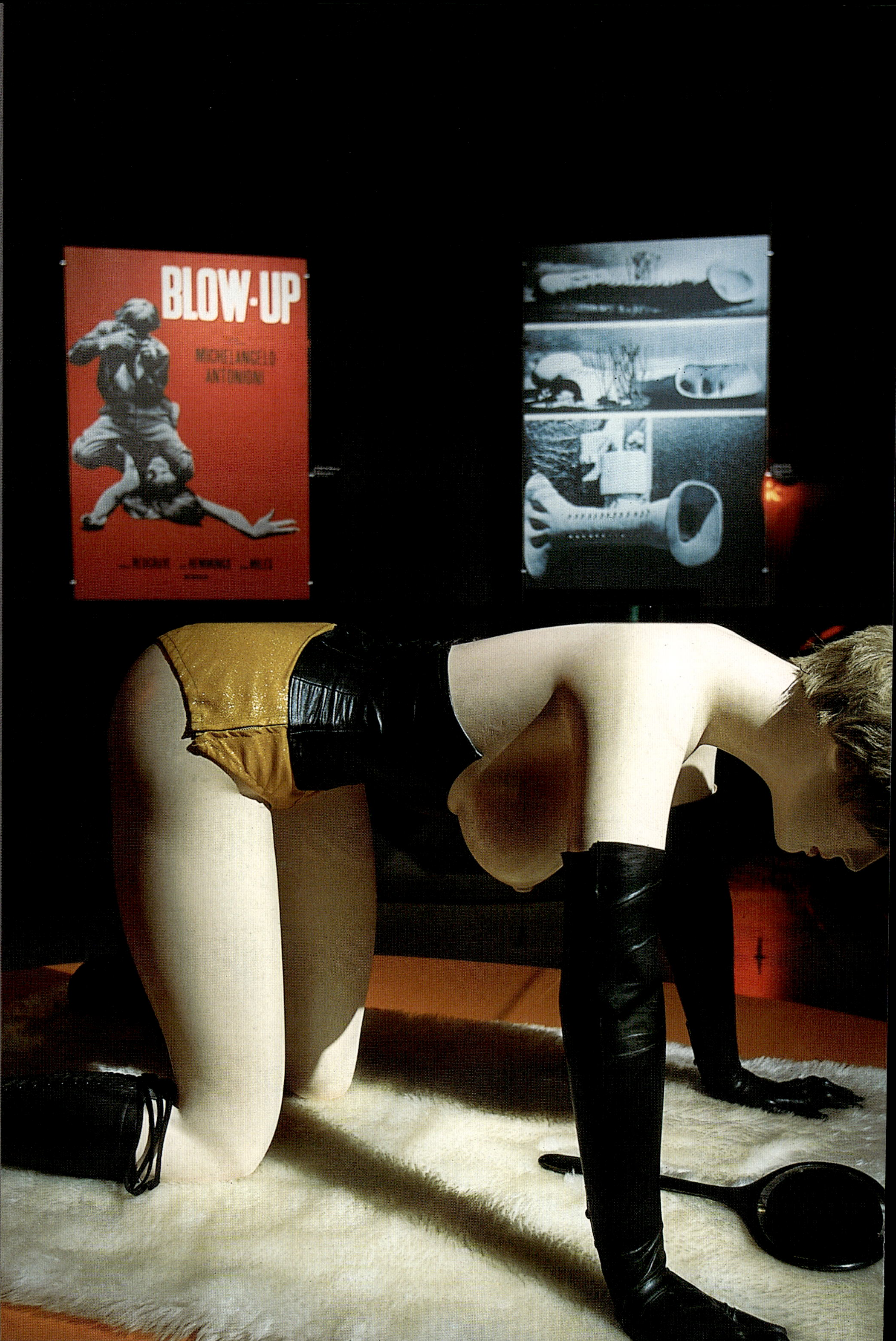

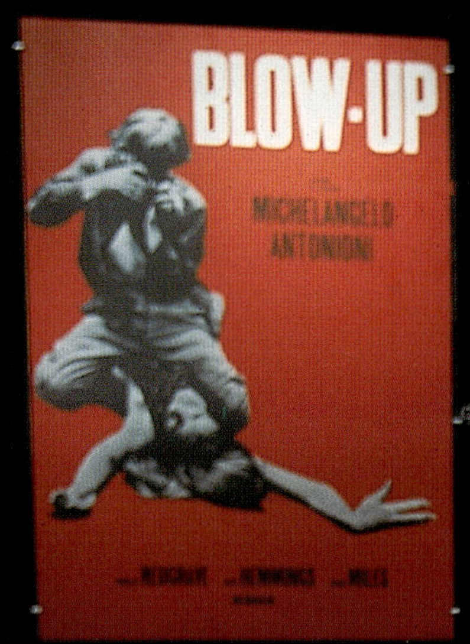

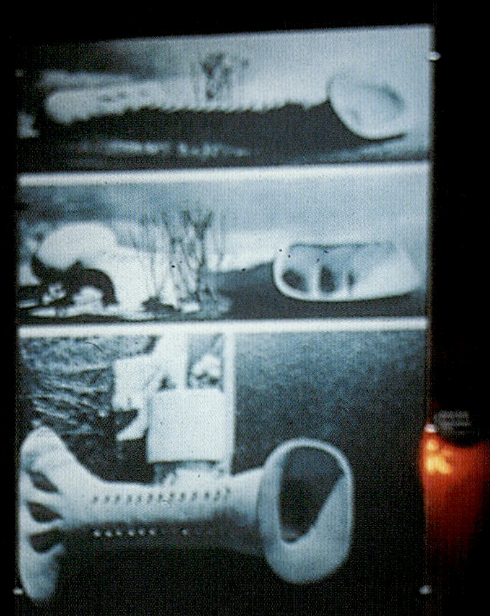

The Power of Erotic Design – Design Museum, London, 1997

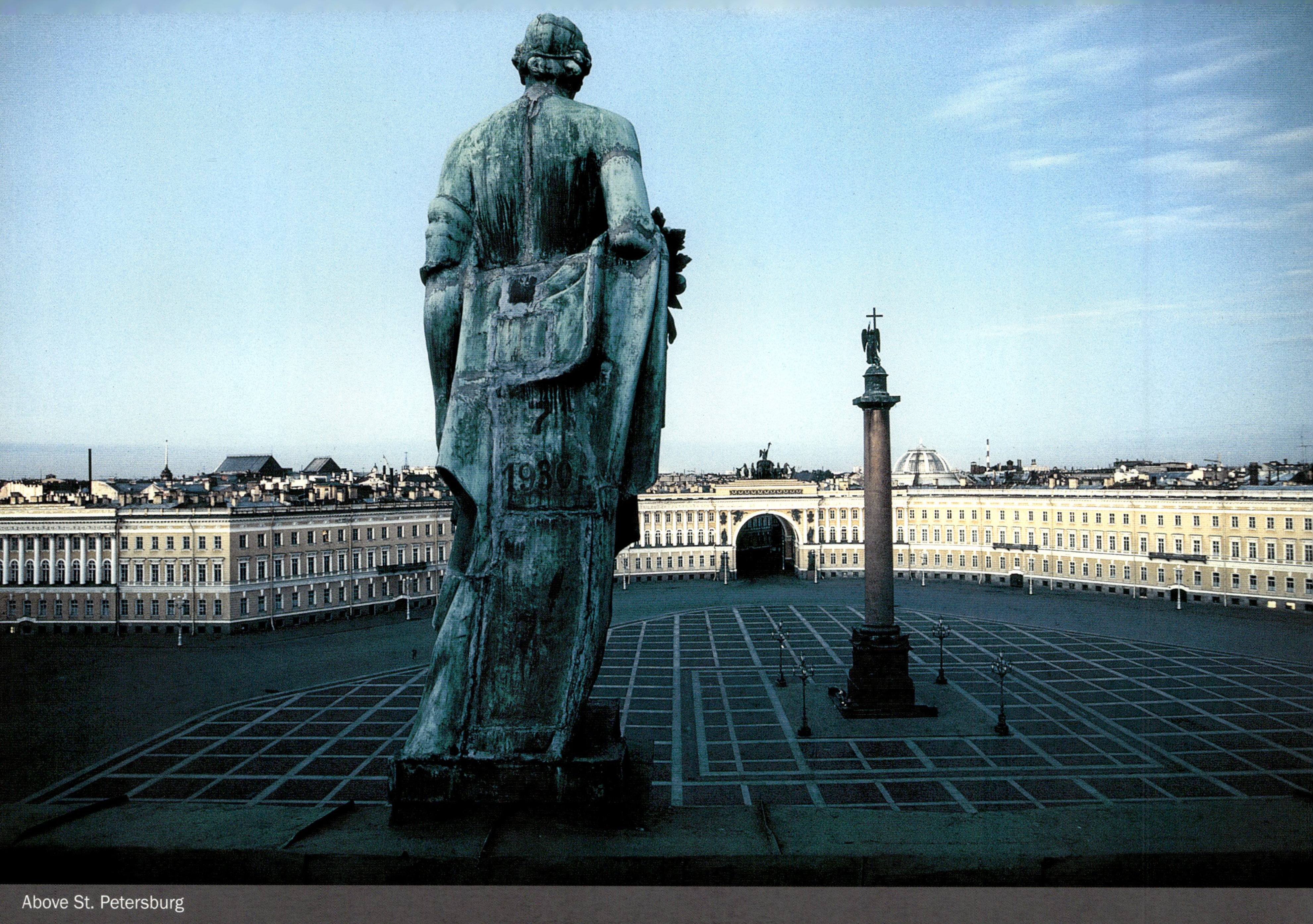

Above St. Petersburg

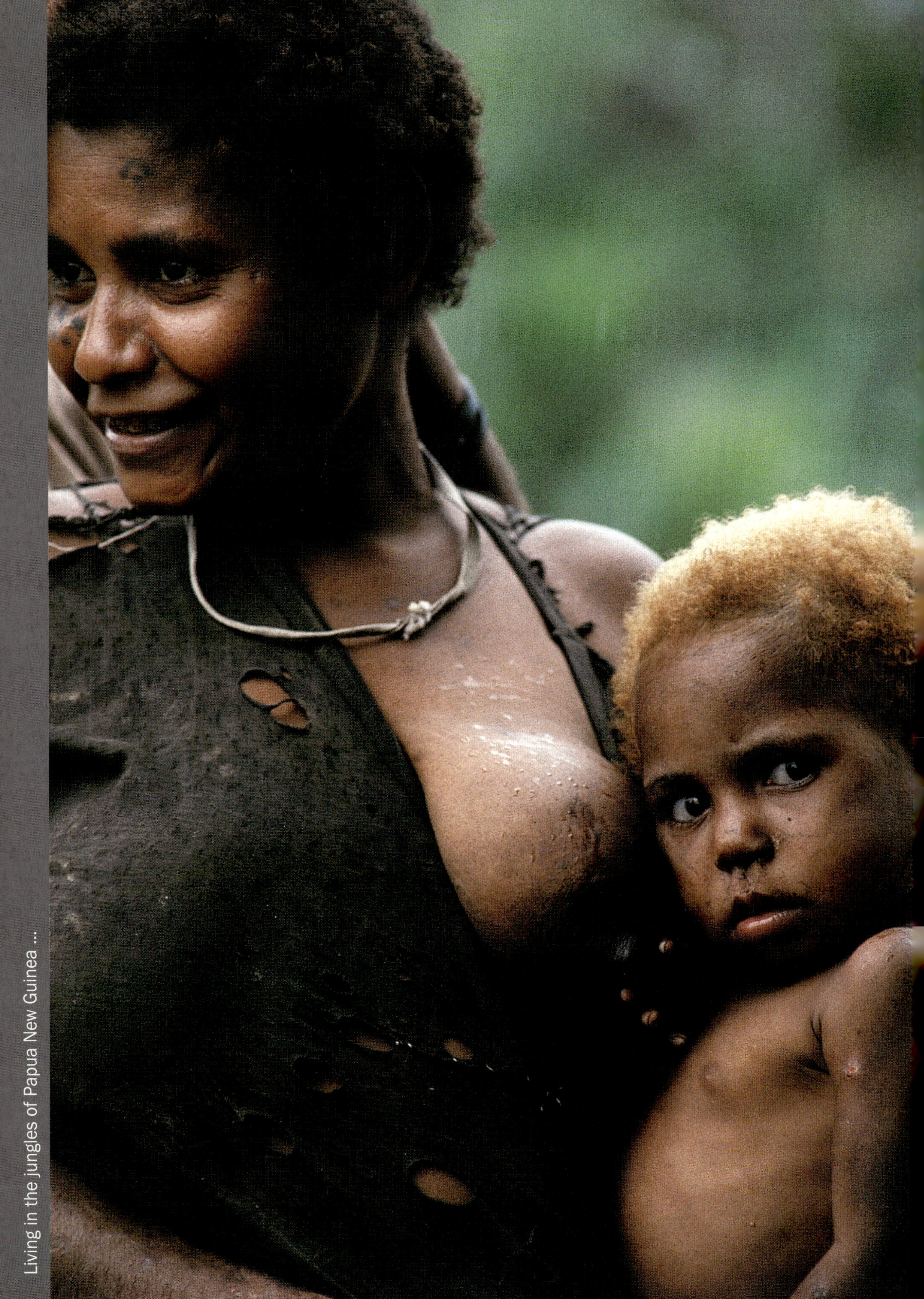

Living in the jungles of Papua New Guinea ...

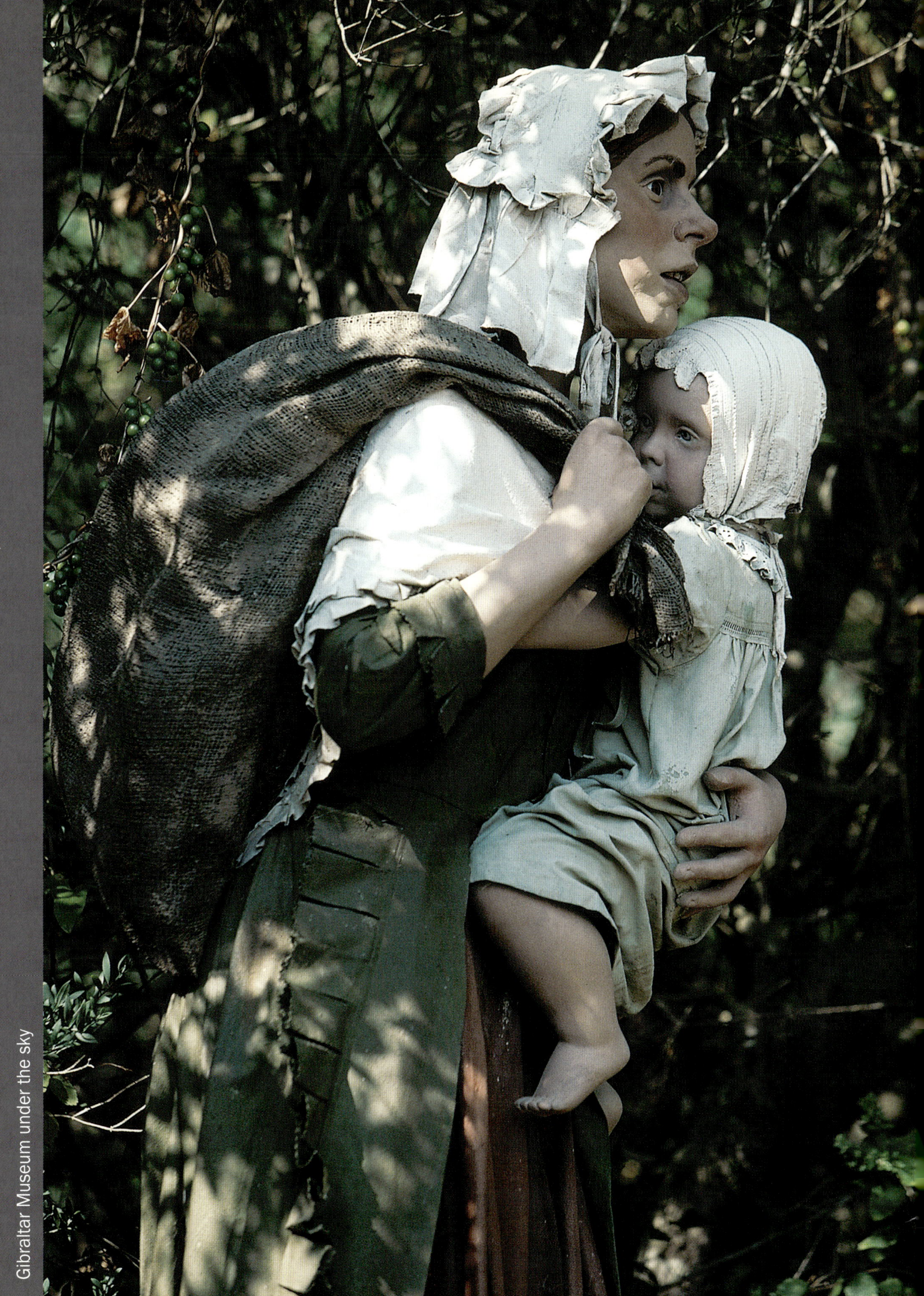

Gibraltar Museum under the sky

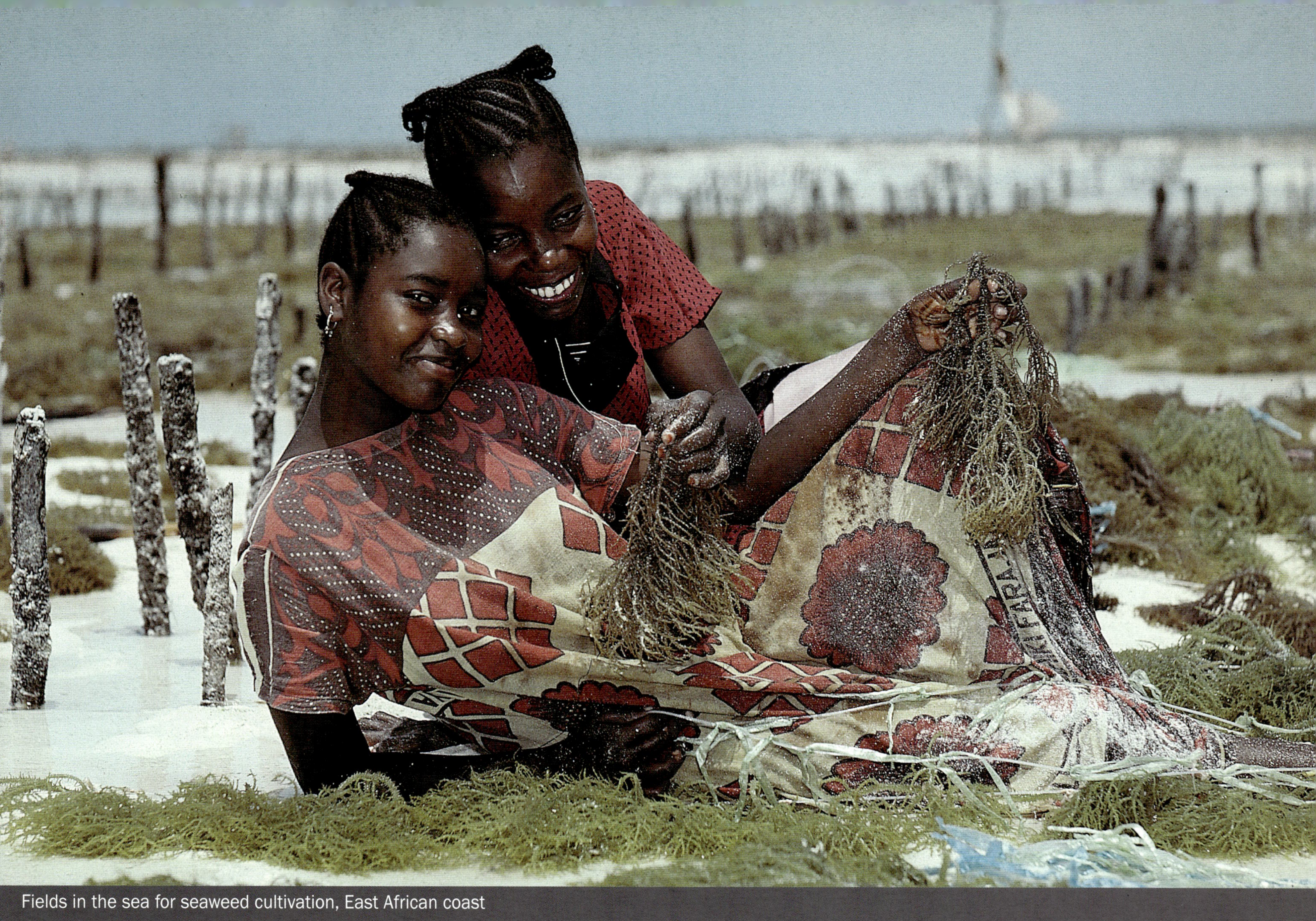

Fields in the sea for seaweed cultivation, East African coast

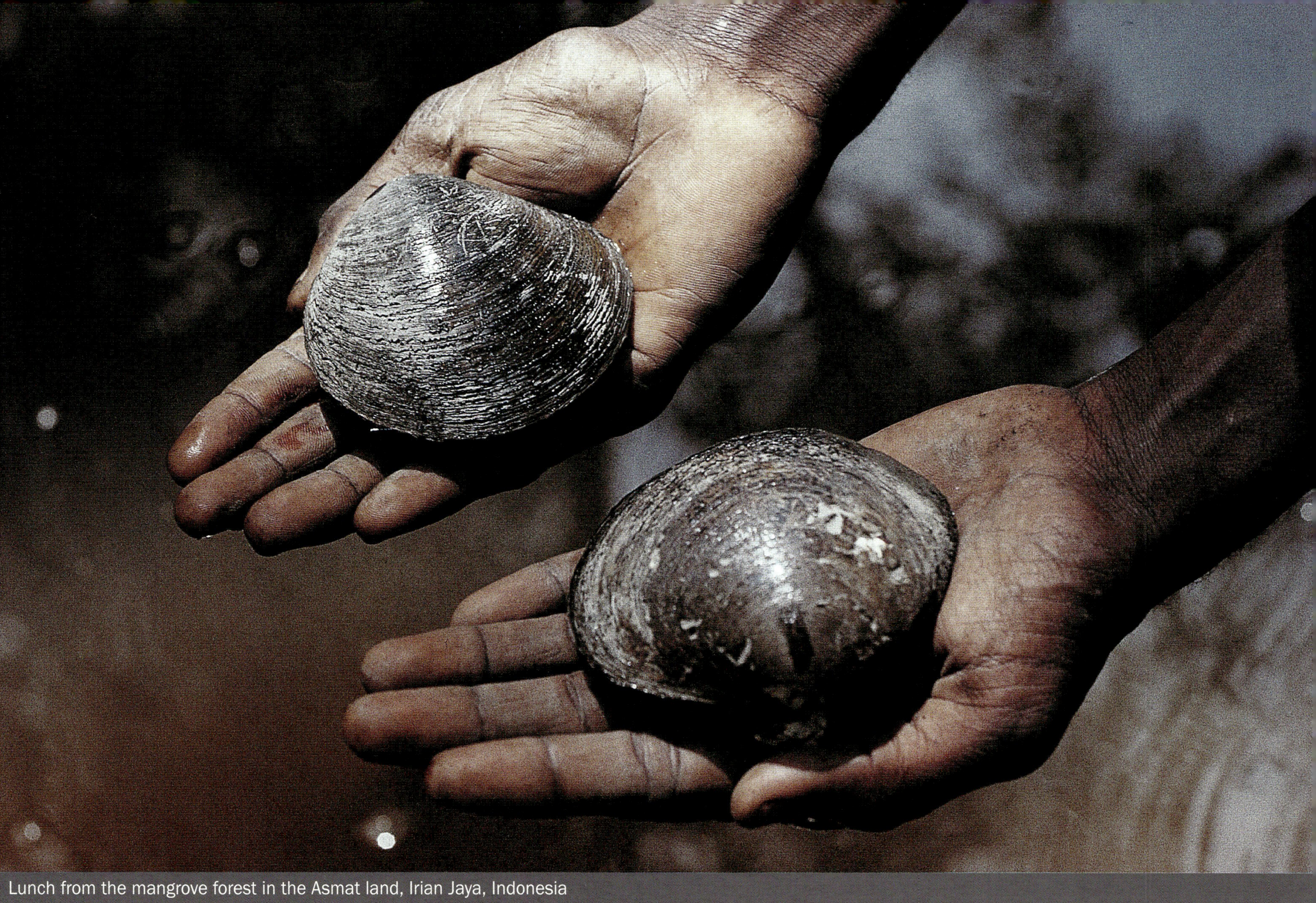

Lunch from the mangrove forest in the Asmat land, Irian Jaya, Indonesia

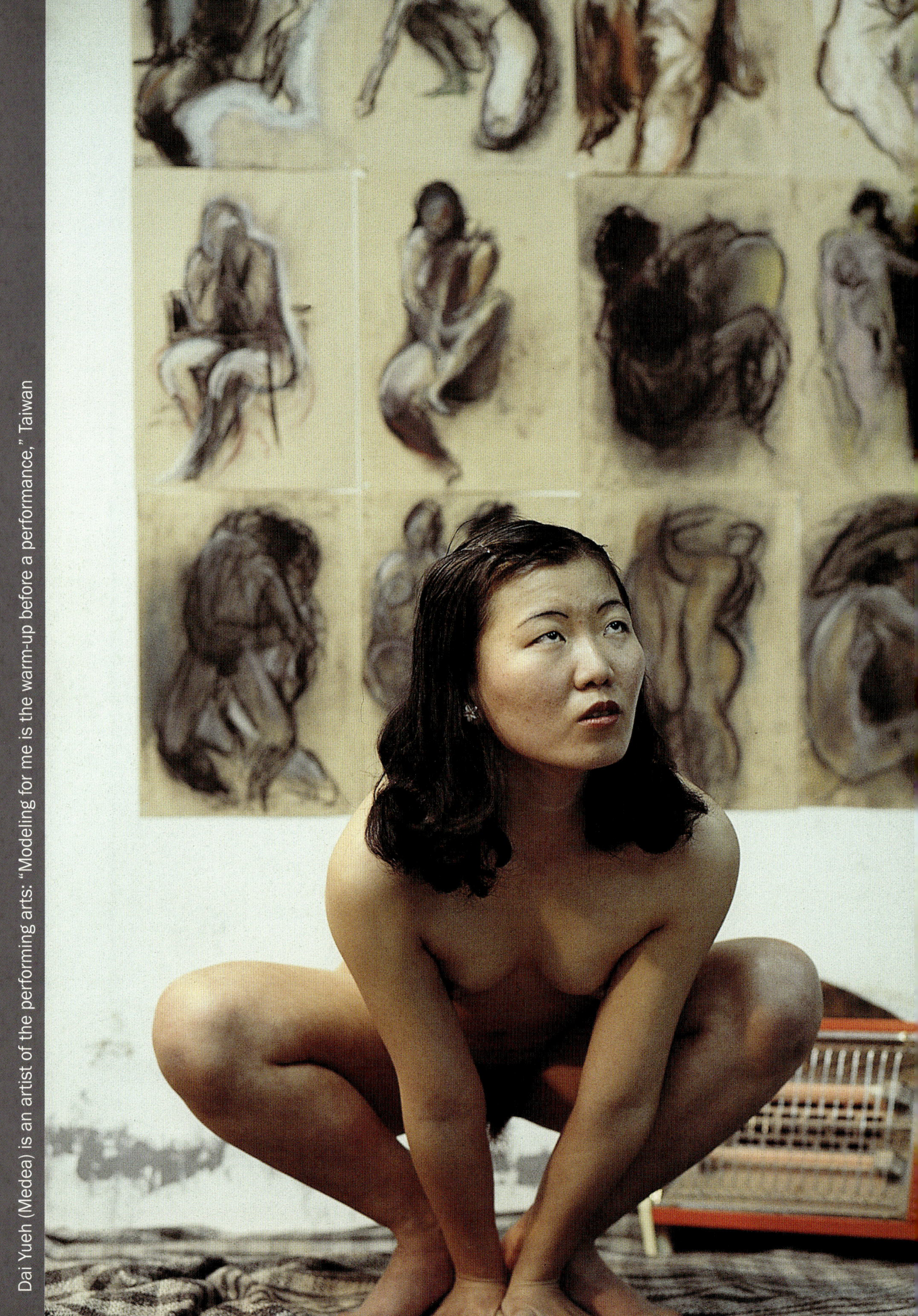

Dai Yueh (Medea) is an artist of the performing arts: "Modeling for me is the warm-up before a performance," Taiwan

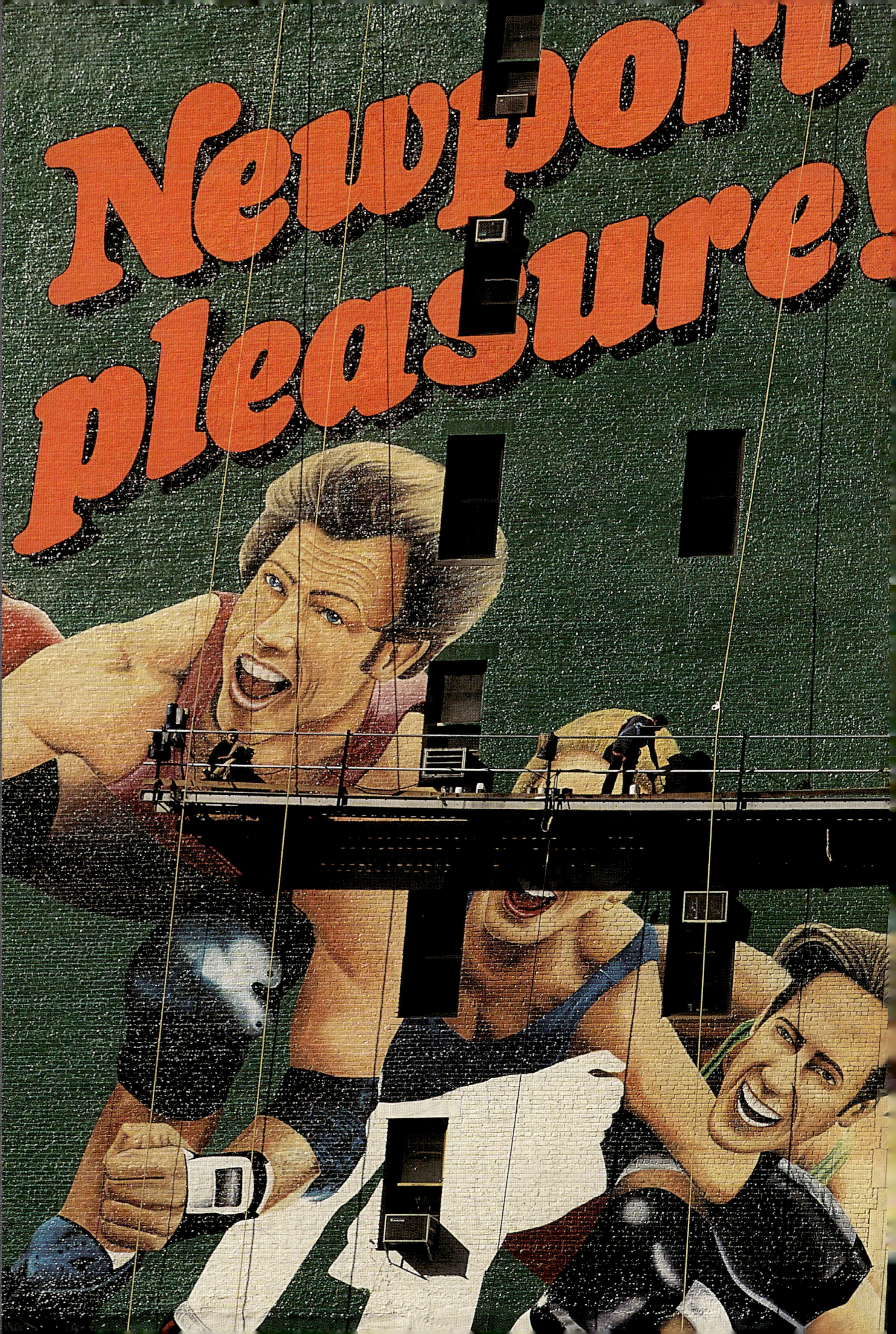

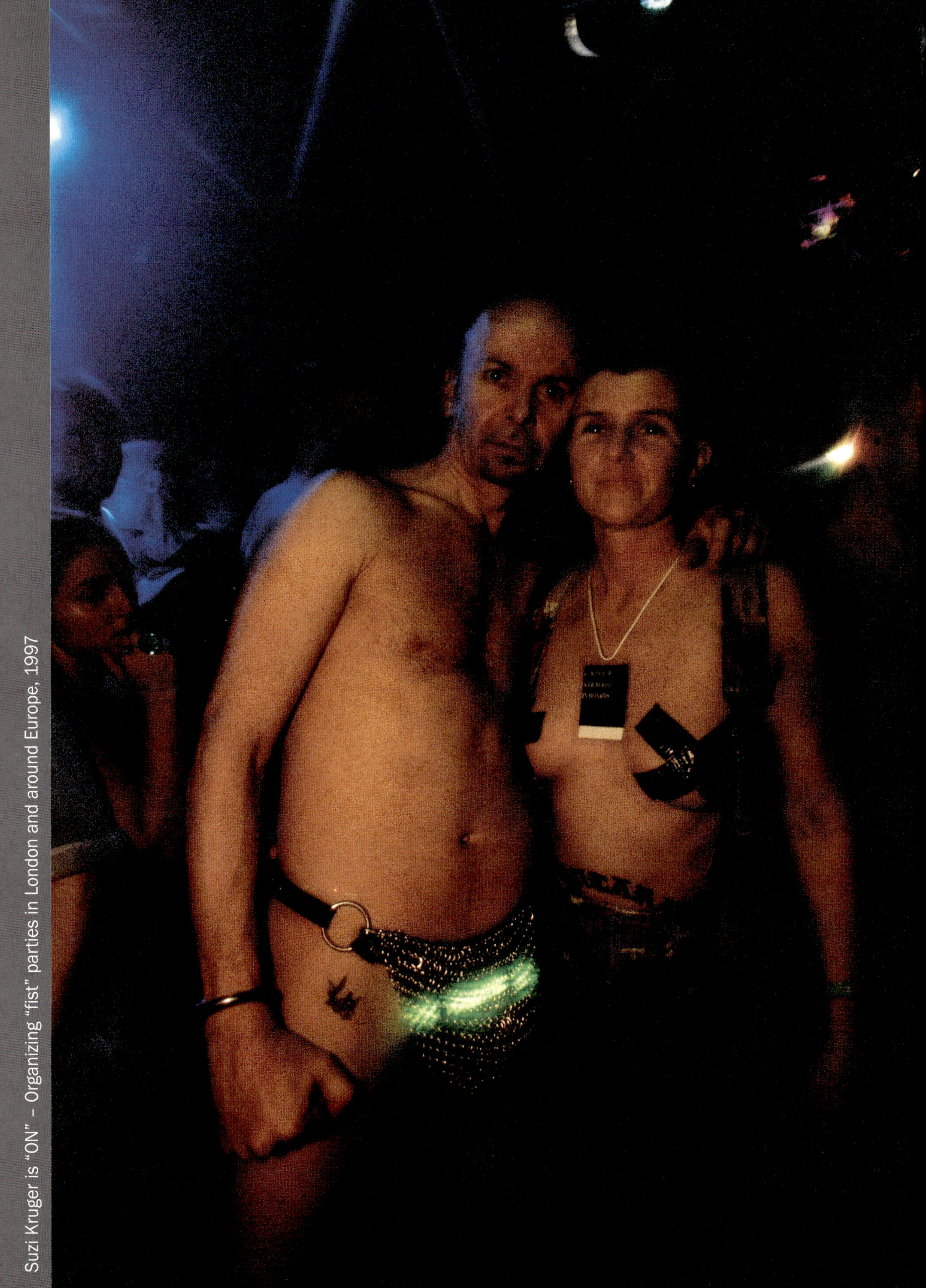

Suzi Kruger is “ON” – Organizing “fist” parties in London and around Europe, 1997

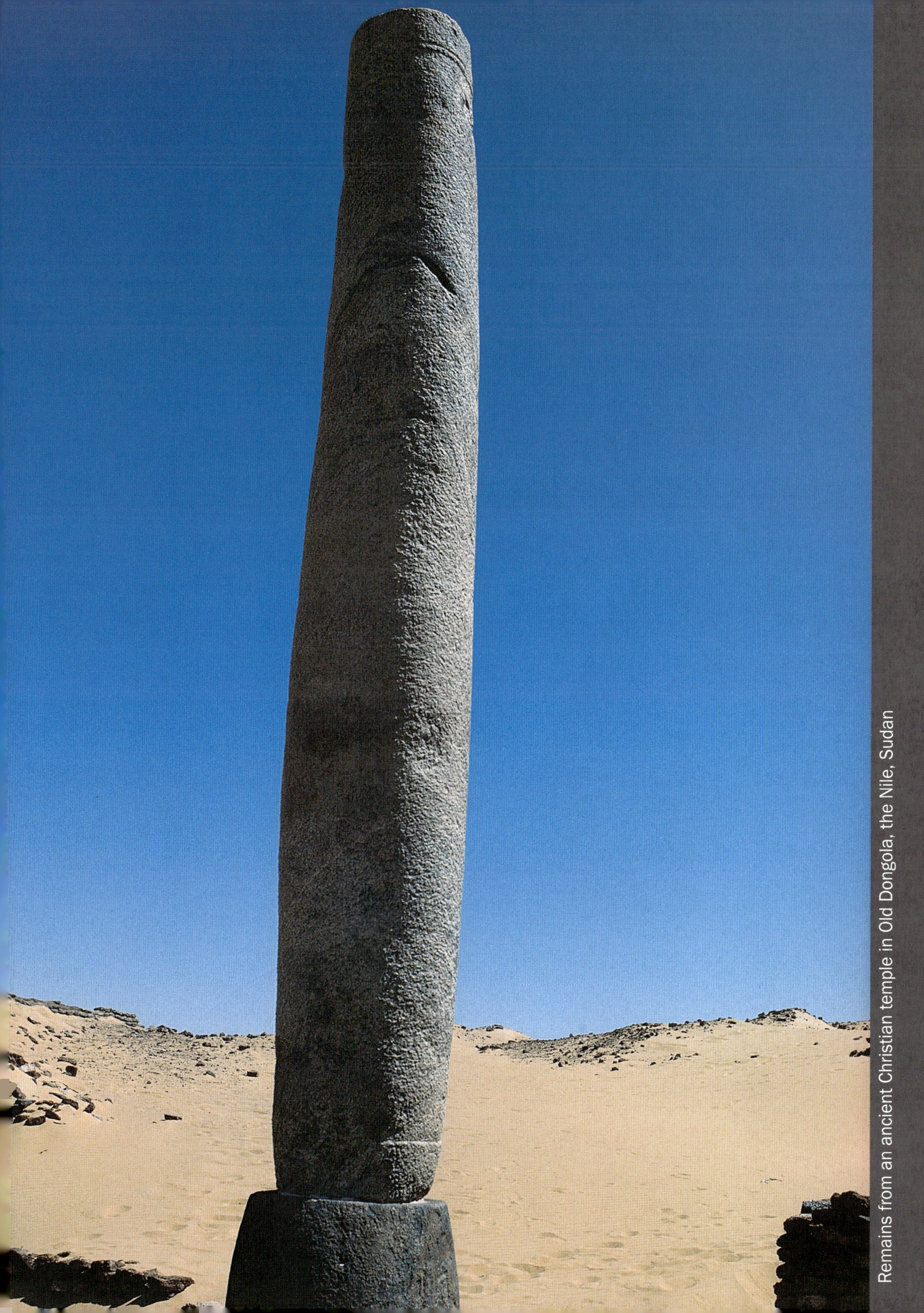

Remains from an ancient Christian temple in Old Dongola, the Nile, Sudan

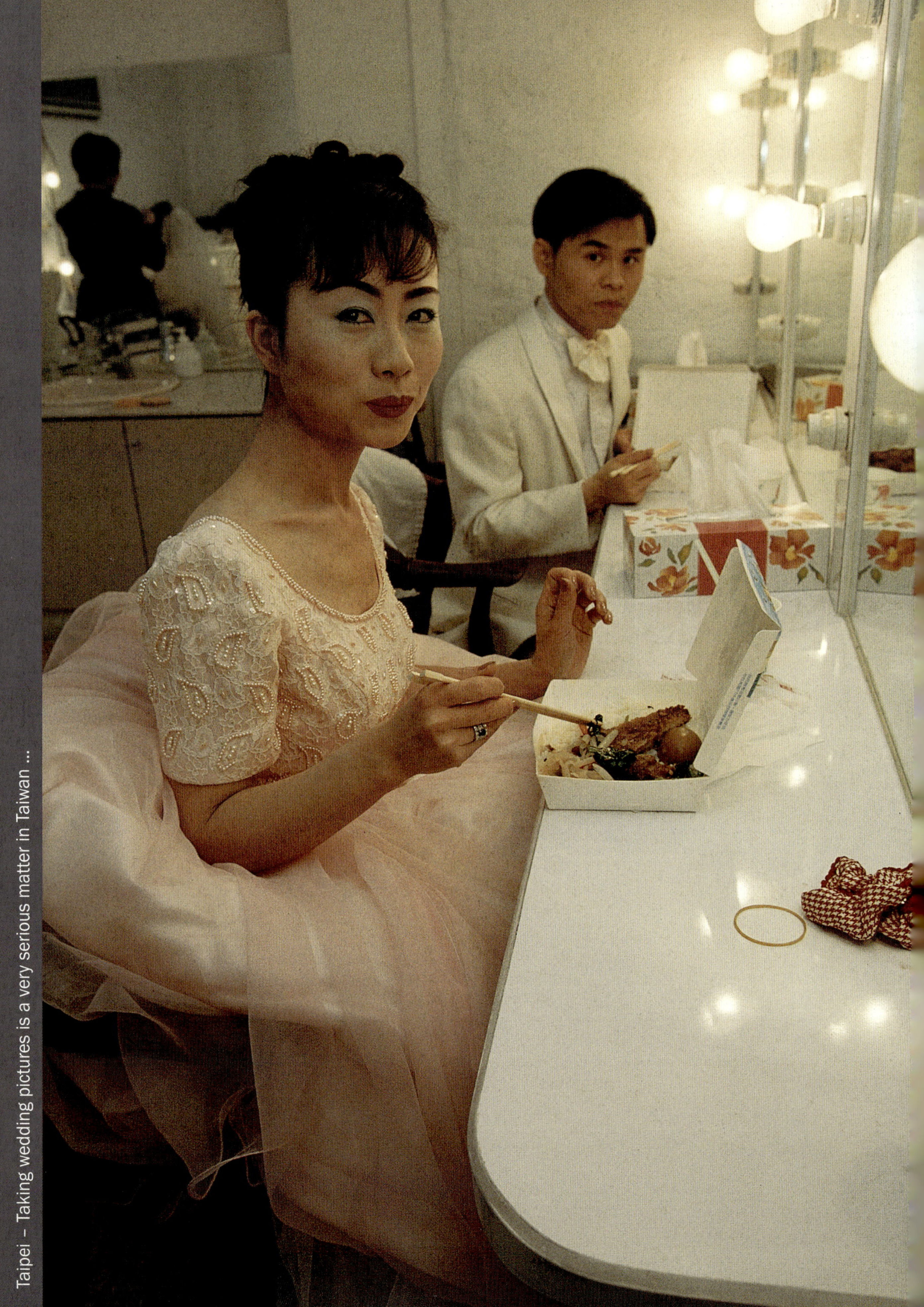

Taipei – Taking wedding pictures is a very serious matter in Taiwan ...

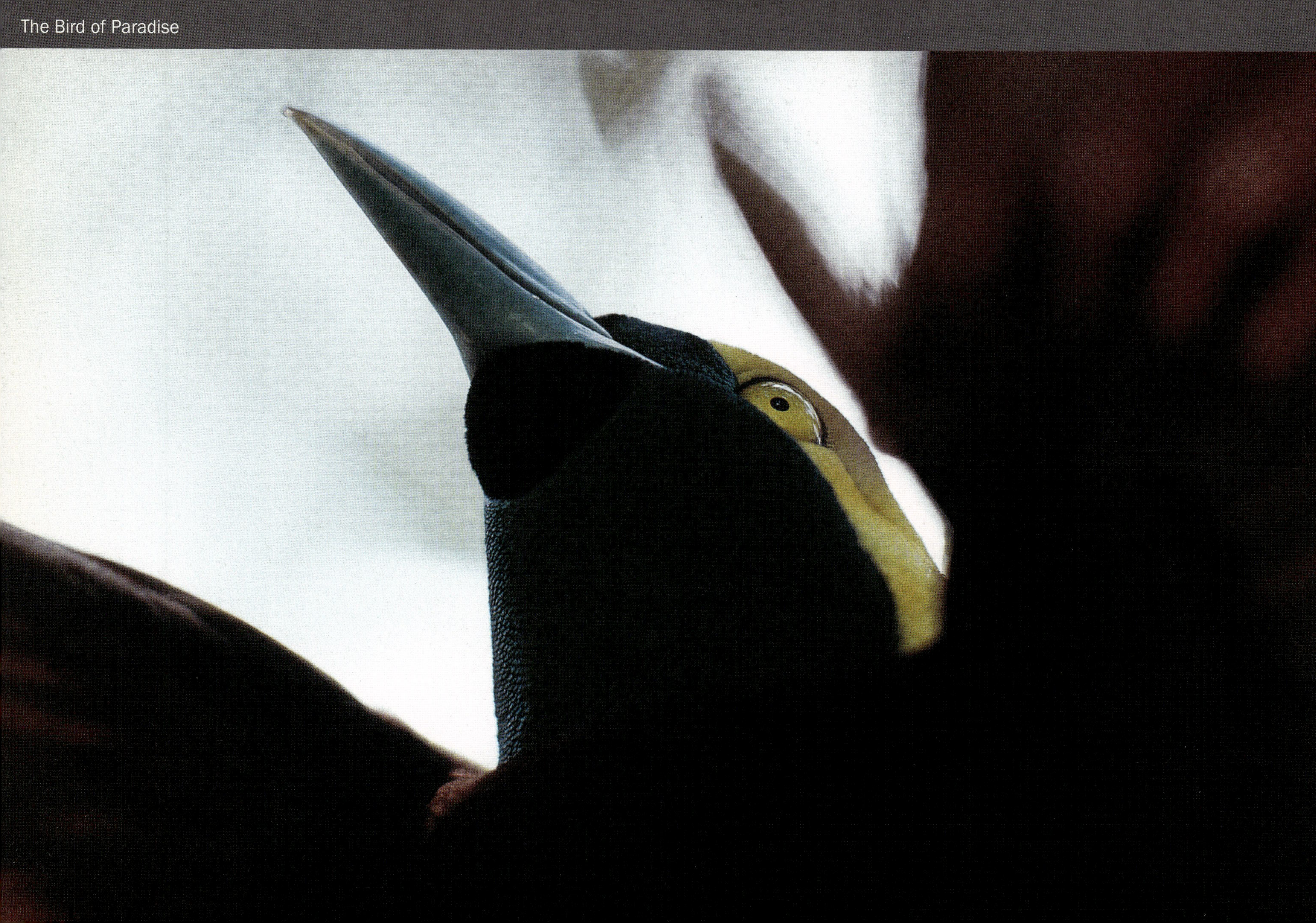

Sudan – Morning

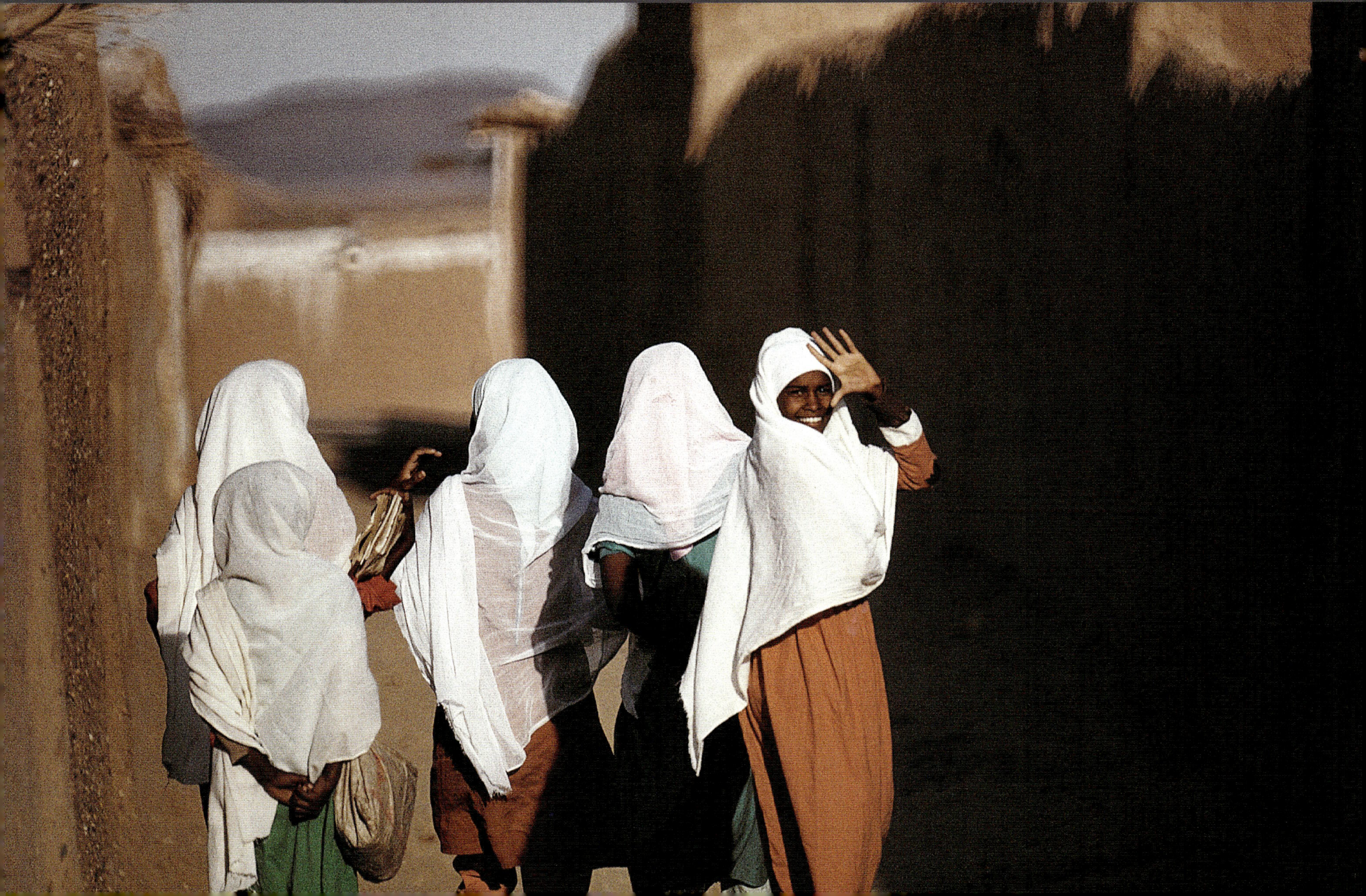

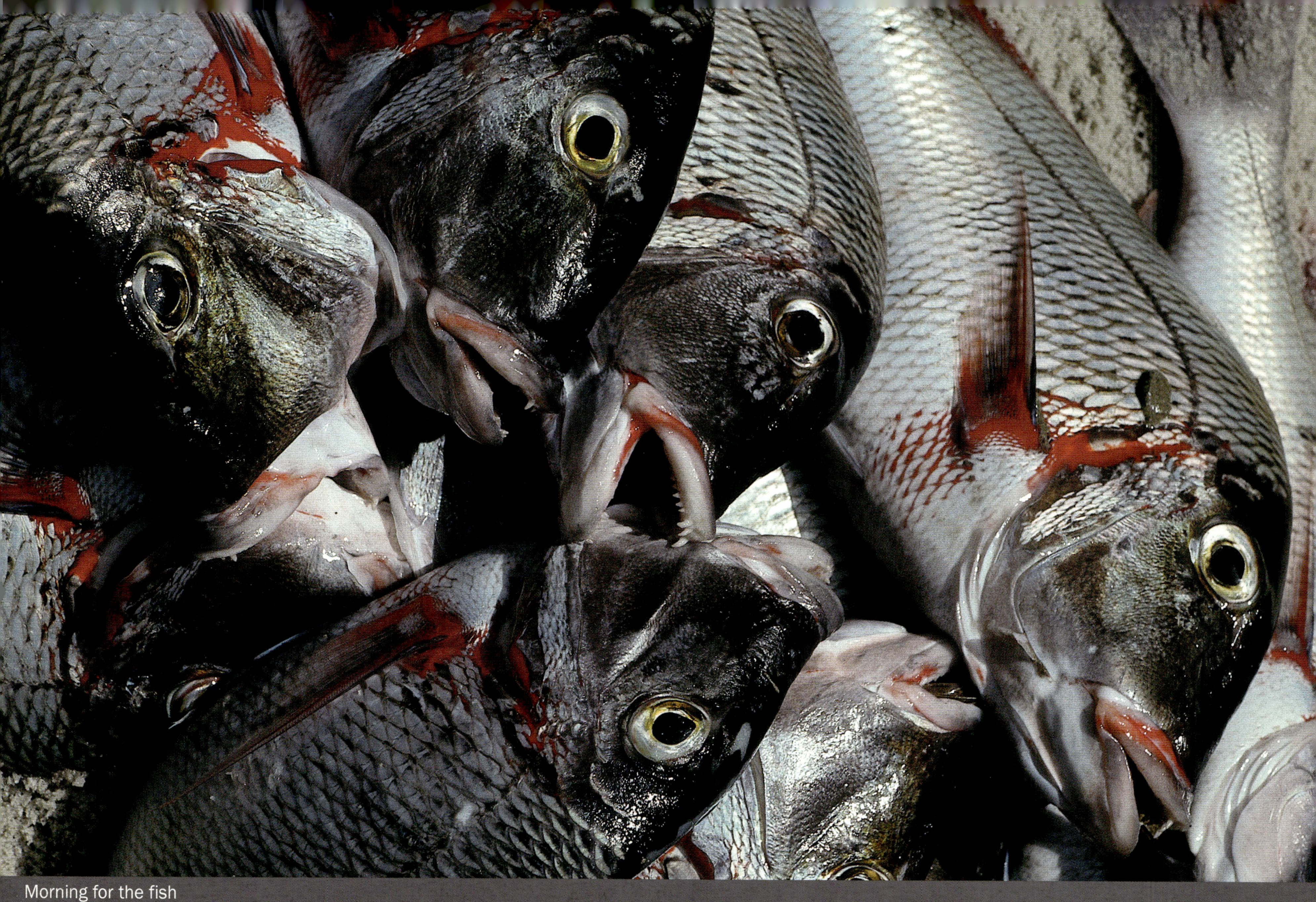

Morning for the fish

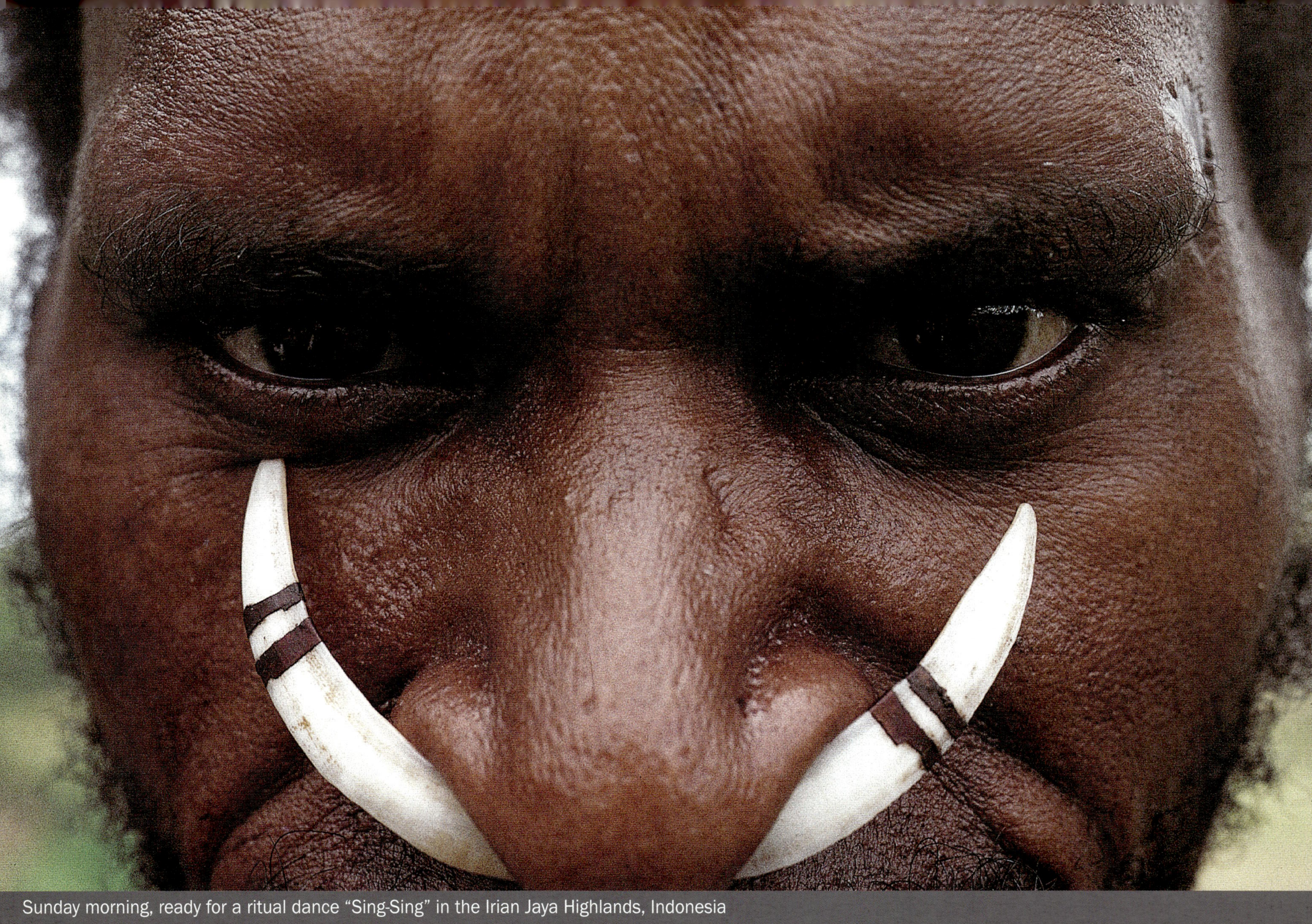

Sunday morning, ready for a ritual dance “Sing-Sing” in the Irian Jaya Highlands, Indonesia

Sunday morning, former USSR

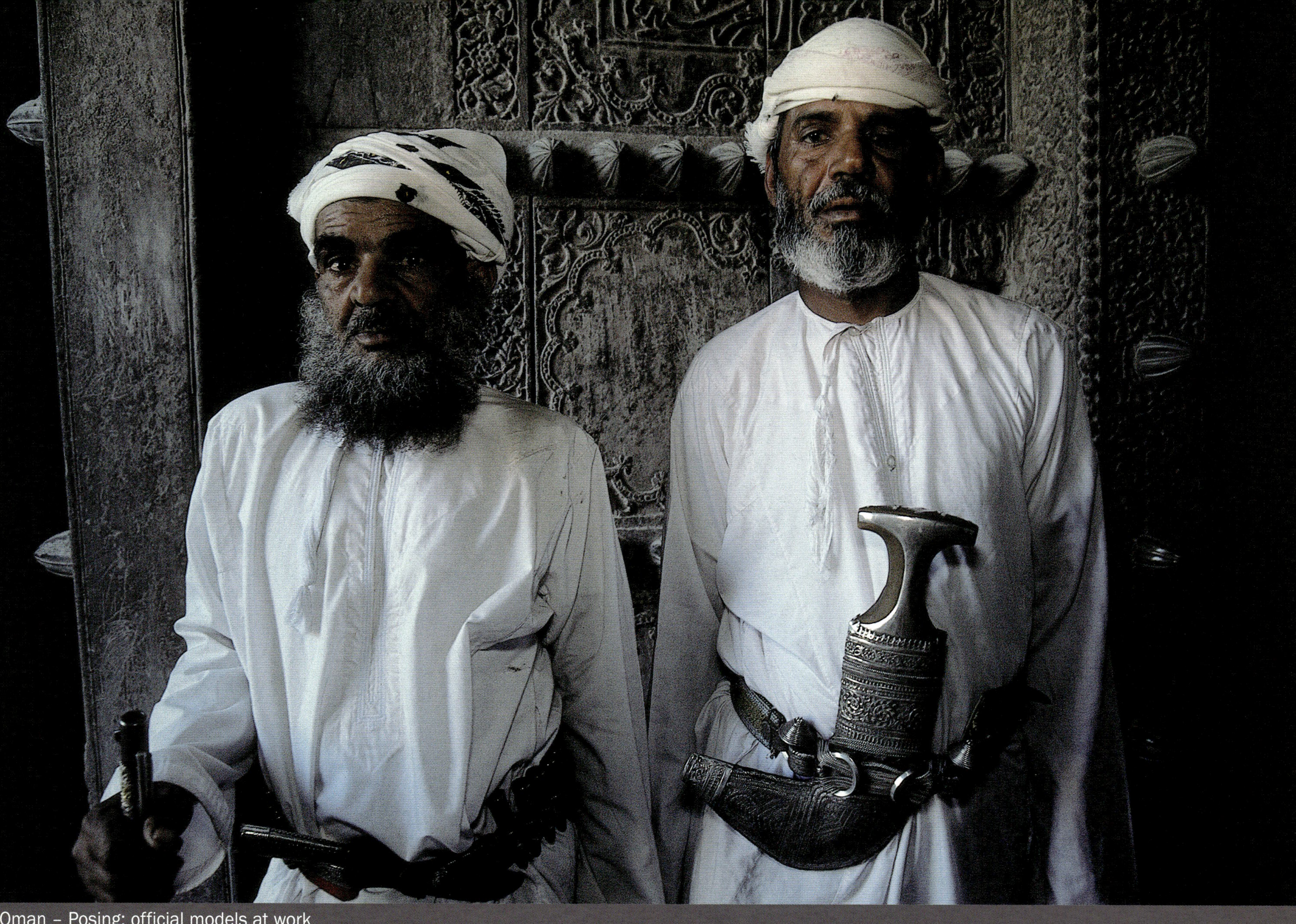

Oman – Posing: official models at work

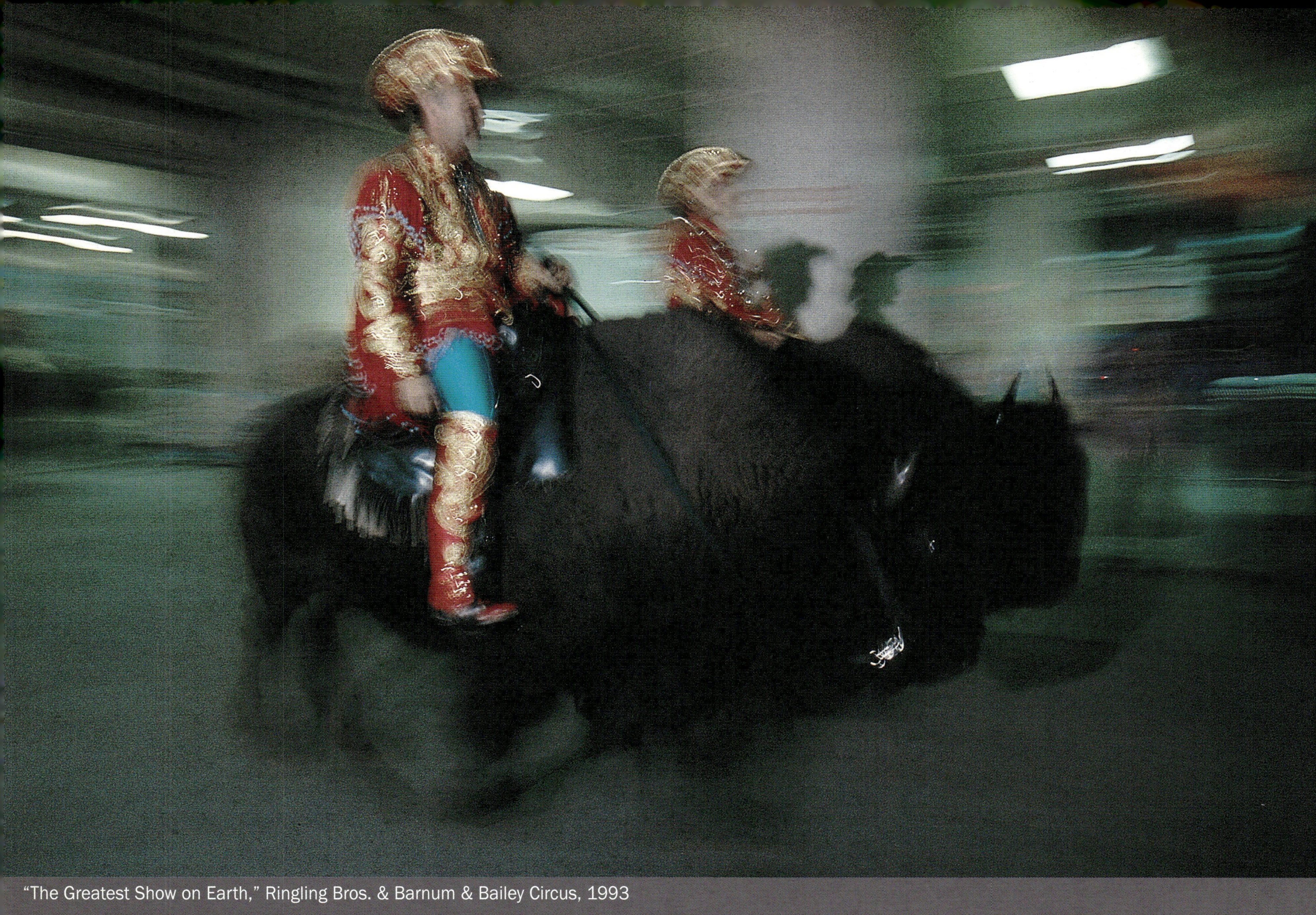

“The Greatest Show on Earth,” Ringling Bros. & Barnum & Bailey Circus, 1993

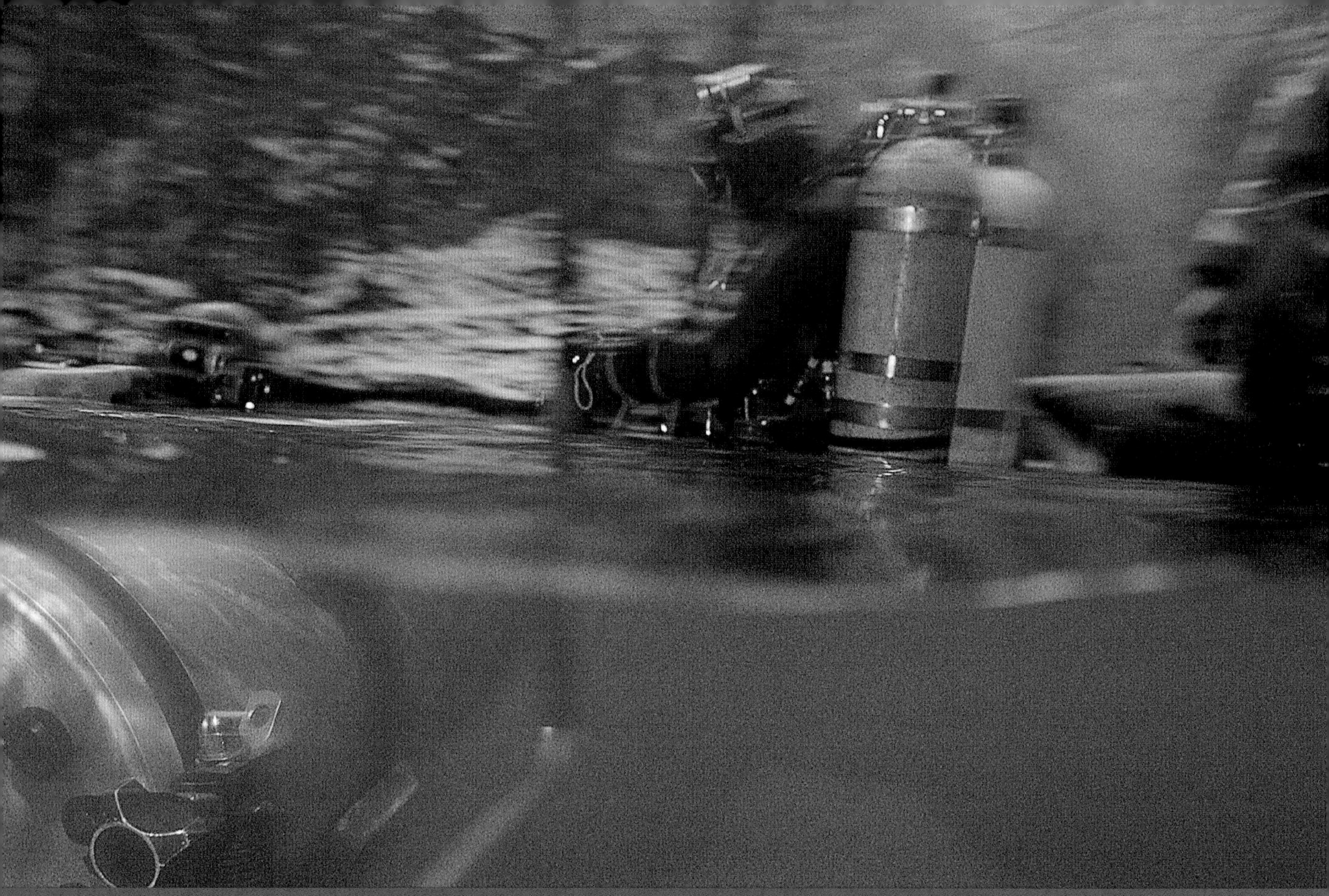
Siphon, Divjak, Slovenia, 1995; Jos Latouche (*Le Grand Bleu* cameraman) getting ready to dive to film the "Human Fish"

"Sing-Sing" – Local dance party in the Irian Jaya Highlands, Indonesia

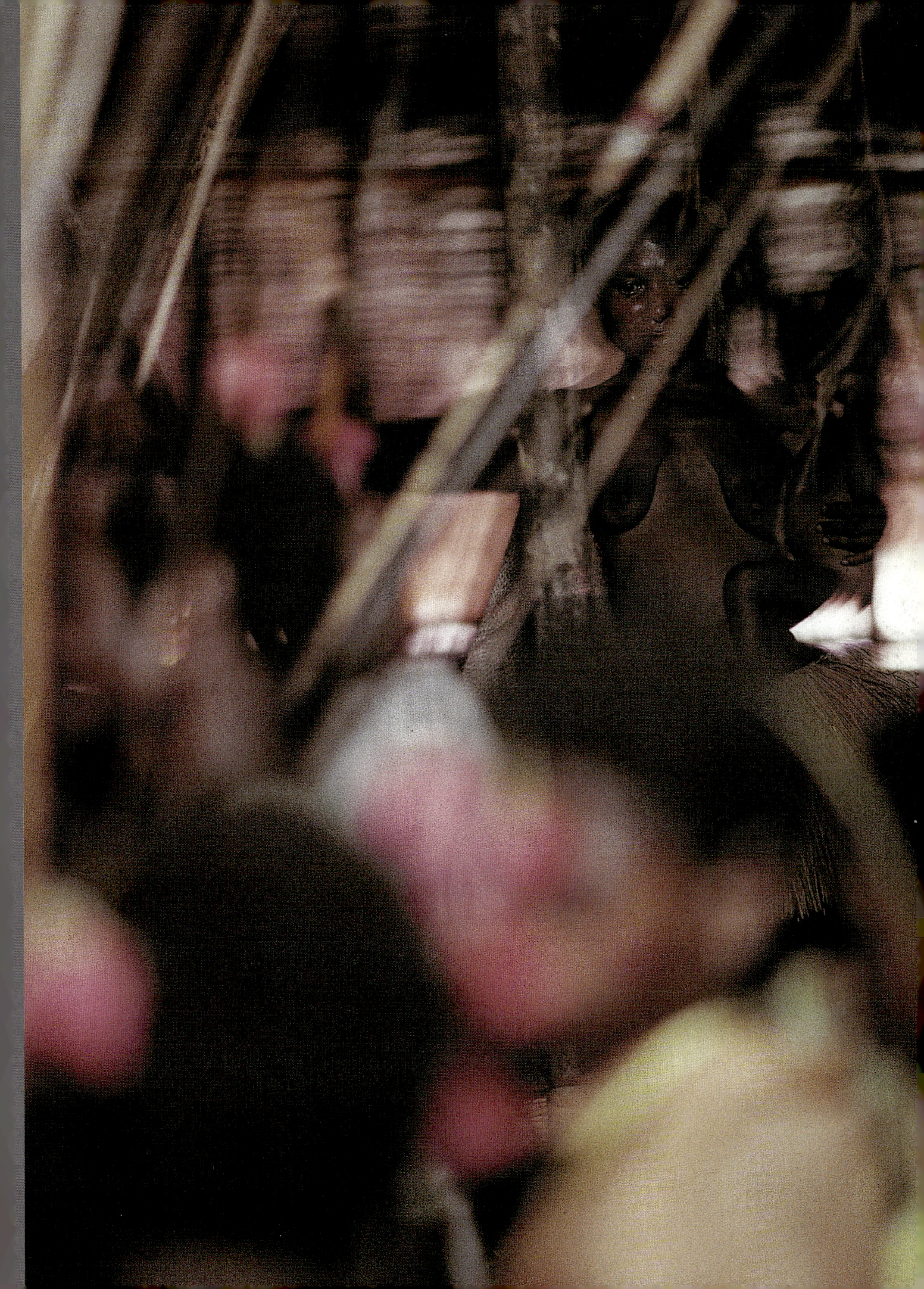

Made by Guarani Indians ... Trinidad Mission in South America

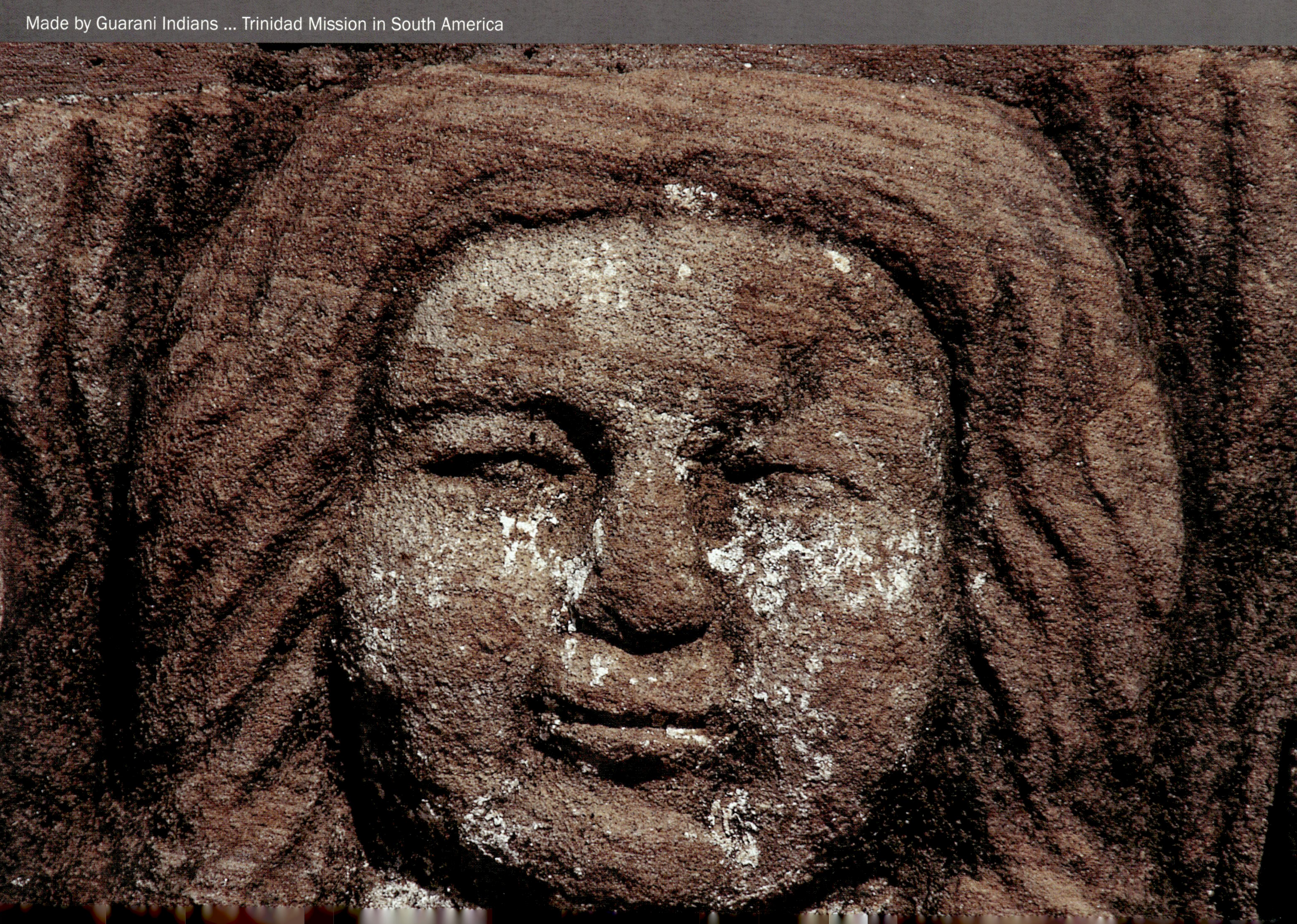

Shanghai, 1993

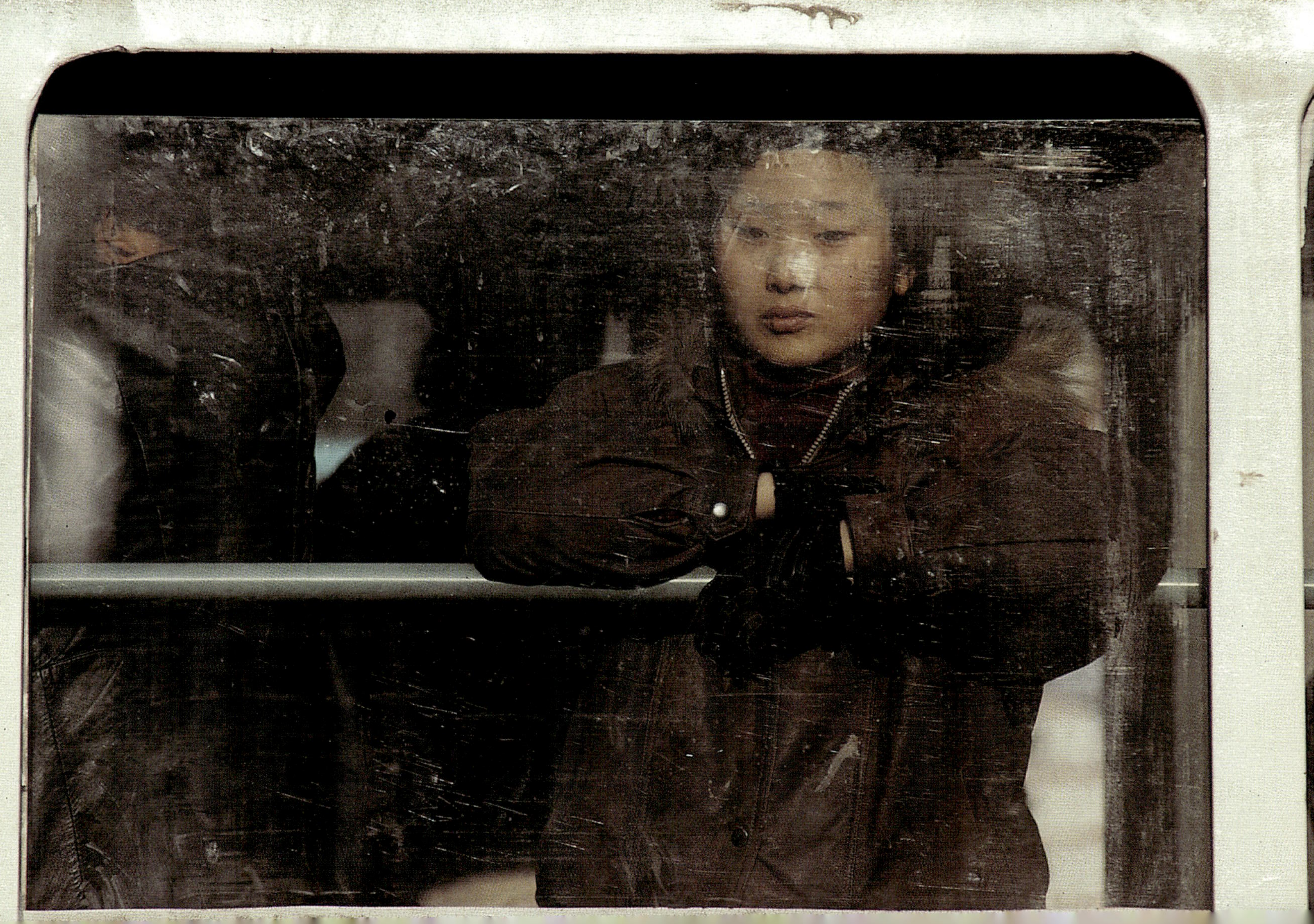

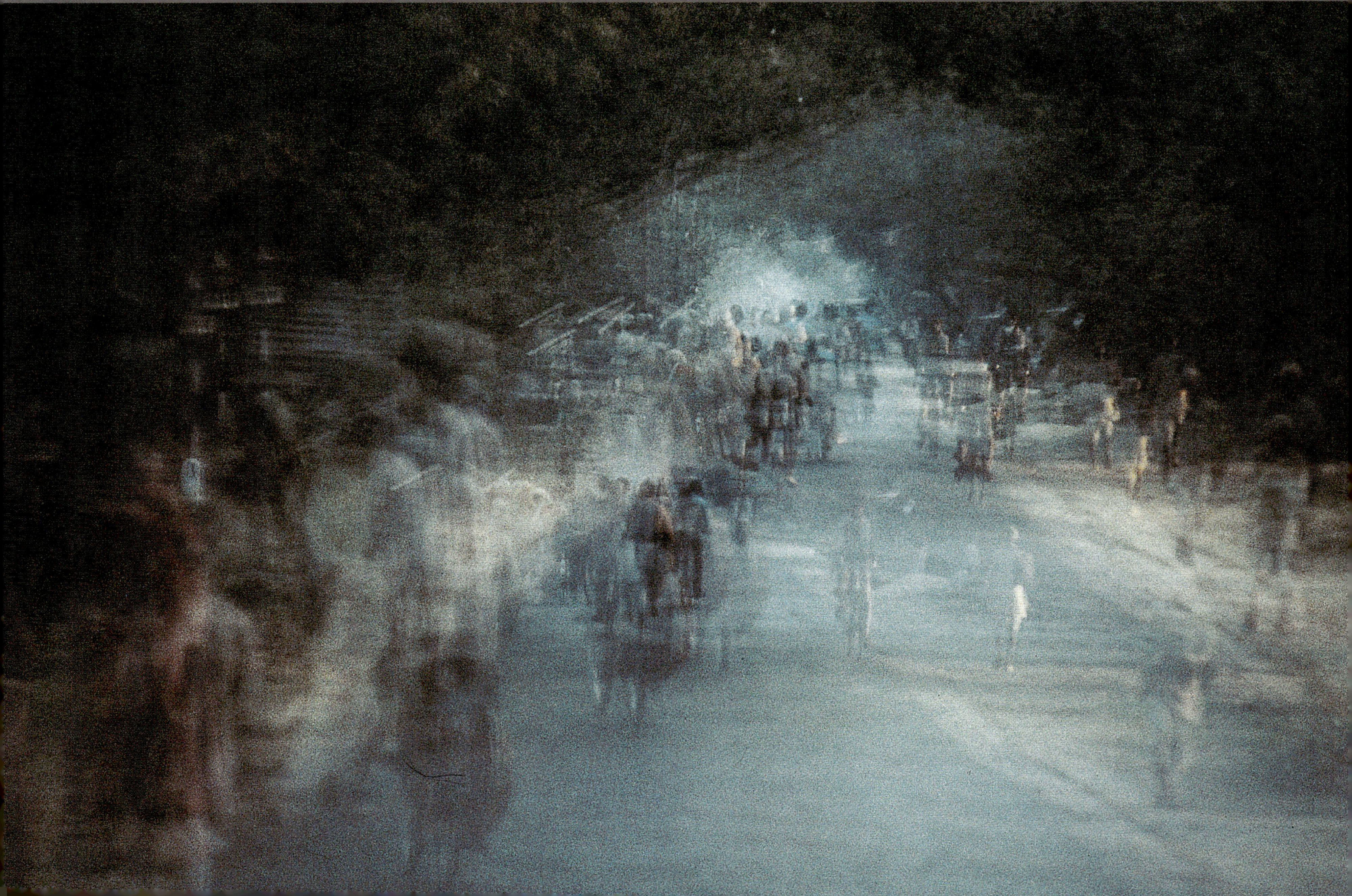

Great Trunk Road, India

Camden Town, the heart of London's market scene

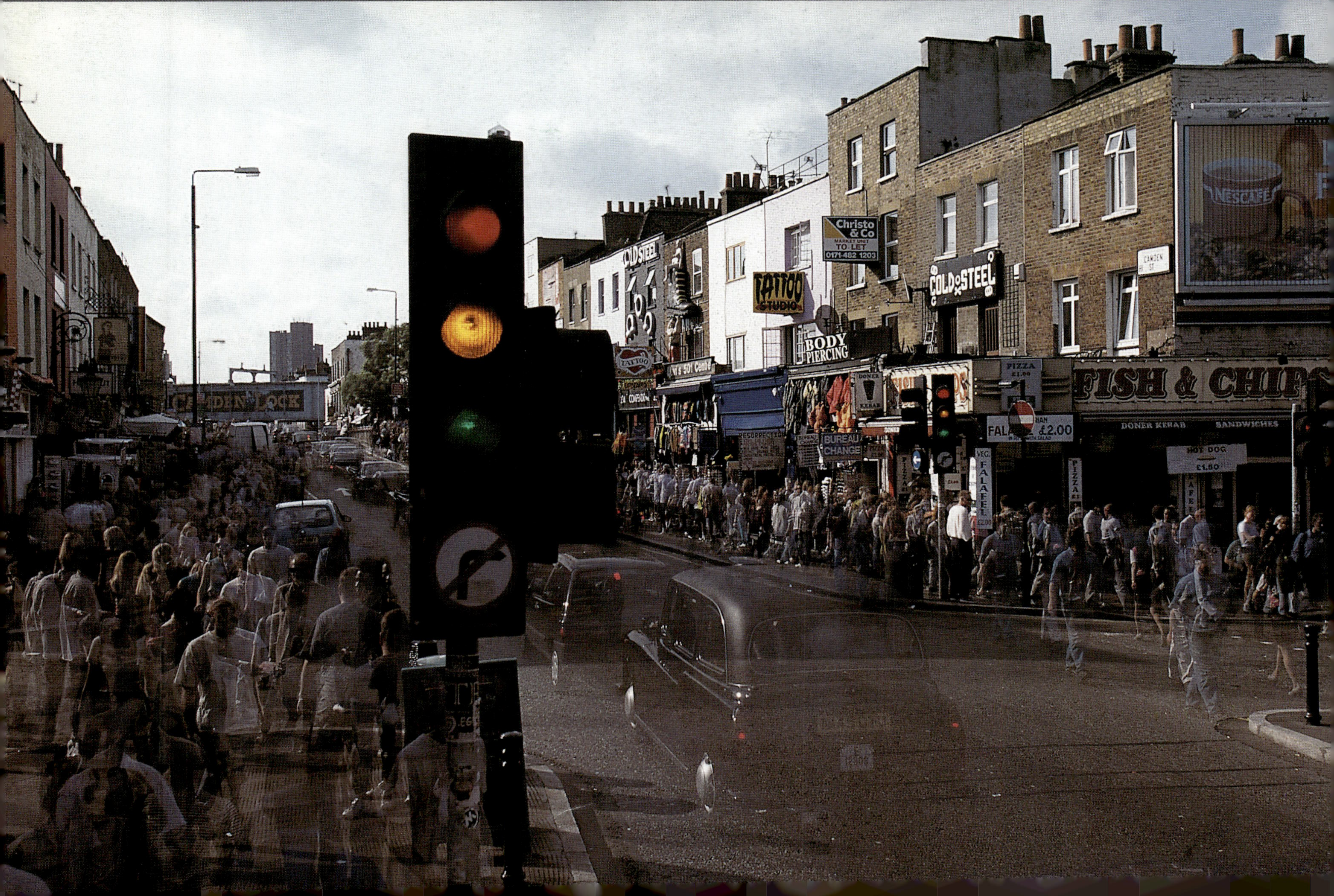

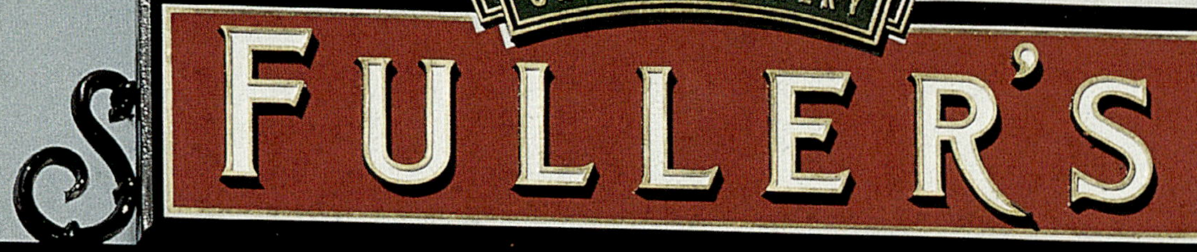
GRIFFIN BREWERY
FULLER'S

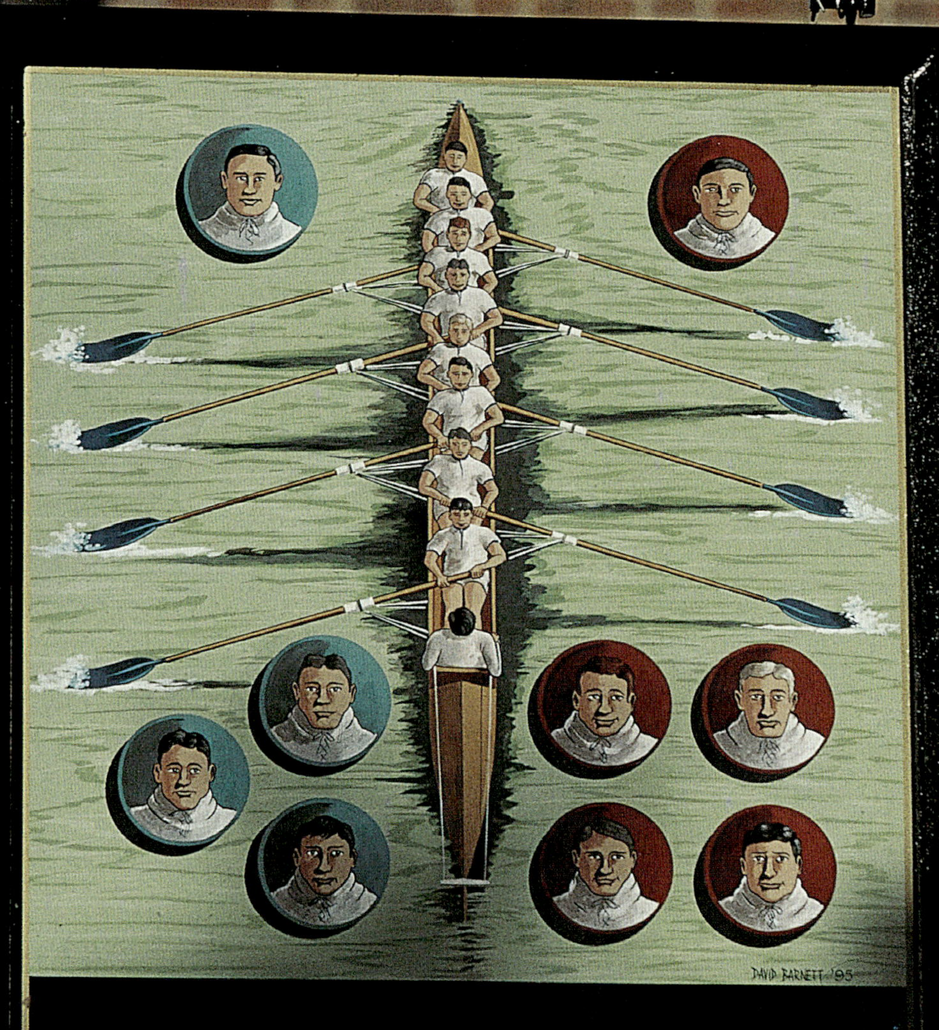
DAVID BARNETT '85
HEAD OF THE RIVER

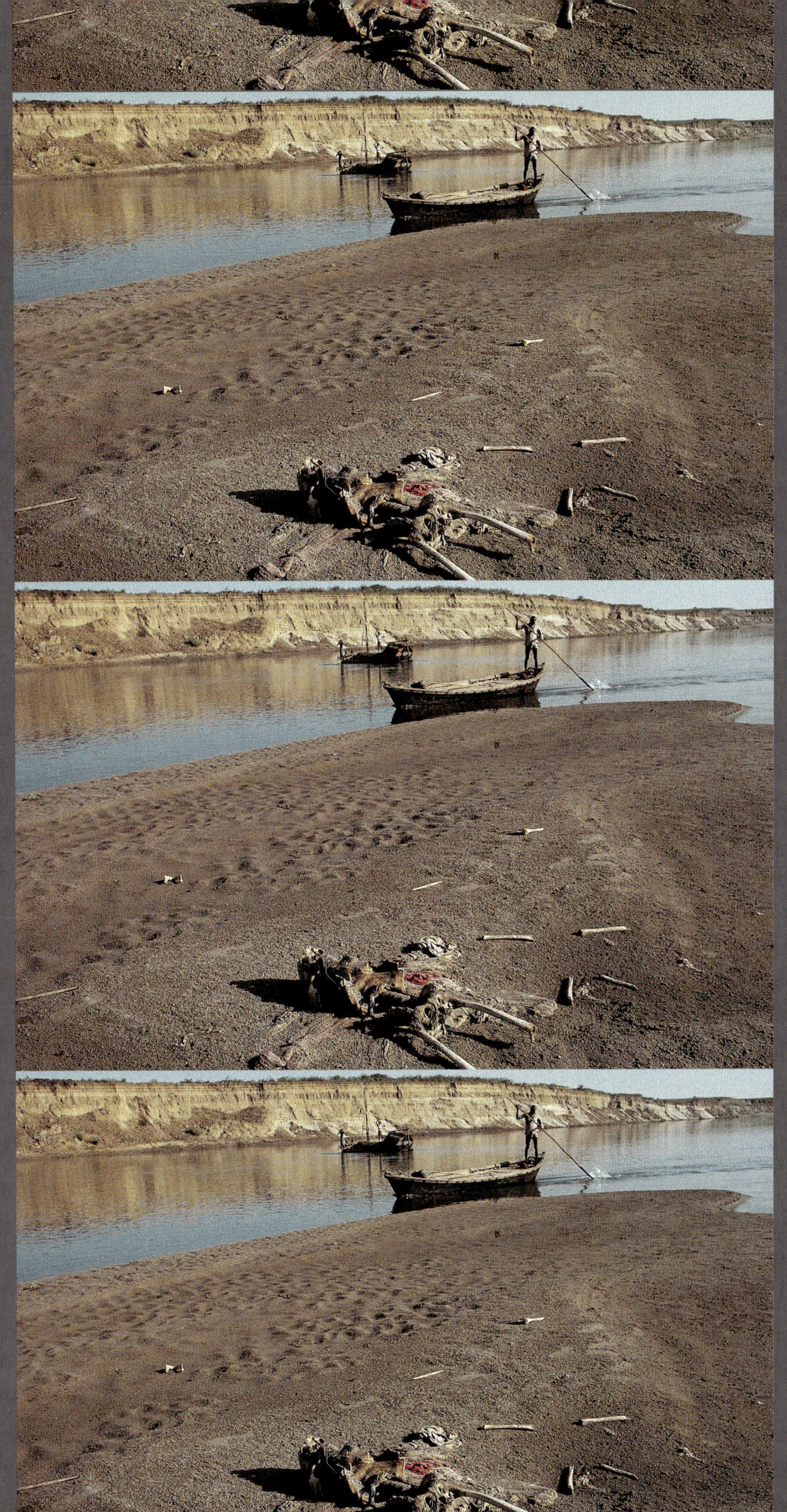

Oxford

Ganges

Trinity College (and the library gargoyle), Oxford

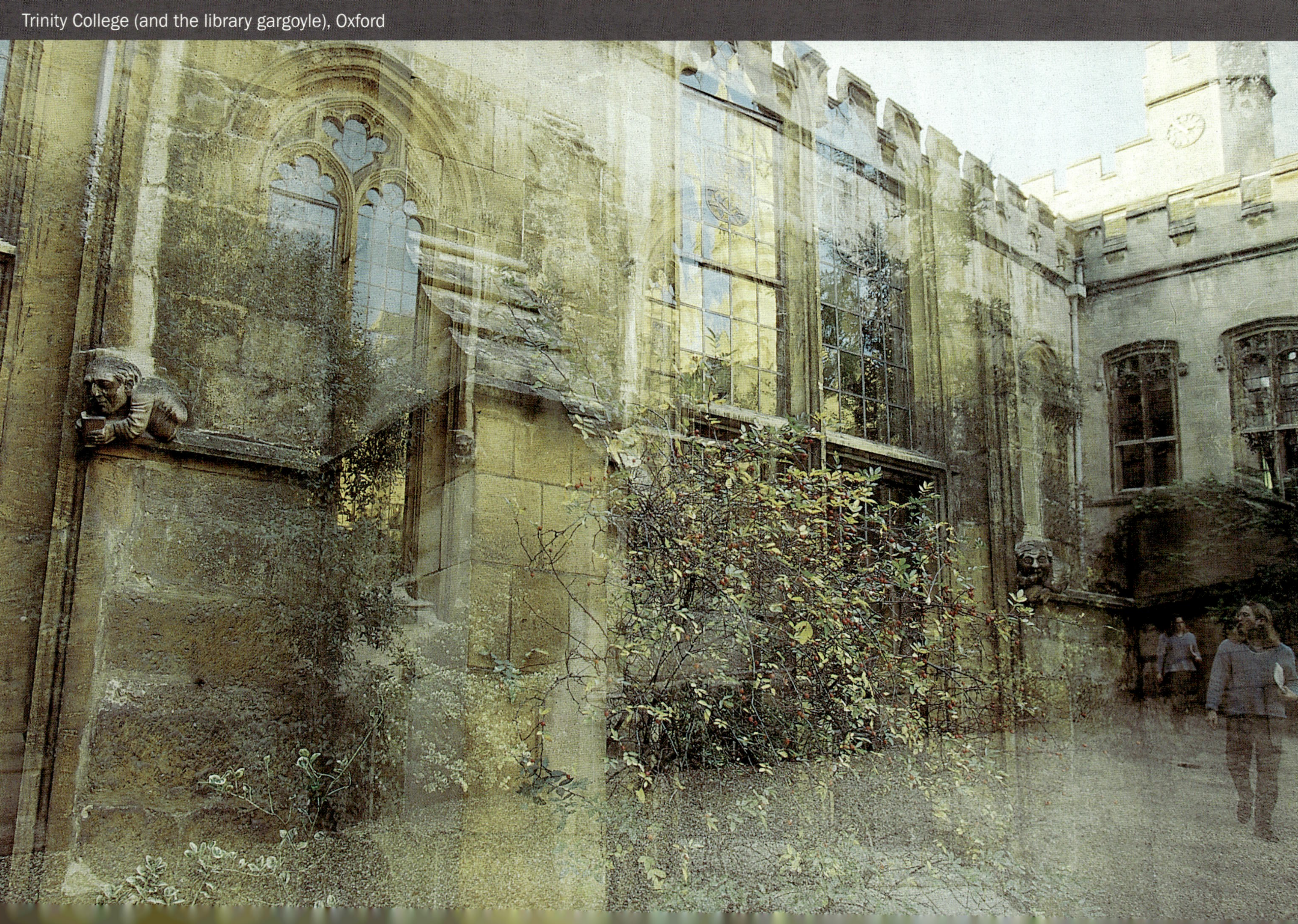

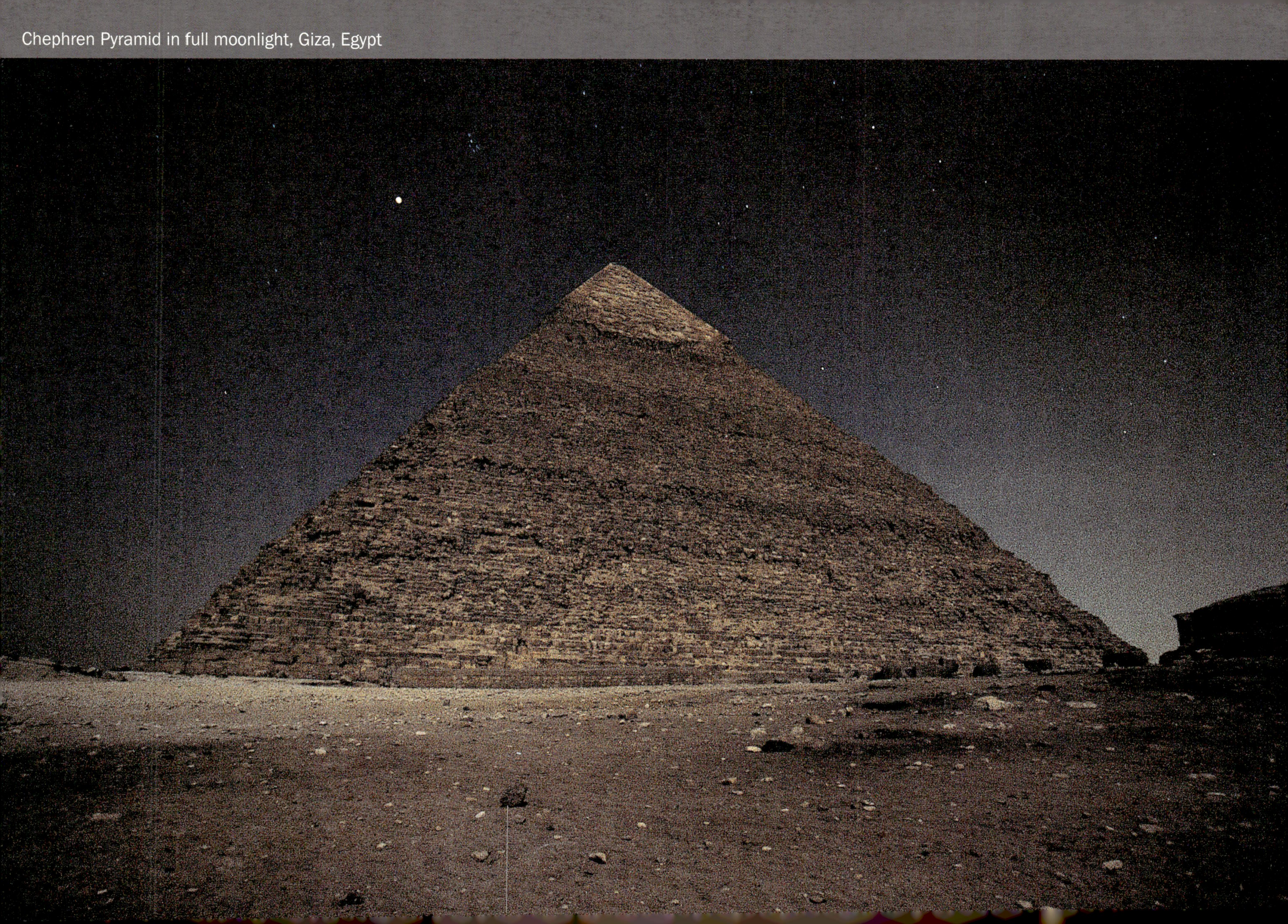

Chephren Pyramid in full moonlight, Giza, Egypt

Shark fin – aphrodisiac

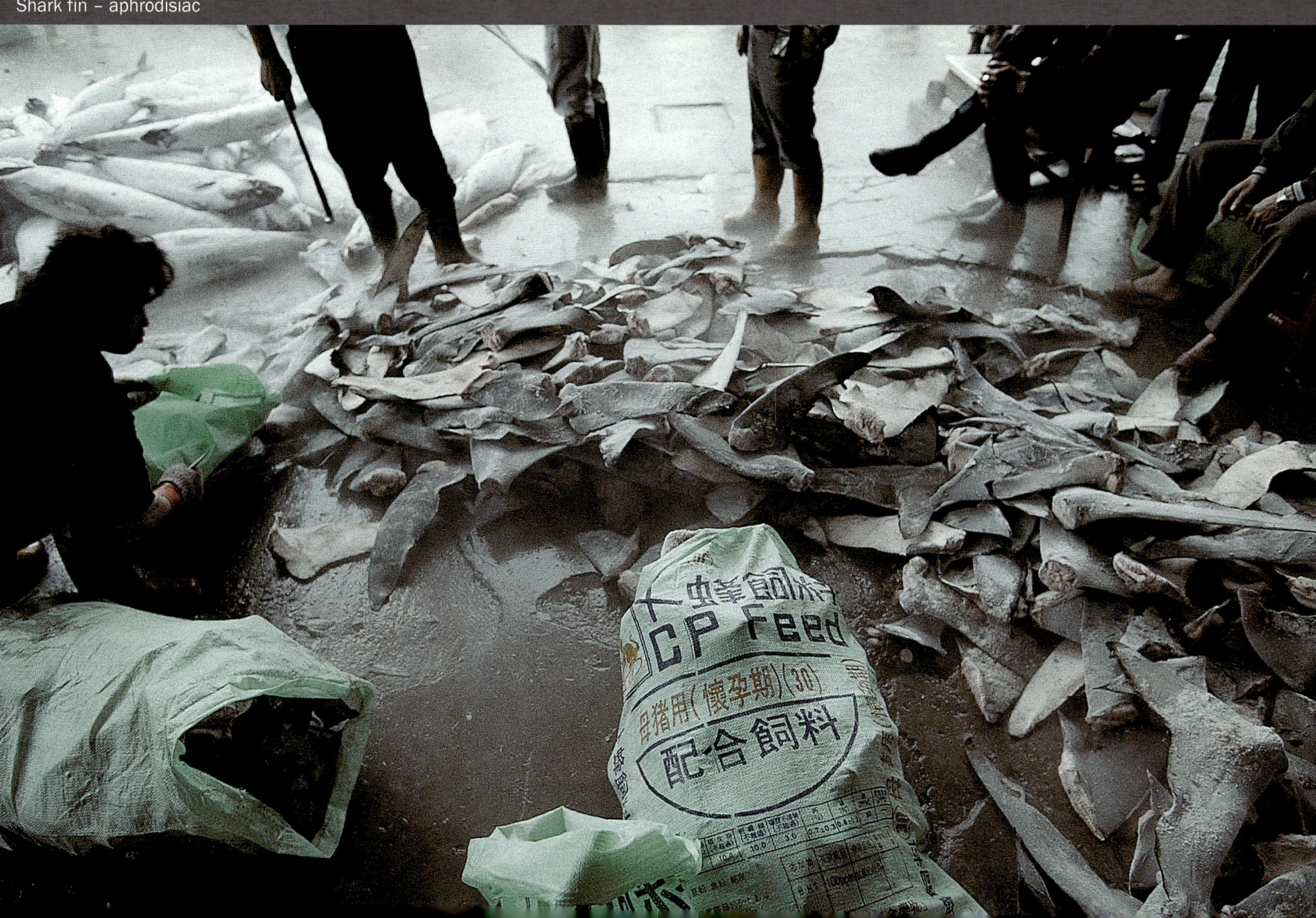

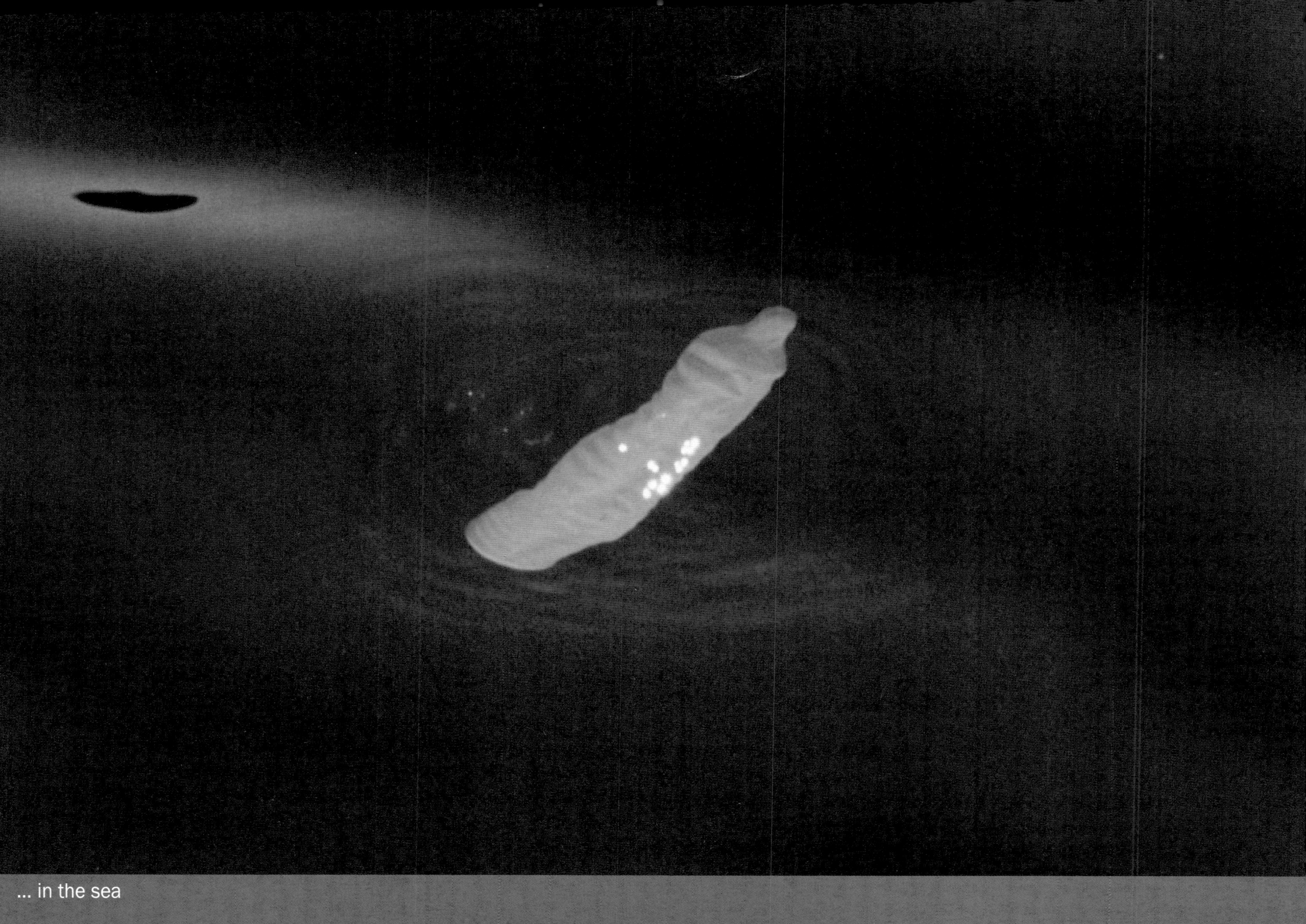

... in the sea

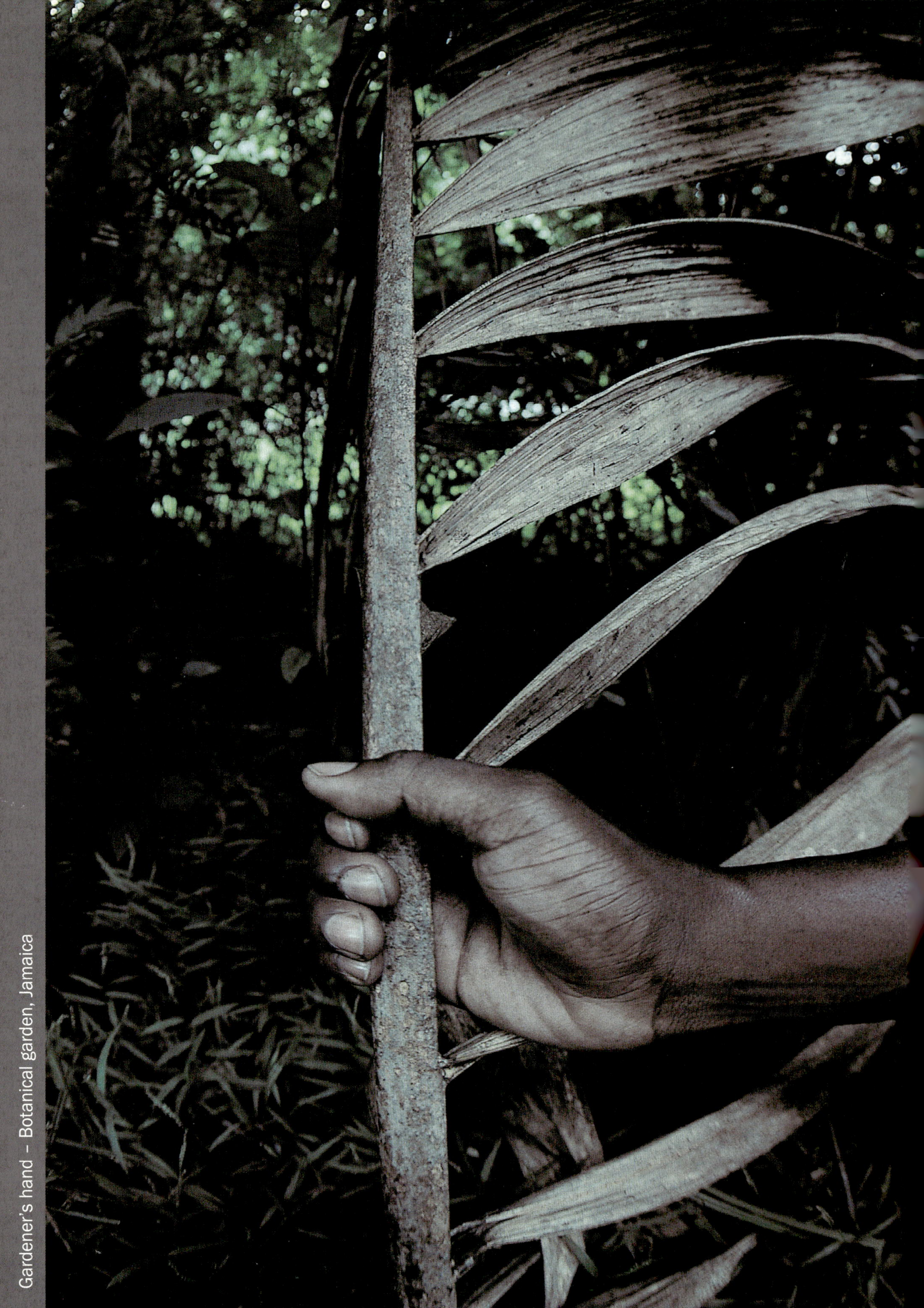

Gardener's hand – Botanical garden, Jamaica

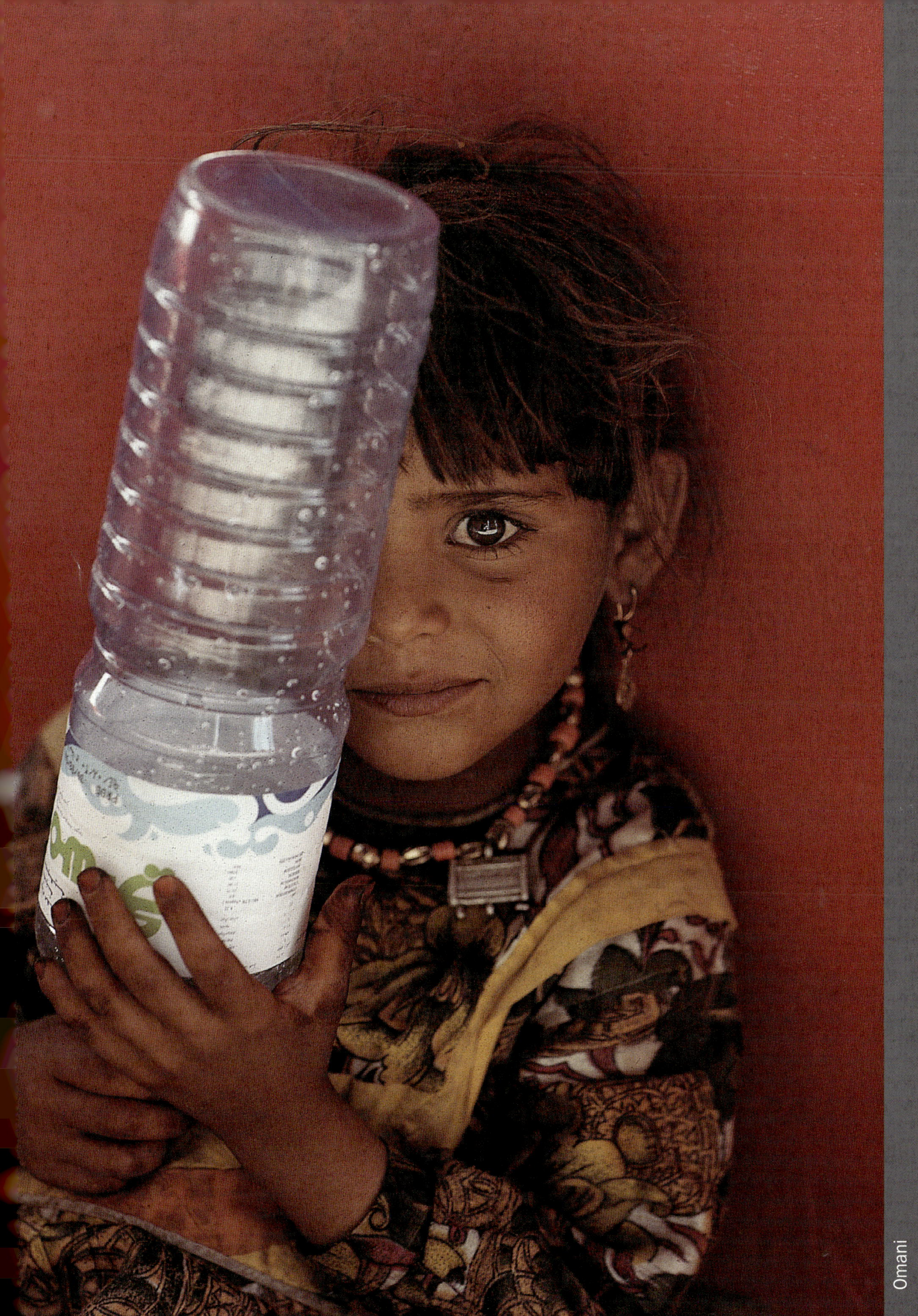

Nile, Sudan

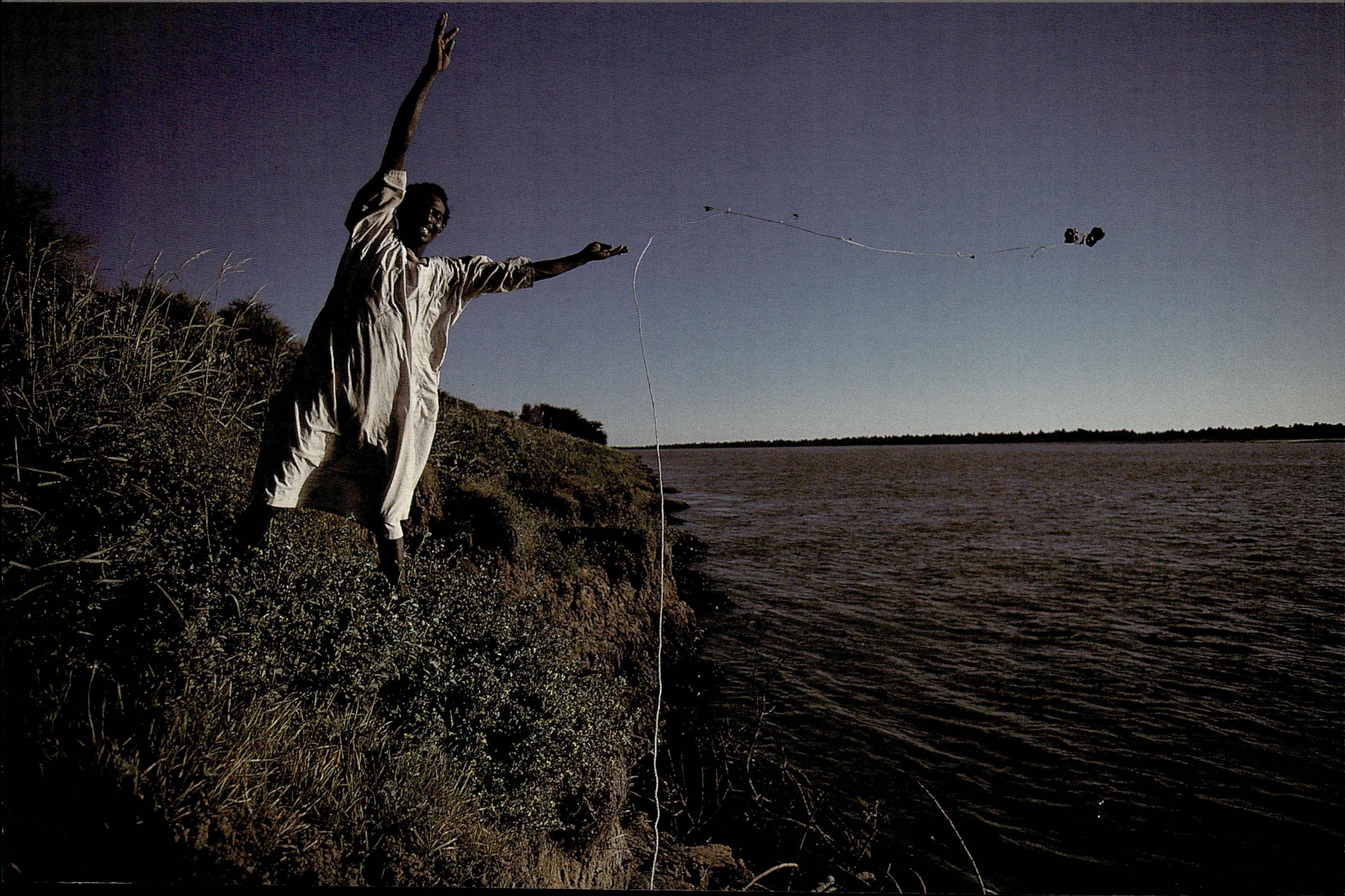

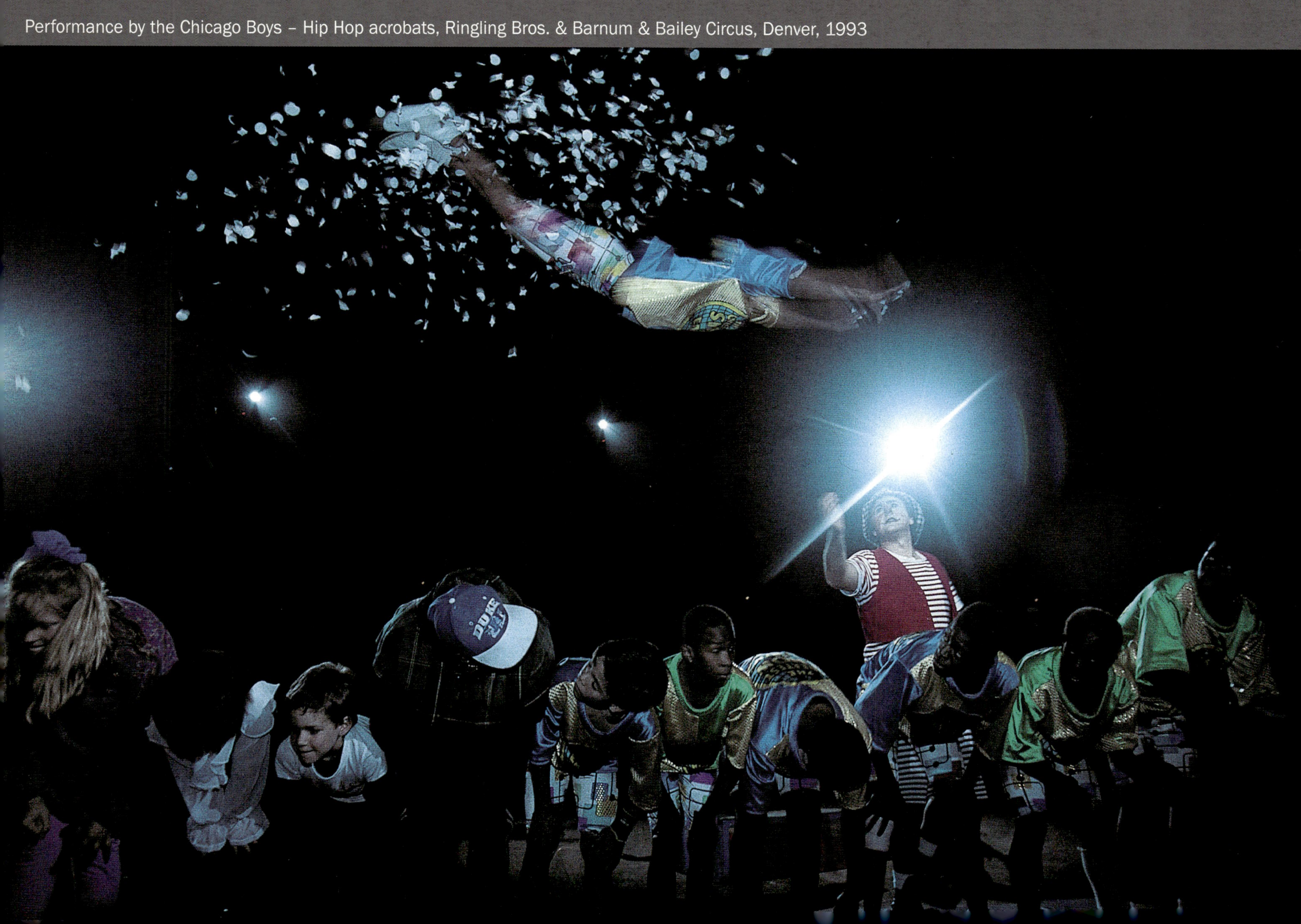

Performance by the Chicago Boys – Hip Hop acrobats, Ringling Bros. & Barnum & Bailey Circus, Denver, 1993

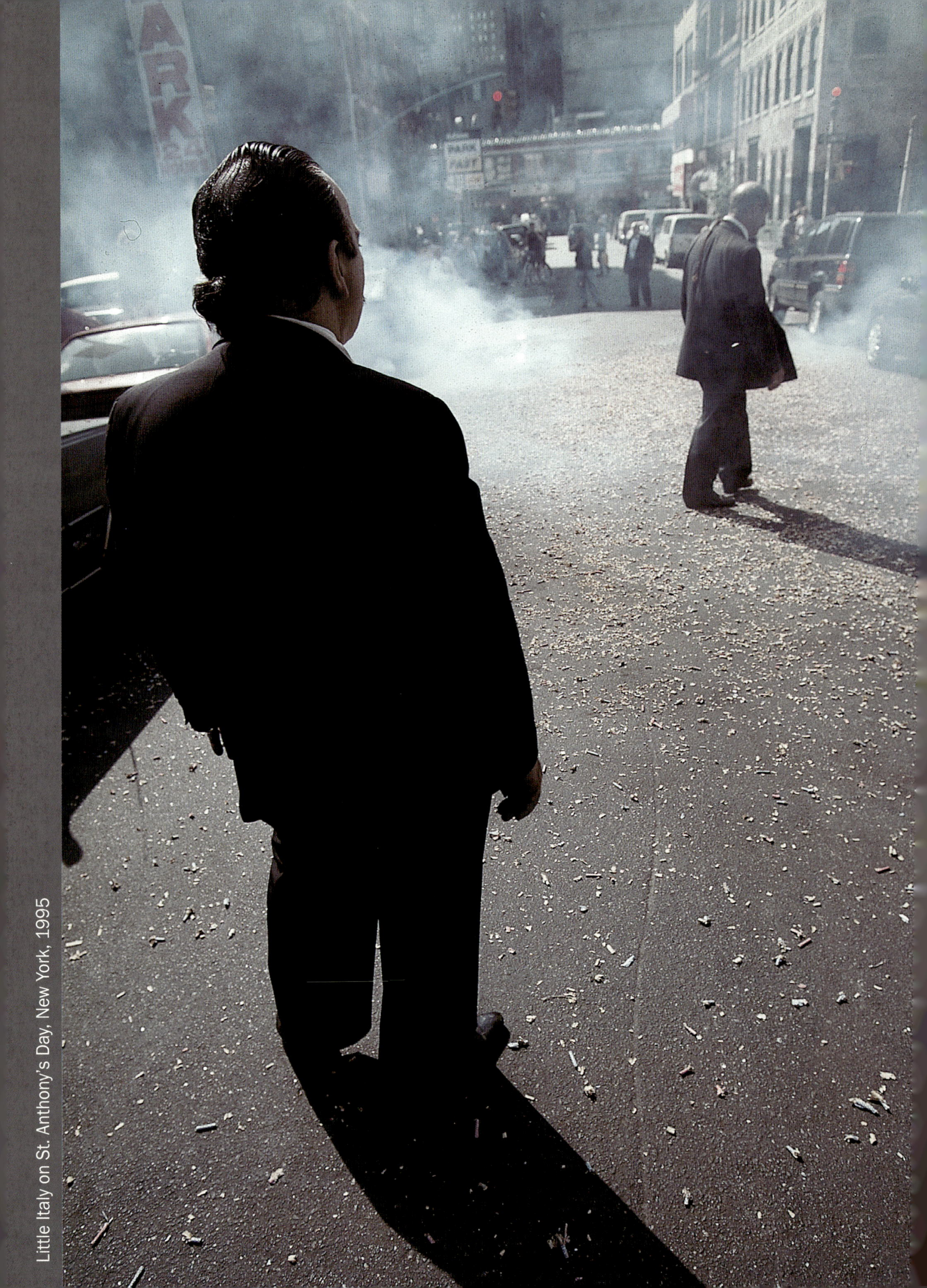

Little Italy on St. Anthony's Day, New York, 1995

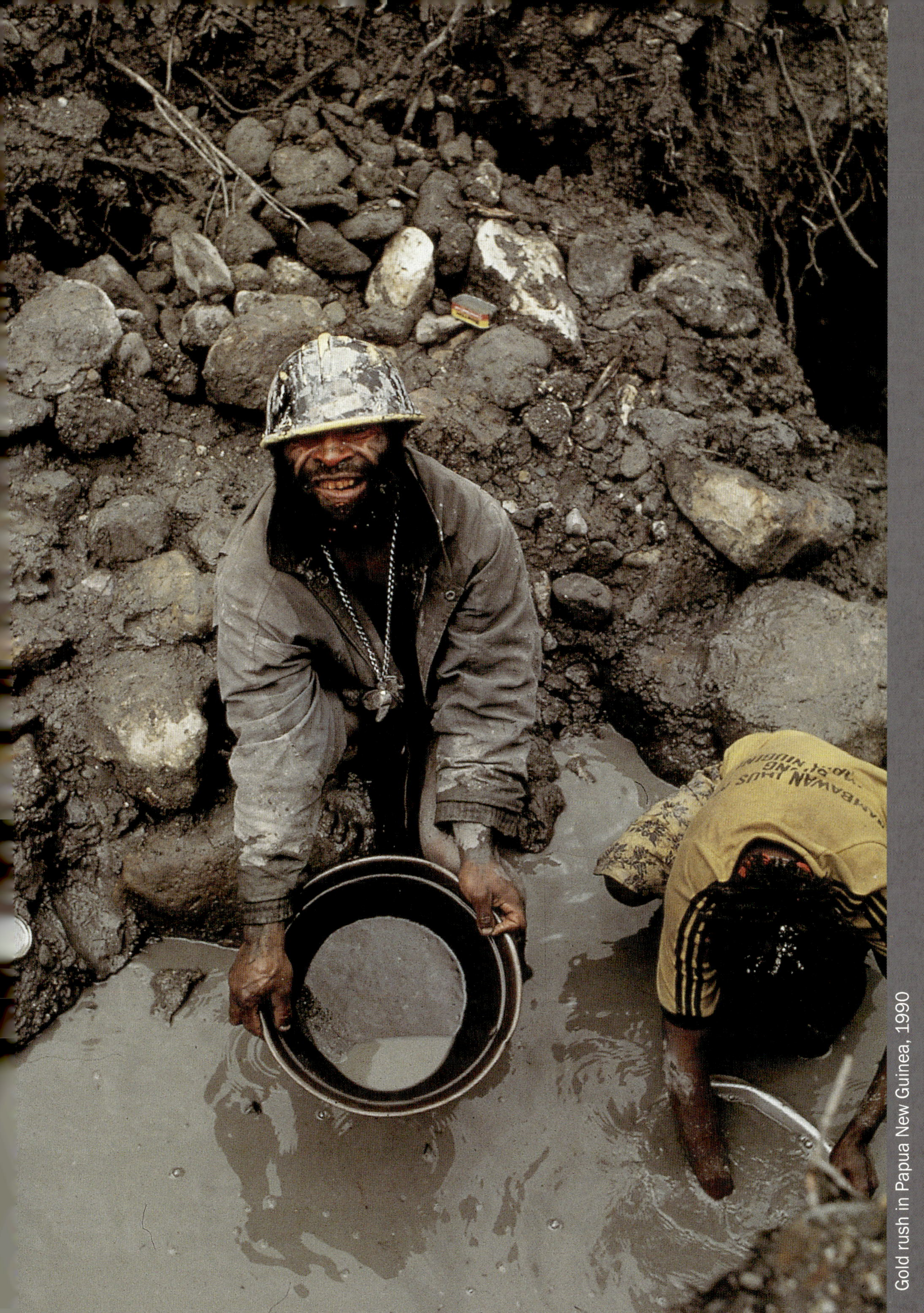

Gold rush in Papua New Guinea, 1990

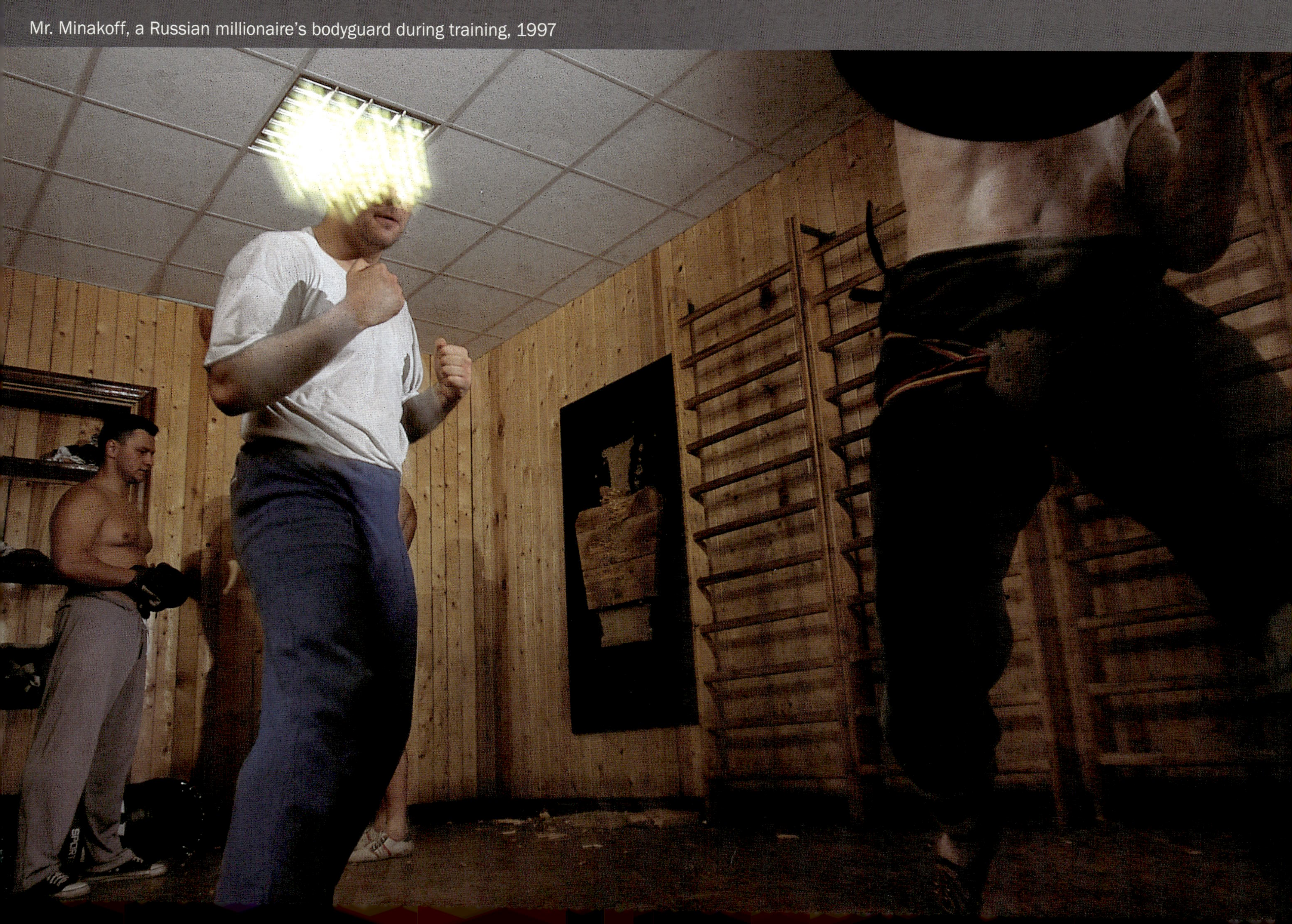

Mr. Minakoff, a Russian millionaire's bodyguard during training, 1997

At the Western Wall during sunrise, Jerusalem, 1994

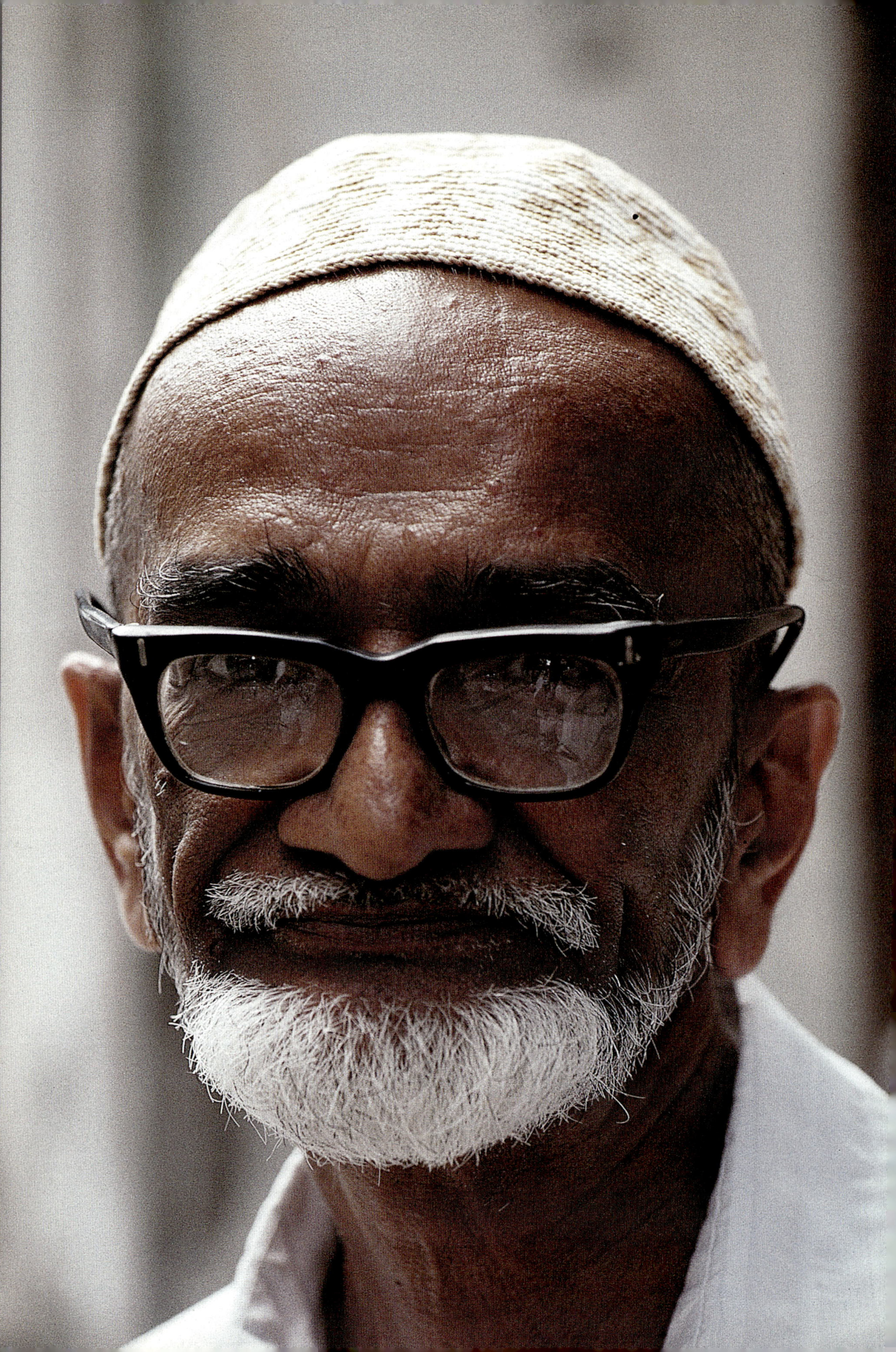

Zanzibar, “Out of Africa”

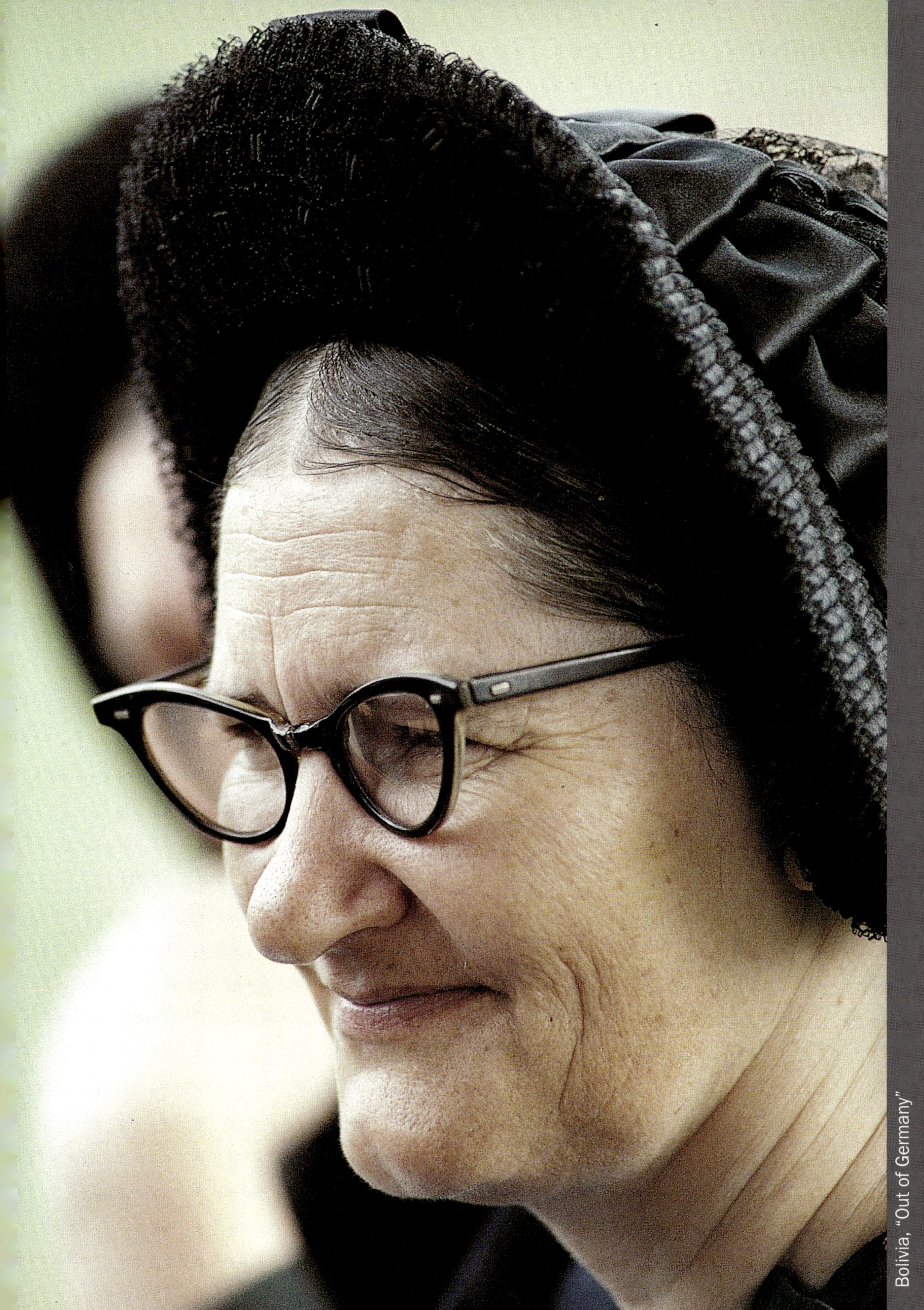

Bolivia, “Out of Germany”

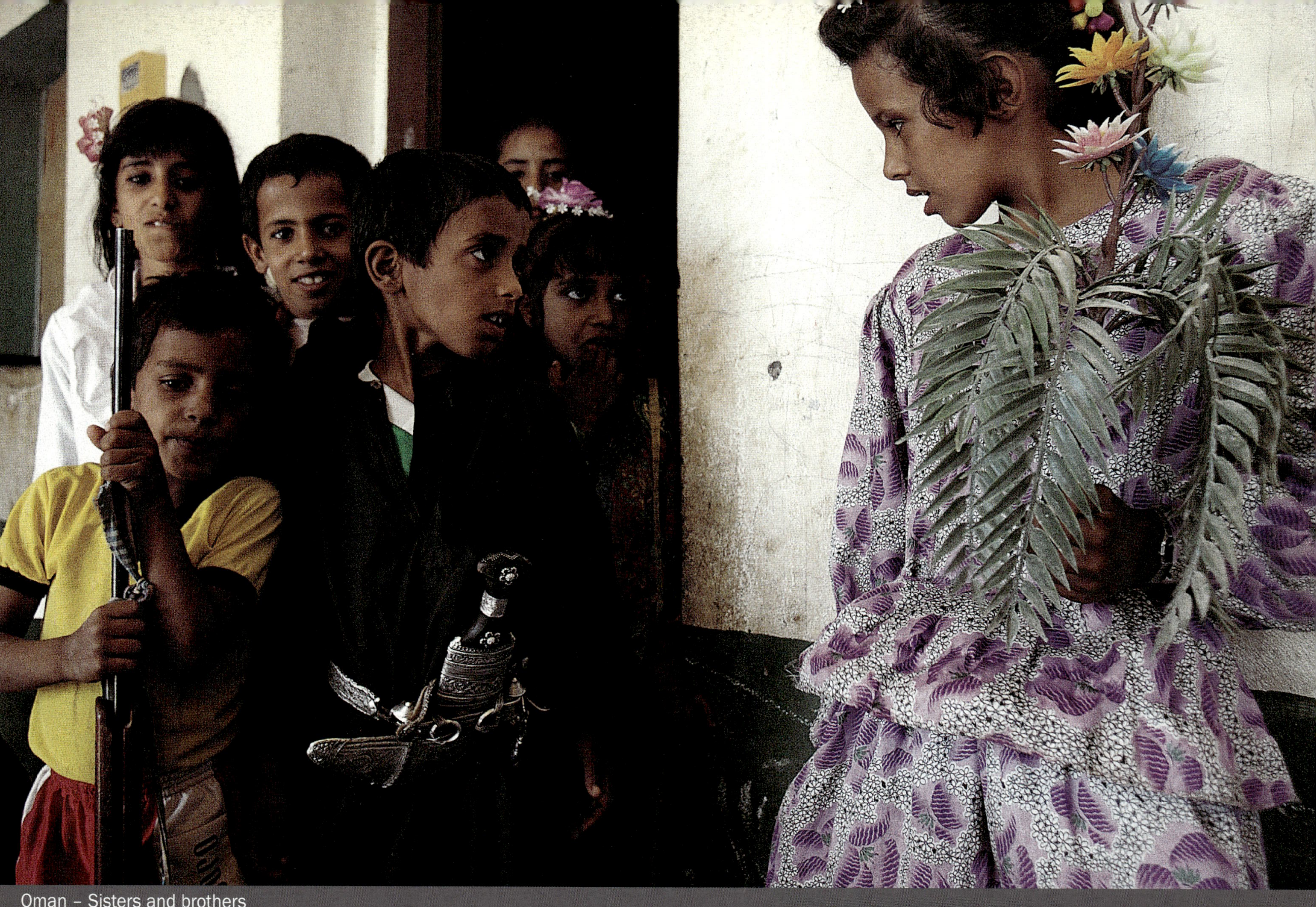

Oman – Sisters and brothers

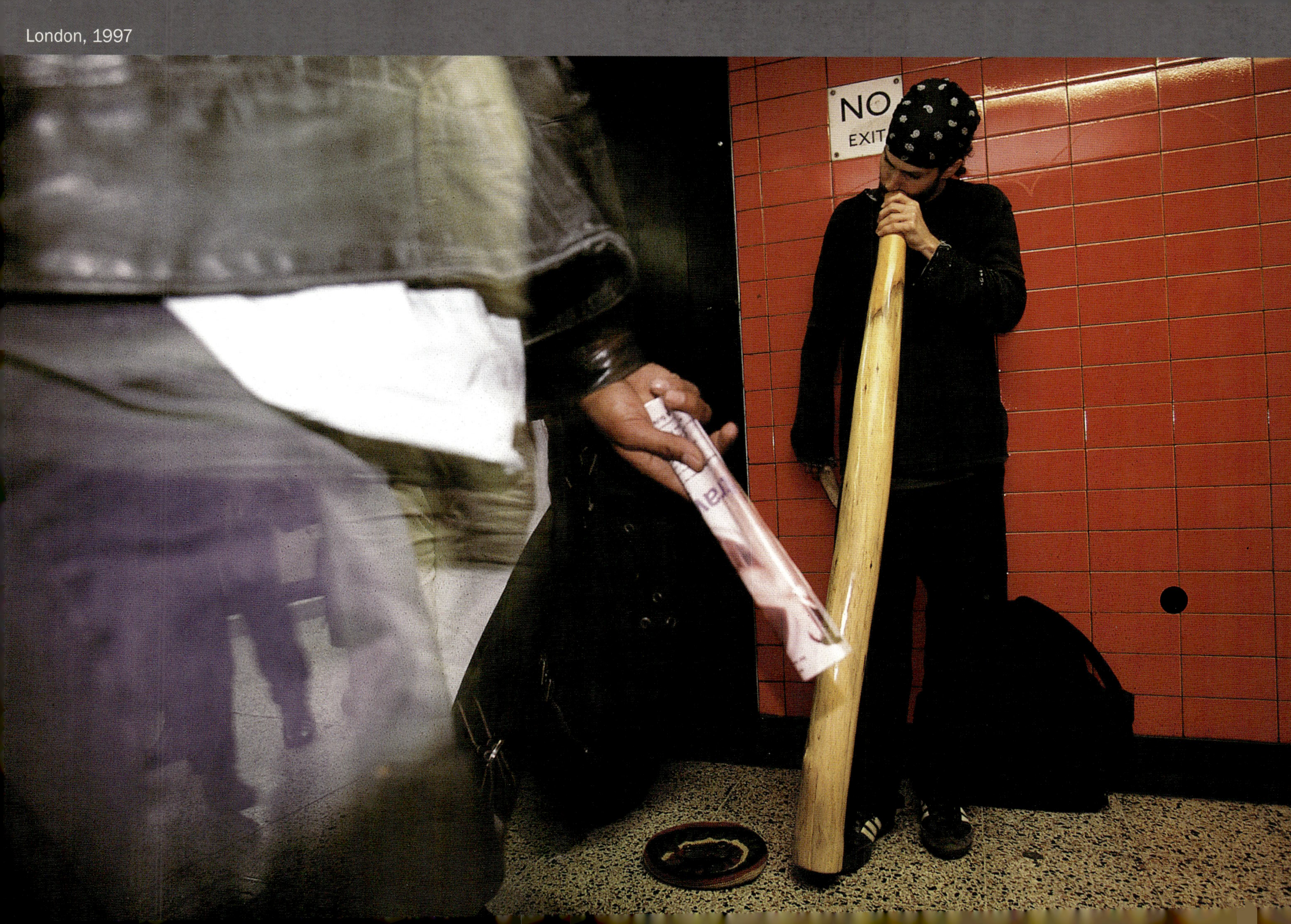

London, 1997

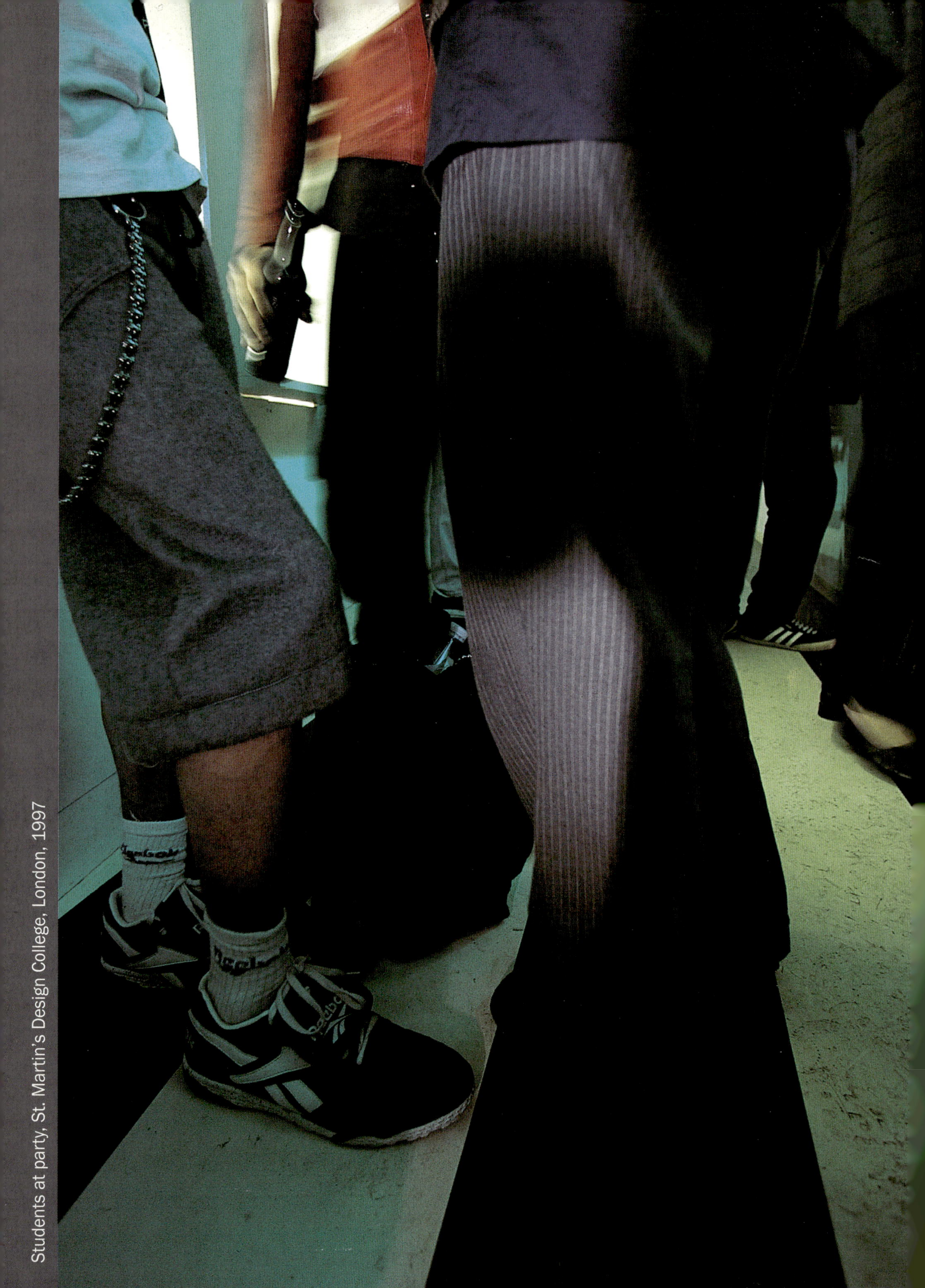

Students at party, St. Martin's Design College, London, 1997

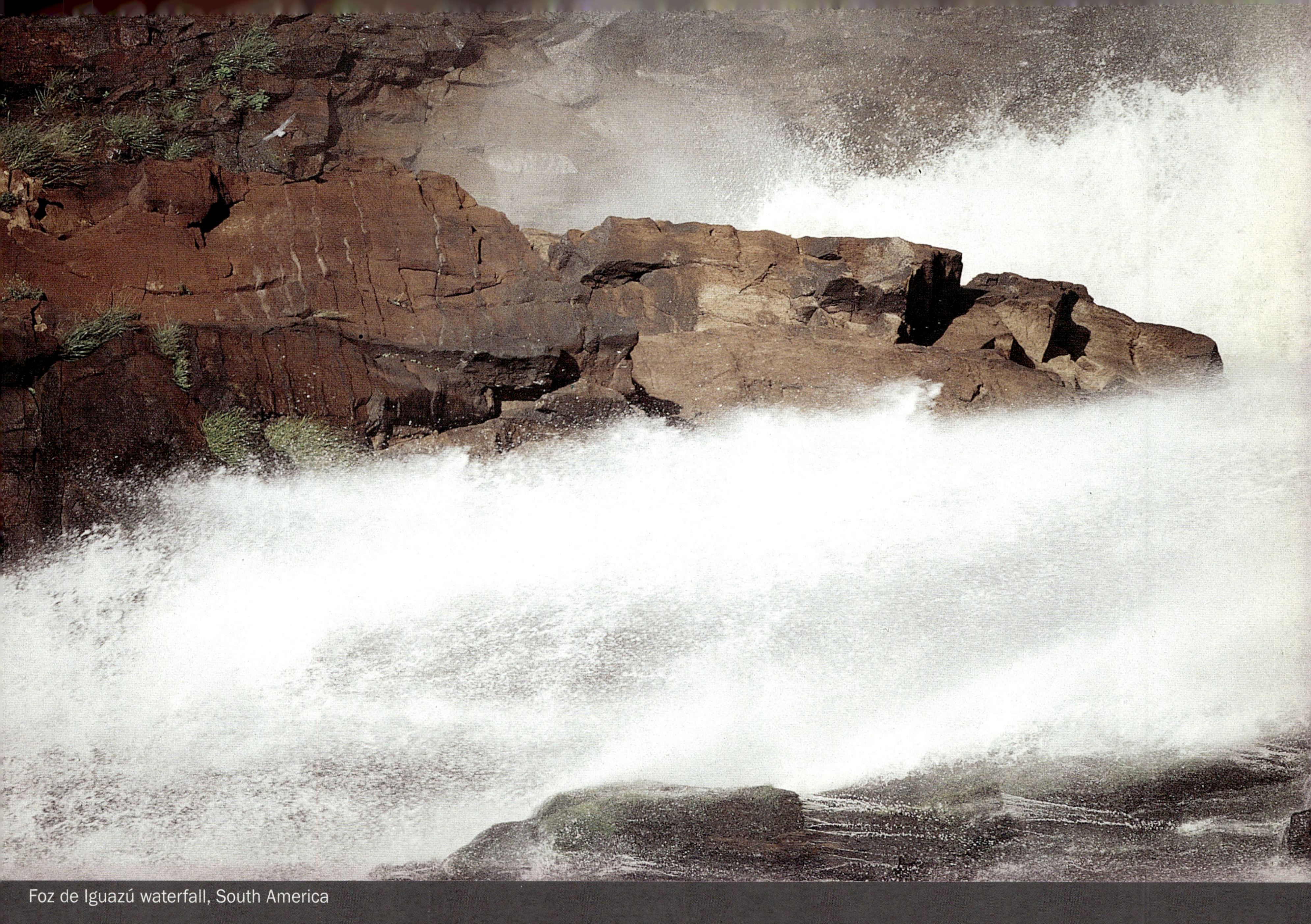

Foz de Iguazú waterfall, South America

Highland forest, Europe

ABC Hispanic district in Manhattan, New York, 1995

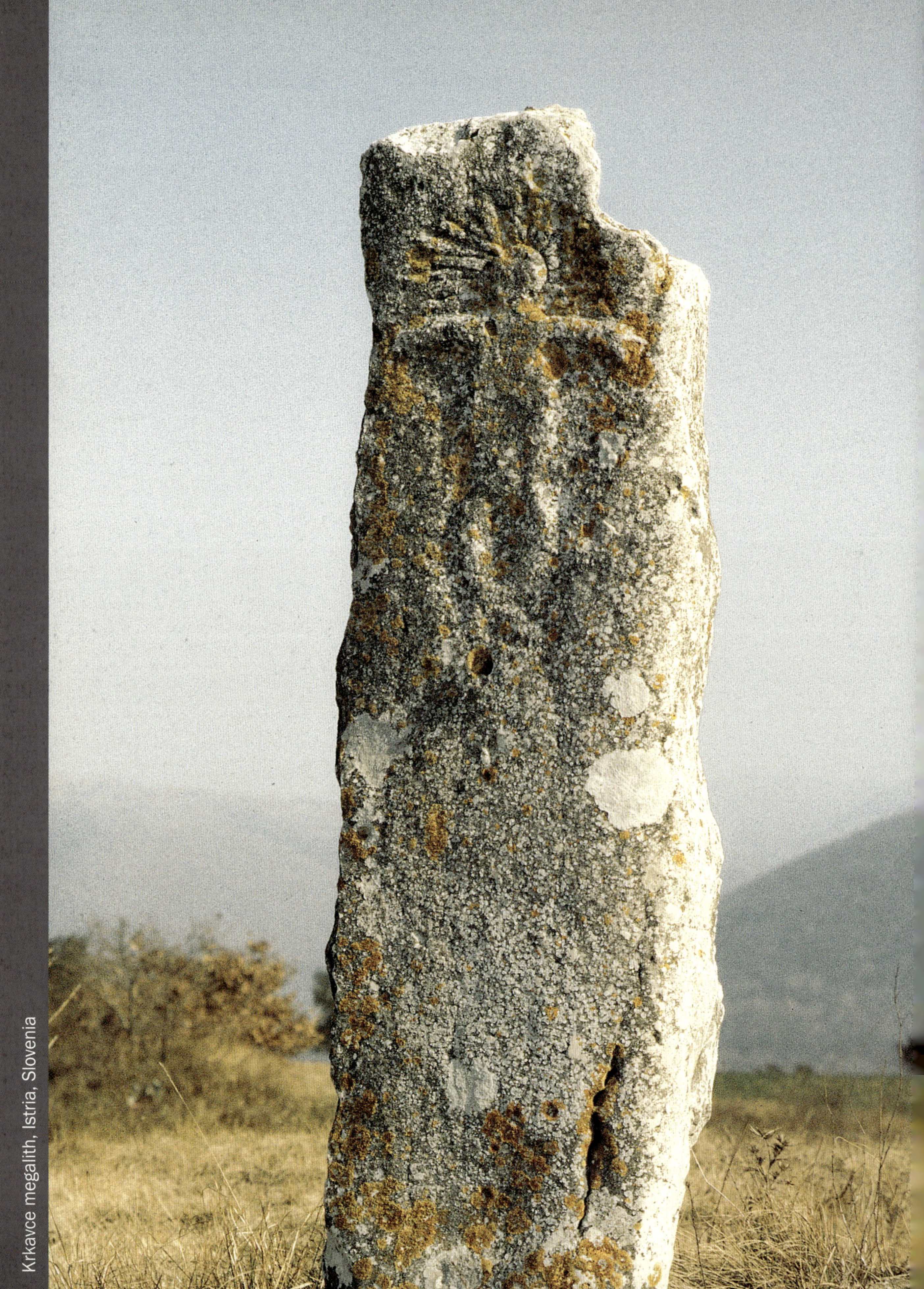

Krkavce megalith, Istria, Slovenia

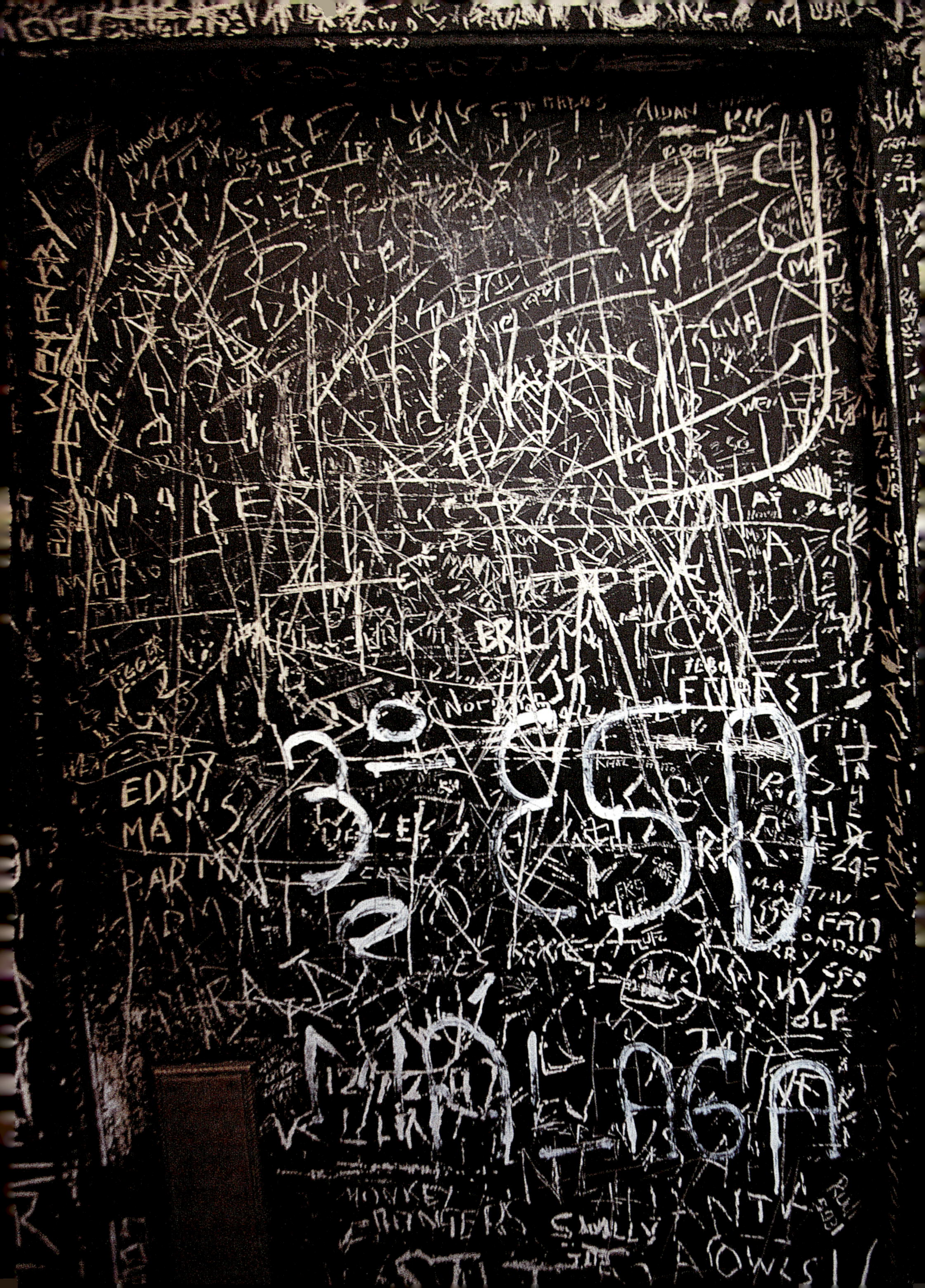
MUFC
BRUM
FOREST
EDDY

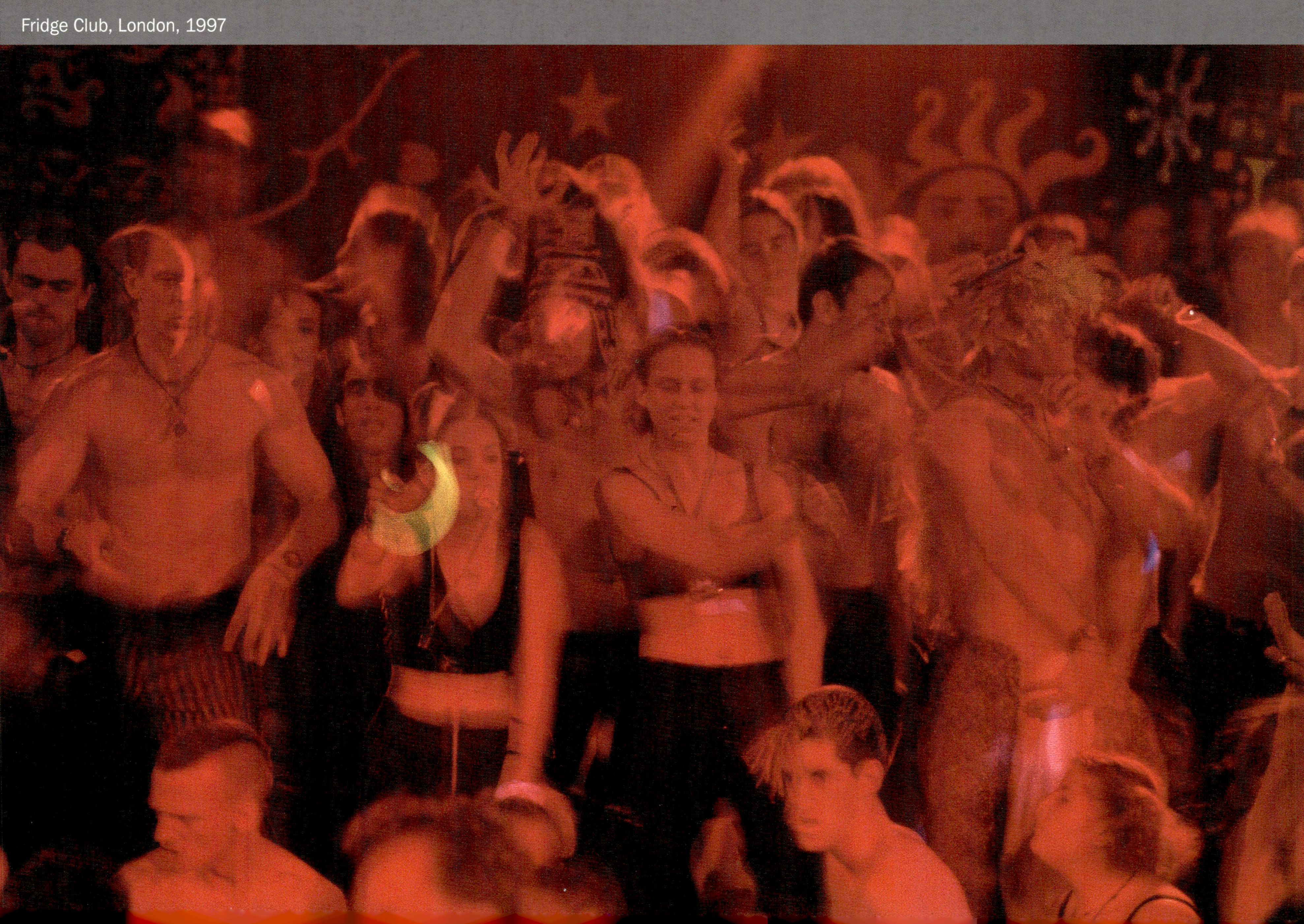

Fridge Club, London, 1997

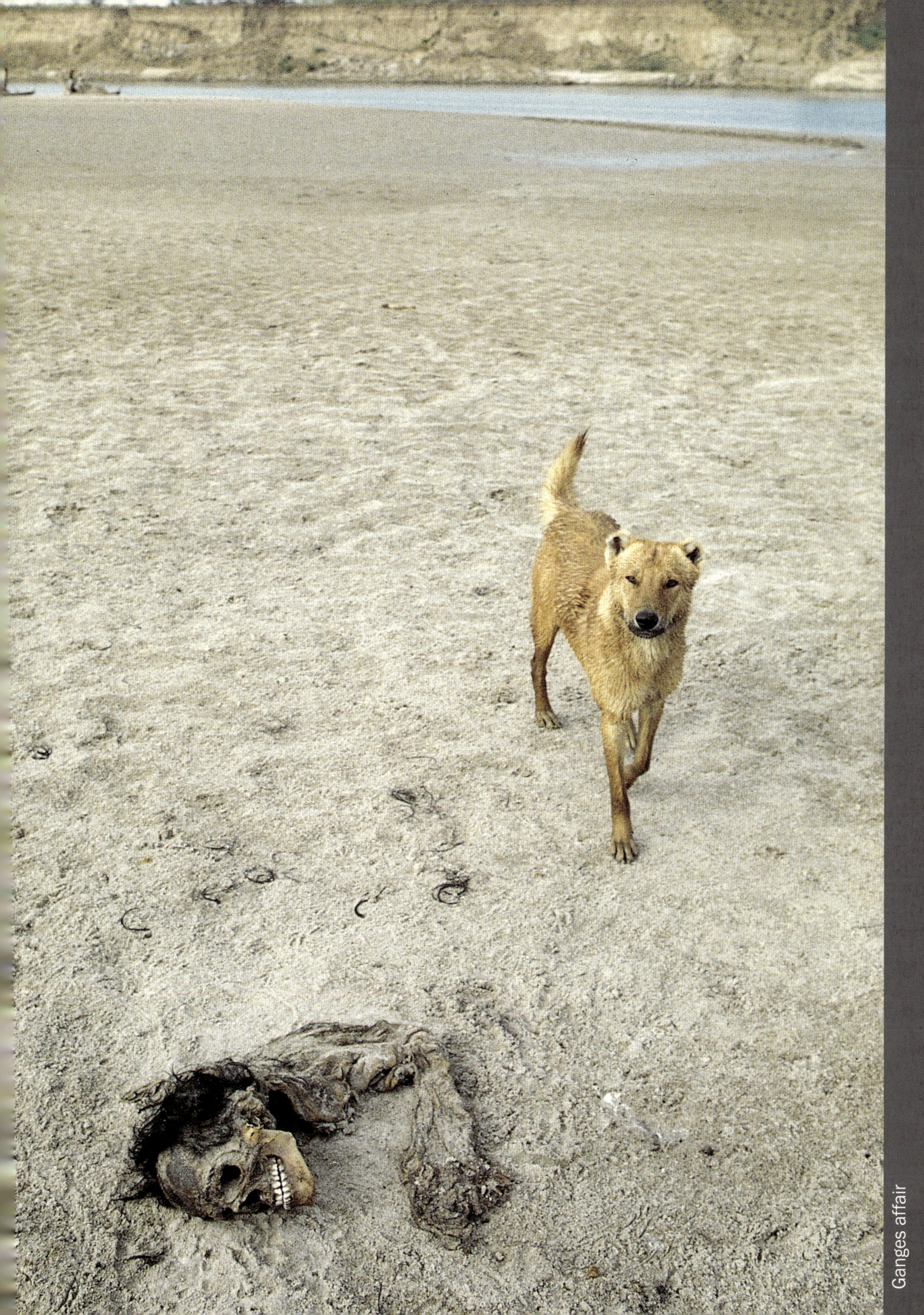

Ganges affair

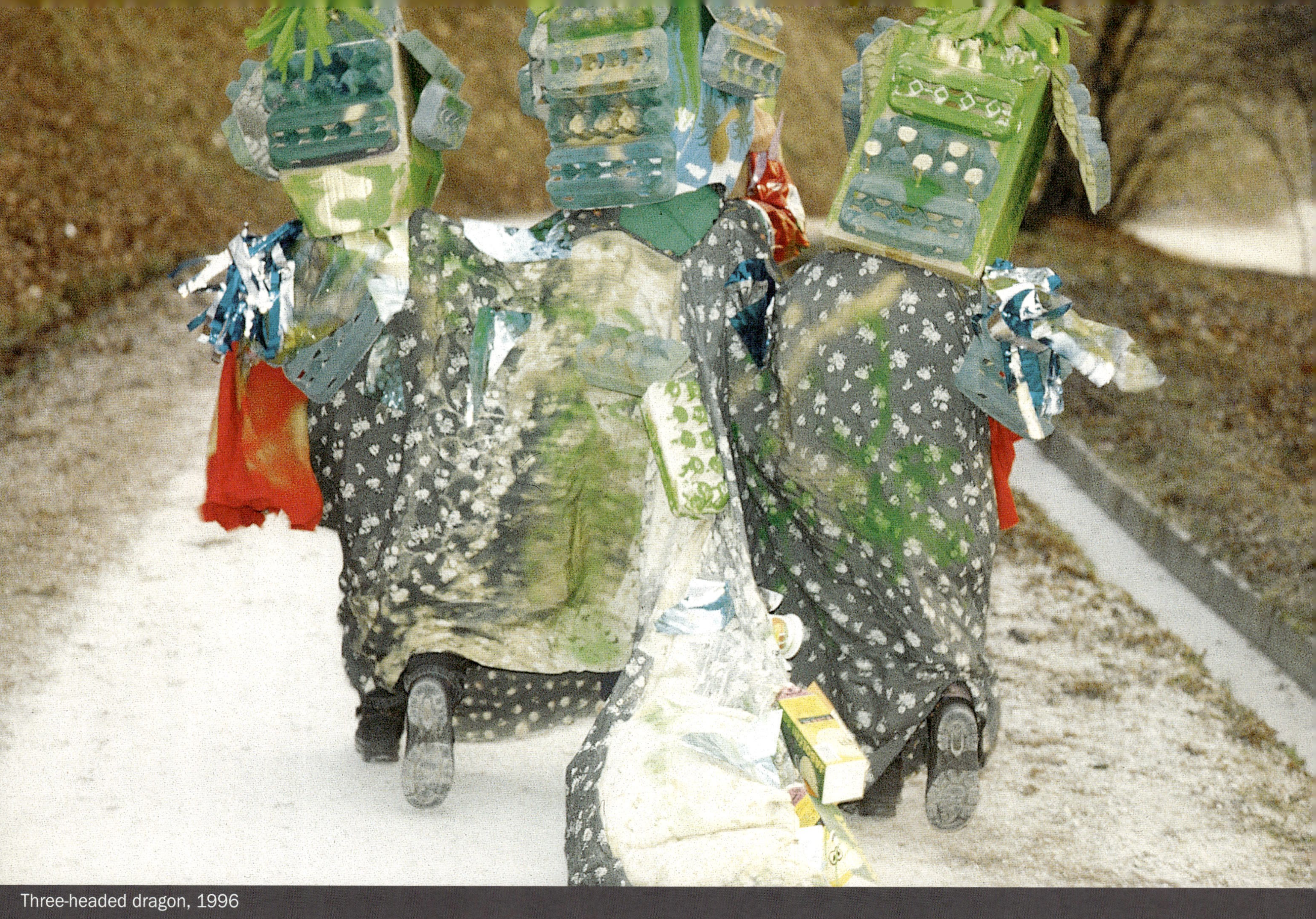

Three-headed dragon, 1996

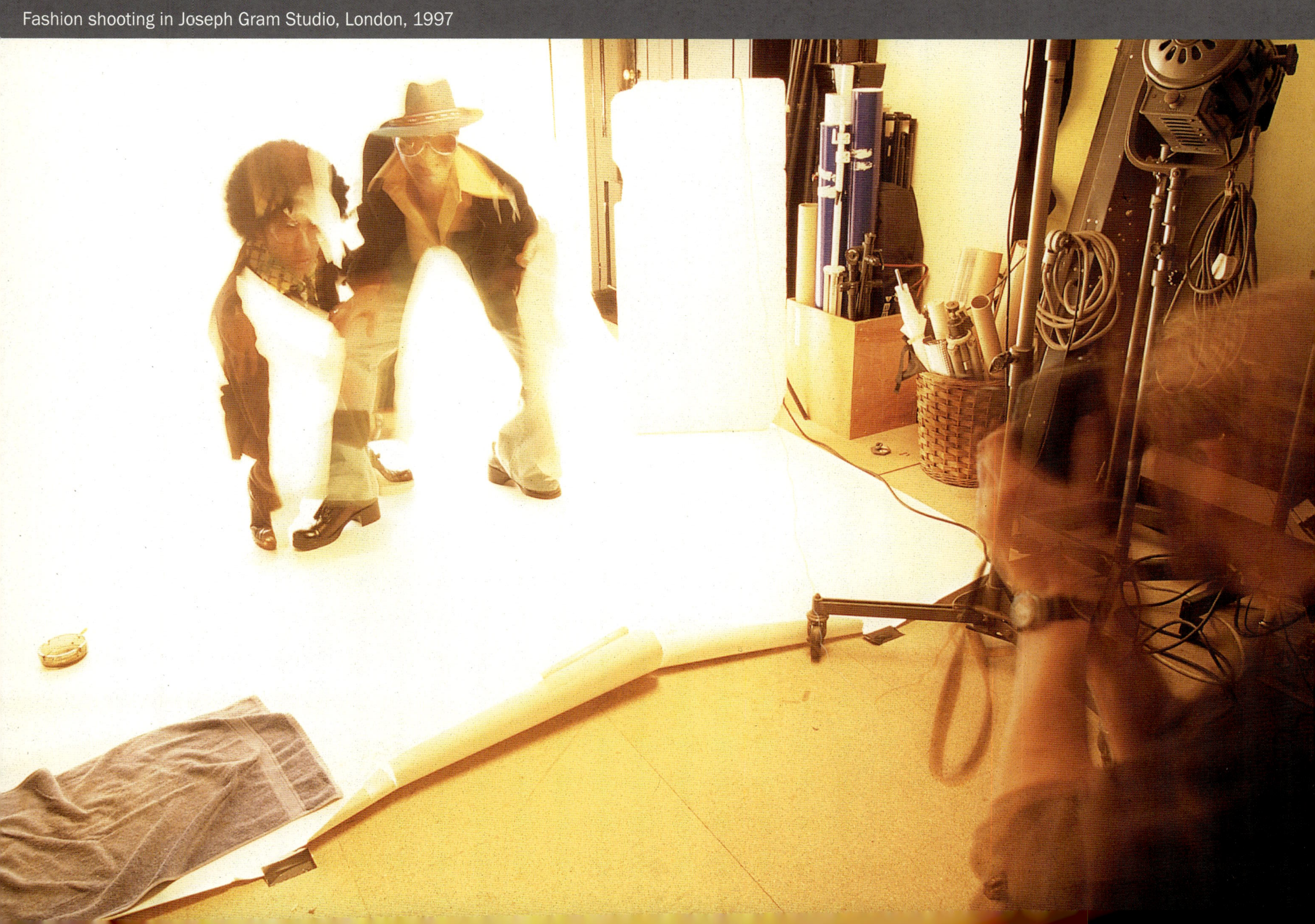

Fashion shooting in Joseph Gram Studio, London, 1997

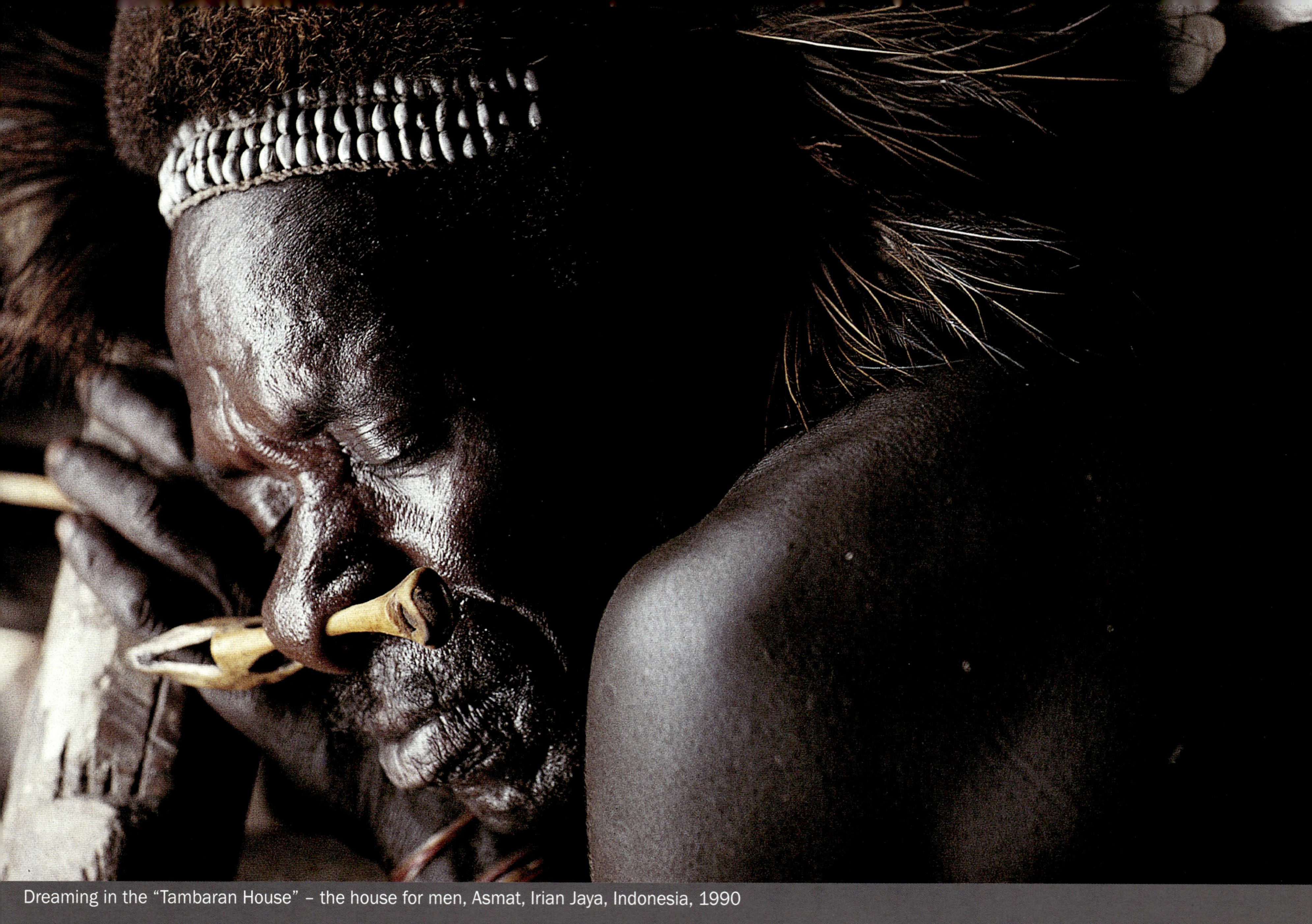

Dreaming in the “Tambaran House” – the house for men, Asmat, Irian Jaya, Indonesia, 1990

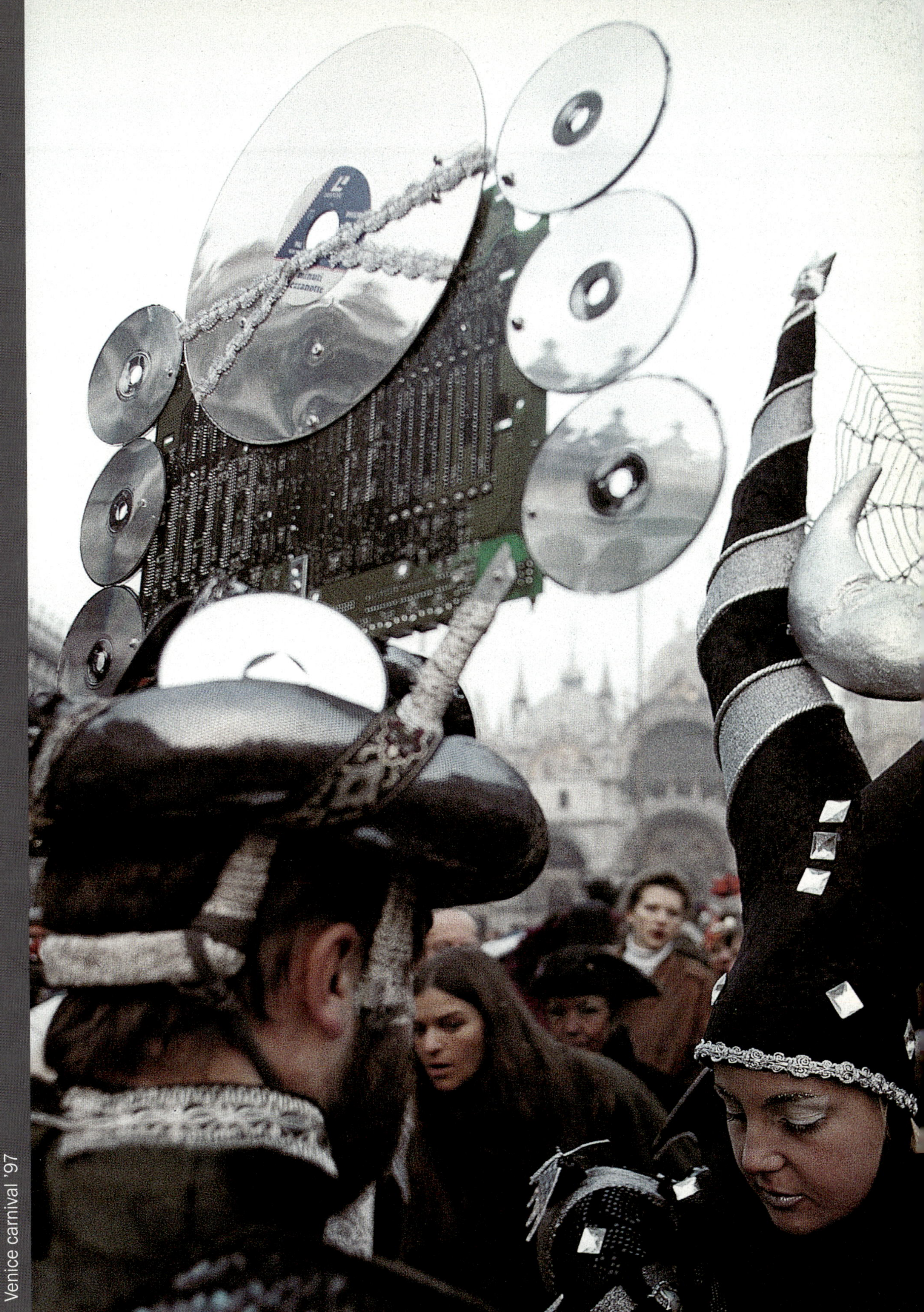

Venice carnival '97

Twin Tower, New York

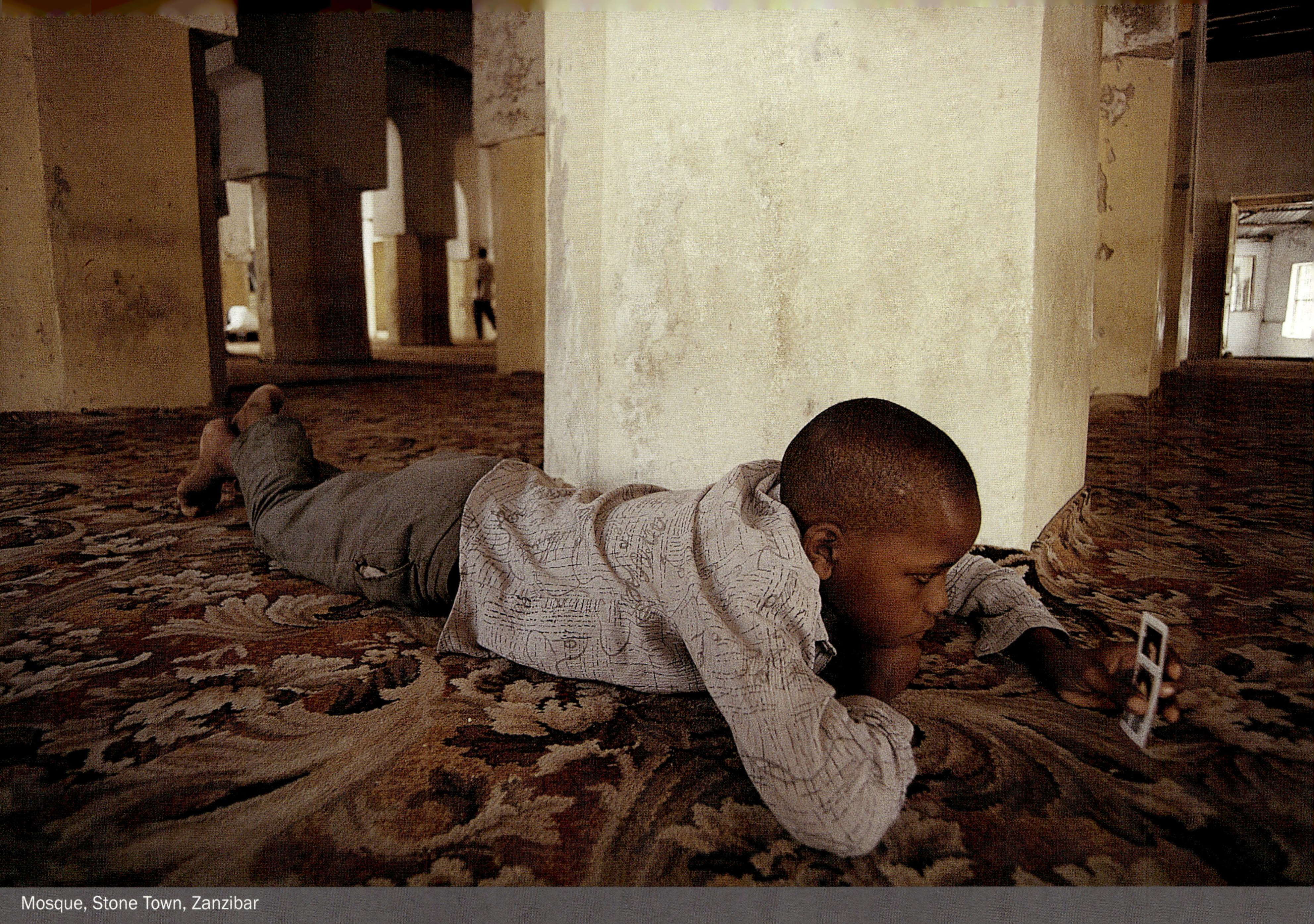

Mosque, Stone Town, Zanzibar

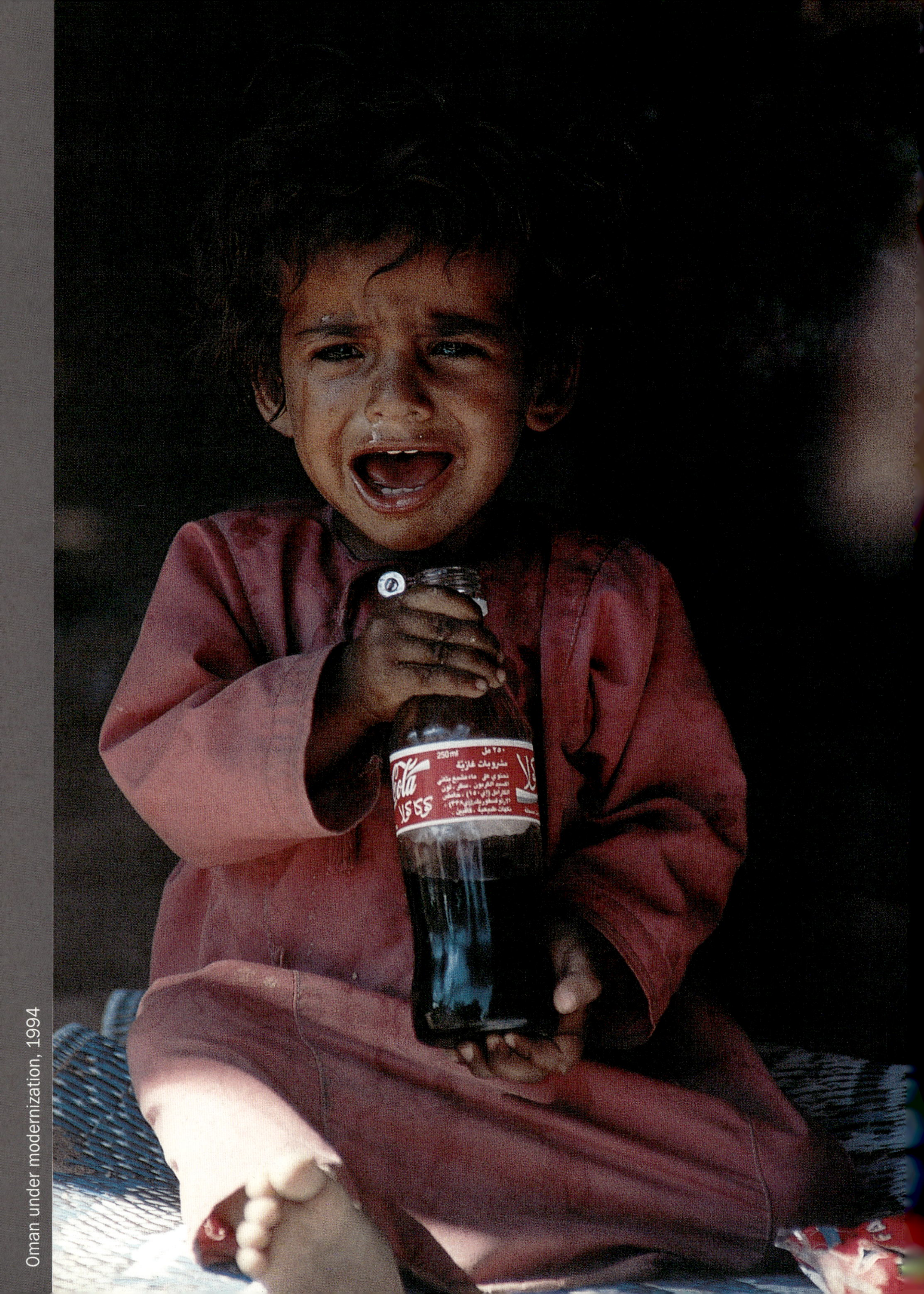

Oman under modernization, 1994

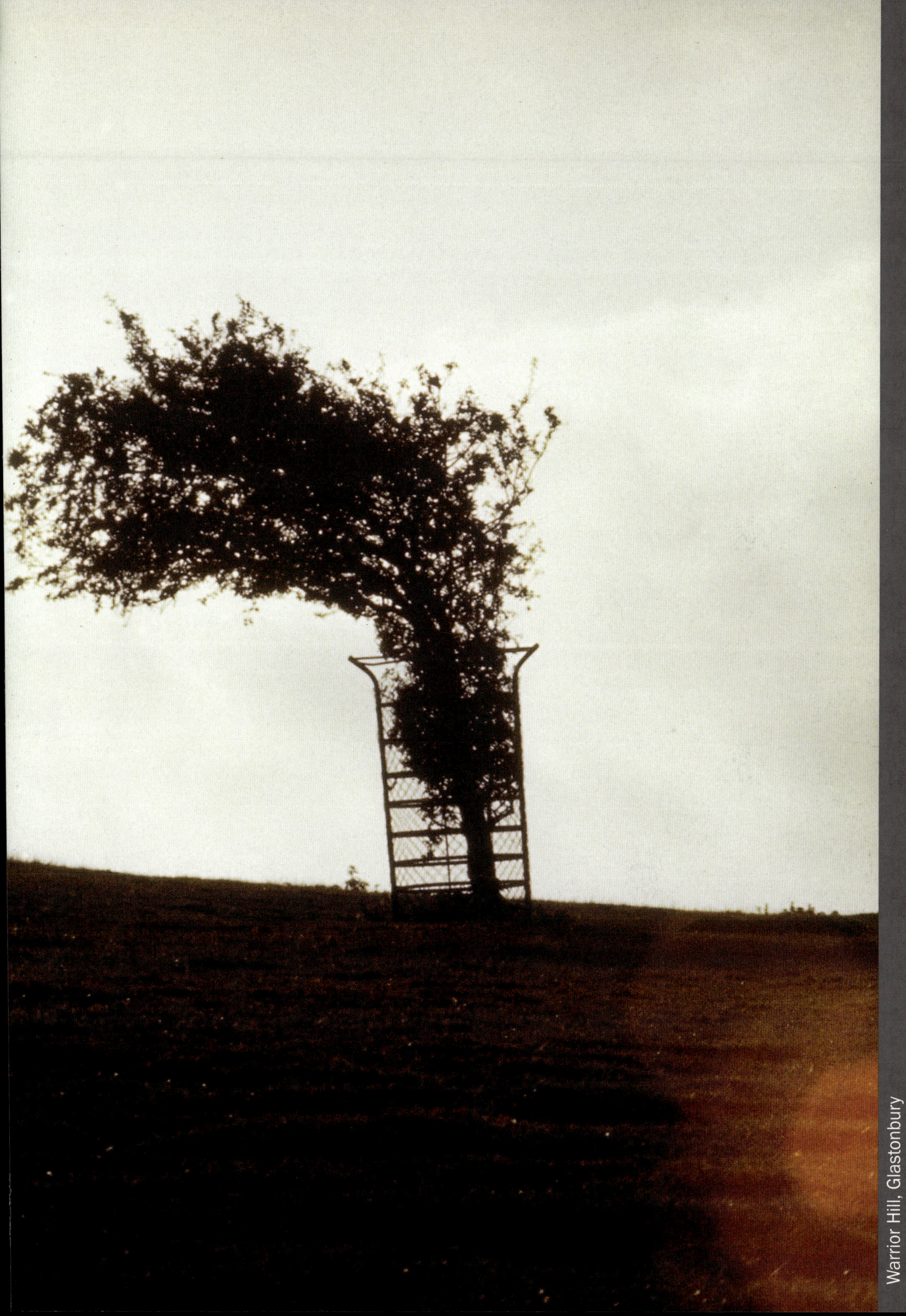

Warrior Hill, Glastonbury

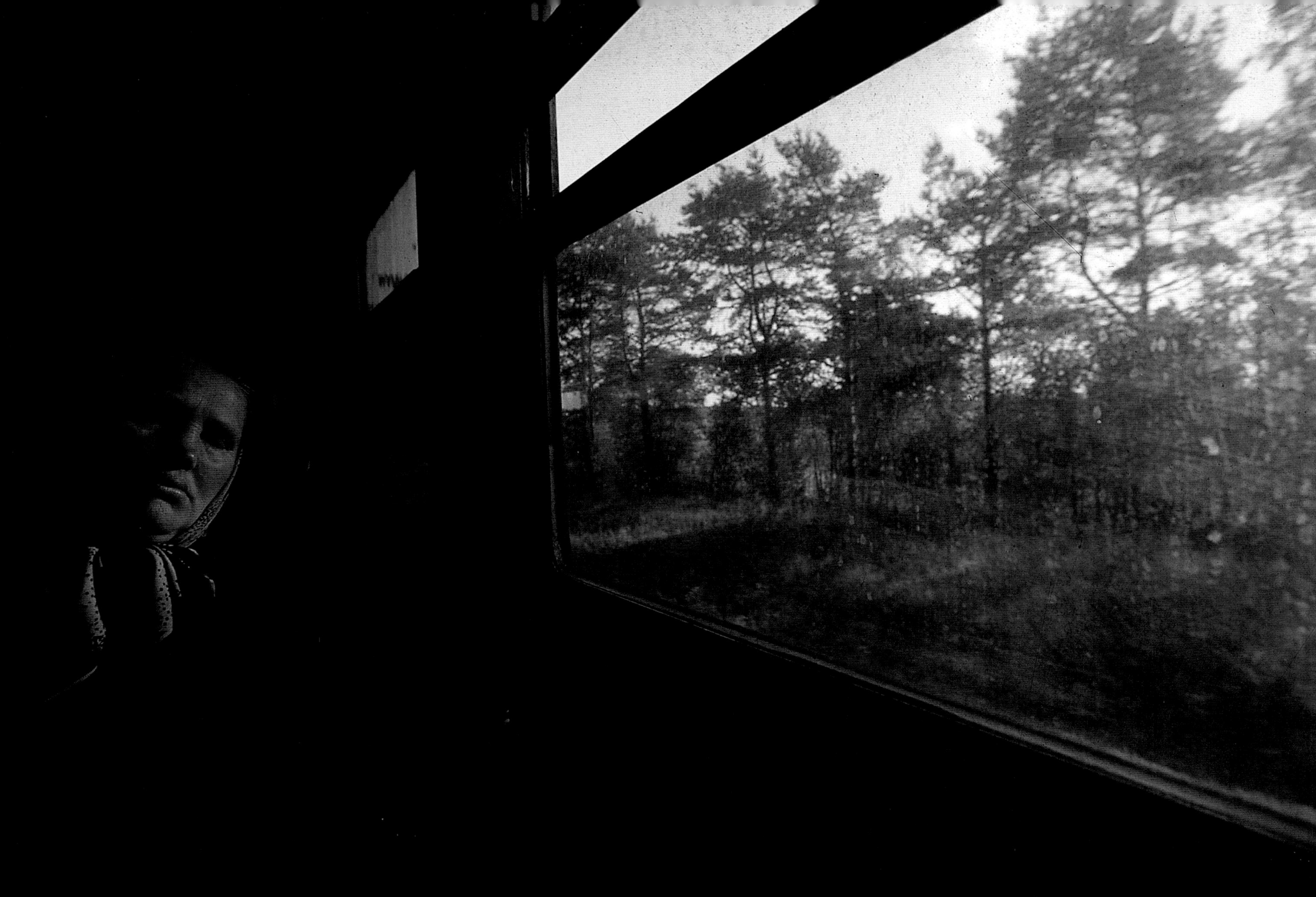

(Tarkovsky) Train to Moscow

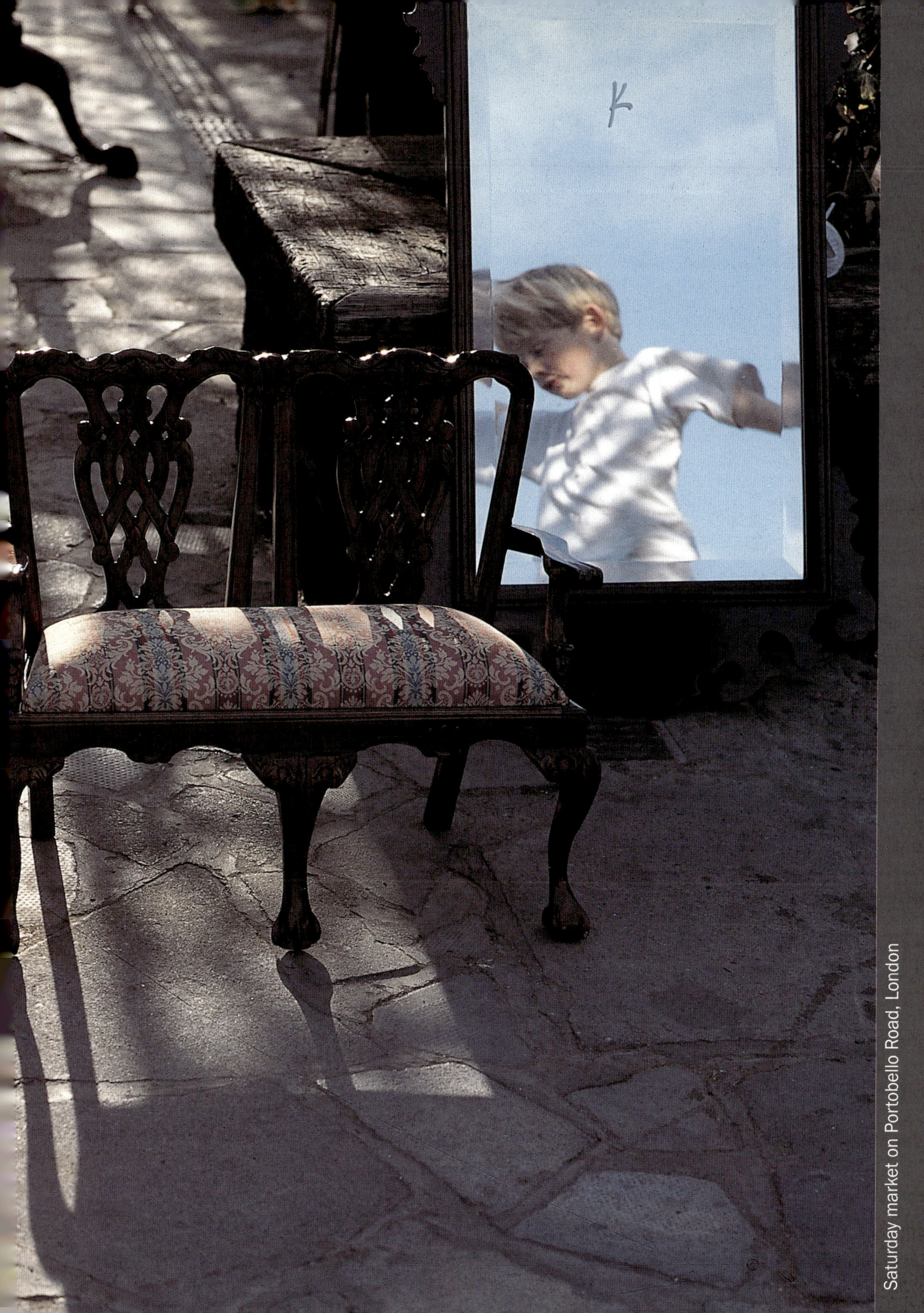

Saturday market on Portobello Road, London

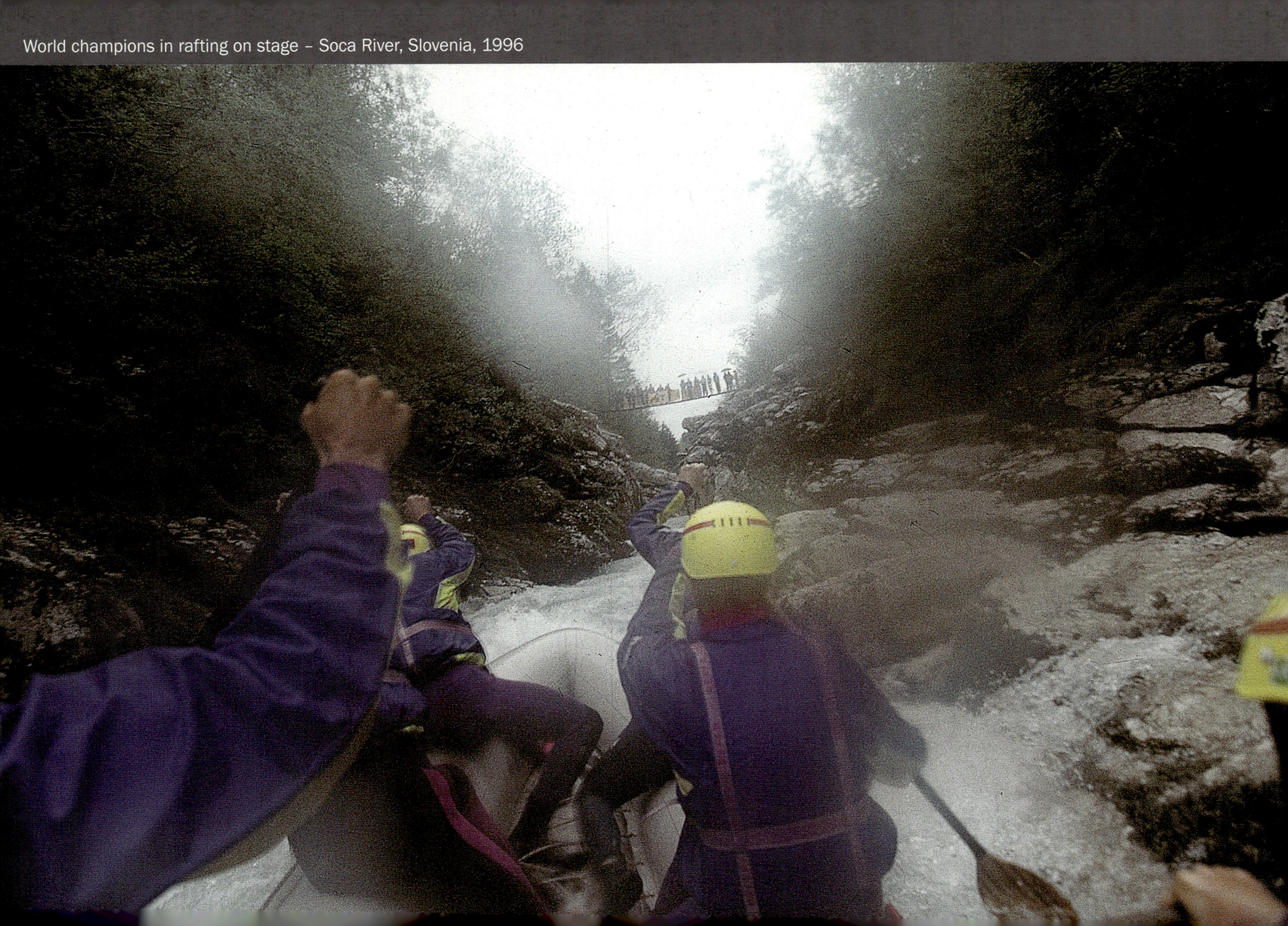

World champions in rafting on stage – Soca River, Slovenia, 1996

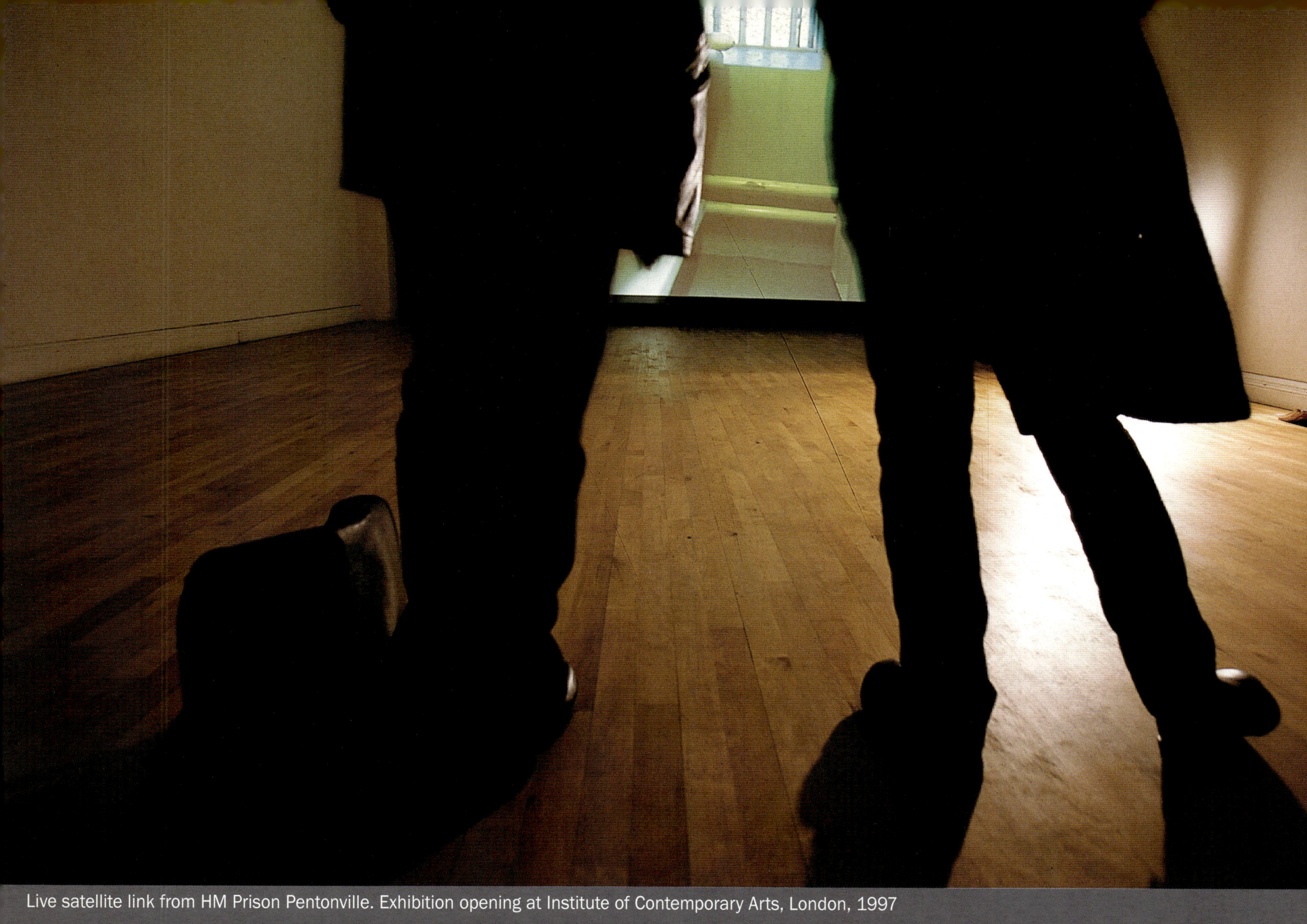

Live satellite link from HM Prison Pentonville. Exhibition opening at Institute of Contemporary Arts, London, 1997

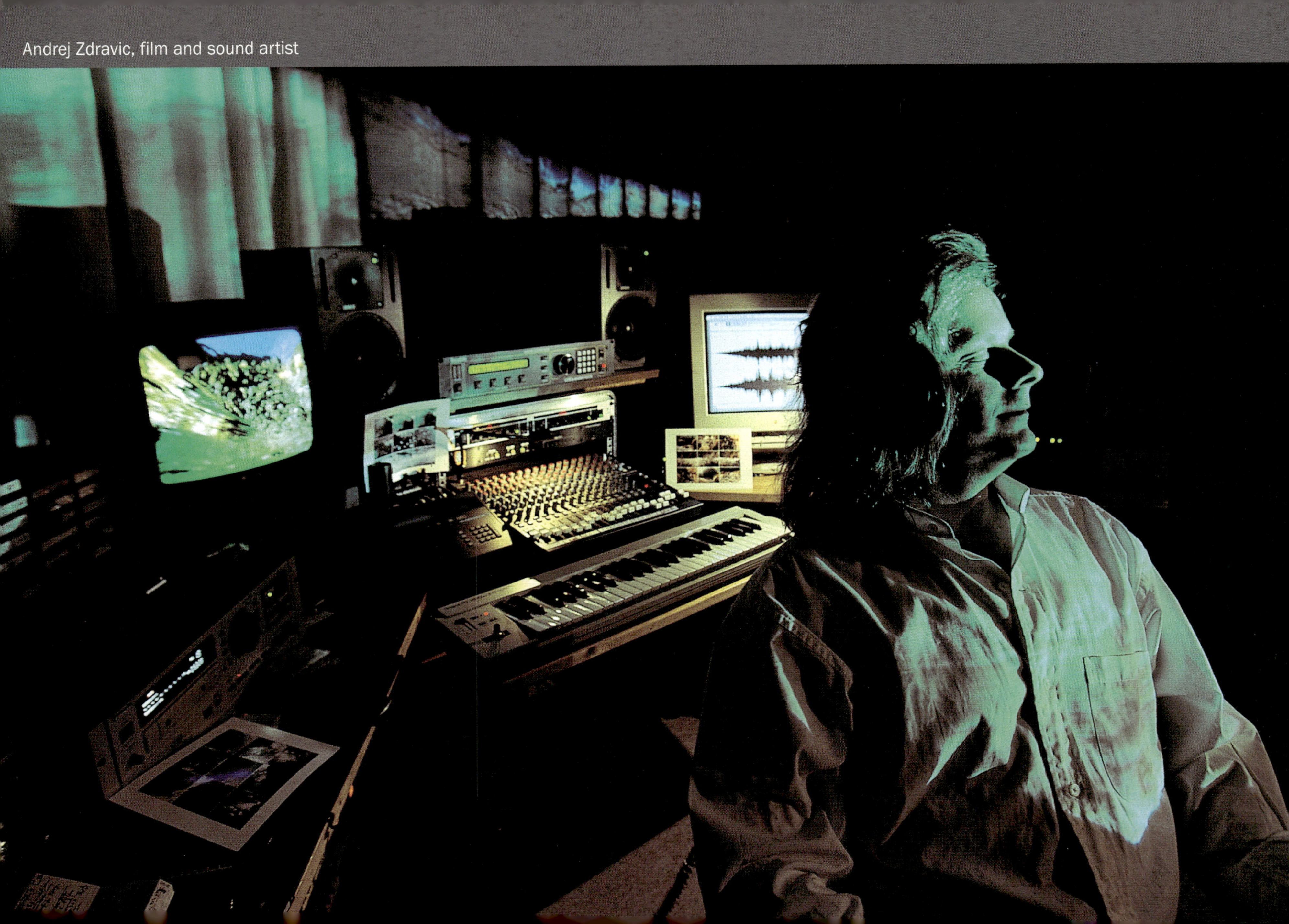

Andrej Zdravic, film and sound artist

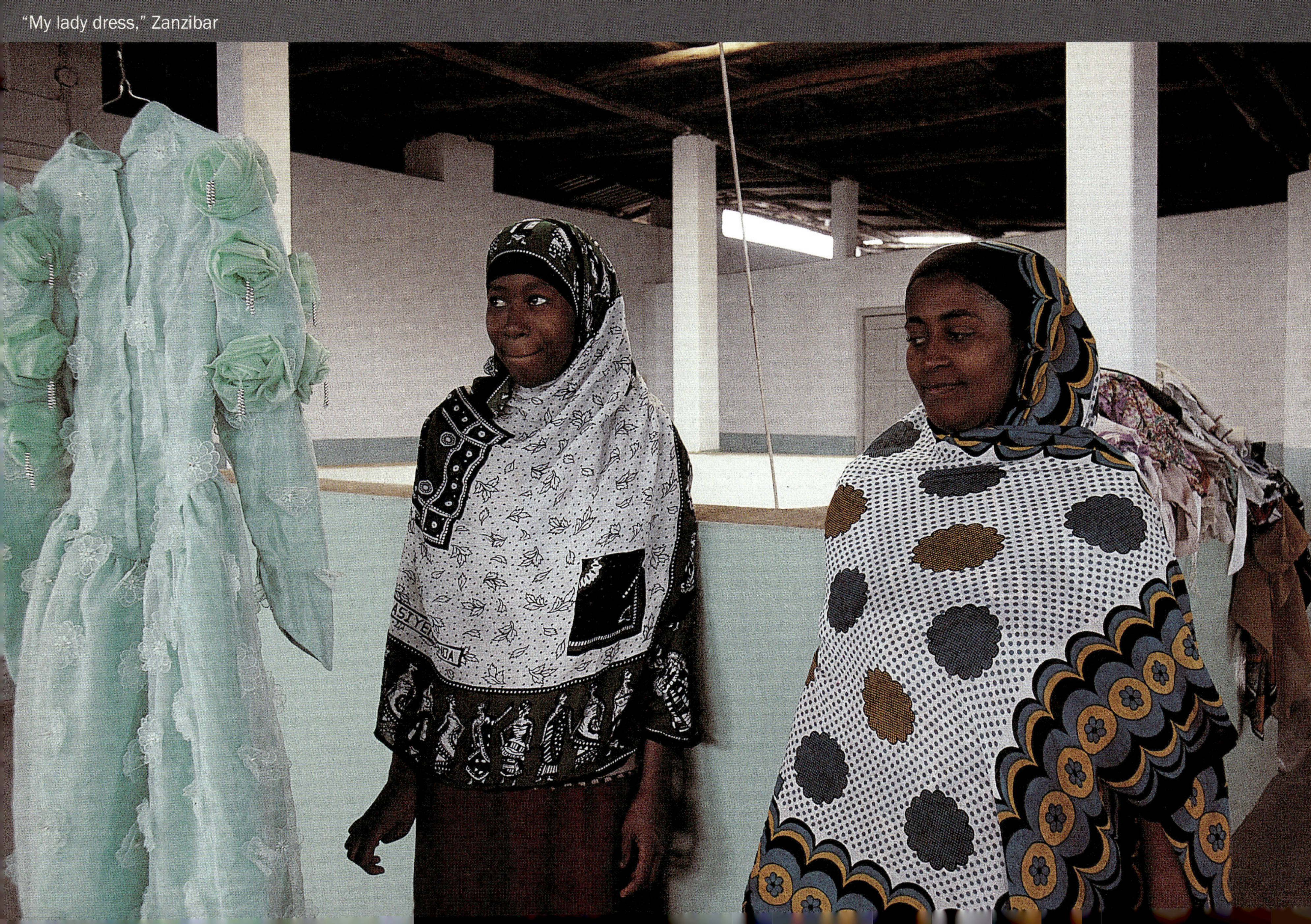

"My lady dress," Zanzibar

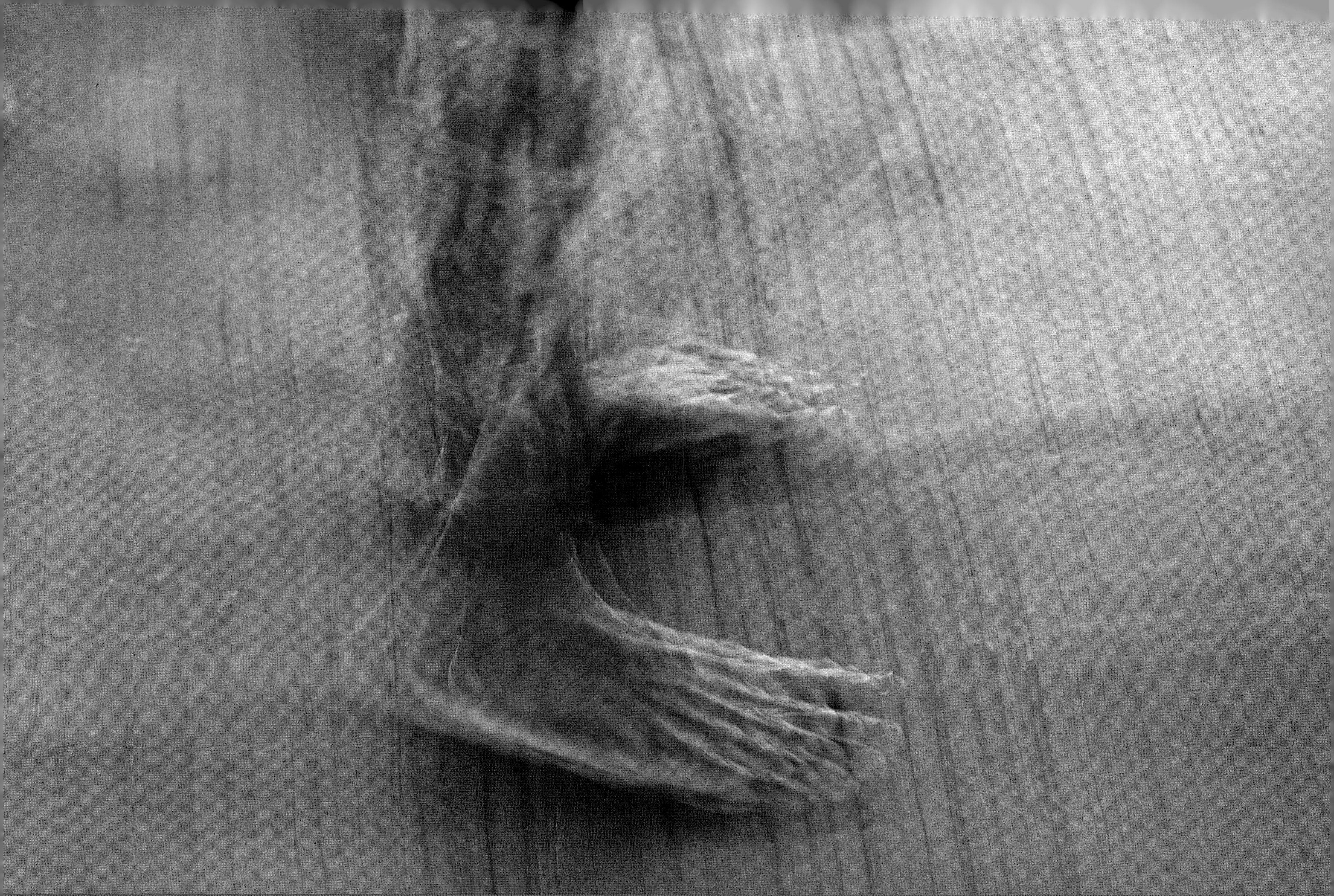

Betel-nut and dance orgy in the “women’s house” – Black River, Papua New Guinea

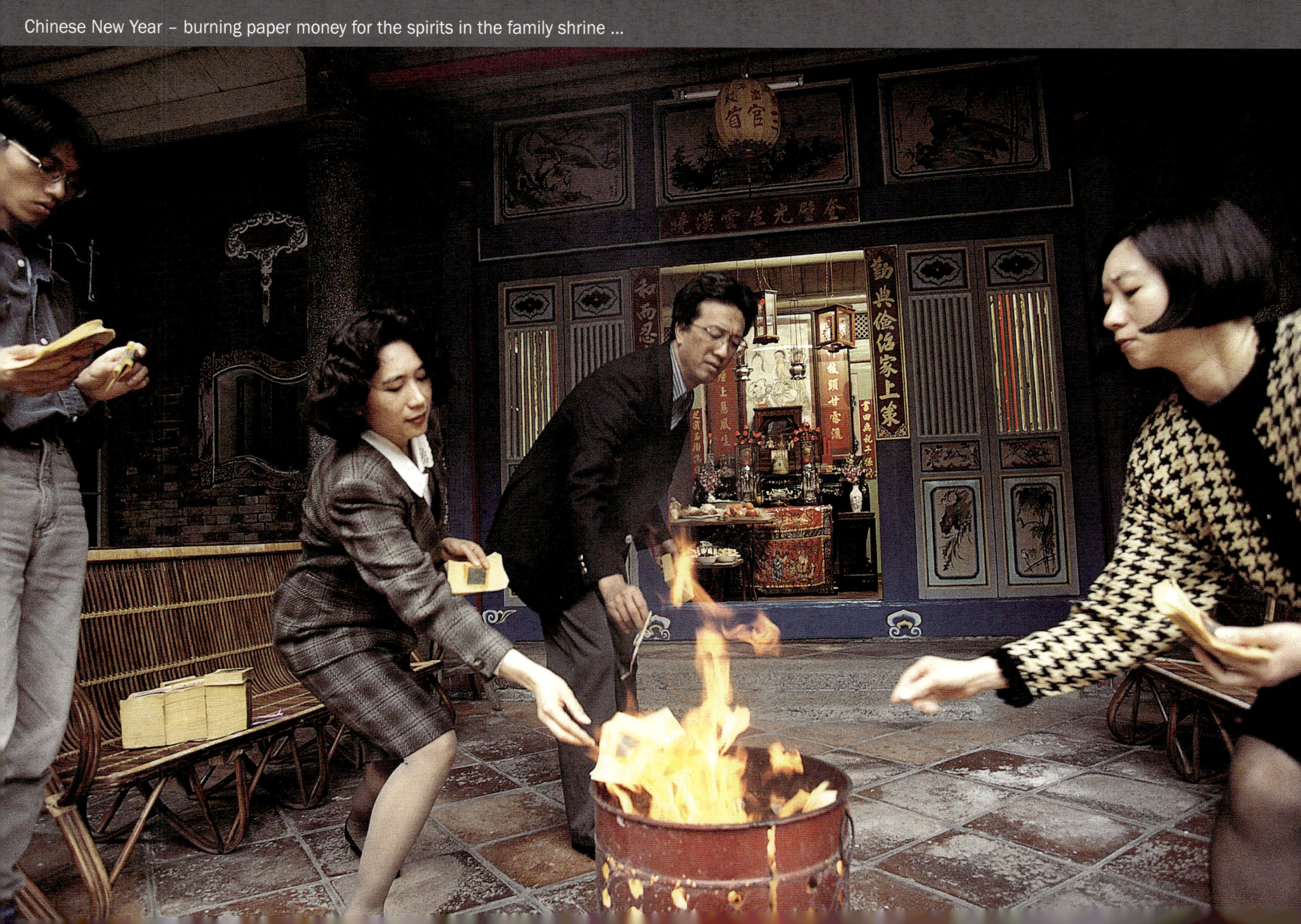

Chinese New Year – burning paper money for the spirits in the family shrine ...

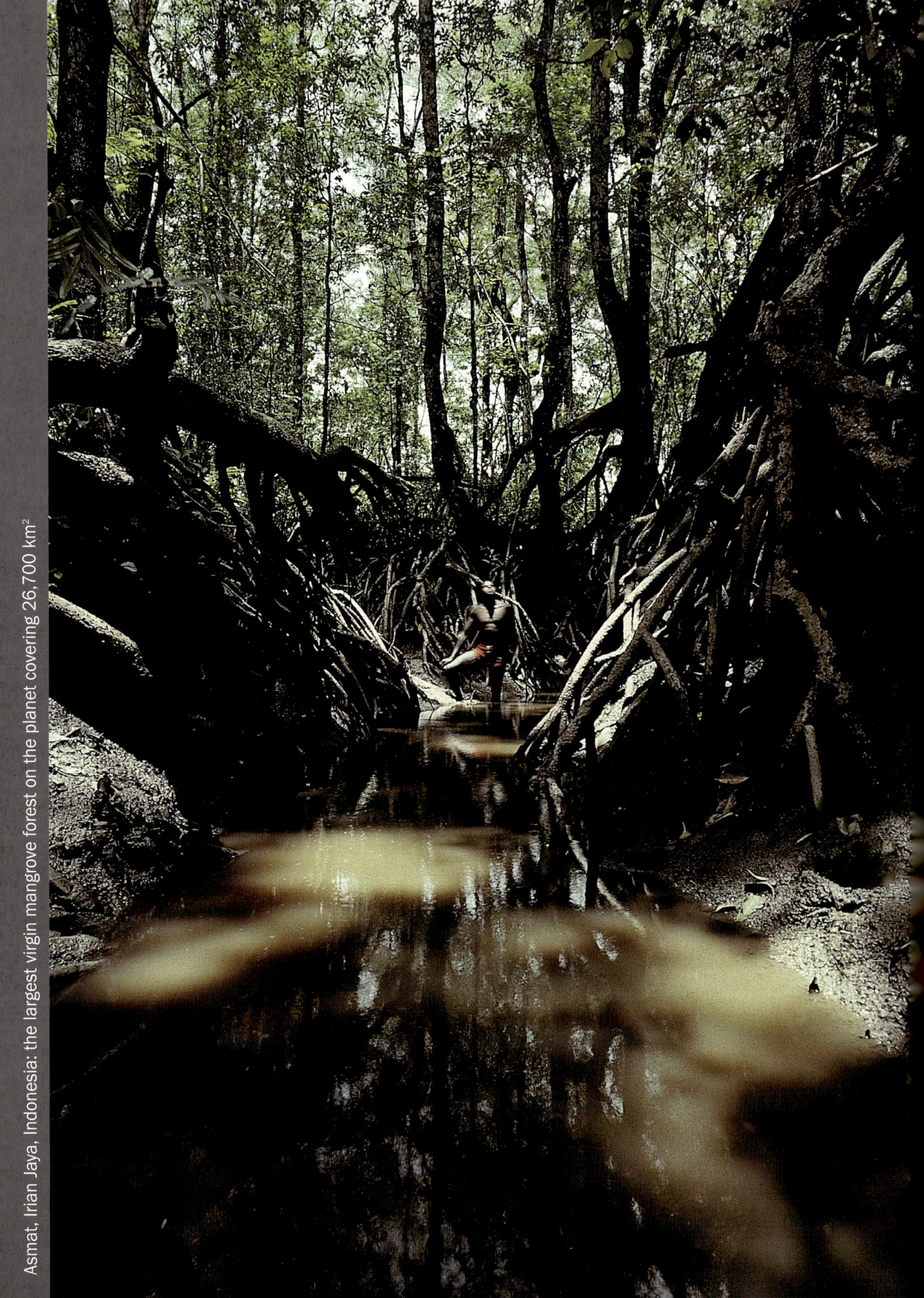

Asmat, Irian Jaya, Indonesia: the largest virgin mangrove forest on the planet covering 26,700 km²

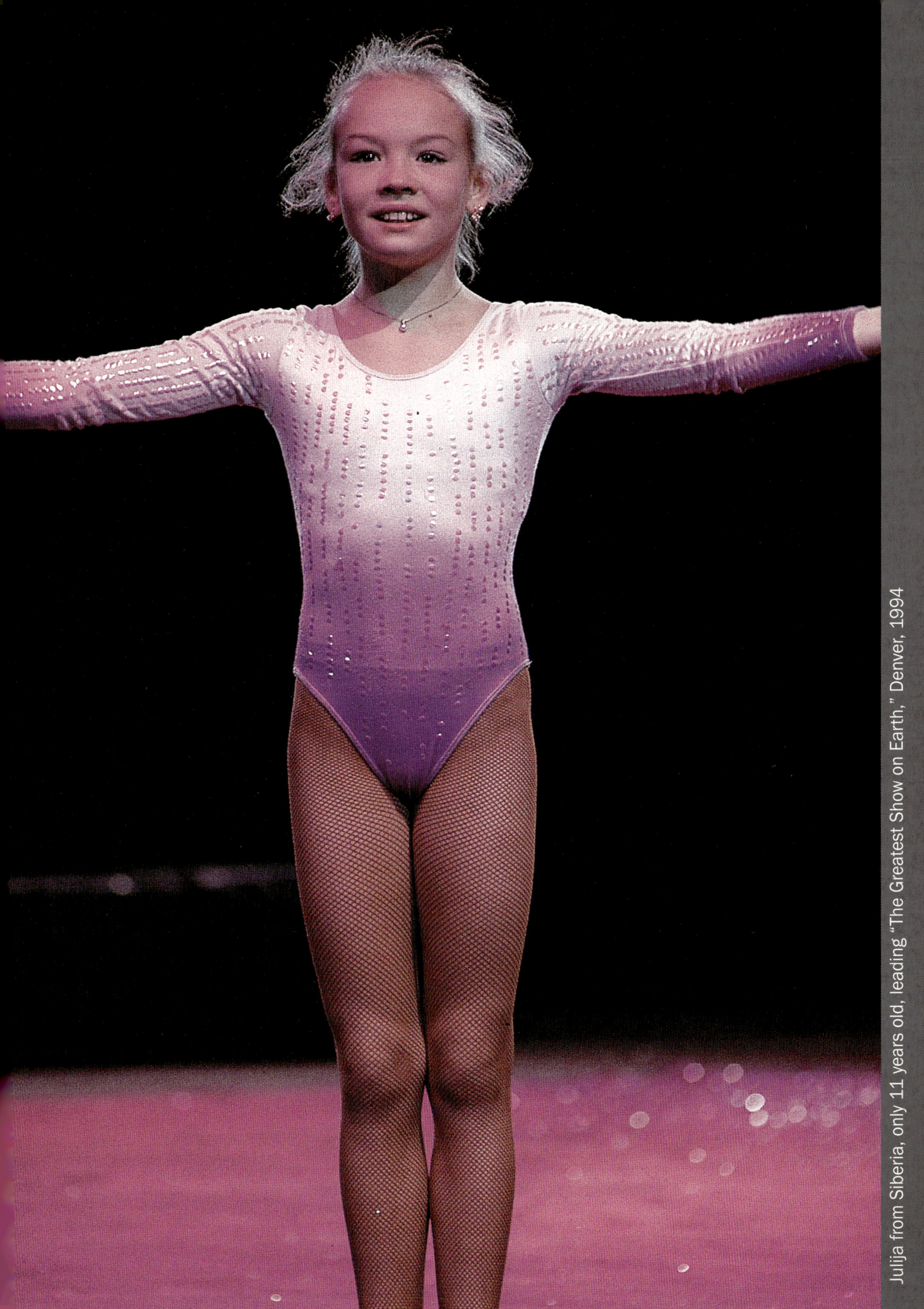

Julija from Siberia, only 11 years old, leading "The Greatest Show on Earth," Denver, 1994

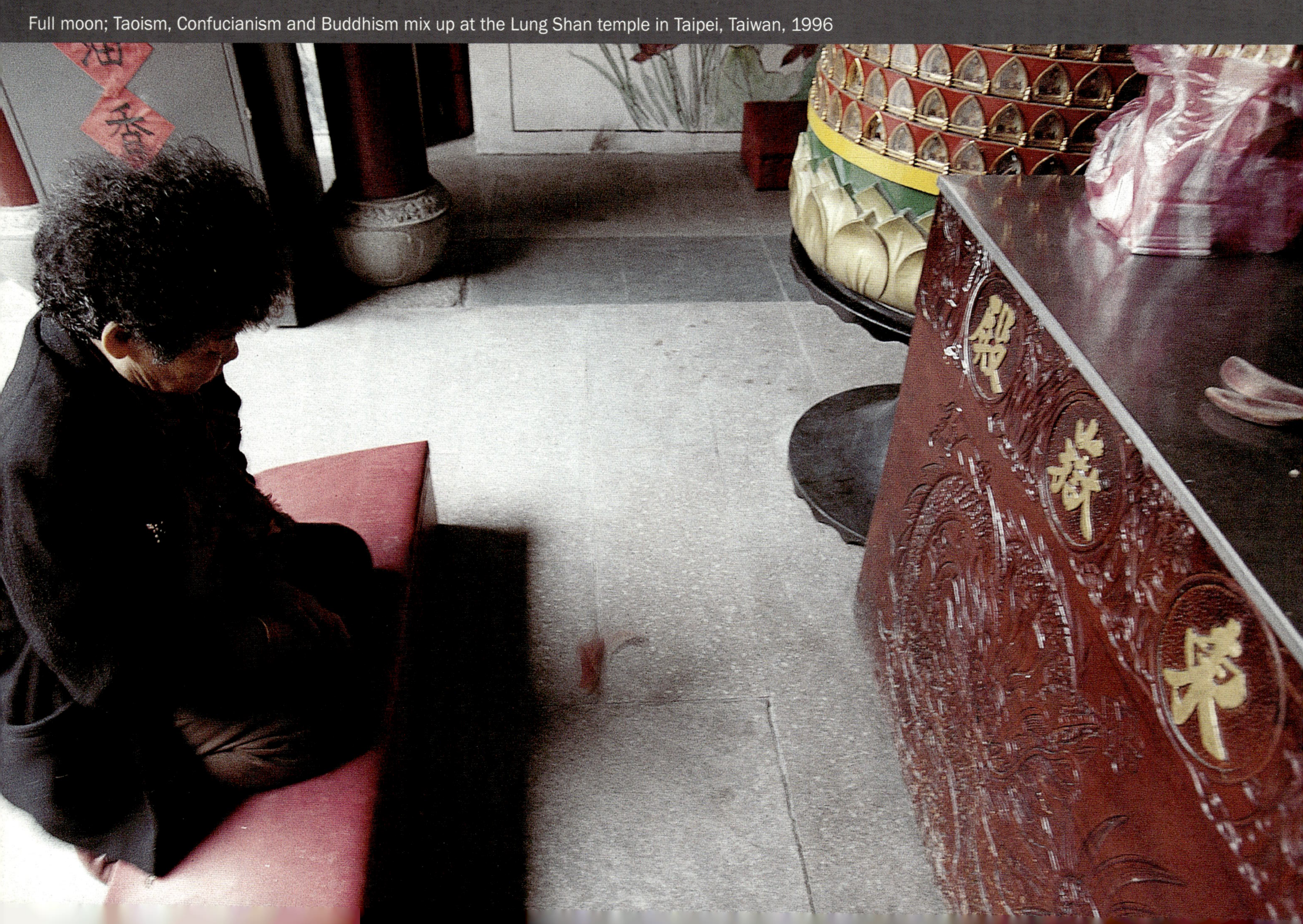

Full moon; Taoism, Confucianism and Buddhism mix up at the Lung Shan temple in Taipei, Taiwan, 1996

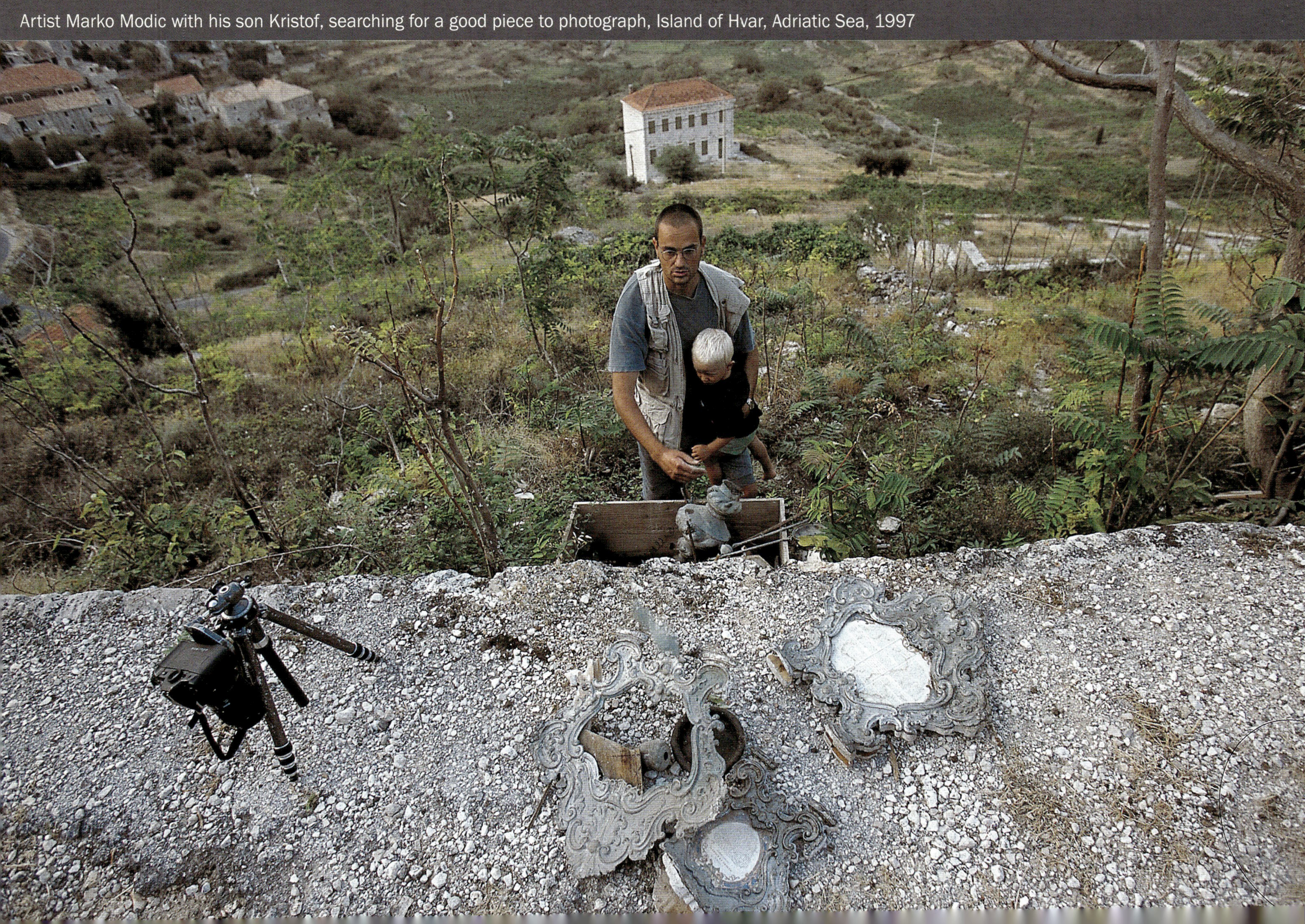

Artist Marko Modic with his son Kristof, searching for a good piece to photograph, Island of Hvar, Adriatic Sea, 1997

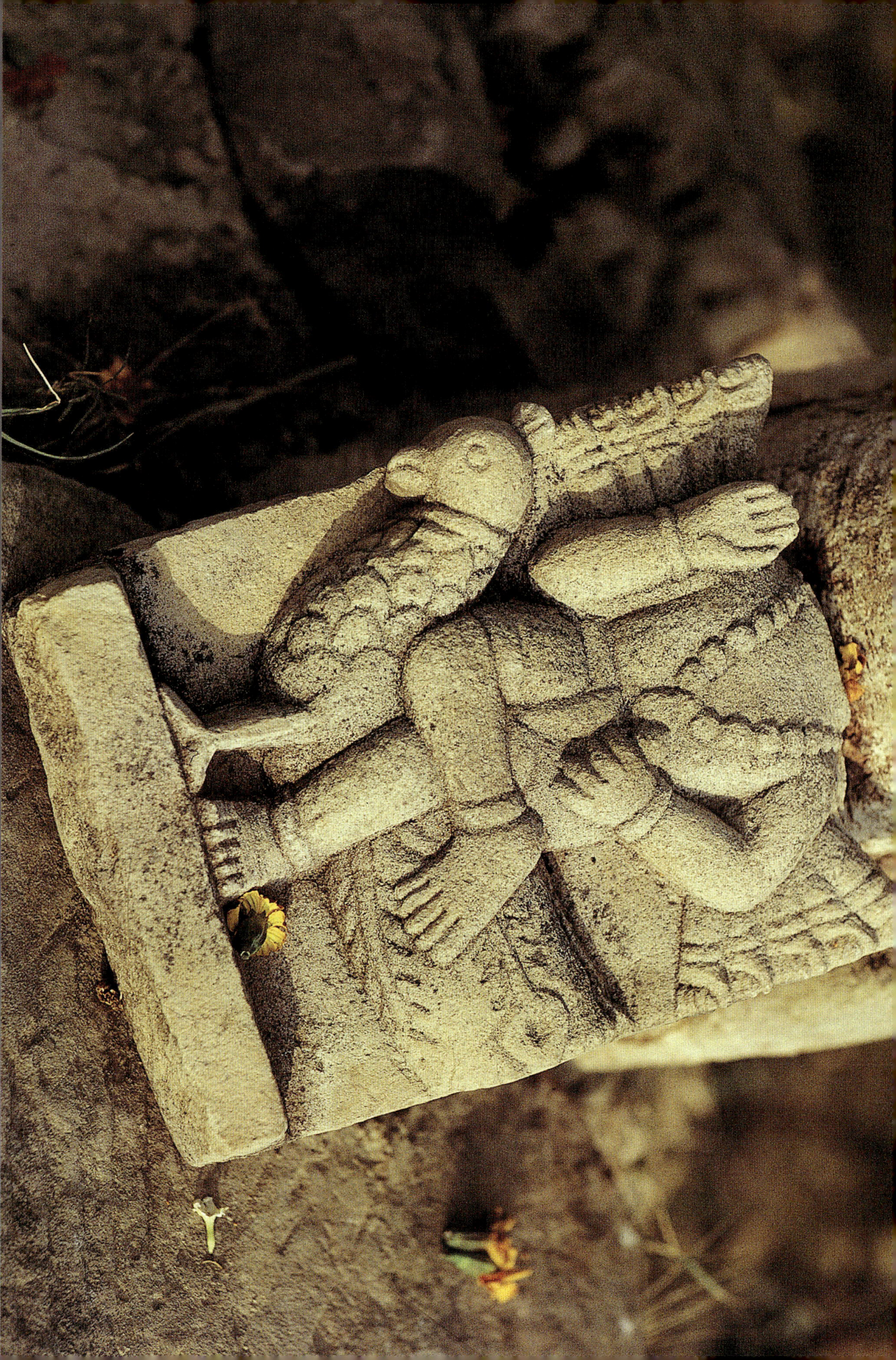

India – Under a tree

Haloze region, Slovenia

"House Tambaran" – men's house, Agri, Irian Jaya, Indonesia, 1990

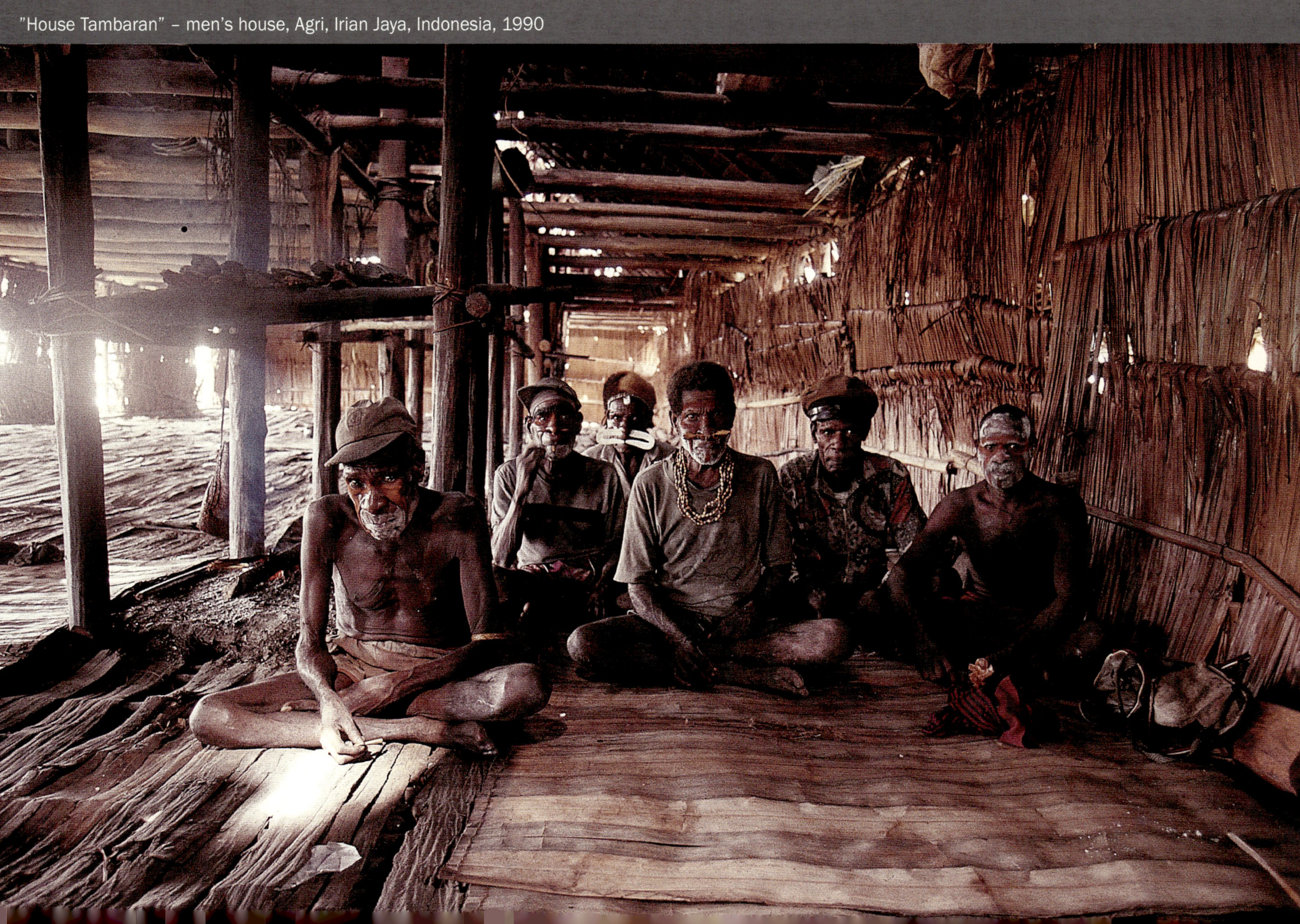

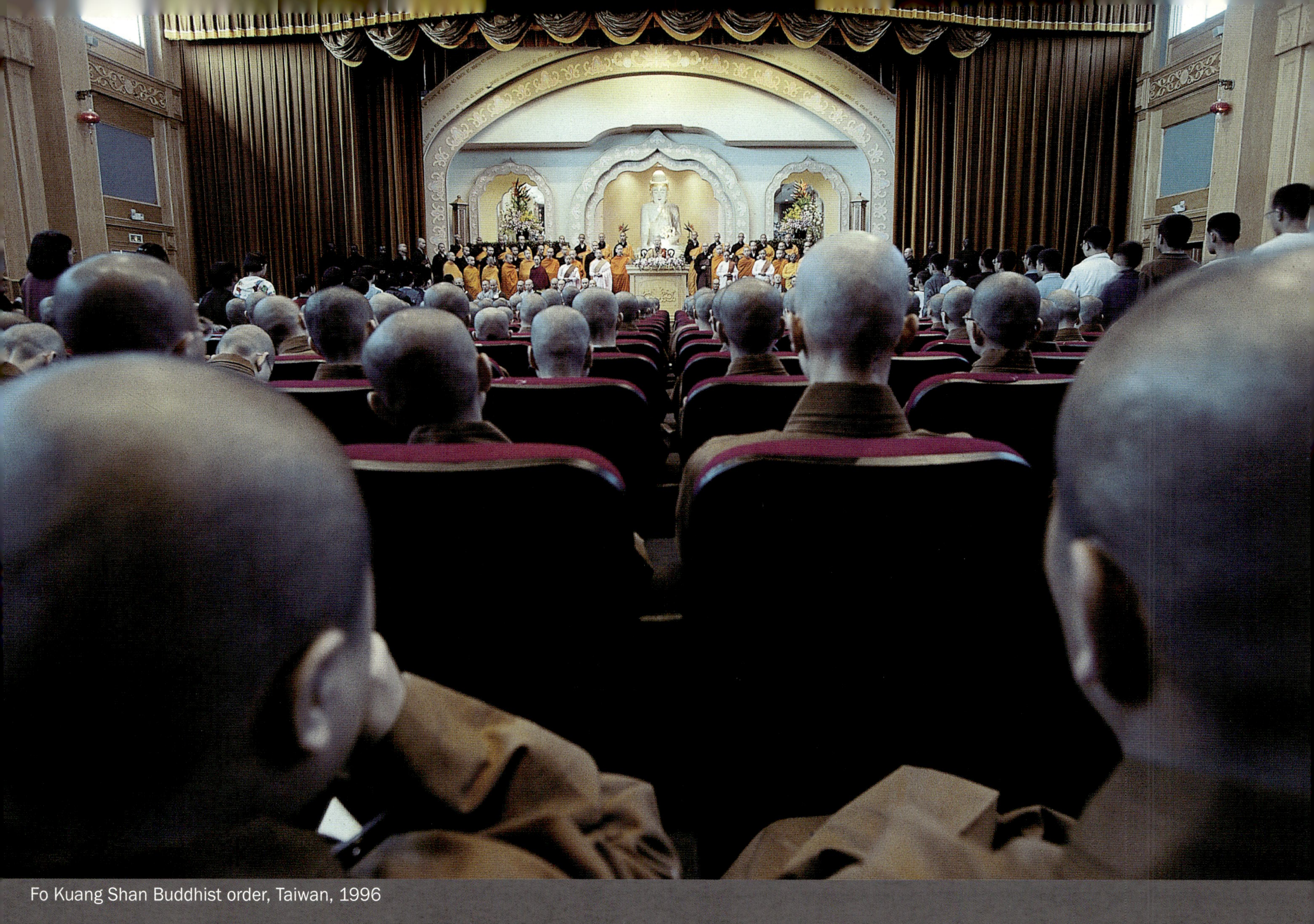

Fo Kuang Shan Buddhist order, Taiwan, 1996

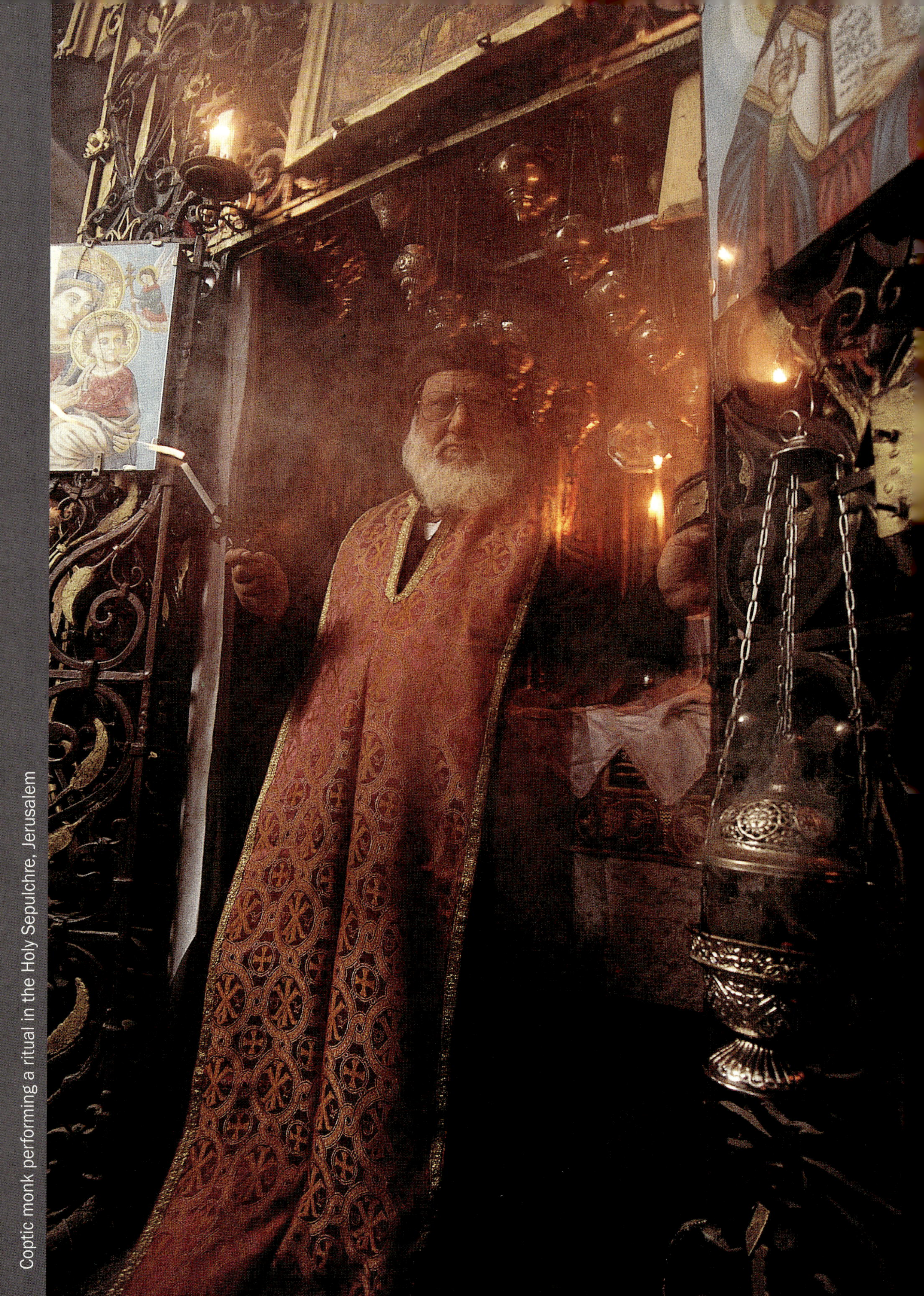

Coptic monk performing a ritual in the Holy Sepulchre, Jerusalem

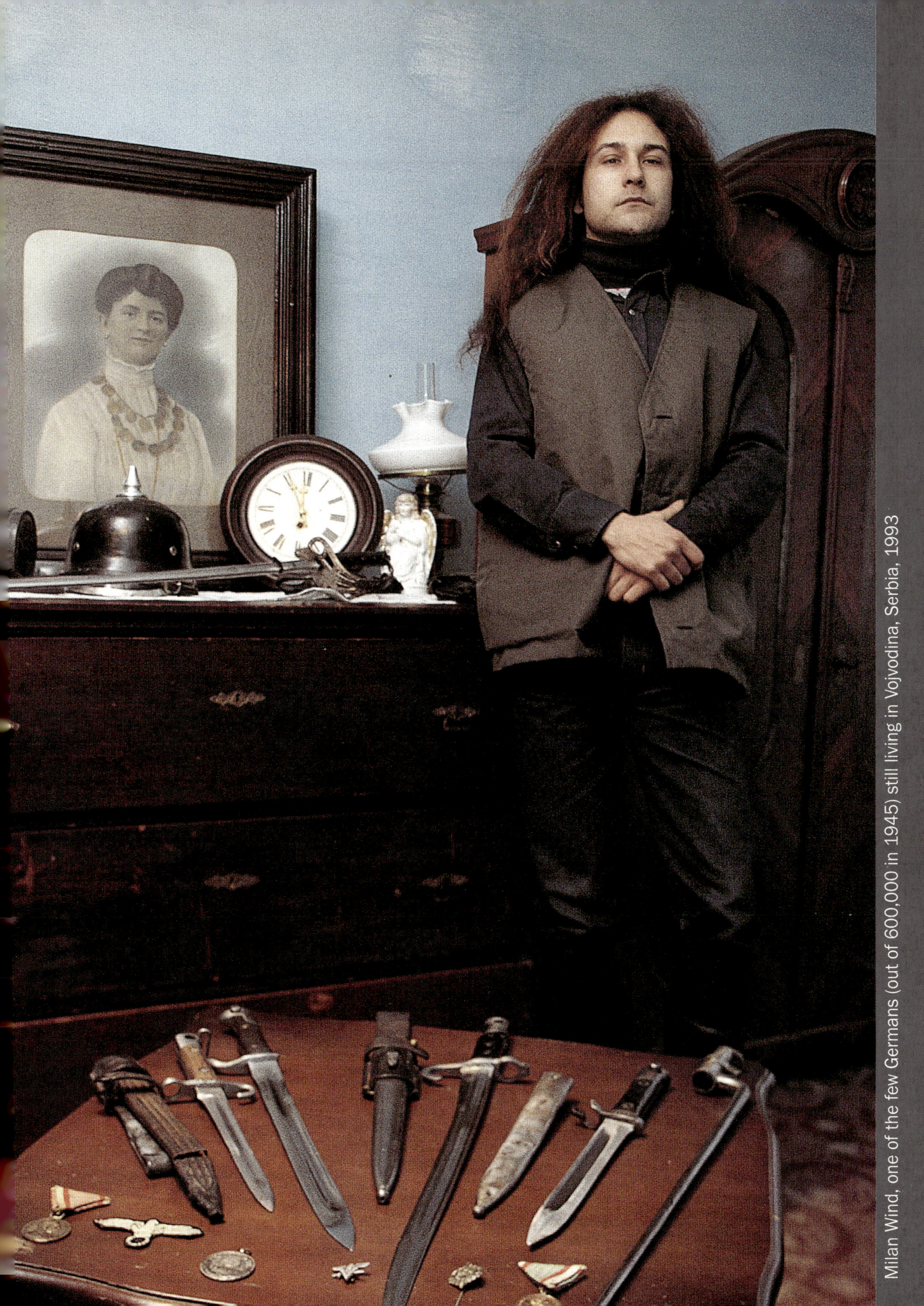

Milan Wind, one of the few Germans (out of 600,000 in 1945) still living in Vojvodina, Serbia, 1993

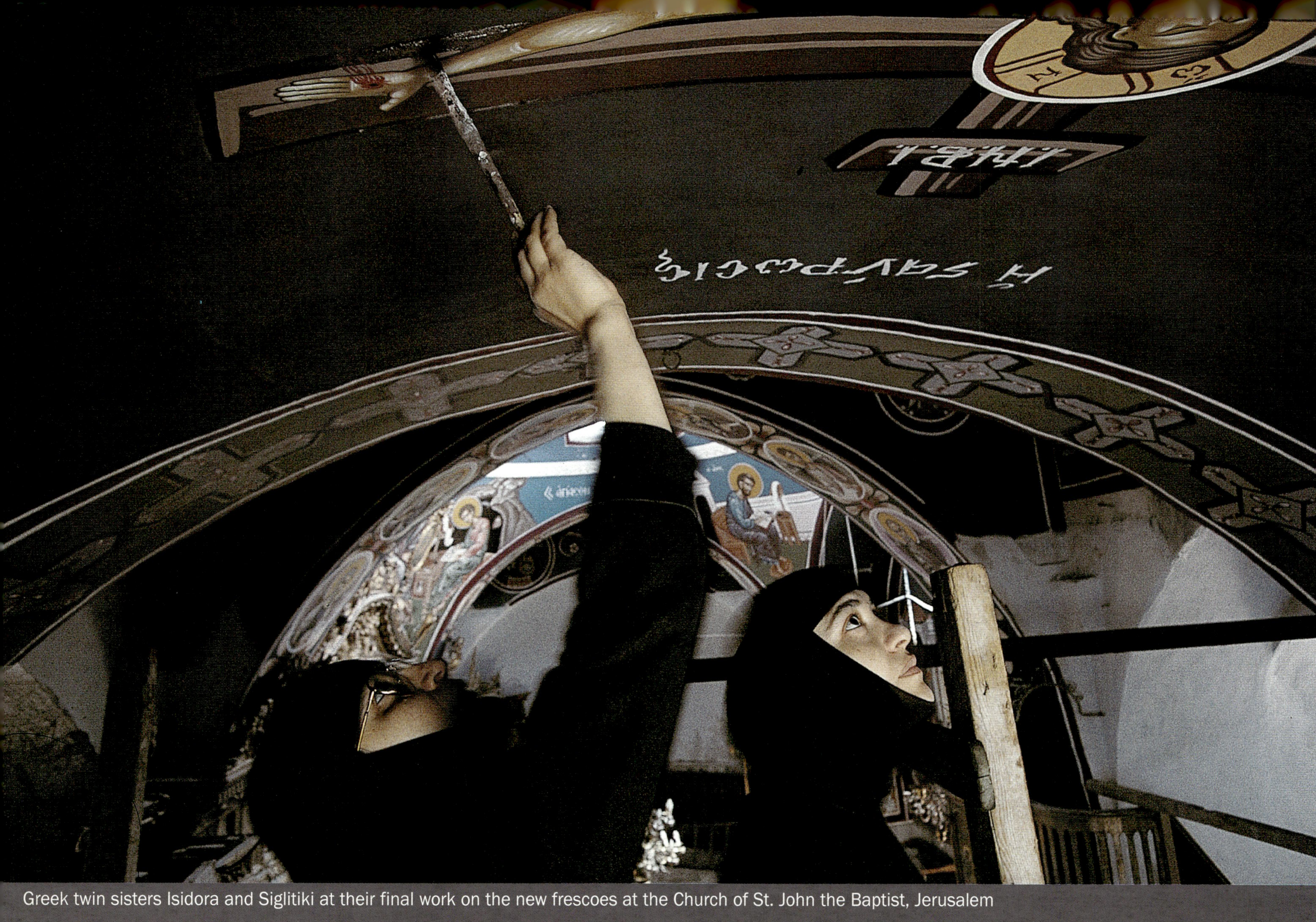

Greek twin sisters Isidora and Siglitiki at their final work on the new frescoes at the Church of St. John the Baptist, Jerusalem

Cheboksary, Russia

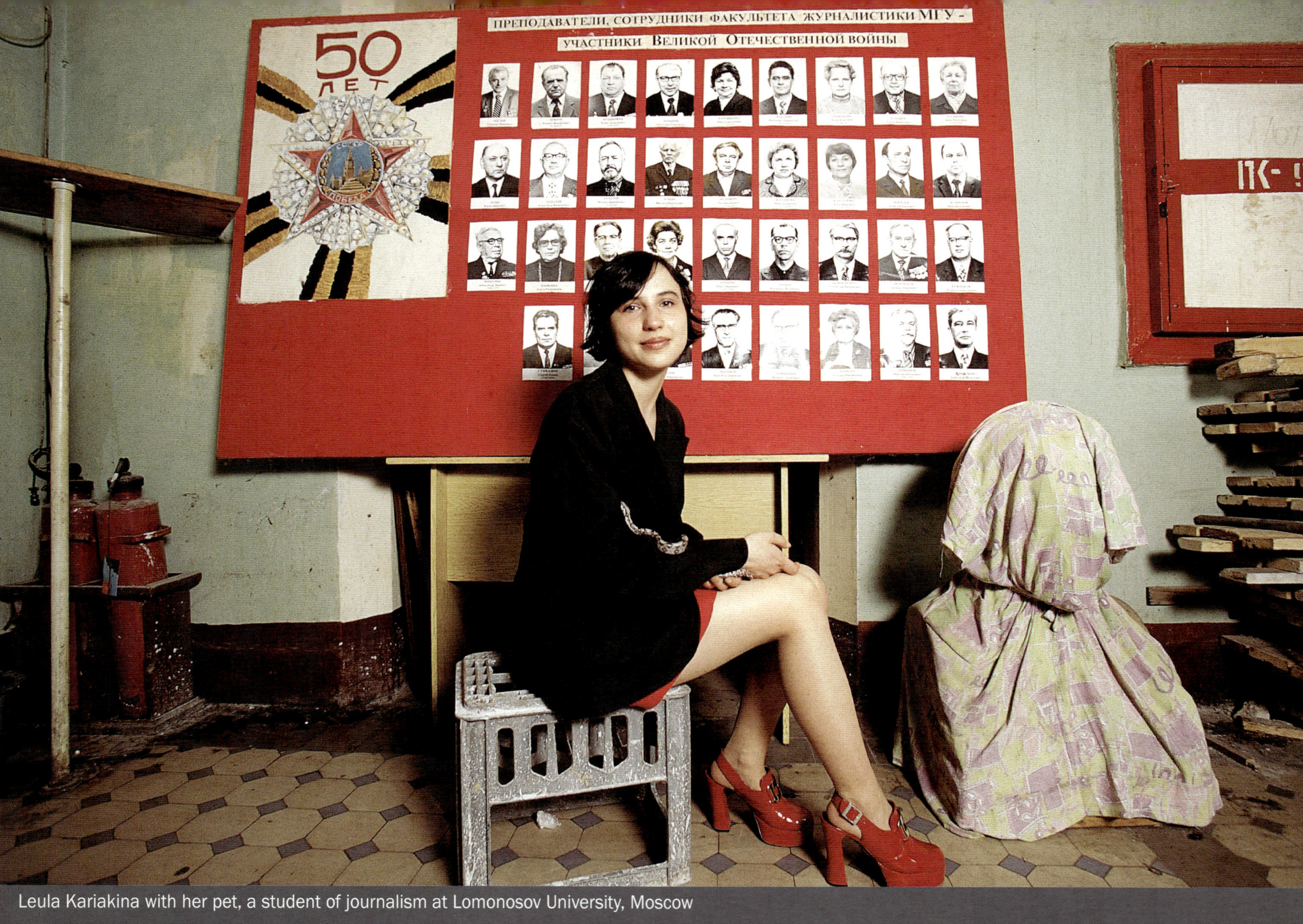

Leula Kariakina with her pet, a student of journalism at Lomonosov University, Moscow

“Lying Buddha” is how the mother calls her son after he became completely paralyzed, Taiwan

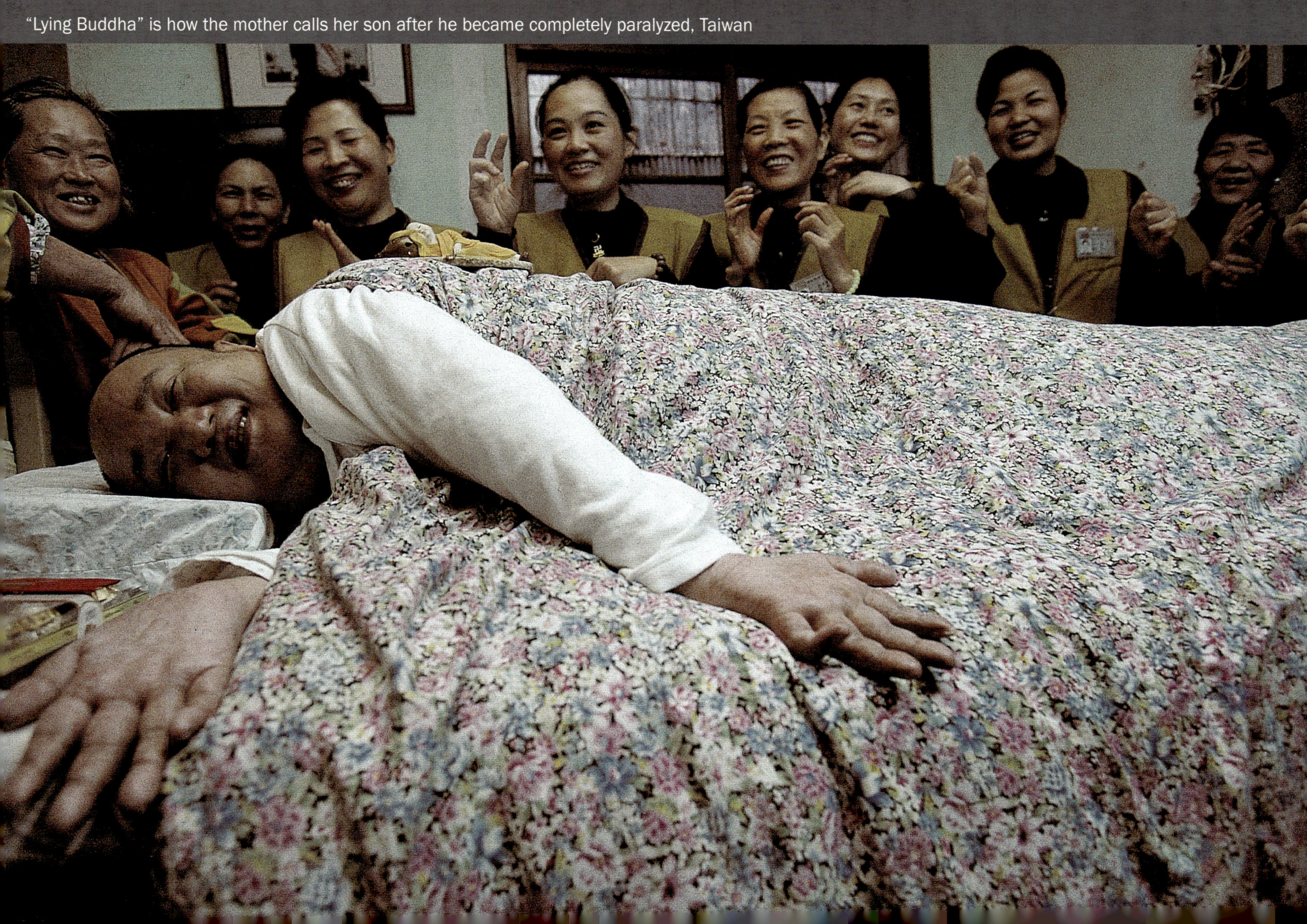

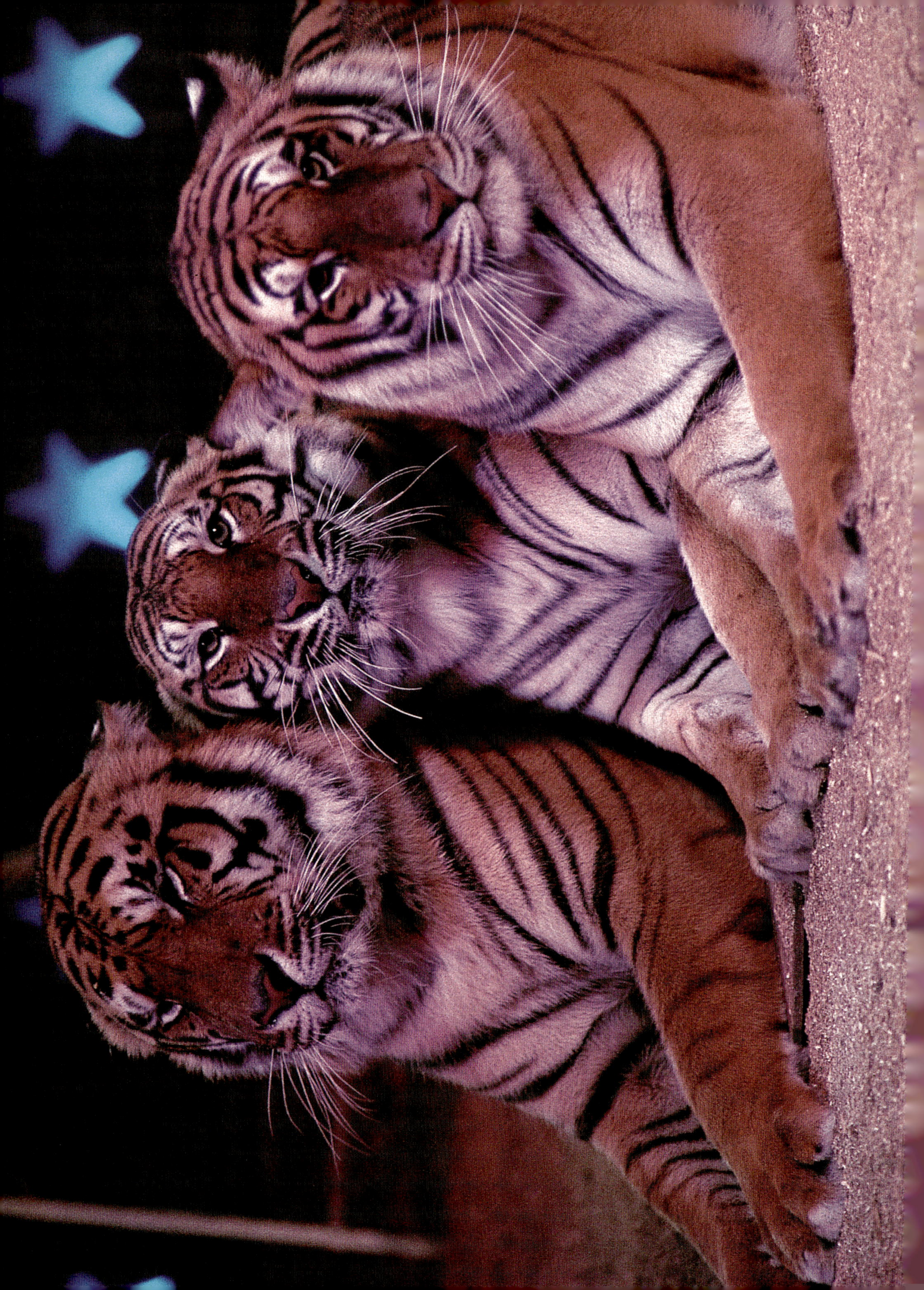

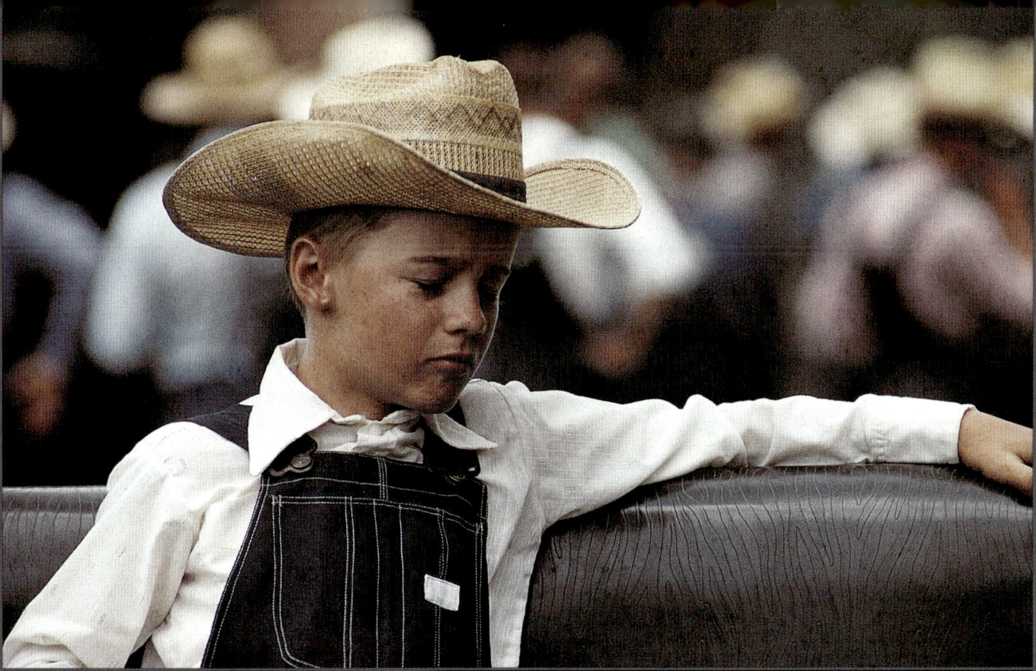

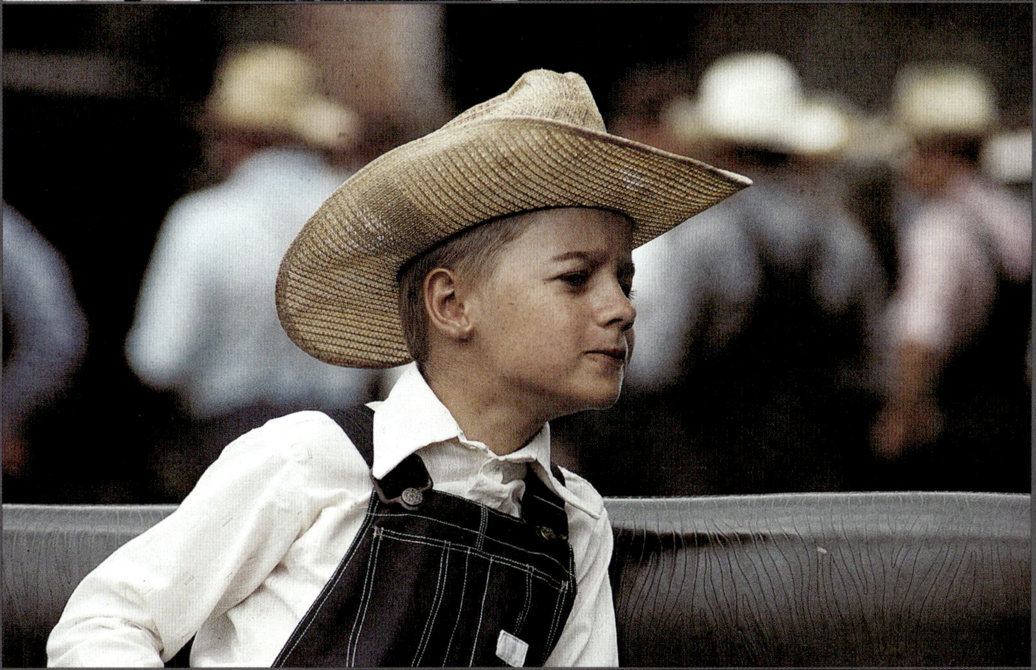

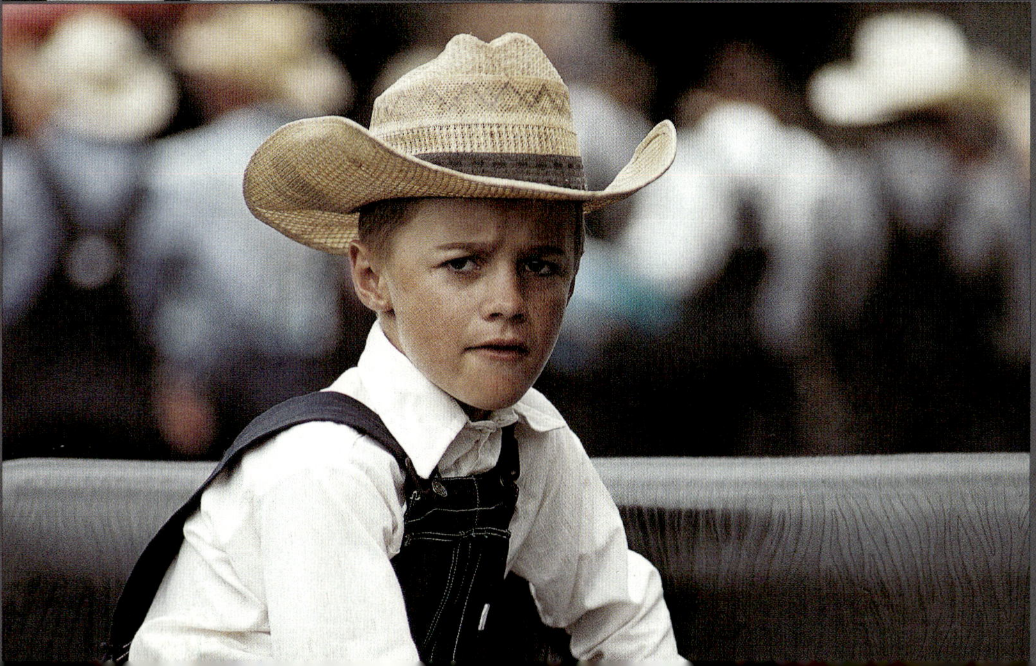

Three...

Mennonites, Bolivia

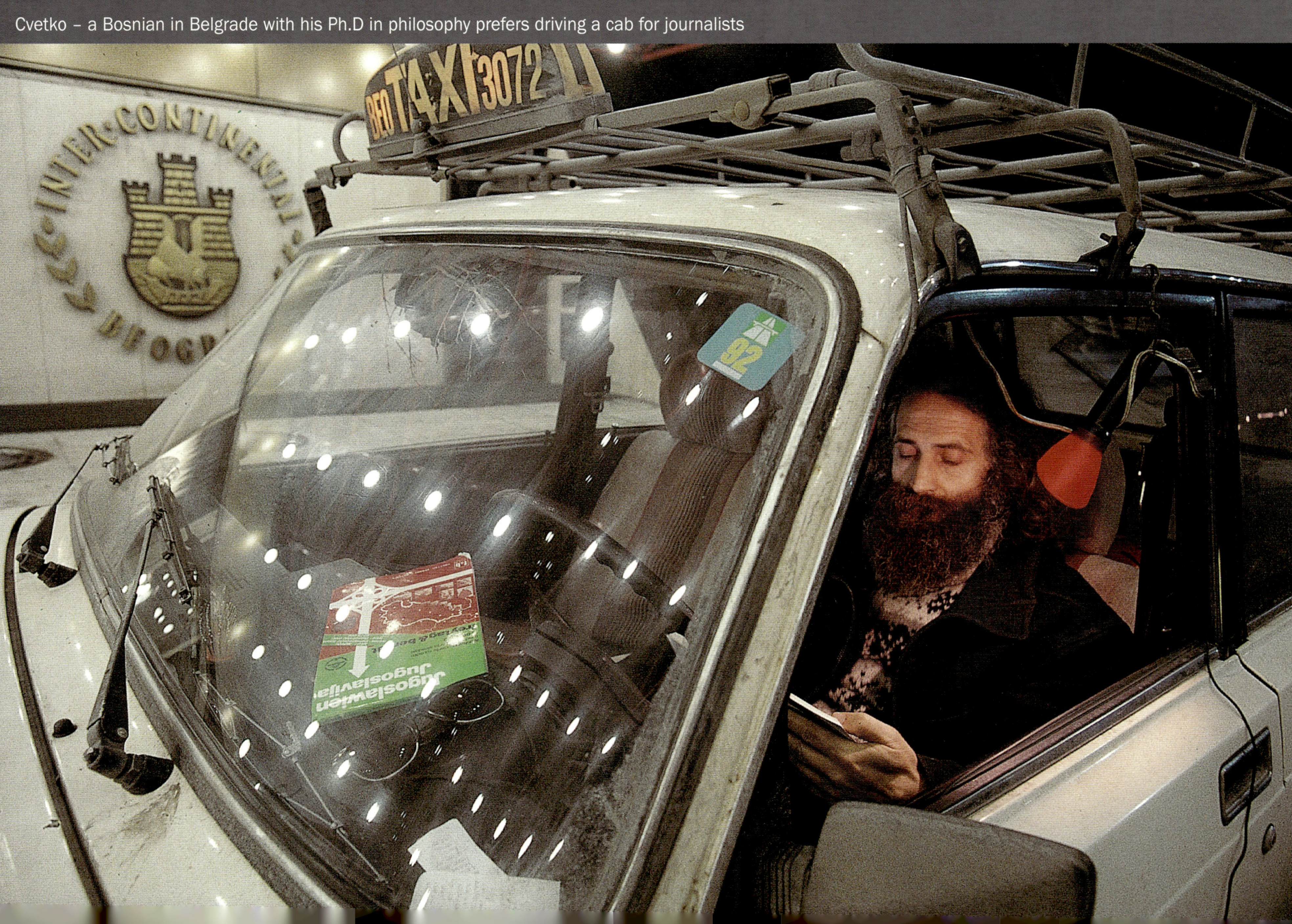

Cvetko – a Bosnian in Belgrade with his Ph.D in philosophy prefers driving a cab for journalists

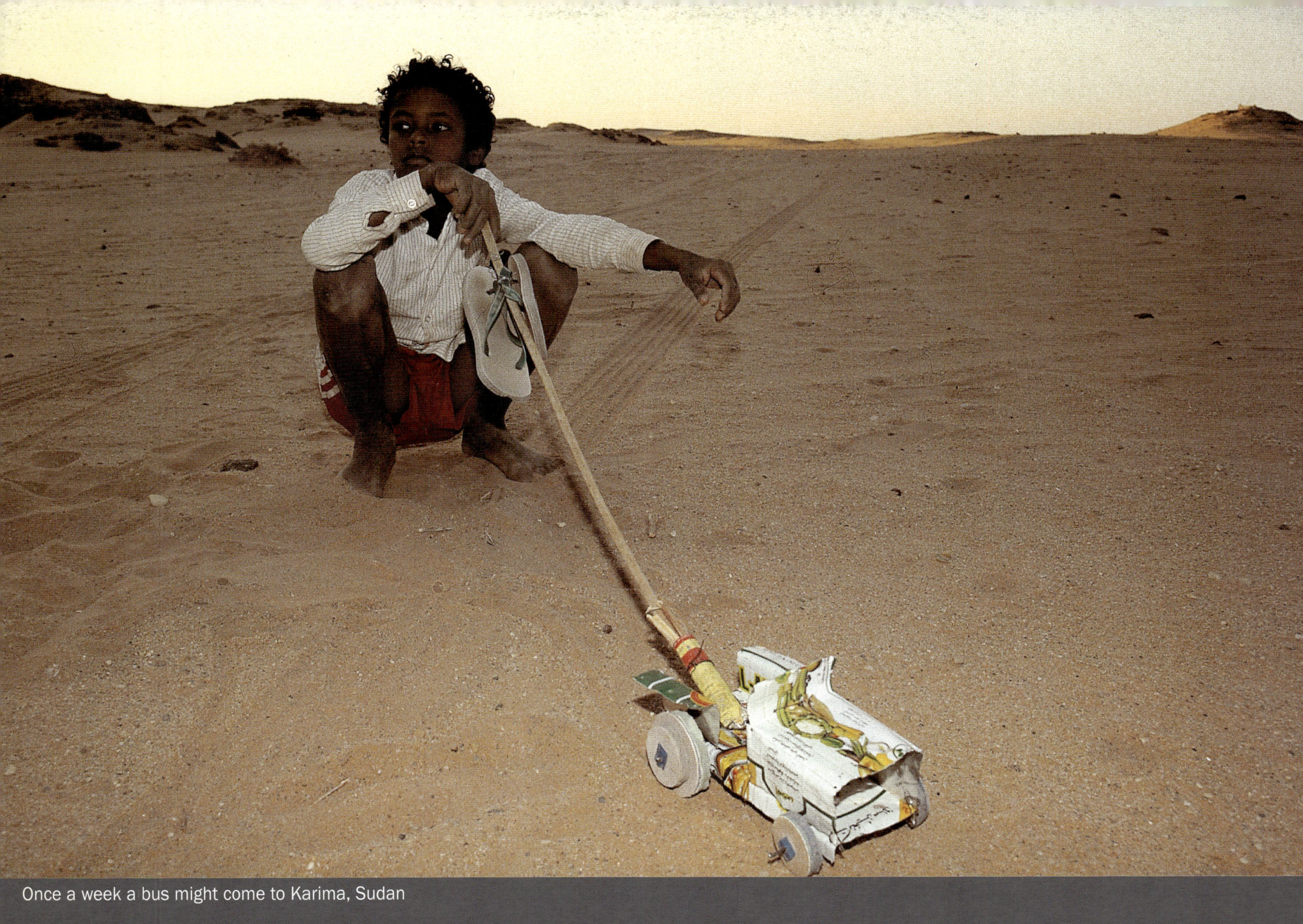

Once a week a bus might come to Karima, Sudan

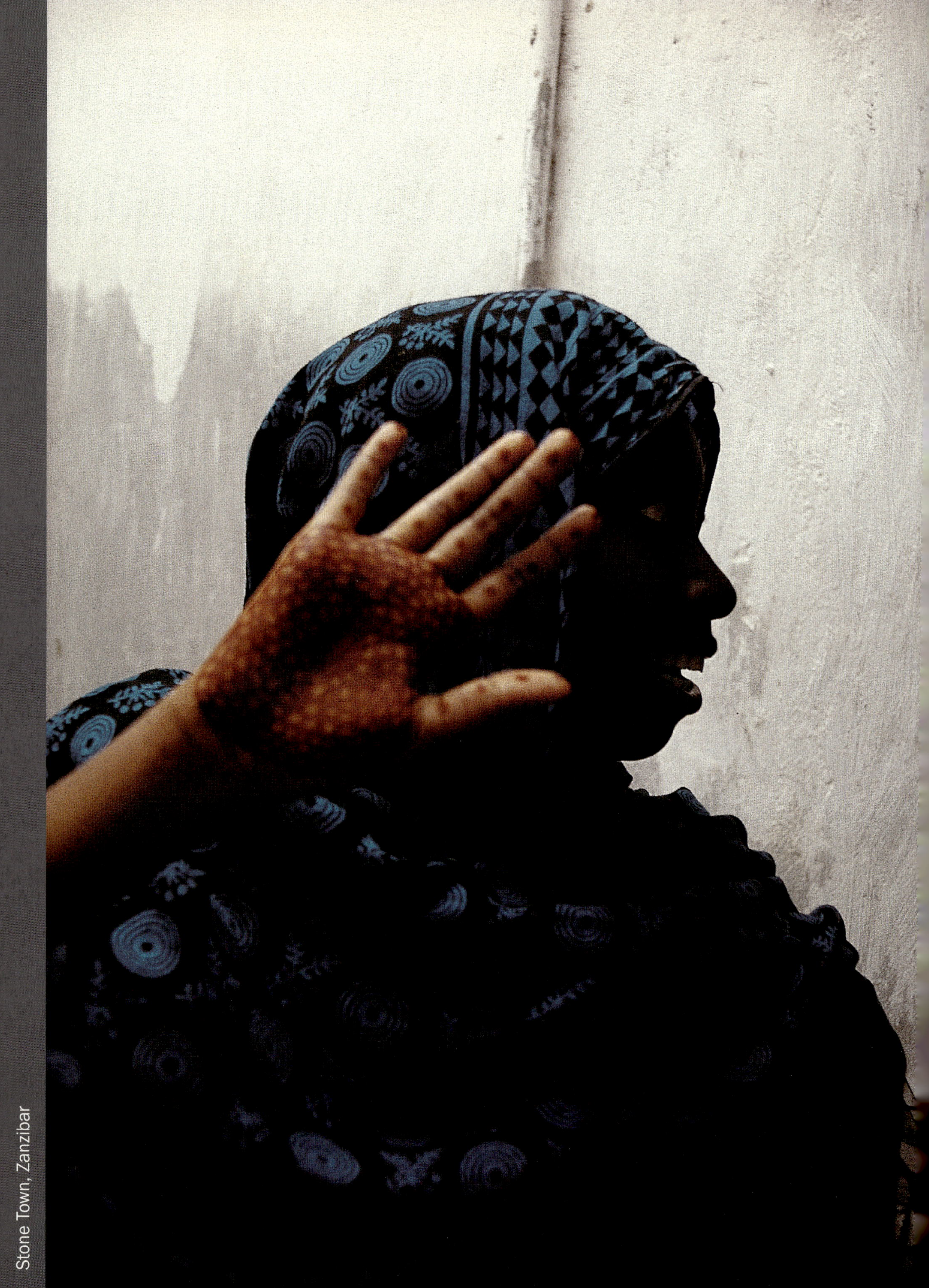

Stone Town, Zanzibar

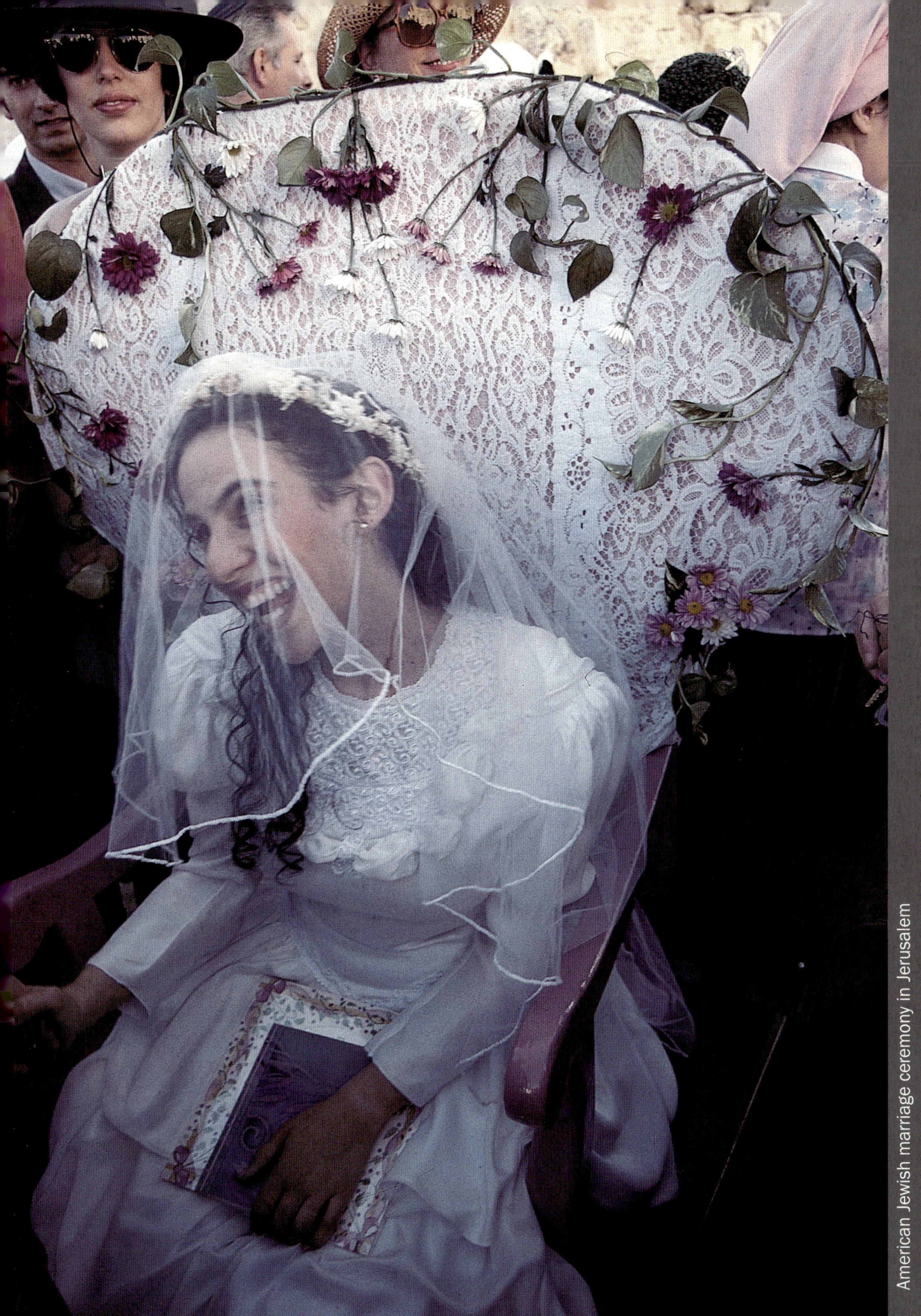

American Jewish marriage ceremony in Jerusalem

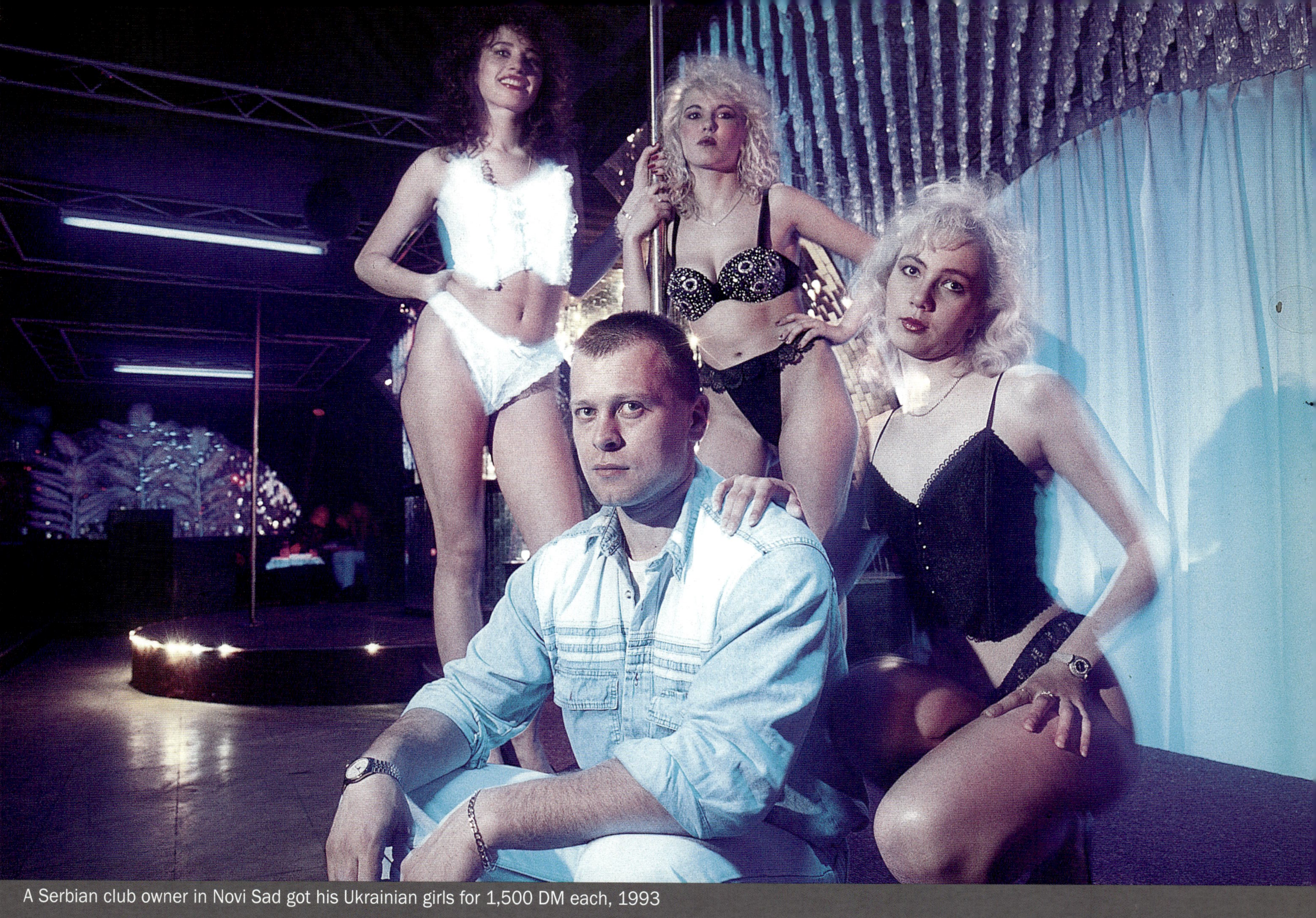

A Serbian club owner in Novi Sad got his Ukrainian girls for 1,500 DM each, 1993

Indian marriage ceremony, London

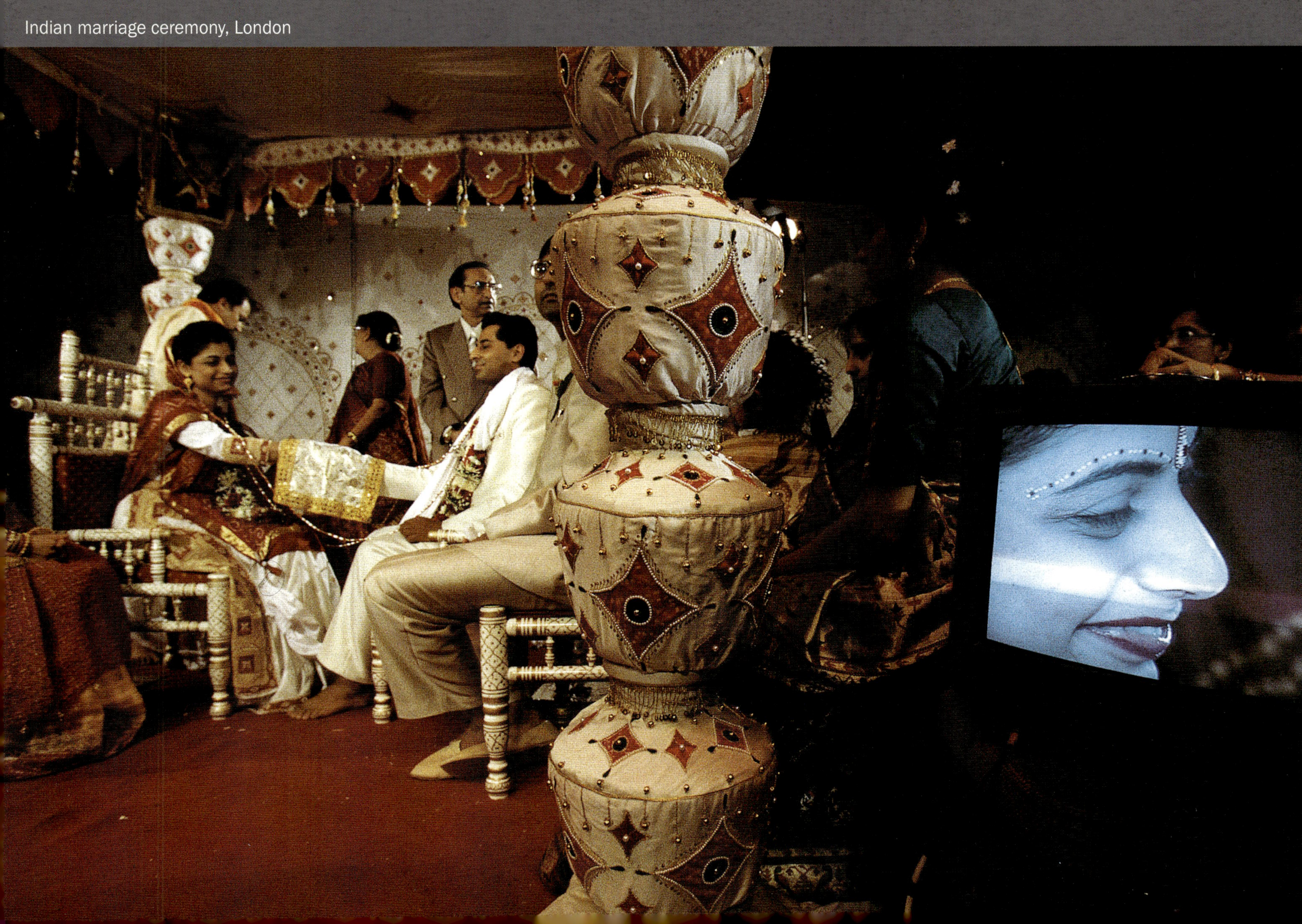

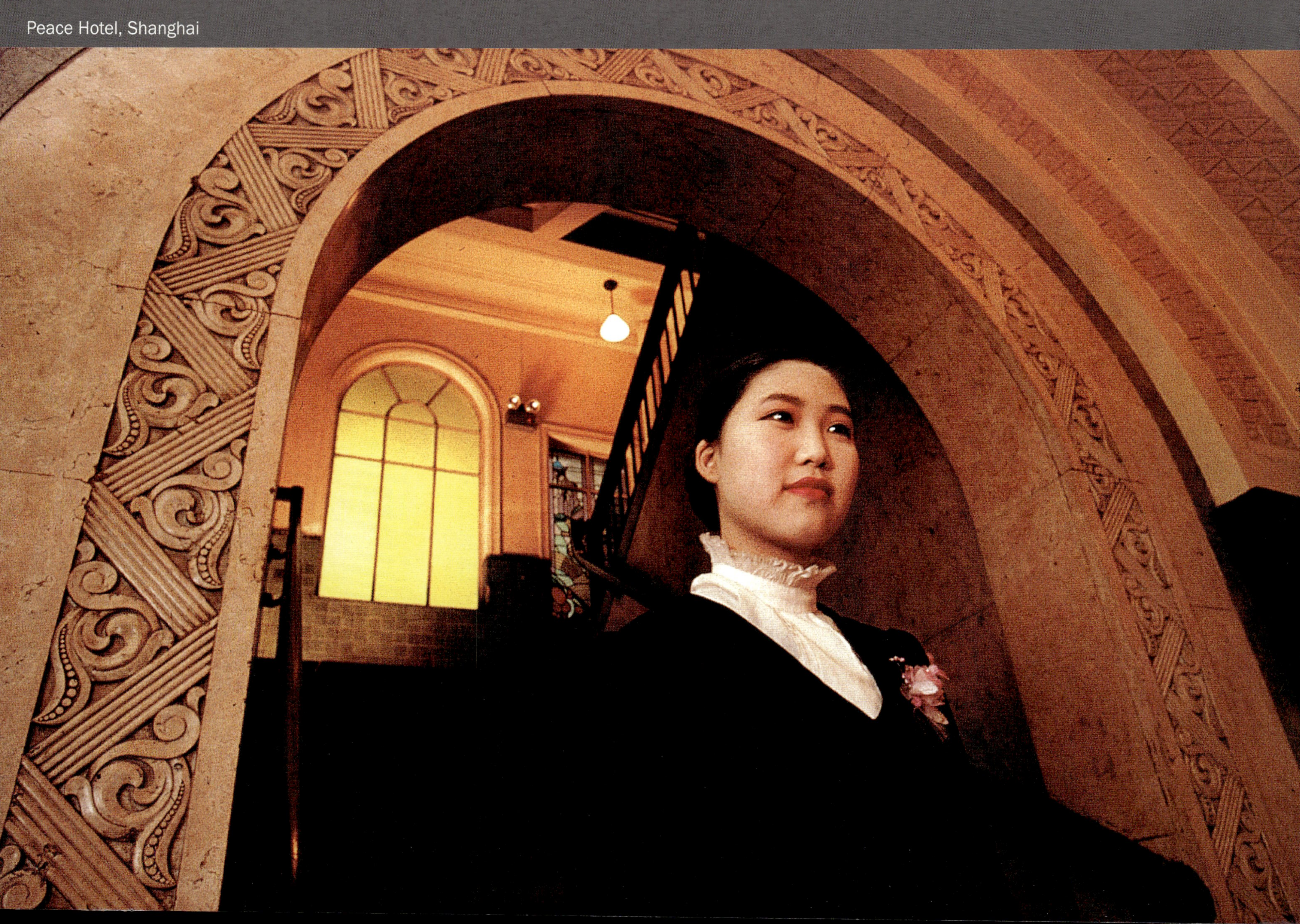

Peace Hotel, Shanghai

Port in Zanzibar

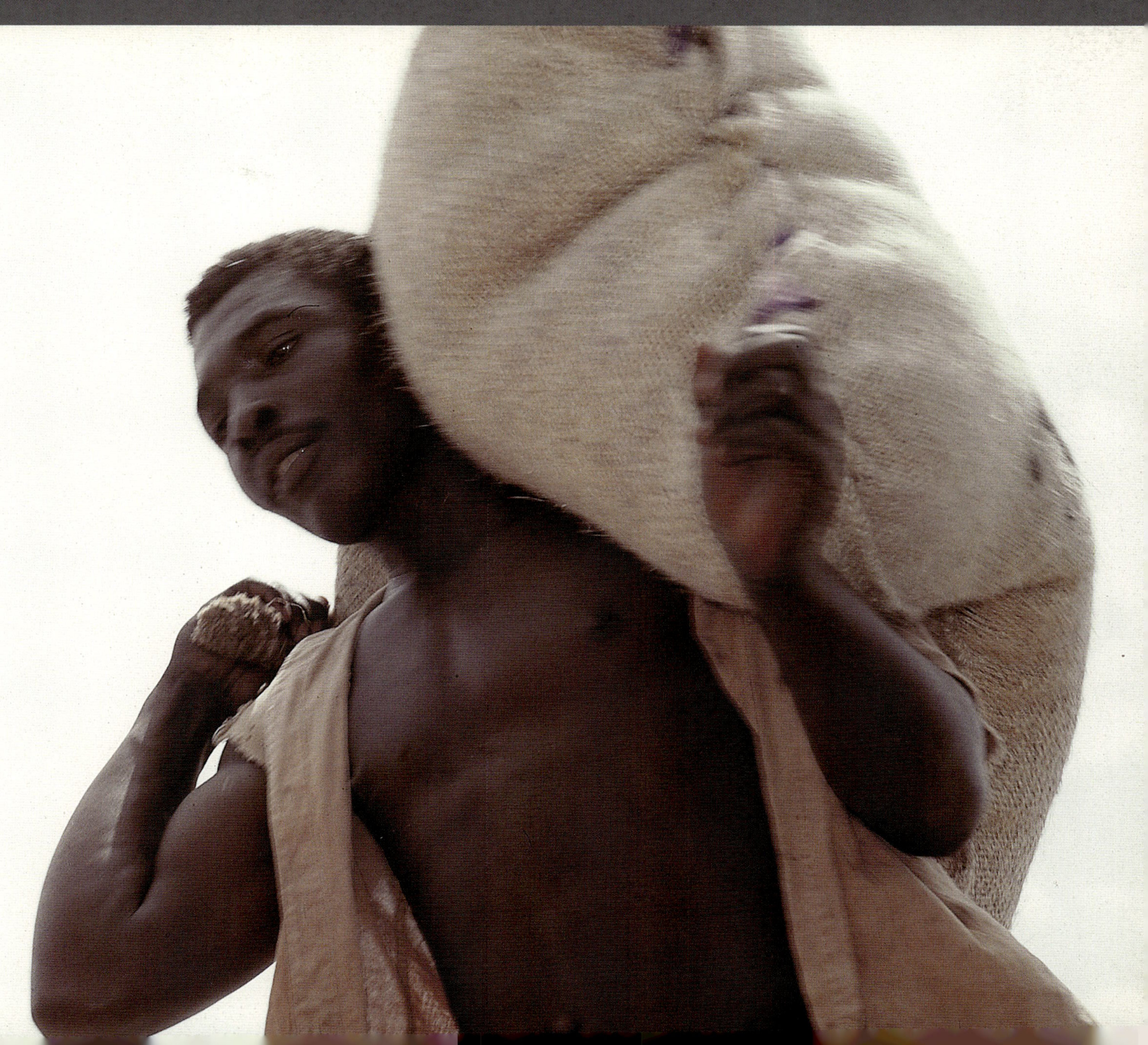

Larry E. Joseph, writer, Brooklyn, New York

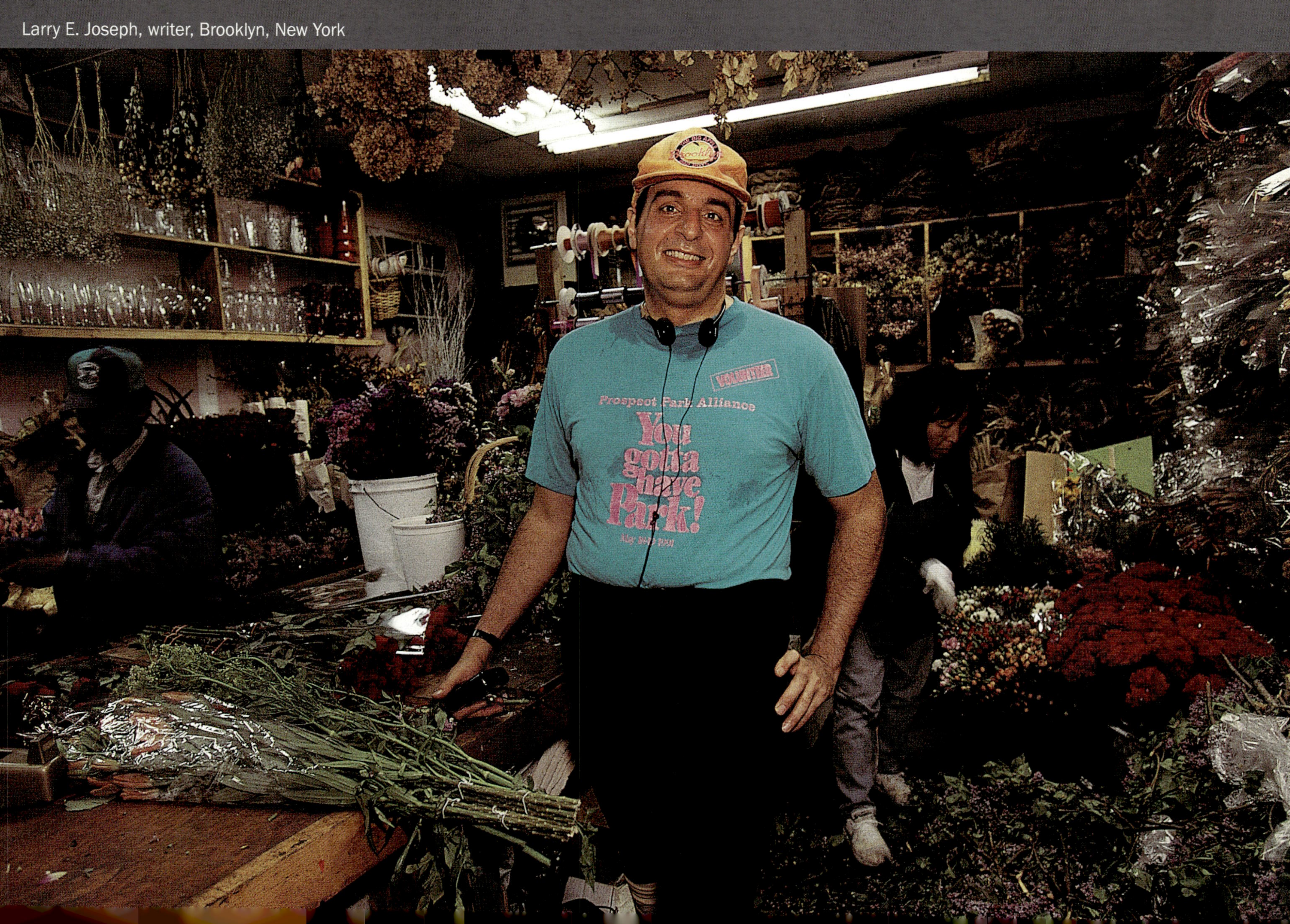

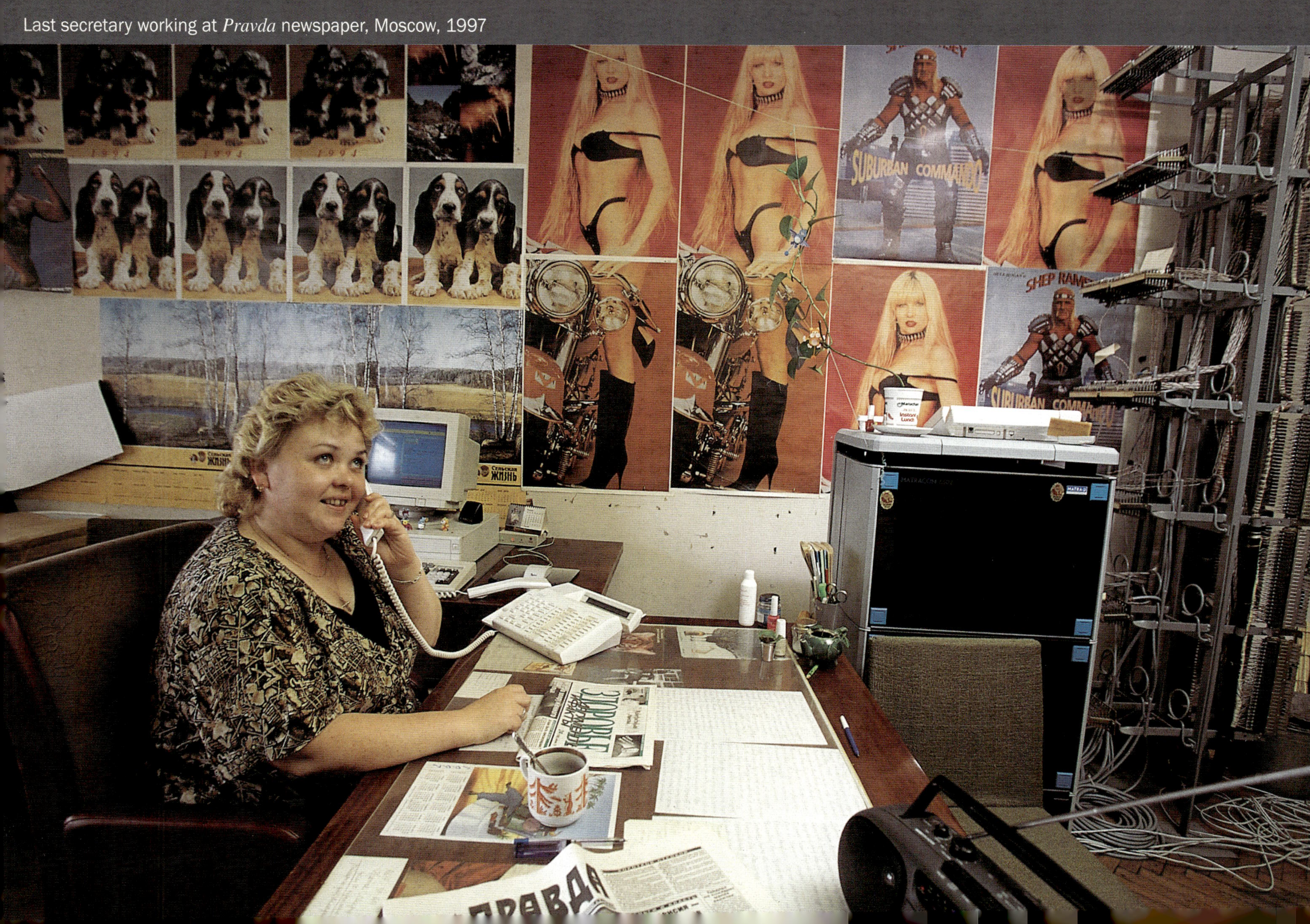

Last secretary working at *Pravda* newspaper, Moscow, 1997

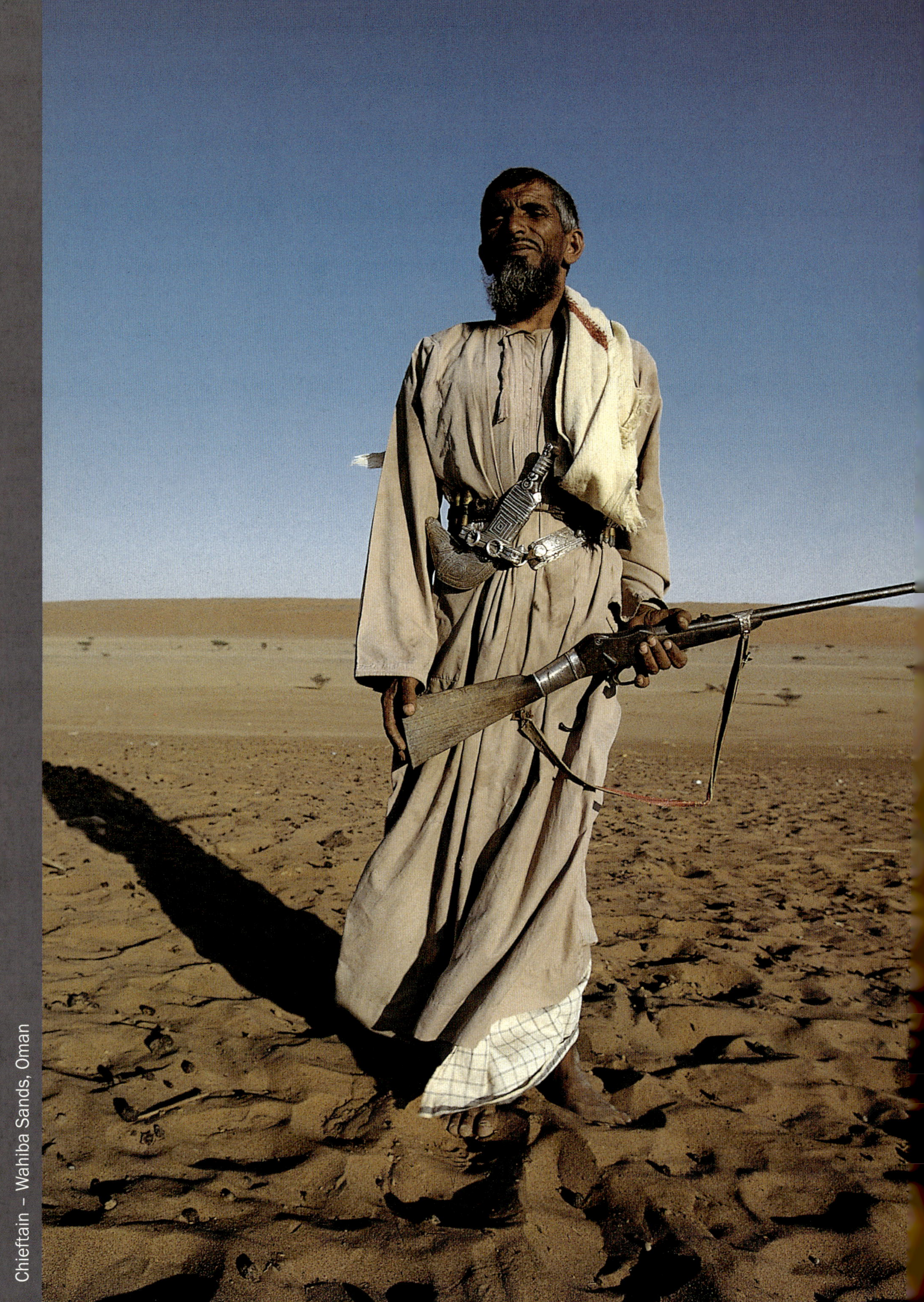

Chieftain – Wahiba Sands, Oman

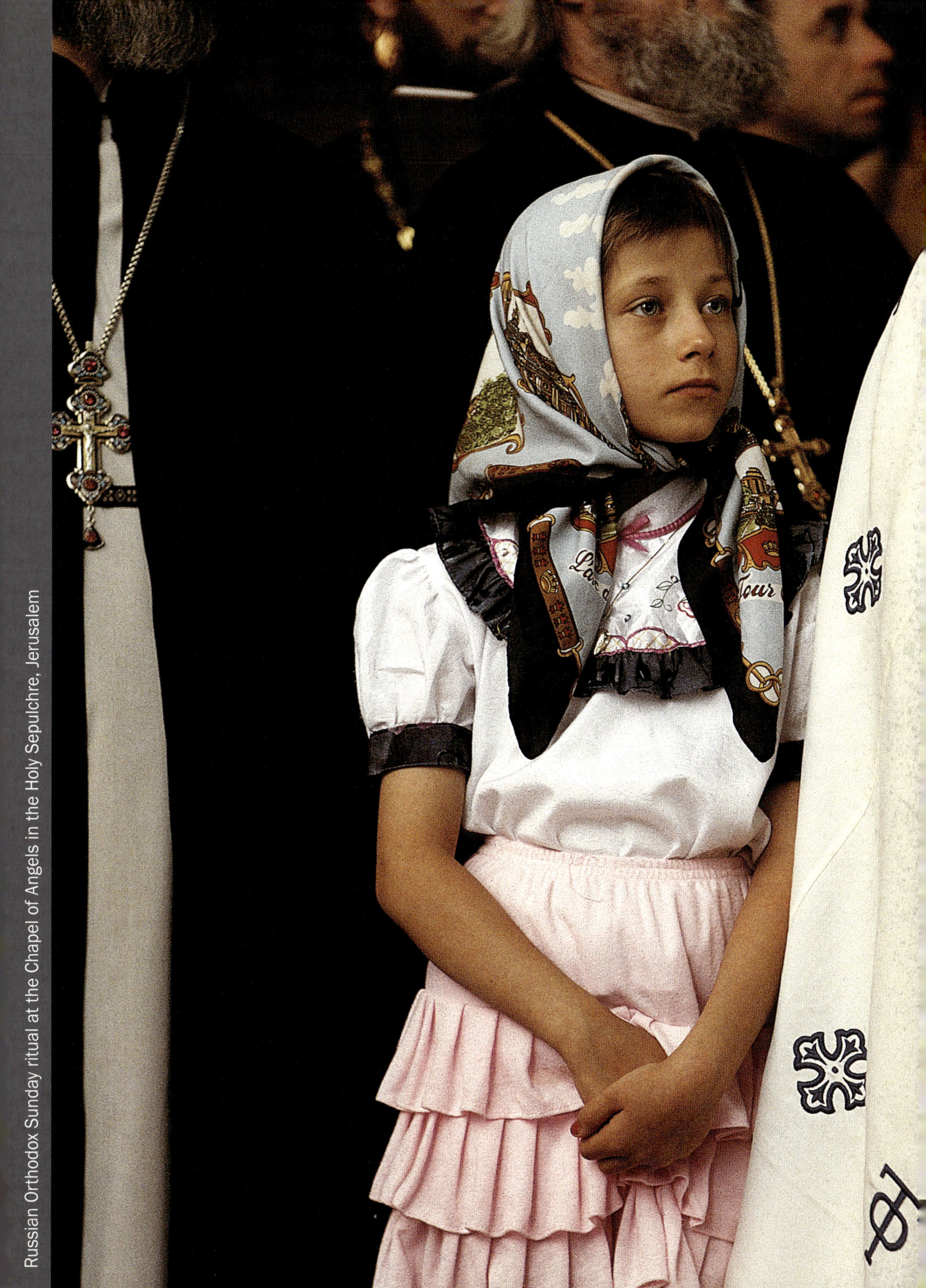

Russian Orthodox Sunday ritual at the Chapel of Angels in the Holy Sepulchre, Jerusalem

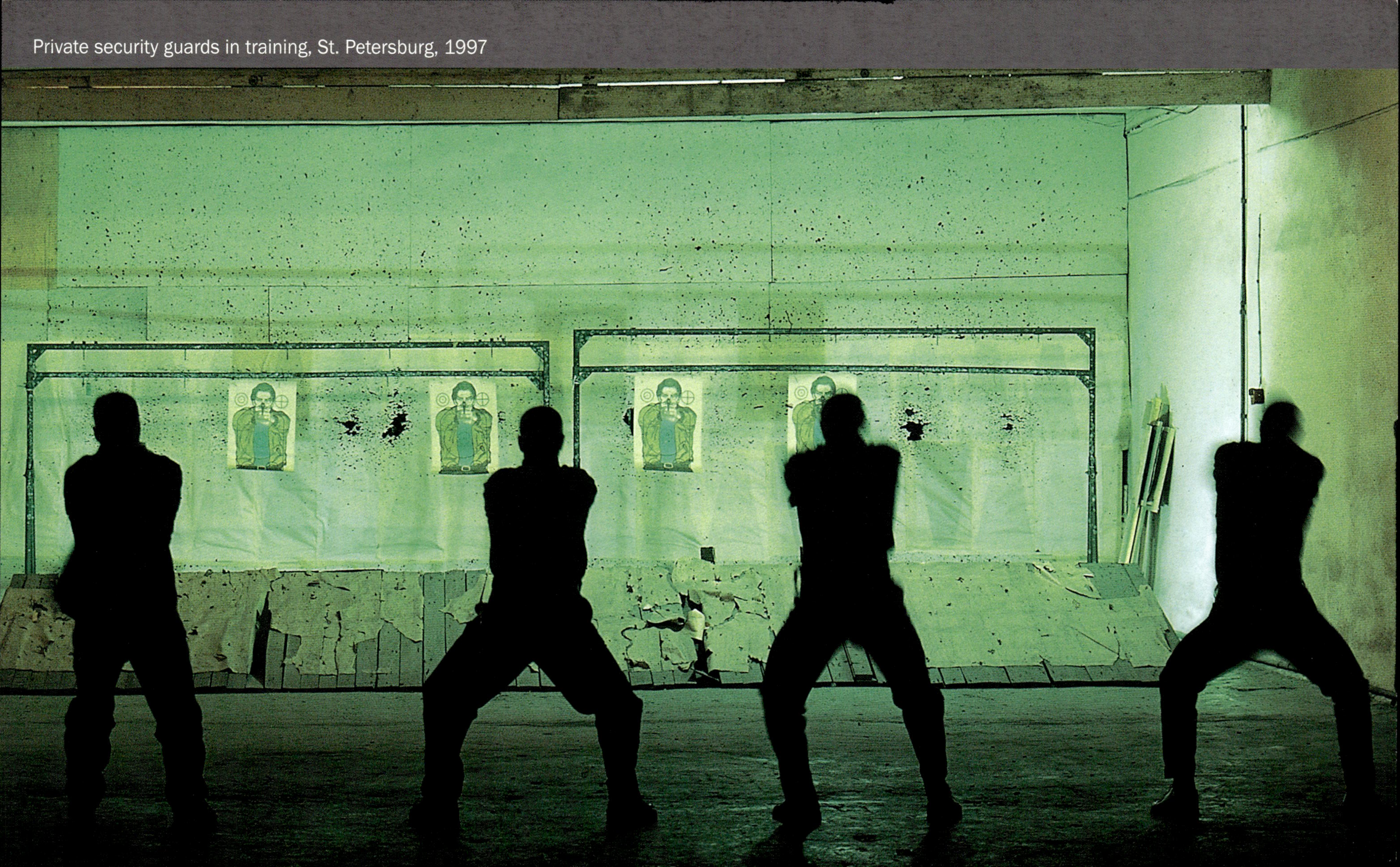

Private security guards in training, St. Petersburg, 1997

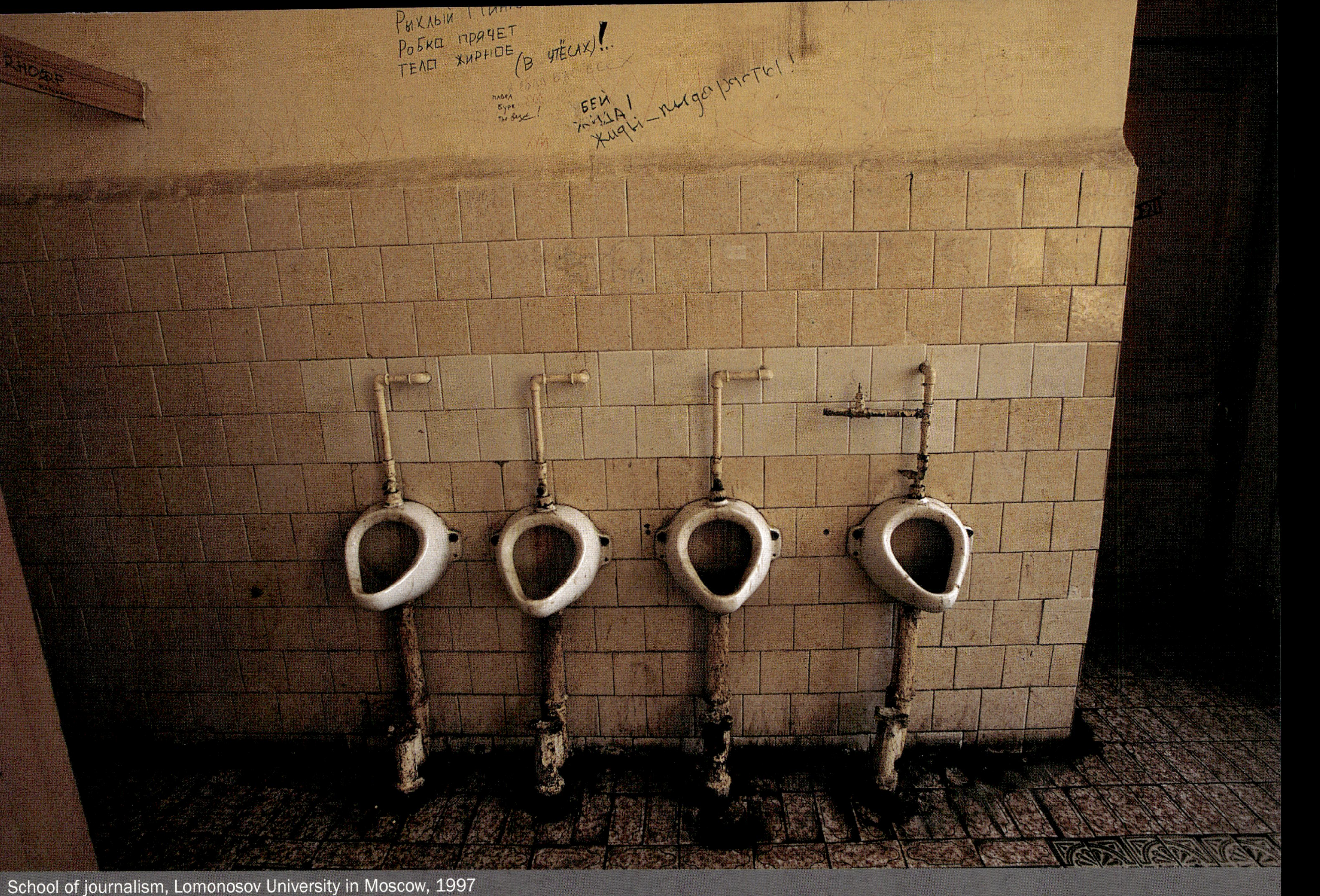

School of journalism, Lomonosov University in Moscow, 1997

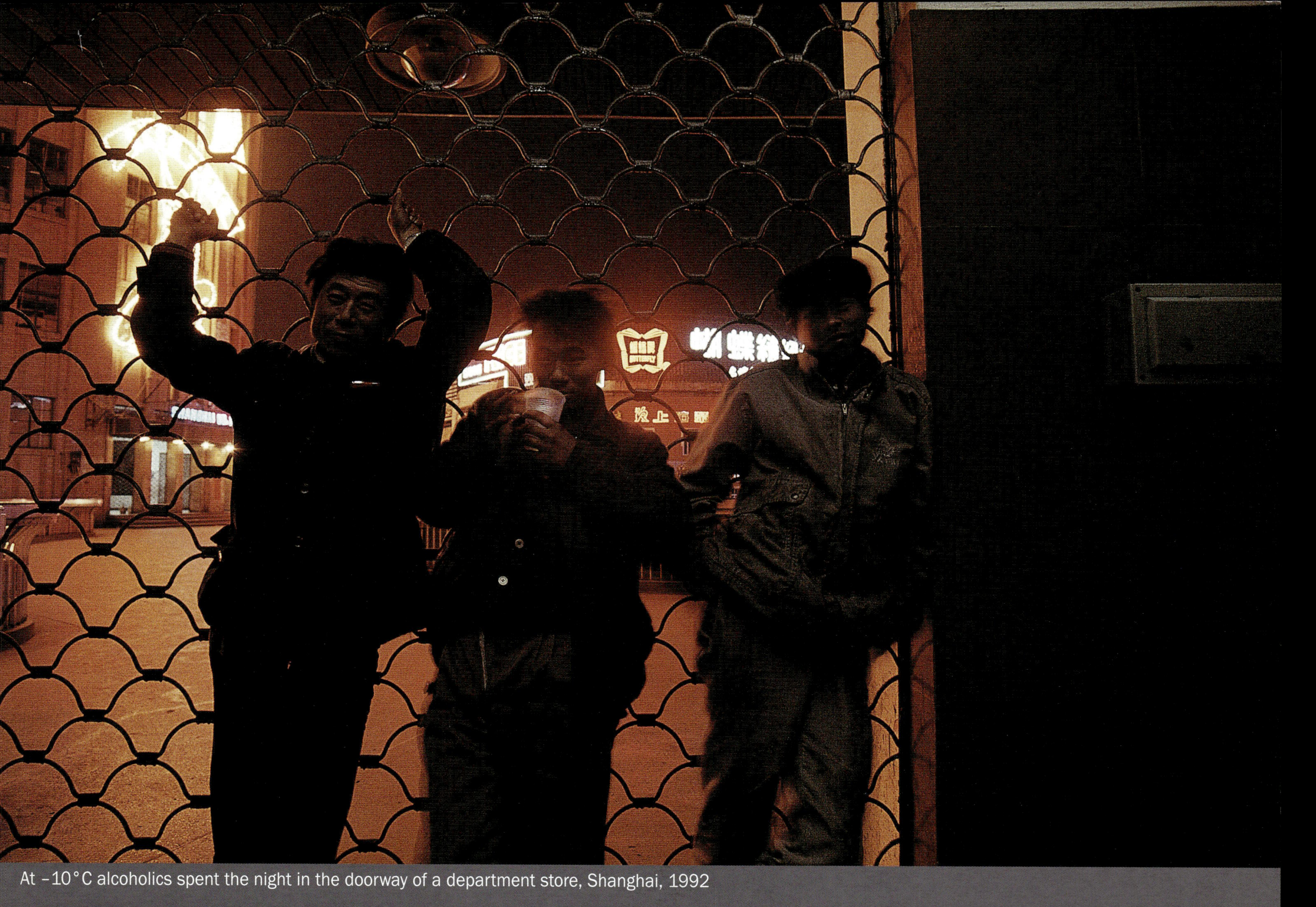

At –10°C alcoholics spent the night in the doorway of a department store, Shanghai, 1992

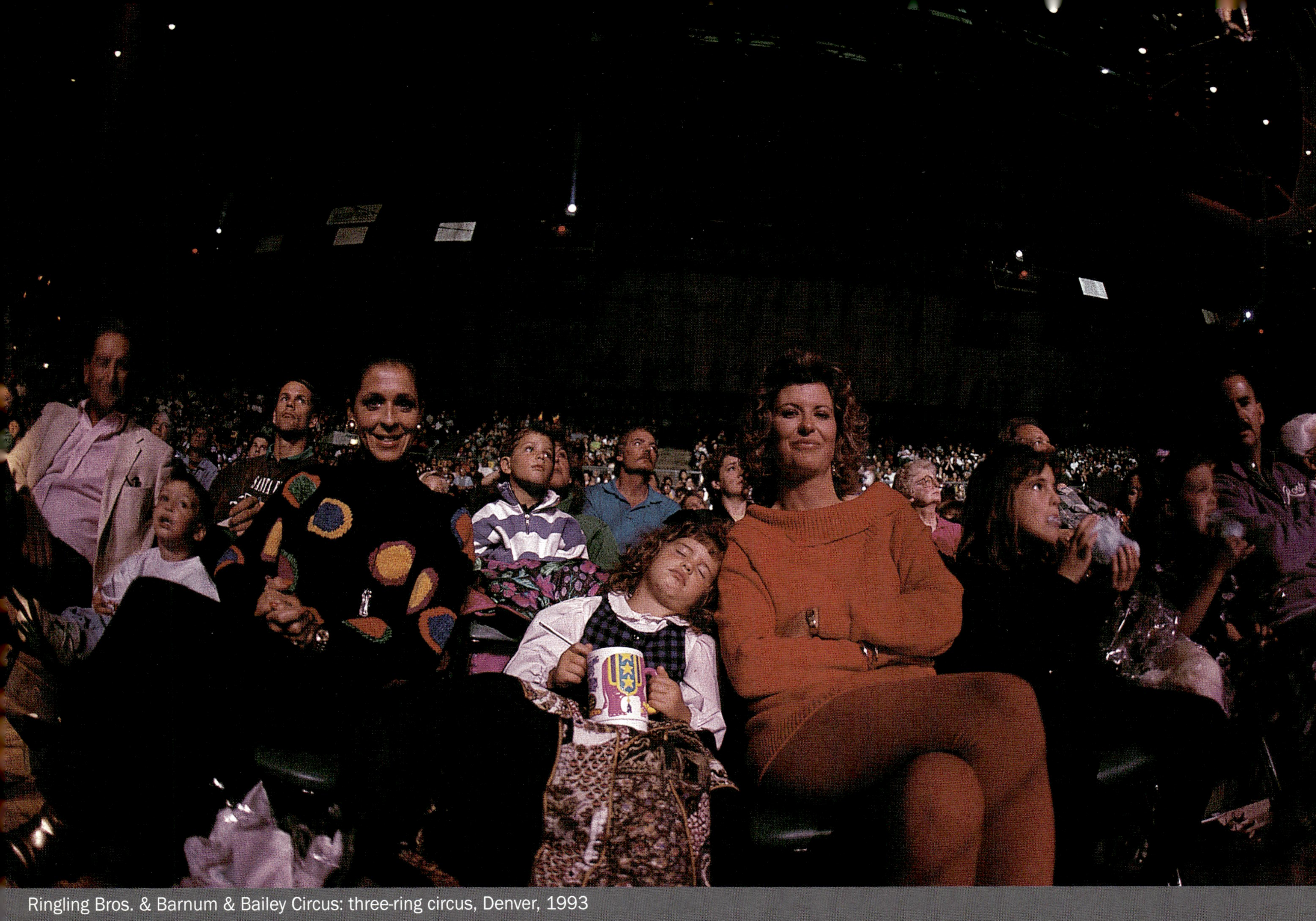

Ringling Bros. & Barnum & Bailey Circus: three-ring circus, Denver, 1993

Cremation – Ganges, India

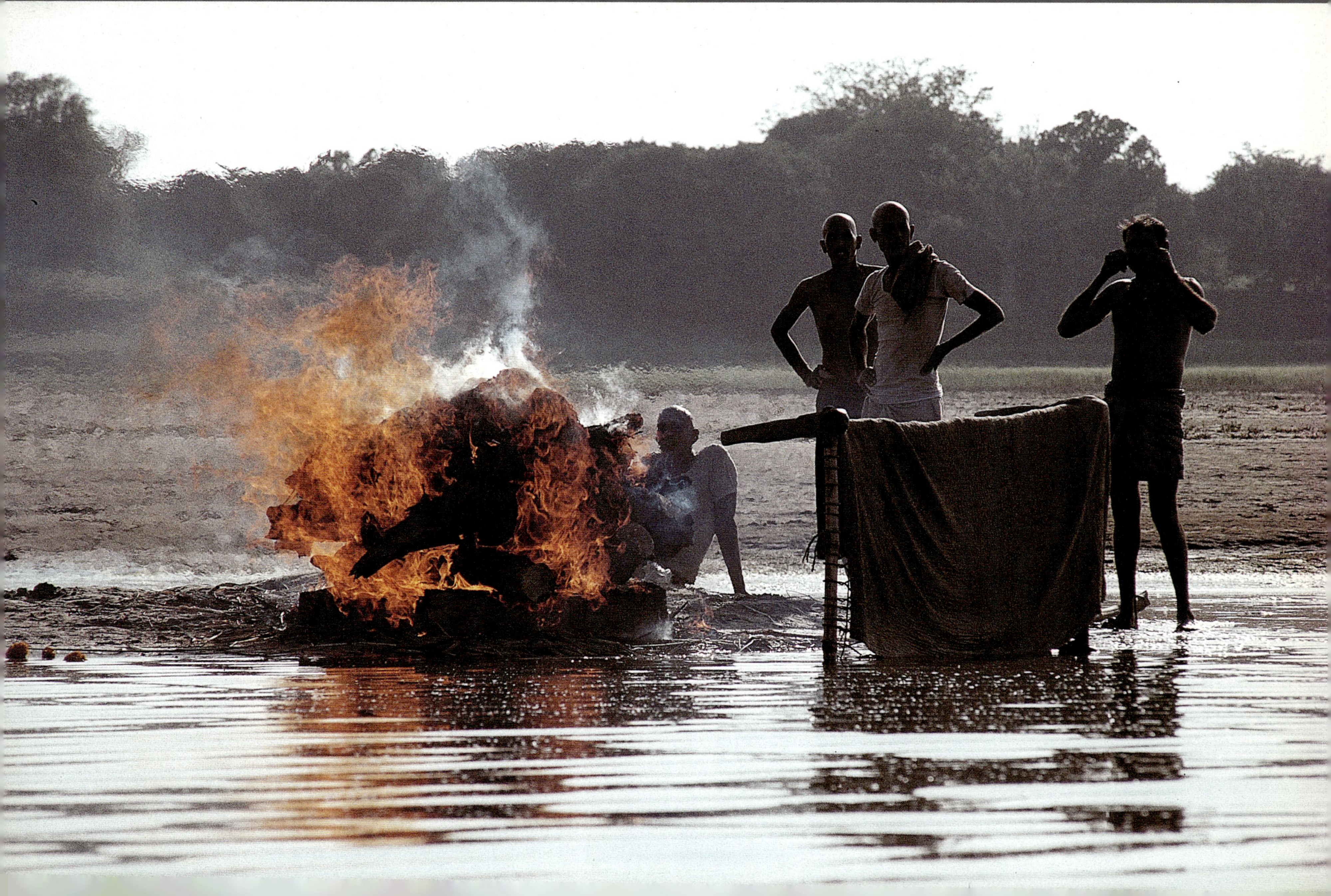

Rankin photographing for *Dazed & Confused*, London, 1997

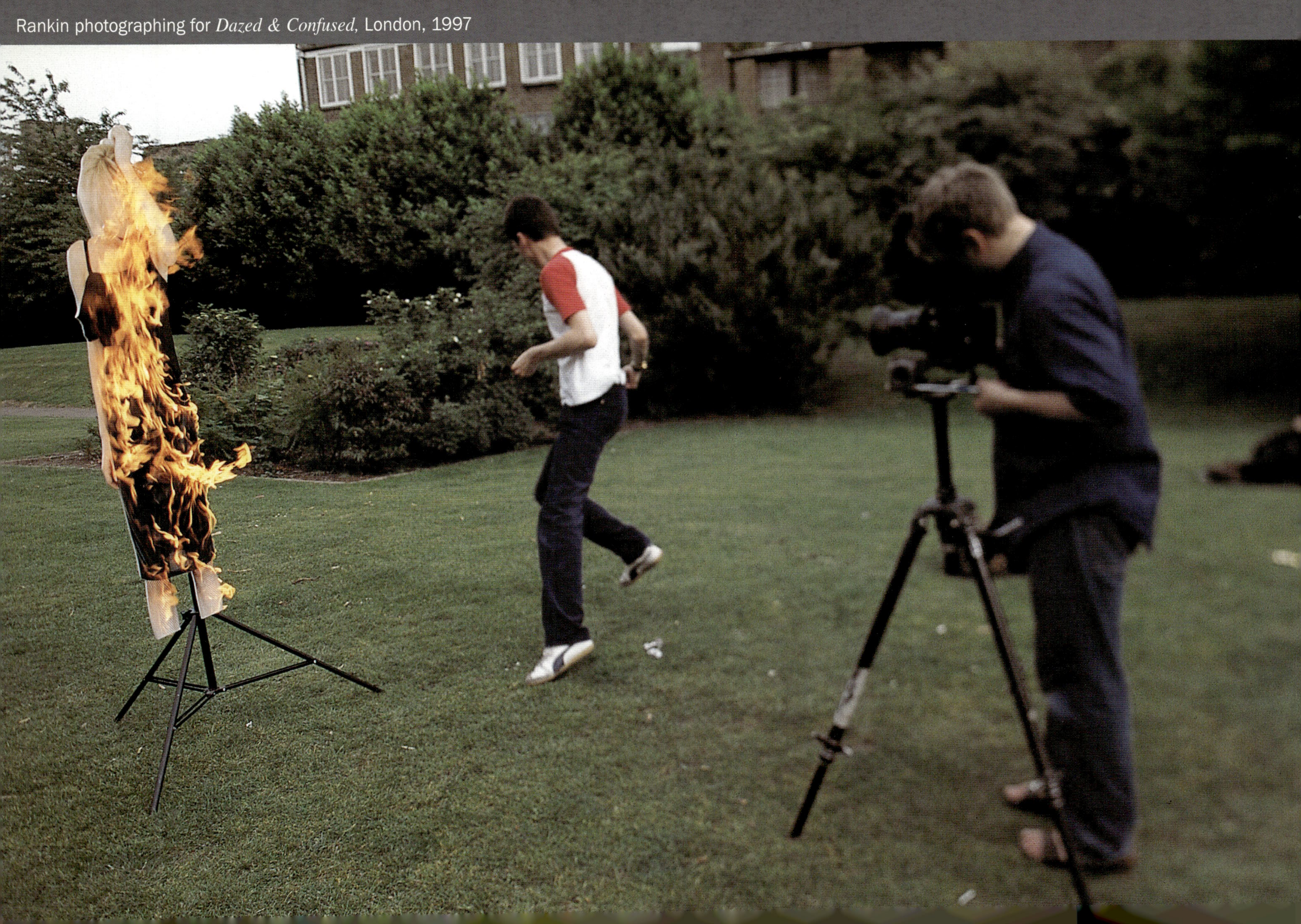

Venice entrance portal; dragon

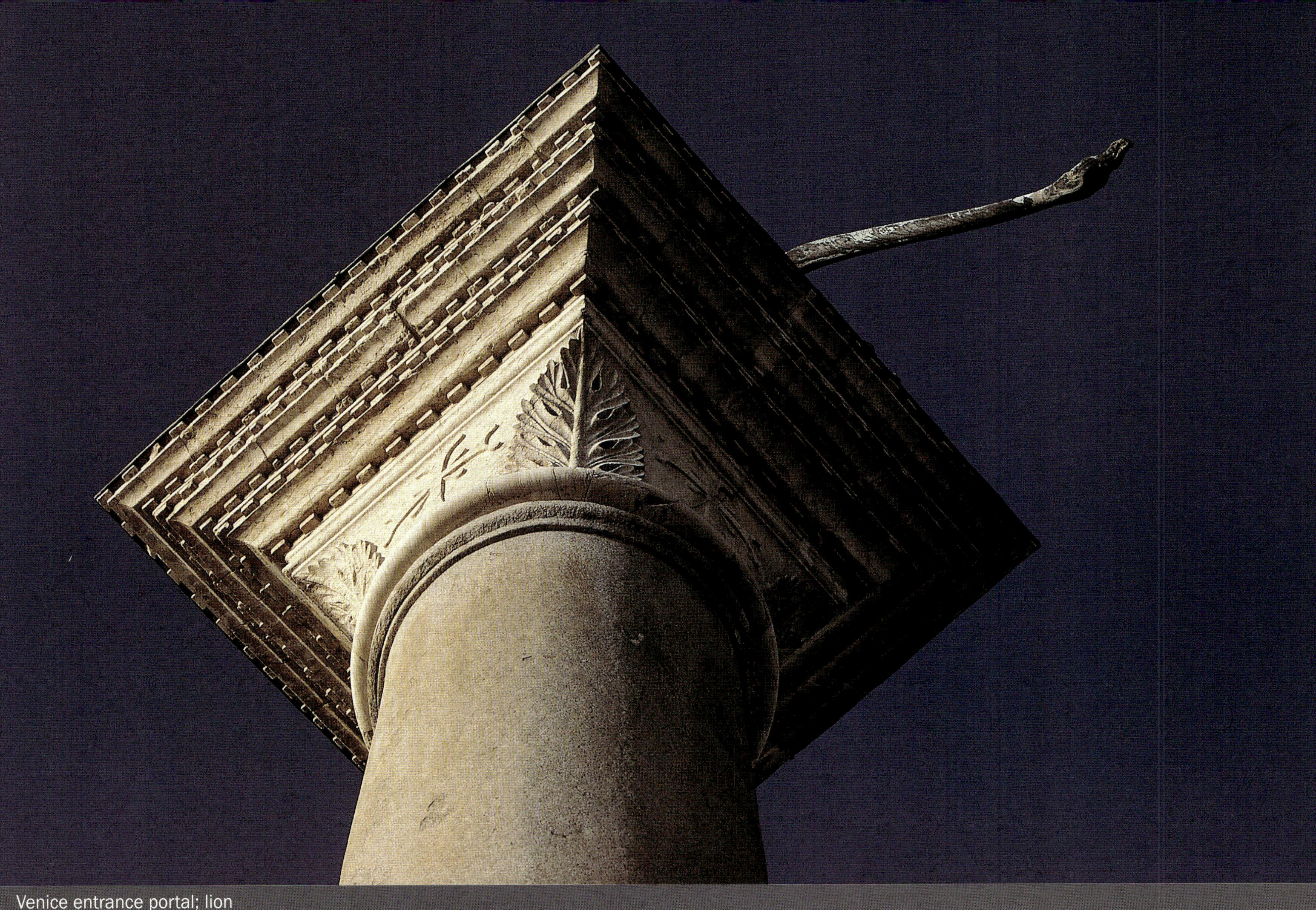

Venice entrance portal; lion

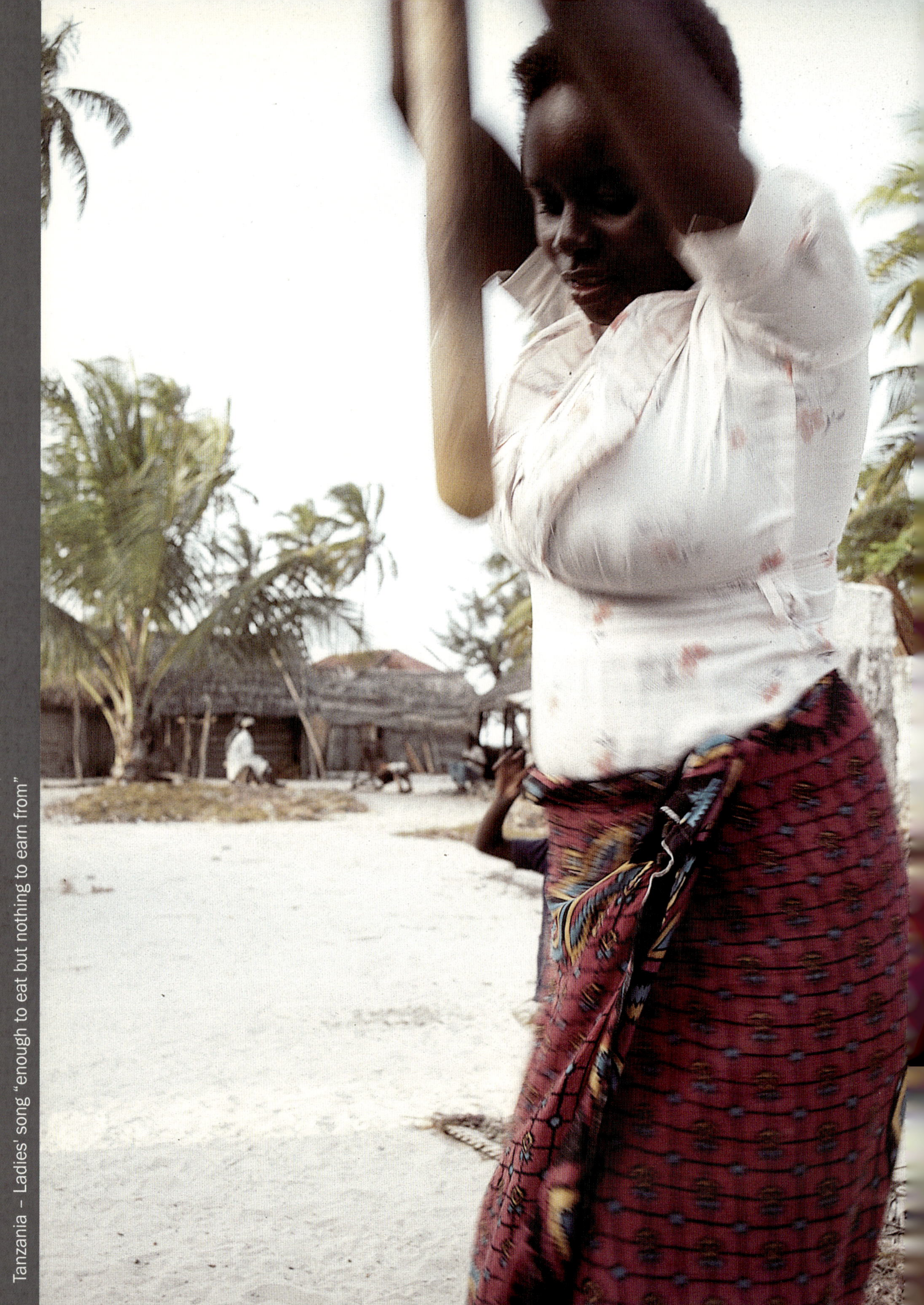

Tanzania – Ladies' song "enough to eat but nothing to earn from"

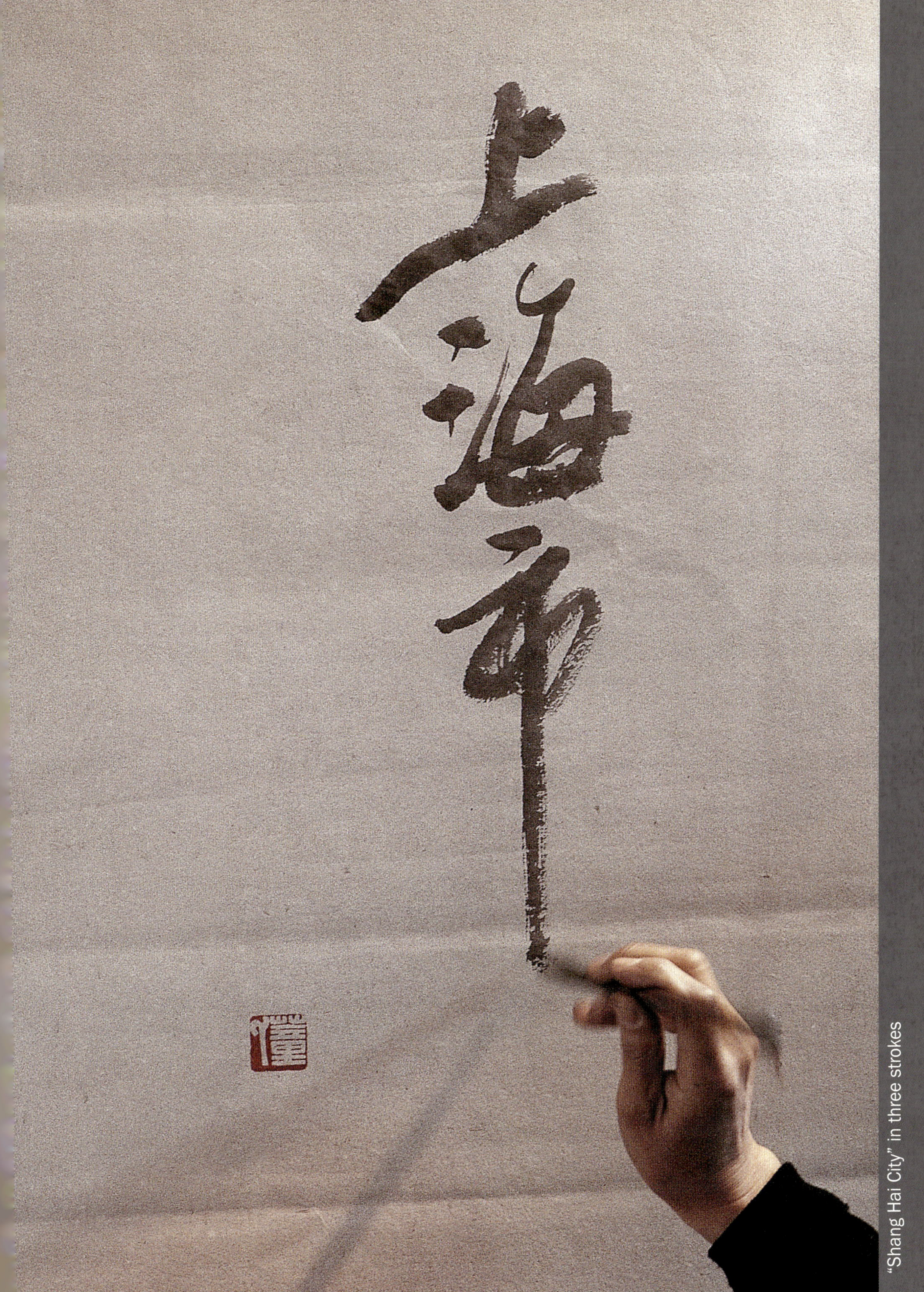

"Shang Hai City" in three strokes

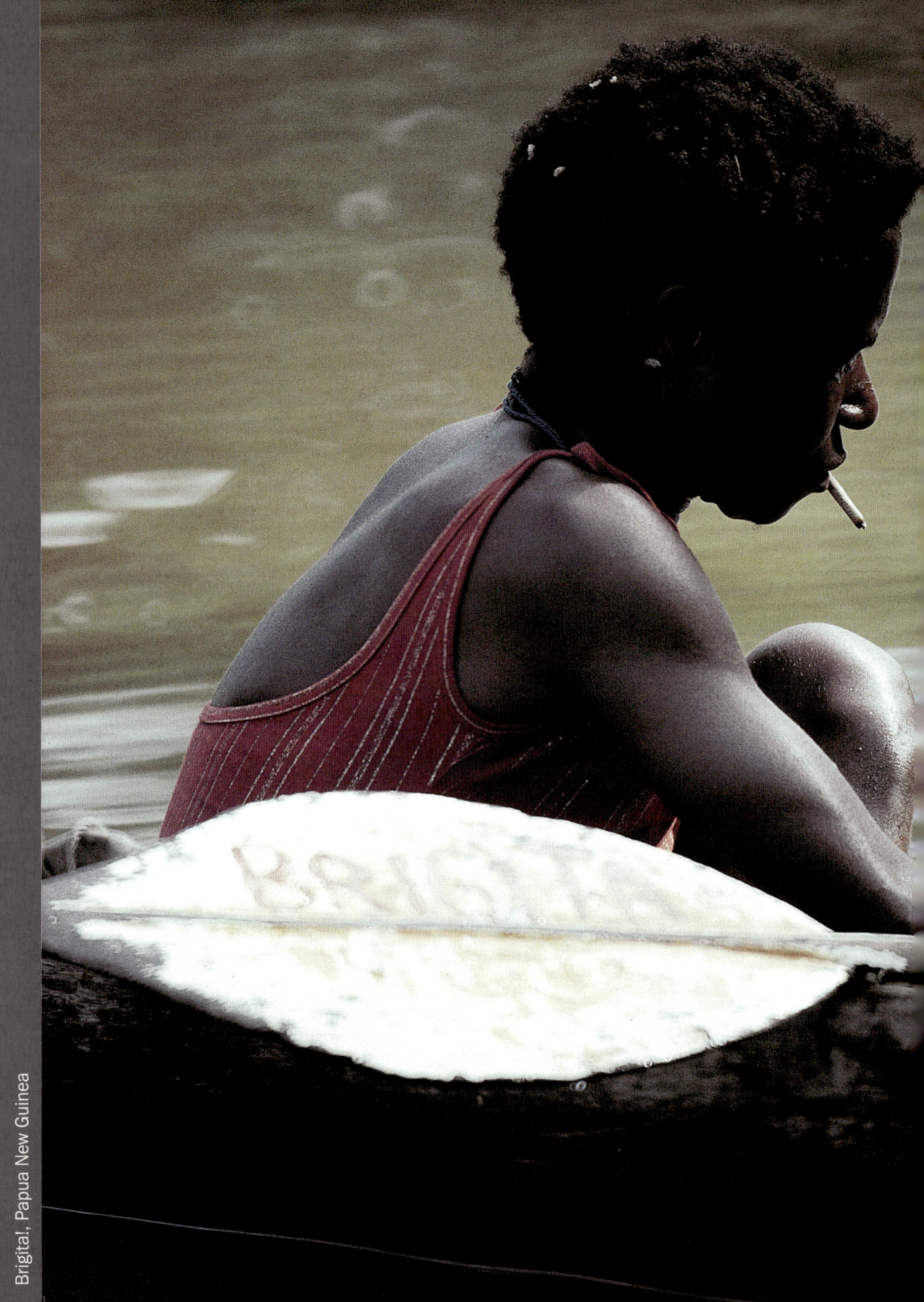

Brigita!, Papua New Guinea

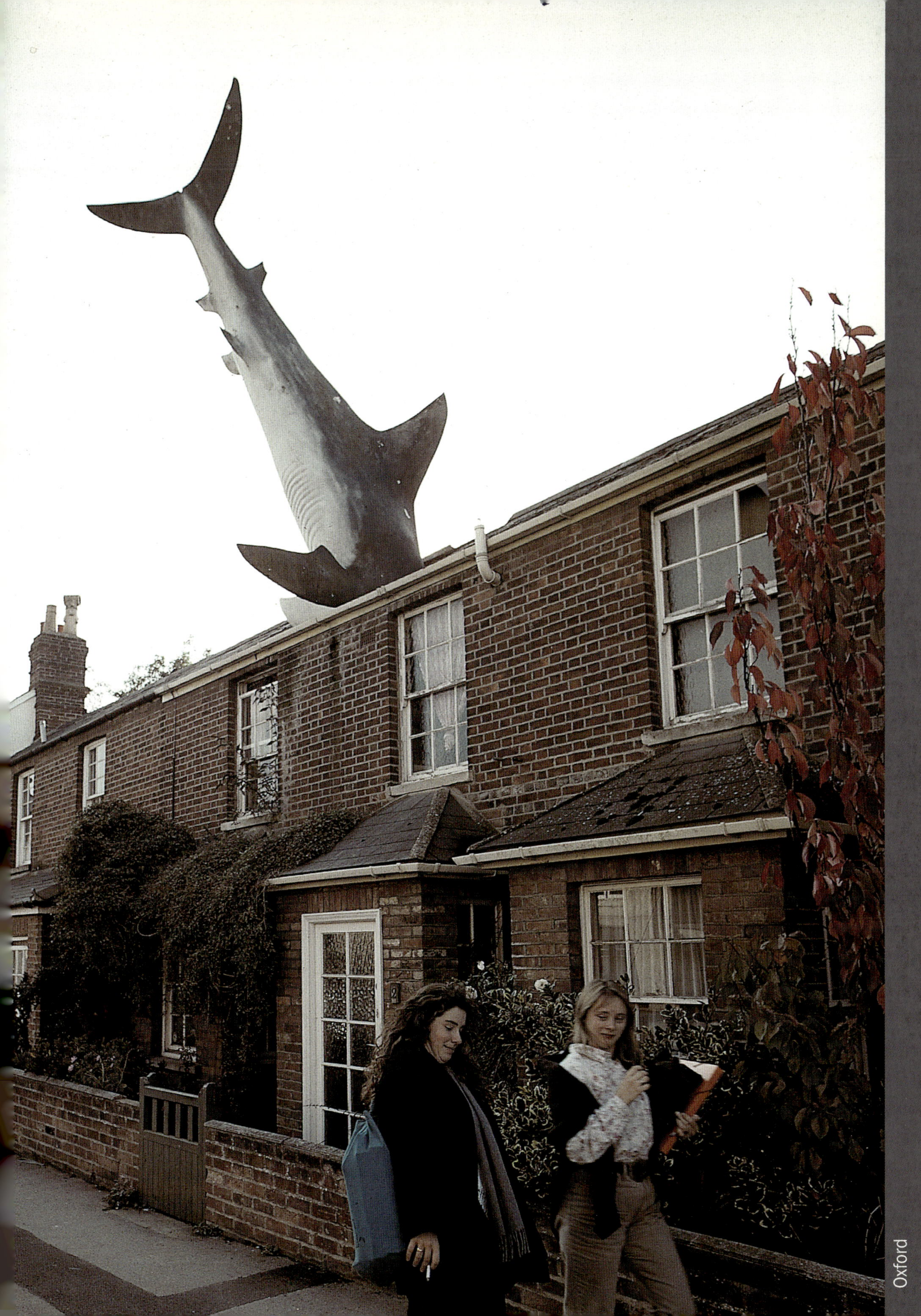

Oxford

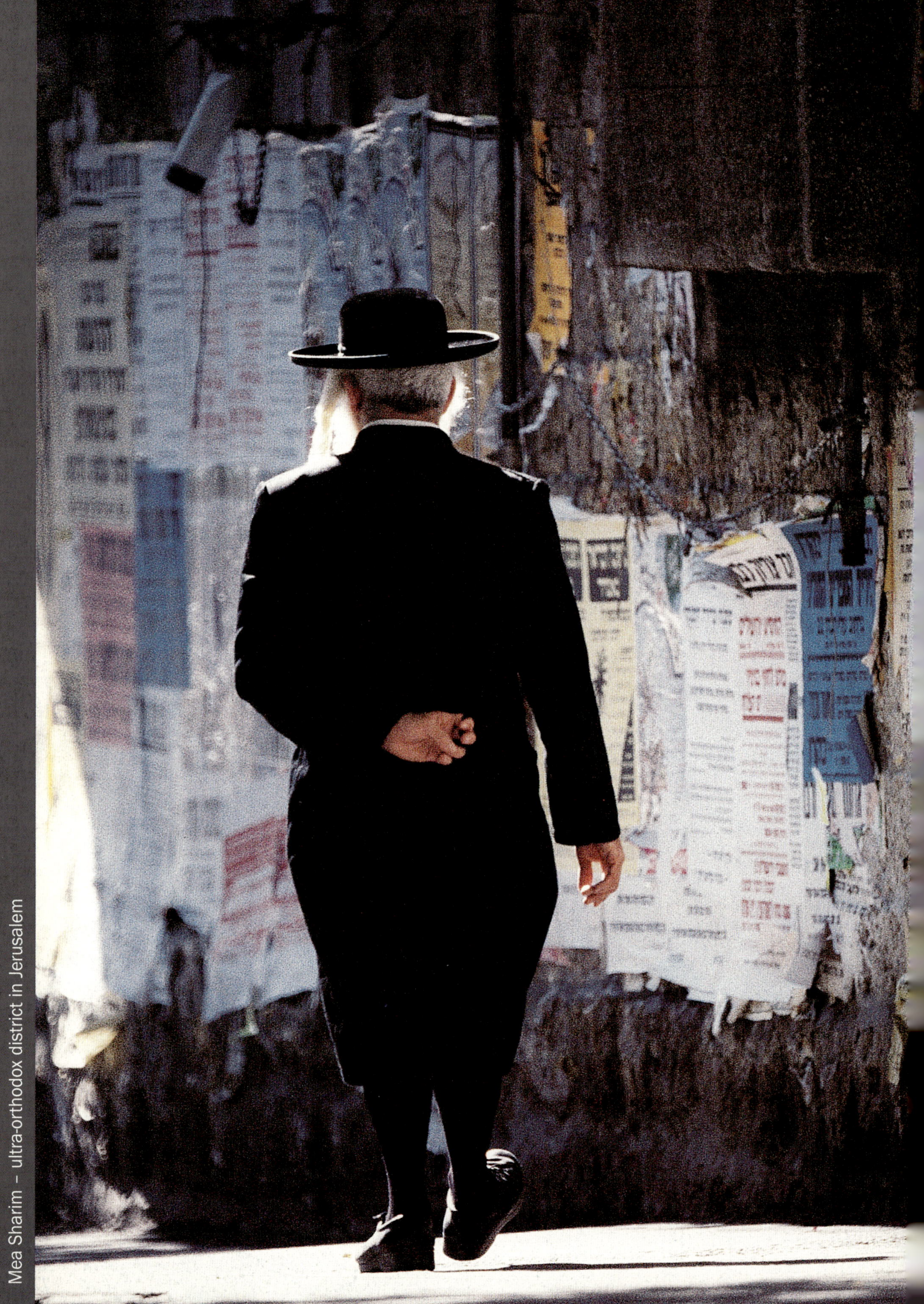

Mea Sharim – ultra-orthodox district in Jerusalem

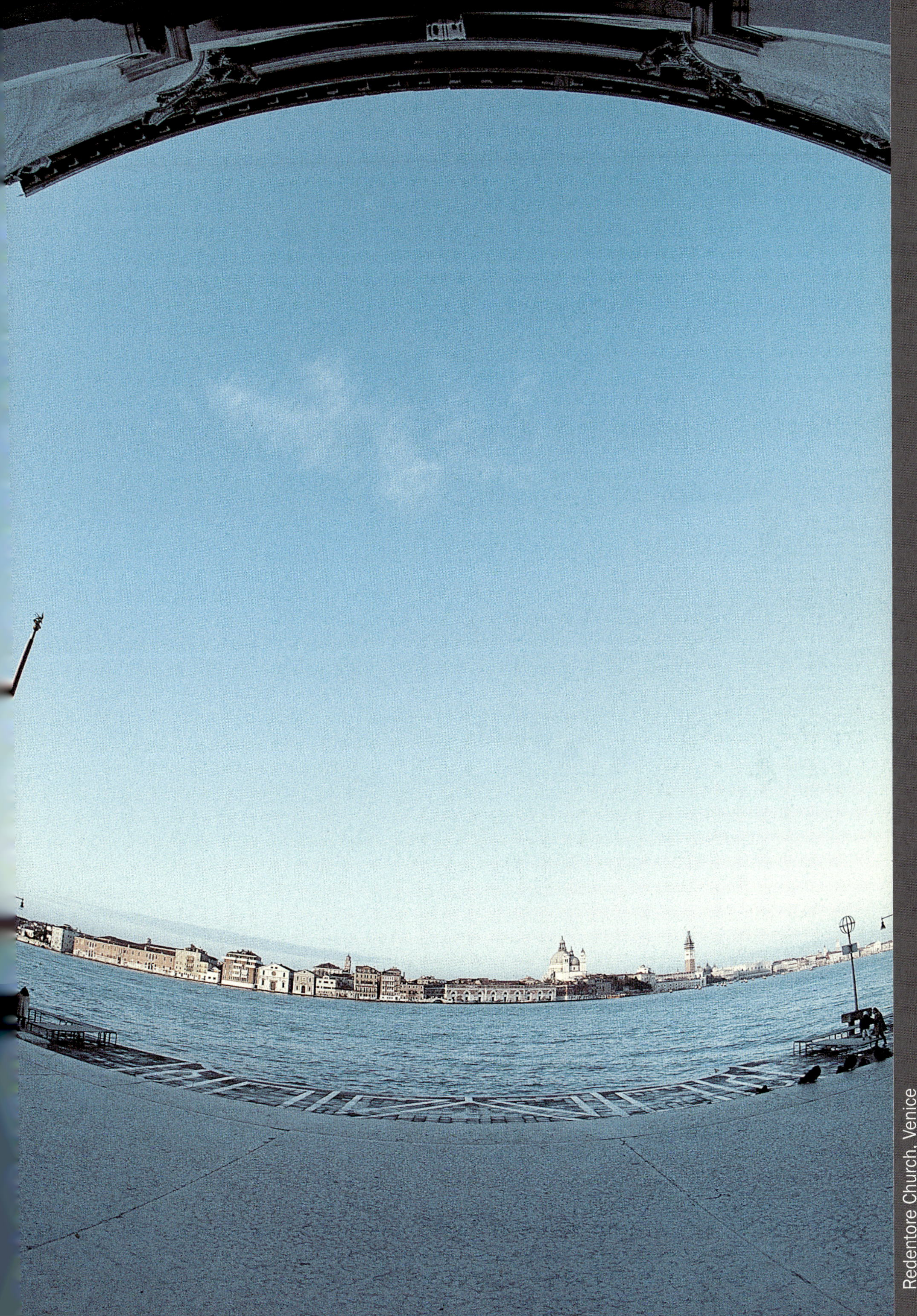

Redentore Church, Venice

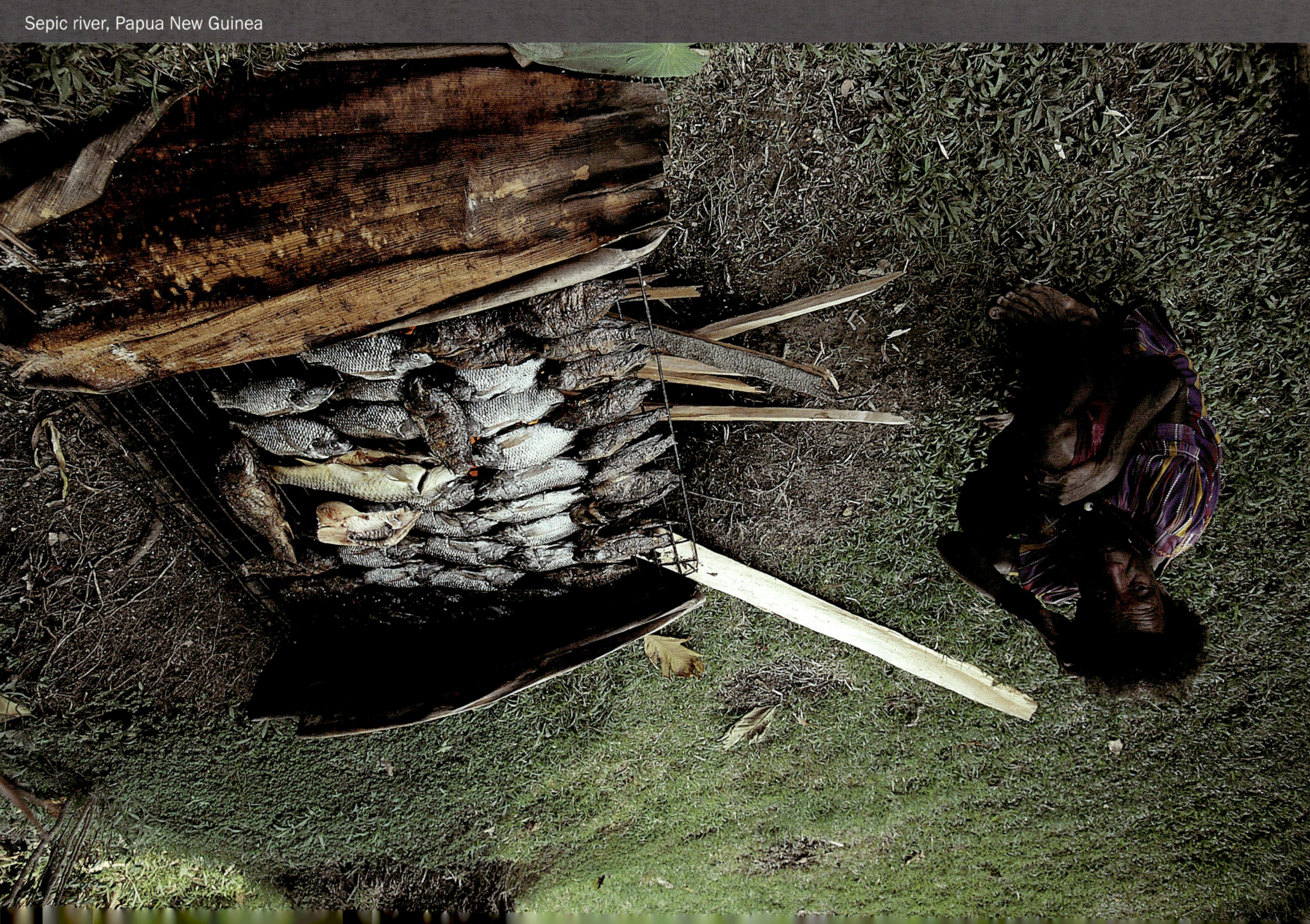

Sepic river, Papua New Guinea

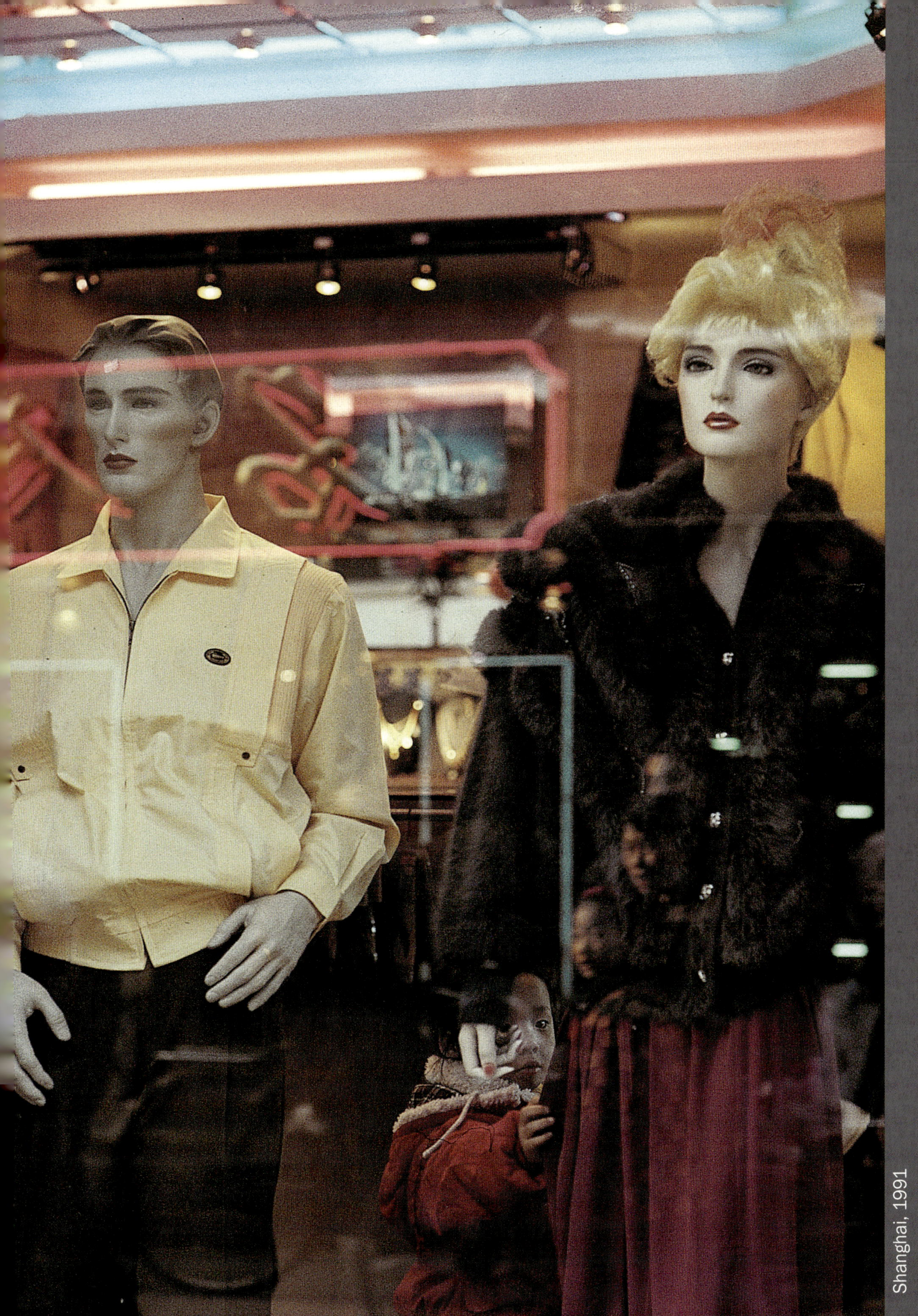

Shanghai, 1991

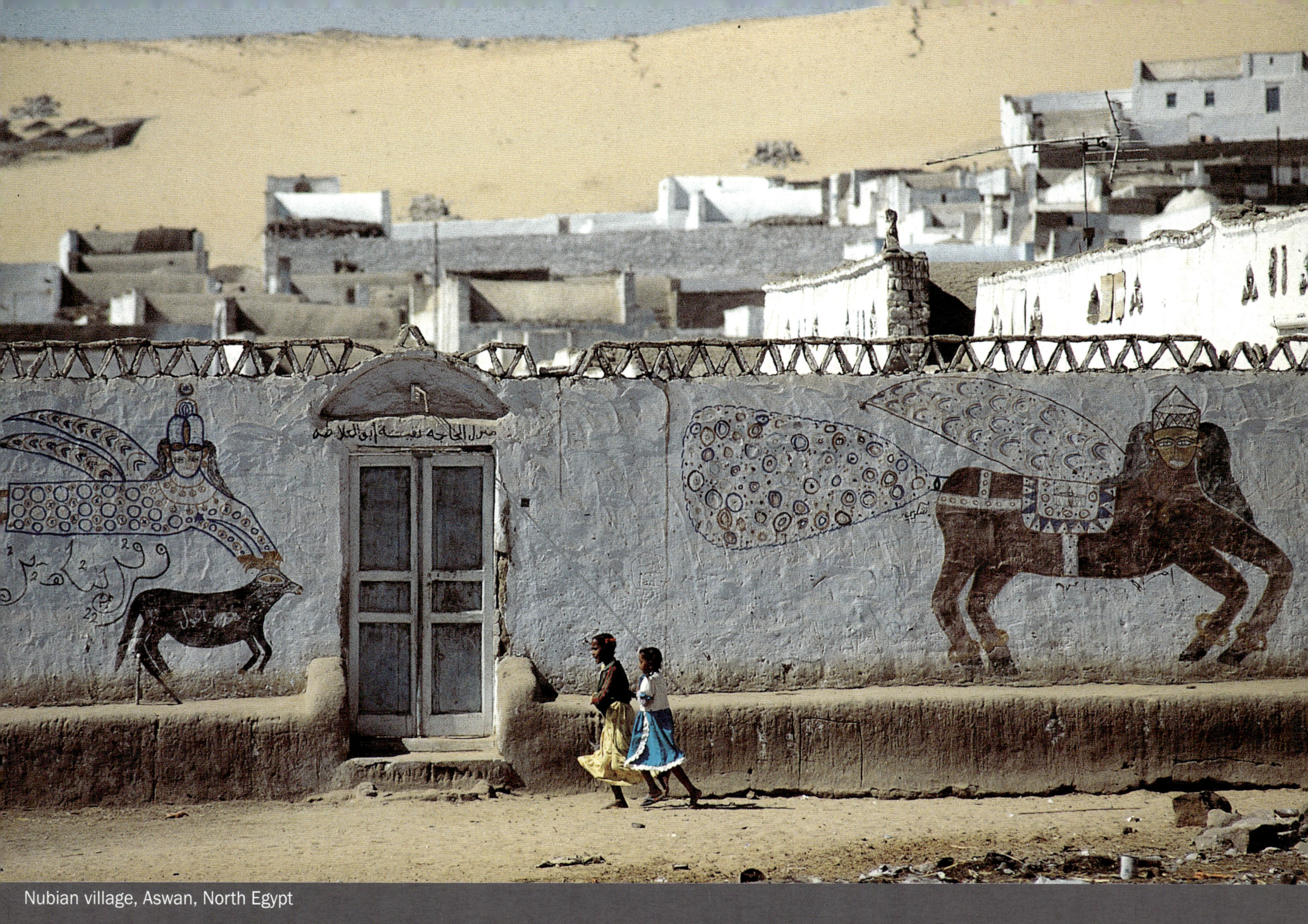

Nubian village, Aswan, North Egypt

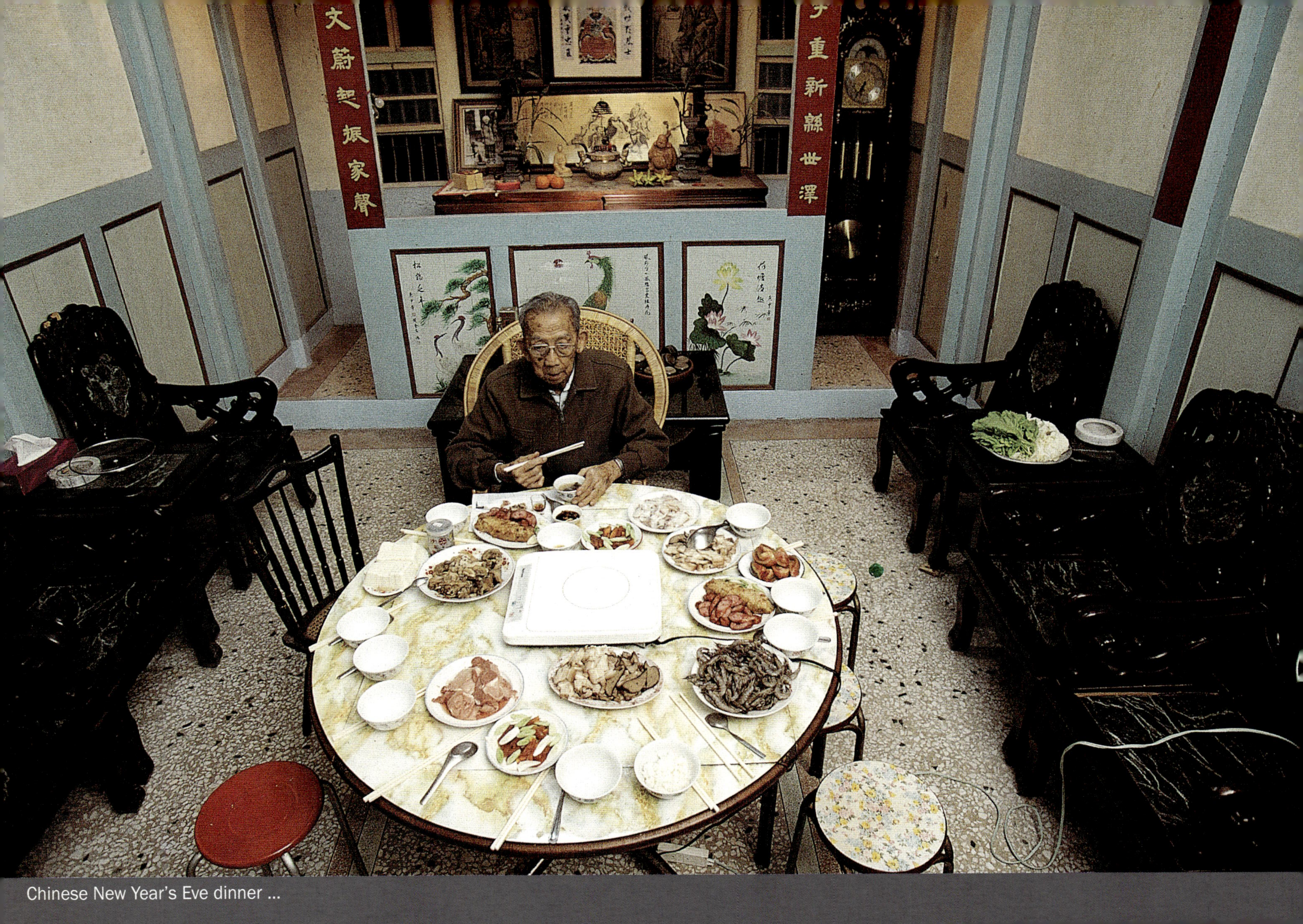

Chinese New Year's Eve dinner ...

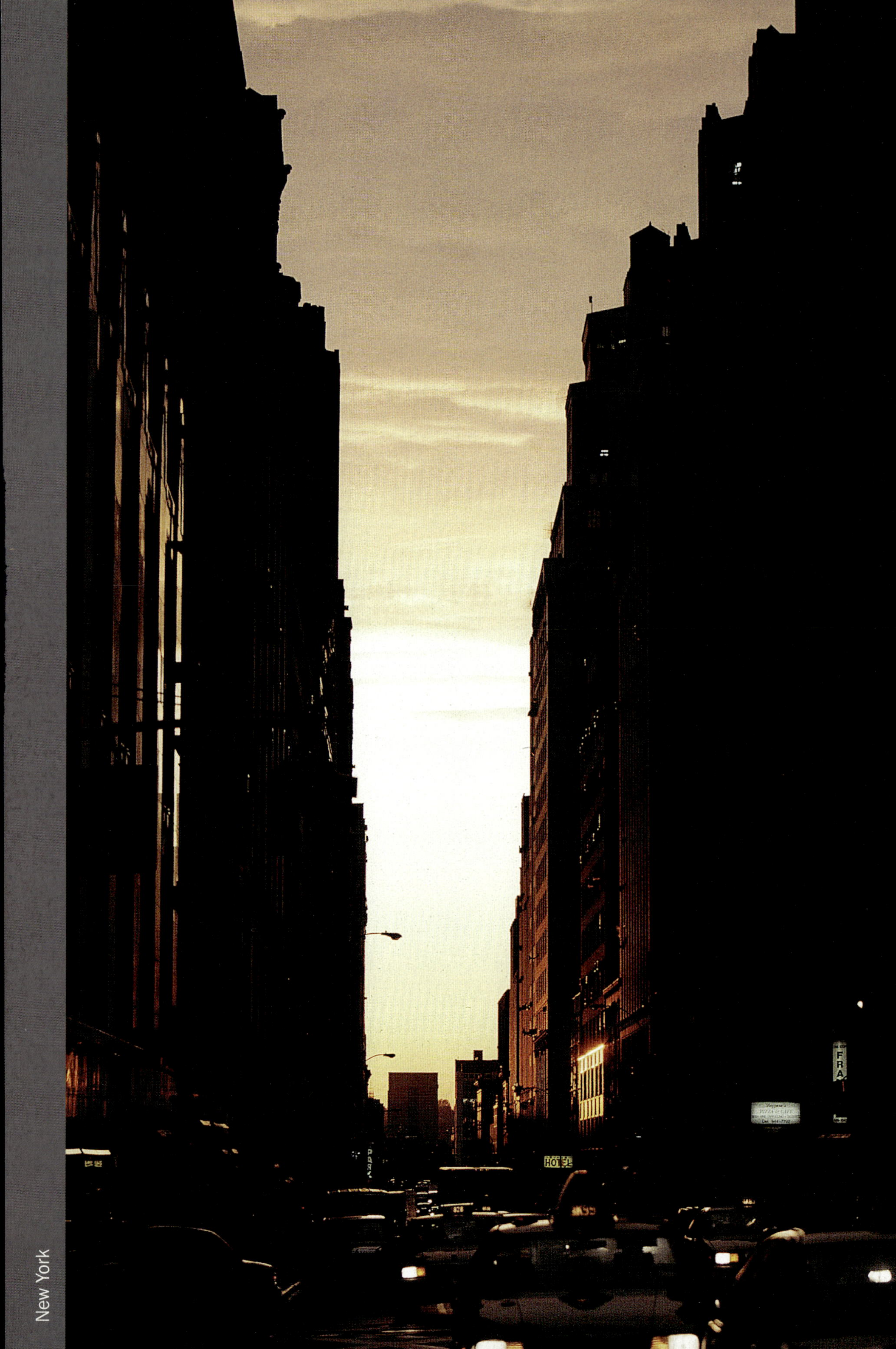
HOTEL

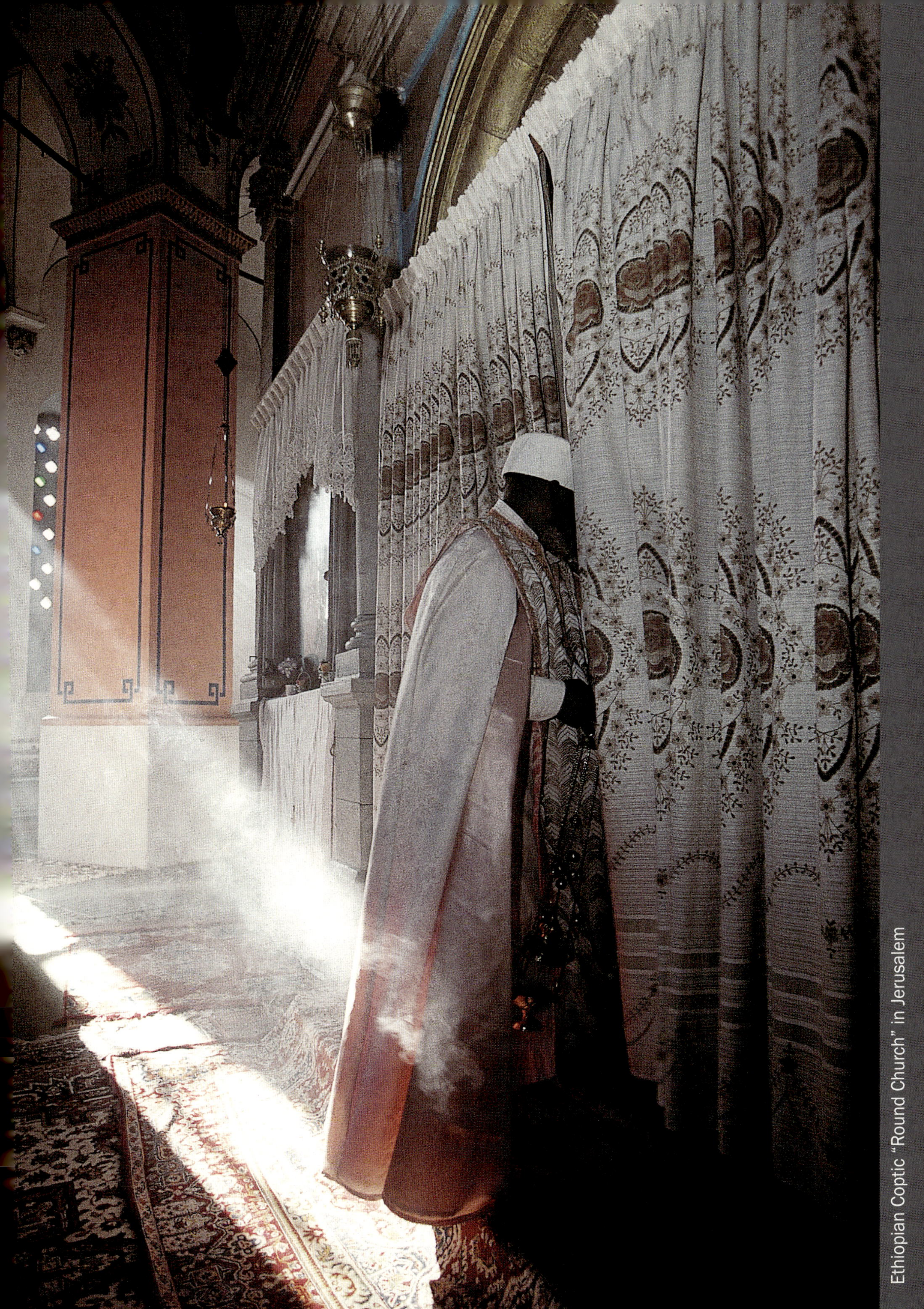

Ethiopian Coptic "Round Church" in Jerusalem

Manhattan Bridge, New York

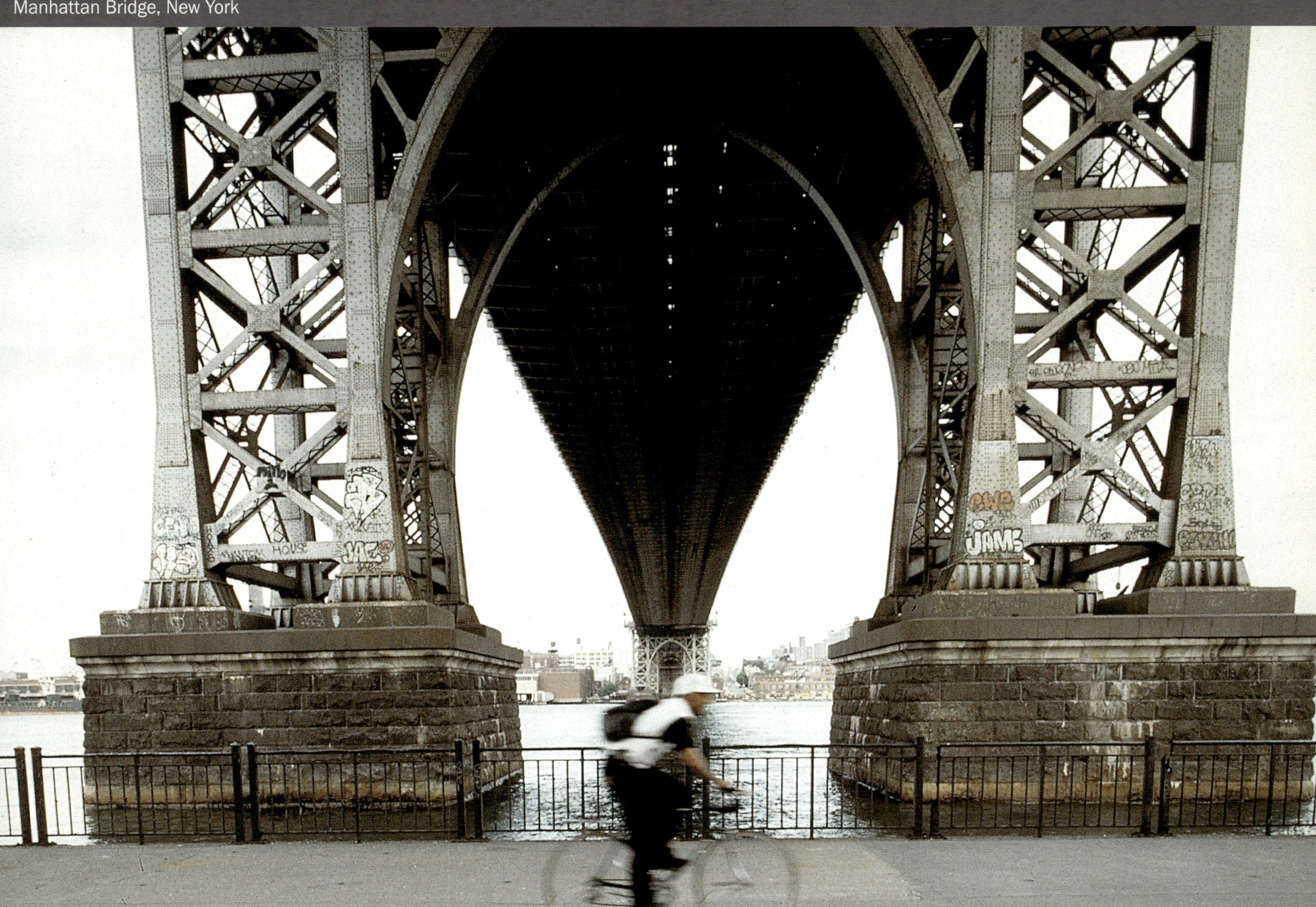

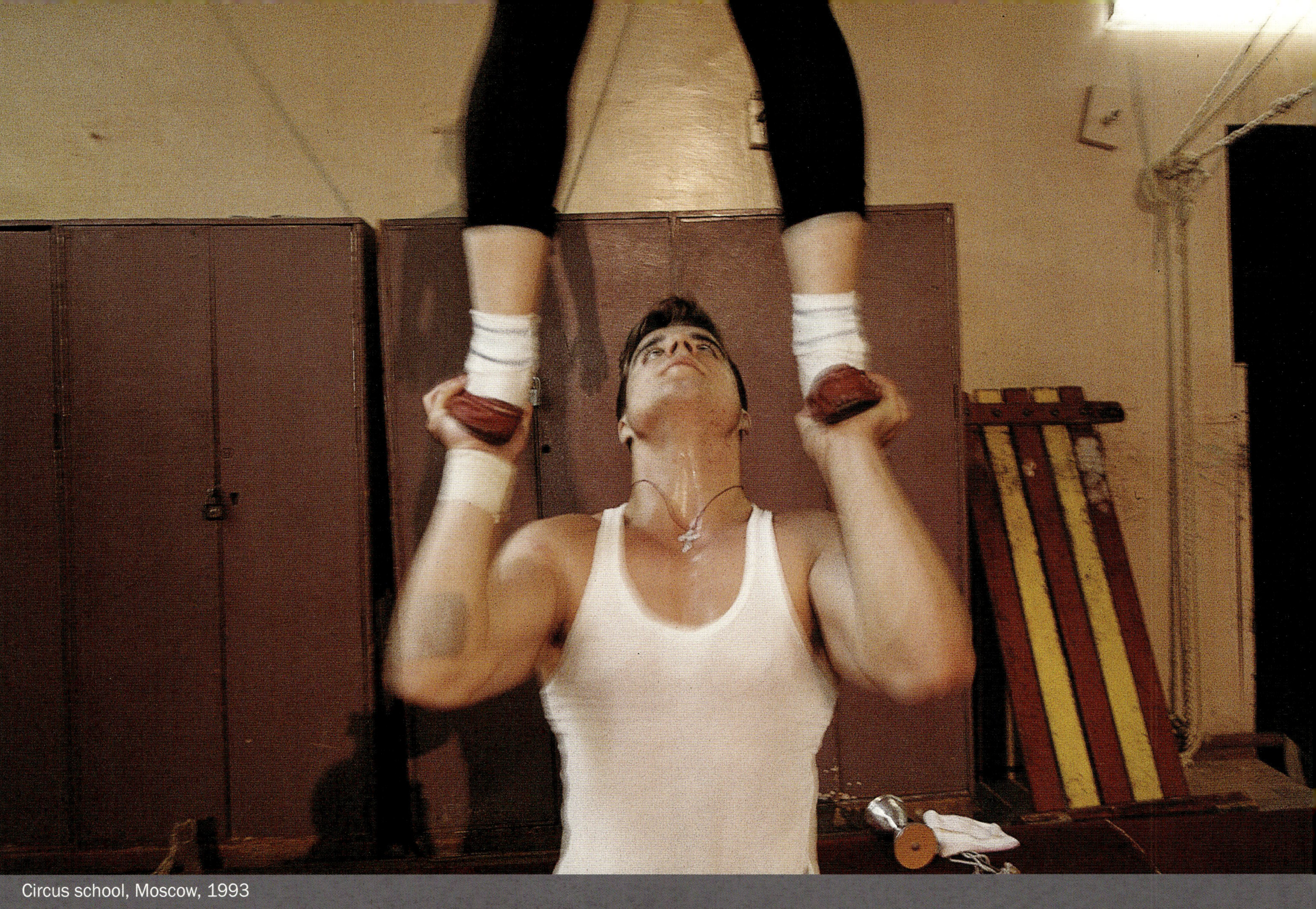

Circus school, Moscow, 1993

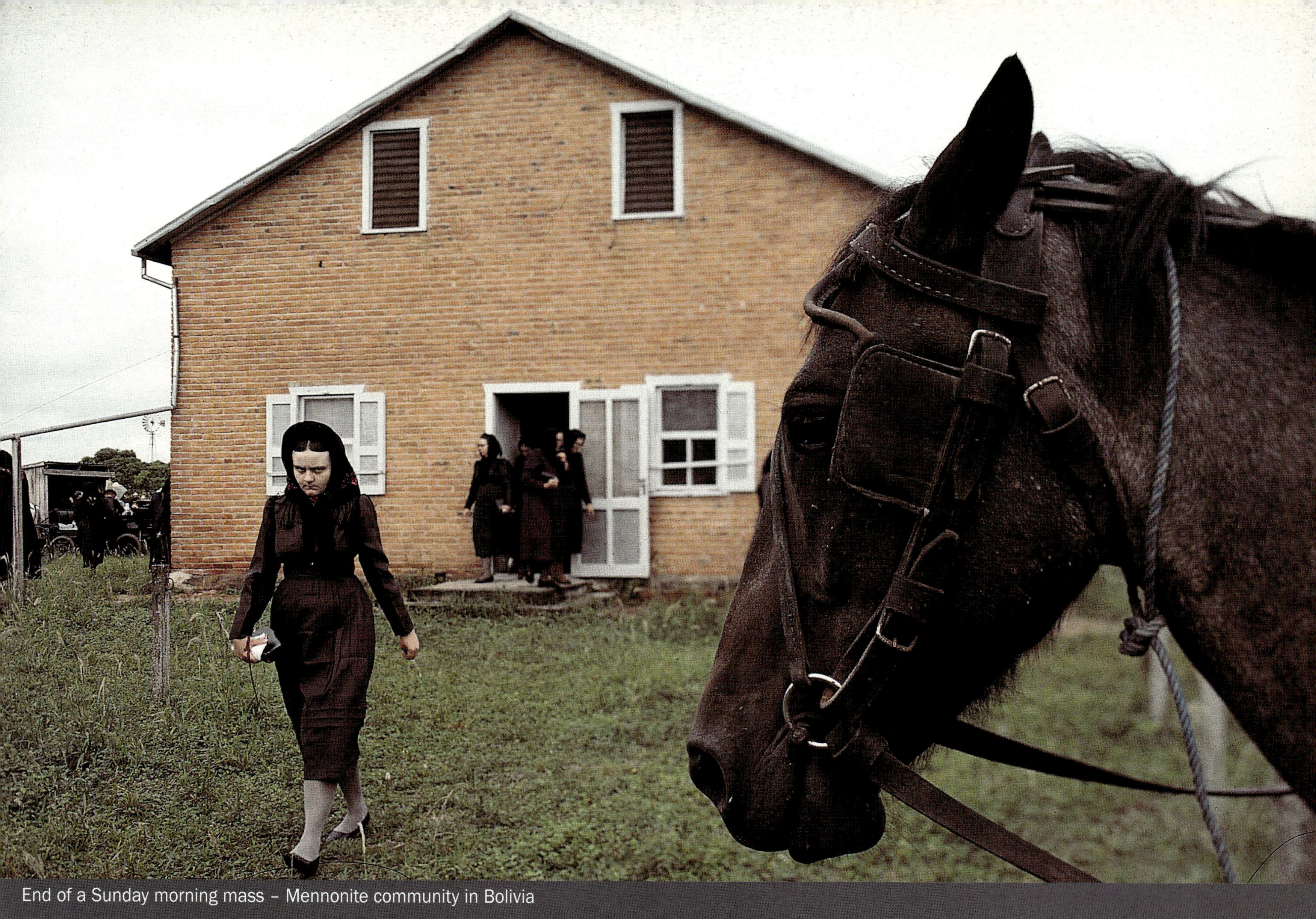

End of a Sunday morning mass – Mennonite community in Bolivia

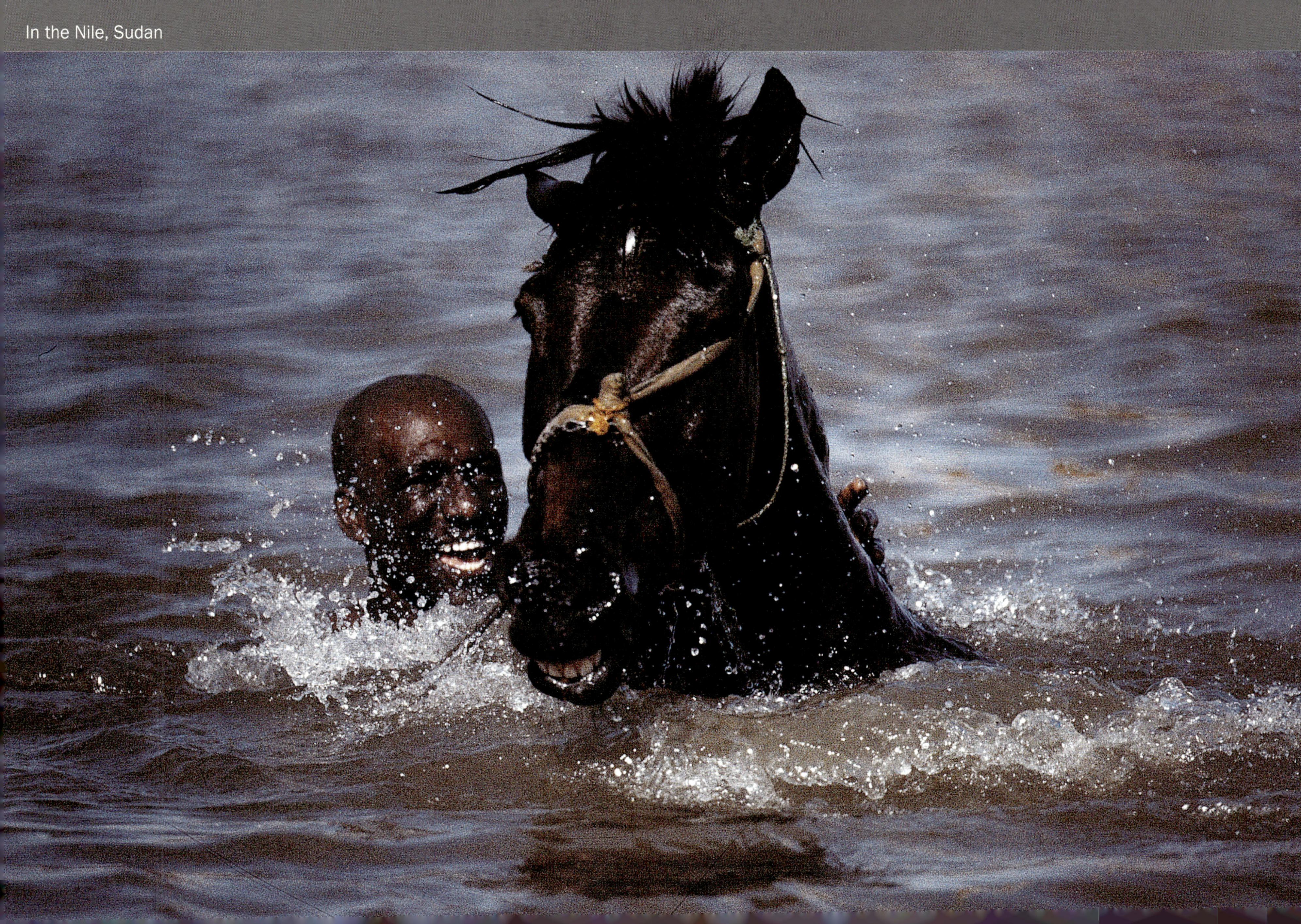

In the Nile, Sudan

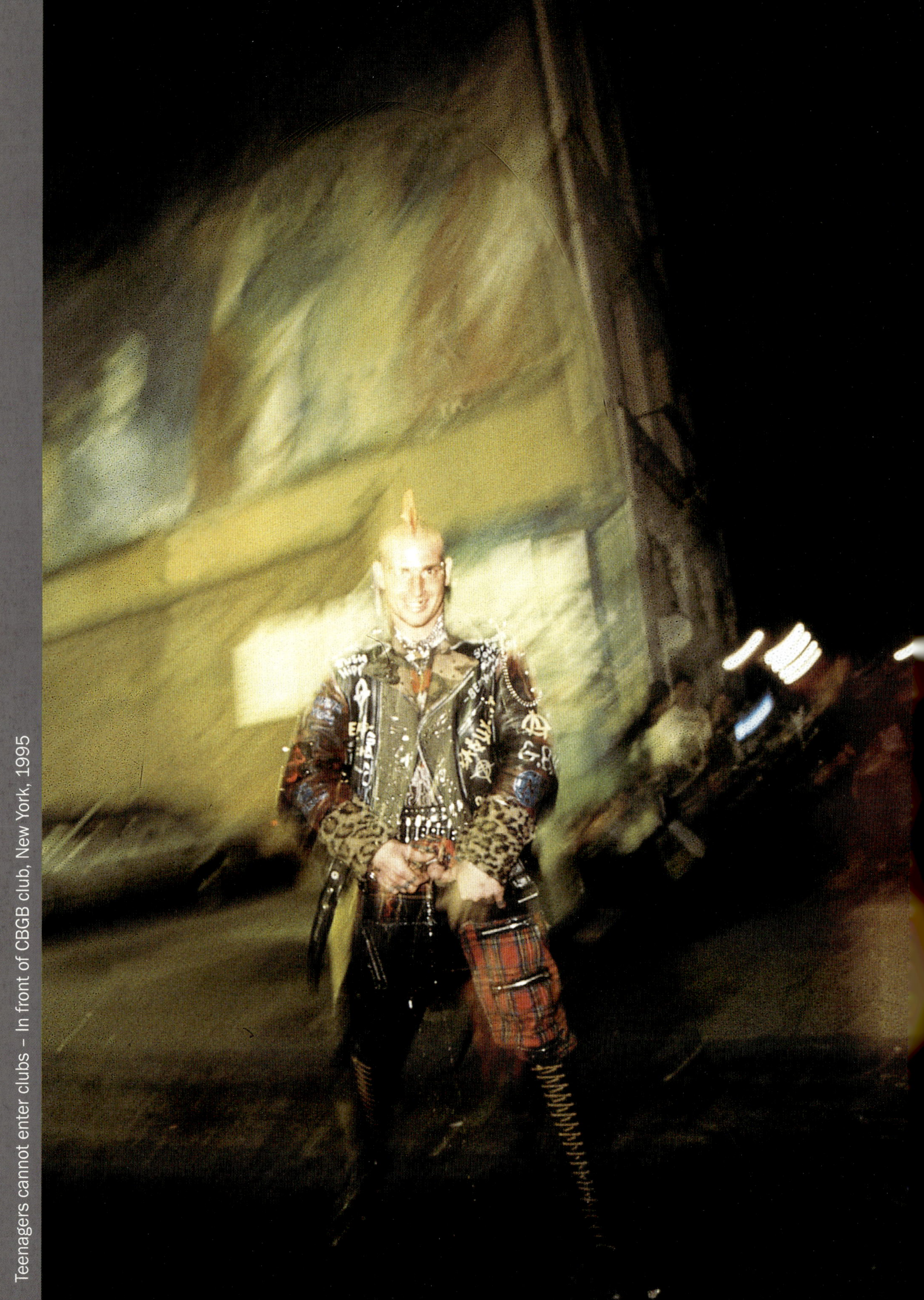

Teenagers cannot enter clubs – In front of CBGB club, New York, 1995

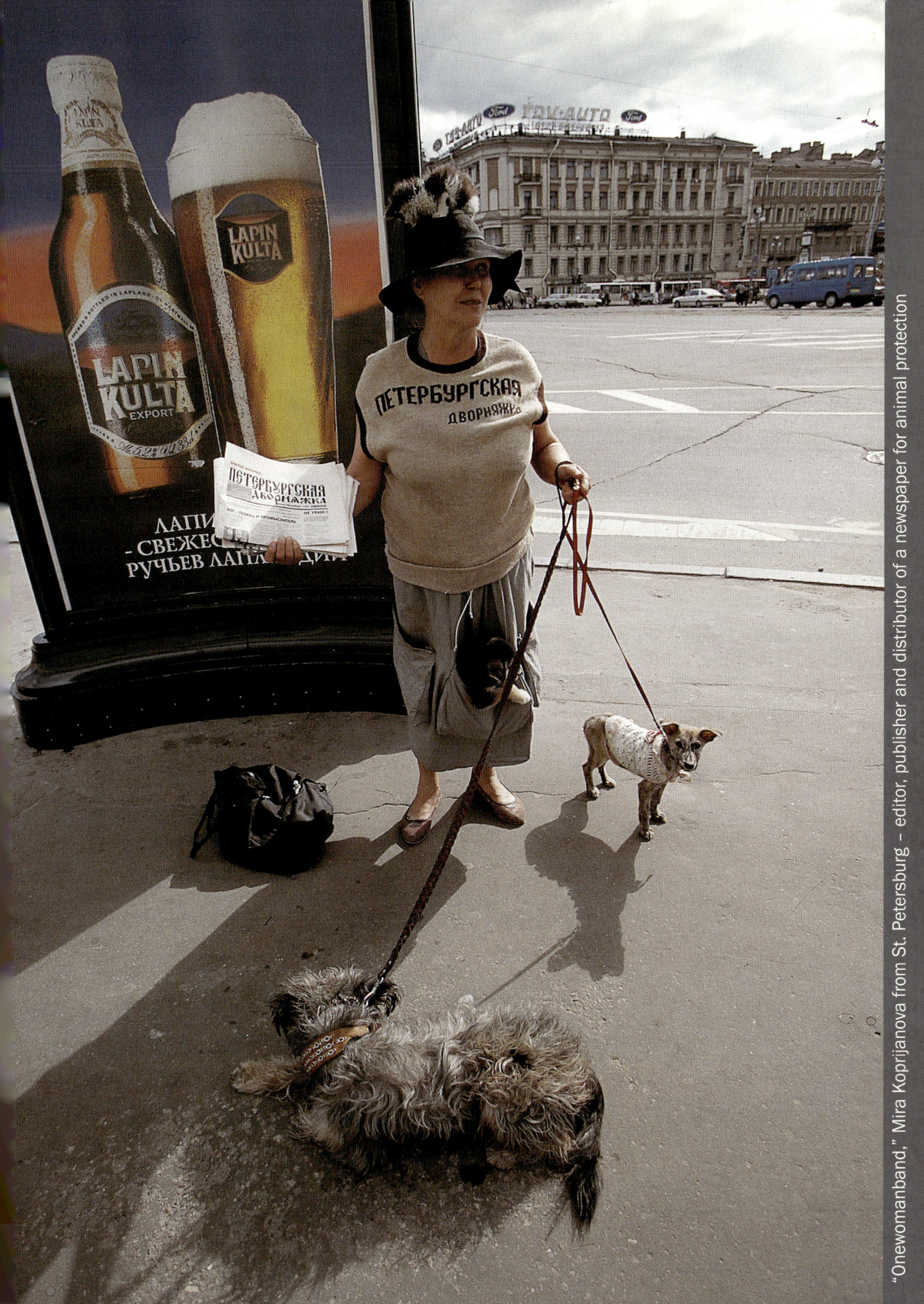

"Onewomanband," Mira Koprijanova from St. Petersburg – editor, publisher and distributor of a newspaper for animal protection

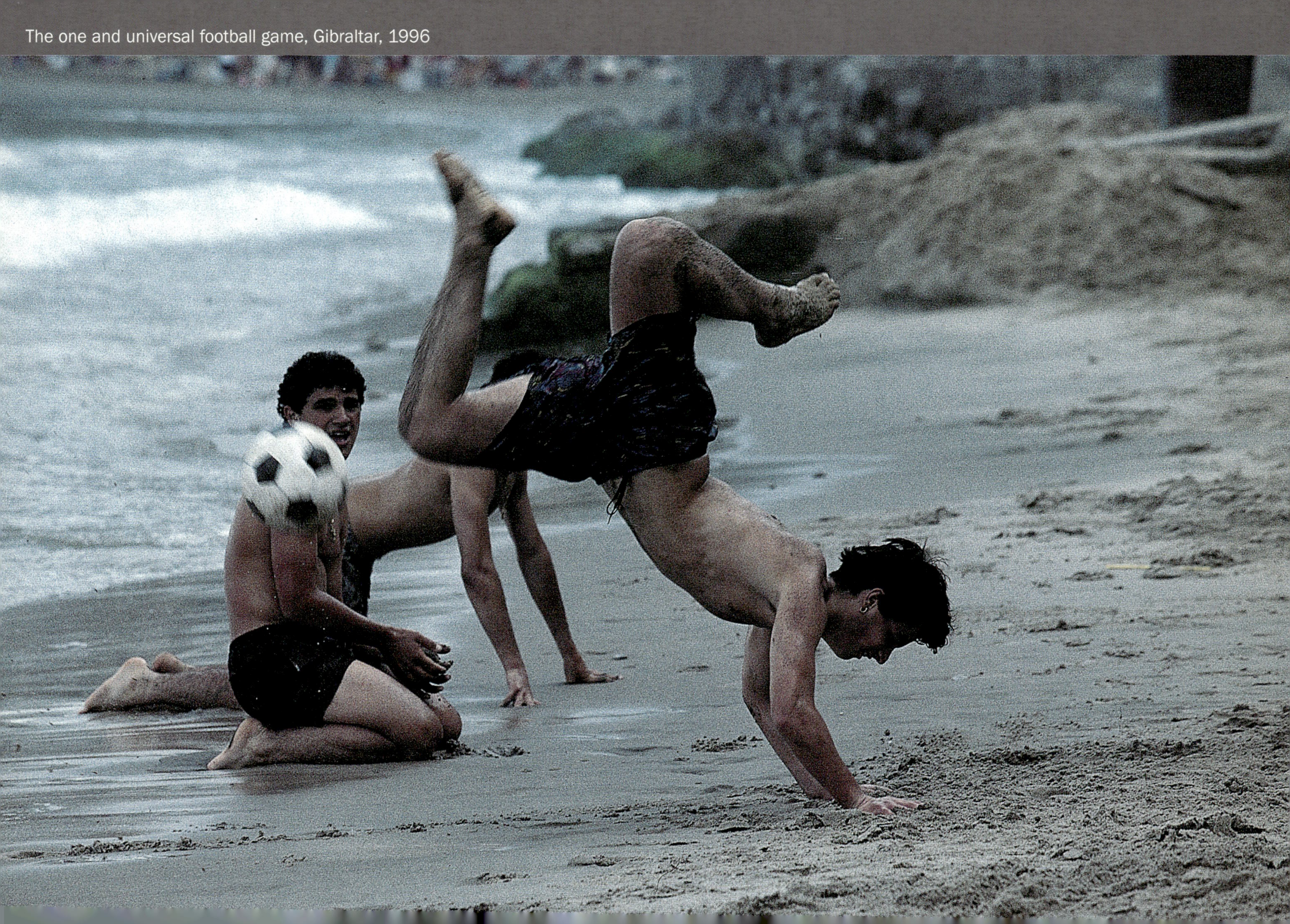

The one and universal football game, Gibraltar, 1996

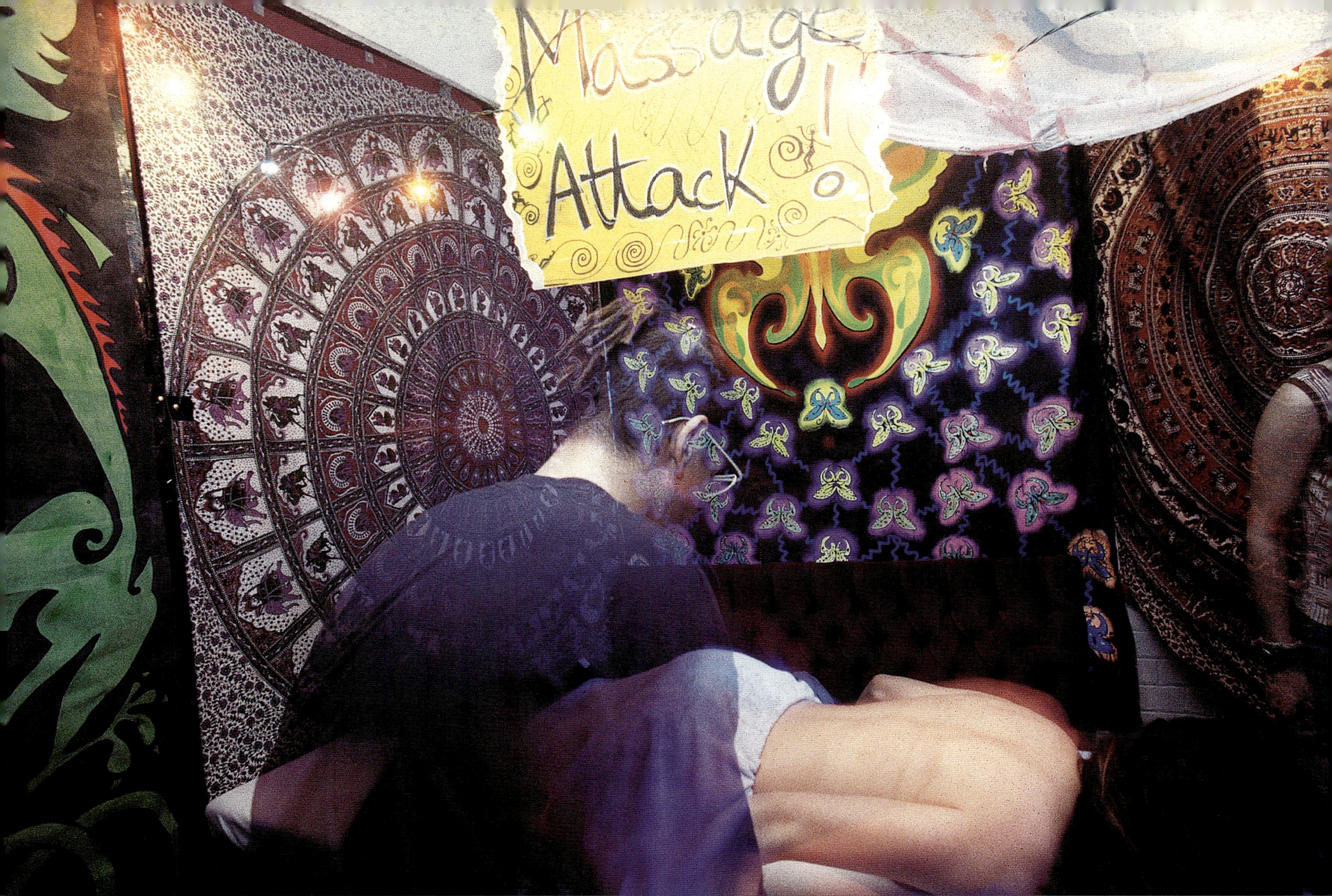

Rave party side room, Pendragon venue, London, 1998

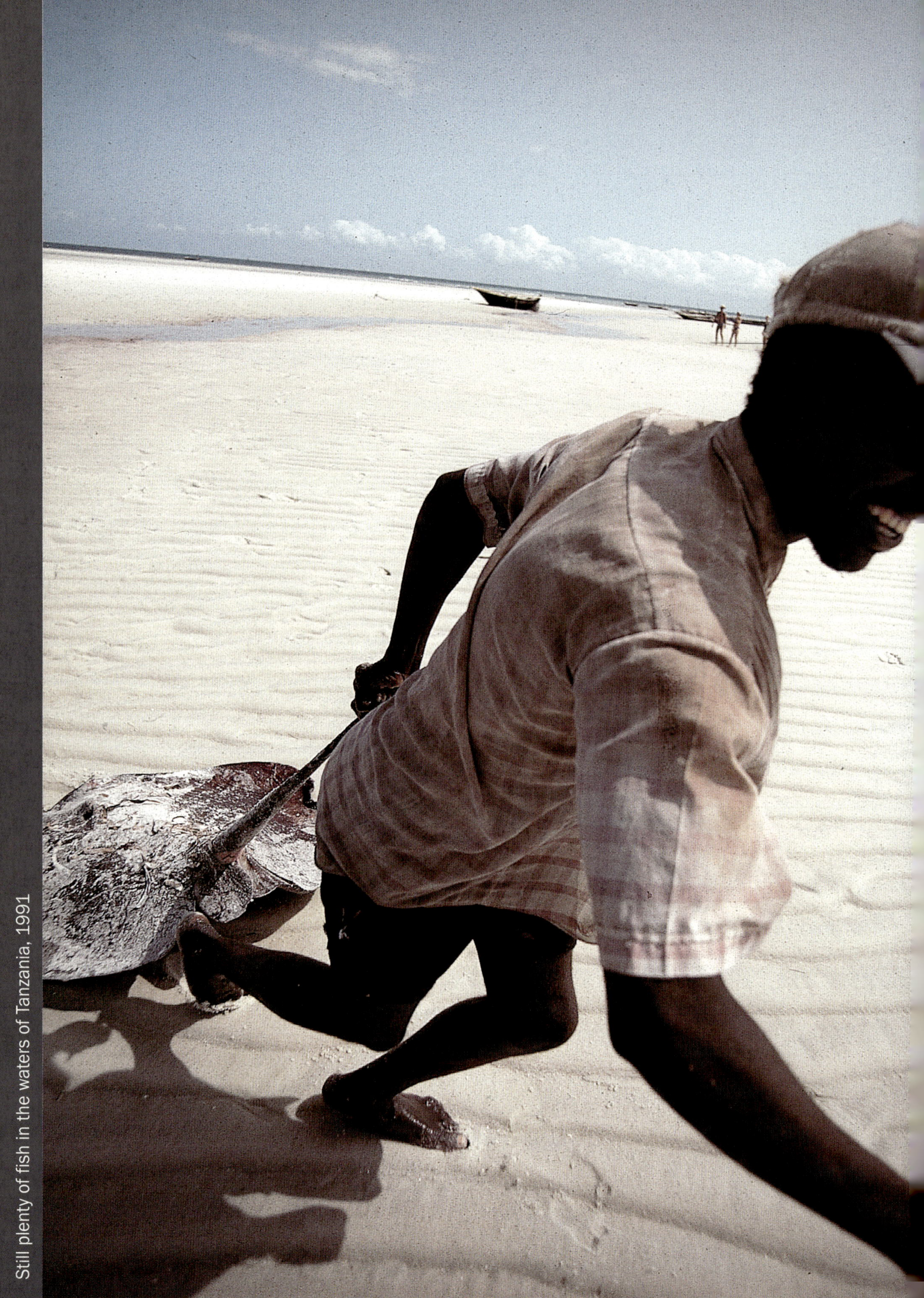

Still plenty of fish in the waters of Tanzania, 1991

Rave party, Ljubljana, Slovenia, 1996

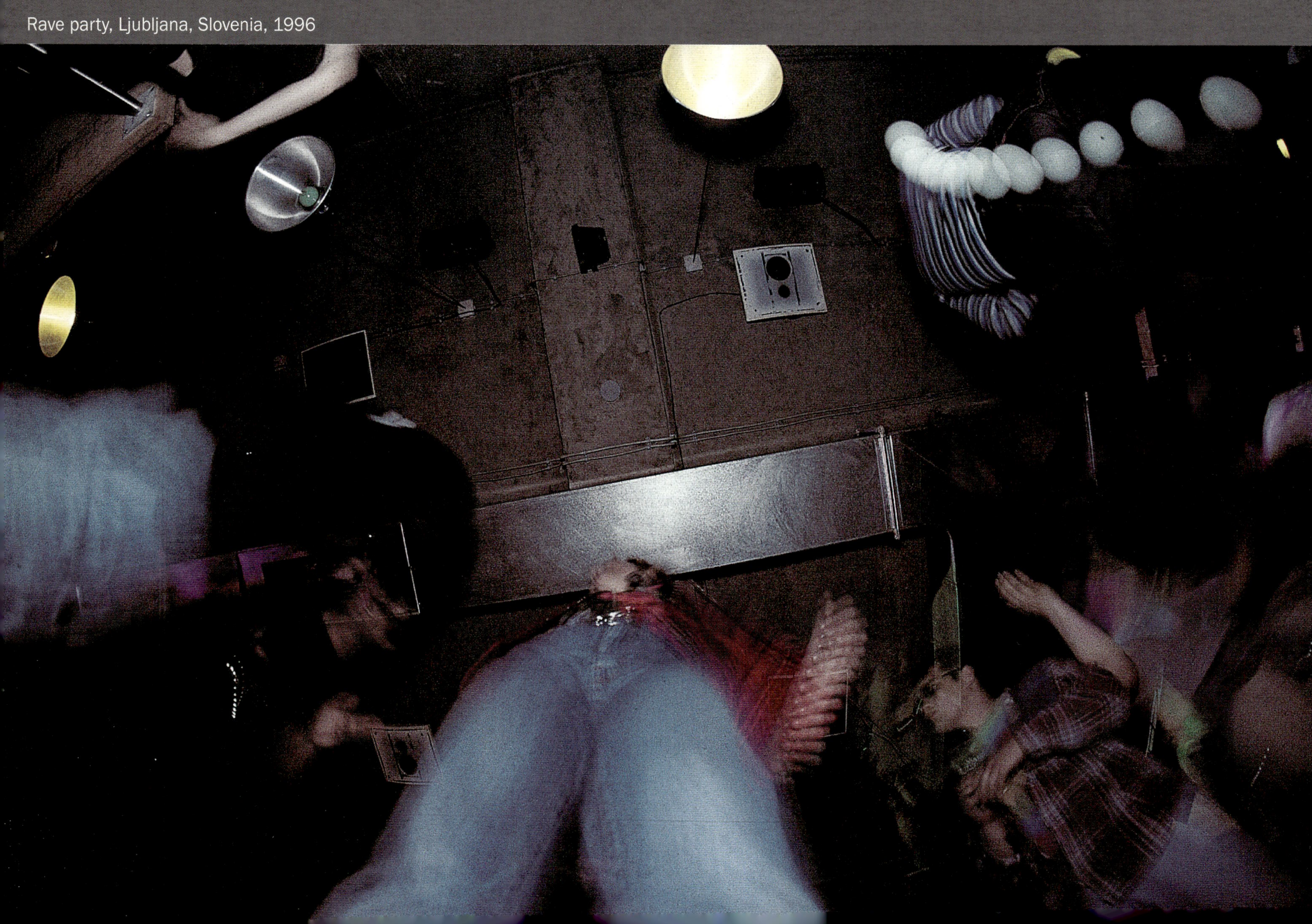

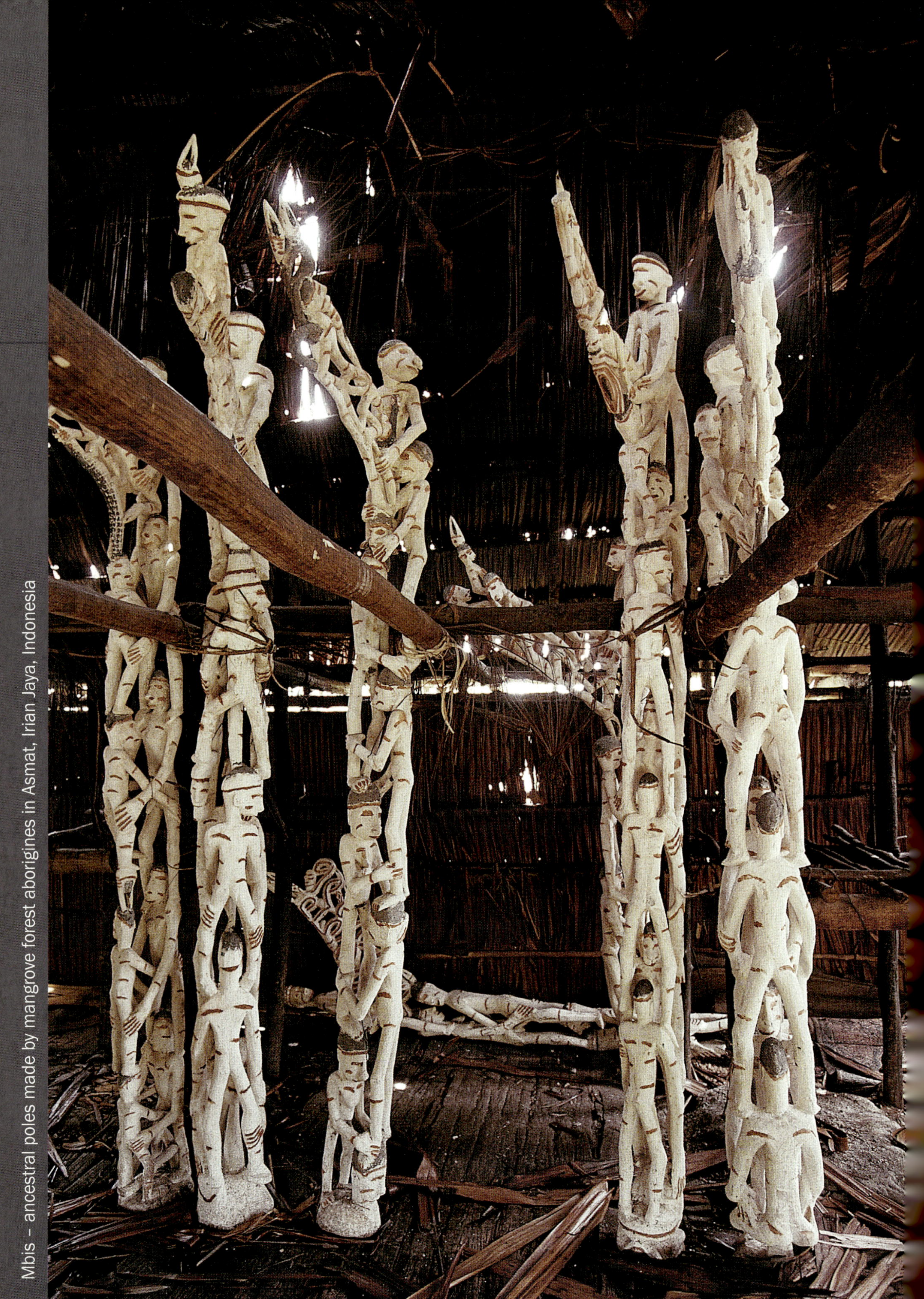

Mbis – ancestral poles made by mangrove forest aborigines in Asmat, Irian Jaya, Indonesia

Perestrojka: Sea lion, from army research program to circus in Moscow

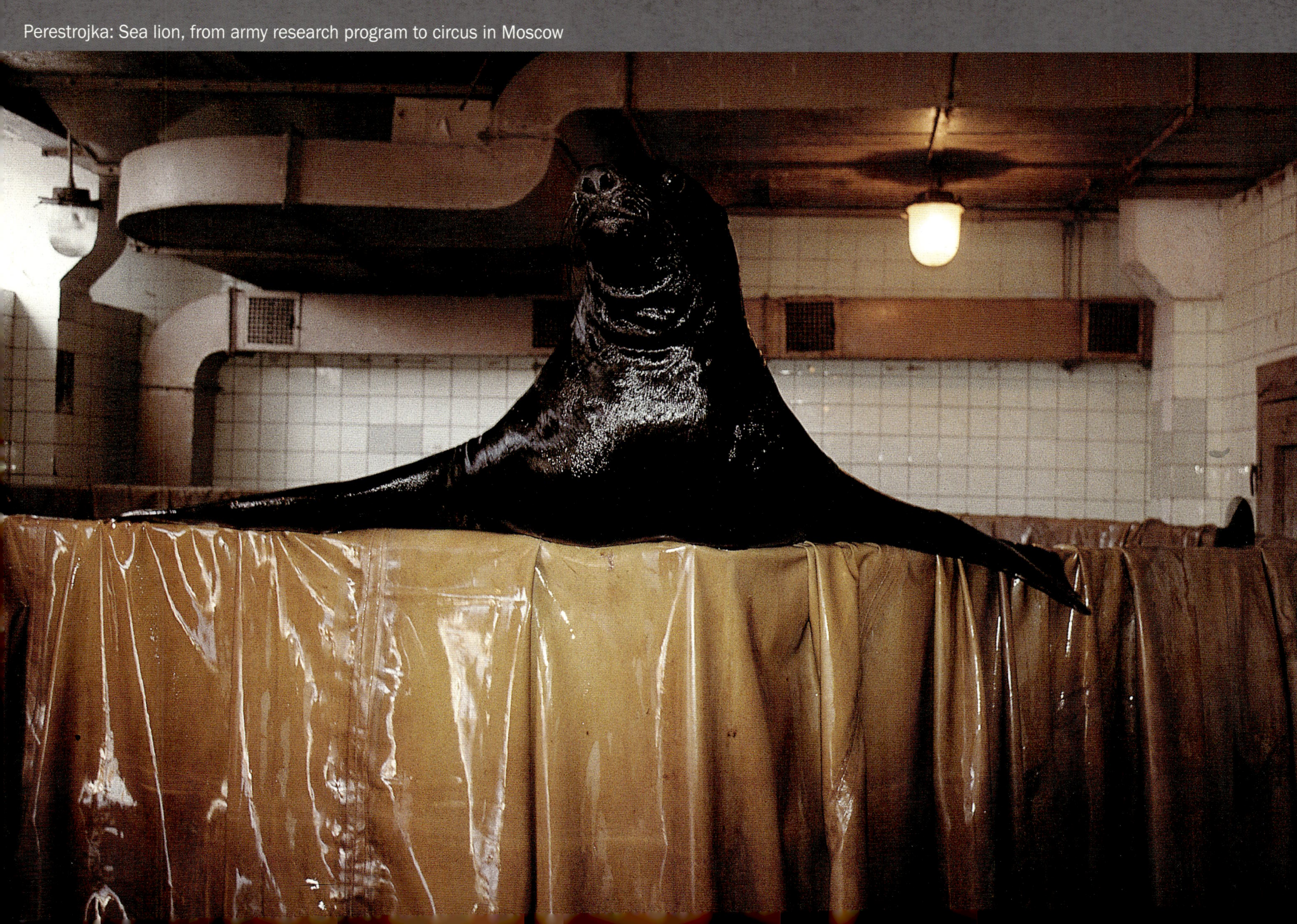

Prehistoric tombs (3rd century B.C.) on Mount Bat, Oman

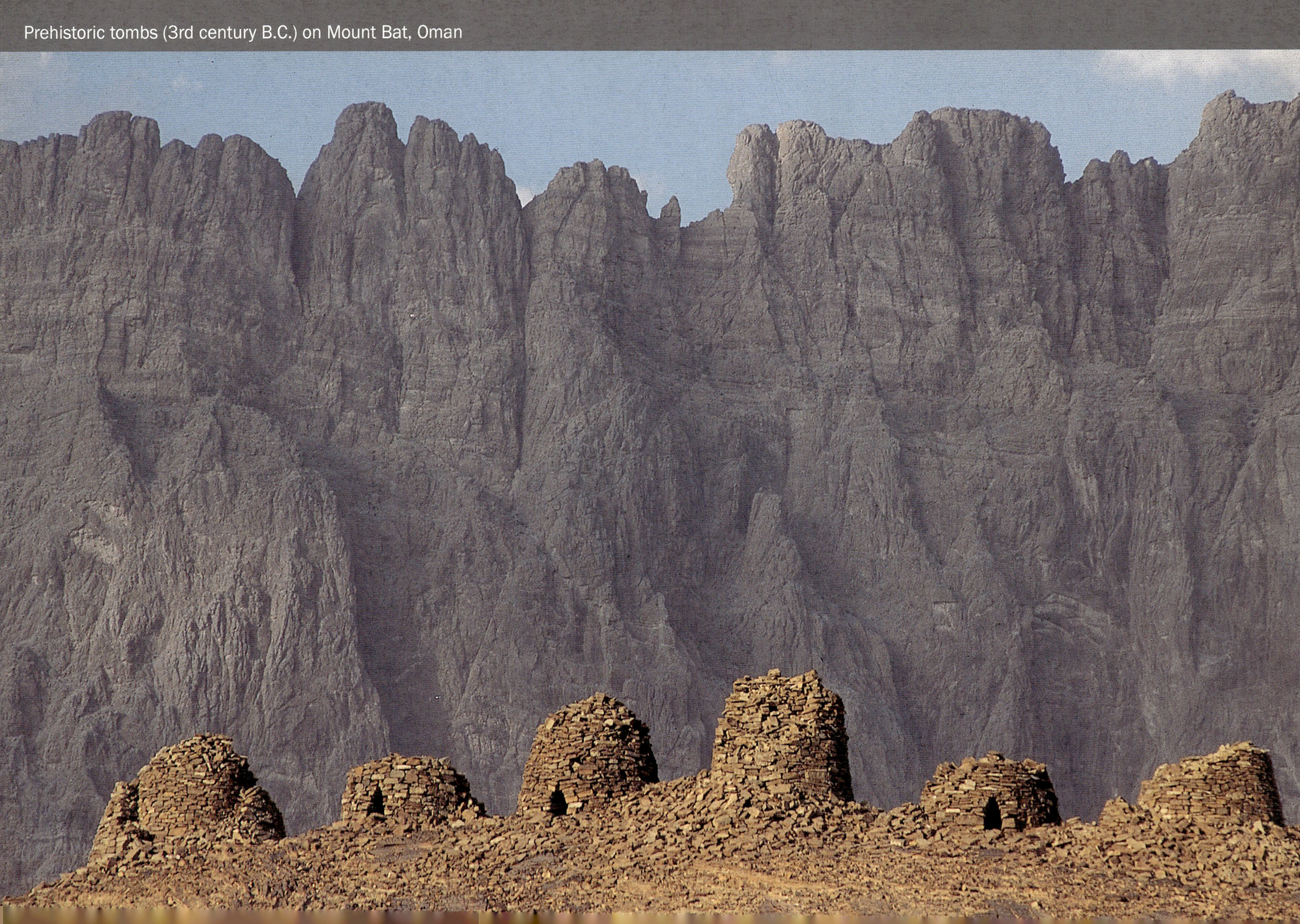

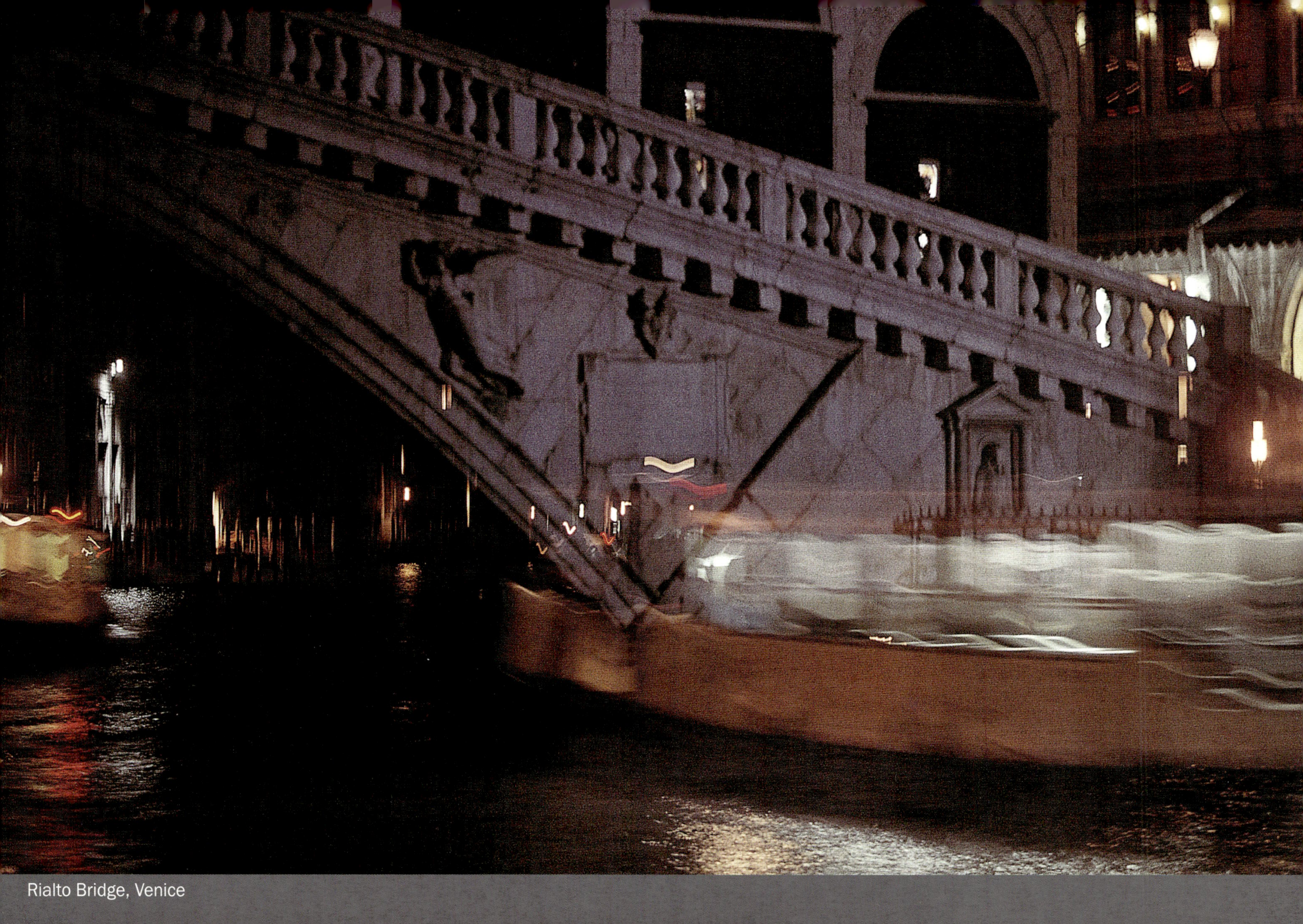

Rialto Bridge, Venice

Frescoes of Santa Rosa, Paraguay

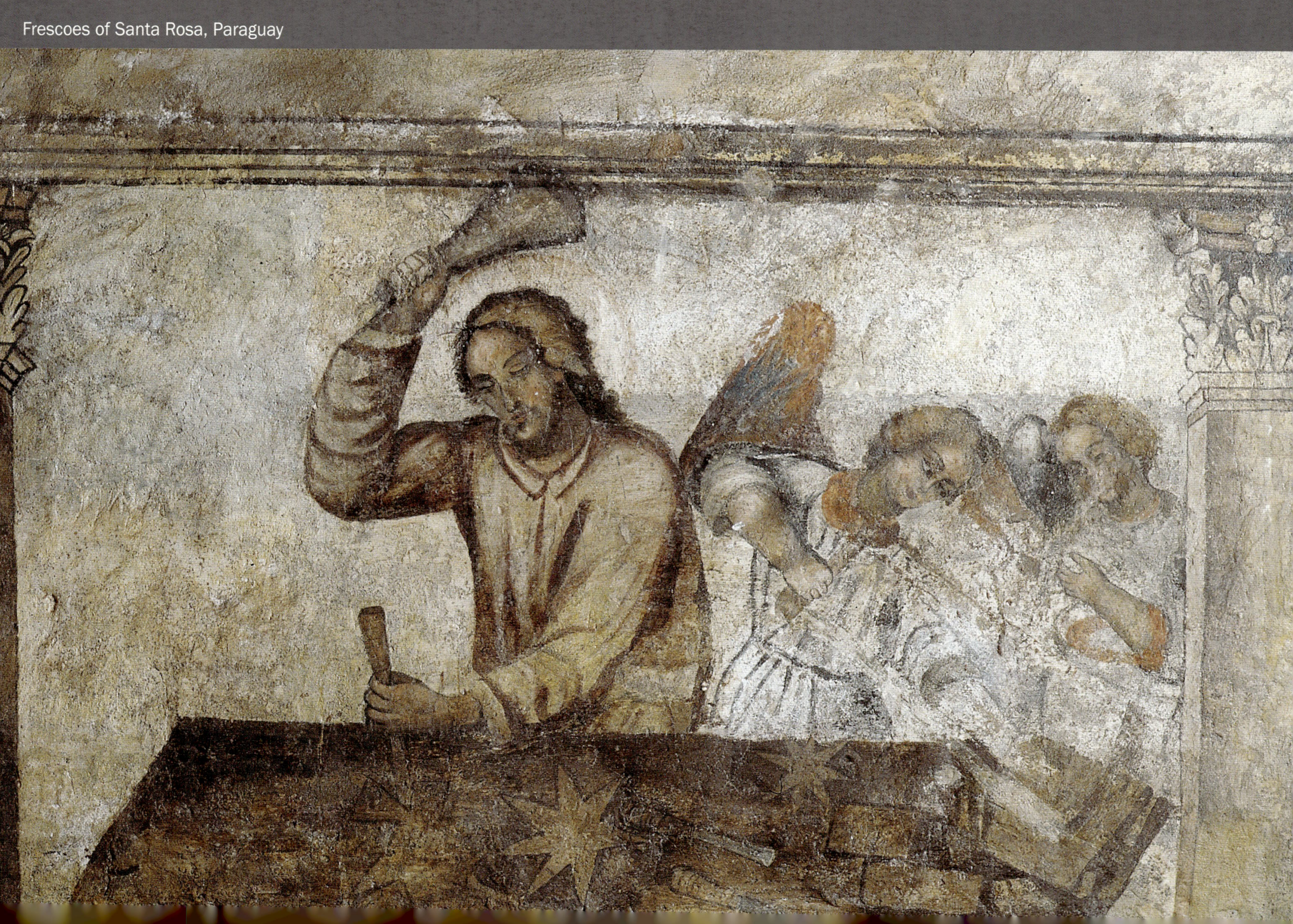

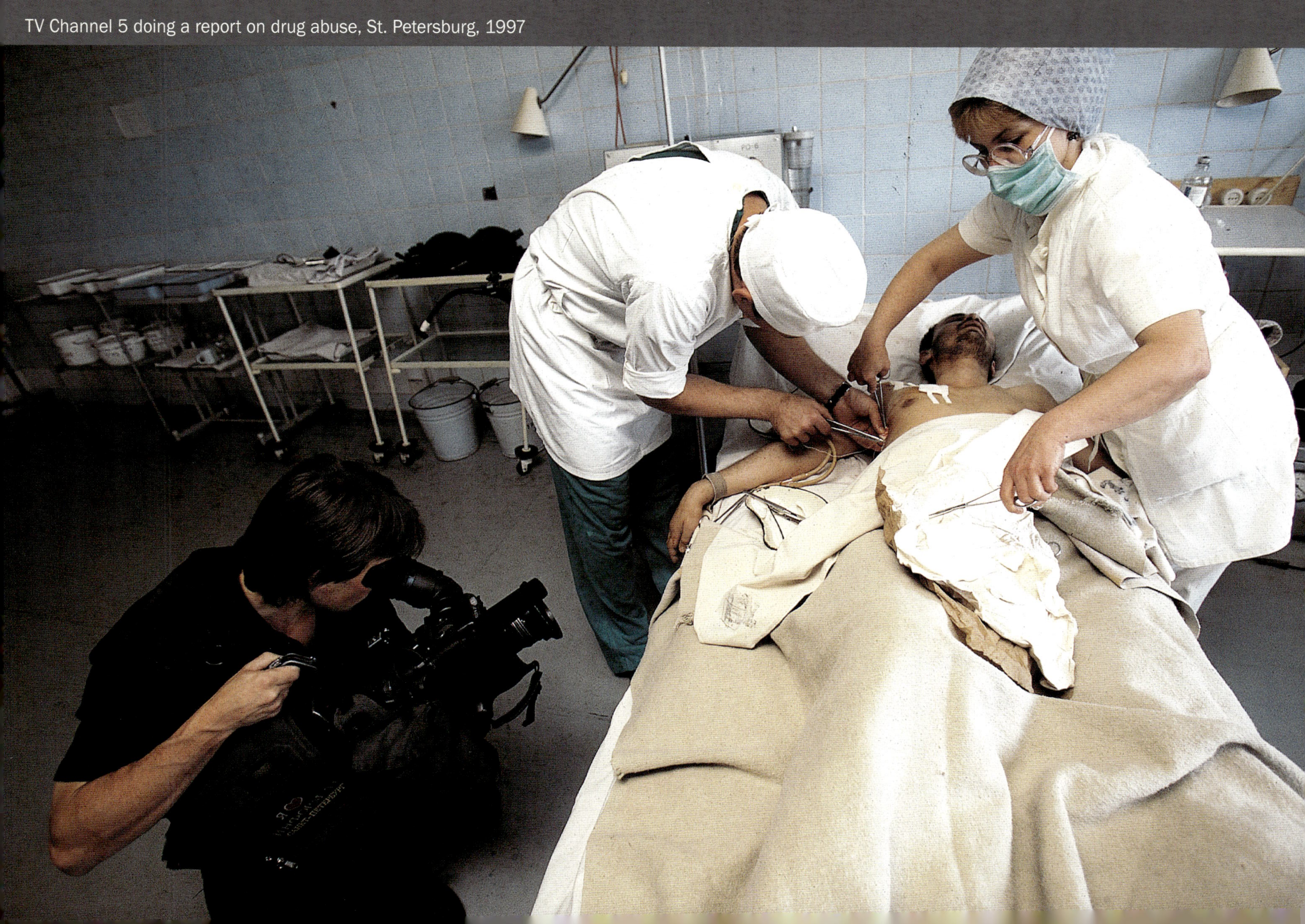

TV Channel 5 doing a report on drug abuse, St. Petersburg, 1997

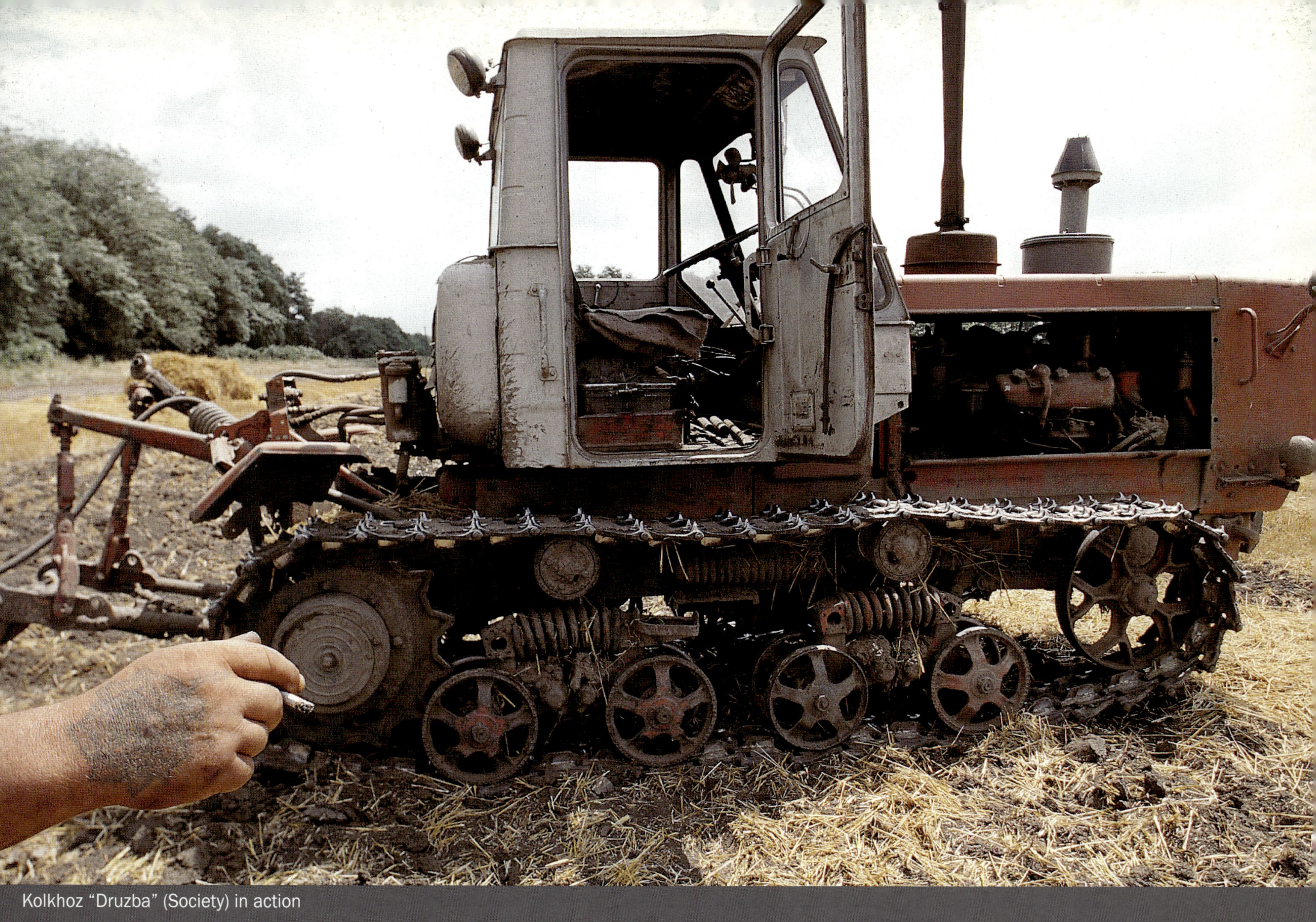

Kolkhoz “Druzba” (Society) in action

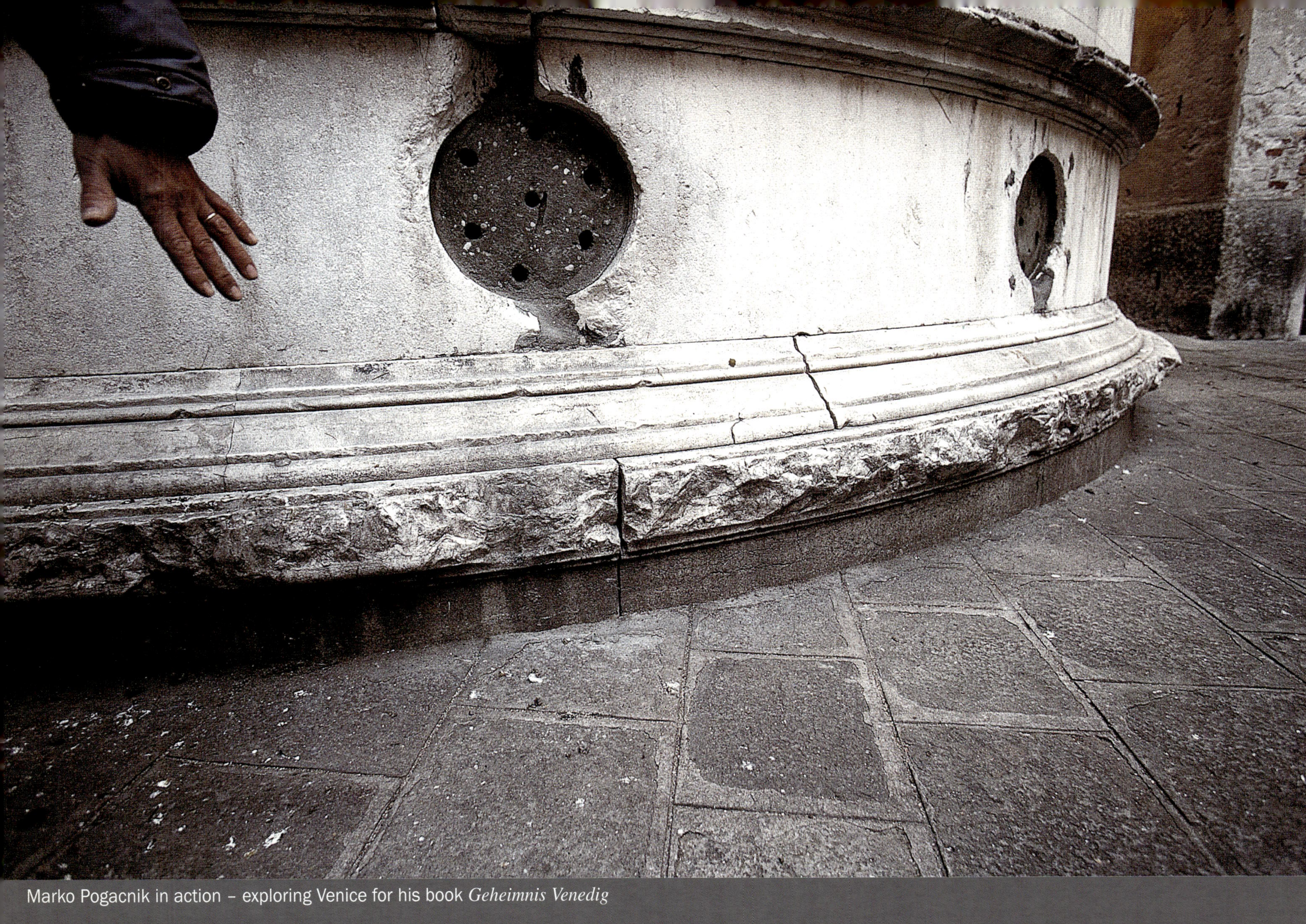

Marko Pogacnik in action – exploring Venice for his book *Geheimnis Venedig*

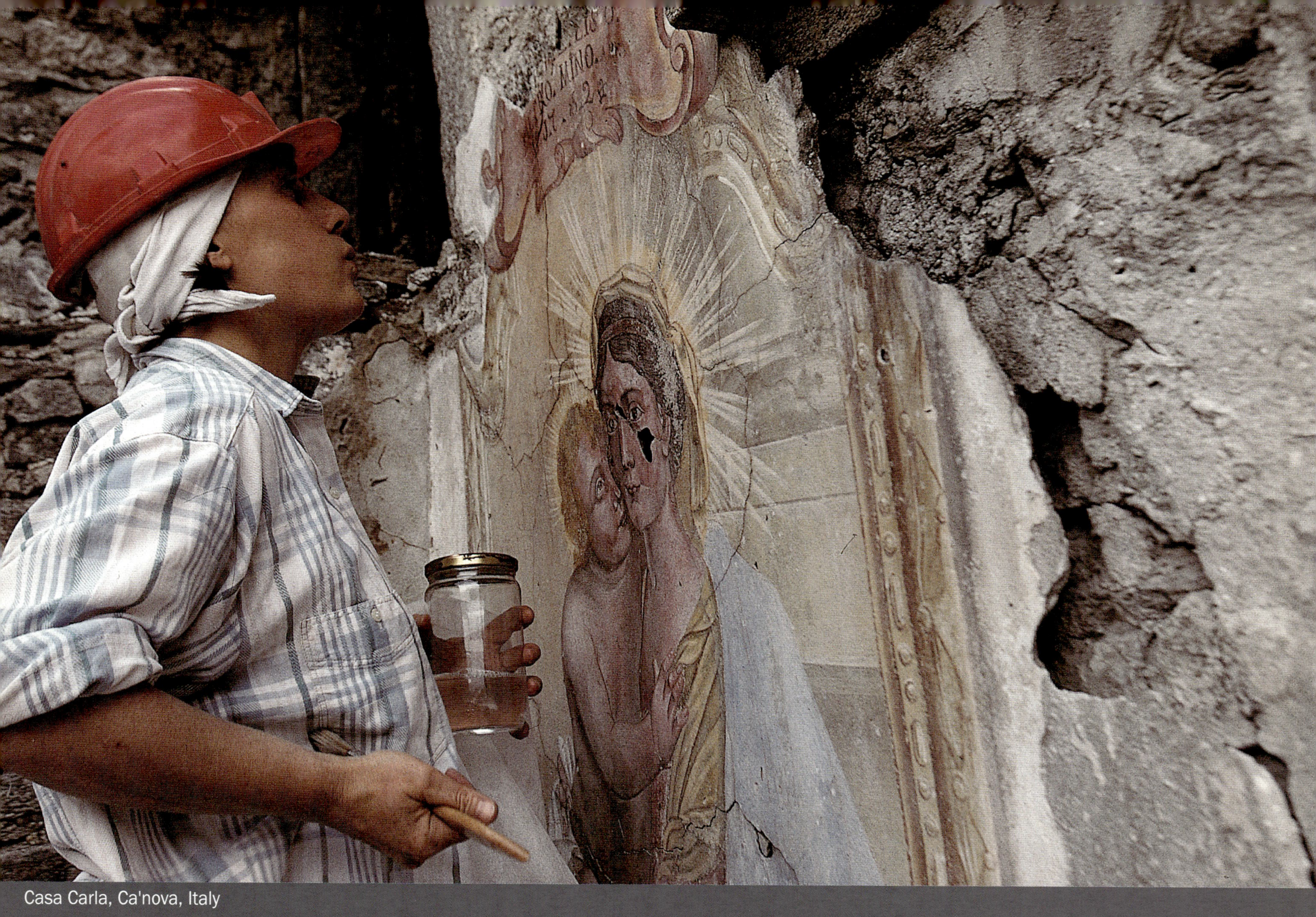

Casa Carla, Ca'nova, Italy

Bosnian refugees, Slovenia, 1993

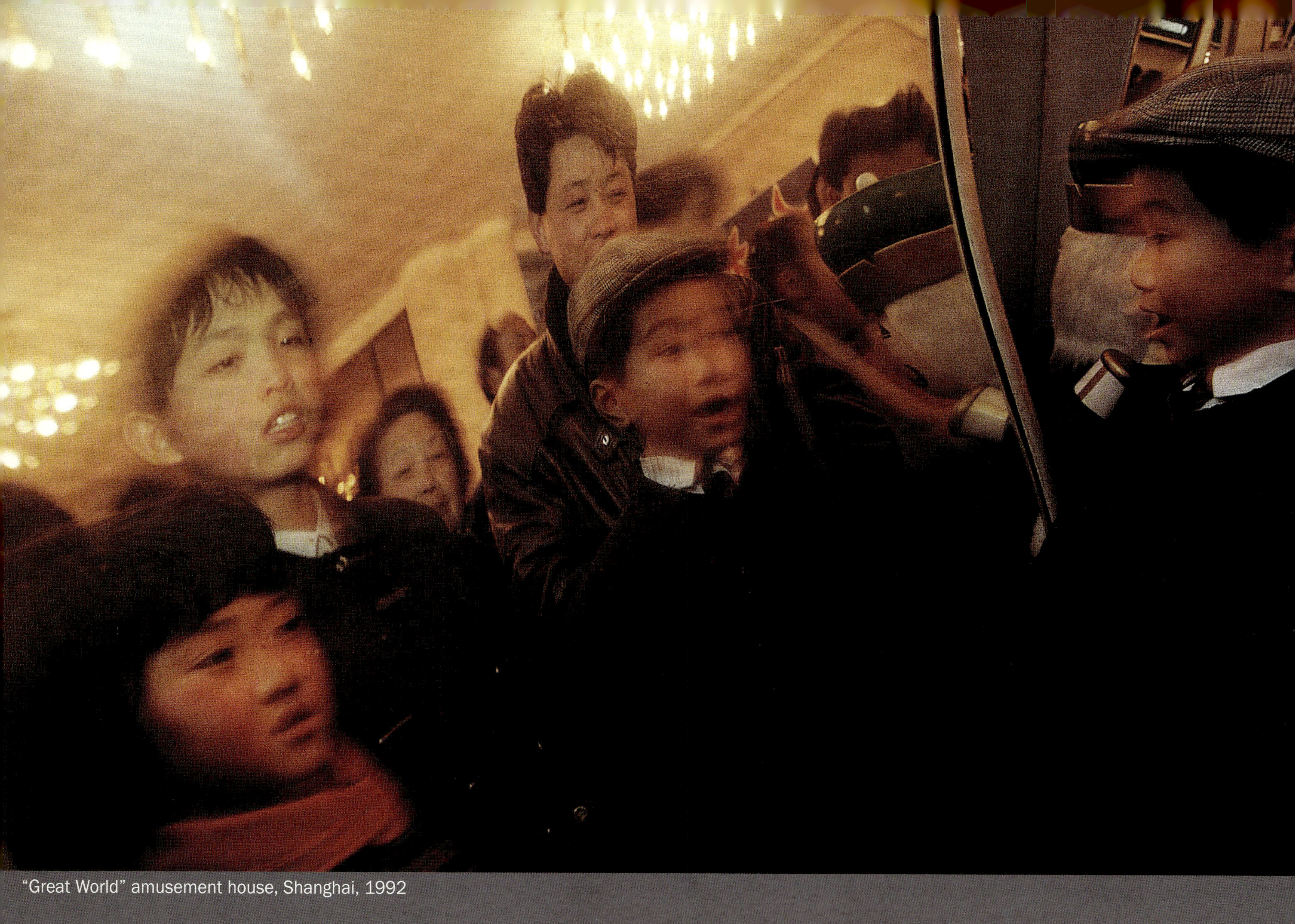

“Great World” amusement house, Shanghai, 1992

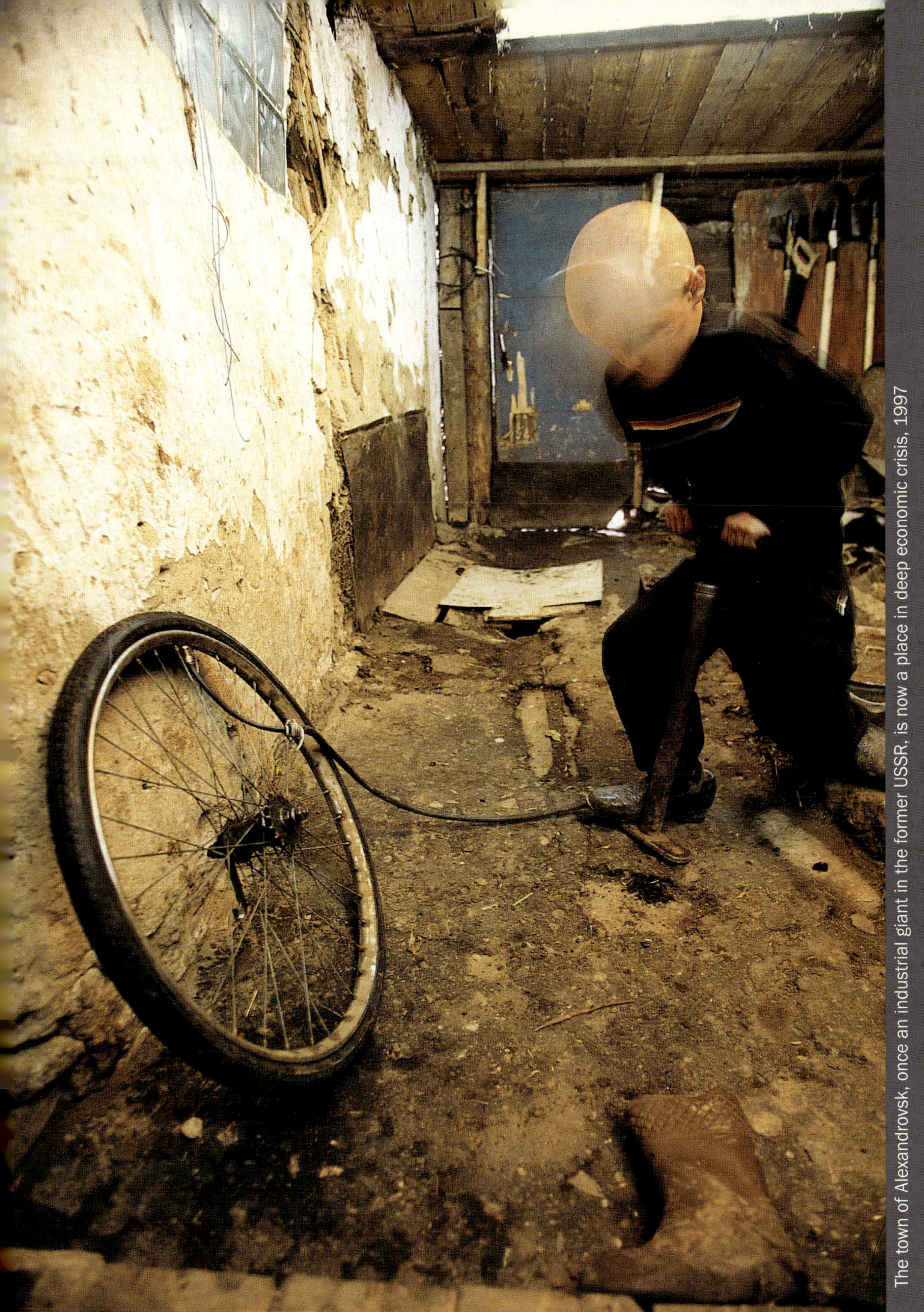

The town of Alexandrovsk, once an industrial giant in the former USSR, is now a place in deep economic crisis, 1997

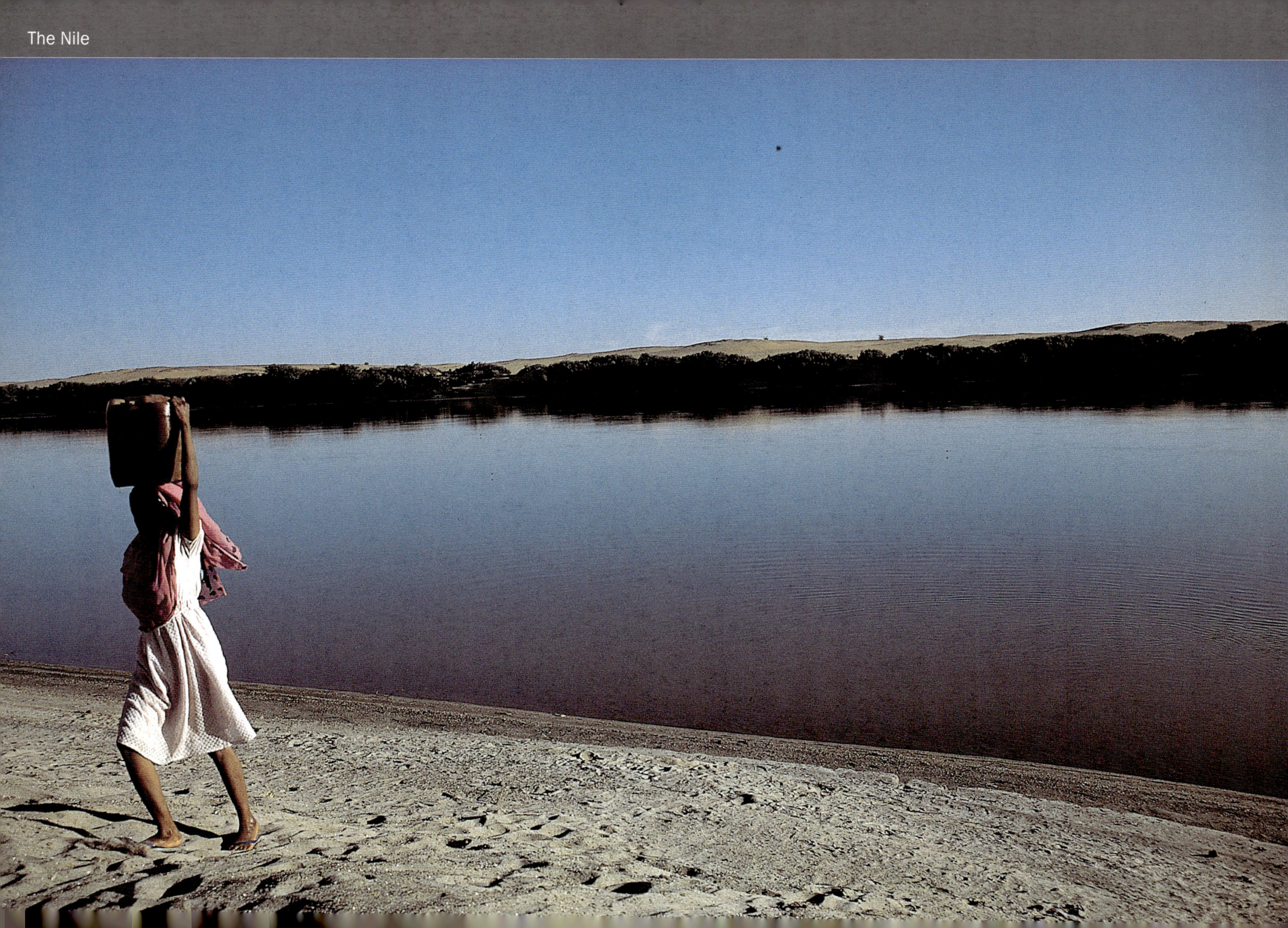

Dhow builder, Sur, Oman

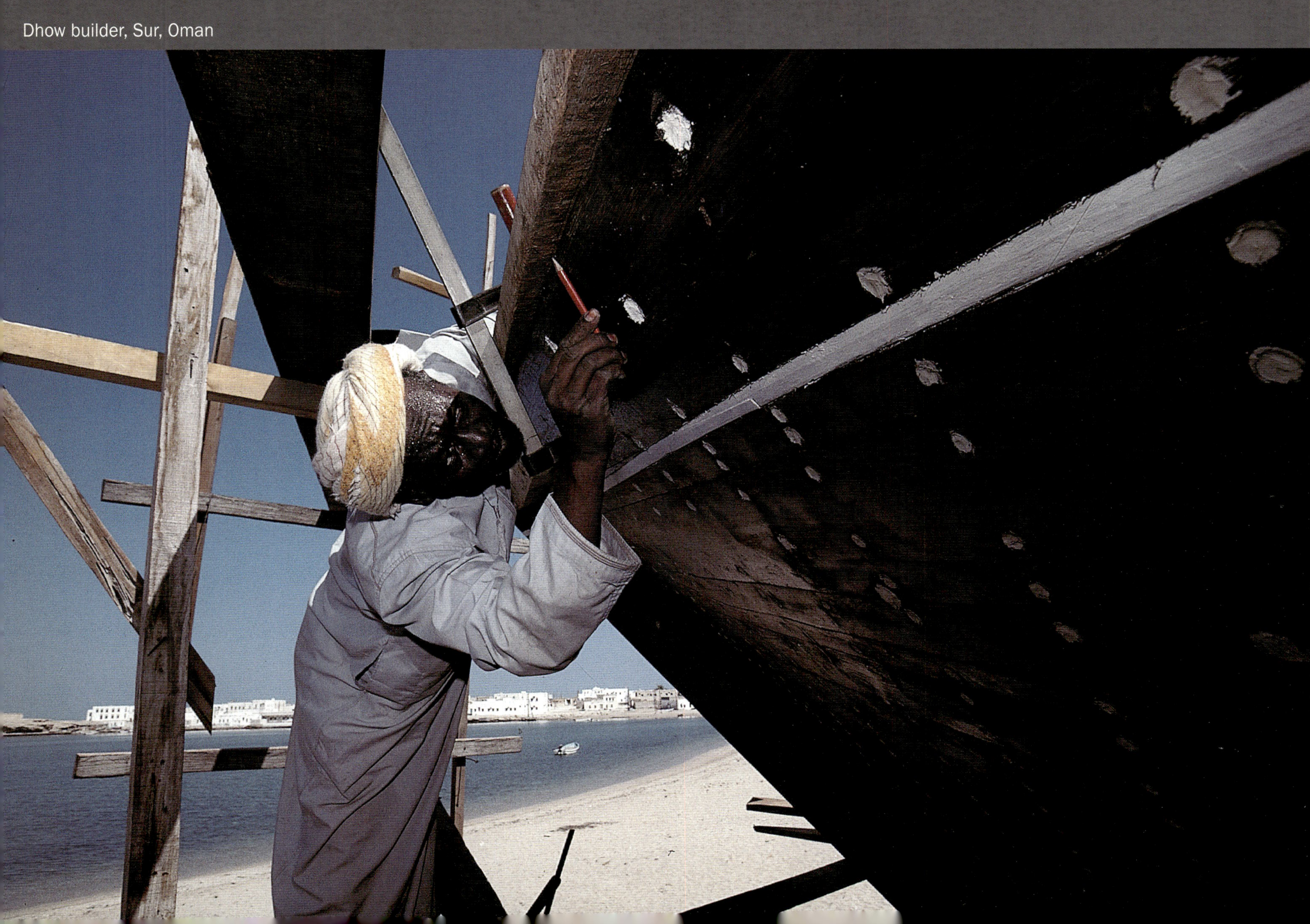

IRWIN – Painters' group sowing during art performance, 1996

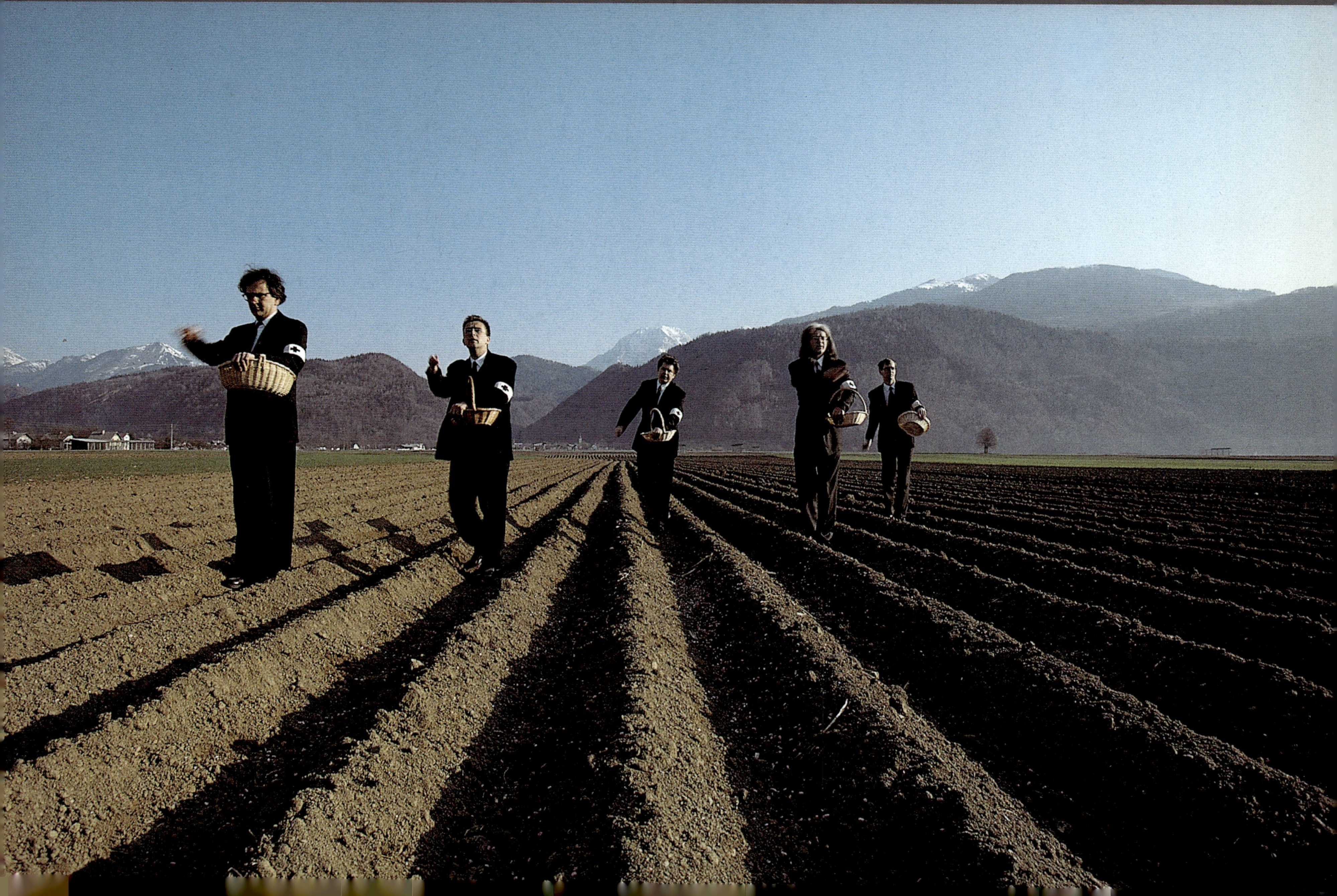

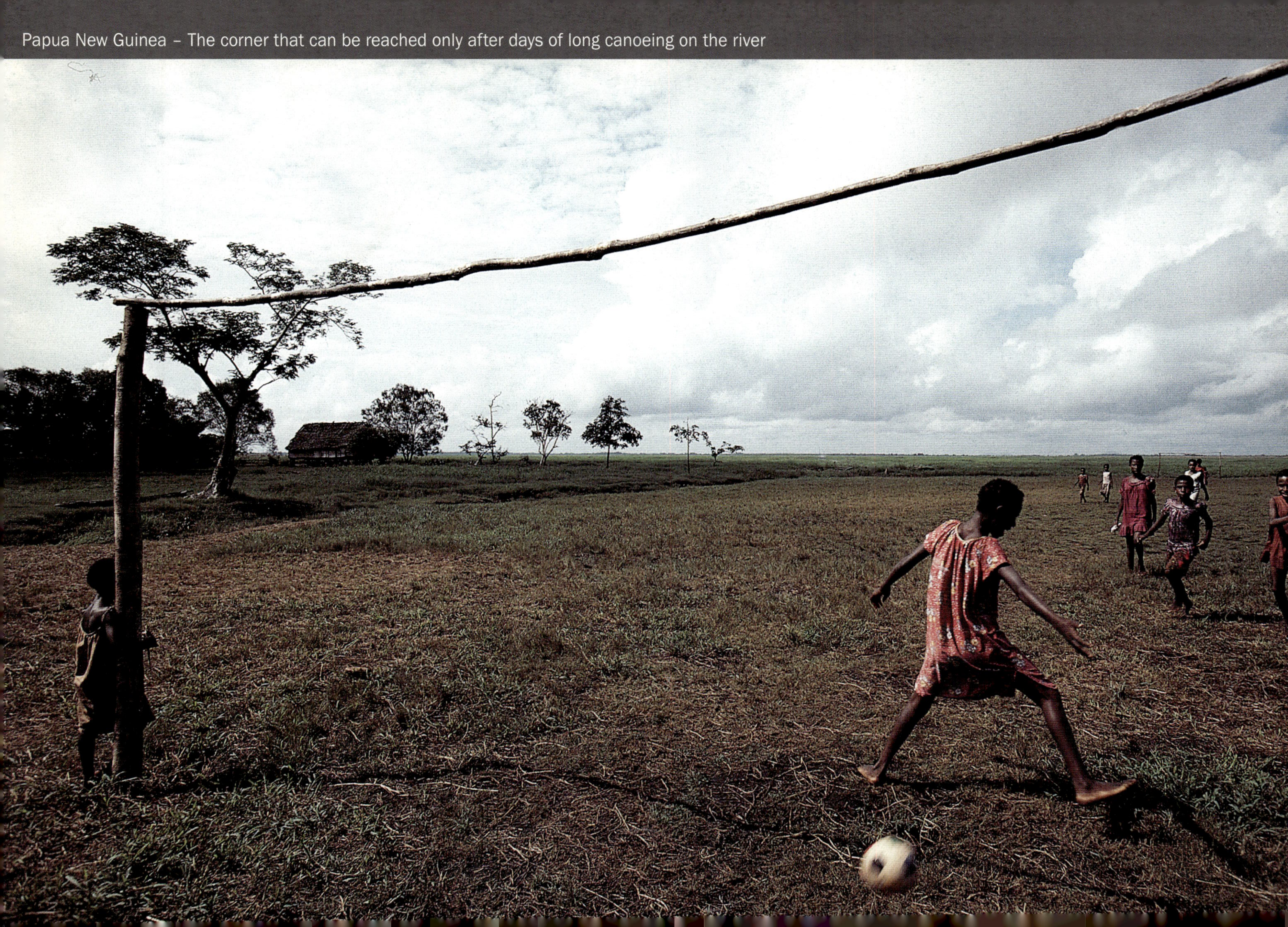

Papua New Guinea – The corner that can be reached only after days of long canoeing on the river

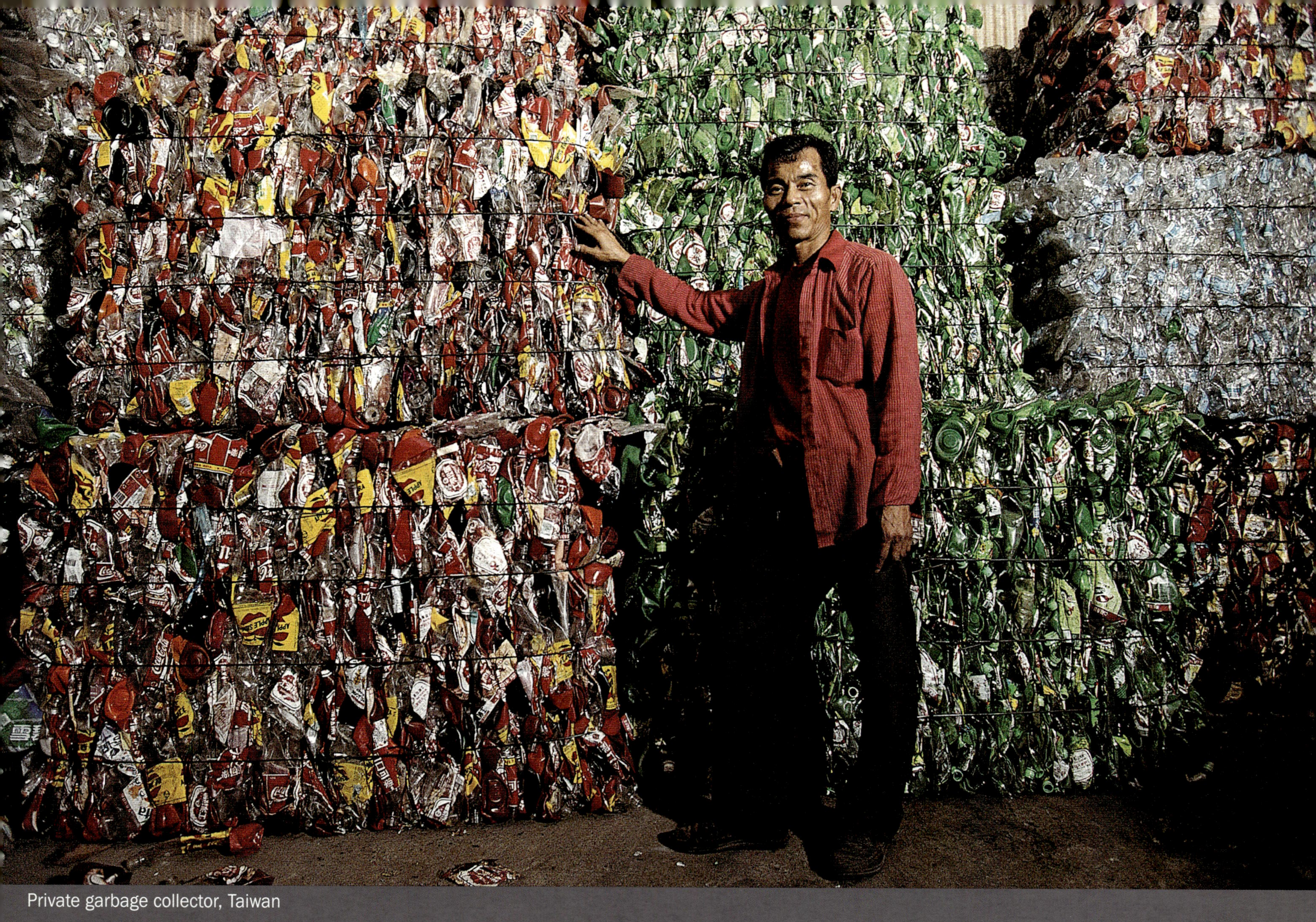

Private garbage collector, Taiwan

Michiko Koshino, London, 1997

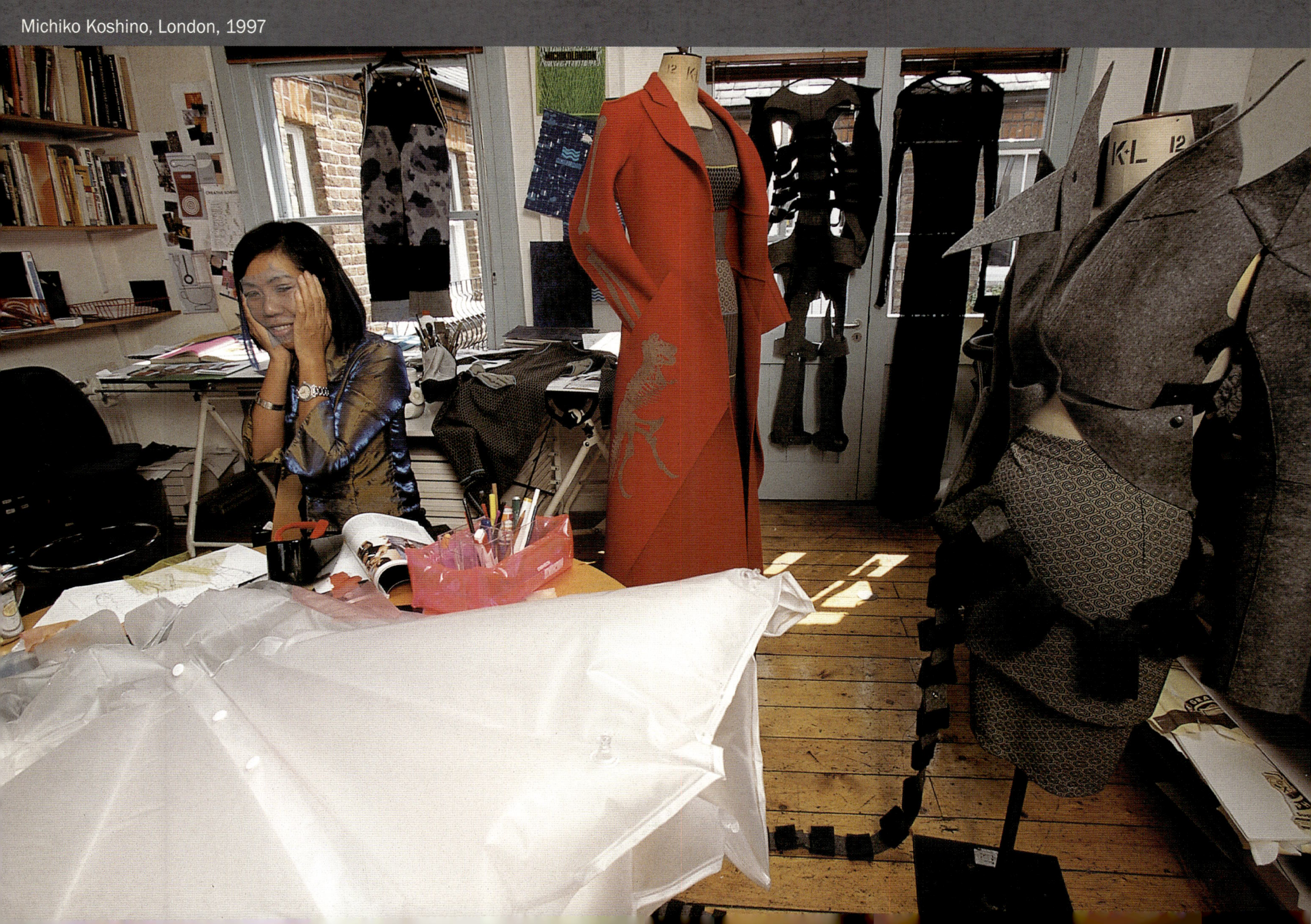

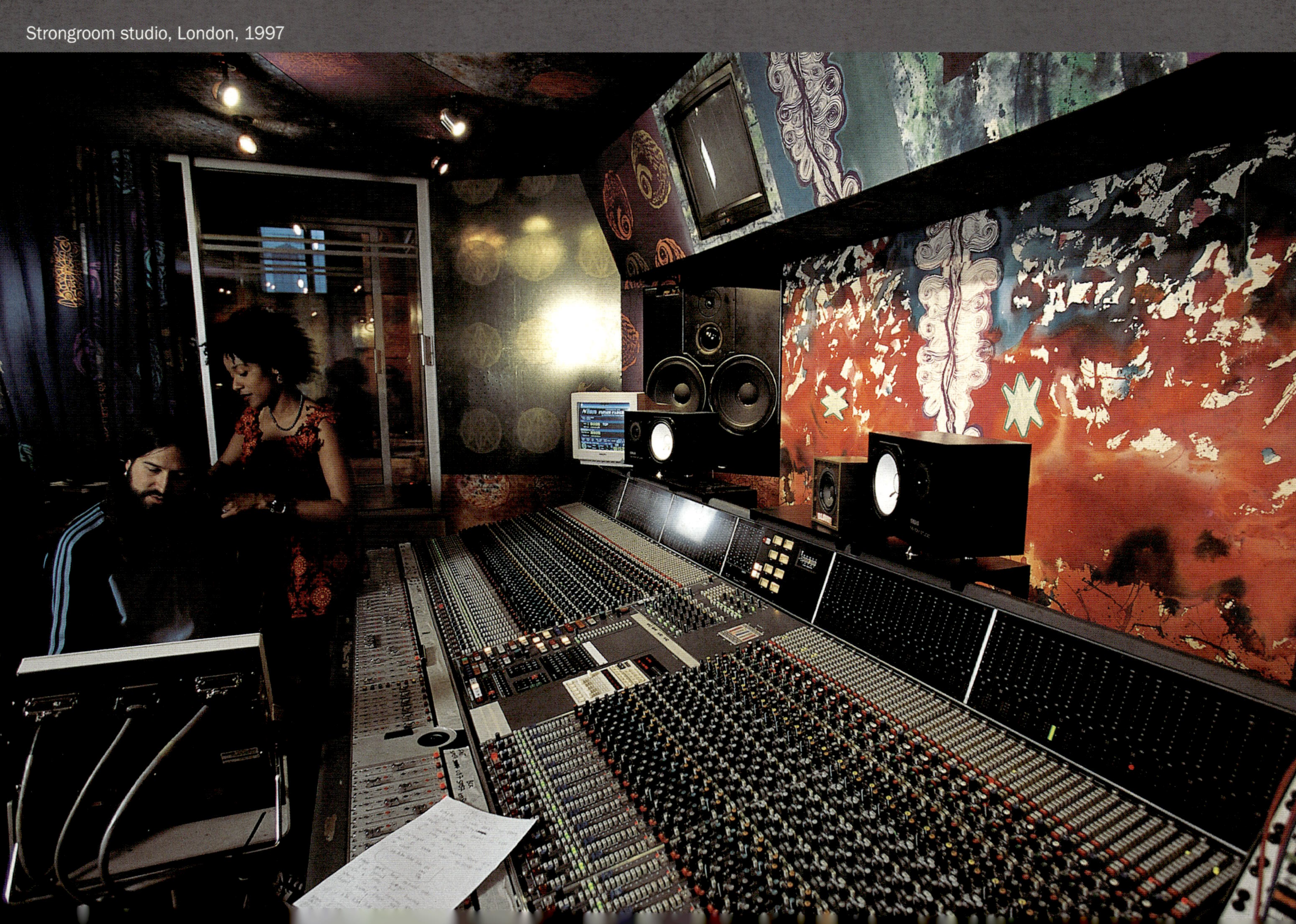

Strongroom studio, London, 1997

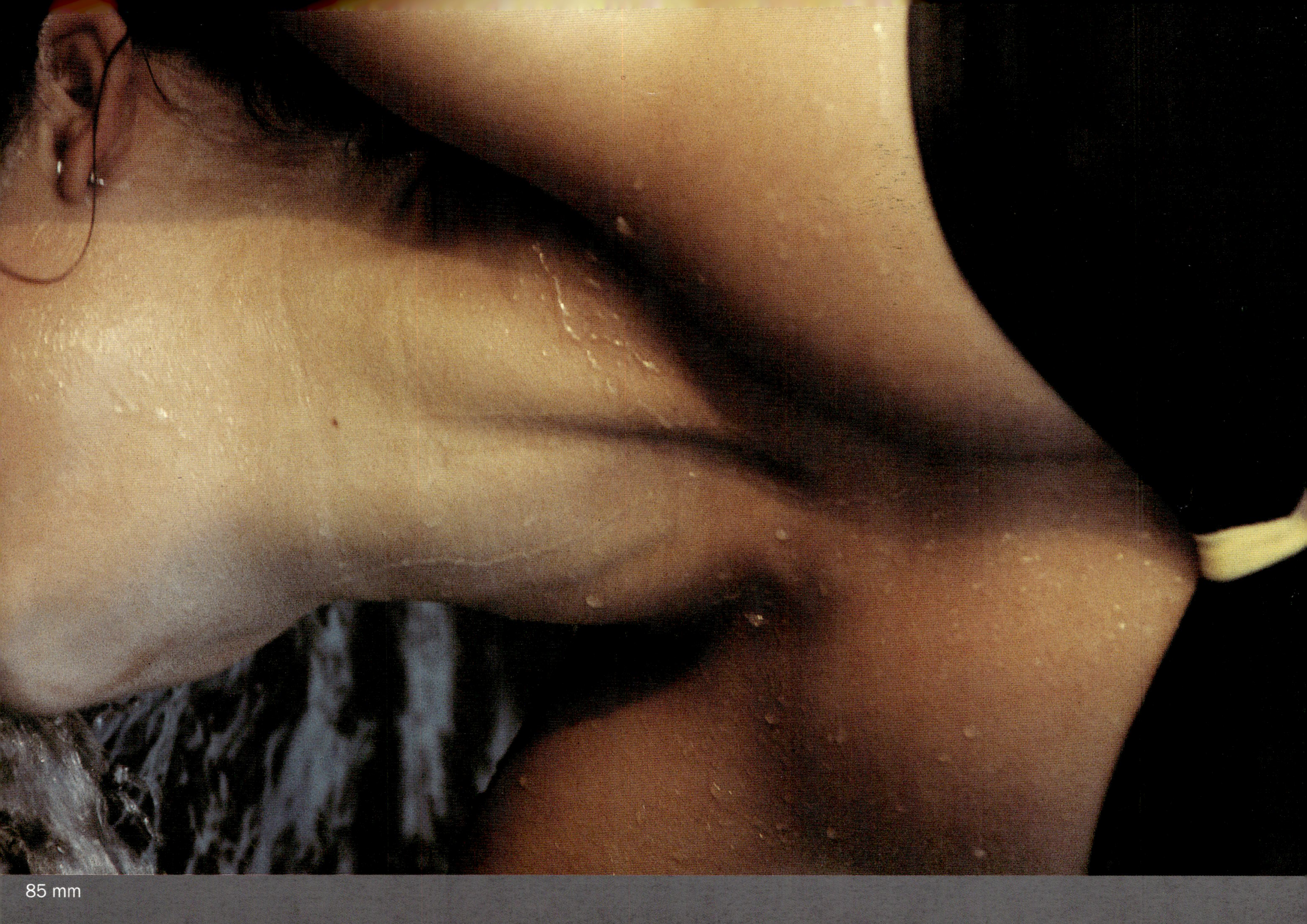

85 mm

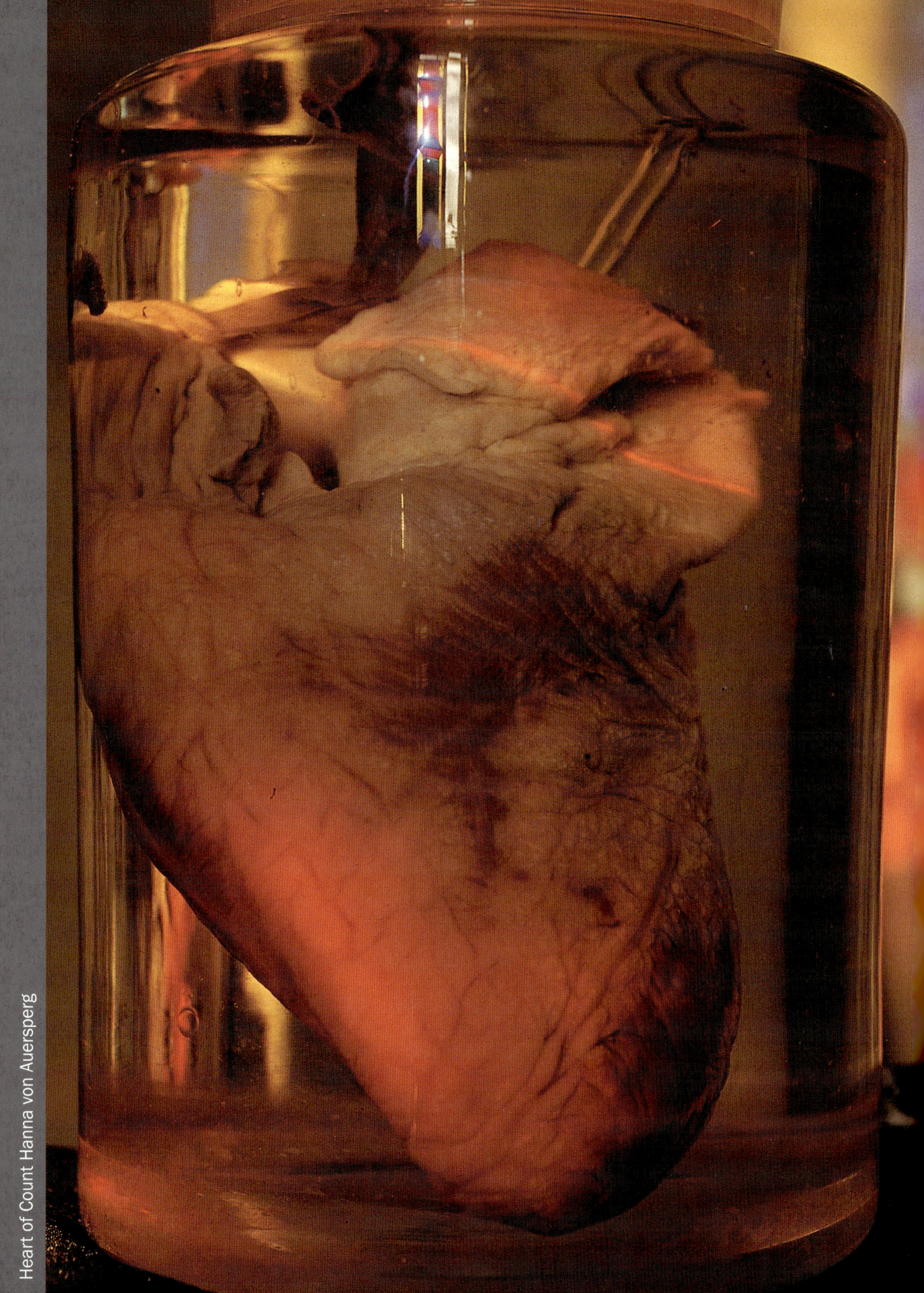

Heart of Count Hanna von Auersperg

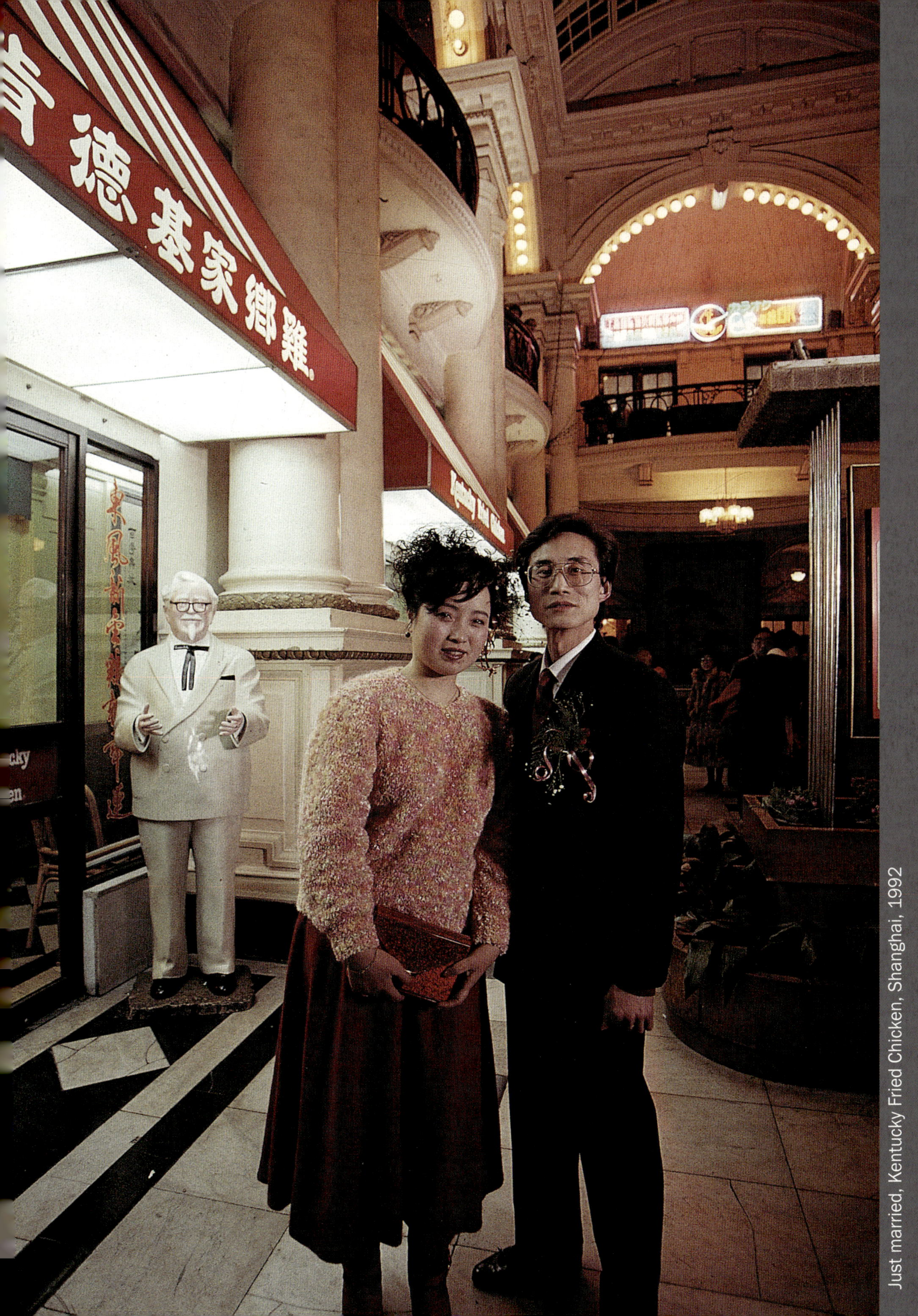

Just married, Kentucky Fried Chicken, Shanghai, 1992

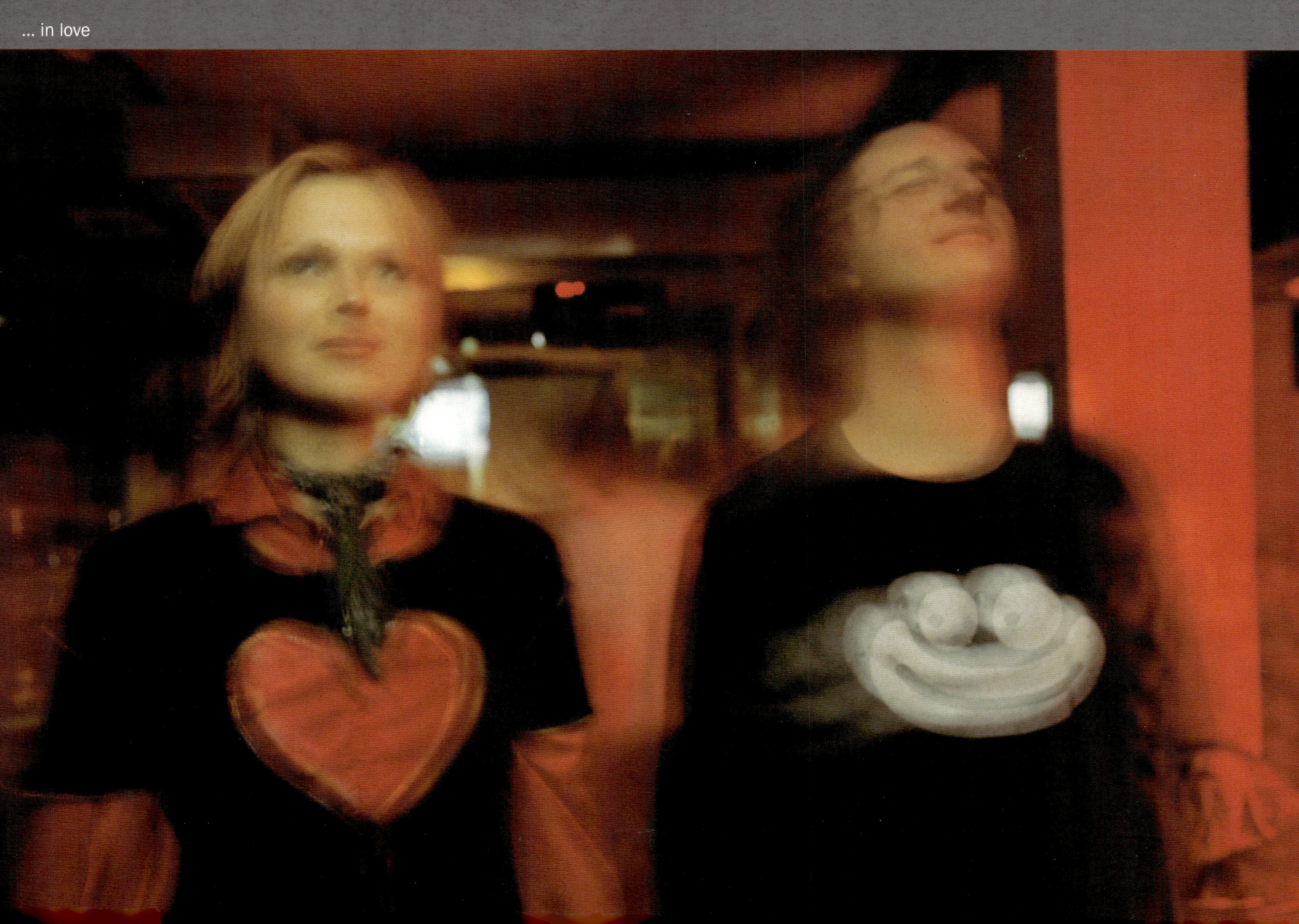

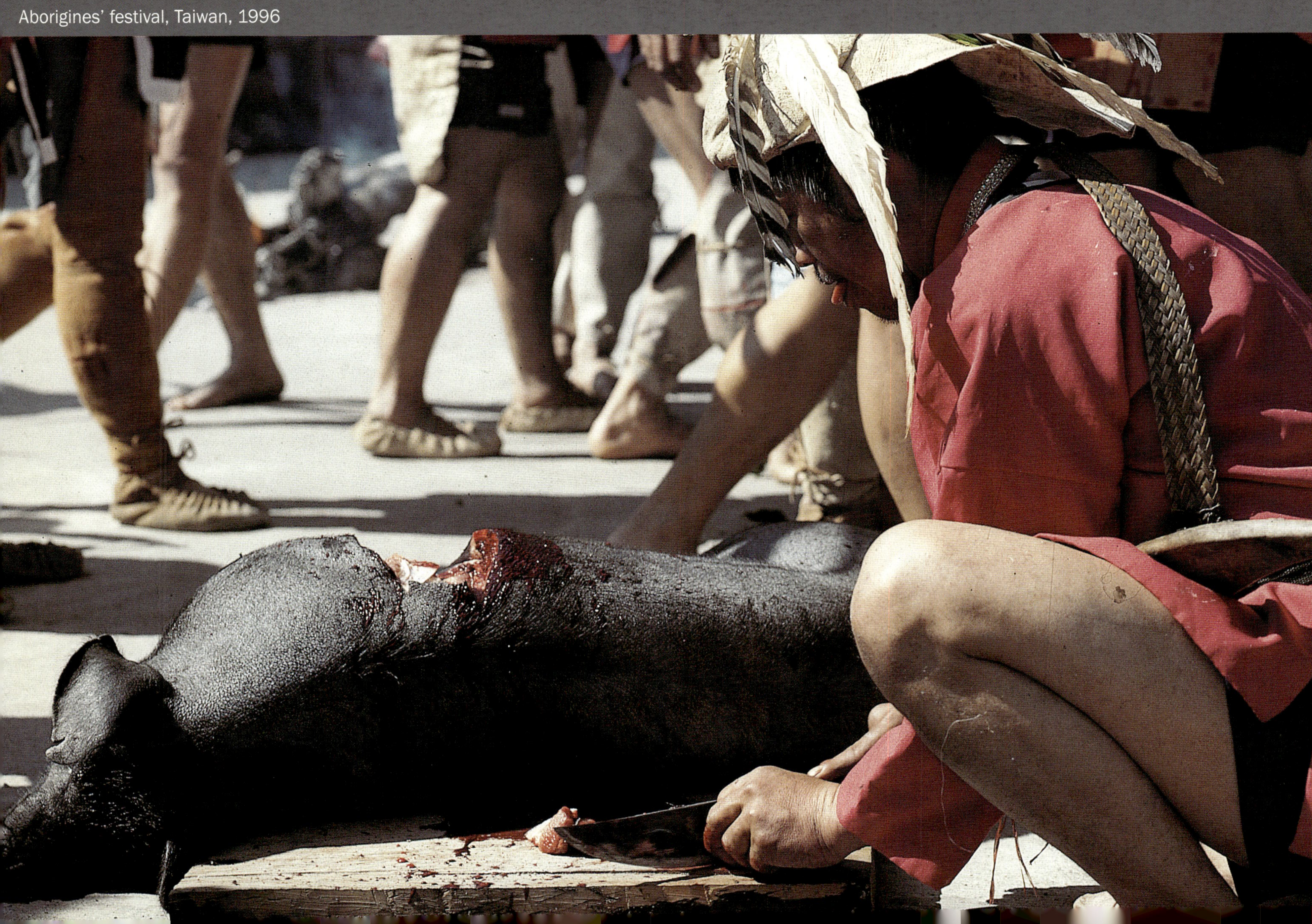

Aborigines' festival, Taiwan, 1996

Robert Traboscia, architect and painter, New York

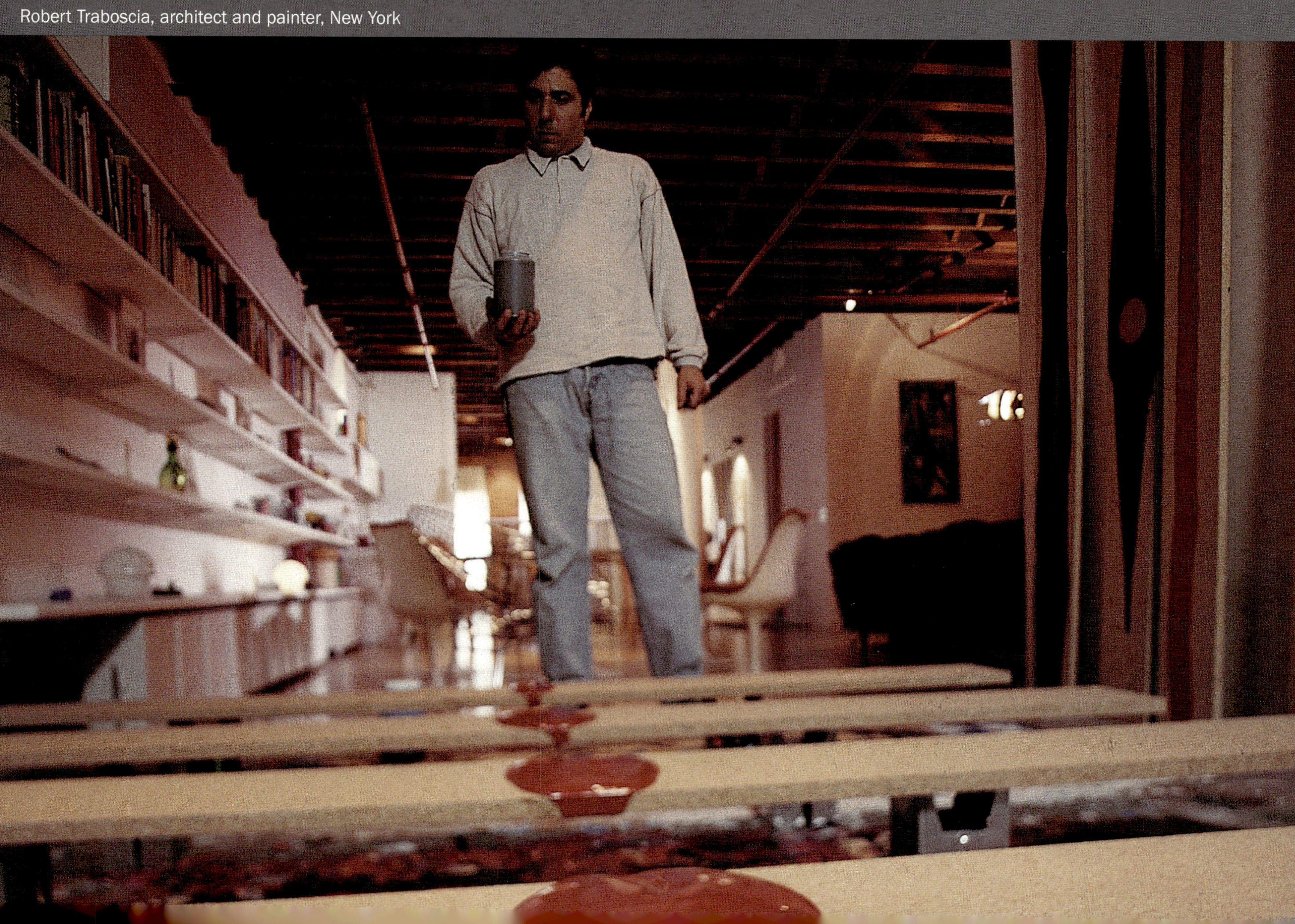

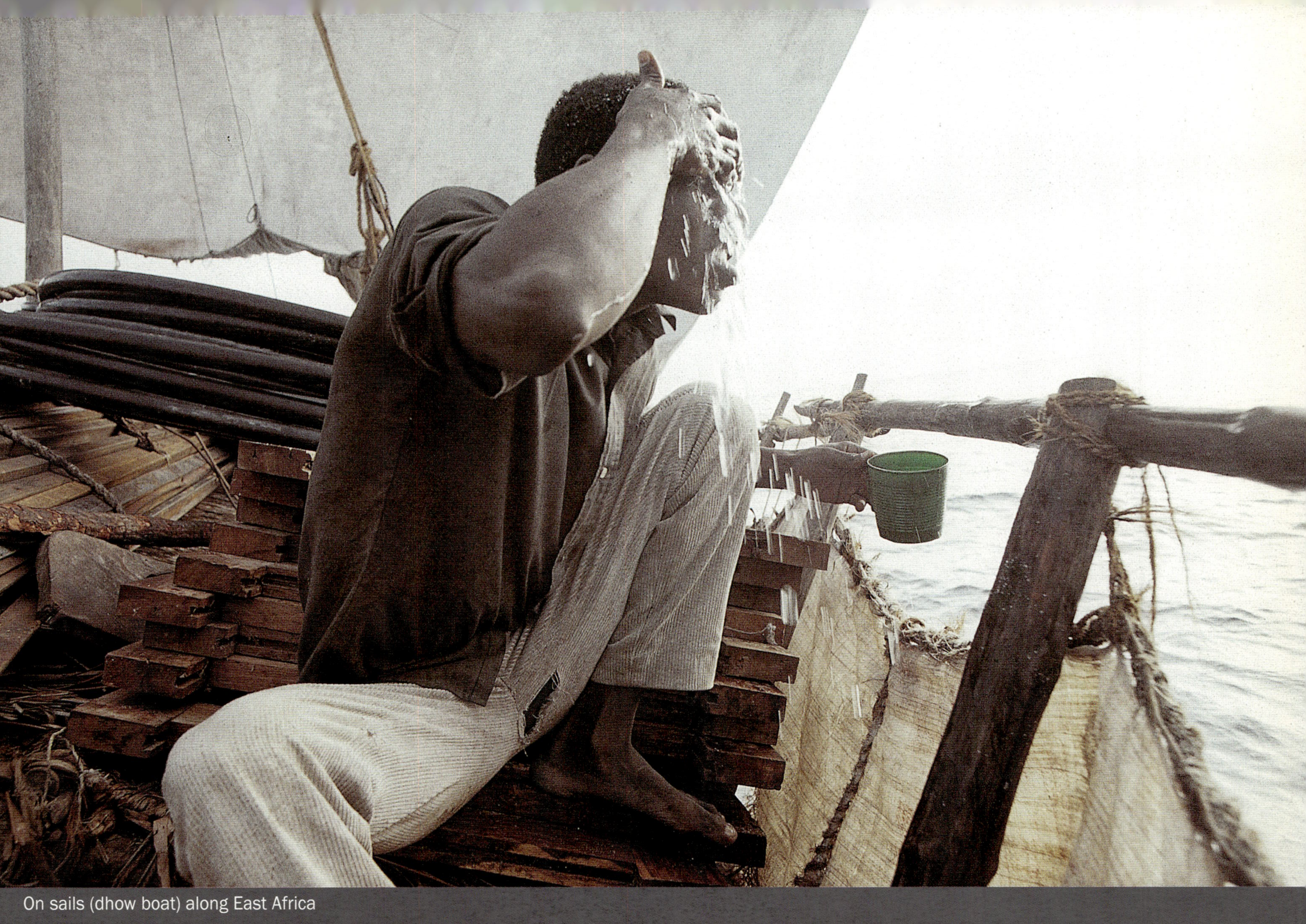

On sails (dhow boat) along East Africa

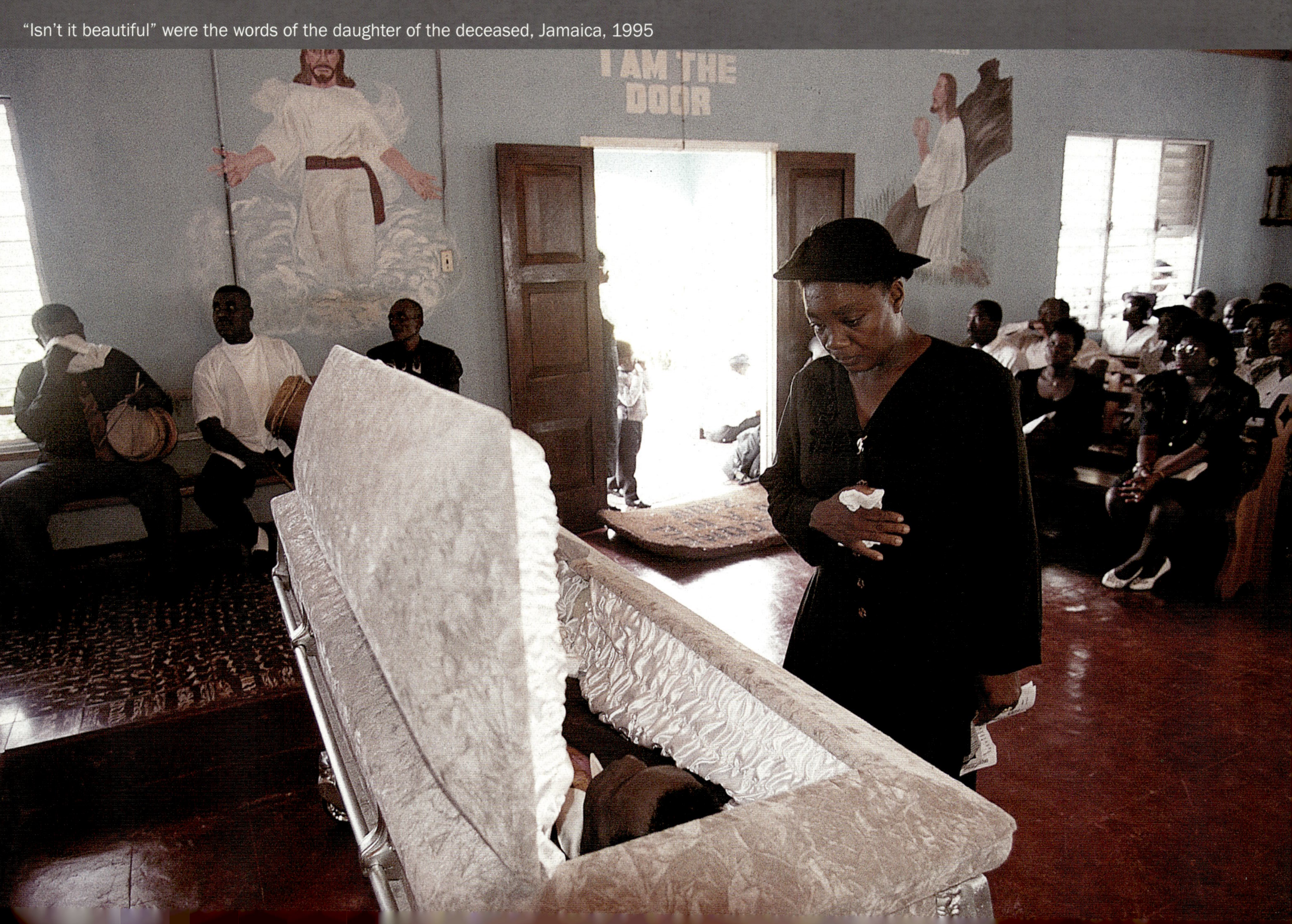

“Isn’t it beautiful” were the words of the daughter of the deceased, Jamaica, 1995

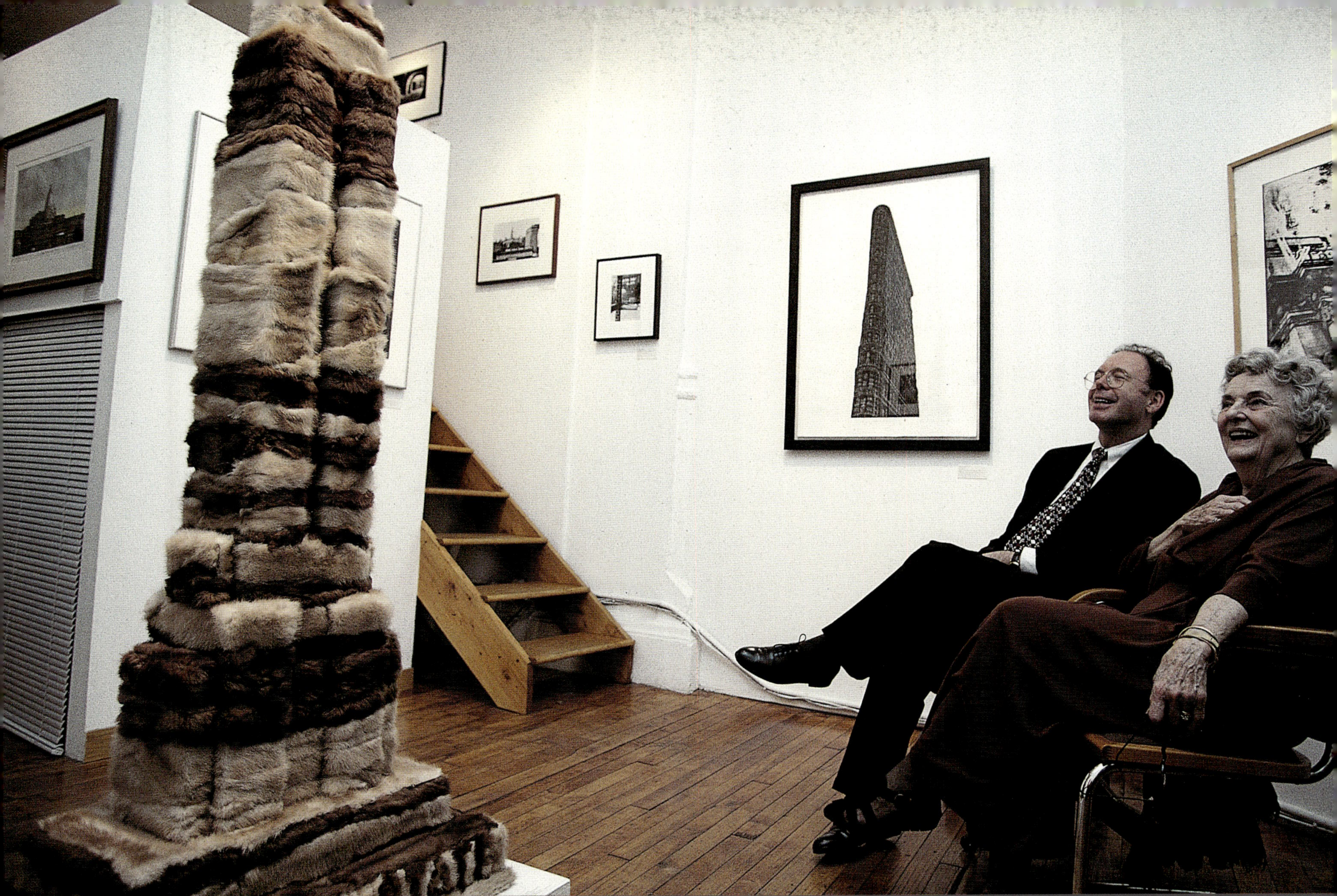

New York City Landmarks exhibition, New York, 1995

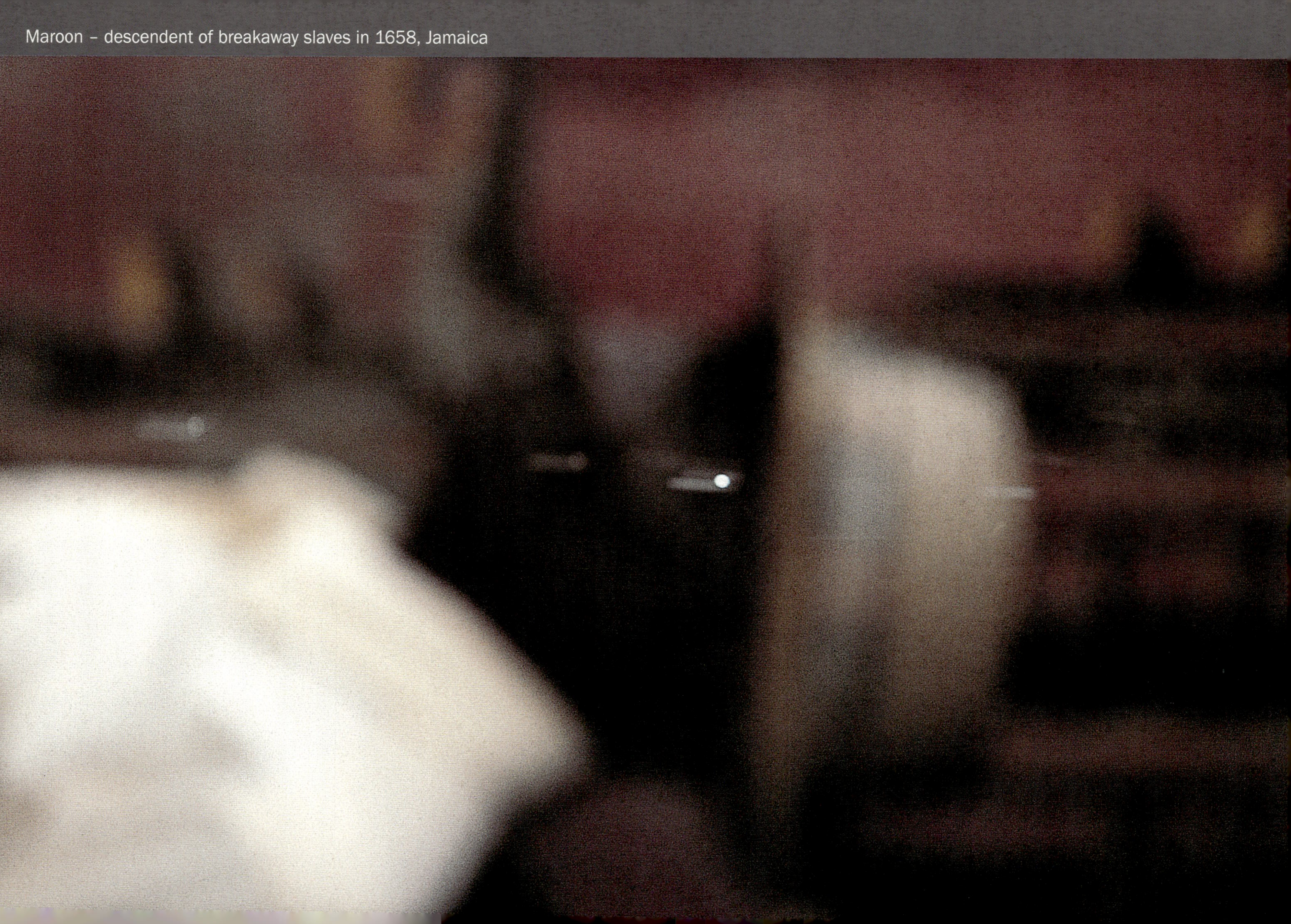

Maroon – descendent of breakaway slaves in 1658, Jamaica

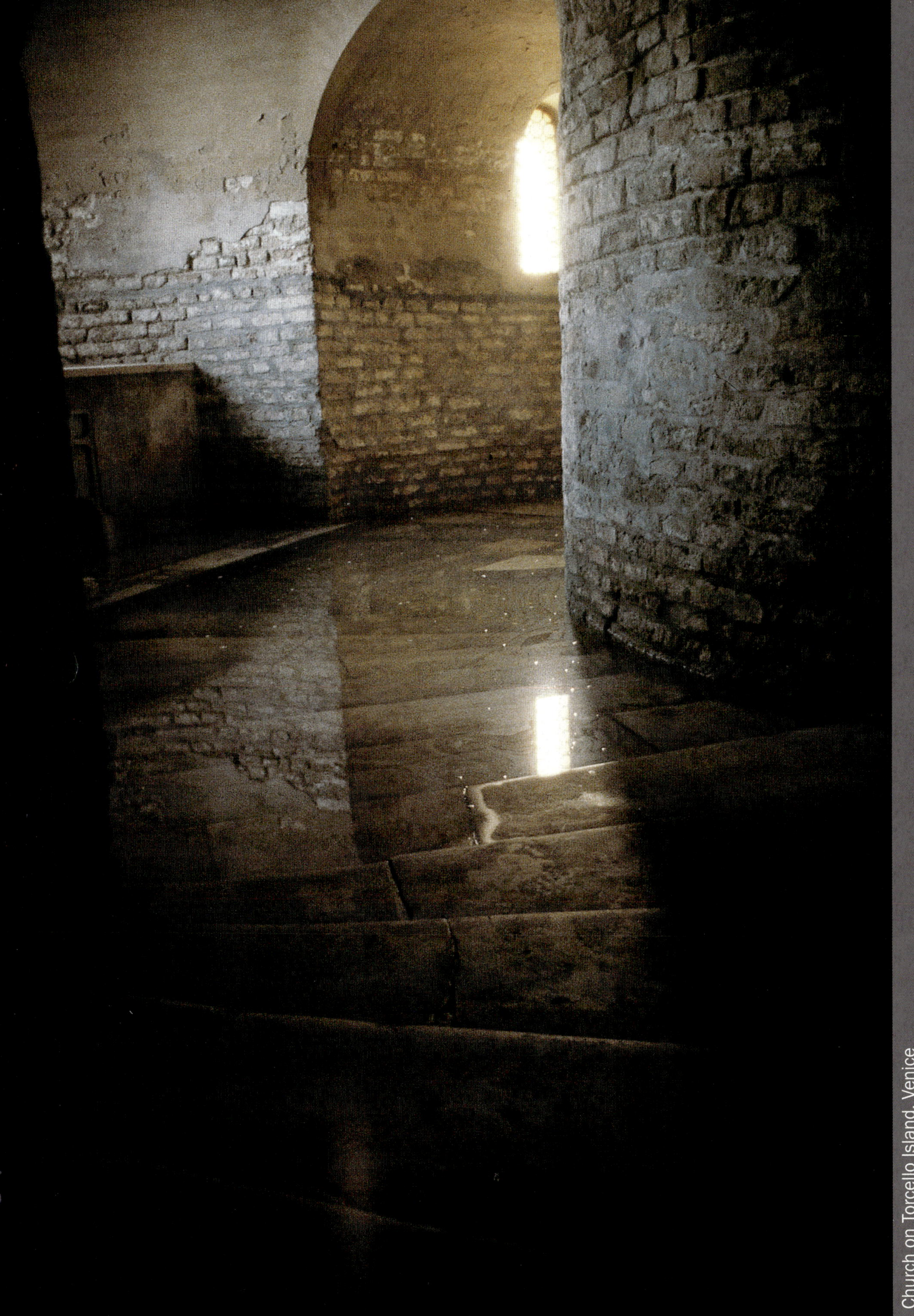

Church on Torcello Island, Venice

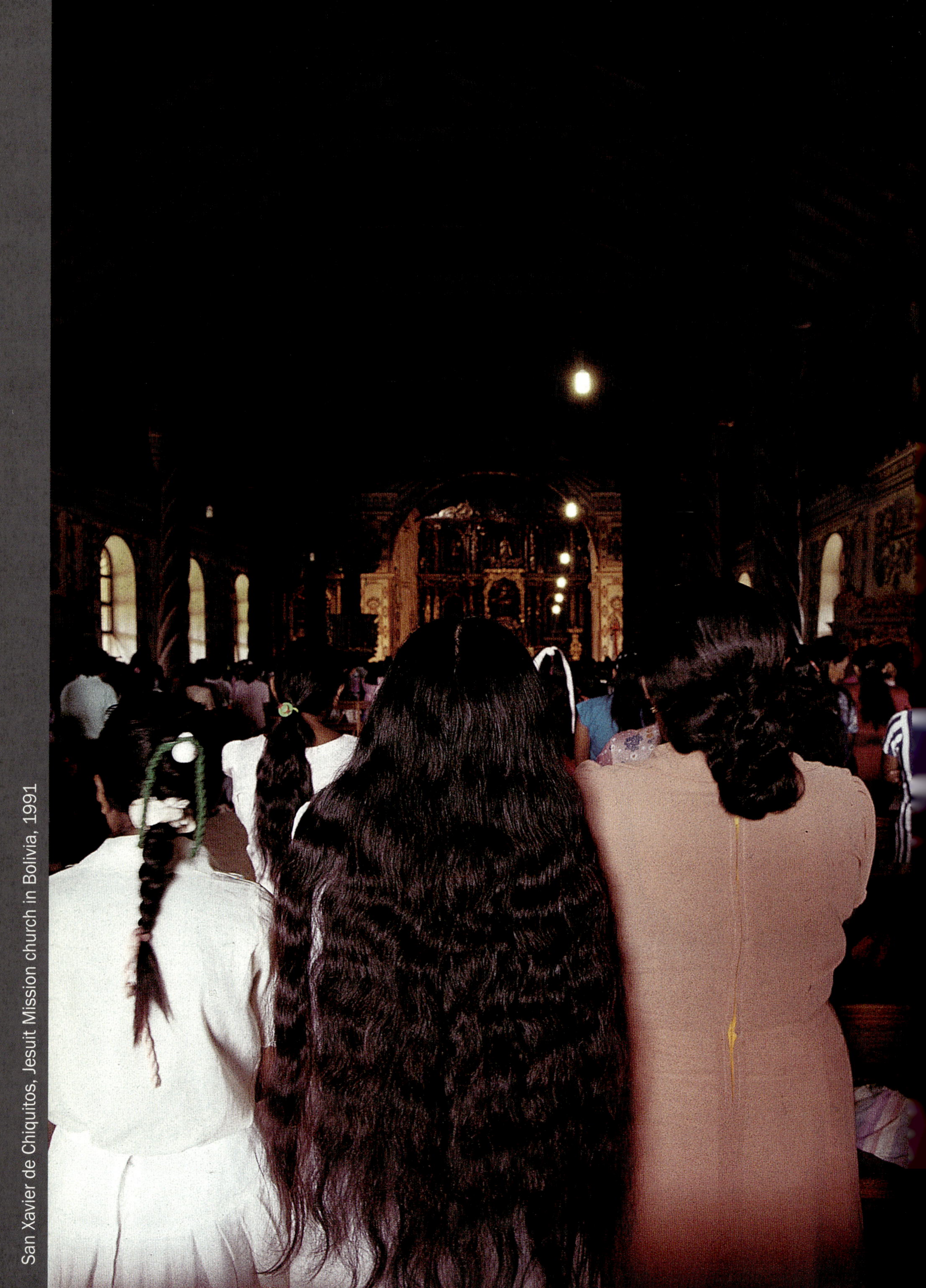

San Xavier de Chiquitos, Jesuit Mission church in Bolivia, 1991

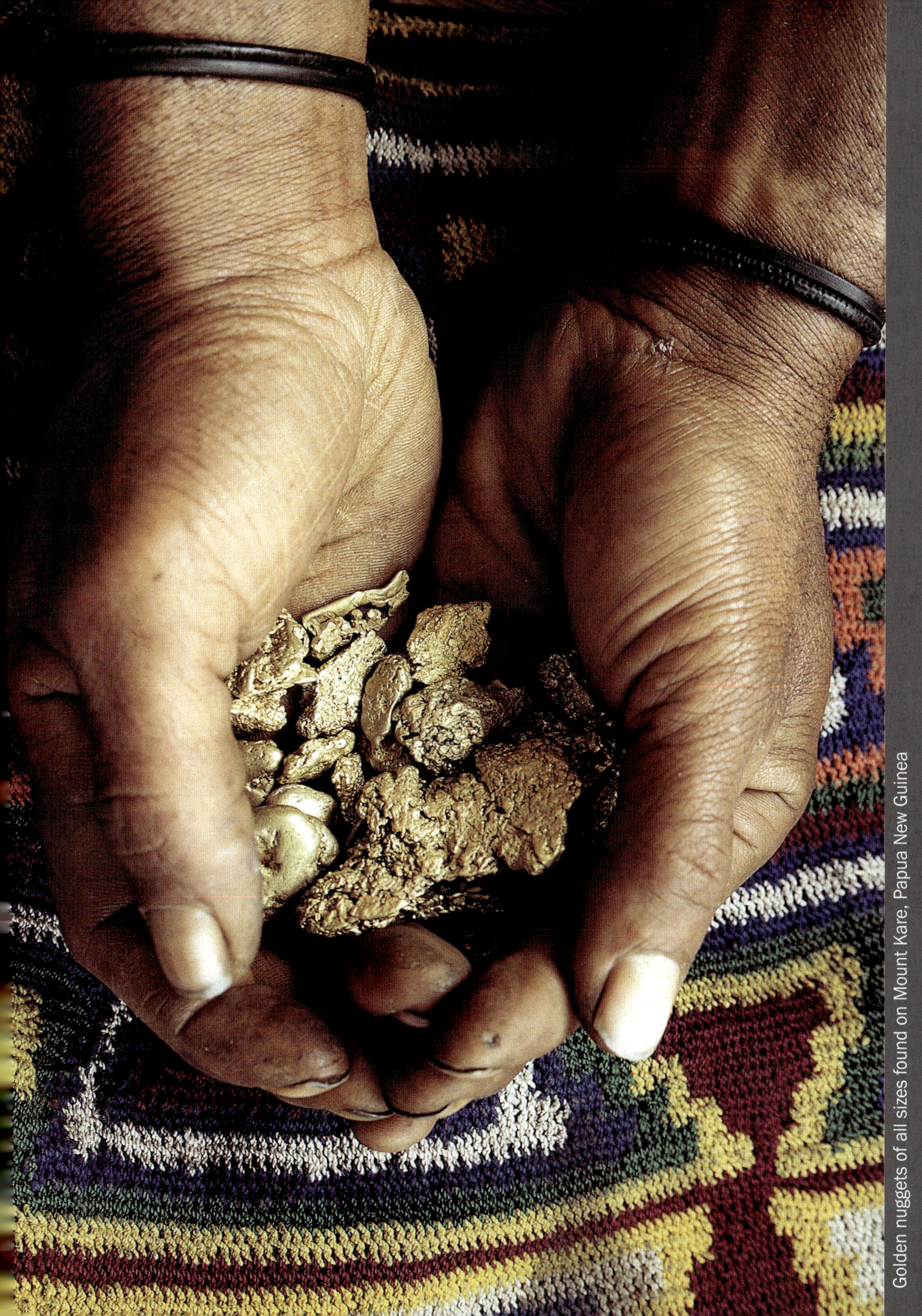

Golden nuggets of all sizes found on Mount Kare, Papua New Guinea

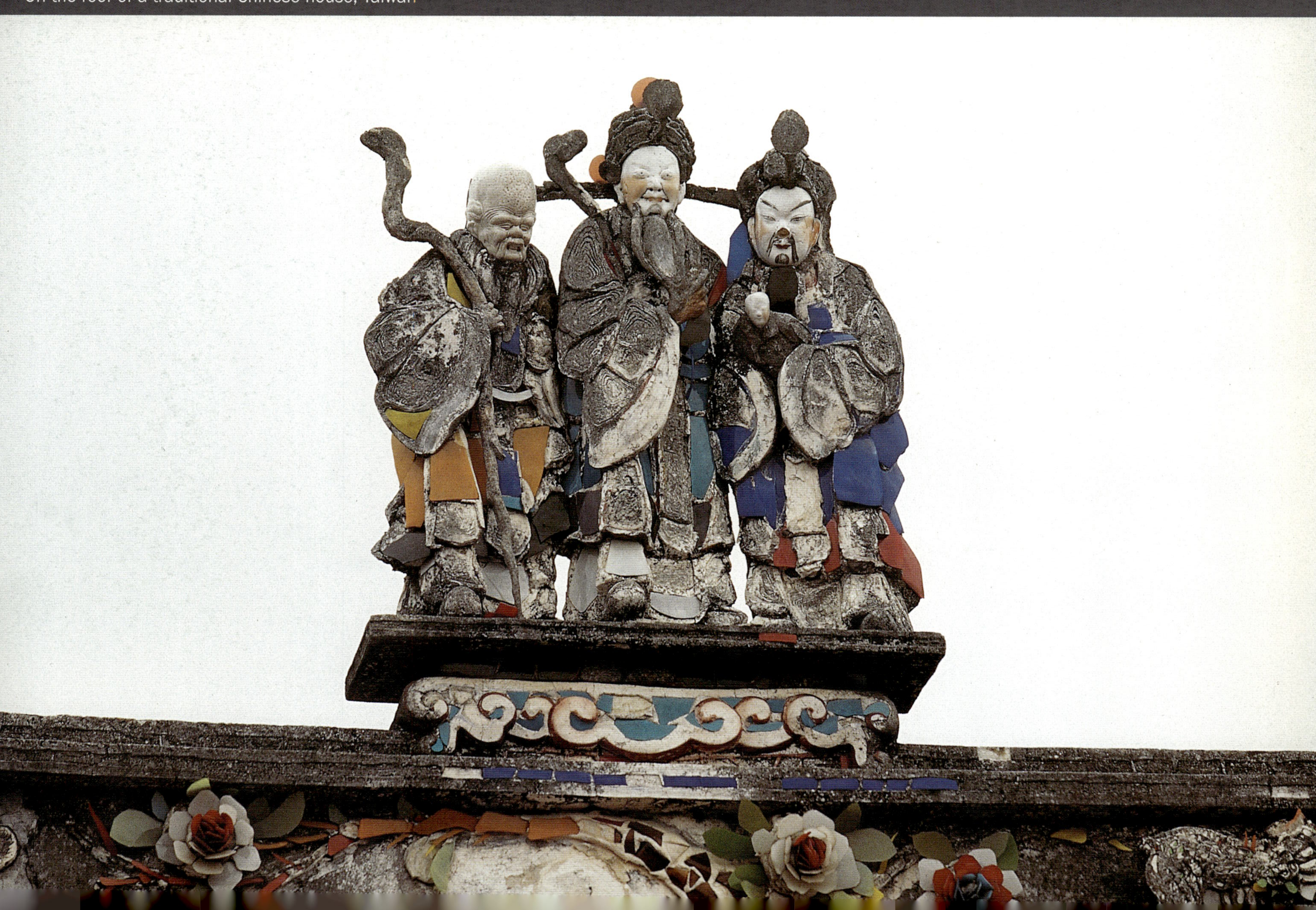

On the roof of a traditional Chinese house, Taiwan

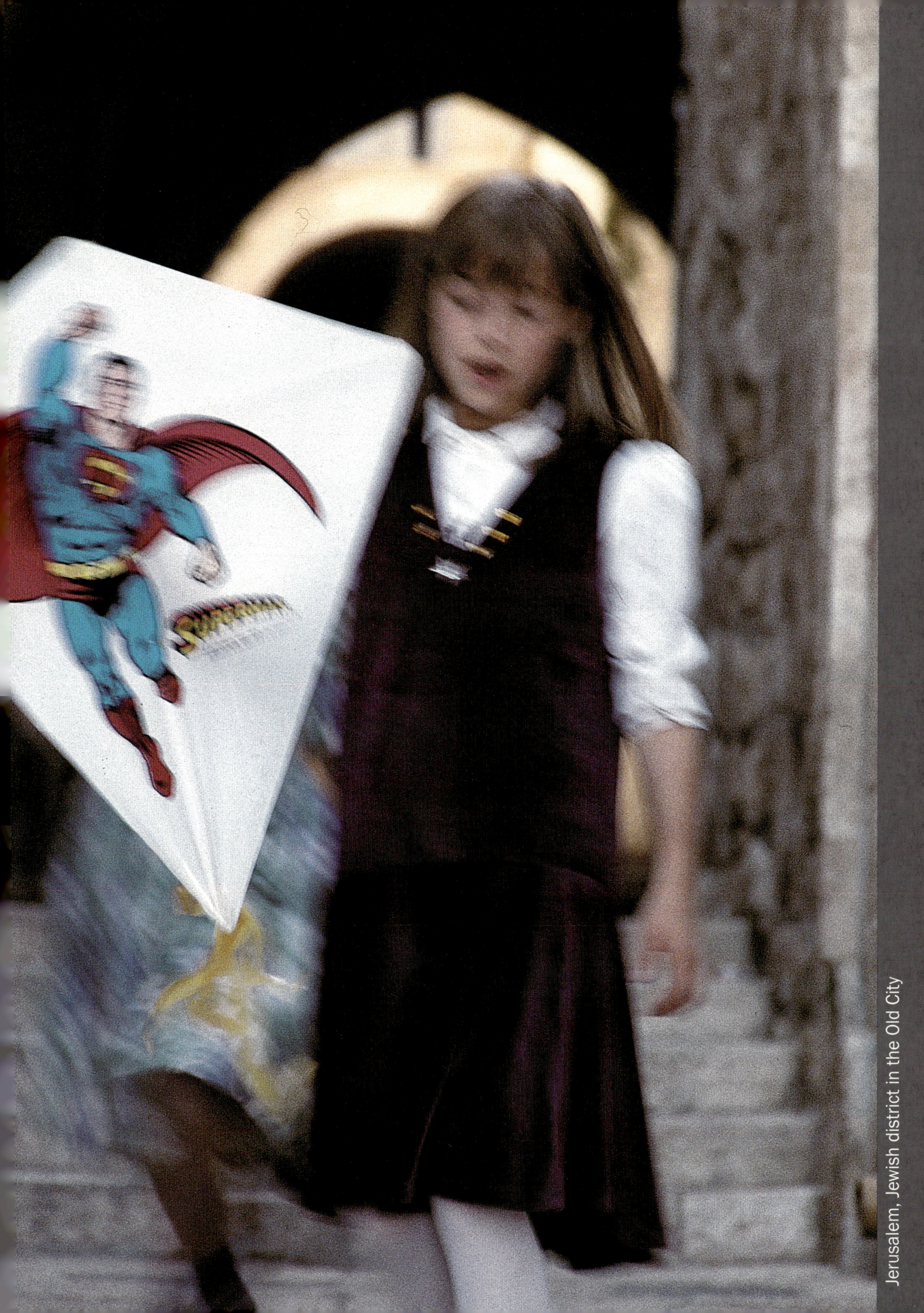

Jerusalem, Jewish district in the Old City

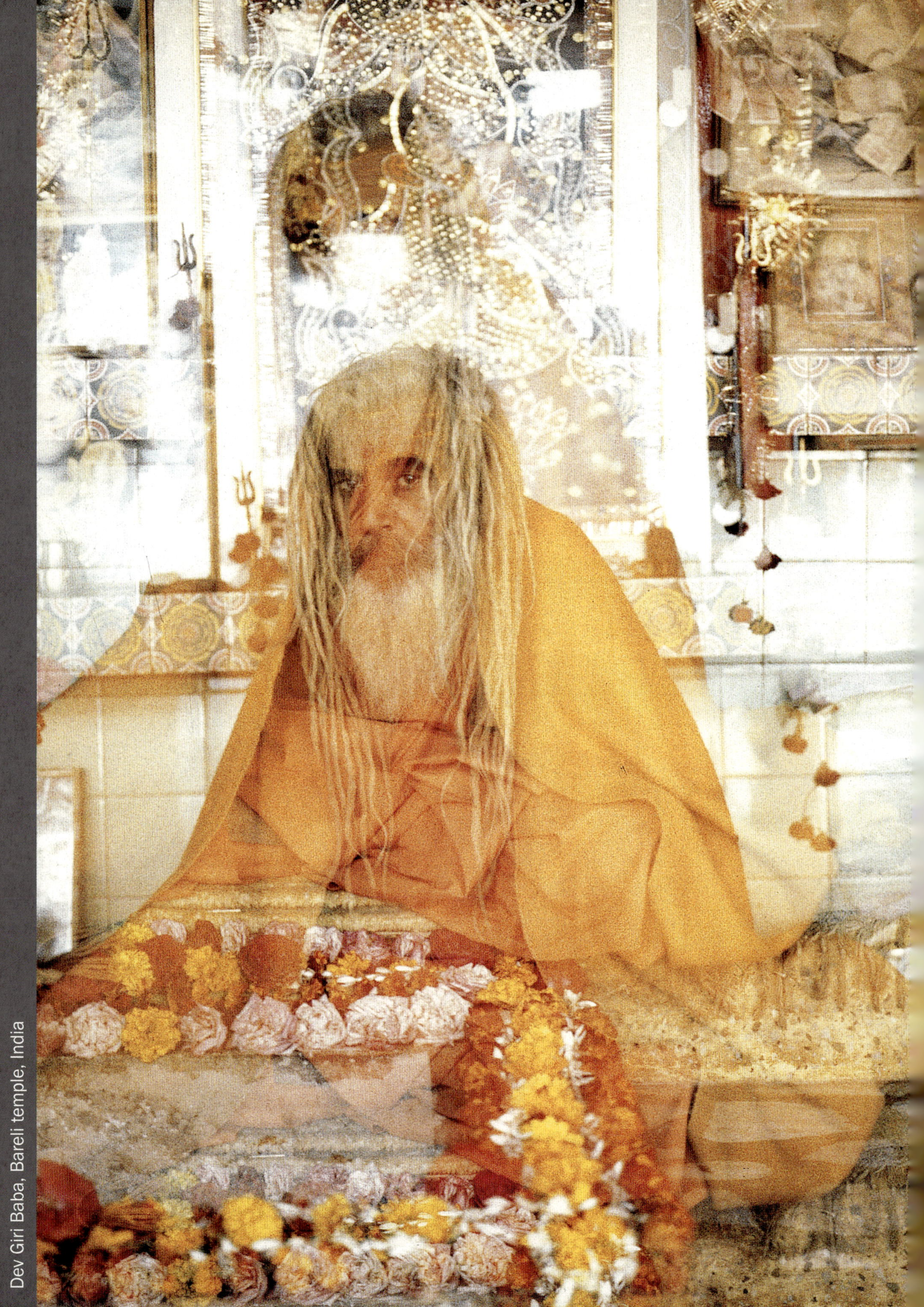

Dev Giri Baba, Bareli temple, India

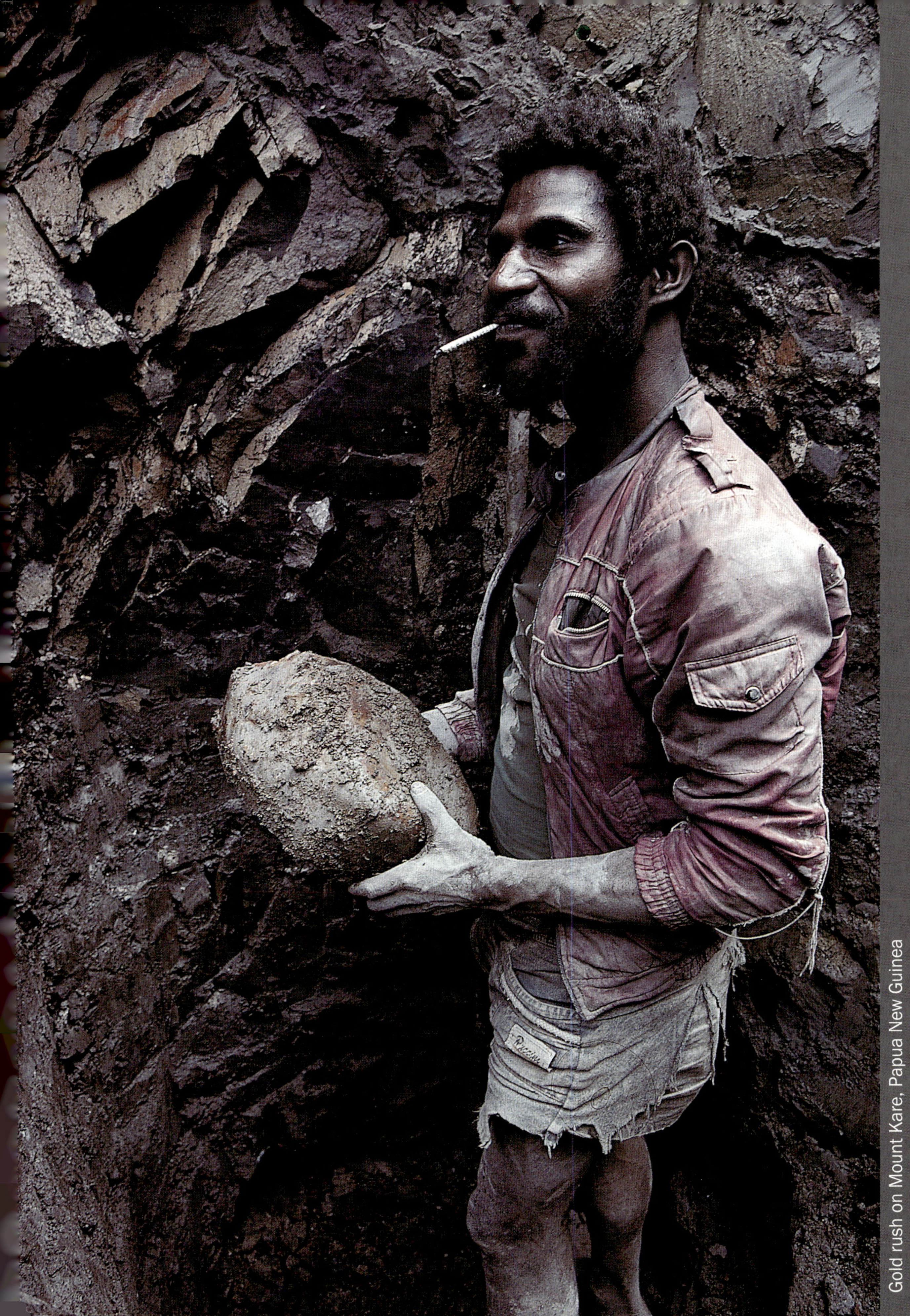

Gold rush on Mount Kare, Papua New Guinea

Venice

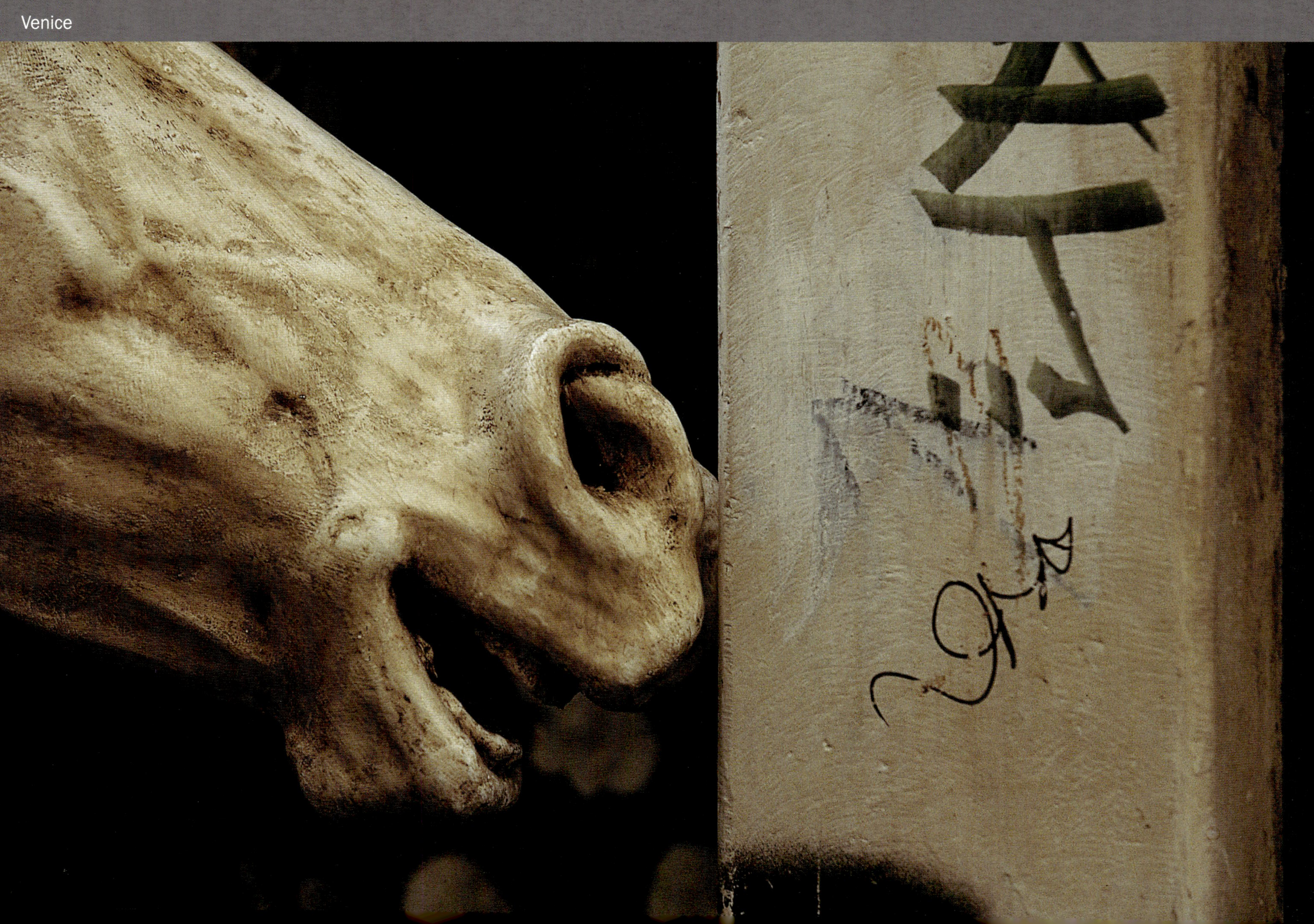

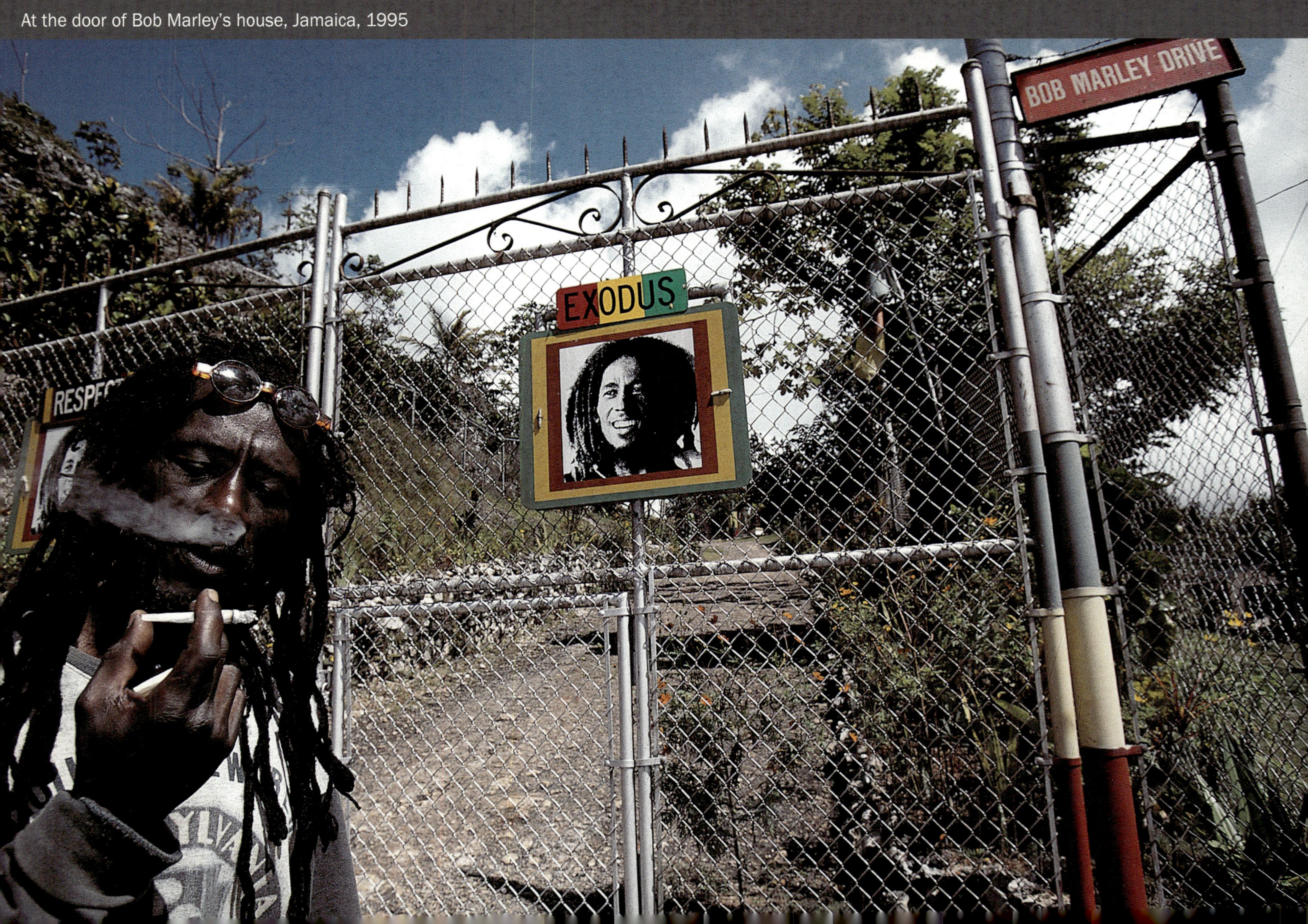

At the door of Bob Marley's house, Jamaica, 1995

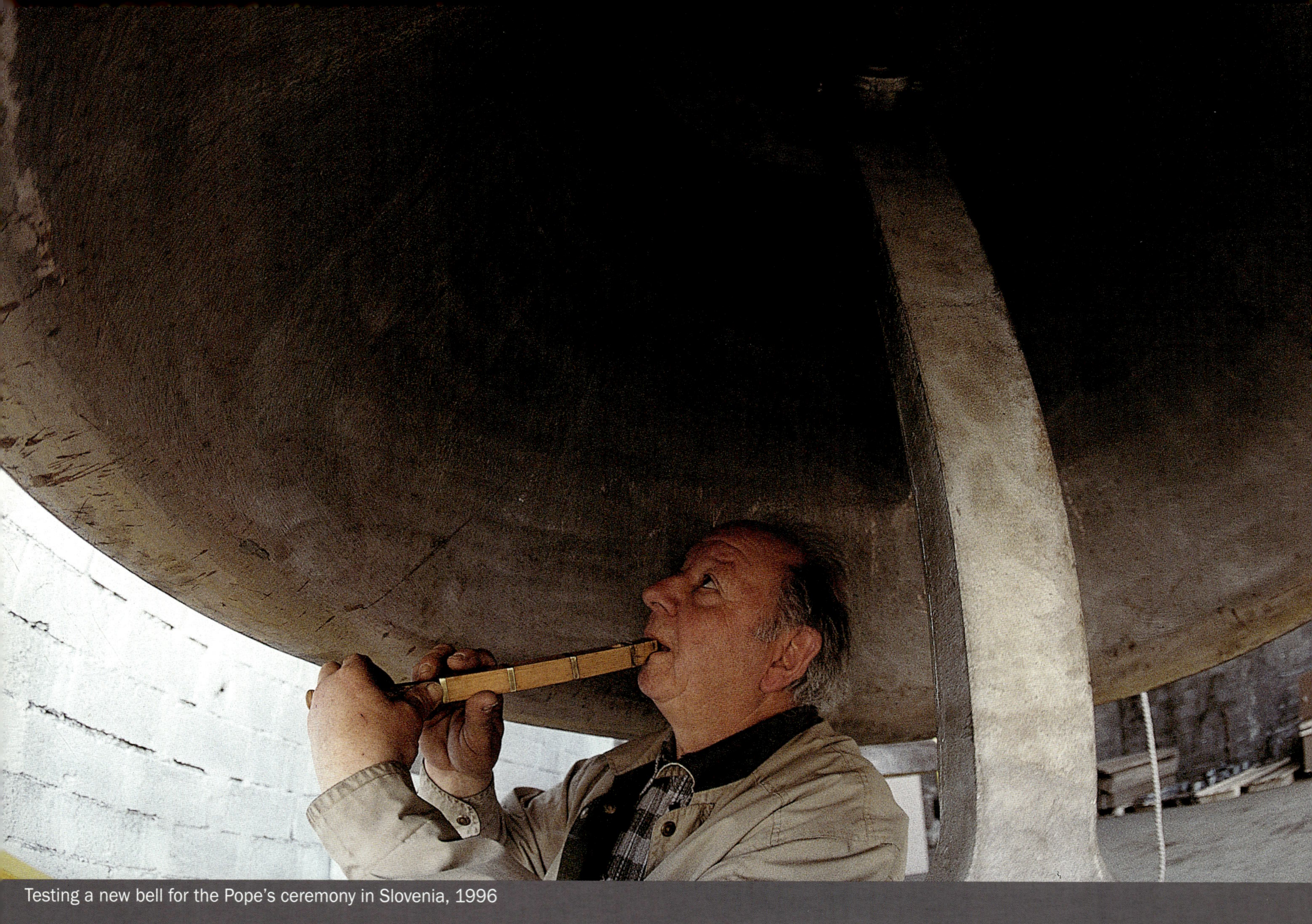

Testing a new bell for the Pope's ceremony in Slovenia, 1996

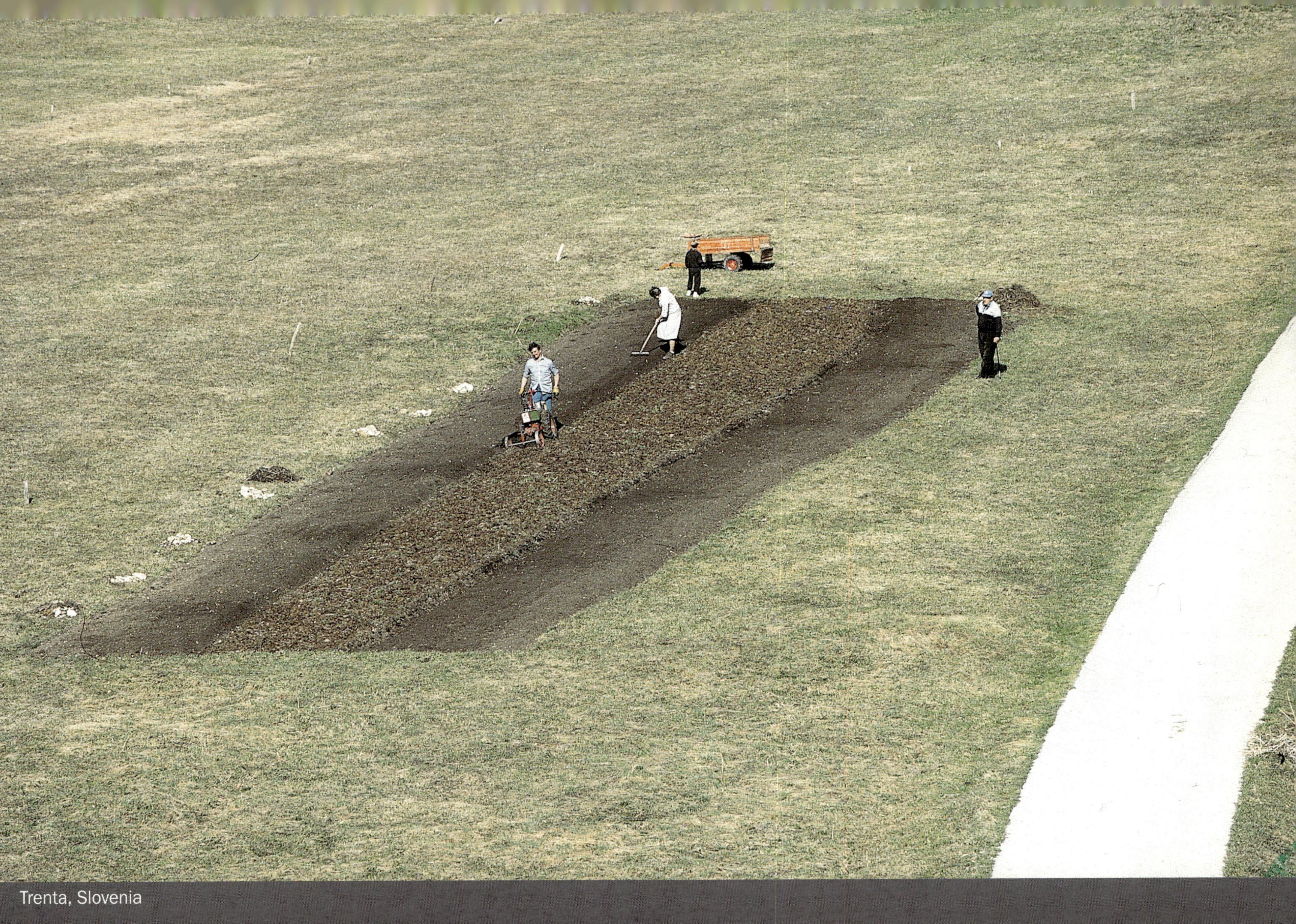

Trenta, Slovenia

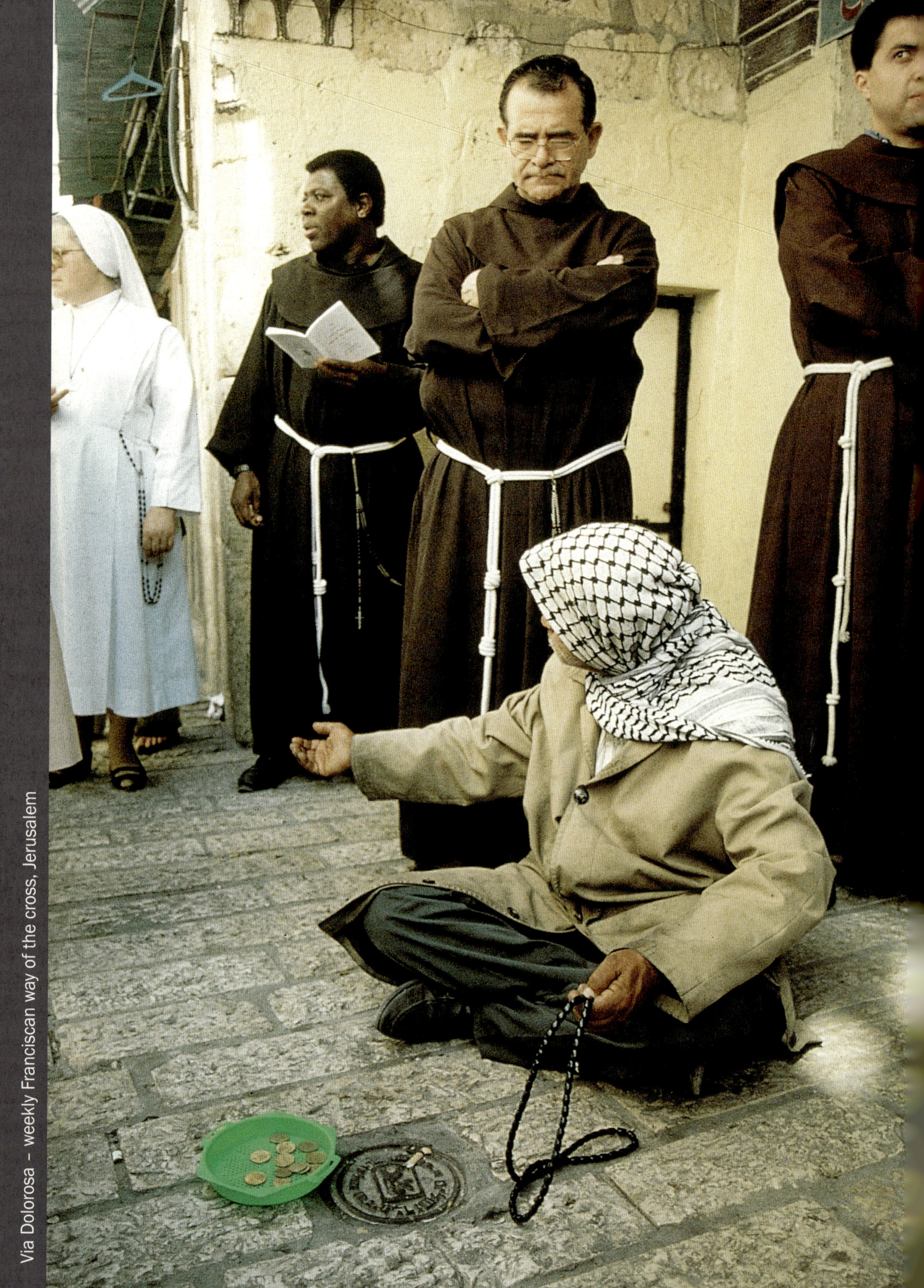

Via Dolorosa – weekly Franciscan way of the cross, Jerusalem

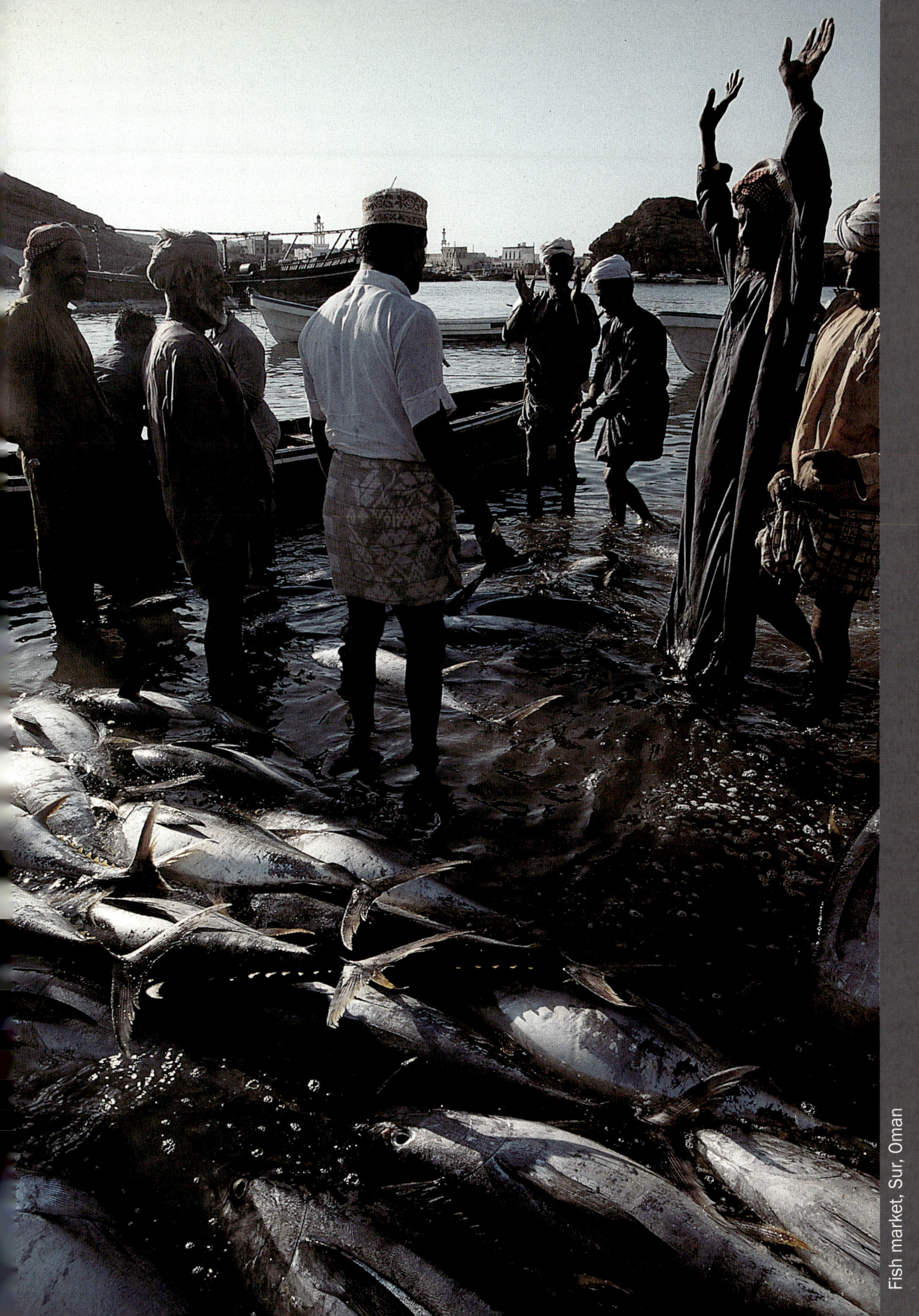

Fish market, Sur, Oman

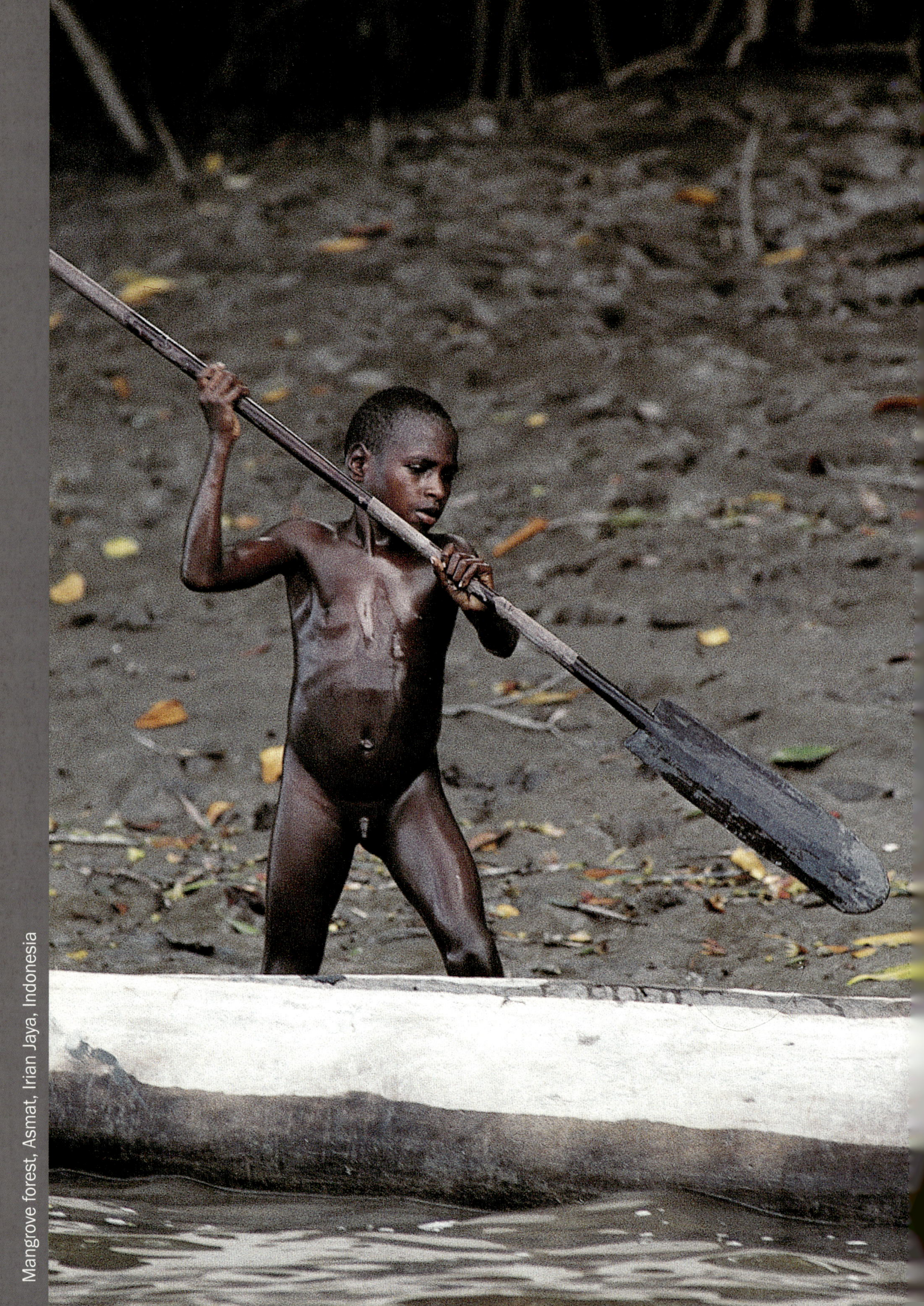

Mangrove forest, Asmat, Irian Jaya, Indonesia

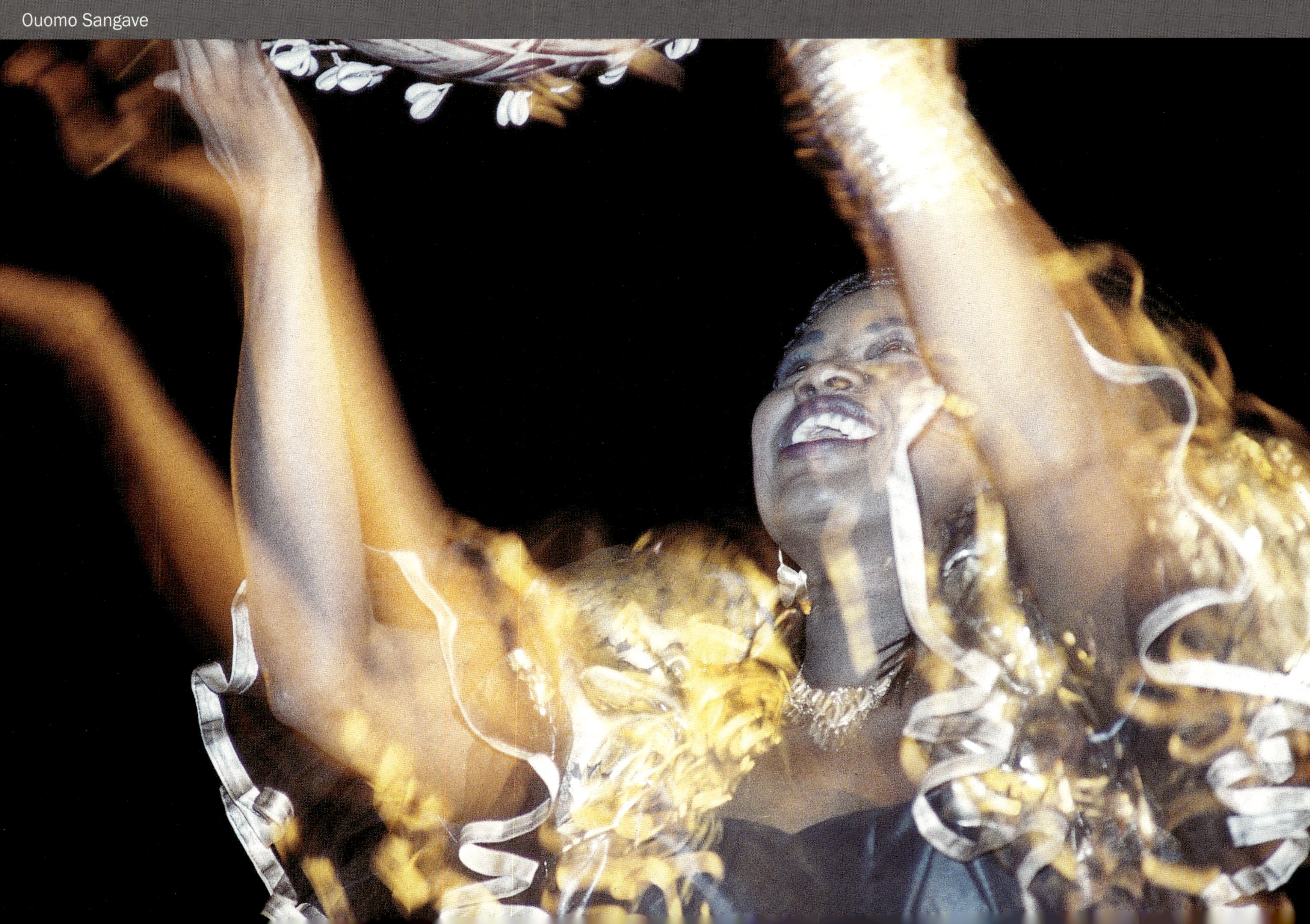

Healing a camel, Oman

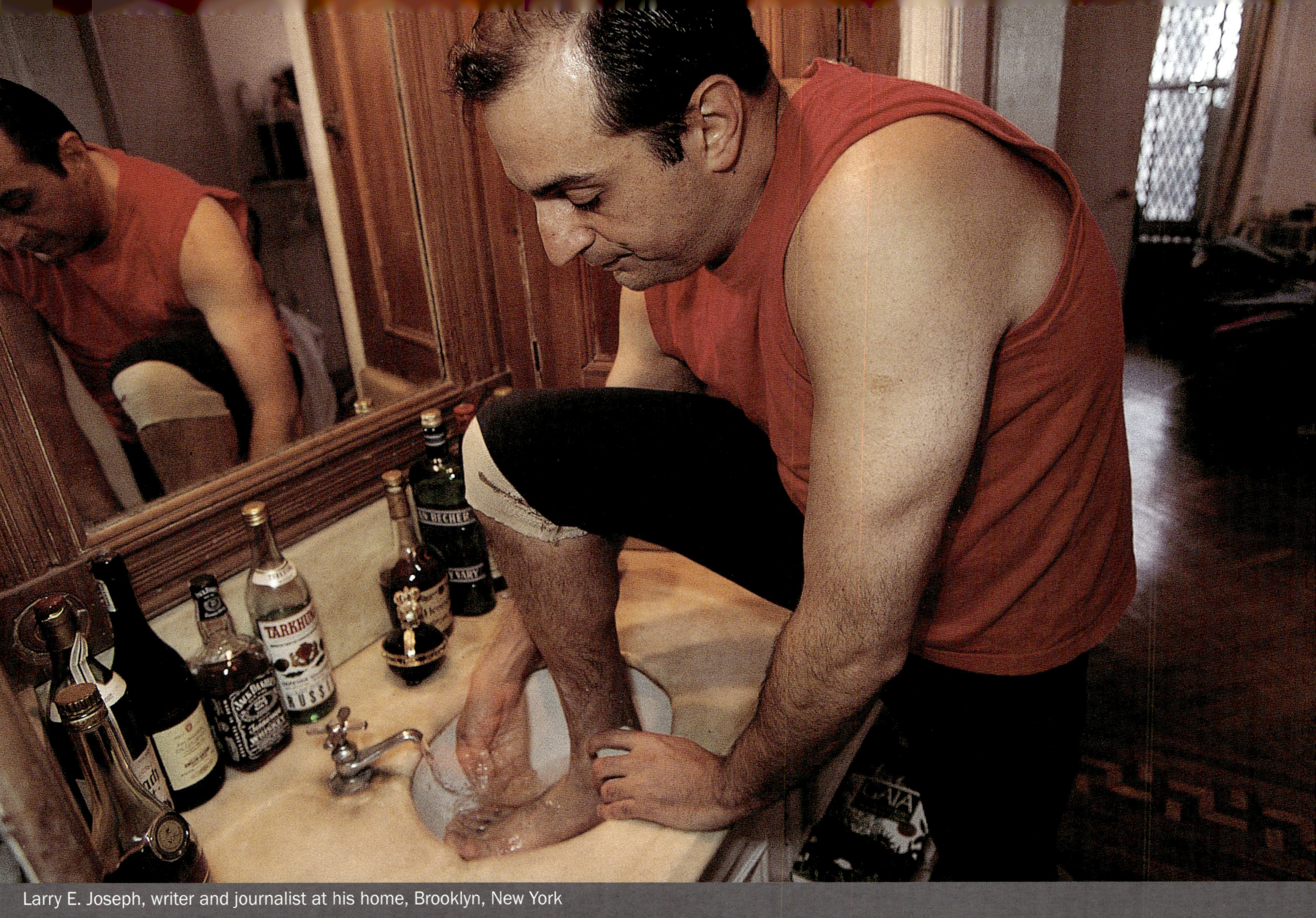

Larry E. Joseph, writer and journalist at his home, Brooklyn, New York

Biennial of Architecture, Belgrade, Yugoslavia, 1993

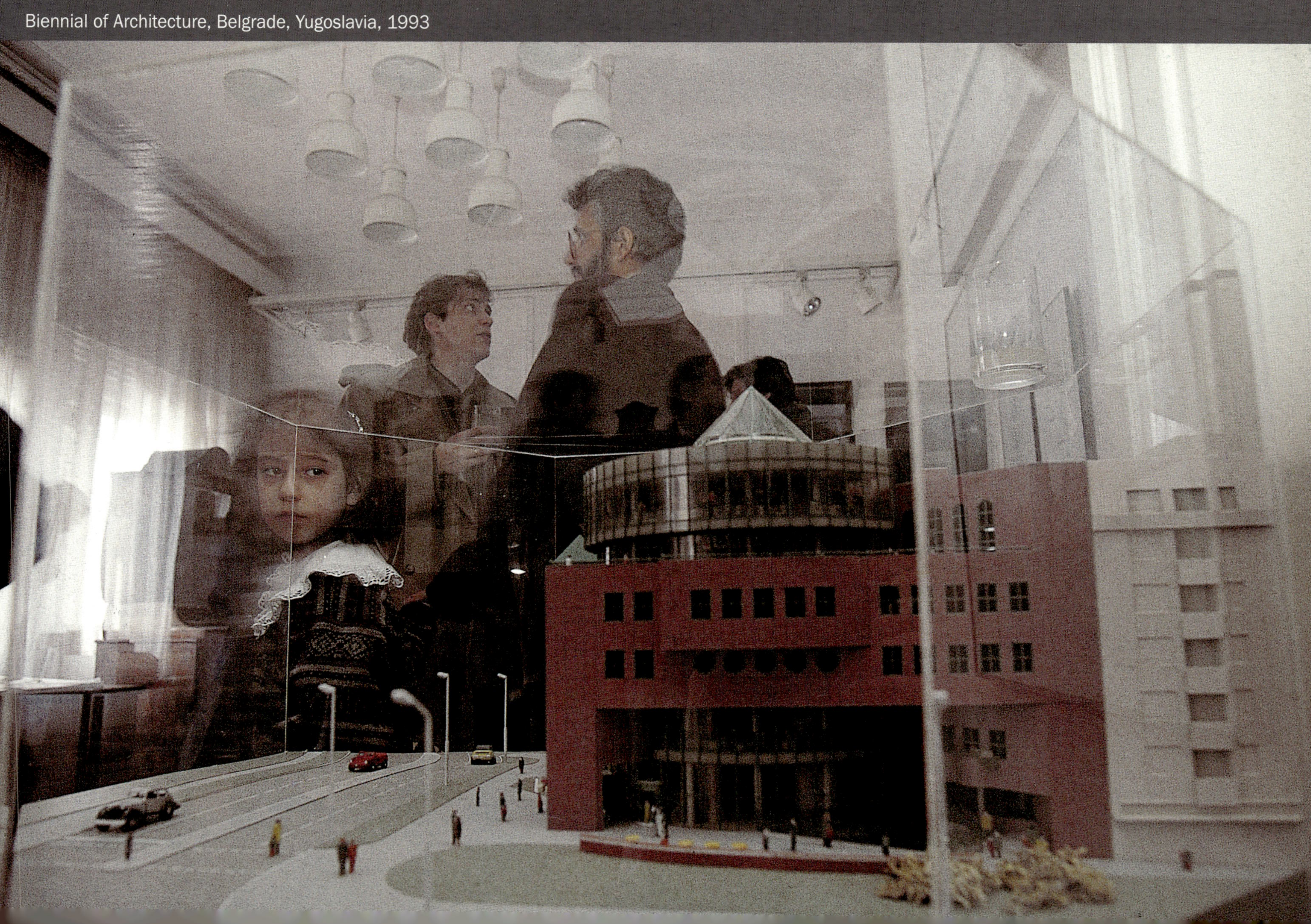

Door to Armenian Quarter, Old Jerusalem

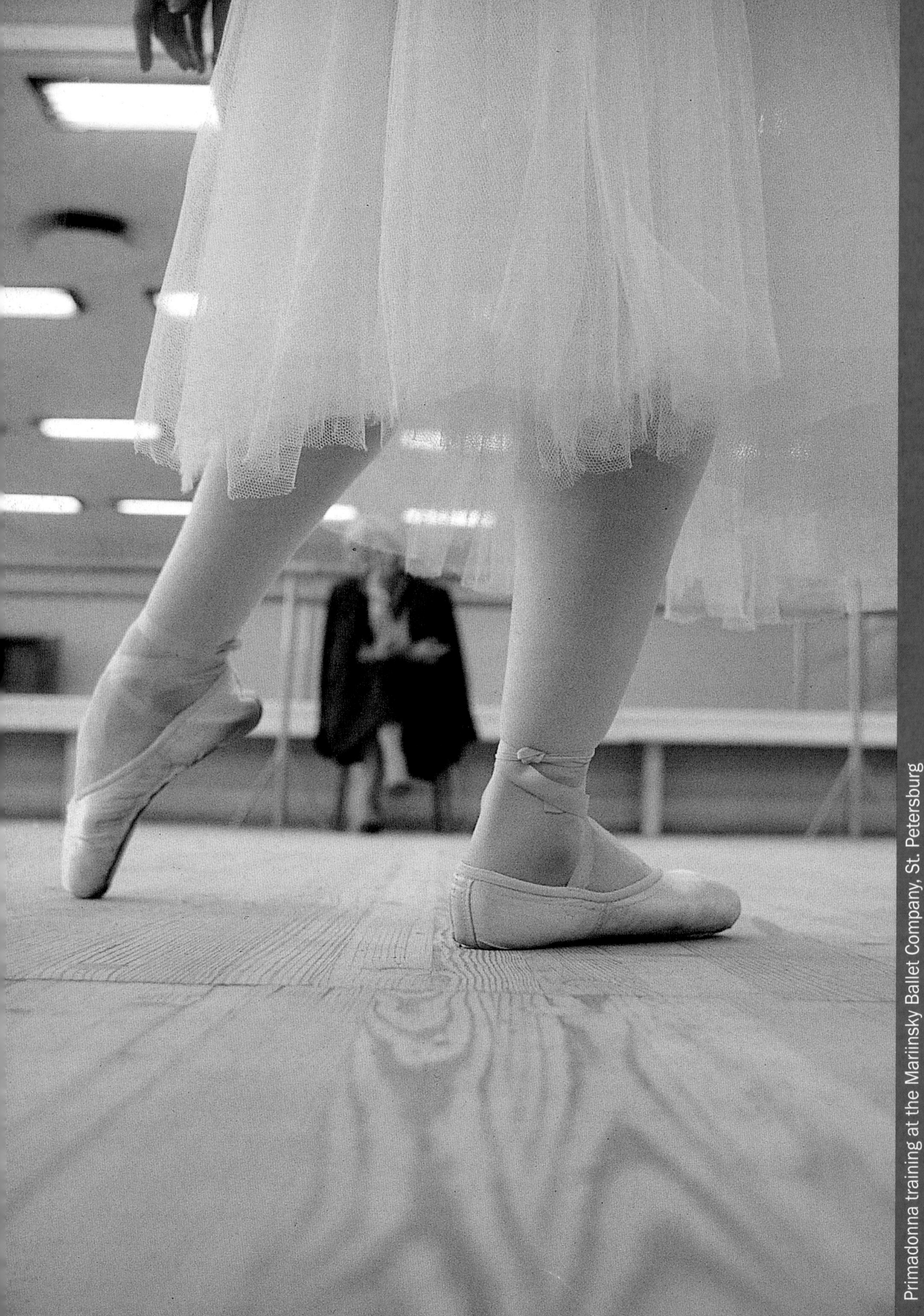

Primadonna training at the Mariinsky Ballet Company, St. Petersburg

Dhow boat's cook, Eastern Africa

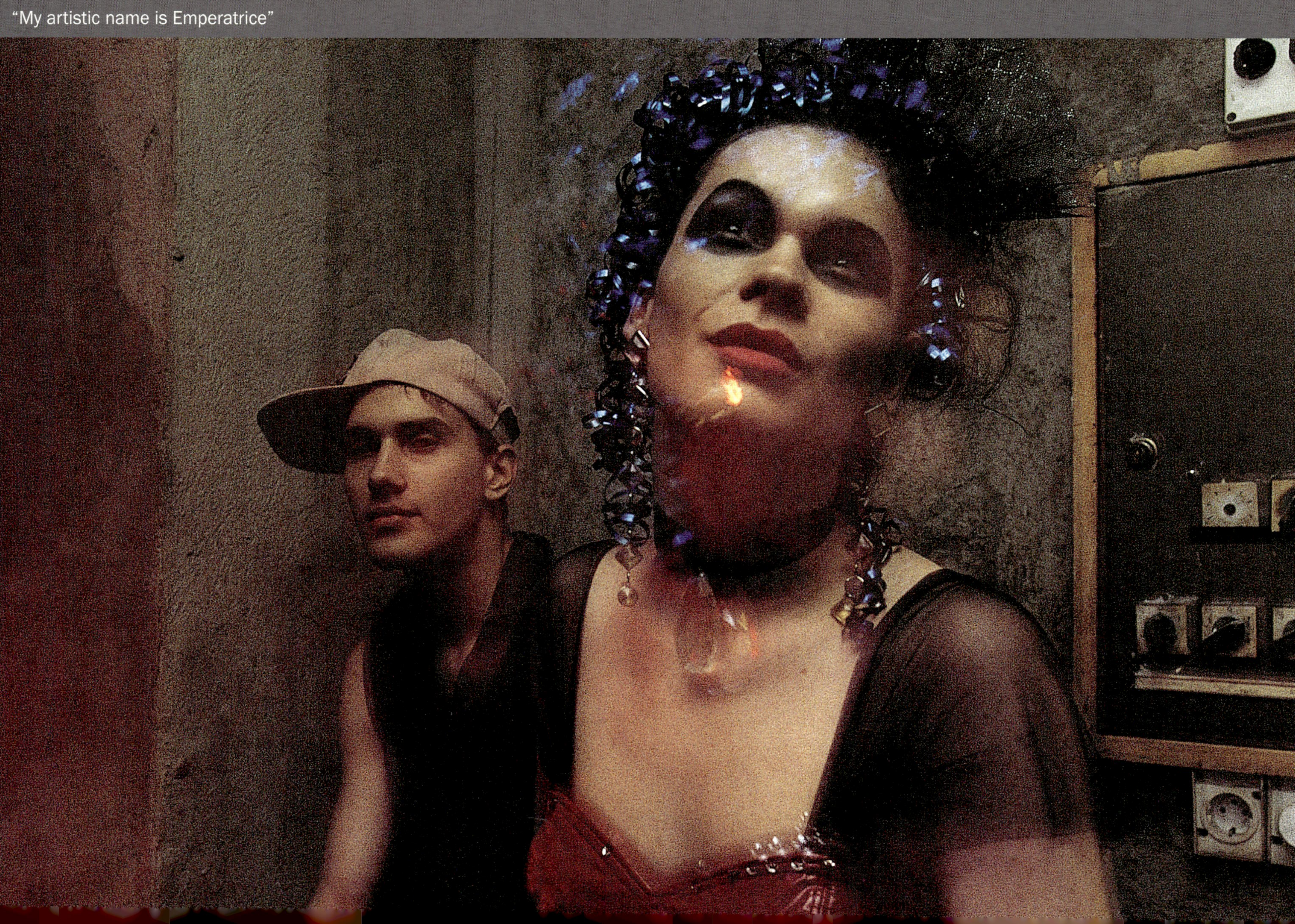

"My artistic name is Emperatrice"

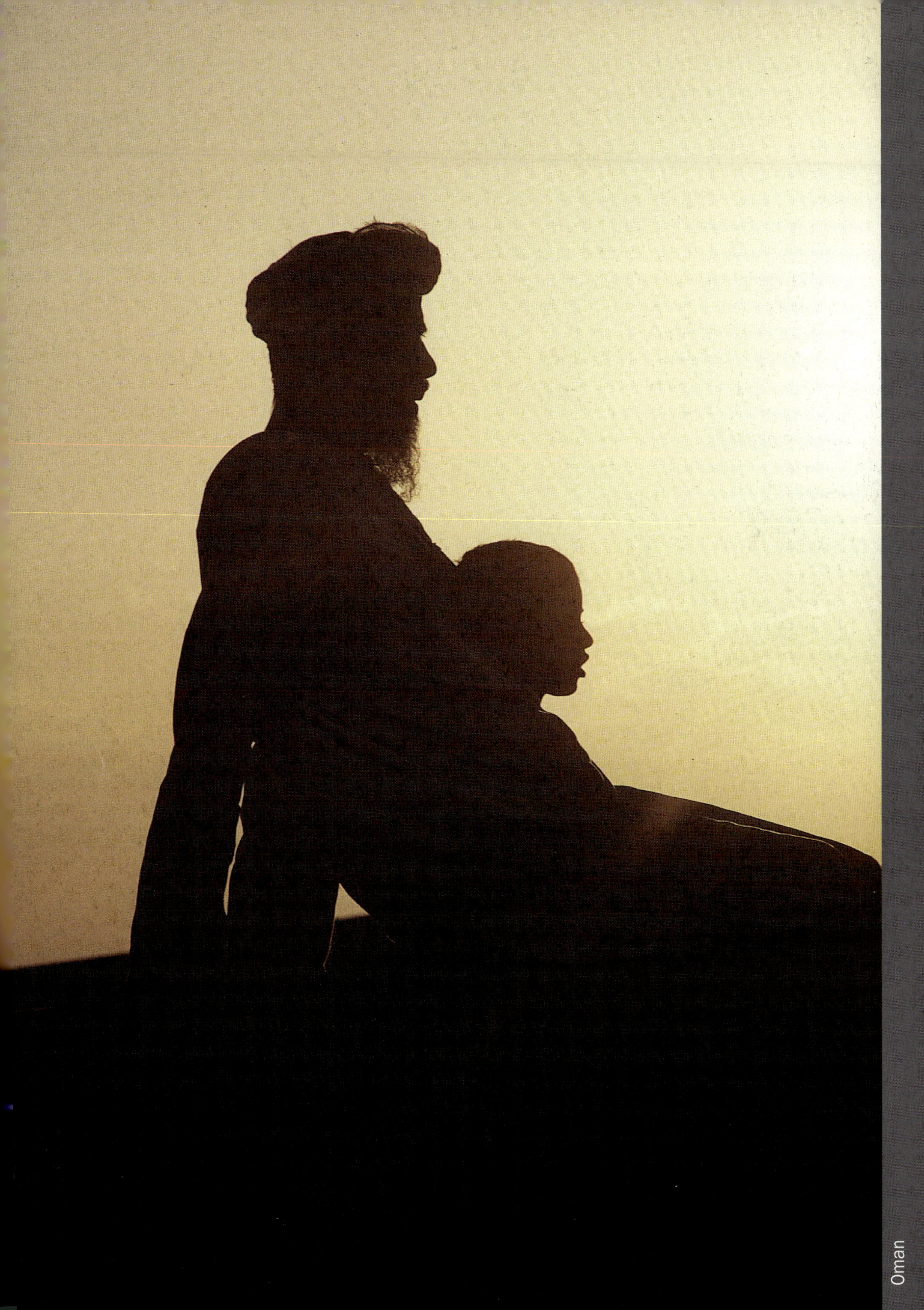

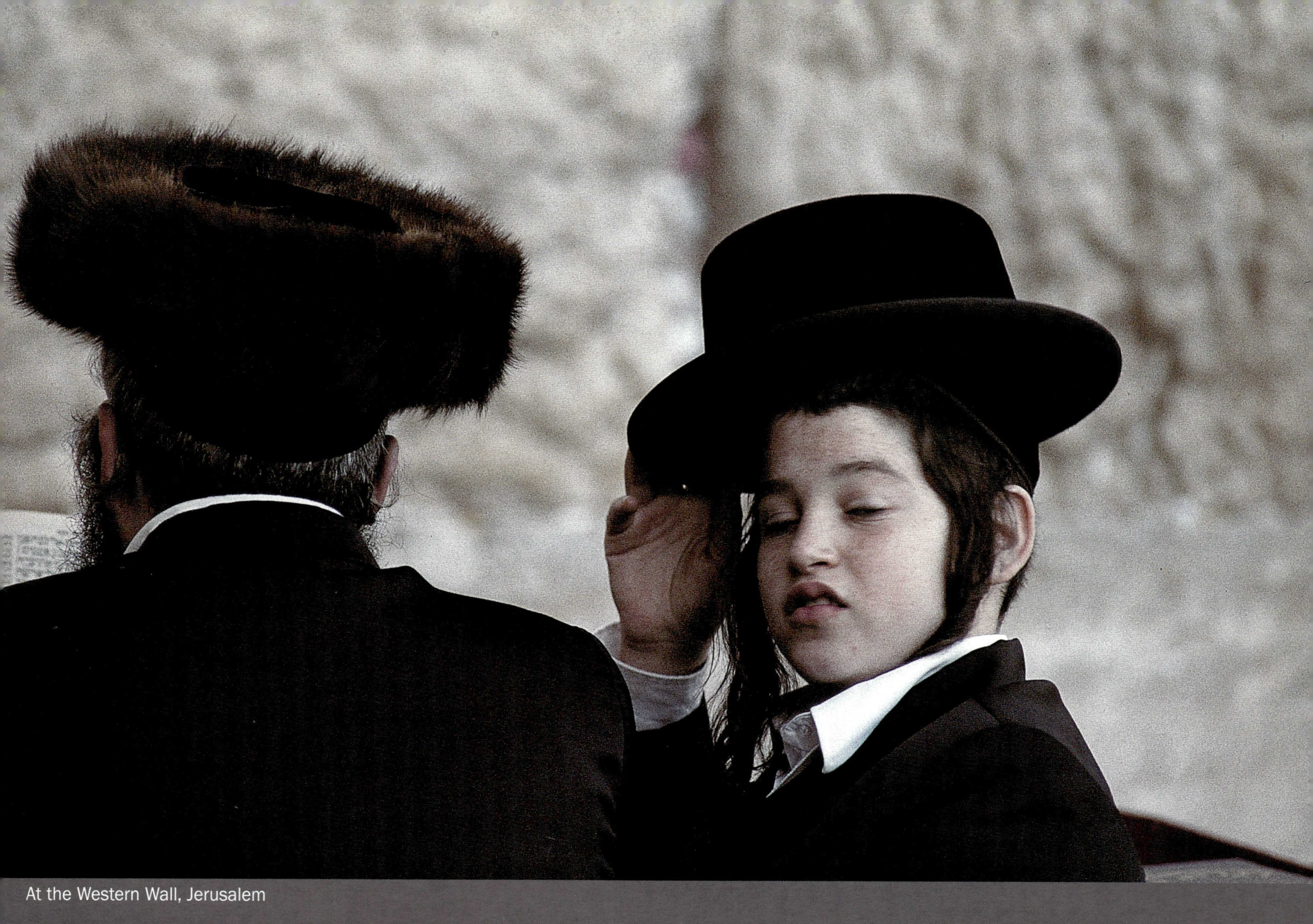

At the Western Wall, Jerusalem

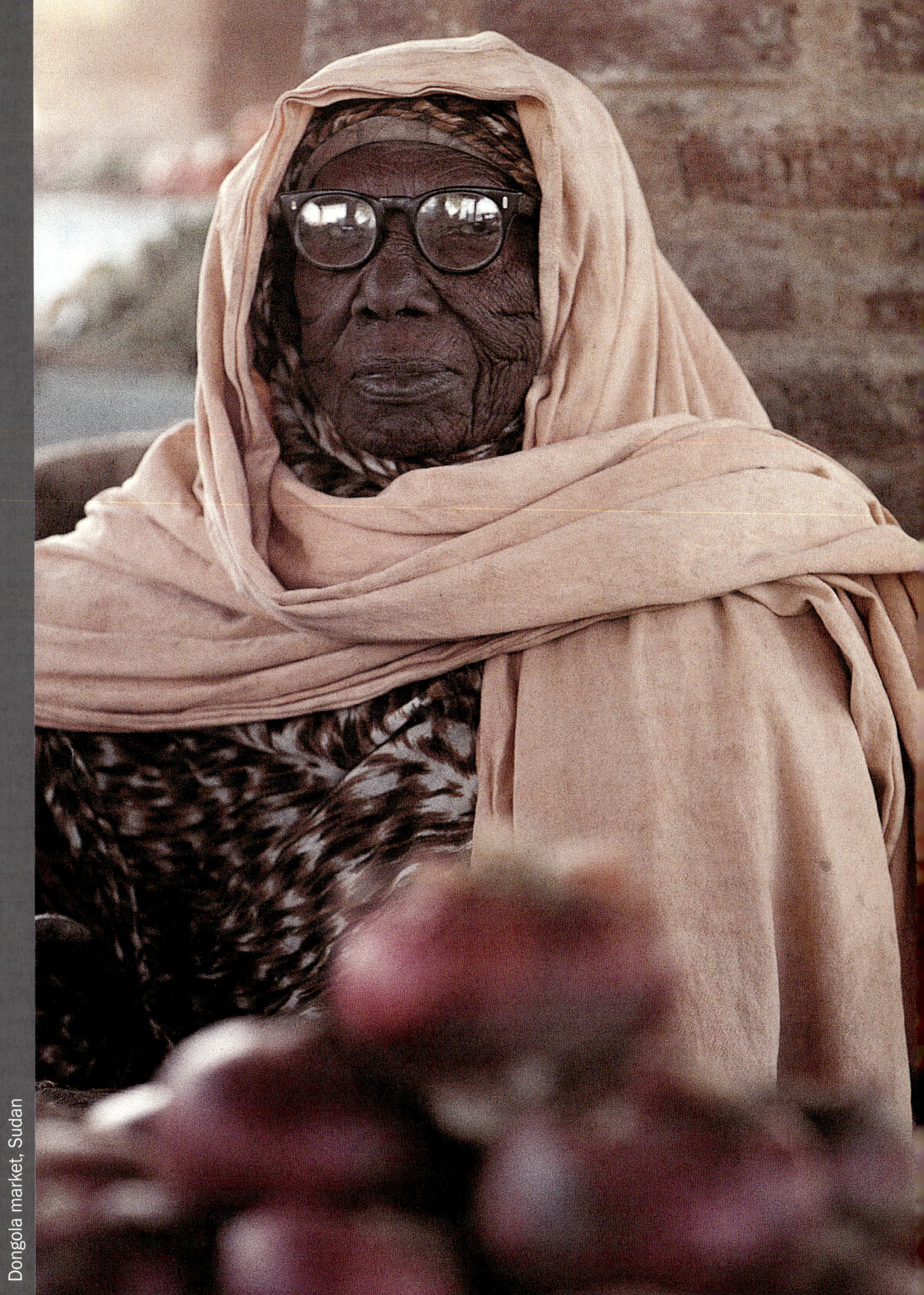

Dongola market, Sudan

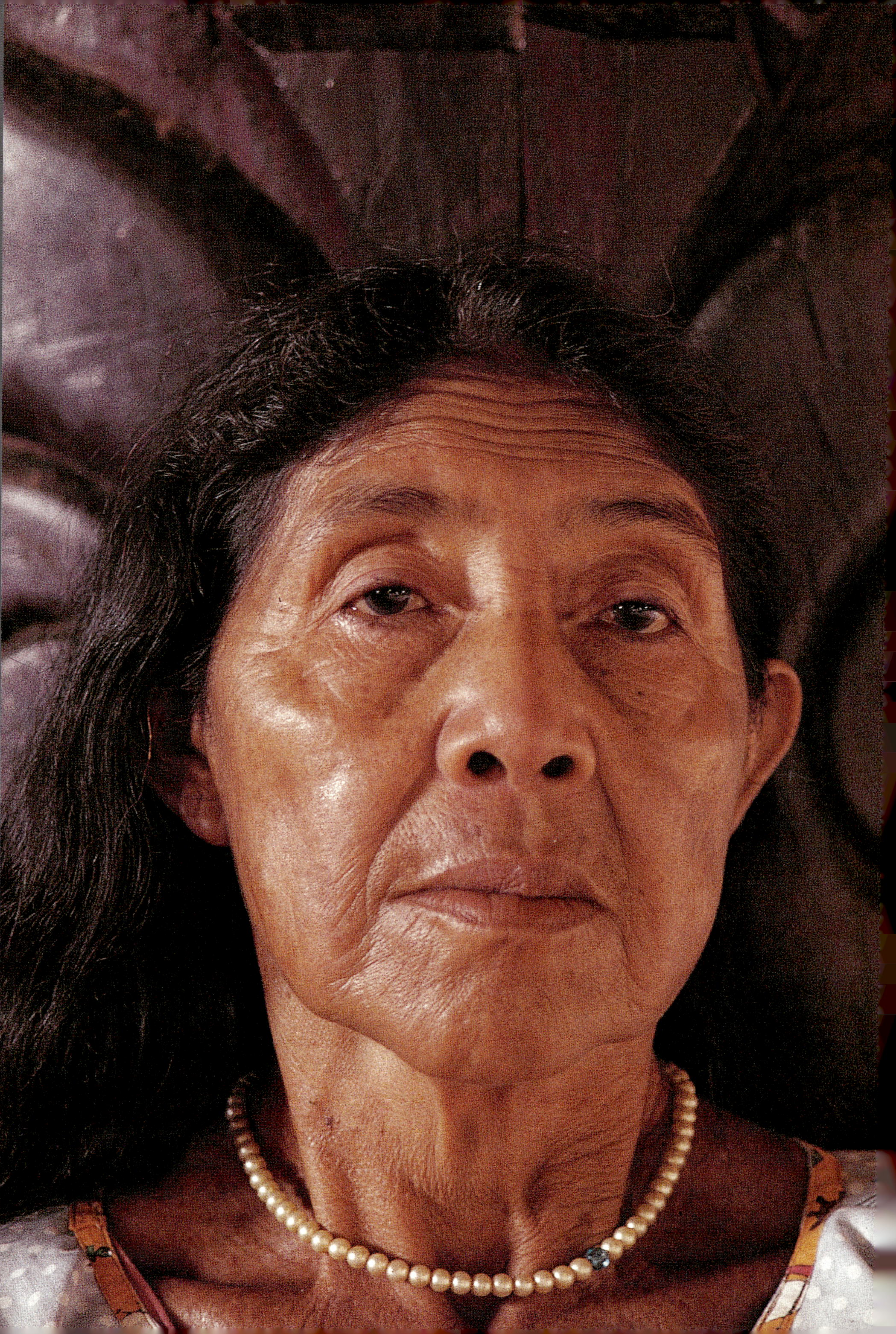

Chiquito Indian, Bolivia

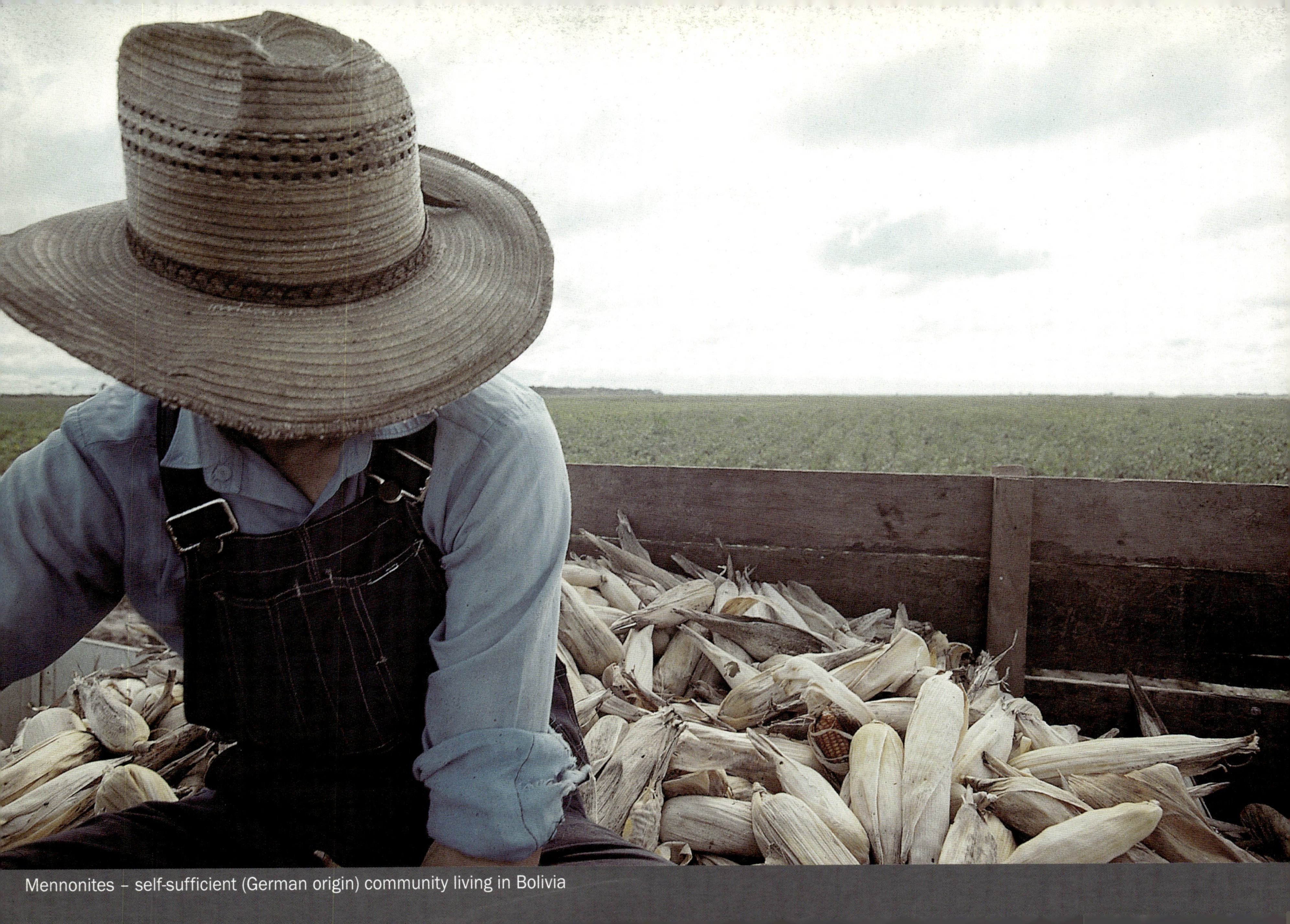

Mennonites – self-sufficient (German origin) community living in Bolivia

Russia, 1997

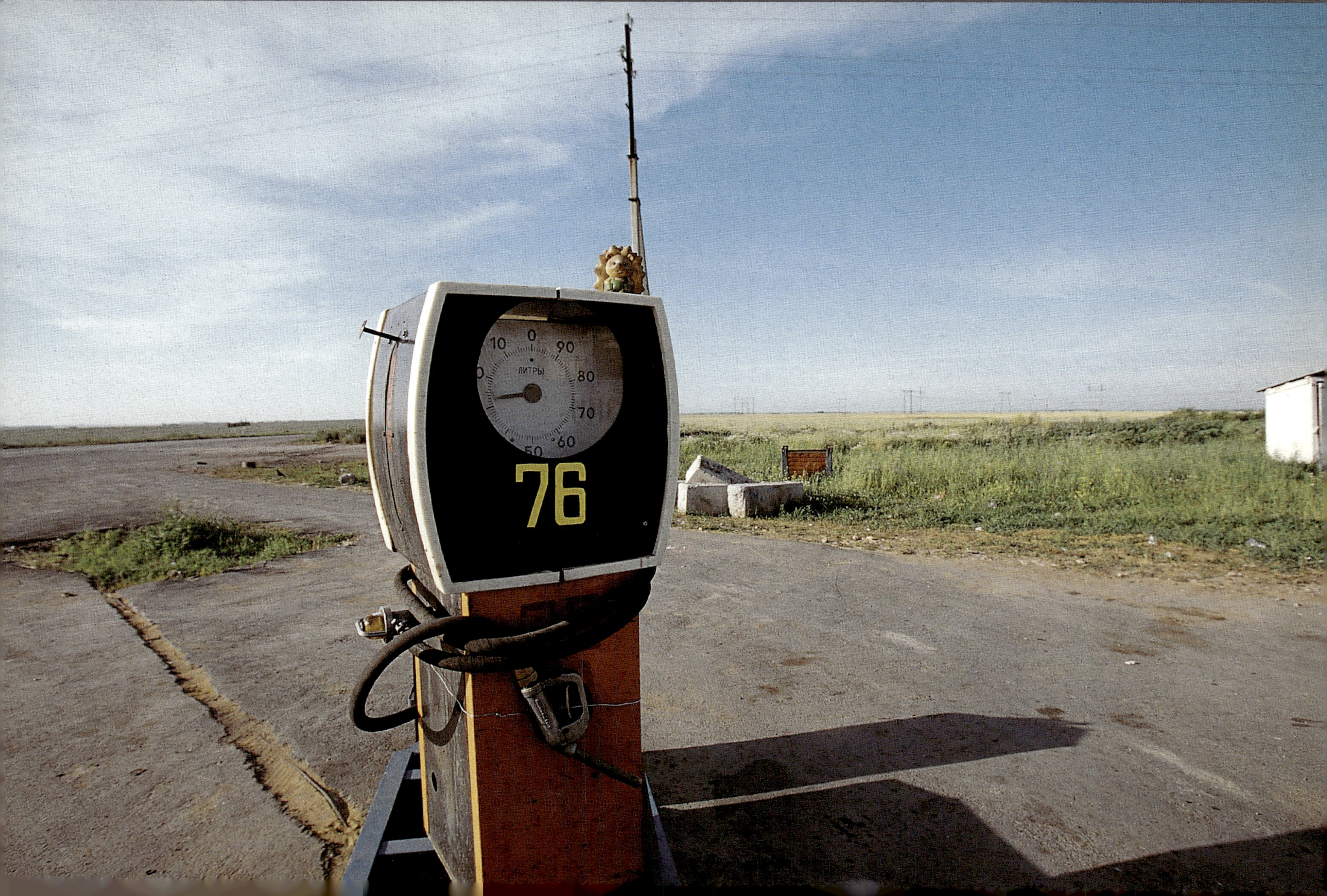

The Red Colobus monkey called Zanzibar Kirkiis, an endemic species, Zanzibar, 1991

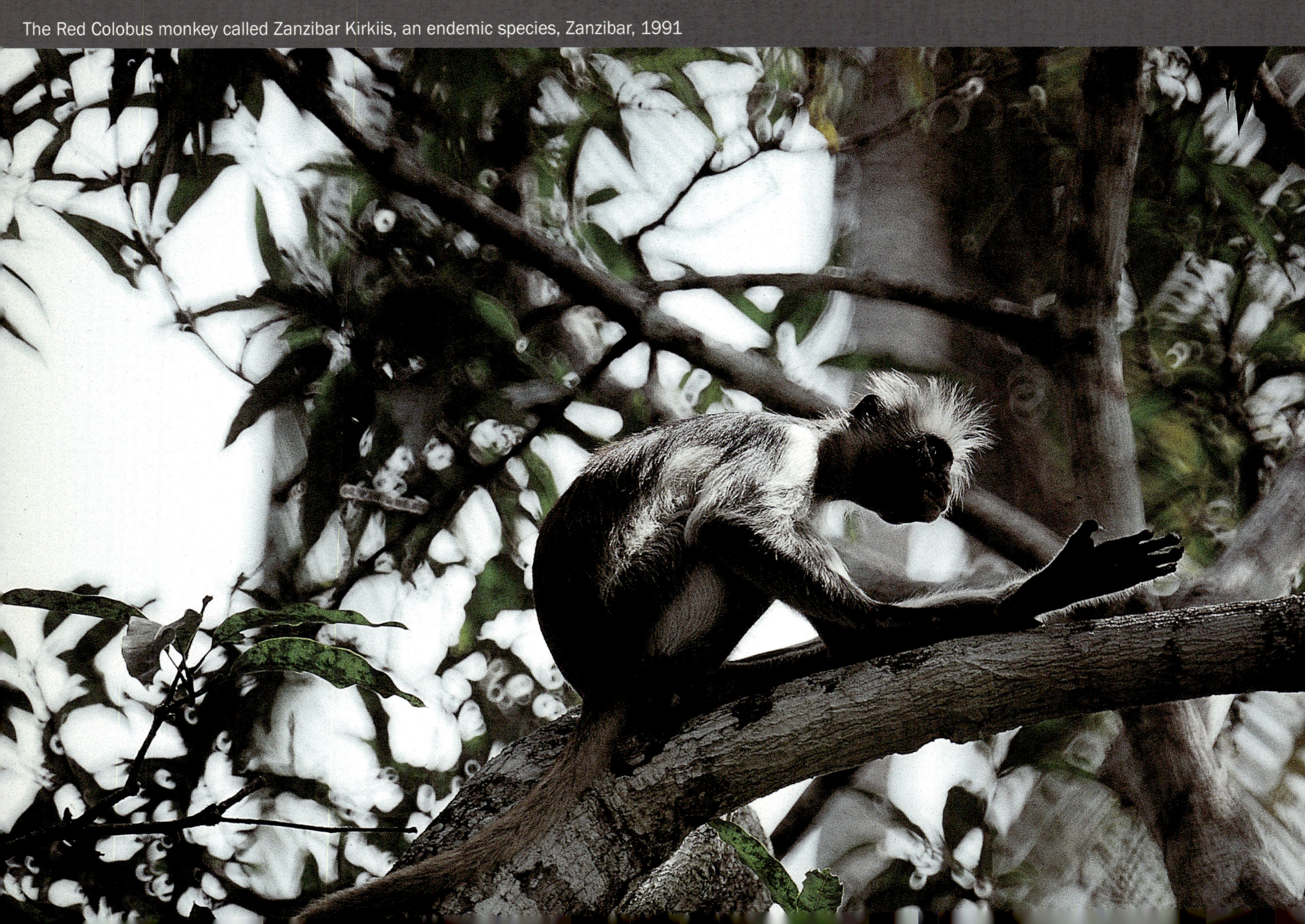

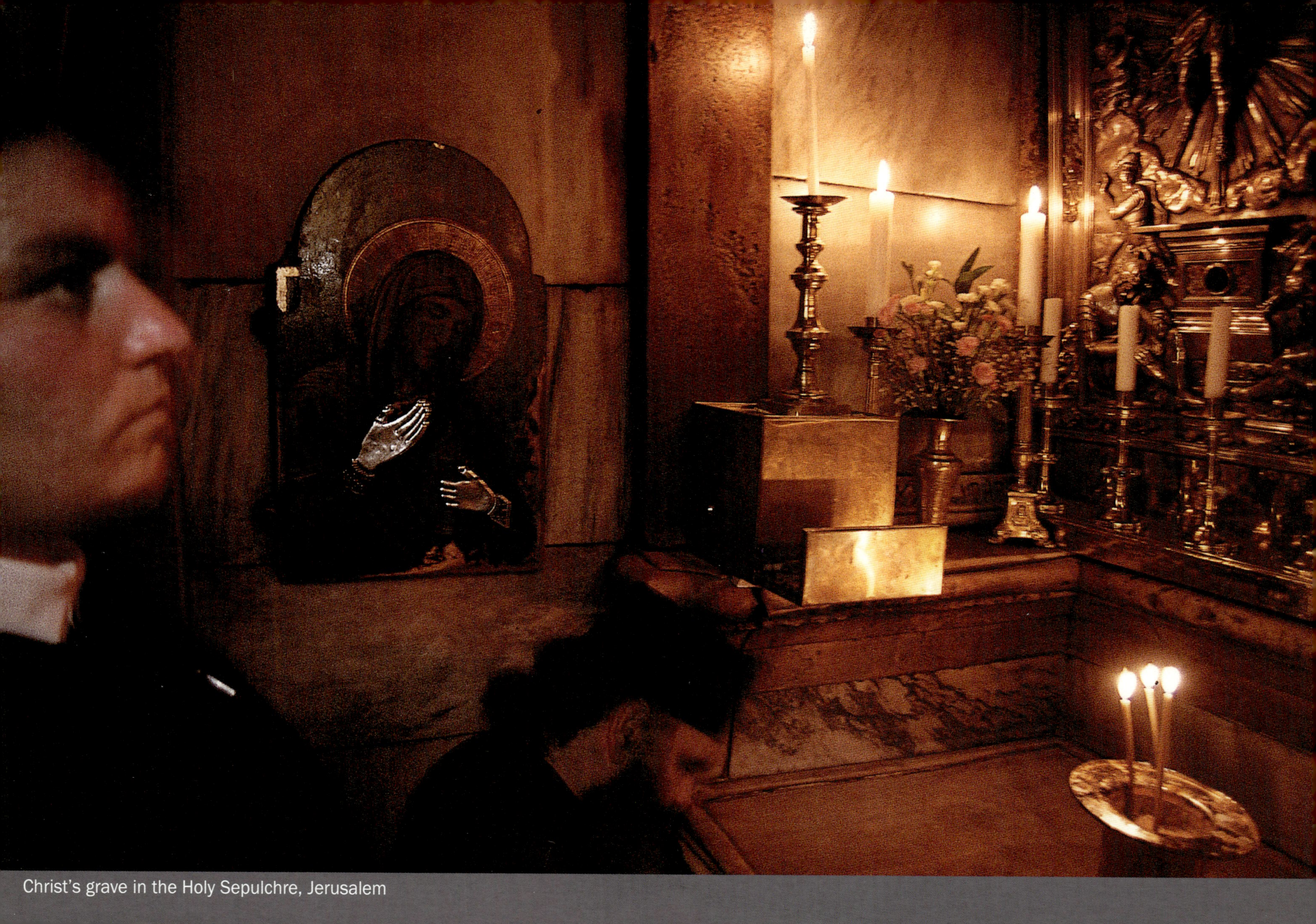

Christ's grave in the Holy Sepulchre, Jerusalem

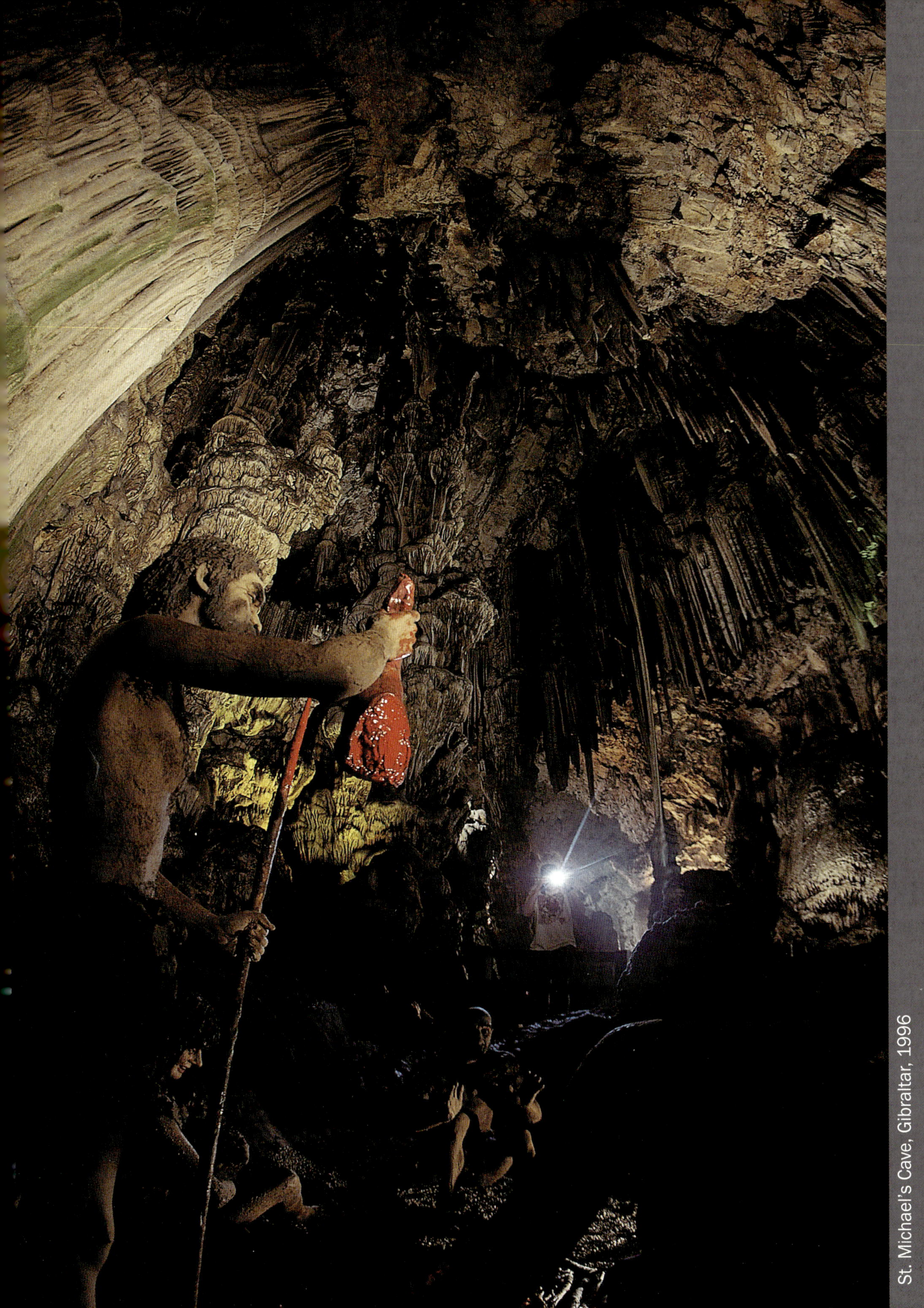

St. Michael's Cave, Gibraltar, 1996

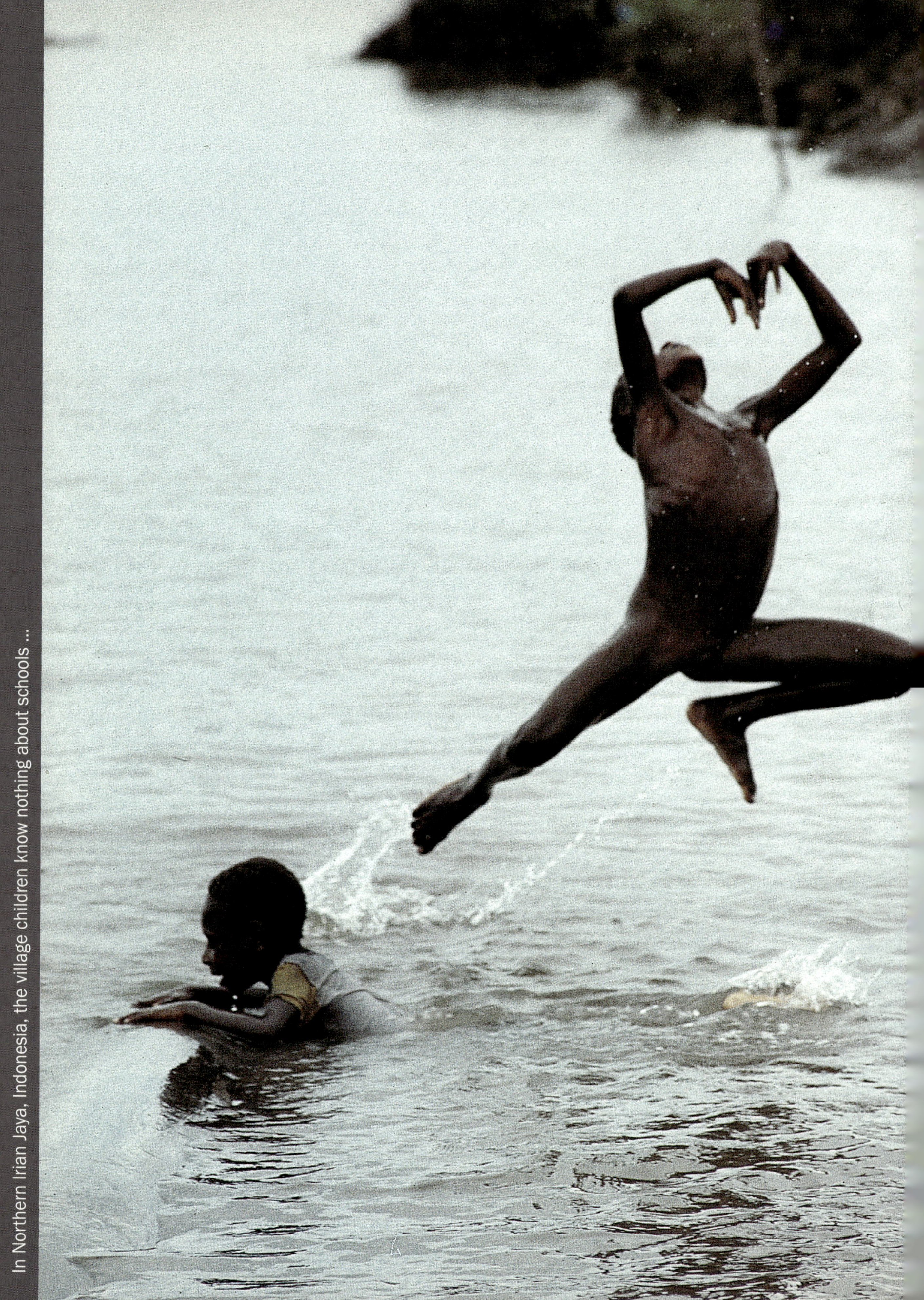

In Northern Irian Jaya, Indonesia, the village children know nothing about schools ...

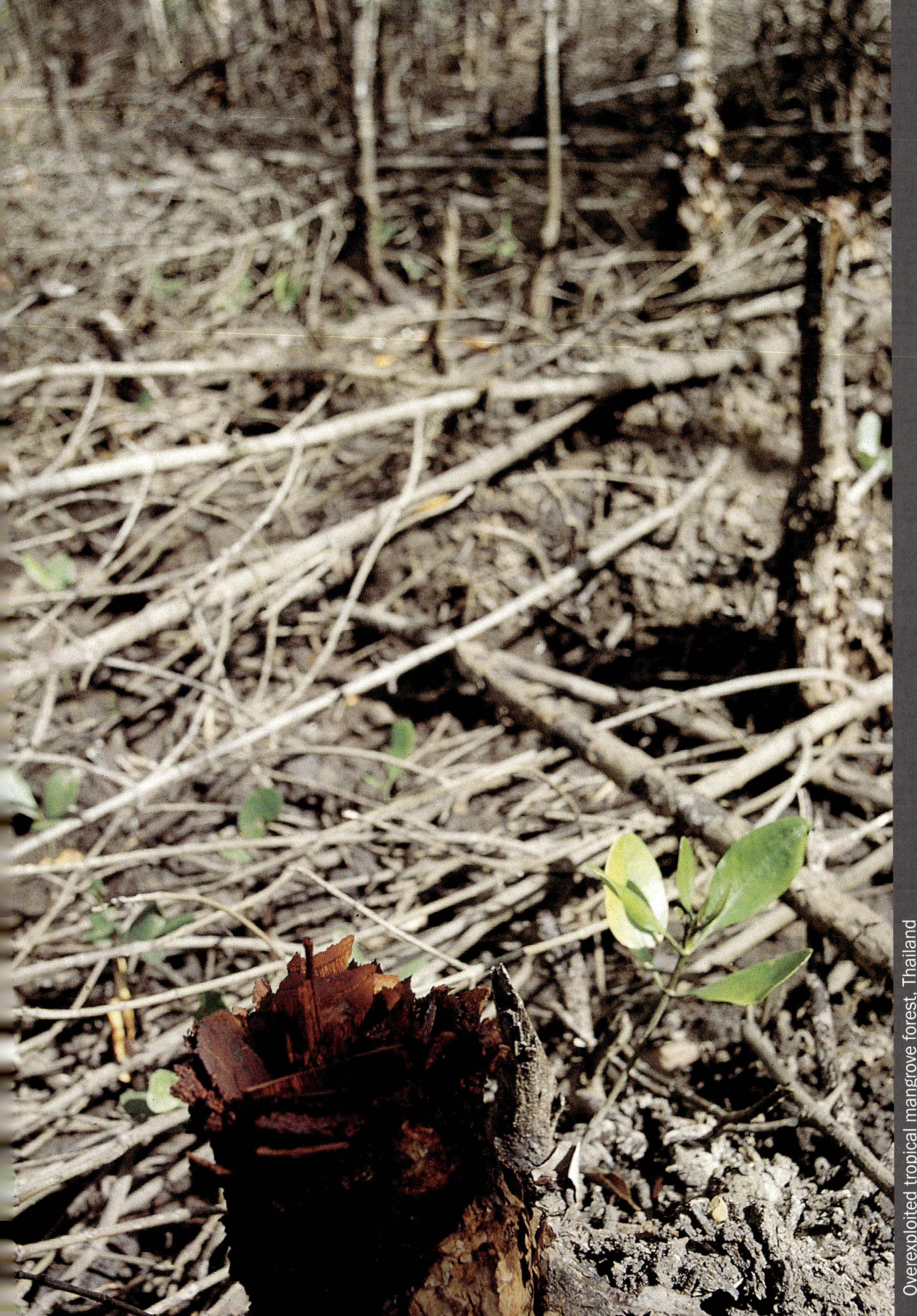

Overexploited tropical mangrove forest, Thailand

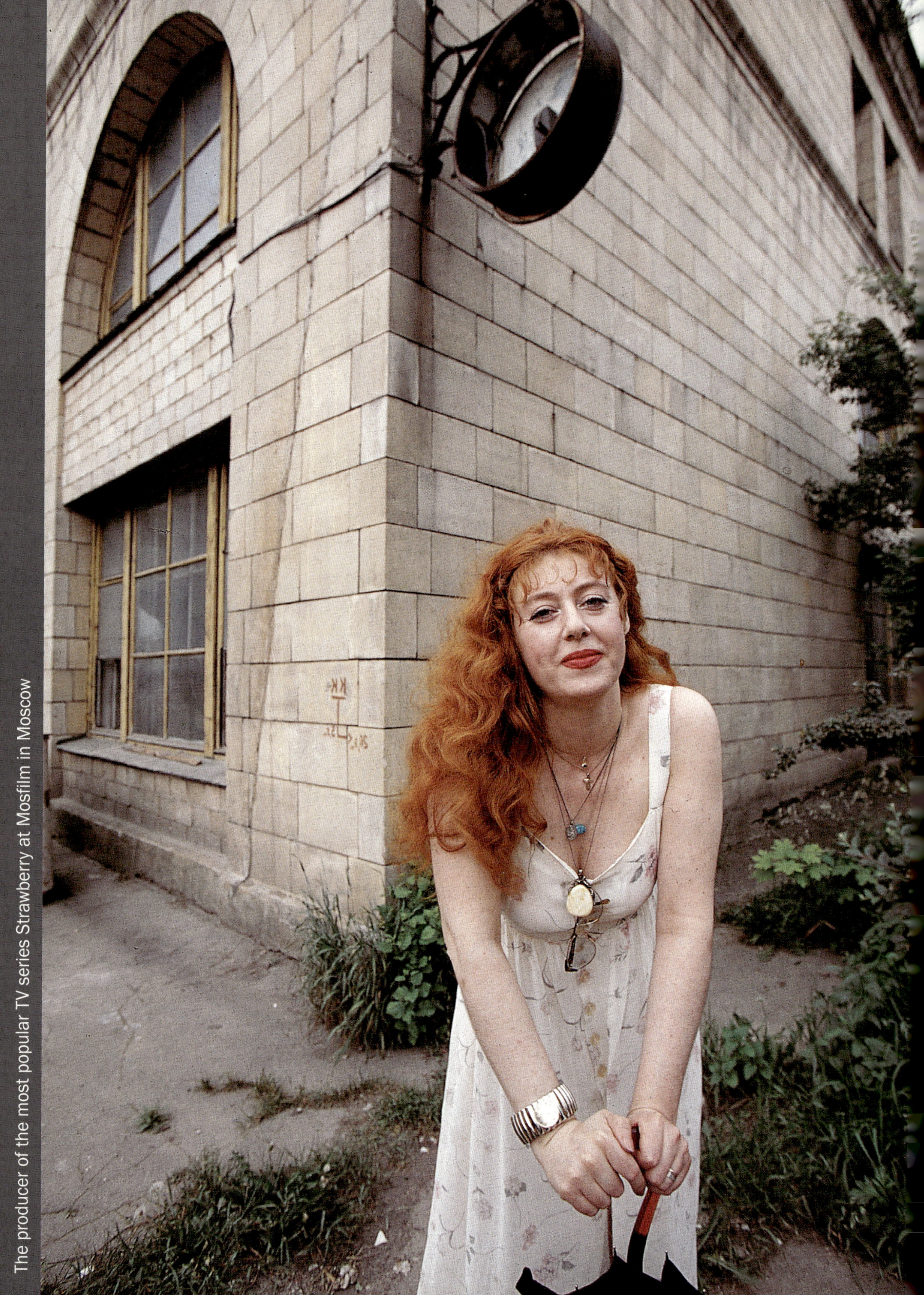

The producer of the most popular TV series Strawberry at Mosfilm in Moscow

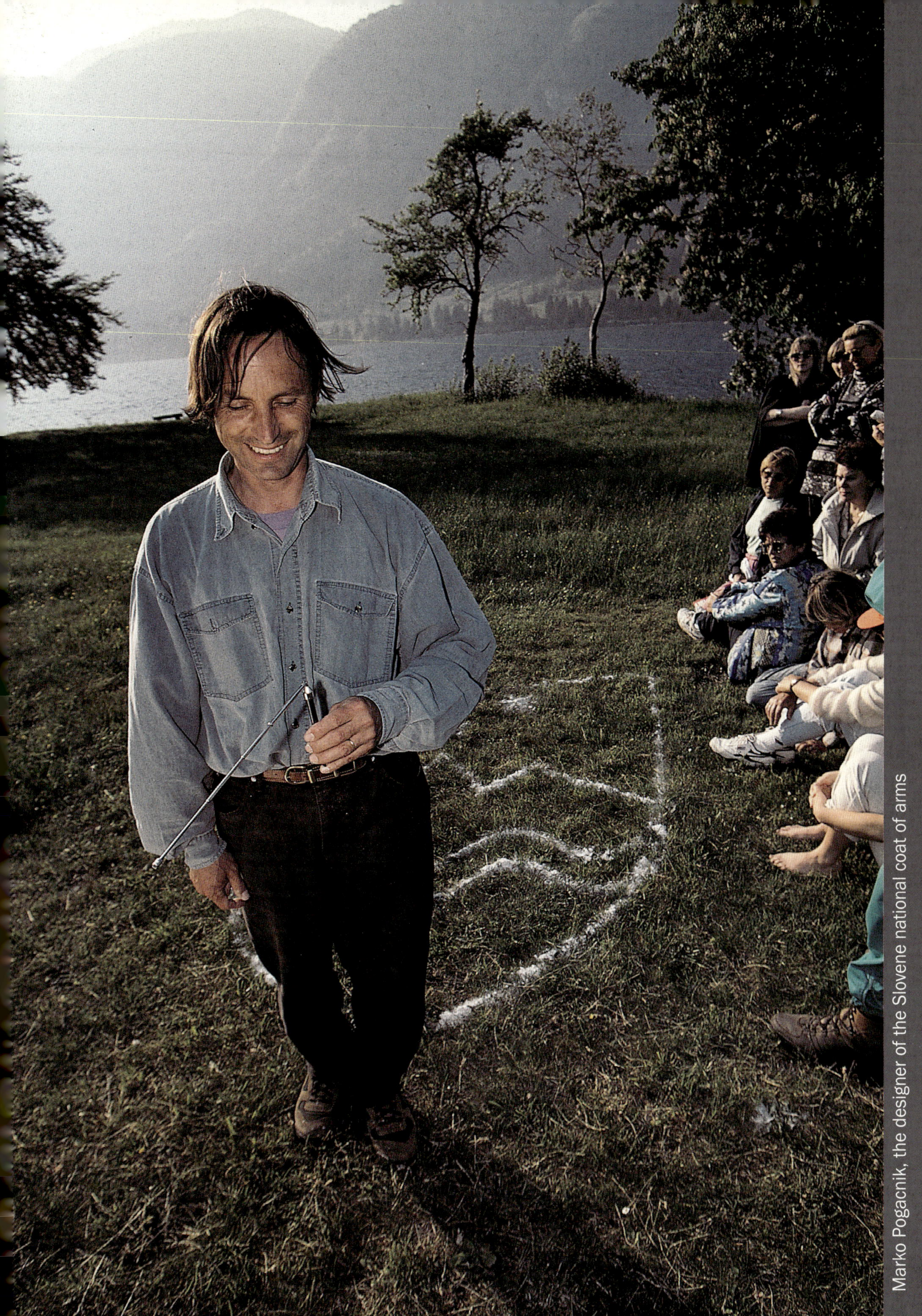

Marko Pogacnik, the designer of the Slovene national coat of arms

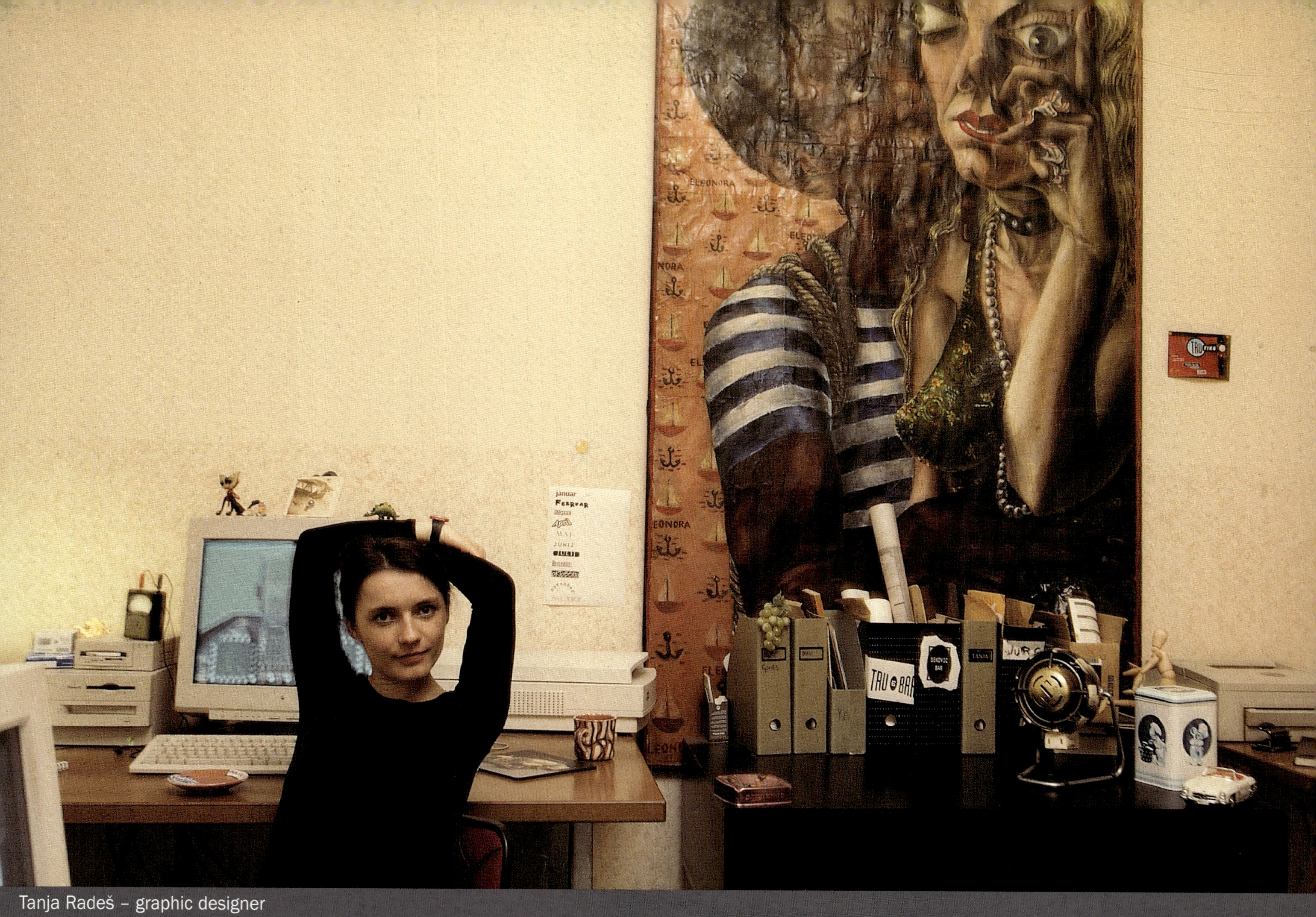

Tanja Radeš – graphic designer

Venice

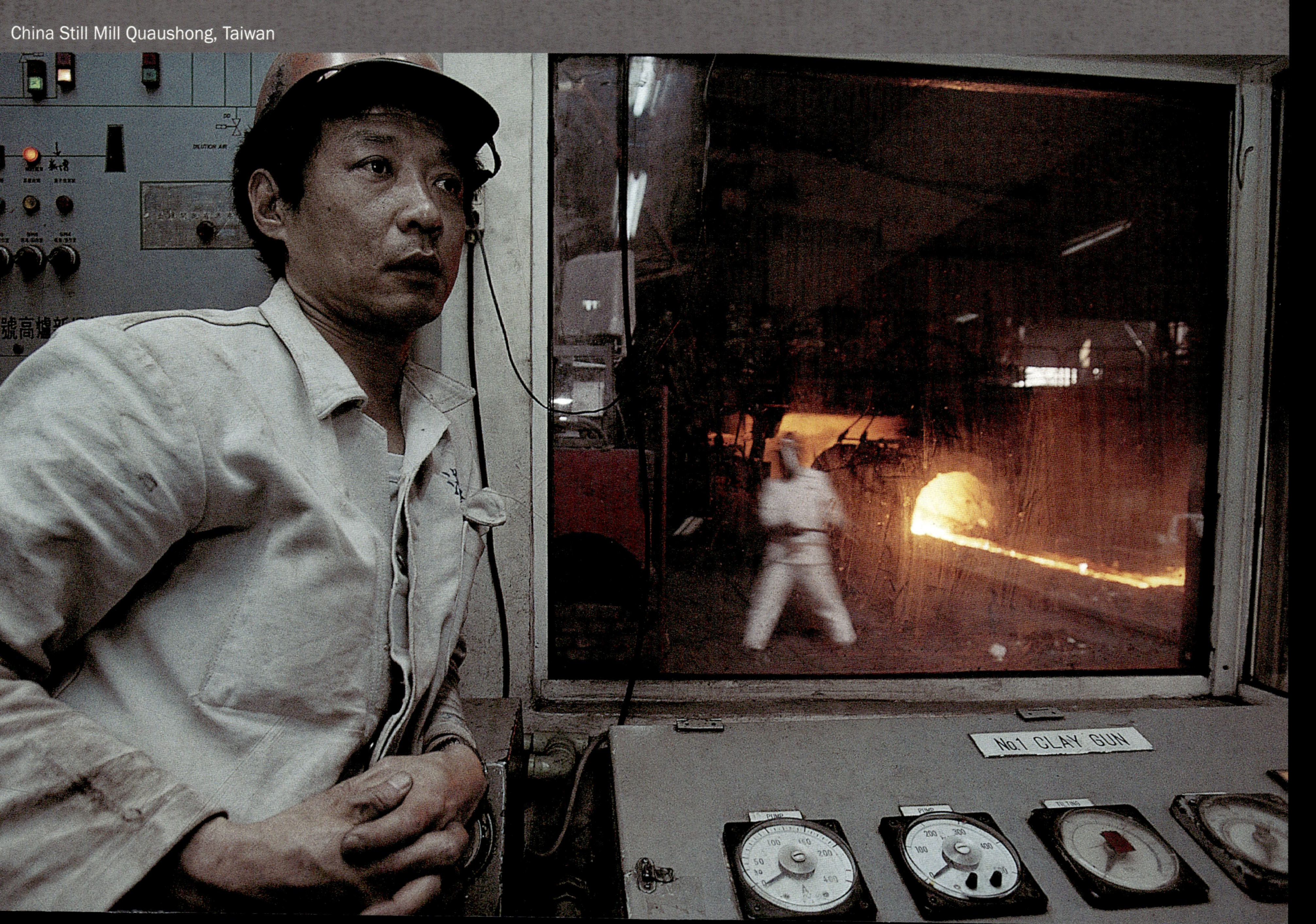

China Still Mill Quaushong, Taiwan

Male Ballet Company, Russia, 1993

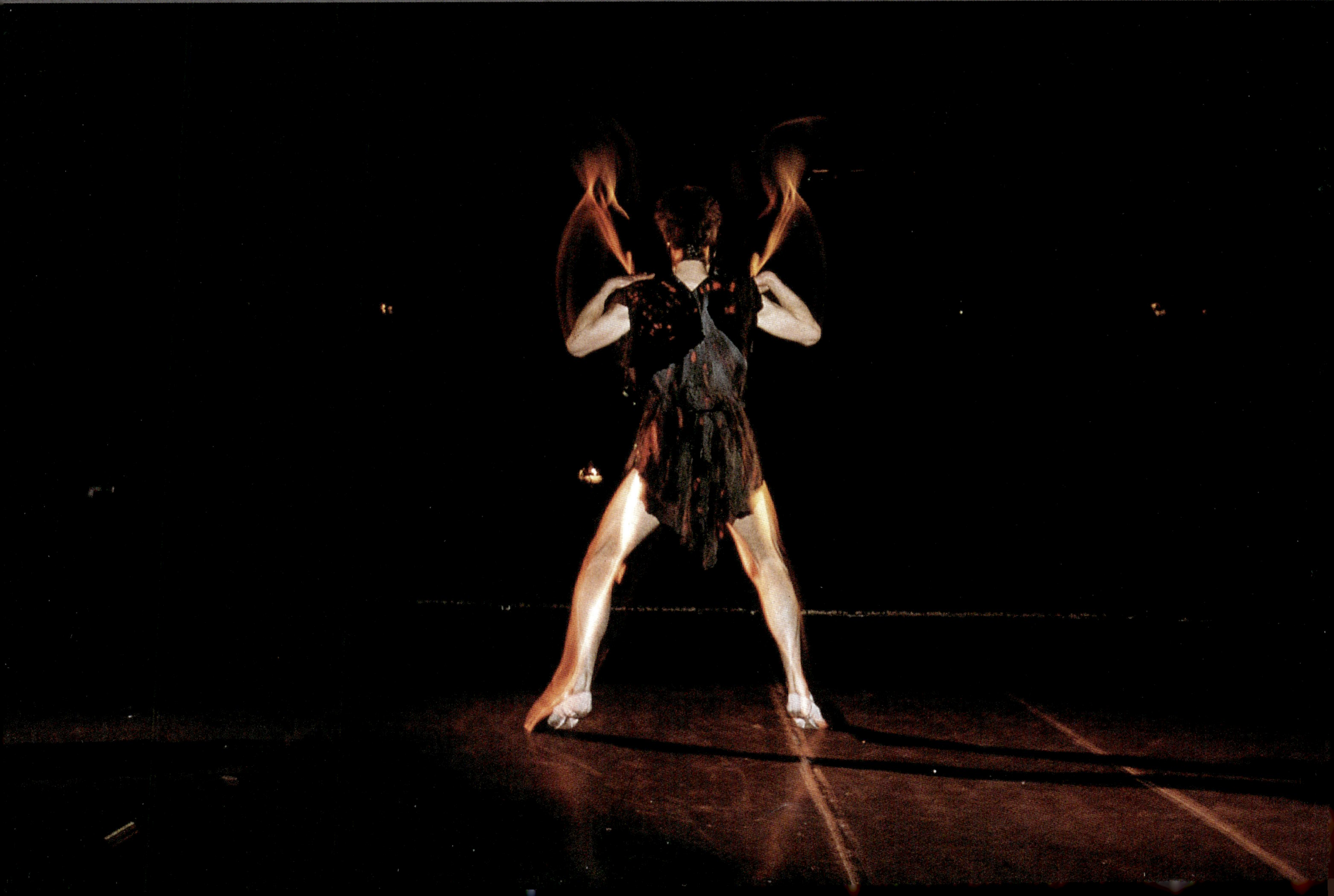

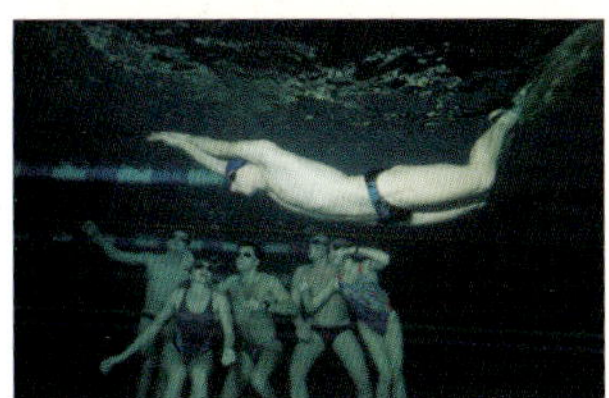

In **1994** I regularly went to a local pool for a quick evening swim, where I constantly ran into a crowd of mono-fin swimmers who were training. They were fun and an easy-going team. One day I brought my photo gear and in an instant they were ready for a show. It was to be the last time I saw Grega, the guy swimming at the forefront. He died shortly afterwards in a car accident, returning home from a European mono-fin swimming competition ...

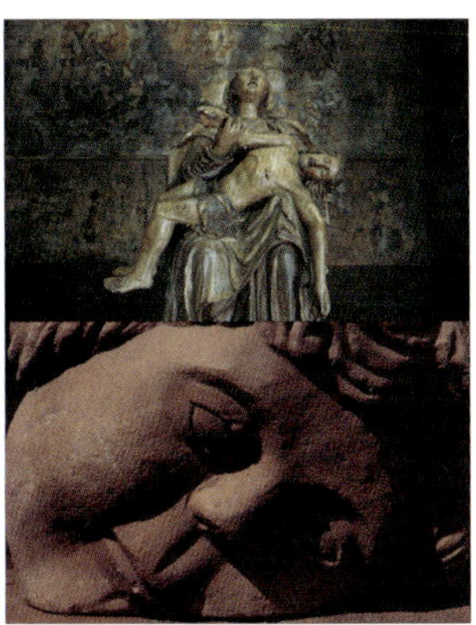

The most significant remains of the entire Jesuit Missions' period (1609–1767) in South America are the objects of art, which are on the same artistic level as contemporary European baroque works. The most appropriate expression for this specific art style is **Guarani-baroque**. Evolving out of a totally different environment, it is named Guarani as a result of being produced by Guarani Indians.

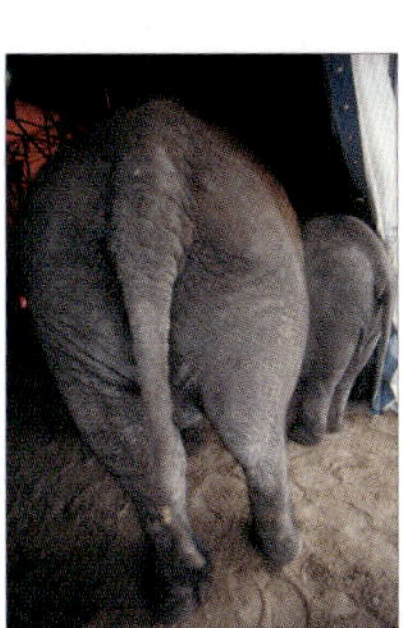

The "real dusty road circus," USA, 1993. Carson & Barns spends each day of its season at a new location. After overnight journeying to the next spot, "the biggest tent on earth" is hauled up with the help of circus elephants at sunrise!

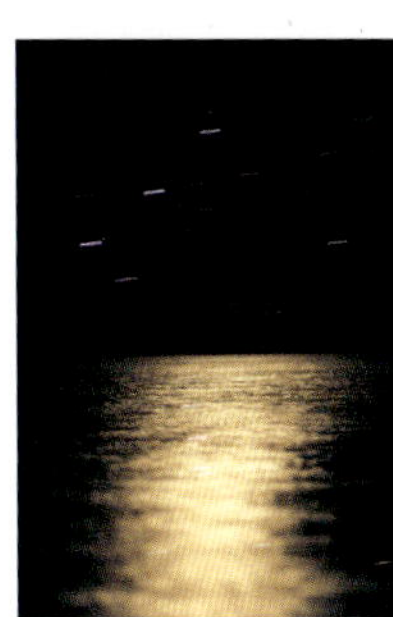

Moon kiss on the Nile, 1990. Days spent in a small boat traveling from the 5th to the 4th cataract in Sudan, and nights sleeping on deserted banks. For how many thousands of years has the river flowed along the same course? What is the Nile? The water that flows or the river bed that remains still? What about the theory of the existence of another, even greater, underground Nile which flows below the overland river bed, following more or less the same water course?

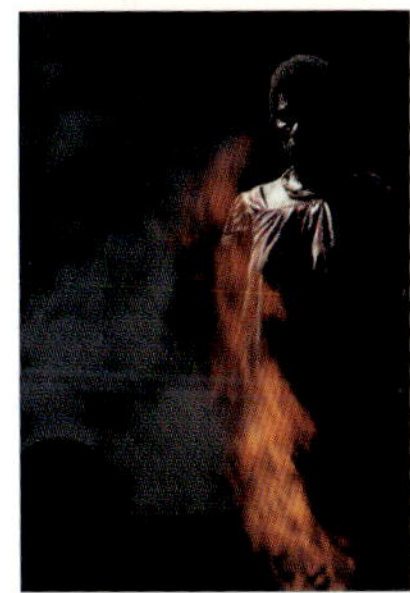

Aibon lady, 1989. The westward flow of the gigantic tropical river system Sepic is the cradle of Papuan Lowland aboriginal culture. The natives live on floating, moving islands. The mystical exception is a unique, inhabited island, which stands on a solid rock. A stone itself is something exceptional here. On Aibon it is the women who rule. They possess fire and are potters. Men are only allowed to trade with the pots ... all over the Sepic land.

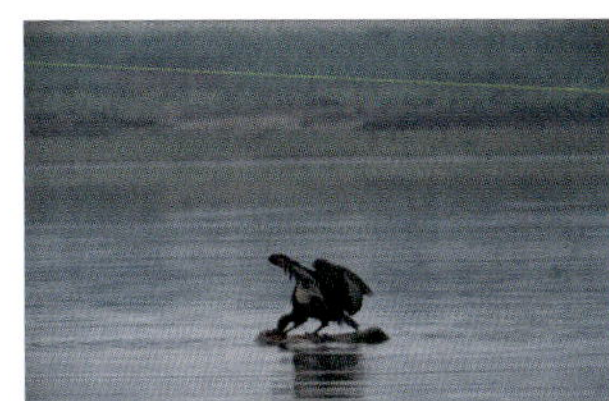

Holy Ganges, 1988. The fatal world in which a chain of associations can become reality. Nobody is after a body but the bird ... There is a clear separation between the body and soul of a man in Hindu civilization.

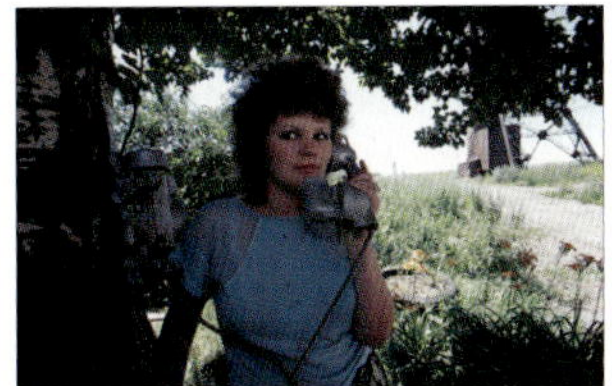

"Broken Russia," 1997. An abandoned mine, a broken telephone ... I asked her to pose for me. She was still (pretending to be) employed as a controller at the mine station (waiting for better times). She had not been paid for the last six months. "God knows who the owner is now." After the first click, my glasses also broke and fell off. No problem! Ljena produced a piece of elastic from her bra to fix my spectacles ...

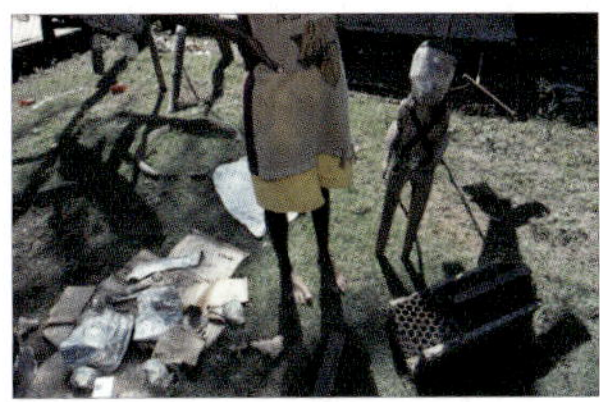

Lost in the middle of trash, 1994. The daughter of an eccentric trash artist in a remote village in Jamaica seemed lost. Not just her – a rat was imprisoned in a cage in the midst of everything which was scattered around the yard ...

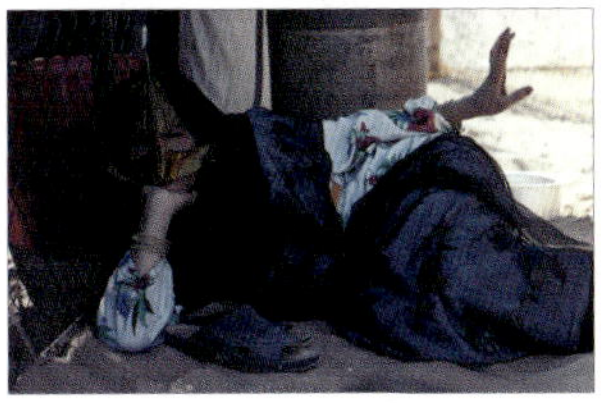

Life became easy in Oman, 1995. I met nomads in the desert just a few hours' drive away from the main road. They do not migrate anymore, government trucks regularly bring them water and the school mini-bus takes the kids to school. As for food, they still prefer camel milk and goat meat.

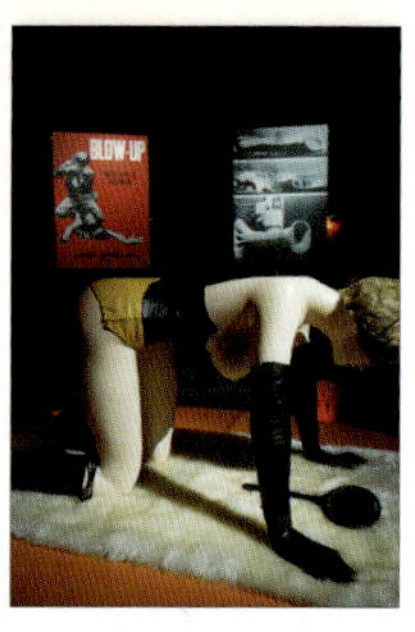

Table by Allen Jones drew the greatest attention at the exhibition "The Power of Erotic Design." Design Museum, London, 1997.

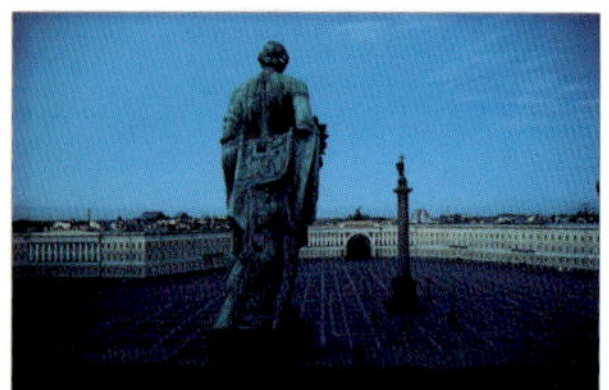

As a **birthday present** in 1994 I got everything I could wish for: the director of the Hermitage Gallery in St. Petersburg allowed me to stay on the roof overnight. This was a time of white nights, with the sun disappearing behind the horizon for an hour only.

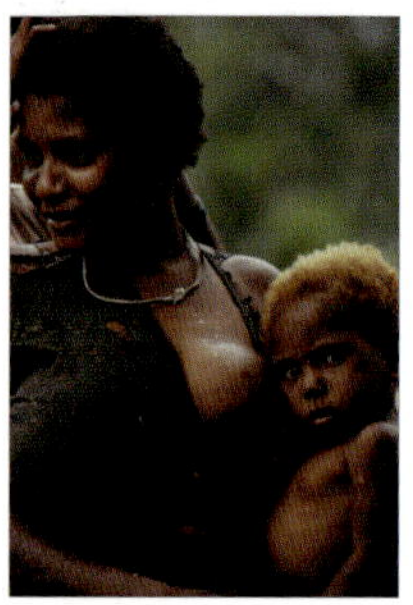

Blondy, 1993. Malnutrition in the Tropics! The equilibrium of survival under the harsh conditions of the tropical climate and swampy land of the jungles of Papua New Guinea means for many a lack of vitamins and proteins ... or a lack of pigment in the children's hair, due to a deficiency of minerals.

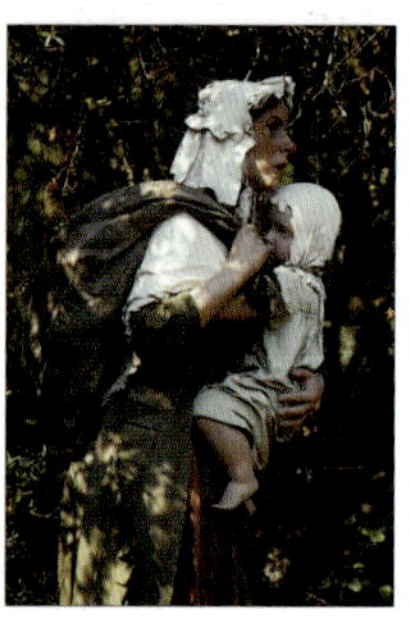

Stoned mother, 1996. Gibraltar Museum under the sky. I wondered: "How many years of rain and wind and sun can such a mother stand?"

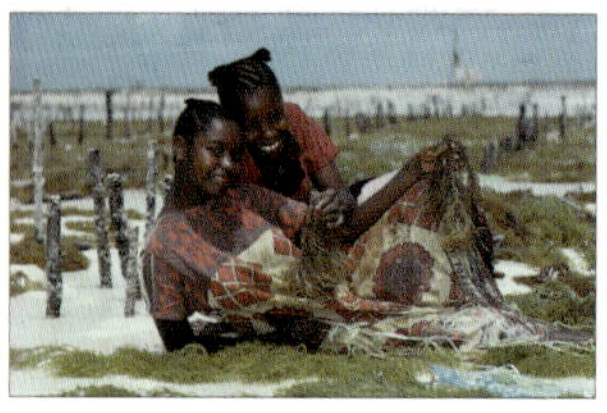

Fortune flash, 1991. For many villages along the Zanzibar coast the results of the Danish ex-navigator Mr. Mortensen's idea of introducing seaweed cultivation to Africa brought prosperity. This cultivation does not harm the ecological system, villagers do not need to change their simple fishing lifestyle patterns, and the profit goes to the farmers selling seaweed on the spot. It was early morning, before the rising tide, before any man could fish ...

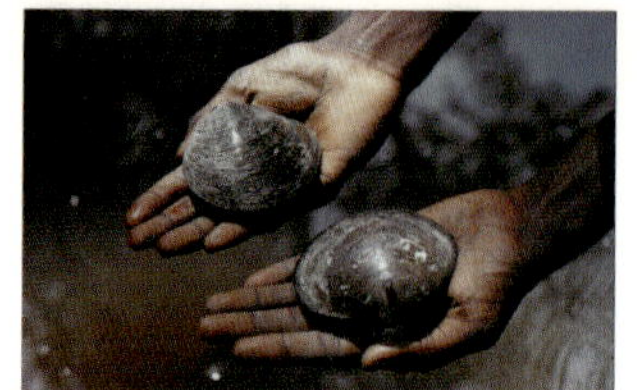

Lunchtime, 1990. None of the natives worried much about the incoming low tide – it meant hours of waiting before we could continue along the canals through the mangrove forest jungle (Asmat, Irian Jaya, Indonesia). Within minutes tasty shells were retrieved from the mud and baked on an open fire ...

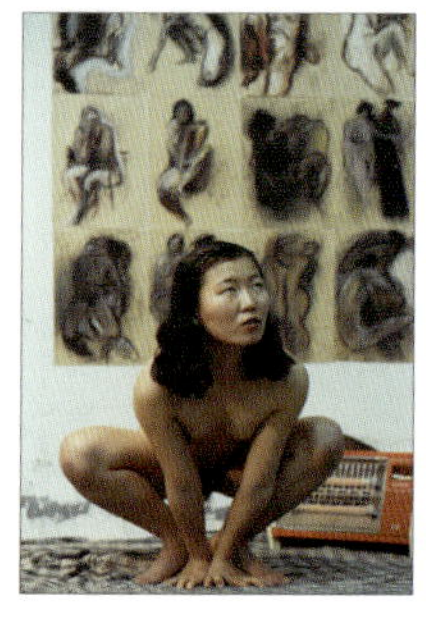

New Models, 1996. In Chinese society one should never uncover or expose the body. Yet in Taiwan, a group of artists – New Models – have recently organized artistic sessions with the aim of acquiring knowledge about the drawing and painting of the naked human body. Dai Yueh (Medea) is an artist of the performing arts: "Modeling for me is the warm-up before a performance, like writing notes before composing a piece of work. It is when I am in my pose that I can feel what existence is all about, when I feel really alive and creative."

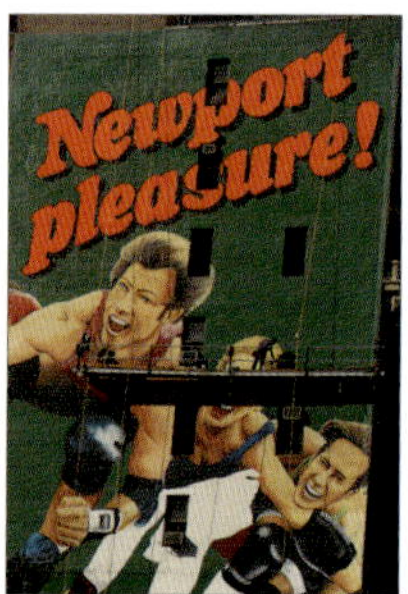

Smoke, 1993, but do not smoke: the antismoking campaign all over the States came to a halt at Manhattan where Newport cigarette pleasure is OK.

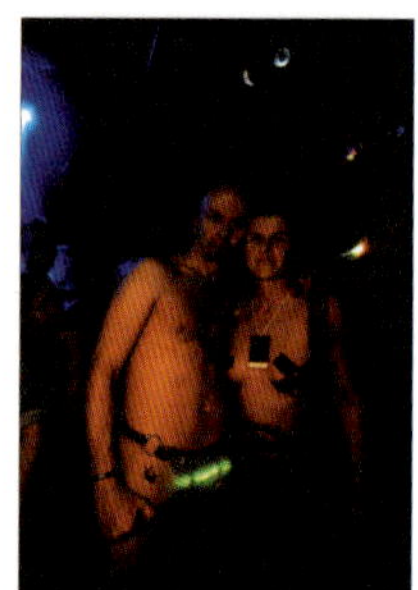

Suzi, 1997: finally, after two weeks of trying, I got her on her cellular phone, what a real business that was ... organizing "fist" parties. She agreed, "cool – but no pictures of fucking on stage, OK?"

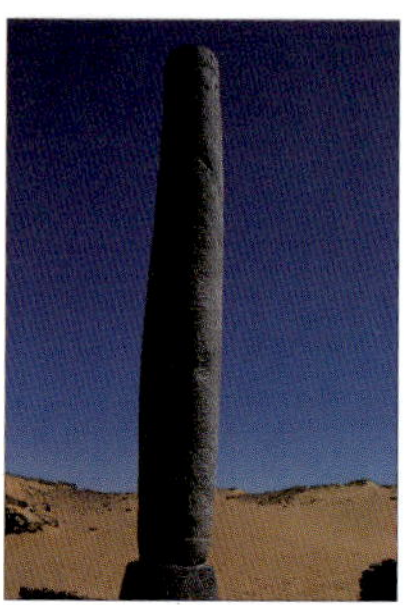

Reminder, 1989. Church stone belonging to the first Christians who lived far up on the banks of the Nile (now Sudan). Nowadays the town of Dongola is merely ruins encircled by Muslim tombs.

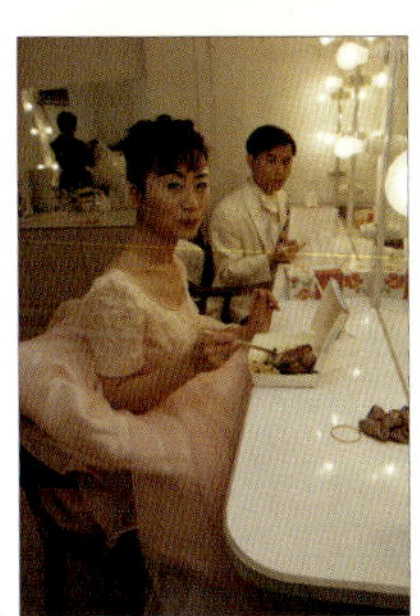

"High China," Taipei: Taking wedding pictures is a very serious matter in Taiwan. Couples have to try on wedding dresses and decide how and where they want to be photographed. The photo ceremony takes a whole day, and involves six changes of costumes, dozens of different poses in a studio and equally on location. Afterwards comes the selection day when photos for enlargement are chosen, which can be hard work for the whole family. The result is a huge album with wooden covers.

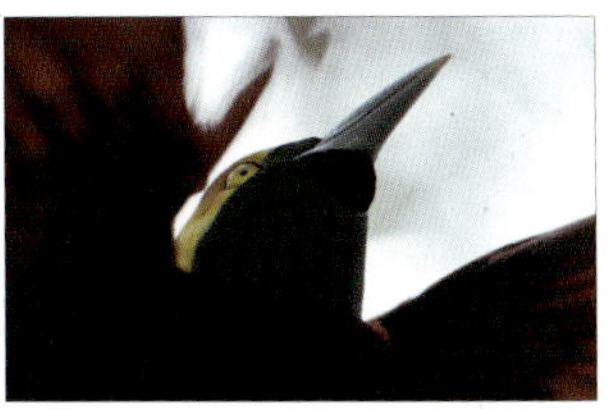

Photographing the Bird of **Paradise** was my **most exclusive** photo assignment ever. For a full three days I went to the bird enclosure in the middle of the tropical forest in the highlands of Papua New Guinea. And the bird got used to me ...

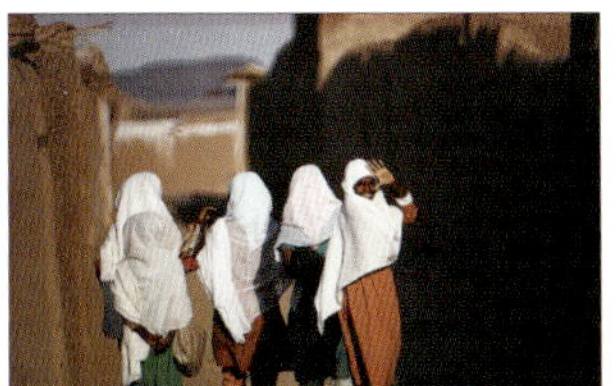

"Where is my coffee?" – an echo in my head ... Morning wandering through a village in Sudan.

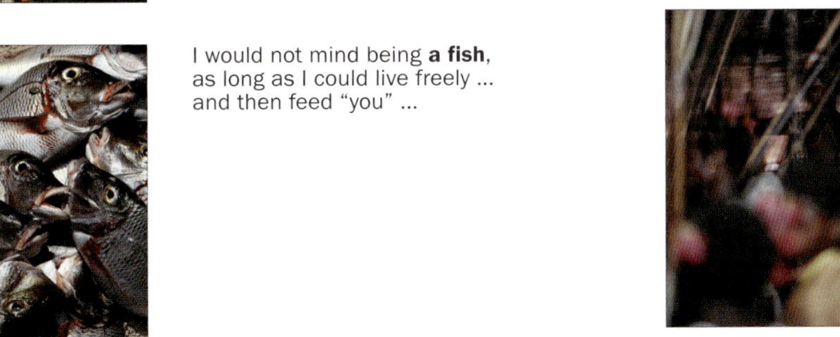

I would not mind being **a fish**, as long as I could live freely ... and then feed "you" ...

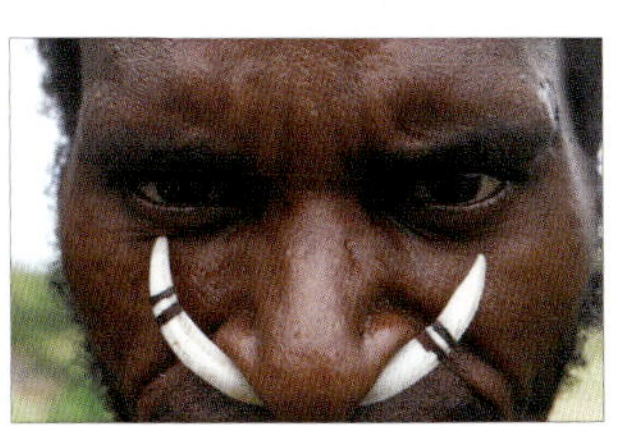

Long days, long houses (men's house), and long parties ("Sing-Sings") are from another world, in which roads, TVs, radios and phones do not exist, but where the imagination rules ... Sunday morning, getting ready for a "Sing-Sing." Irian Jaya Highlands, Indonesia.

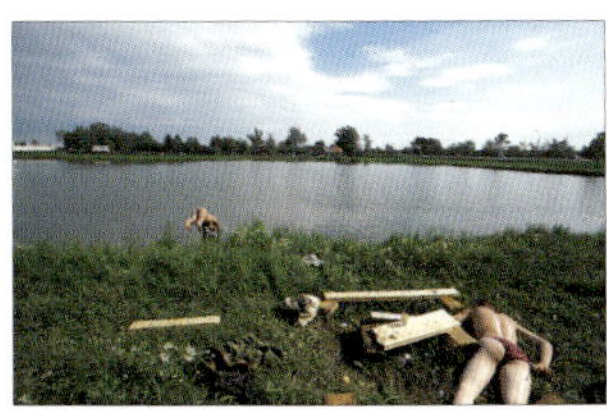

Sunday morning Vodka, former USSR, 1997.

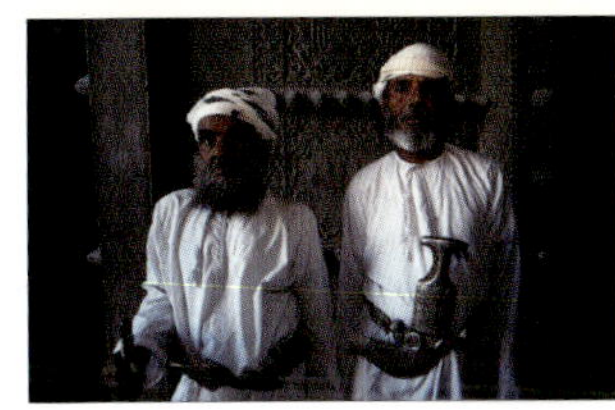

Oman – Posing: **official models on duty.** During the last 20 years the country has rapidly changed to a rich Arab country, having attained Western standards. In order to remember history, many old forts in the country are now being restored.

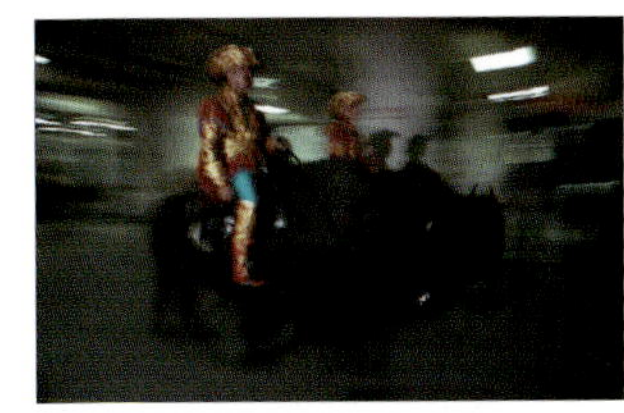

Riding bisons! **Real US act** at the Ringling Bros. & Barnum & Bailey Circus – "The Greatest Show on Earth," 1993.

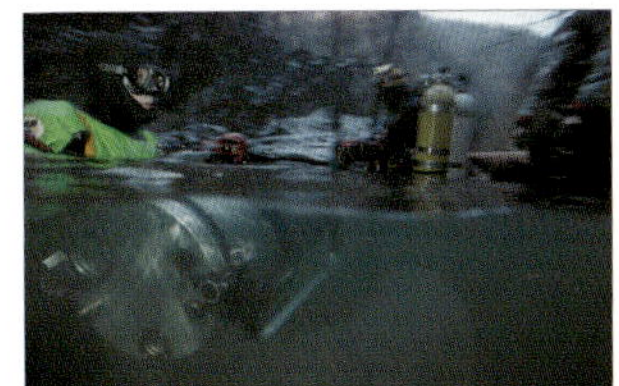

Jos Latouche ("Le Grand Bleu" cameraman) – preparing for a dive to the siphon to film the "Human Fish," an endemic animal which lives in the Karst cave systems. His encounter with a creature which lives in the dark for up to 100 years came to an abrupt end. It was winter and his dry suit broke in the cave. Within a few minutes he was out, fighting for his life.

"Sing-Sing:" local dance party which can also be interpreted as a ritual dance – if the BBC reaches them. Irian Jaya Highlands, Indonesia.

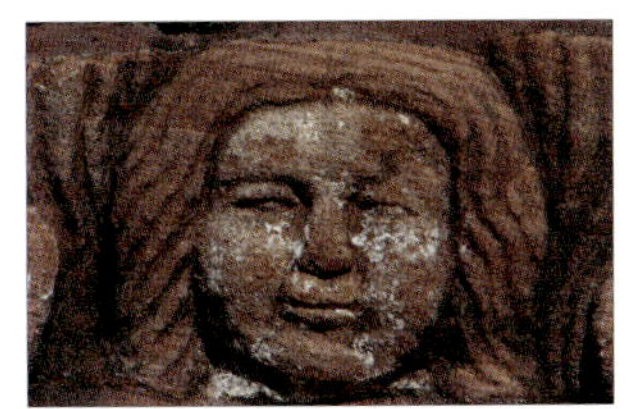

In the early days of the Missions, there was a lack of white paint for the statues, so the Indians produced it from snail shells crushed together and burnt. This white pigment proved to be extremely durable, and one can still see traces of it on the stone relief. **Trinidad Mission,** in today's Paraguay.

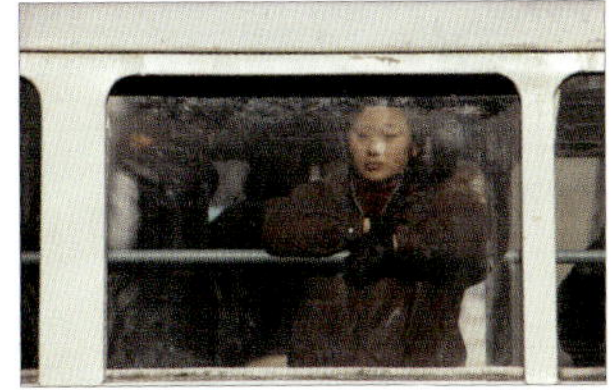

Shanghai rush hour, 1993: "The worst time of the day involves spending two hours in a crowded bus where people become aggressive."

Never ending flow wherever you go, goes as far as roads go, from place to place and all the way in between ... Great Trunk Road, India.

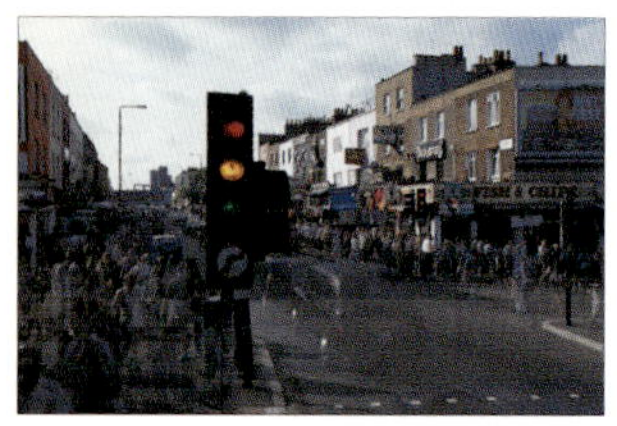

Camden Town, the heart of London's market scene.

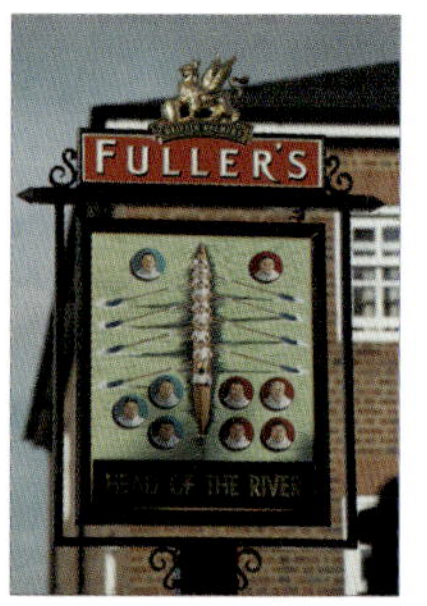

Two sides of the river: in Oxford I got the message – the students there are really determined to study!

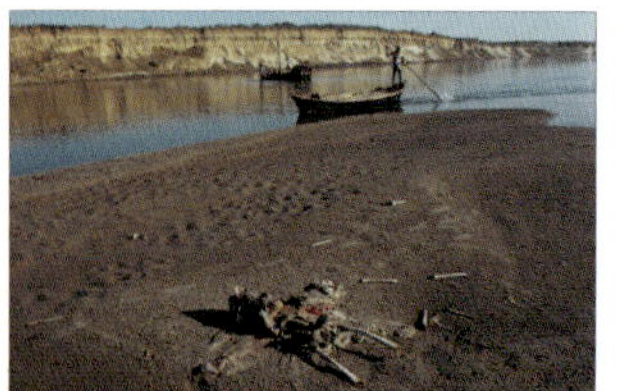

Ganges – for Hindus the best place to **leave your body behind.**

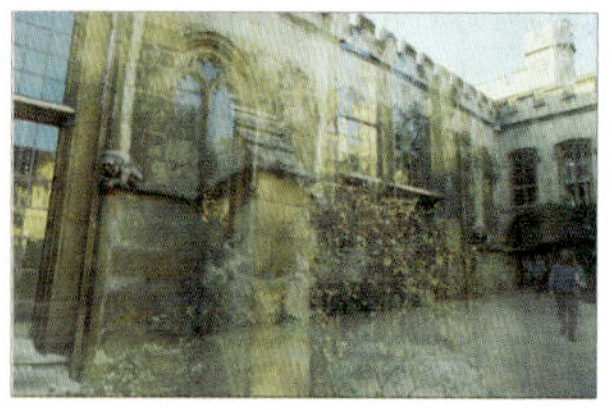

This Oxford **library gargoyle** is one of many around the university buildings – summoning strength from the underworld.

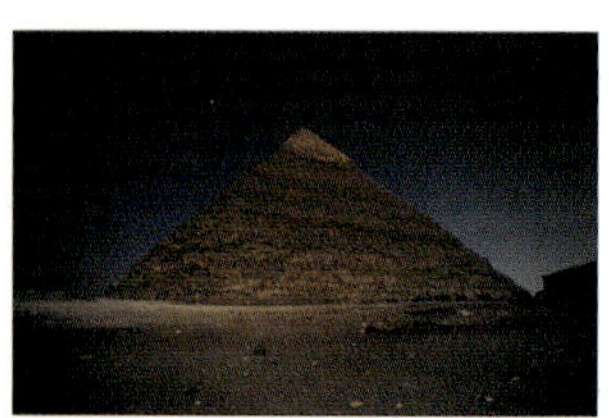

Full moonlight on the Chephren Pyramid, once covered with a crystalline, perfectly smooth granite stone wall. It could probably be seen from the moon.

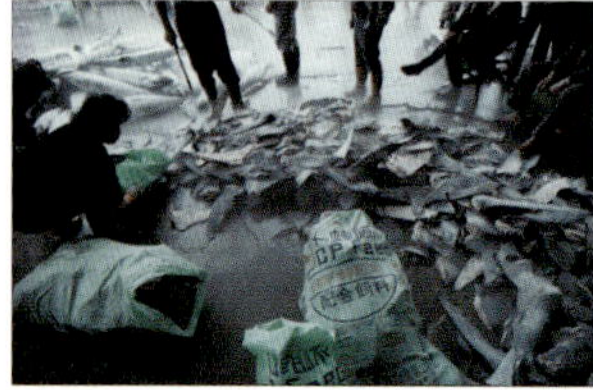

Shark fin – aphrodisiac. The demand for shark fins has increased dramatically over the last few years. Fins are used to make traditional Chinese soup, which is considered to be a powerful aphrodisiac. Large quantities of various sharks are caught, only to have their fins cut off – the remains are later thrown overboard. Taiwan, Suao fishing port.

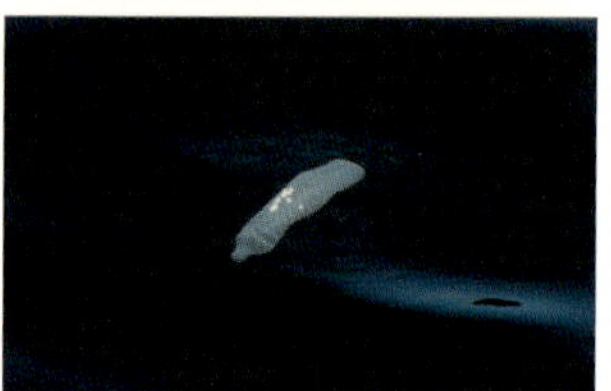

... in the sea

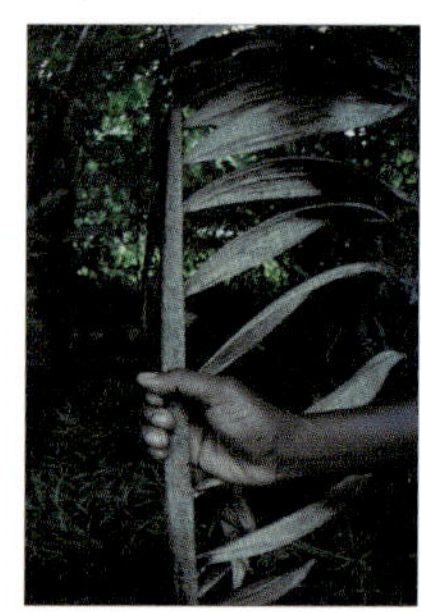

"If you come at midnight and write your wish on a piece of paper under the cotton tree and leave it there, the spirits will help you."
Gardener's hand. Botanical garden, Jamaica.

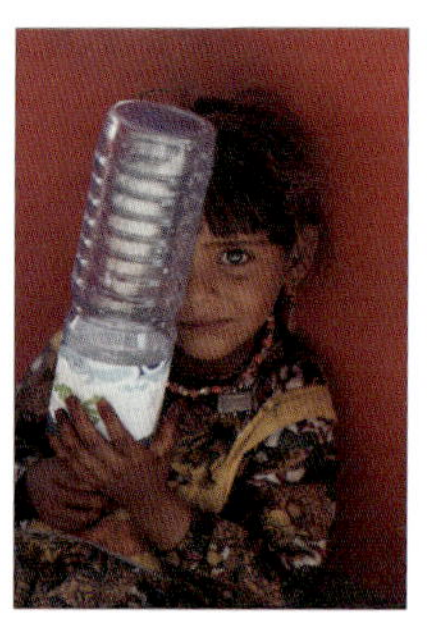

Omani in the once remote mountain valleys (wadis) of the Hayar Mountains. The government of modern Oman supports the local people (schools, roads, electricity, agricultural machinery) in order to prevent migration to towns and preserve the existence of agriculture.

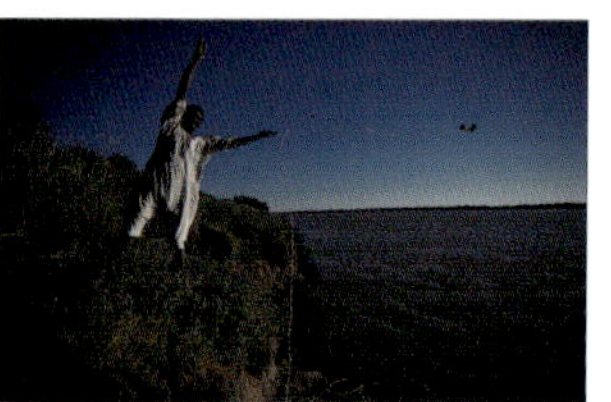

Fisherman on the Nile, Sudan. According to the legend, God sneezed and as a result Earth appeared. In Heaven a goddess cried and the Nile was born.

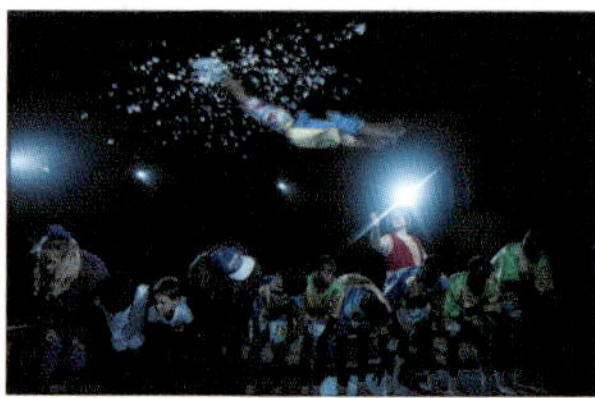

Performance by the **Chicago Boys** – Hip Hop acrobats – the stars of the children's show. "They were picked up on the road and went through eight months of intensive training led by Russian acrobatic experts." Ringling Bros. & Barnum & Bailey Circus, Denver, 1993.

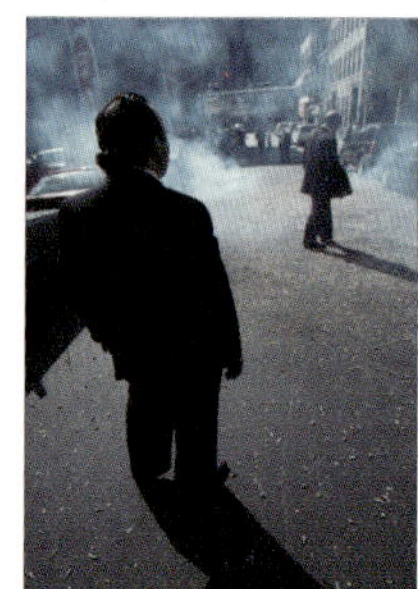

Little Italy on St. Anthony's Day, New York, 1995. I felt Hollywood did not need to invent much, it was all there. Aged machos playing their power games – a massive firecracker explosion at the end of the road was "a warning" for the Chinese, and marked the border between the Italian neighborhood and the engulfing Chinese community. Ironically, the firecrackers were actually bought in Chinese shops ...

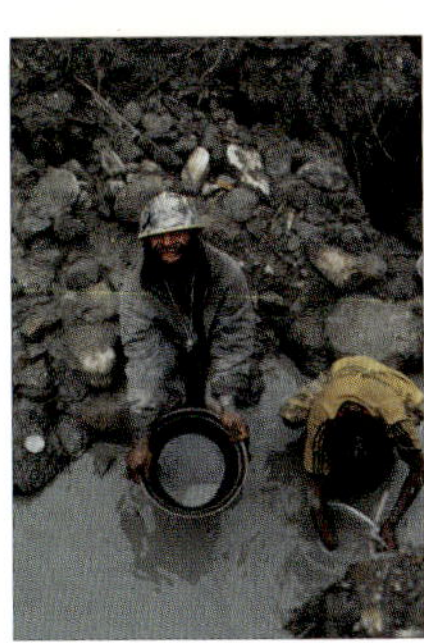

Gold rush in Papua New Guinea, 1990. The Papuans are born power hunters. Hunting is a means of life preservation but it also augments the power which a good hunter gains in the clan hierarchy, the social status. The power of the white man, as they see it, is money. Consequently gold is a means of acquiring the white man's power. In the past they were disinterested in gold!

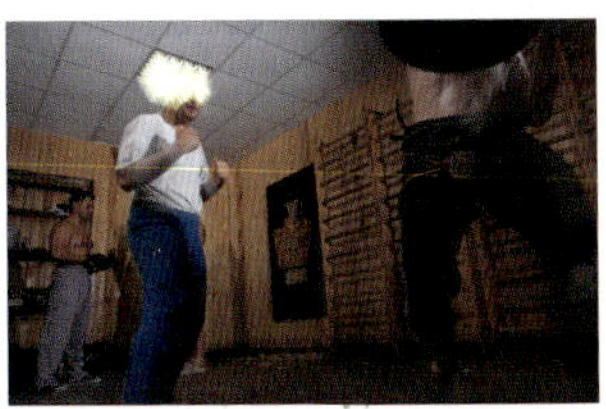

The **bodyguard** of Mr. Minakoff, a millionaire from St. Petersburg, during training, 1997.

Jerusalem: The most sacred **moment at the Wall** had not been revealed to me until I came there one day before sunrise. A mere dozen, very spiritual men, were offering their morning prayers, combining them with the ecstatic swinging of the body back and forth and the turning of the head left and right. Shortly after sunrise they collectively greeted the day, toasting it with schnapps, and within a moment made their silent disappearance.

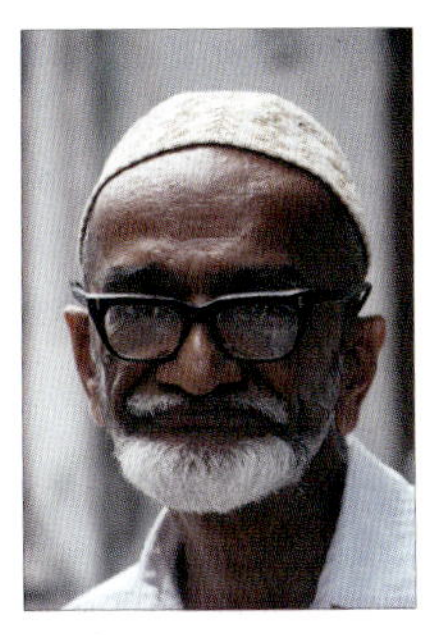

Zanzibarian – A fantastic mixture of many races of different cultural and religious backgrounds is expressed in the faces of the Zanzibar people. The only real bond between them is their Swahili culture and language which is based on this mixture.

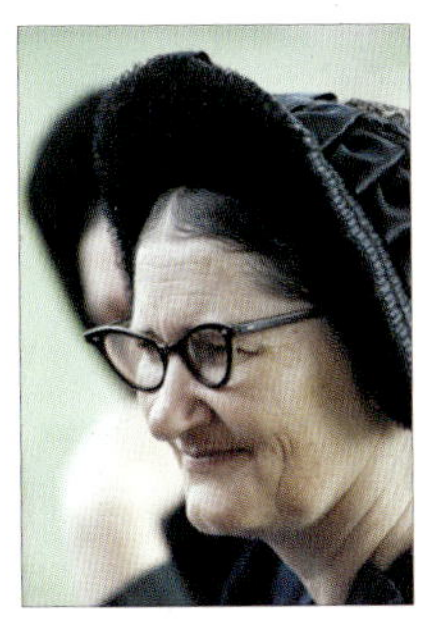

A Mennonite lady from Bolivia. The Mennonite church split from the Amish in 1693 as a consequence of a disagreement over the strictness of discipline. The Amish insisted on the strict practice of shunning excommunicated members, whereas the majority of the Swiss Brethren repudiated this cruel practice.

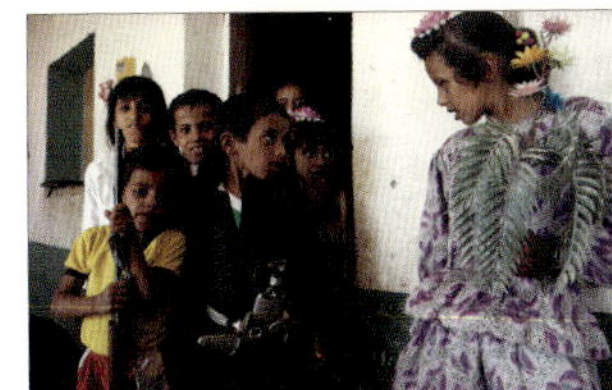

Oman – Sisters and brothers. "It is very simple. If these people did not get all they do now (machinery, electricity, irrigation systems, telephones etc.) they would come to Muscat, but the Sultan knows that we need these people here for the tradition to continue." Oh, my guide was so fat, all he could do was smile and sweat!

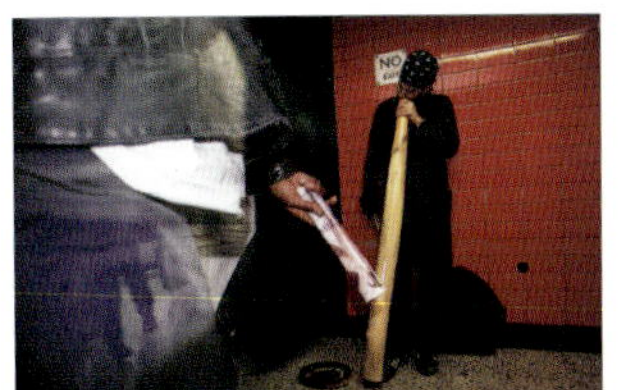

An **American** playing an Australian aboriginal instrument made by himself, London, 1997.

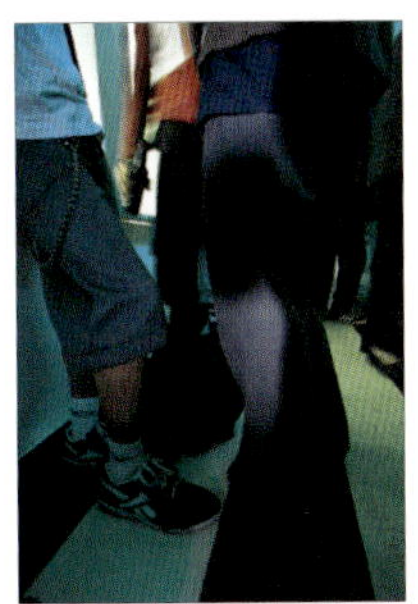

I like bicycles ... **the chain** "pulled" my camera out of the bag. It was a hardcore party for the fashion students at St. Martin's Design College, London, 1997.

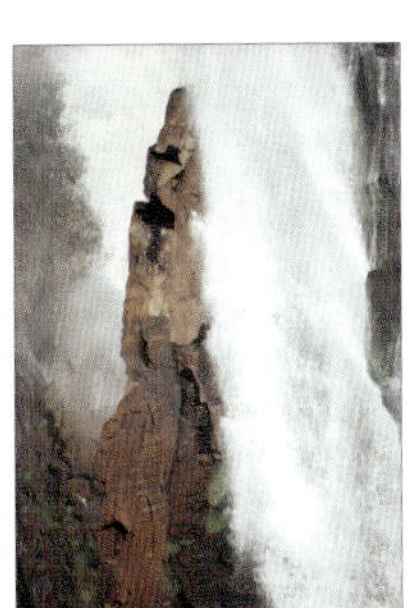

Foz de **Iguazú** waterfall is one of the top five tourist spots in South America. 500 years ago Guarani Indians tried to hide here to escape a destiny of becoming Portuguese and Spanish slaves.

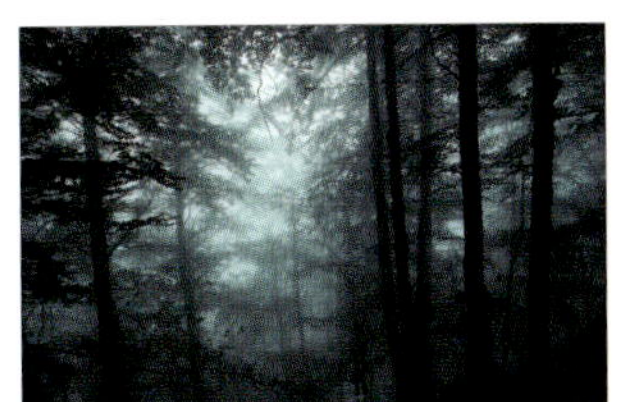

Highland forest, Europe.

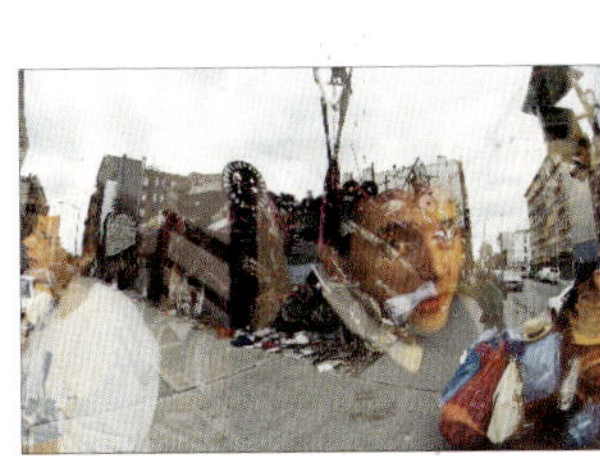

An **ex**-pub, an **ex**-trash place, an **ex**-art place. ABC Hispanic district in Manhattan, New York, 1995.

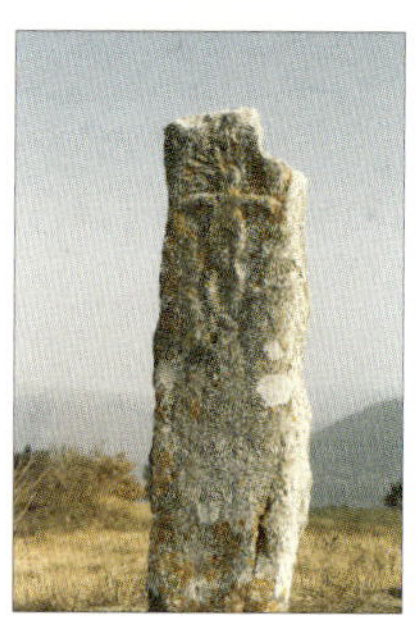

“Fire from the head.” A man with an aura, a different one. Krkavce megalith, Istria, Slovenia.

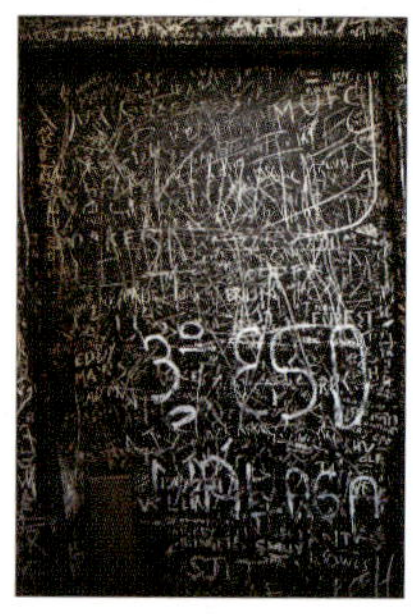

OLE, EDDY MAY’S, FUREST, CONDON, UTF, BRUM, MONKY MANTEOS, EAKE, MALAGA ...

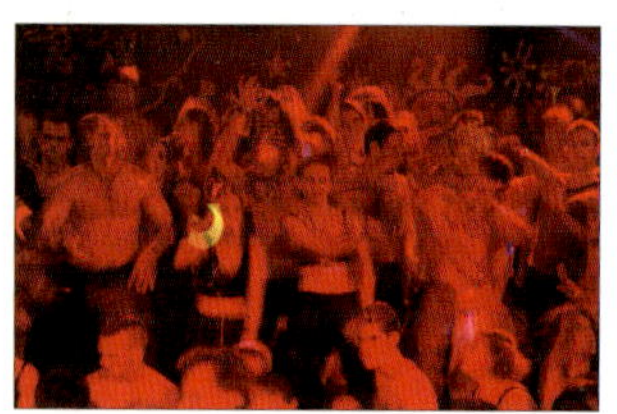

Afro-Celt venue – rave party at Fridge Club. The 17- gigawatt reflectors and super cooling system made it possible without ecstasy. London, 1997.

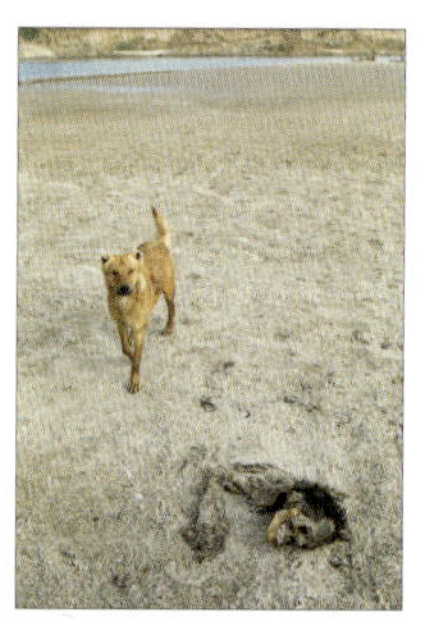

Ganges – Soul and body **(and dog)** are only a temporary affair.

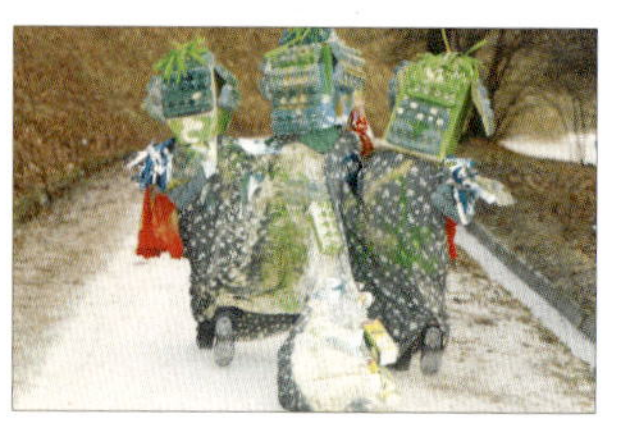

Three-headed dragon, 1996, was a “masterpiece of design” by friend Barbara who actually worked on the layout of this book.

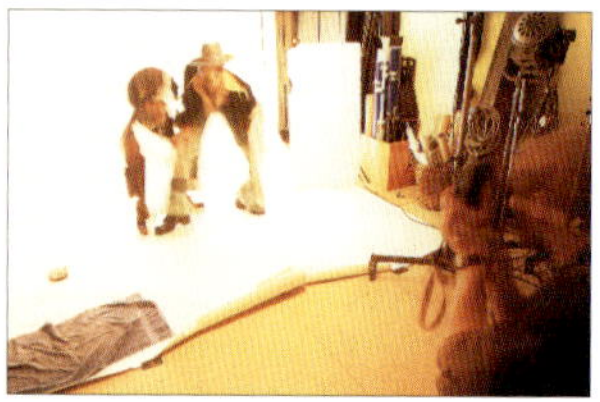

Back to the sixties. Fashion shooting in Joseph Gram Studio, London, 1997.

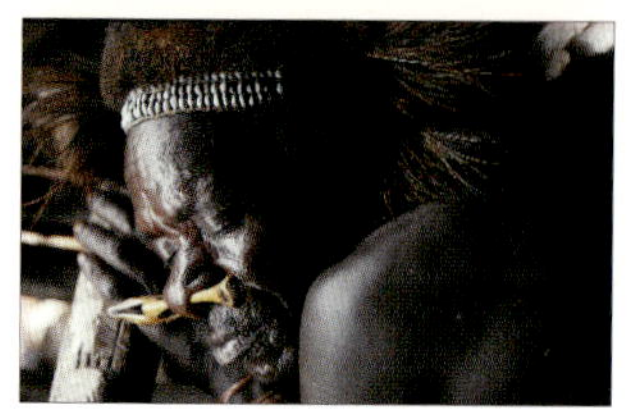

I spent the whole day in a long canoe moving through a labyrinth of water ways in mangrove forest. Finally reached a village with no other access to it ... On approaching “Tambaran House” – the **house for men** – dogs barked, people gathered and the guy still did not wake up. Asmat, Irian Jaya, Indonesia, 1990.

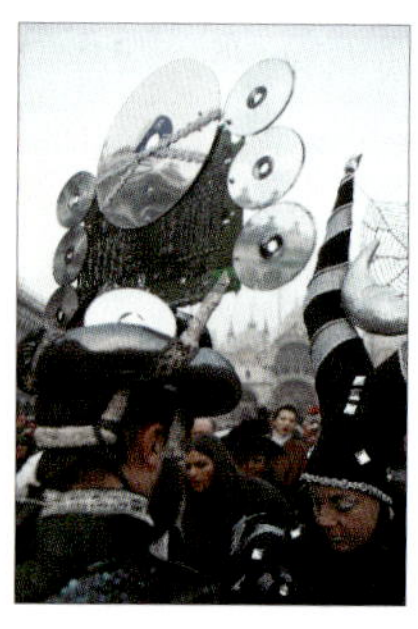

Cyber king & queen. German favorites at Venice carnival ’97.

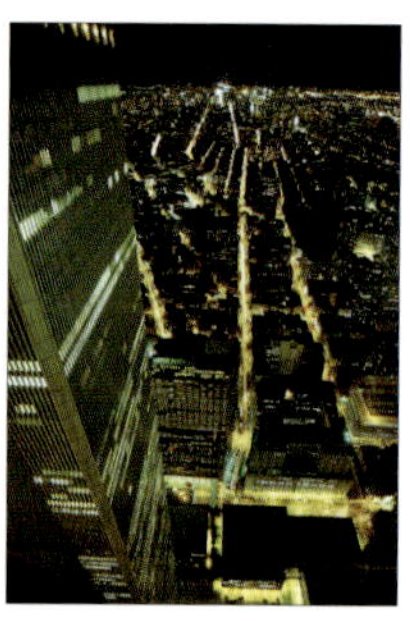

Twin Tower of WTC, New York, where big meets small ...

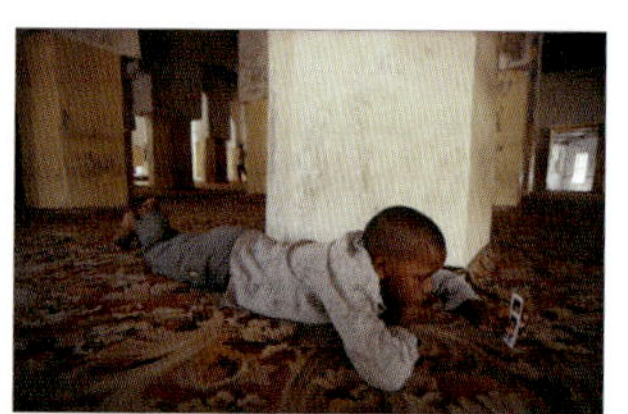

Enjoying a cool breeze, wafting through the mosque in Zanzibar, a boy **playing cards** made me feel as if I was in his living room somewhere in the sky ...

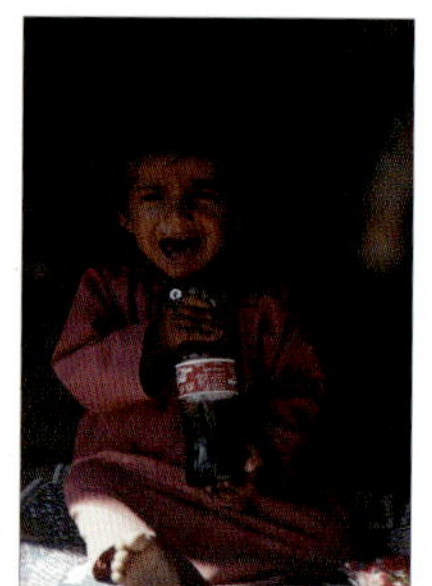

O, man, Oman ... Over the last 20 years the country has changed into a rich Arab country by Western standards, but just a kilometer off the main road family life cannot catch up with the pace of change.

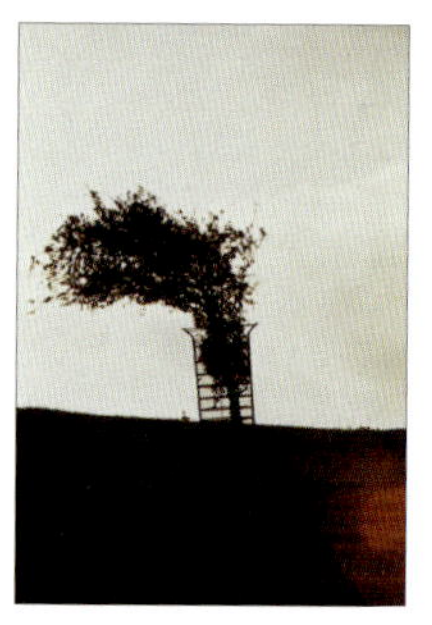

The **Magic spot,** Warrior Hill, in Glastonbury, England, has been marked by the same fragile wild pear tree for 2,000 years.

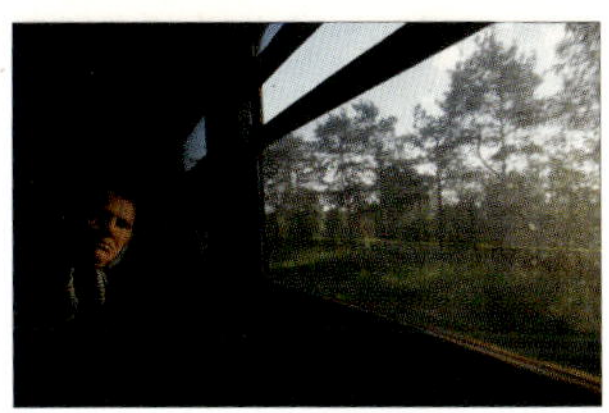

Dreaming on, 1997. Once an important industrial town, Alexandrovsk attracted workers, even from Moscow. Nowadays people go to Moscow to try and sell anything they can.

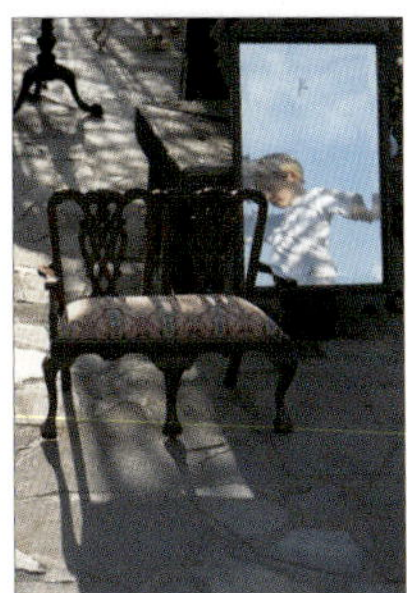

Saturday market on Portobello Road, London. I promised a parent to send a photo of a boy playing, but I'm not sure I kept my promise!

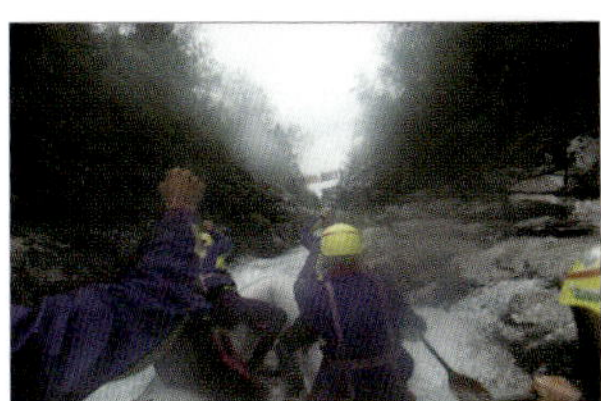

World champions in rafting **on stage.** The members of the Slovene rafting team are not professional rafters. They all have jobs and professions but the skills and experience they have acquired on the Soca River makes them a real team. In 1995, 1996 and 1997 the team won the first prize at the World Rafting Competition on the Zambezi River.

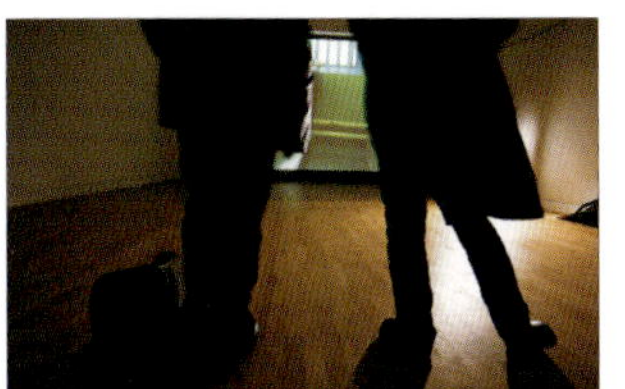

Off stage, Darren Almond, Live satellite link from HM Prison Pentonville. Exhibition opening at Institute of Contemporary Arts, London, 1997.

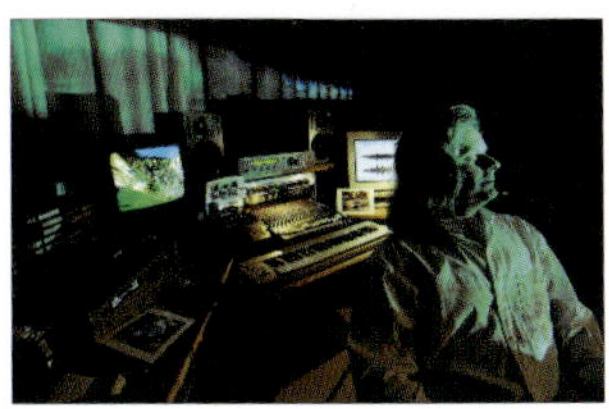

Dreaming Andrej Zdravic, 1996 – film and sound artist: "No doubt, I get excited by the chaotic churning of water, these moments when energy is directly manifested. But underneath all this chaos there is a system, there are laws. On the other hand, chaos such as we see it in nature, is self-regenerative. Chaos creates, even in destroying: just as lava consumes an entire forest, it brings forth, at the same time, minerals, gases, air and water from the depths of the earth ..."

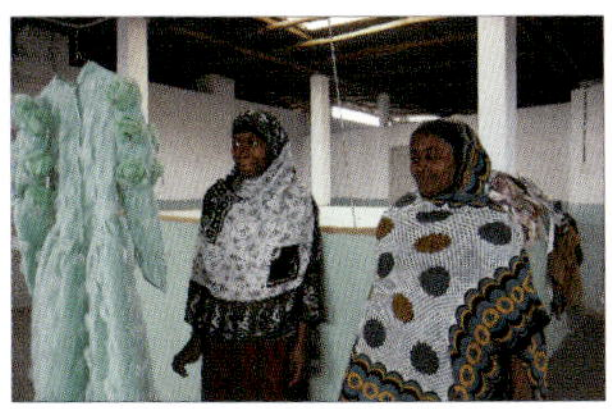

"My lady dress." If Zanzibar uses its incredible potential in the future, it will not be very far from the glory and fame of its old days. Anything that is done in Zanzibar influences a larger area. This is reflected in the famous ancient Arab saying: "When one pokes into Zanzibar, they dance on the Great Lakes."

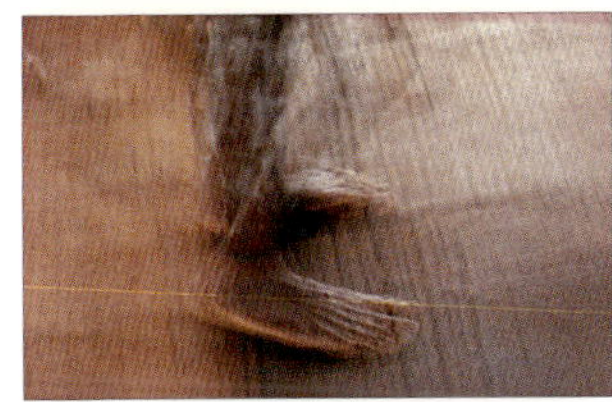

On the third day: Since I left before the betel-nut and dance orgy of the "women-only allowed" in the "women's house," the orgy has never ended for me. Black River, Sepic river system, Papua New Guinea.

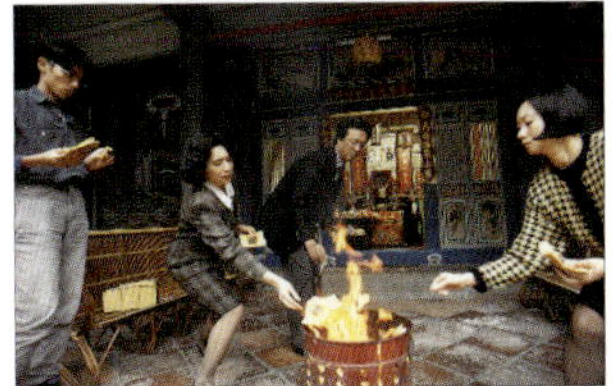

The two sisters – Mei Fang, a surgeon living in Japan, and Tsung Fang, in business in the USA – come home annually to celebrate the Chinese New Year. It starts with the burning of paper money at the family shrine in the morning of the last day of the year.

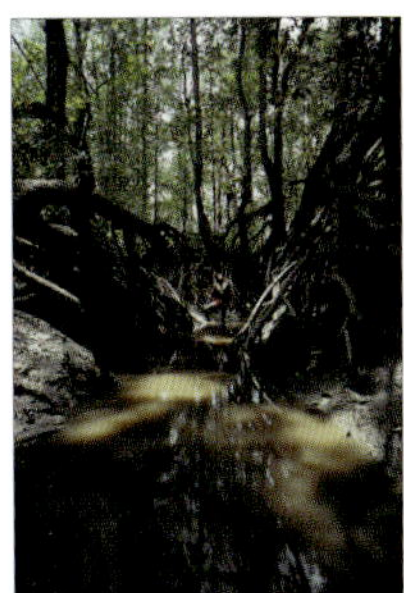

Finally I was **in the forest** ... the authentic virgin mangrove forest that is so hard to imagine. Mangrove trees can really grow big! But it takes time, and Asmat (Irian Jaya, Indonesia) is almost the last corner of the earth where people still live with and from the forest.

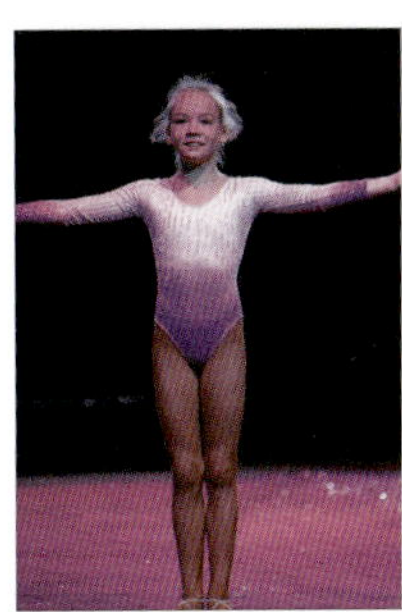

Julija from Siberia is only 11 years old. The little blonde has enormous talent, and "uncle Petya" – nickname Sorutchan – has been training her for two years. Together they are performing a classical Russian circus act (girl and athlete). "The Greatest Show on Earth," Denver, 1994, is taking place in front of an audience of 20,000. Julija was the main star of the show.

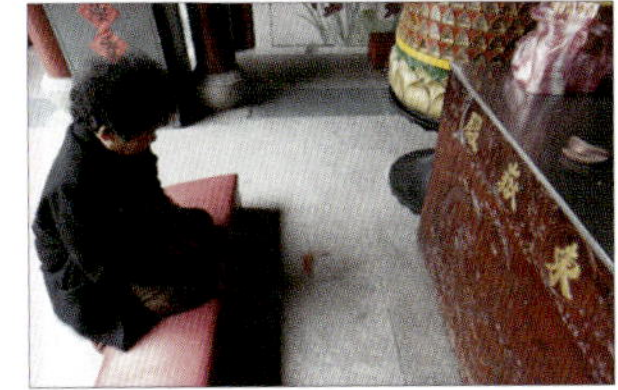

Taoism, Confucianism and Buddhism mix up at the Lung Shan temple in Taipei, Taiwan, 1996. **"Good luck,"** "for good luck," "not to cross good luck." All you do should bring you good luck, everything you do should be done with respect to certain laws in order to gain good luck, and to find out about your good luck, it is popular to throw wooden pieces in the temple.

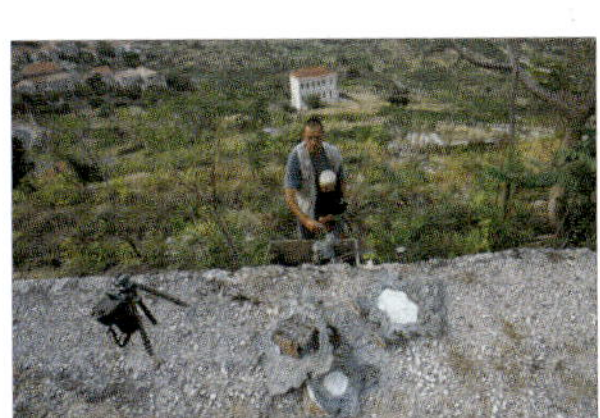

In search of a **good piece** to photograph, artist Marko Modic and his son Kristof. Island of Hvar, Adriatic Sea, 1997.

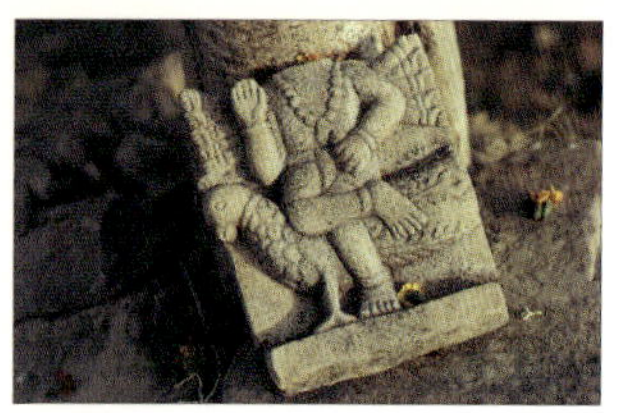

There are many carved stones simply lying around India and each of them has a special meaning for the local people. My explanation for this one was simple: to be **as free as a bird** you have to be a master of that thing first.

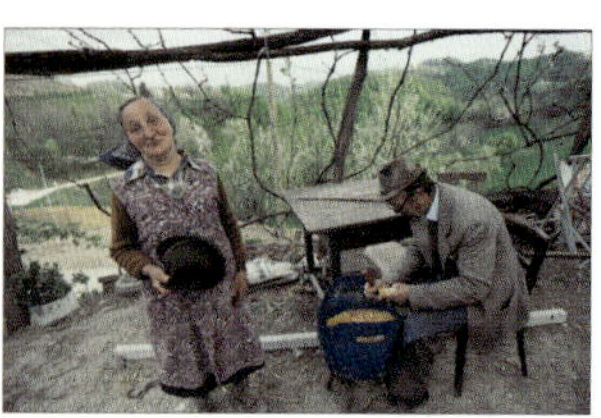

"Let me change his hat ... I bought it for him for special moments." Such beautiful people will stay in my heart forever. I could not leave without her gift of thirty fresh, superorganic eggs. Haloze region, Slovenia.

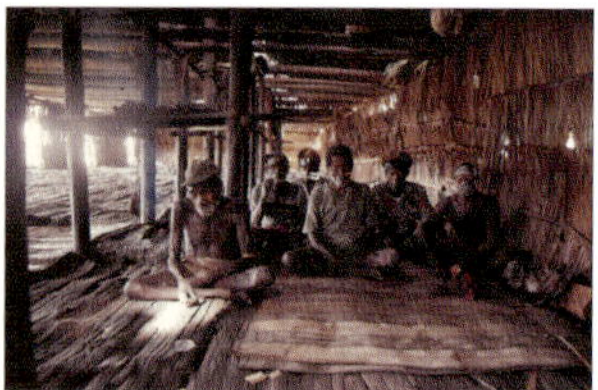

Carving crew: All men in Agri (Irian Jaya, Indonesia) carve to some extent. Everyone learns to make his own paddles, canoes, spears ..., but when something more elaborate is required, men turn to the best carvers in the village, who are highly respected and have a status equal to that of important headhunters. Carvings connect the life of this world with the world of the spirits. They are the medium through which the Asmat remain in contact with their ancestors.

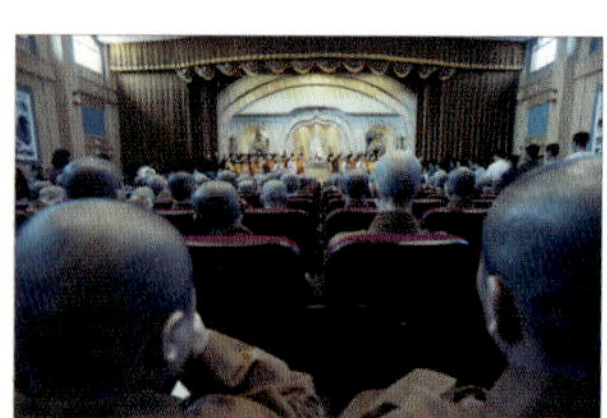

Holidays in Fo Kuang Shan winter camp. In 1949 the Venerable Master Hsing Yun arrived in Taiwan from China. In his lifetime he established more than 100 branch temples on all 5 continents, 6 Buddhist colleges, 2 high schools, Hsi Lai University in California, several kindergartens ... Fo Kuang Shan is the largest Buddhist monastery in Taiwan, providing all sorts of educational programs (from kindergarten to university), social and medical care programs for people, from birth till death.

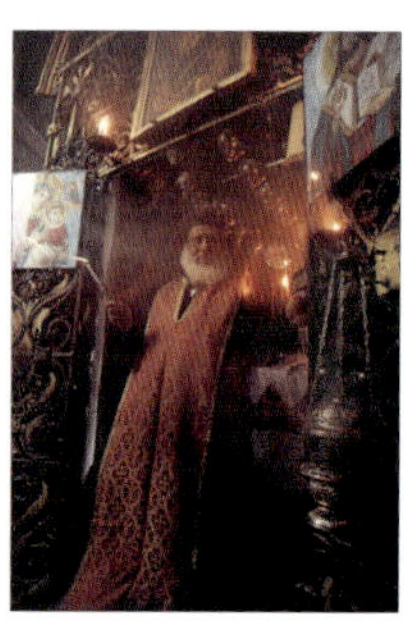

Holy Sepulchre in Jerusalem ... The high morning energy, through the dark spaces of the huge shrine, can be as long as a three-hour ritual with the three monks singing, filling the church with incense, reading the Bible in front of one of several small chapels which are spread all around the sanctuary. The masses formally follow a fixed pattern but it adapts well to special religious occasions. With such dynamics, the scene is actually never repeated, and whenever you enter the Holy Sepulchre there seems to be a whole new pattern of different rituals. A true example of the Theory of Chaos?

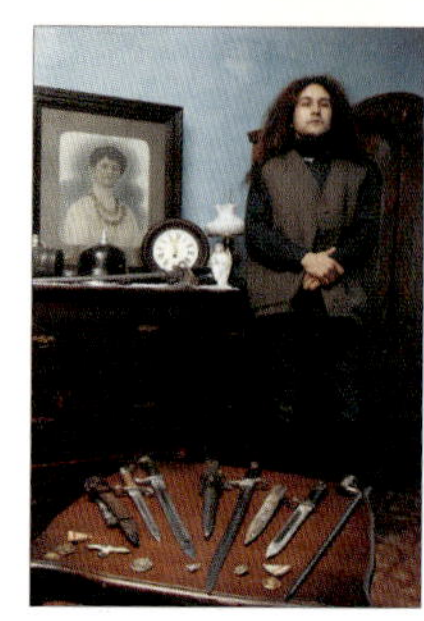

In 1945, 600,000 Germans were expelled from Vojvodina – ethnic cleansing in former Yugoslavia. Milan Wind is one of the rare descendants living there, who do not want to forget their family roots.

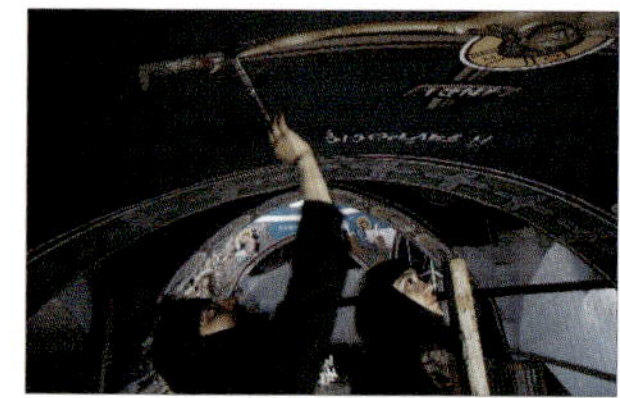

Greek twin sisters Isidora and Siglitiki Giorna, busy with their final work on the new frescoes at the Church of St. John the Baptist in Jerusalem. During the photographing the scaffold construction collapsed. It happened slowly enough for the falling sisters, cameras and flashes to be caught up; by a miracle all was held together by the edges of the broken construction. Nobody got hurt, nothing broke! That same day many friends phoned my home in Ljubljana, to ask if it was me who had crashed in an army helicopter in the woods of Slovenia. It was my namesake.

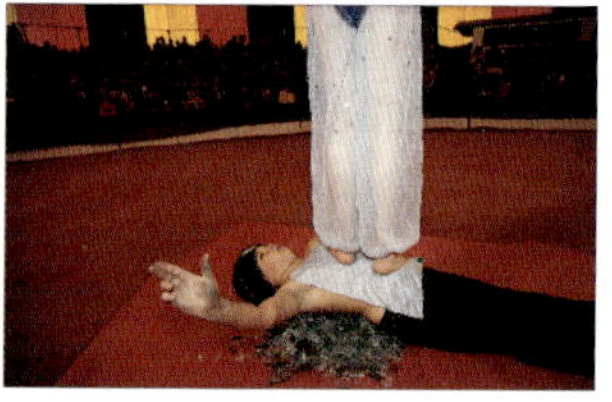

Magician. Shapito Circus in Cheboksary, Russia, 1993.

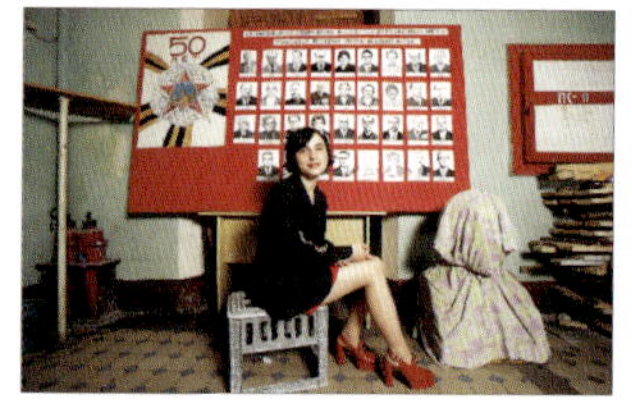

Leula Kariakina with her pet, a boa snake. The school of journalism hasn't changed much from the old regime – it is still a school for the elite. Lomonosov University, Moscow.

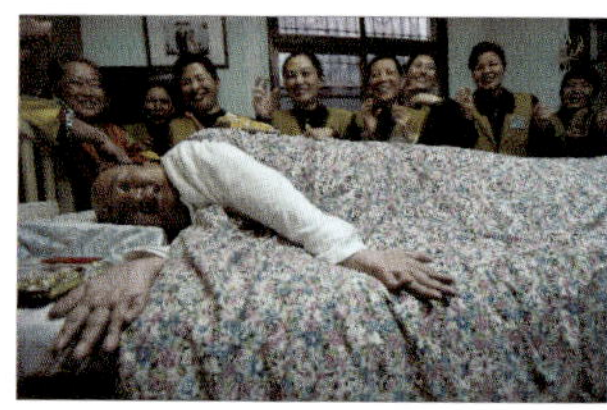

"Lying Buddha" is how the mother calls her son after he became completely paralyzed. A Buddhist nun of Cheng Yen's faith, determined and hard working, started a non-profit charity mission out of nothing but ideals and love for the poor and needy. Today, their relief services have covered all corners of Taiwan and extended to the USA and several other countries.

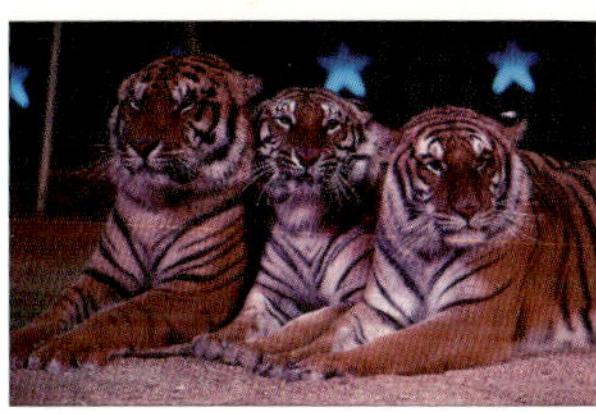

Three ... Mary Chaperfild from England – the most famous name in animal training. The family goes back to the times when they established the zoo. Knie Circus, 1993.

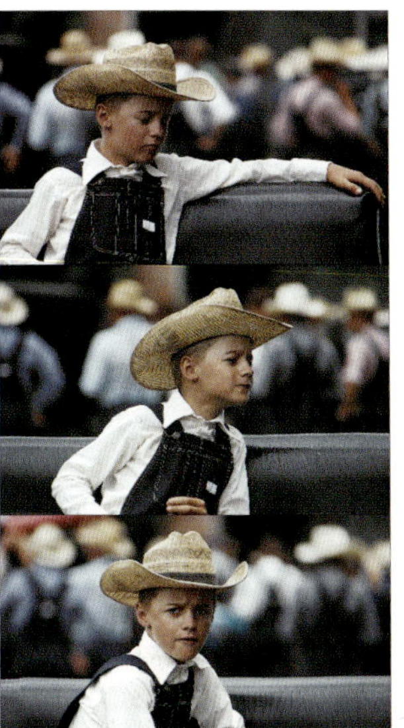

Swift Current, Mennonite colony in Bolivia. Historically Mennonites are the descendants of Teutonic tribes originating from what is now Switzerland, Germany and the Netherlands, and sharing the faith of the Roman Catholic Church until the time of the Reformation. The most radical of all the Reformists were the Swiss Brethren. Due to their uncompromising way of thinking, most of the early Brethren leaders died as martyrs, while their followers were sentenced and sold to serve as galley slaves and executed in their hundreds. The Count of Alzey was once heard to exclaim: "What shall I do, the more I kill them, the greater becomes their number!"

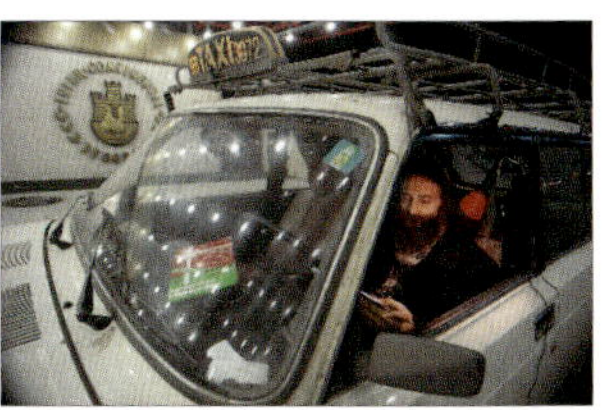

1993, **free lance angel.** "Cvetko, the taxi driver" was ready to go through sniper fire to any location or "side" in Bosnia. With a Ph.D in philosophy, Cvetko Novicic worked as a guide and translator for foreign journalist crews reporting from the battle fronts in Yugoslavia. When he was not working he spent his income on smuggling food, clothes and medication to any side of troubled Bosnia.

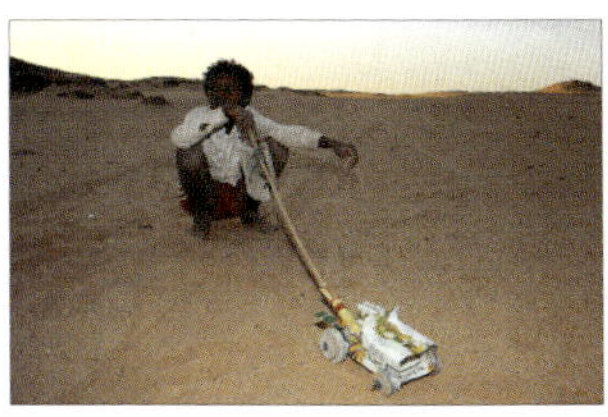

Fantasy driver ... Once a week a bus might come to Karima, Sudan.

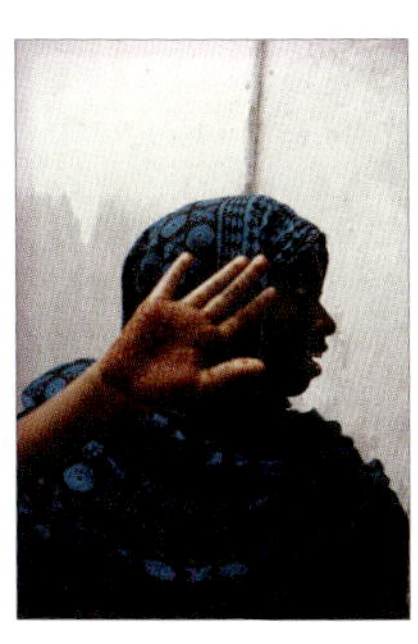

The **lady** standing at the door saw me from afar and didn't want to wait, since I looked like ... a photographer. I peeped through the door of her house into the yard ... where she agreed to be photographed. Stone Town, Zanzibar.

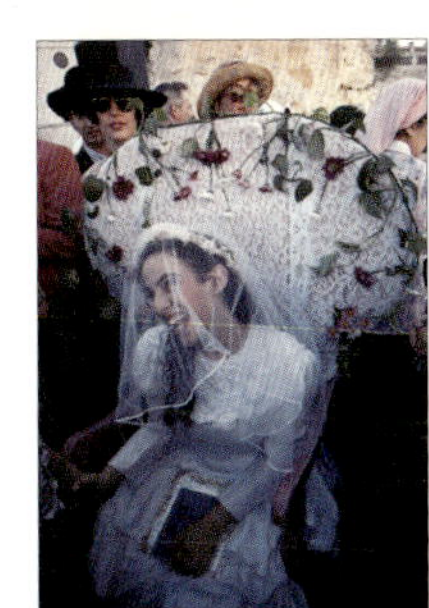

An American in Jerusalem. The Jewish marriage ceremony usually takes place in a synagogue but for greater exclusivity this one was arranged in the central square of the Jewish quarter of the Old City.

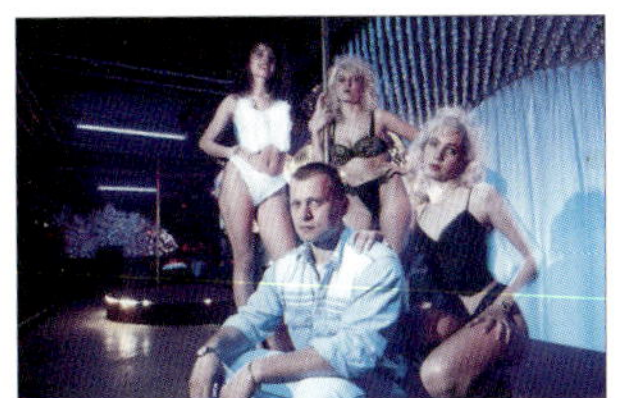

1993, UNPROFOR troops inspired a night club owner in Novi Sad, Serbia, to start a business with **Ukrainian beauties.** He paid 1,500 DM each to get them over the border, and the girls, without money and passports, were forced to do any kind of deal he wanted.

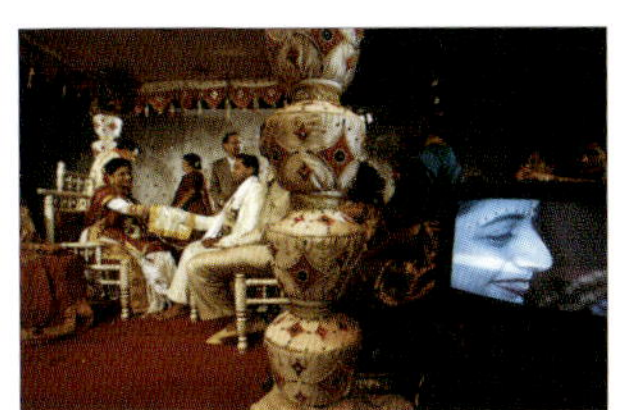

A 5- to 6-hour-long **Indian marriage** ceremony, London, 1997.

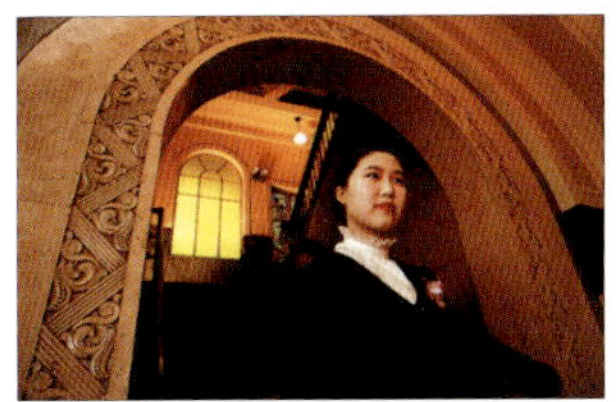

Peace Hotel, 1992. In 1929 it was known as the Cathay Hotel. It was then – and is now once more – the most fashionable meeting place for foreigners in Shanghai.

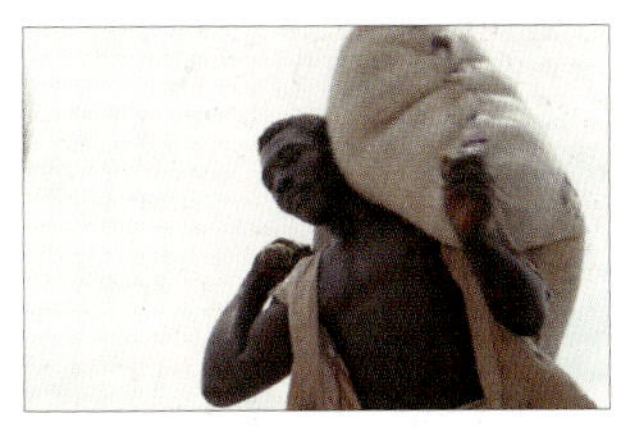

Zanzibar – **the Land of the Blacks,** as could be translated from ancient Persian.

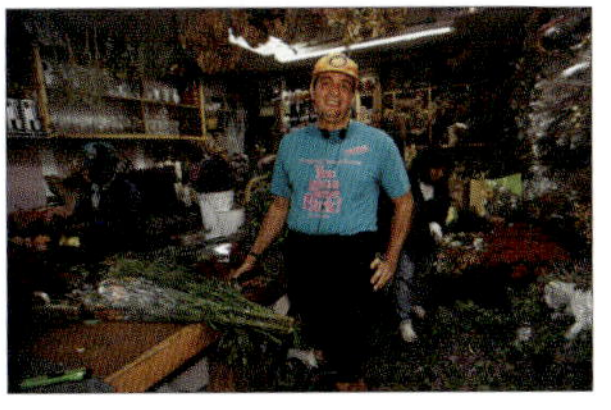

Lawrence E. Joseph is an independent writer, actively involved in the global ecological movement. **Larry** is also a very sociable guy with a lot of friends of differing profiles. On my arrival I rang him up and he announced with that positiveness so unique to Americans: "Great to see you in New York. Let's go to a private party!"
It was a closed reception at the home of Doe Lang, once a star in the musical "West Side Story," now a renowned expert on the possible effects of charisma in people's lives. I found myself in the midst of invited critics, writers, musicians and film directors. Brooklyn, New York.

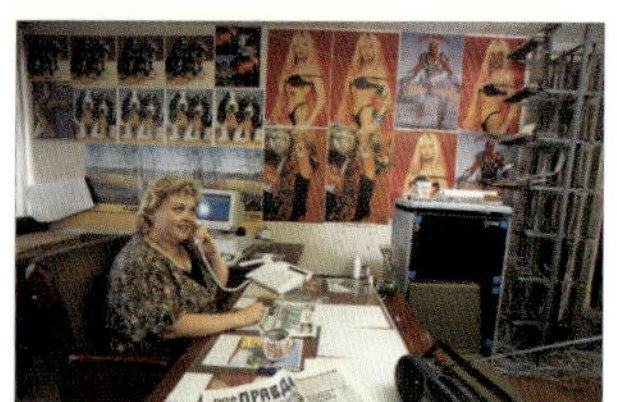

Last secretary working at "Pravda" newspaper, Moscow, 1997.

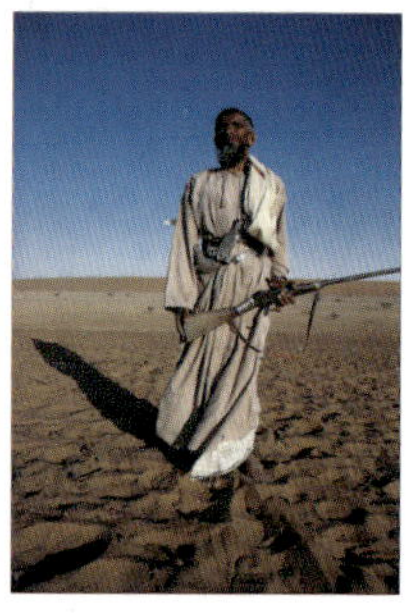

Chieftain of the tribe which lives in the desert of Wahiba Sands, Oman.

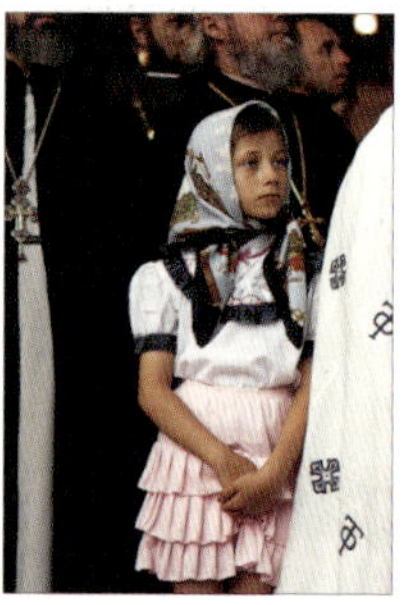

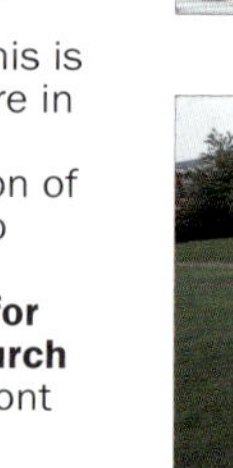

Jerusalem, 1994: "Look up, already for decades the central dome has been under reconstruction. Churches holding their services here cannot agree who will pay for it. This is proof that the Christians are in conflict even in their own house," was the explanation of an official (Jewish) guide to tourists exploring the Holy Sepulchre. It was **the day for the Russian Orthodox Church** to hold morning mass in front of the Chapel of Angels.

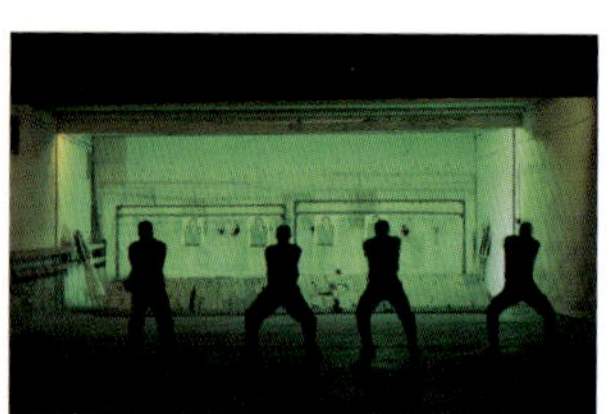

An **ex-policeman** from St. Petersburg, 1997 – Mr. Minakoff's private security guards in training. He made his first million with a security service which employed ex-policemen. His money now circulates in many other businesses. As a conscientious citizen of St. Petersburg, and in collaboration with the municipality, he is trying to establish special police forces, "which would thoroughly clean the town of Mafia, corruption and crime – the order will reinstate trust in the town, so that its citizens might live fully ..."

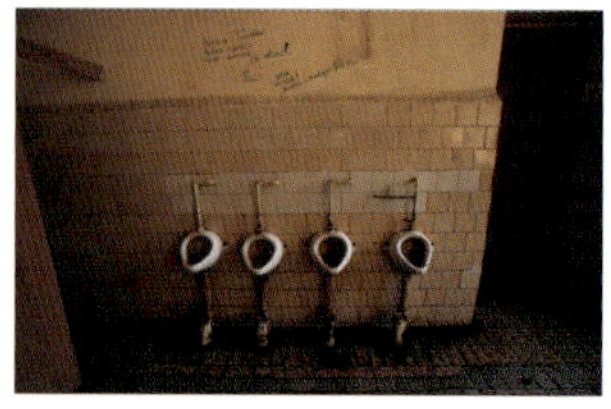

Toilet at Lomonosov University in Moscow, 1997.

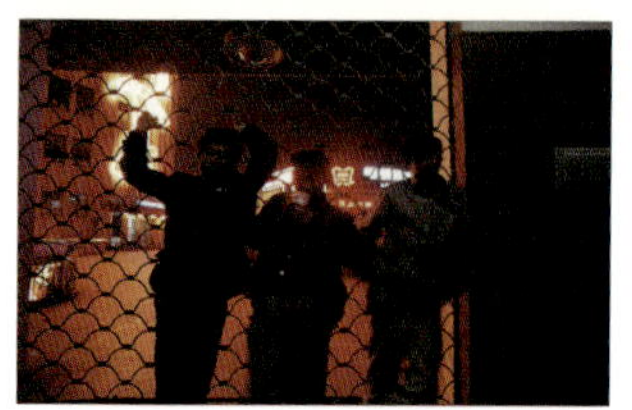

Shanghai, 1992. At –10°C alcoholics spent the night in the doorway of a department store.

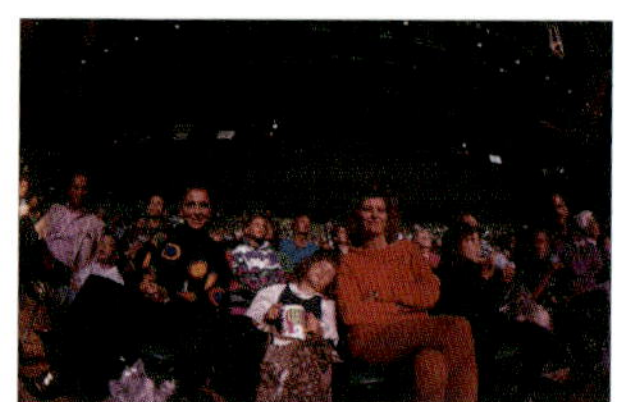

"The Greatest Show on Earth:" three-ring circus, 20,000 spectators ... and a lot of **trash food.** Denver, 1993.

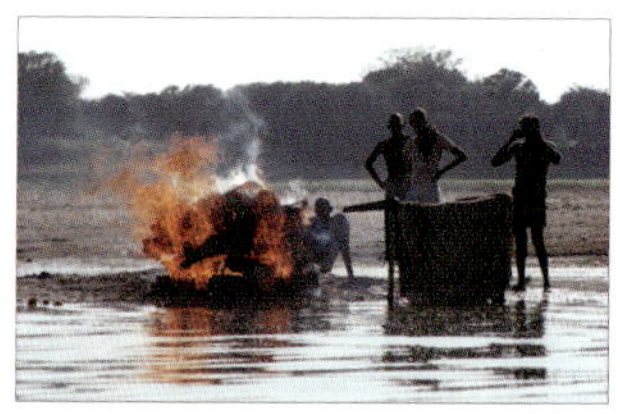

Cremation – Ganges, India.

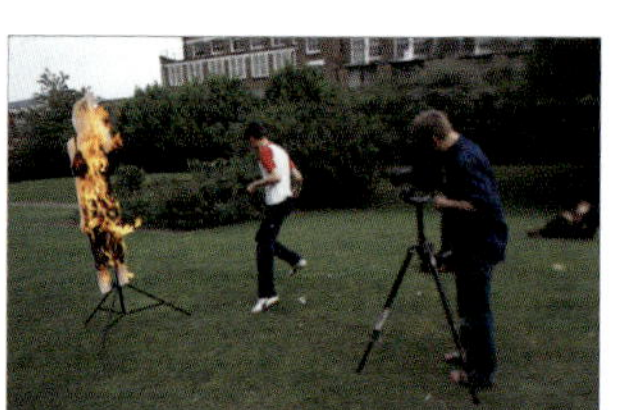

Fashion shooting. Rankin photographing for Dazed & Confused, London, 1997.

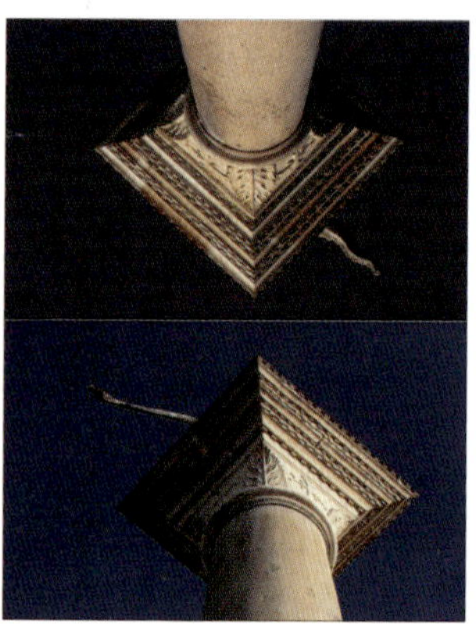

Basic: the dance of two polarities, two principles – **heaven and earth,** the perpetuum mobile of Venice.

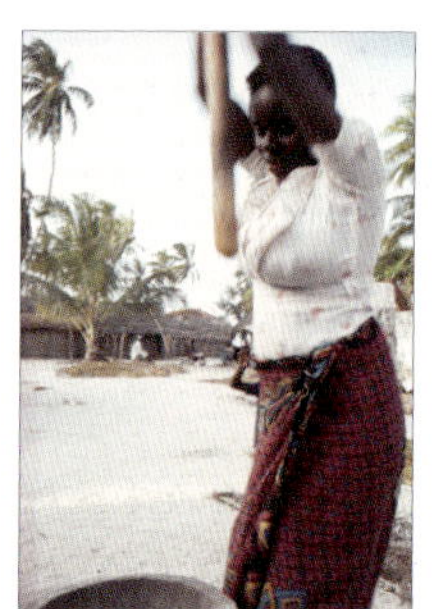

Tanzania along the coast seems idyllic, with **enduring healthy tropical life** ... but soon one realizes that having enough fish and grain is not enough to make a living today. Fish has no price here, and the men have gone searching for work in town, leaving the women behind. Living without any income is impossible even under a palm tree!

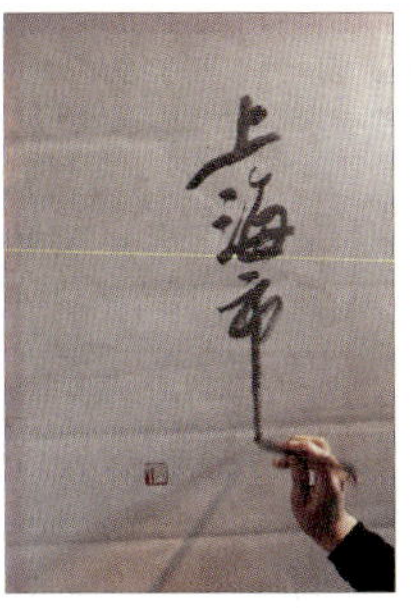

Working on the article about Shanghai I got the idea for a title photo: **"Shang Hai City"** in three strokes.

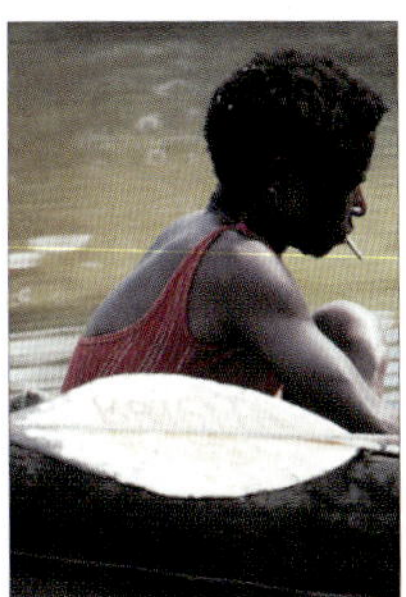

According to the mythology of the Sepic people, Papua New Guinea, there were only **women** at the beginning, and they invented men. Even today women do everything to ensure the smooth running of everyday life, and men stand aside, trying to control the spiritual side of life. It seems that people here are ever threatened by nature ... on a different track ... far from man's ways of controlling nature and creativity.

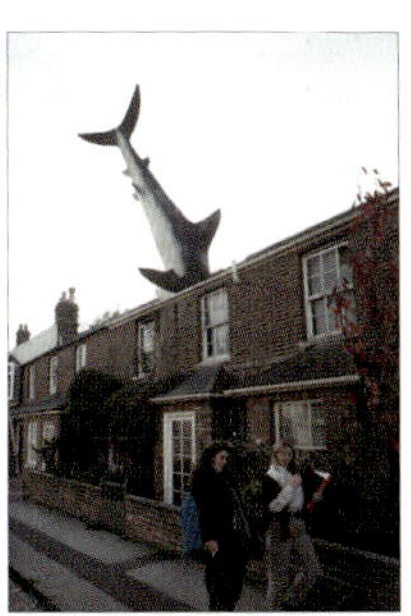

Probably **one gets used** to it. At first the neighbors got mad, now it is becoming a new symbol for Oxford – an artist's house.

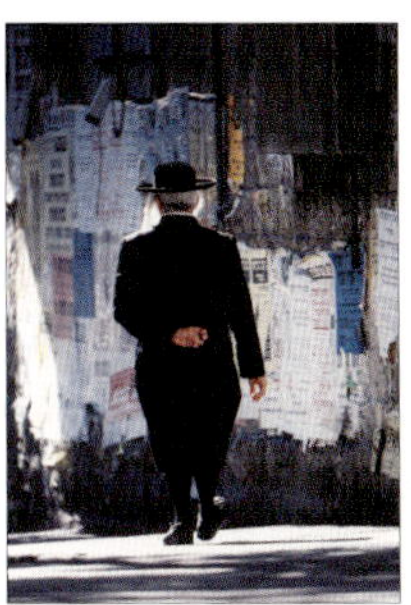

Mea Sharim – ultra-orthodox district in Jerusalem. It took me a while to understand that all these paper-posters are actually obituaries ...

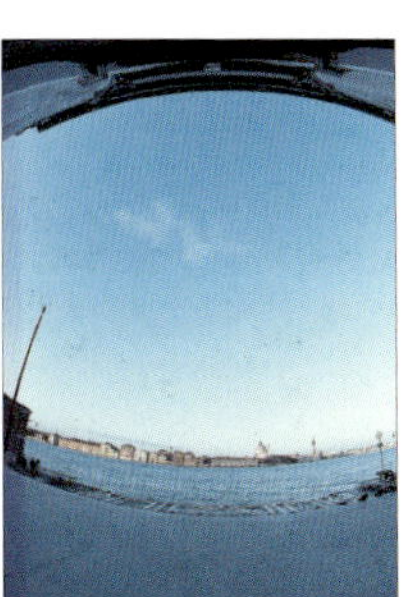

Palladio's Redentore Church in Venice is for many (books) one of **Palladio's** architectural riddles. I was here twice, both times due to a book by my friend, the sculptor Marko Pogacnik. His explanation of the Redentore Church being an instrument which, together with another two Palladio churches, creates a court of sound, in which the outside vibrations approaching the town are brought in tune with ... caught me.

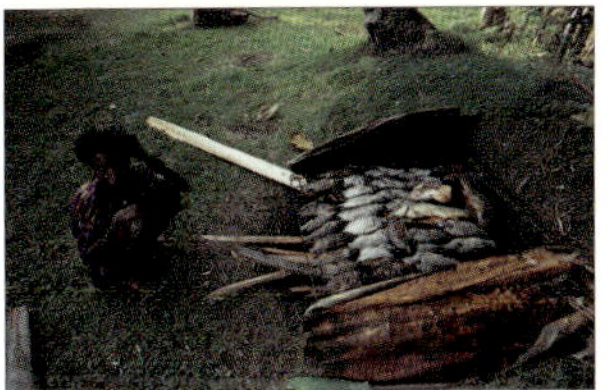

Drying fish as well as fishing is a woman's task in the land around the Sepic river, Papua New Guinea. There are plenty of fish in the Sepic river but fishing is dangerous as there are plenty of crocodiles waiting to attack.

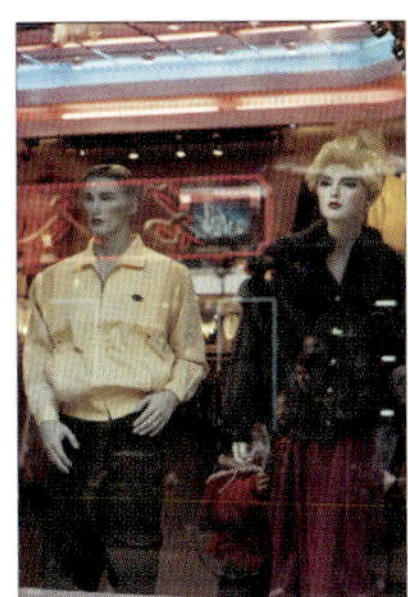

Sweet beginning, Shanghai City, 1991. For the second time capitalism is entering China through Shanghai ...

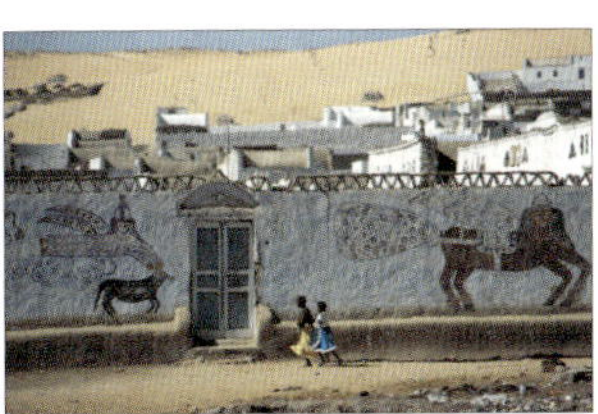

Only the river Nile divides Aswan, North Egypt, from a **Nubian village,** which is being modernized; but the Nubians still insist on their own lifestyle of isolation.

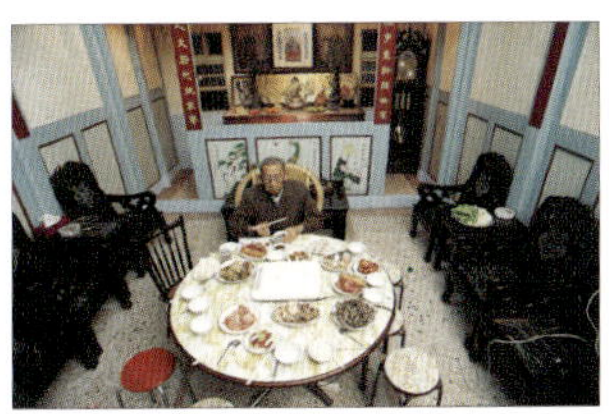

Over a hundred members of the Chiang family live in the village of Lukang, South Taiwan. The family has maintained ownership of the land for the past 300 years. On New Year's Eve, four generations of the direct descendants of the Chiang family gathered in the family shrine for a dinner consisting of the traditional dish – **hot pot.**

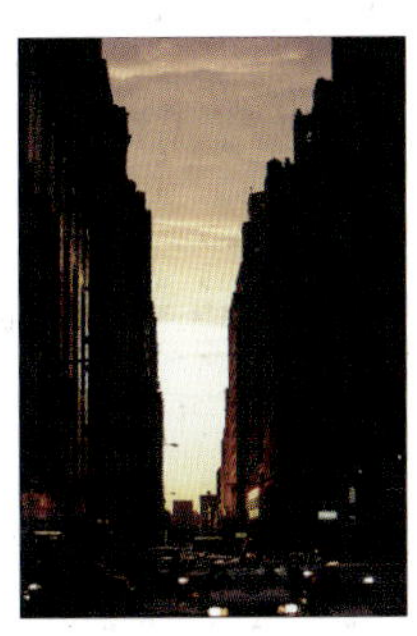

The Ethiopian Coptic **"Round Church"** has an altar in the middle. The church is divided into sections for women and men, who are separated by a curtain, but rituals are performed in front of both sides simultaneously.

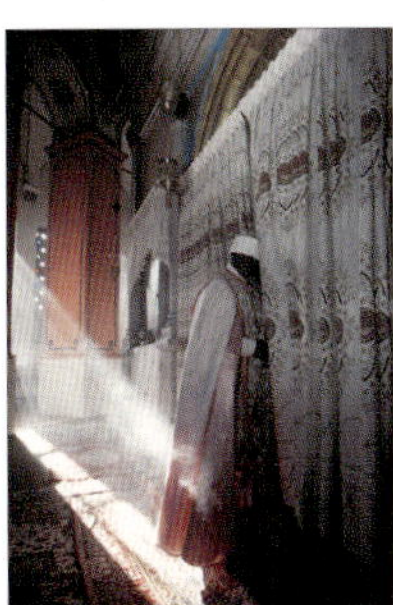

In a precise parallelogram, the grid of **Manhattan avenues,** one can gaze from East to West and from North to South, New York.

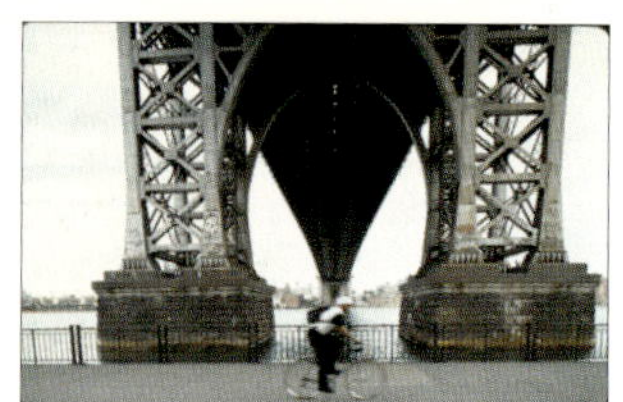

Most of the coast around Manhattan is a **walking & biking area** only, New York.

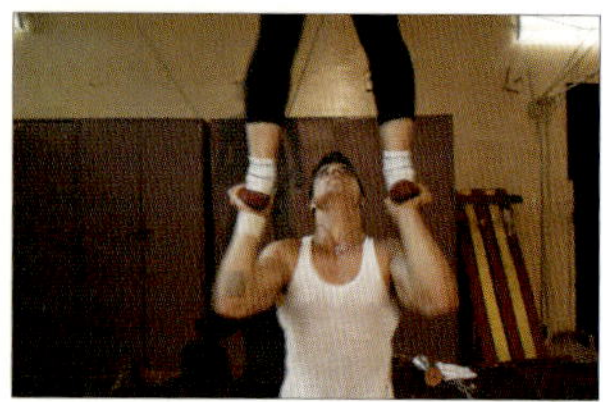

At one time Moscow's famous **circus school** was only for the best (who came from all over the USSR, Eastern Europe, China ...), for those who passed difficult exams and were selected – 1 out of every 600 candidates. Today, interest in working for a circus has decreased, but the school still tries to remain elite amongst the few left in the world. Vanjicka during her 1st class training hours, Moscow, 1993.

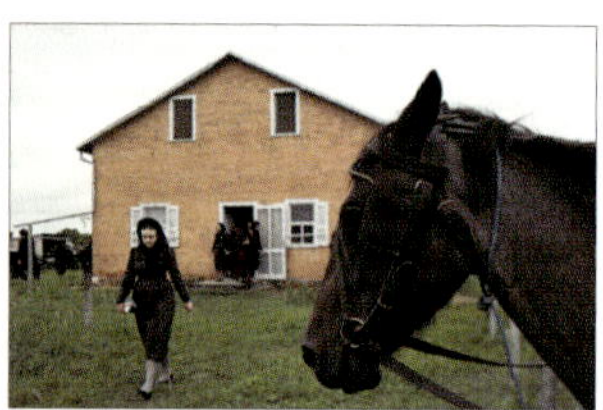

It won't be easy – but if you are a virgin, prepared to have a lot of children, you desperately want to stop reading, listening to music, watching TV and driving a car, and if you want to use the Holy Bible as the ultimate and only source of information for the rest of your life, you might have the chance of becoming a **Mennonite**. End of a Sunday morning mass – Mennonite community in Bolivia.

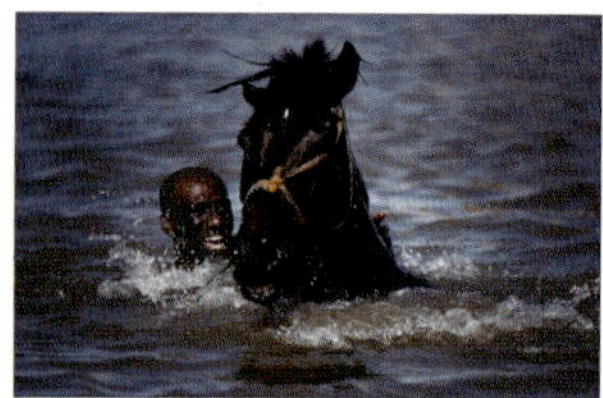

In the Nile, Sudan.

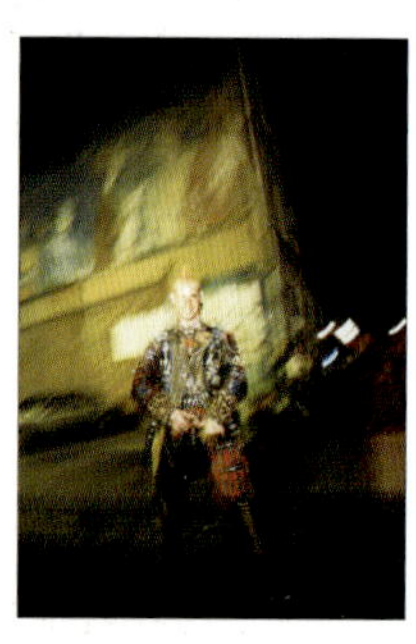

CBGB club & motherland **for punks**. However, as teenagers are not allowed to enter clubs, they mark their territory outside. New York, 1995.

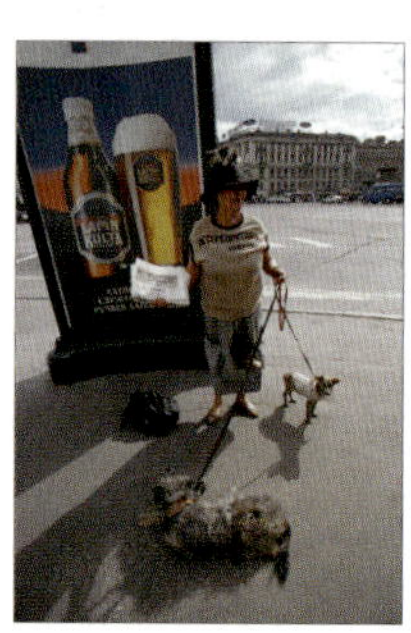

"Onewomanband," Mira Koprijanova, editor, publisher and saleswoman for her own independent newspaper for animal protection, distributes free copies to everyday passers-by, at Nevsky Prospect, St. Petersburg's main street. The project is financially subsidized by a religious organization, but this only covers the printing costs, all the other work, she says, is her mission in life.

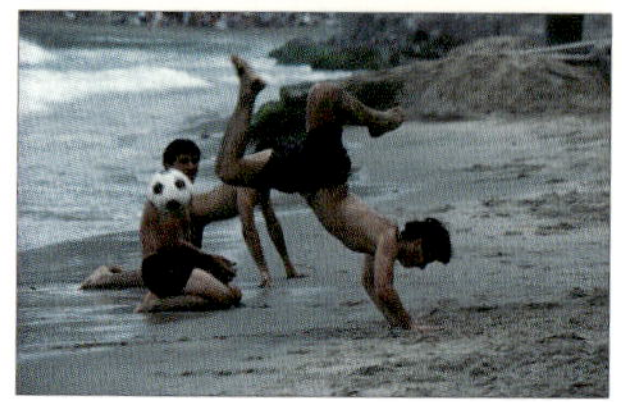

This picture could have been taken anywhere around the globe ... The one and only, universal **football** game. Gibraltar, 1996.

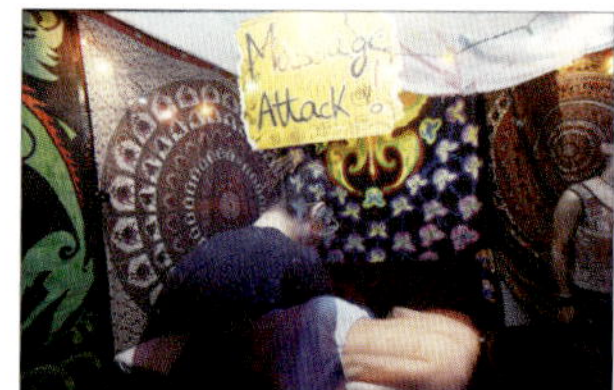

Rave party side room, Pendragon venue, London, 1998.

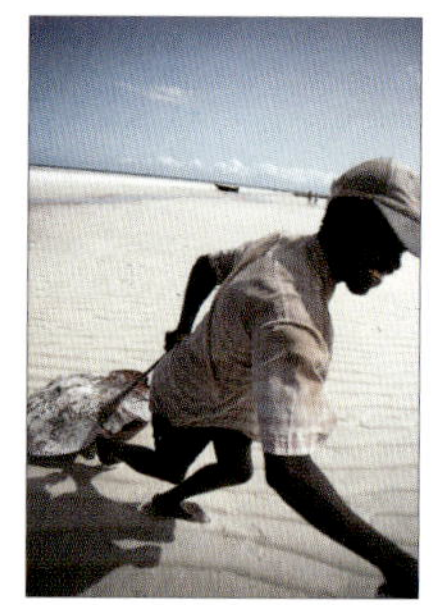

There are **still plenty of fish** in the waters of Tanzania. The rhythm of fishing is dictated by low and high tide. The coral reef is a good place to fish but also an impassable obstacle when the low tide comes in. Any boats which don't make it back before the end of the high tide are trapped in the open sea outside the reef. The fish are sold at small outdoor "markets," on the beach, and are later transported to the main markets in town.

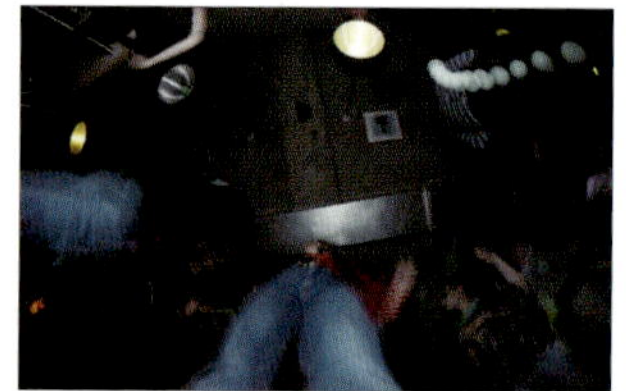

Make love not war on ecstasy. Rave party, Ljubljana, Slovenia, 1996.

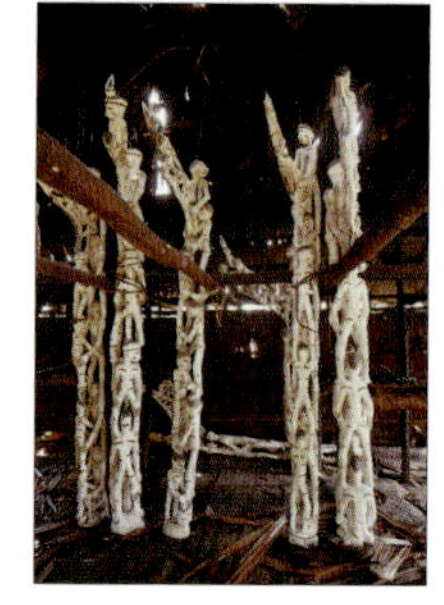

On the 18th of November 1961 Michael Rockefeller, a millionaire's son, went to collect ancestral poles, **Mbis**, for American museums in the Asmat – the swampy mangrove forest region of Irian Jaya, Indonesia, at the time still known for rituals involving head hunting. He never returned, and most probably his skull was one of the last that the Asmat used for the ritual installation of the Mbis. It was an unfortunate coincidence that the Otjanep, after months of hard work, had just finished several Mbis to protect their homes, underneath which they needed to position the skull of a white man, in order to be able to revenge the death of warriors who had been killed by the Dutch peacekeeping forces.

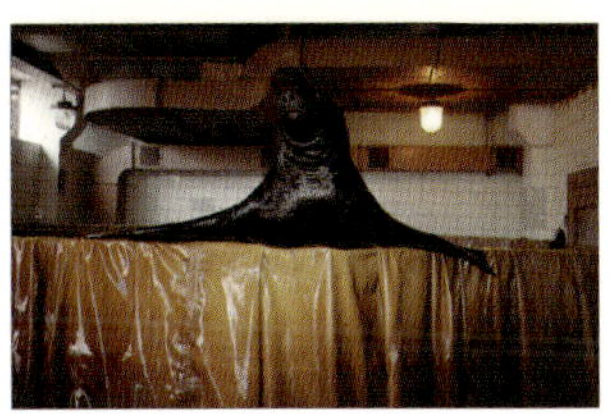

Perestrojka in Russia brought sea lions into the circus ... together with their trainer, scientist Nikolay Timchenko, who had previously been engaged in an army research program to detect nuclear weapons in the sea, with the help of his sea lions.

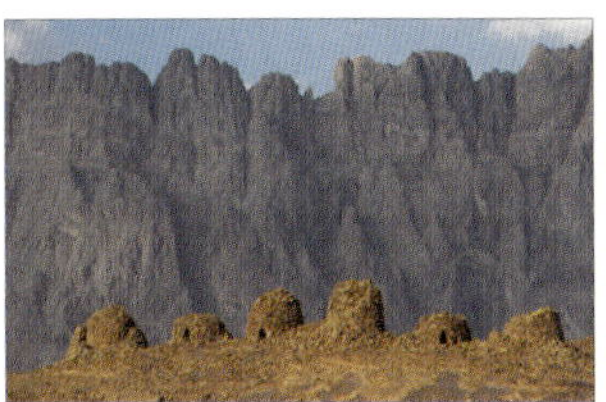

Nobody really knows the origin of the prehistoric tombs (3rd century B.C.) on **Mount Bat**, Oman.

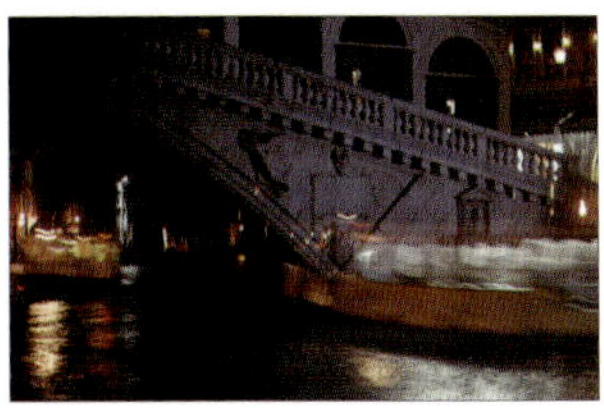

Rialto Bridge ... as one is able to feel it, but in reality it cannot be seen as such. This view is a composition of reflections and reality.

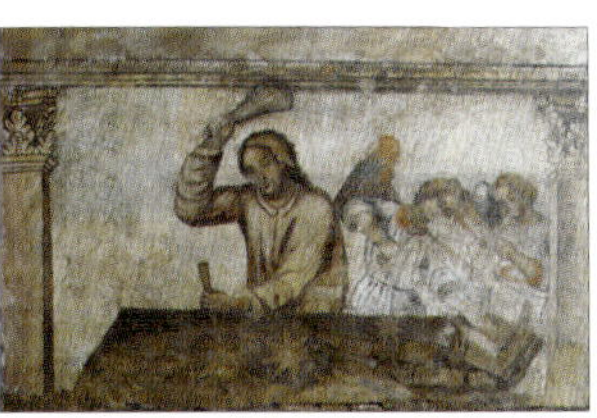

The poorly preserved frescoes of **Santa Rosa** in Paraguay are just a simple illustration of the former excellence which could be seen on the walls of Jesuit Mission churches in the 17th and 18th centuries.

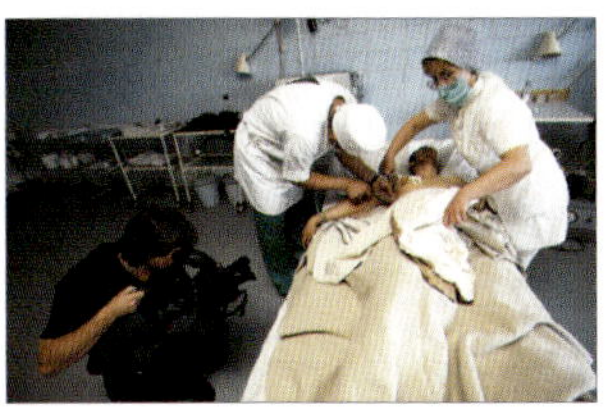

TV Channel 5 doing a report on drug abuse, St. Petersburg, 1997. **A man lying in a coma** as a result of an overdose of heroin. Heavy drugs are easily available in clubs and cafes, especially in St. Petersburg. Three reanimation beds are the only chance for those who have overdosed on drugs, bad alcohol or pills. Work with patients is proclaimed as a research program.

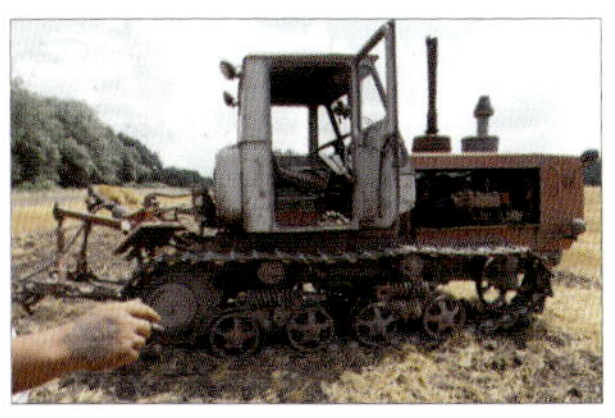

Flower power in Russia, 1997: Kolkhoz, collective agriculture, is still alive: "In practice we now have more problems with selling, storing wheat and maintaining all this old machinery ... not to mention the overall changes taking place in the agricultural system."

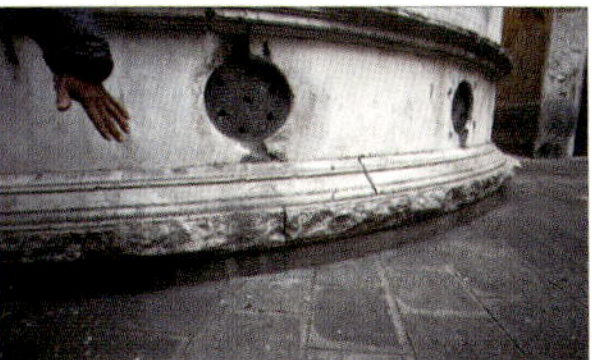

Through the hand. Marko Pogacnik, a sculptor and writer can actually feel the energy patterns of the place ... Venice, San Fantin, 1997.

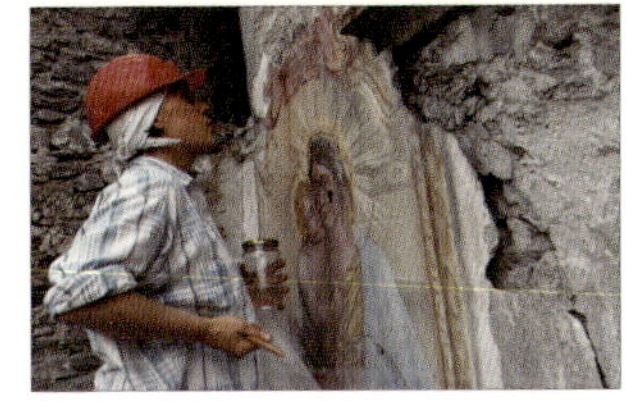

"At least the **frescoes** should be preserved," was the decision of Ken Marquardt, who moved, together with his family, from the States to Italy and started a restoration project in the small historical village of Ca'nova.

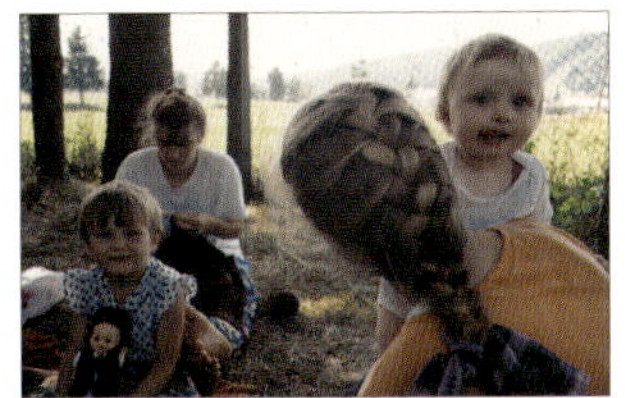

When I sent photos of Bosnian refugees in the camps to my agent, his comment was, "No good, no guns, no tension, no tragedy." My argument for this photo was: blond and blue-eyed people, which is contrary to the stereotypical image of a dark-haired and dark-skinned **Balkan people.**

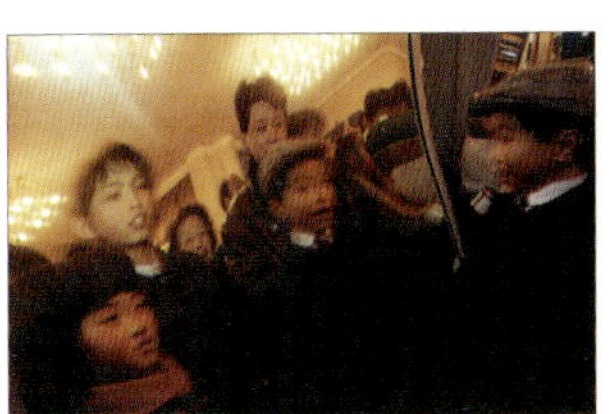

"Great World" in Shanghai, 1992, before the "New World" inherited the charisma of being the best amusement place in town.

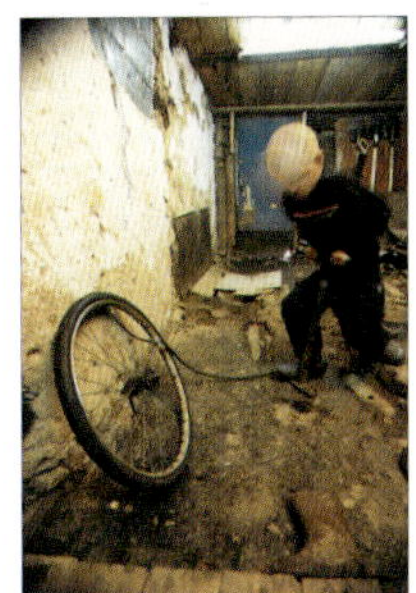

For children life goes on ... Alexandrovsk, once an important industrial town in Russia. After the closure of the TV factory "Record," it became a place where the majority are unemployed and desperate in the everyday struggle for survival, 1997.

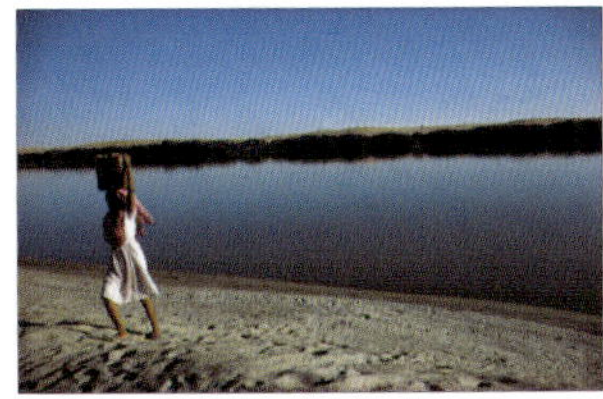

Why are there no hydroponic food cultivation farms along the desert land of the Nile in Sudan, or solar water pumps to bring water to the houses? It seems that the **equilibrium** of the input and output of living is different in this part of the world.

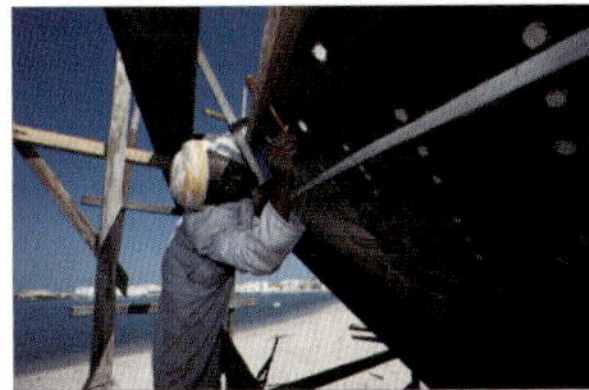

A dhow builder's yard in Sur, Oman, is famous for its long tradition of building Arab dhow sailing boats, which once navigated as far afield as India and the Cape of Good Hope. The masters do not use plans for construction.

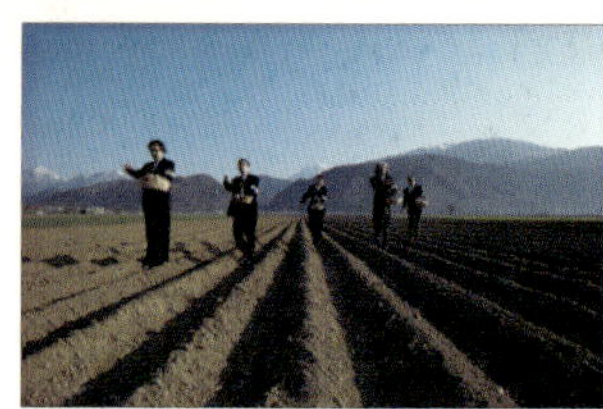

IRWIN – group of Slovenian artists-painters. In 1992, in collaboration with fellow NSK (Neue Slowenische Kunst) groups, IRWIN opened several "NSK Embassies" throughout Europe and the world and redefined itself as a "State," as opposed to an "Organization:" the NSK State in Time. For NSK, as a State in Time (a state without territory), the Internet is naturally an ideal medium. Thus, "NSK Electronic Embassy Tokyo," whose first virtual embassy corresponds perfectly with their wish that different groups be linked together within the NSK collective and offered the possibility of opening links to an even wider audience.

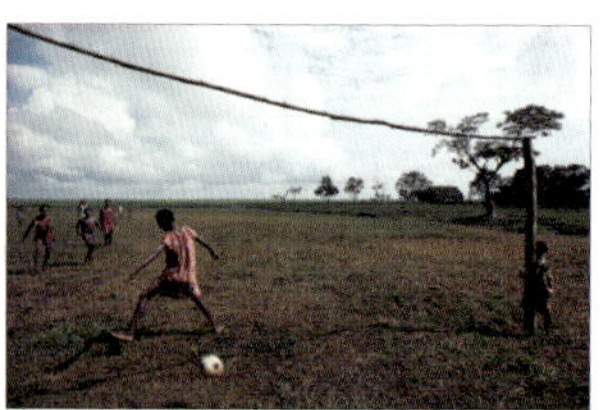

Village Kaminabit on the Black River ... of the Sepic river. A destination which can be reached only after days of canoeing on the river, Papua New Guinea.

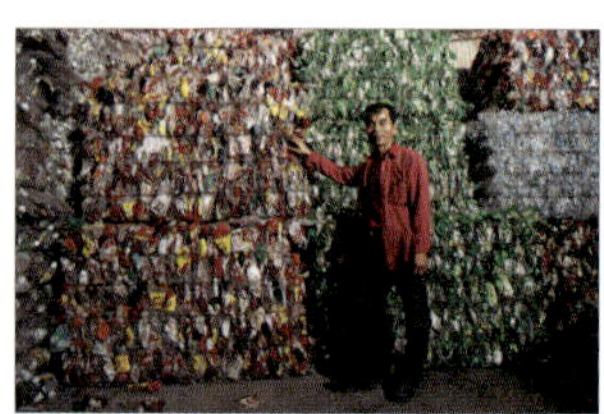

Taiwan, 1996: On an island of 36,000 km^2 and 21 million people, garbage has been a problem for many years. Four years ago the government started an expensive campaign of selective **garbage** collecting. Separate colored bins (for glass, plastics, batteries, paper, various garbage ...) were positioned all over the towns, but the recycling of materials was not well organized; everything ended up on the same rubbish heap, and the program failed. Now some of it (collecting and recycling) is done on a private basis.

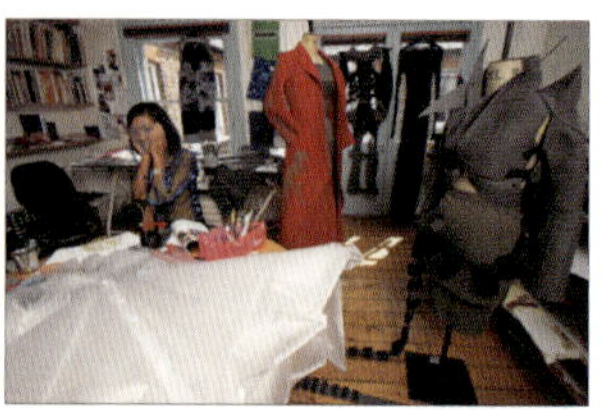

Michiko Koshino in her studio: running two studios simultaneously, one in Tokyo and one in London, moves her to the top of the fashion world where an agile mind is a must.

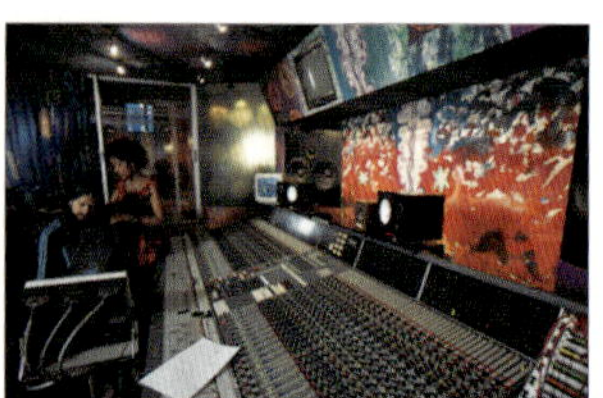

Strongroom (studio 1) sound studio in London, 1997, is known to be at the cutting edge of the state-of-the-art sound with its latest equipment.

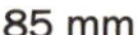

85 mm

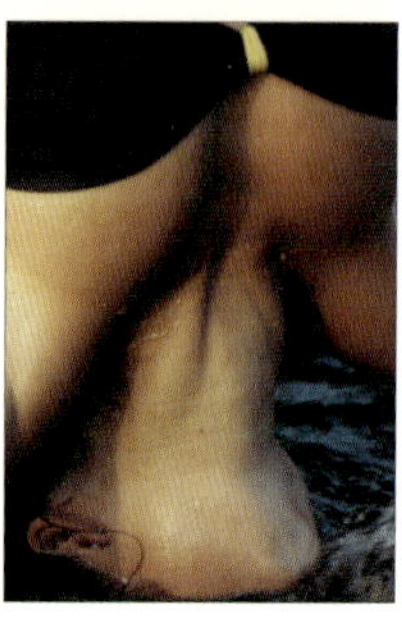

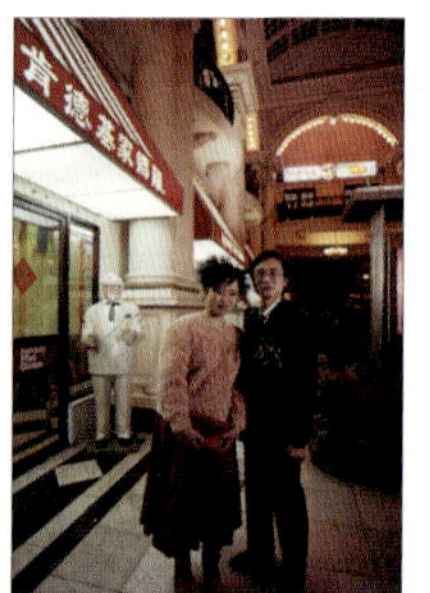

The Heart of Count Hanna von Auersperg: according to the legend he fell in love with the "wrong" (peasant) girl. His family objected to this relationship and sent him to the army. He could not bear the loss and killed himself on duty. His heart, embraced by the girl's red ribbon, is conserved and locked in the family's graveyard chapel close to the castle.

A complete melange of time and space – in the French Club, the old Shanghai building left over from the Concession times, cheap intrusion of American lifestyle – Cornel Sanders of **Kentucky** Fried Chicken, where a newly wed Chinese couple enjoyed their ceremonial lunch, 1992.

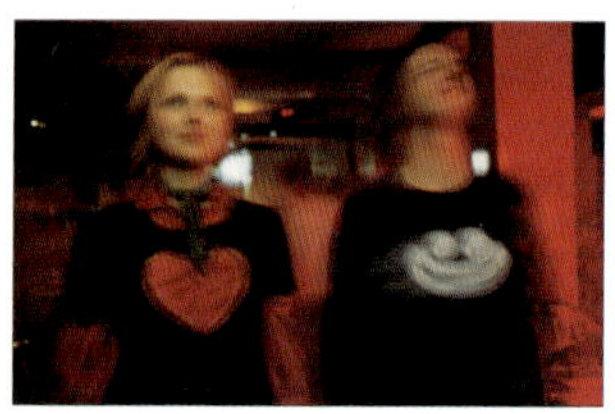

Robert Botteri **"in love"** is a journalist. For nine years he has been chief editor of "Mladina" (Youth), the leading, outspoken, independent weekly magazine, that openly played an essential role in Slovenia's gaining independence.

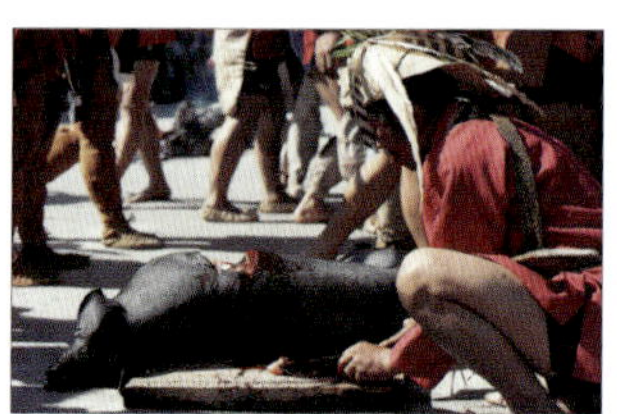

Respect was the message from the government, starting programs to support a small aboriginal community to preserve their culture. Aborigines in Taiwan have been living there for at least 11,000 years, but nowadays they are not able to compete within the aggressive modern society. Like native American Indians they suffer from poverty and alcoholism.

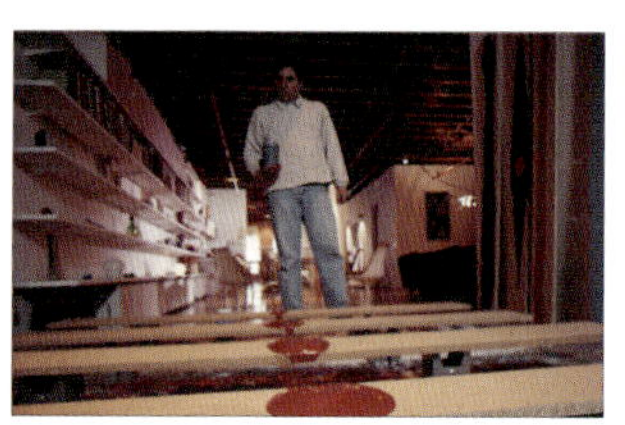

Robert Traboscia, an Italian architect in his Soho loft, home and studio, 1995. I came back Friday evening as Bob invited me to accompany him to a regular gathering of Soho community members. Caterina (also an architect) explained: "Having free time for the community is very American. In Italy nobody would give up Friday evenings for the community."

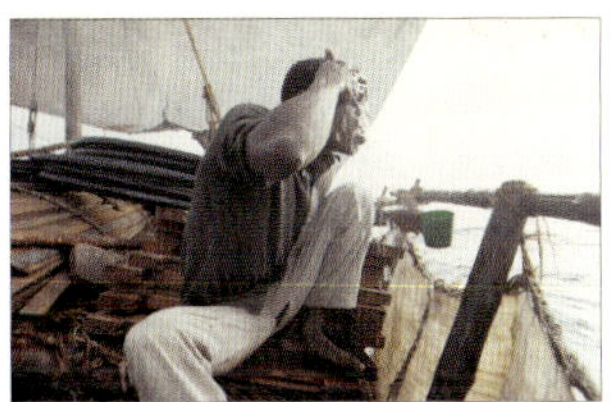

Ancient sailing boats – **dhows** are still used for cargo transport along the east African coast. Daily life on a dhow is a monotonous routine. The winds are fairly steady, and once sailing, the crew members are busy with their own small activities such as fishing, cooking, repairing sails, napping, searching for a shadow under the hot tropical sun, reading the Koran ...

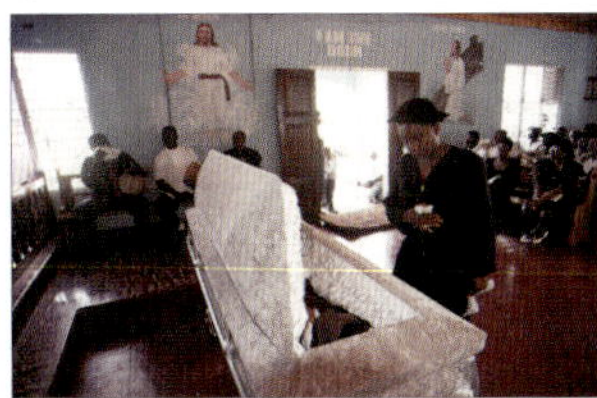

The last stop before the funeral was to hear the morning singing in the church. "Isn't it beautiful" were the words of the daughter of the deceased when the procession entered the church. For them, dying and death is a process for which the departing person needs a song and good spirits to depart in peace. "Hallelujah, hallelujah, hallelujah my lord!" the family and friends were singing all night (it should or could also be nine nights). It was a time to share love and unity for one of them.

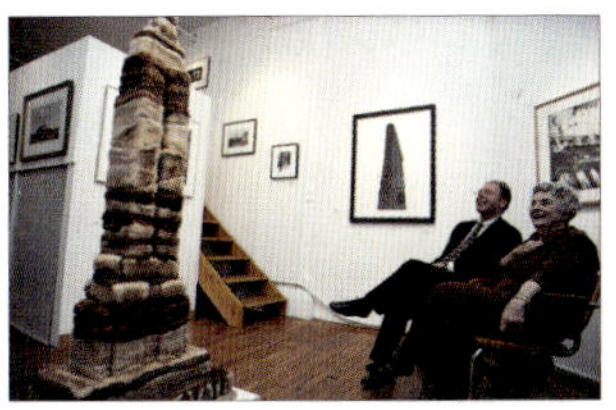

New York City **Landmarks** exhibition, New York, 1995.

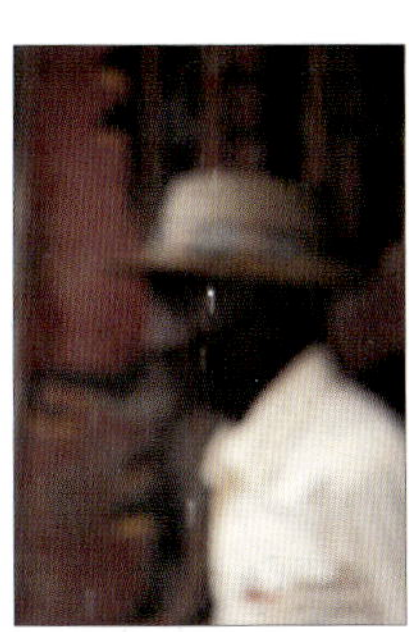

Maroons – mostly of Afro-Spanish origin, the breakaway slaves in 1658 established a base in the mountains, from where they attacked the English. After 100 years they gained independence and they still have their own rights today, living in the same areas as they did during the times of slavery.

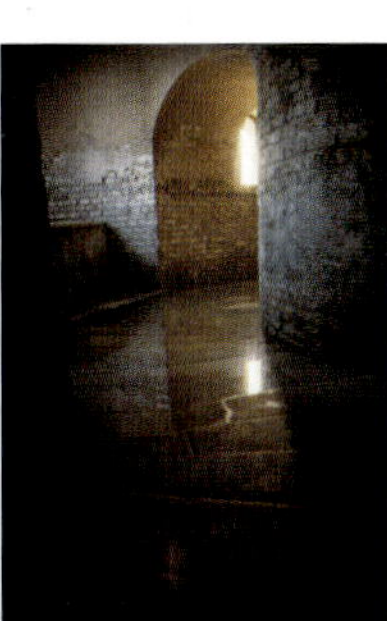

Torcello Island is the place where Venice was born. The church still has the original sacristy as a round corridor around the altar which one crosses over on the water.

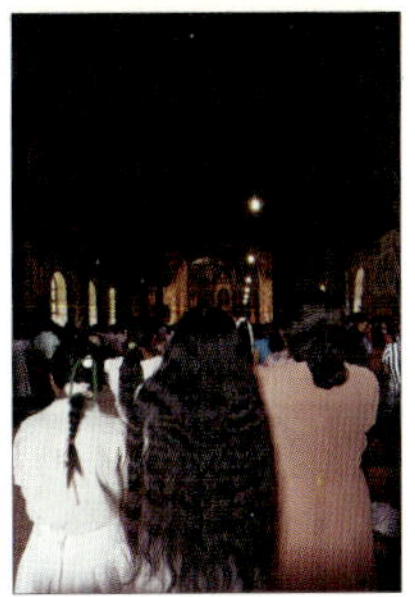

1991: **Mystery** or a mistake? After the "War of the Triple Alliance" between Argentina, Brazil and Paraguay in 1865–1870, only the Jesuit Mission's ruins remained ... an exception from this period are the few Chiquito tribal churches in remote parts of Bolivia which are still thriving. Lately, they were recognized by UNESCO as part of the World Historical Heritage, and careful restoration of these few churches continues.

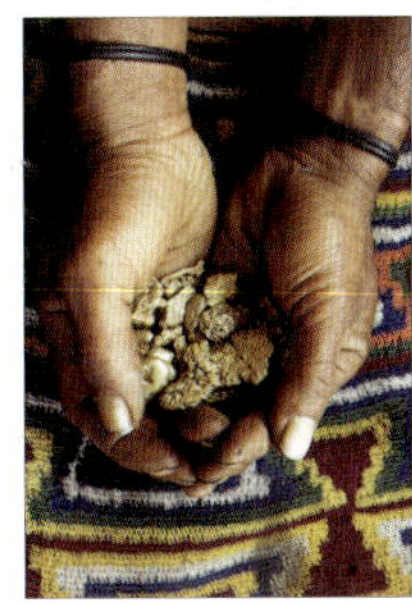

Golden nuggets of all sizes found on Mount Kare, Papua New Guinea. The biggest one was worth 1,700,000 US dollars.

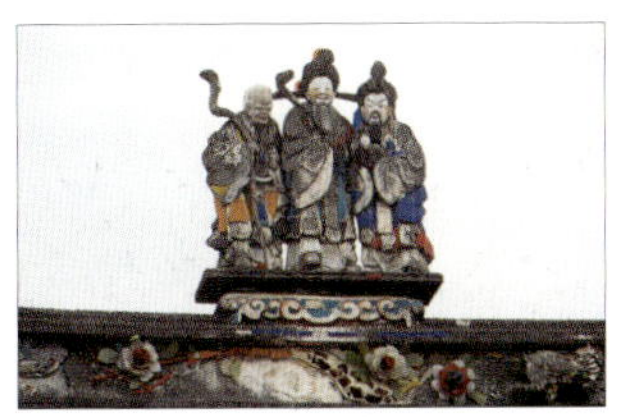

Patron saints on the roof of a traditional Chinese house, Taiwan.

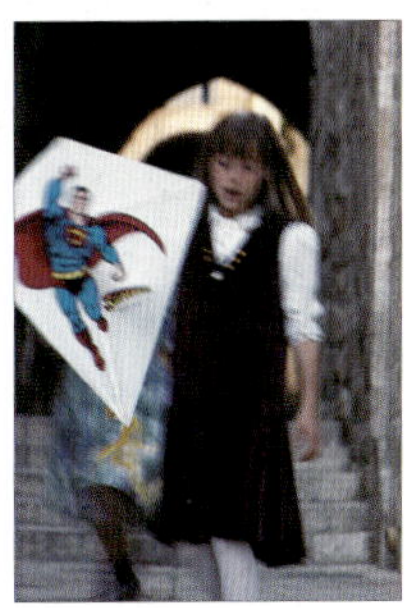

Shabbat in Jerusalem. At sunset on Friday you have to stop all your activities in respect for Jewish tradition, which is very much present, especially in the Jewish quarter of Old Jerusalem where even as a foreigner you insult merely by pressing the button on your camera ... so this was my last photo in the sunset light of the day.

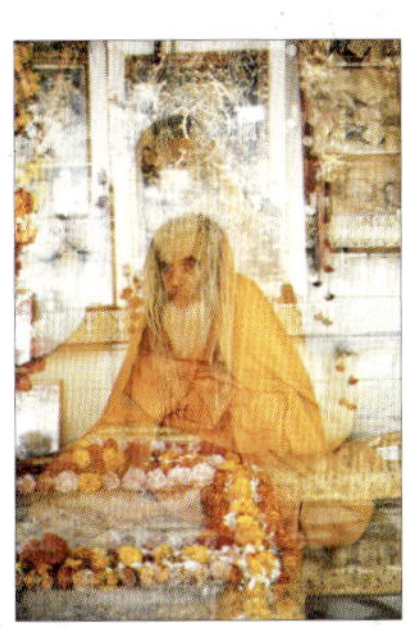

Dev Giri Baba, a spiritual person (naga baba) with no material belongings or worldly interests ...

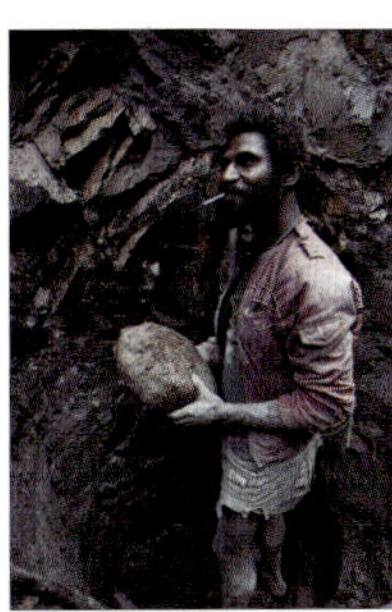

Gold rush, Papua New Guinea: for the Papuans, money itself (as a physical object) has an incredible "power." In their minds, money is still something one needs to collect or take, not simply a reward for work. Gold is just something in between.

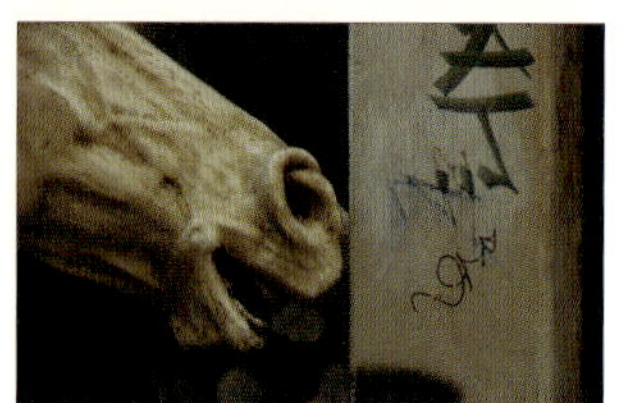

Venice: the **horses** protruding from San Marco's facade were always an enigma for me ... it appears as strange as if the horses were leaping out of a coral reef. Well, this one was in a shop which sold Venetian carnival masks.

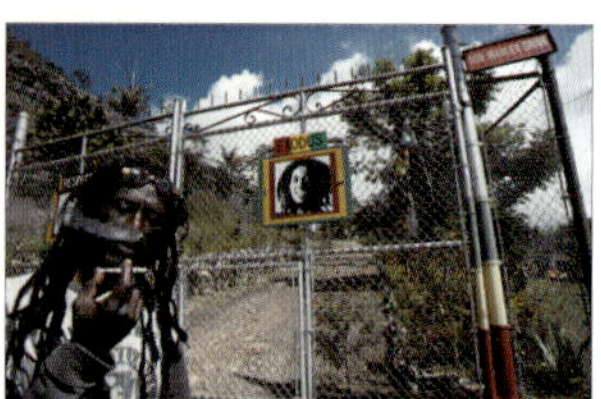

Mr. **Guardian** at the door of Bob Marley's house, which is actually Bob's birth place, Jamaica, 1995.

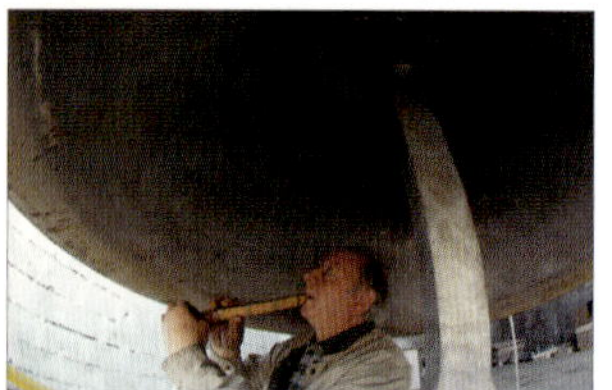

In 1996 the **little country** of Slovenia was totally stressed: the Pope announced he was coming. A new set of enormous church bells was made for the occasion ...

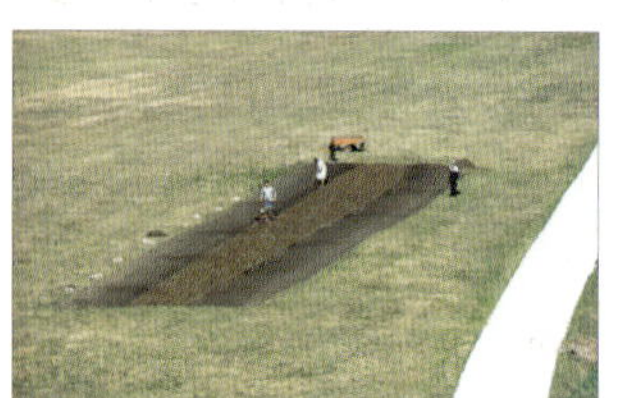

Trenta valley in Slovenia, **potato spring.**

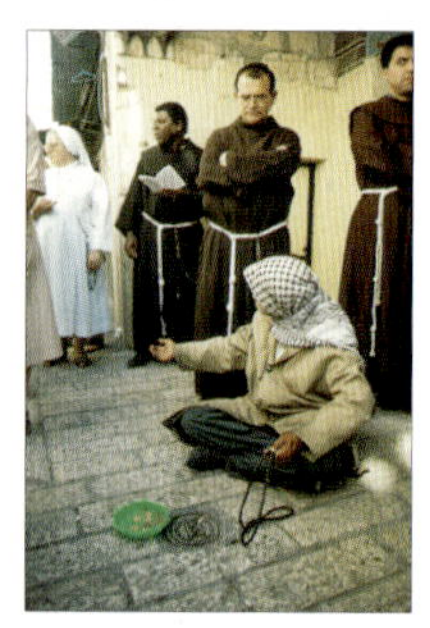

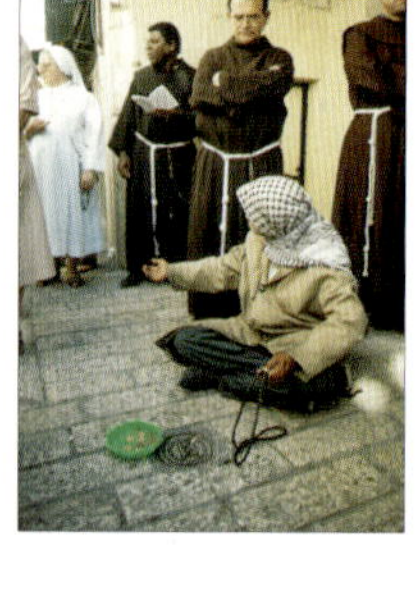

The regular weekend procession along Via Dolorosa which is considered to be the authentic **way of the cross** taken by Jesus.

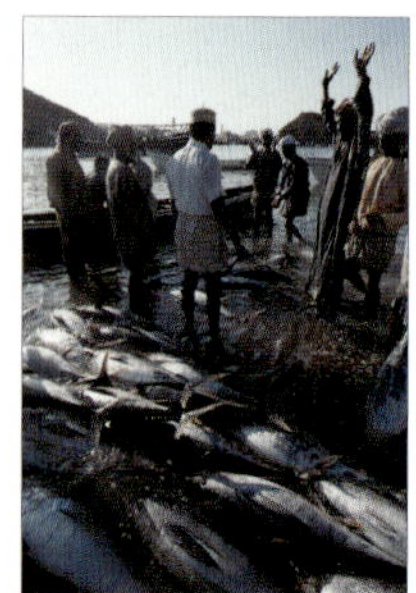

Plenty of fish in the Arabian sea ... **Allah** ...

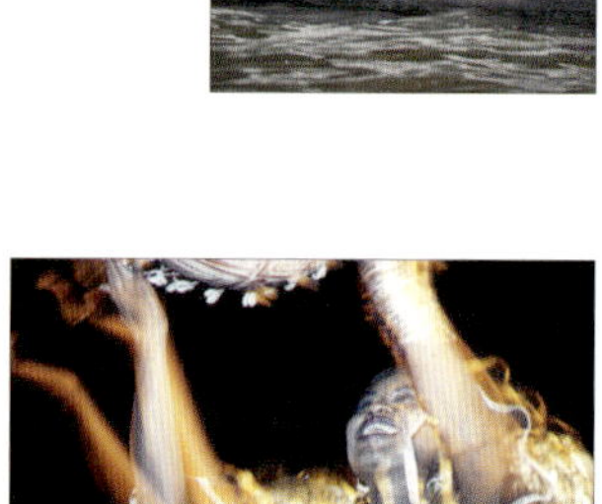

Meat, as any other meat, is distributed among all members of the tribe. It is known that Chinese meat is more tasty than the Indonesian, whilst the toughest is the white one. The constant conflict with the Indonesian army has once and for all ended, but head hunting only came to an end with the passive persuasion of the missionaries. Asmat, Irian Jaya, Indonesia.

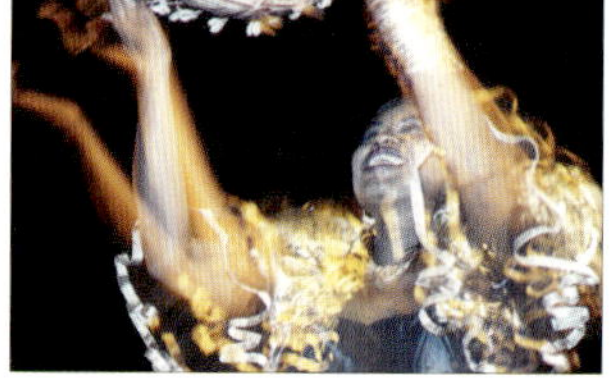

Ouomo Sangave, black mother, black beauty, black heart and a rainbow voice – on her European tour, 1995.

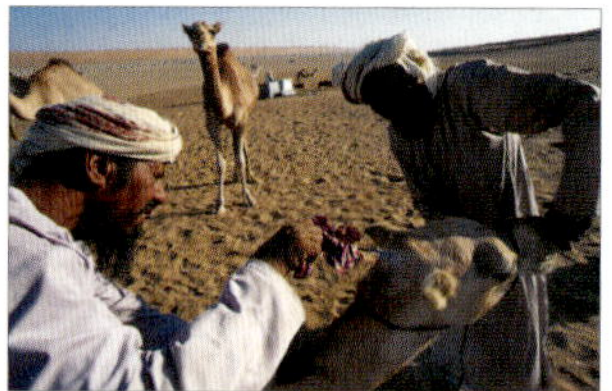

"Doctor was here!"
Acupuncture with a red-hot needlelike iron prod inserted into the head was a kind of instant treatment for her disease.

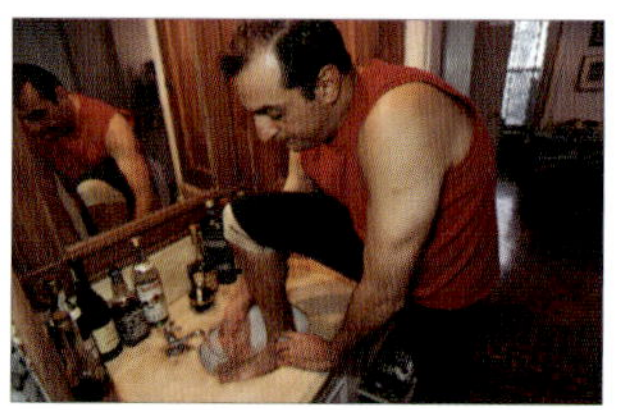

L. E. Joseph for the 2nd time.
As a writer it was easy for him to understand ... my wish to photograph him washing his feet after a jog.

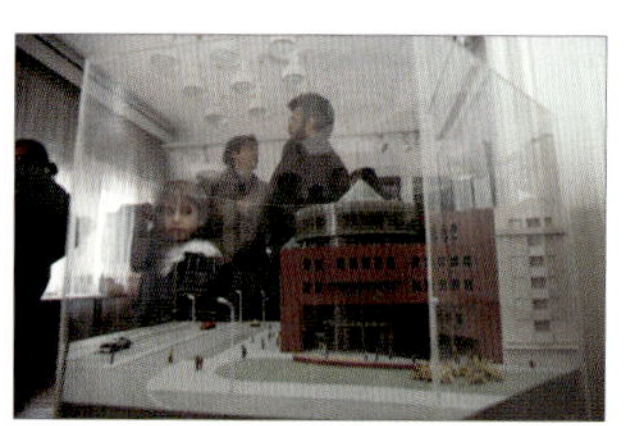

Belgrade, Yugoslavia, 1993. It was like in a dream ... the opening of an architecture exhibition in the days of no hope for the future and of desperate war propaganda.

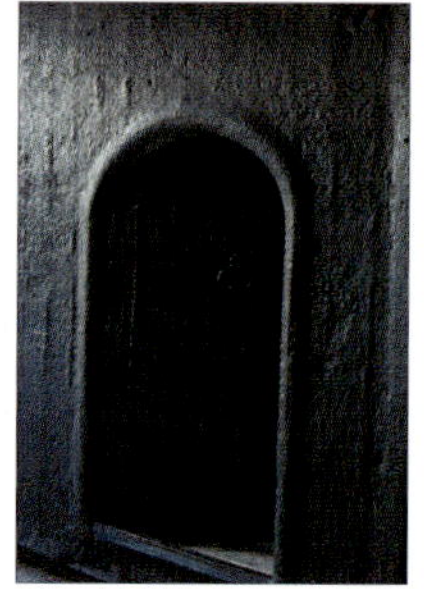

Main **entrance** to the Armenian Quarter, which is separated by a high wall within the town walls of Old Jerusalem.

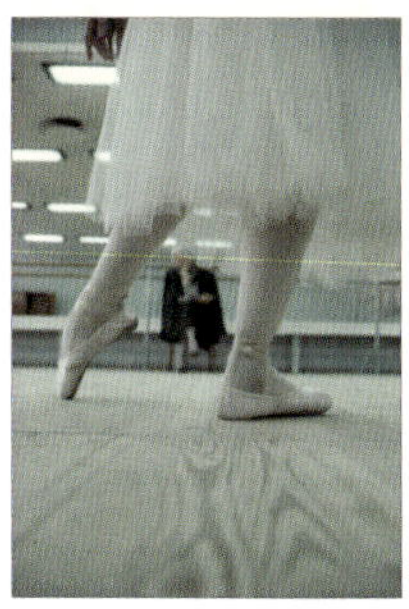

Mariinsky Ballet Company in St. Petersburg, 1993. **Primadonna** ballerina during her long training hours, with a tutor or two correcting her.

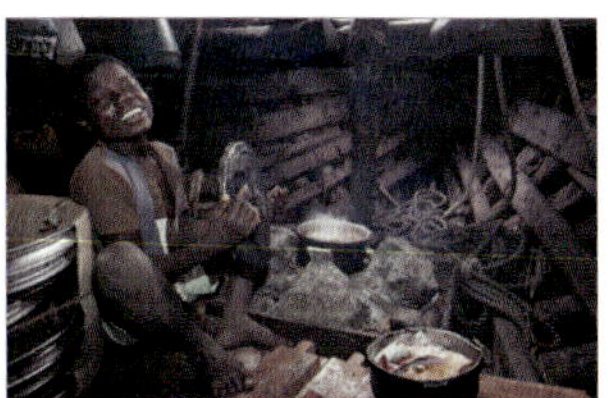

So young and **already cooking** meals for the ten people of the cargo sailing boat crew. It is a responsible task to cook on an open fire on a wooden boat, Tanzania.

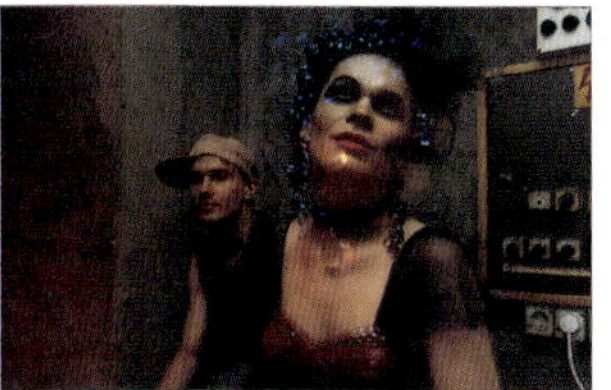

"My **artistic name** is Emperatrice" – During the day she is a he ...

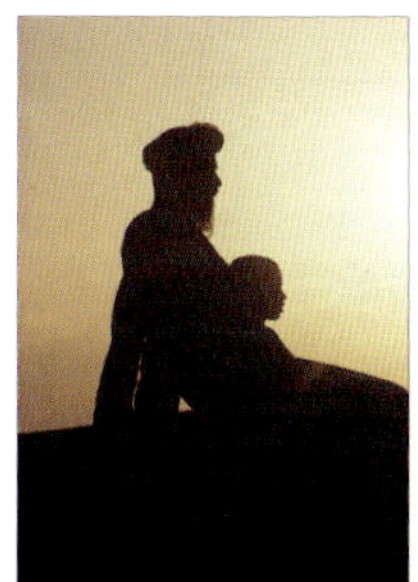

Growing up in the sand, Oman.

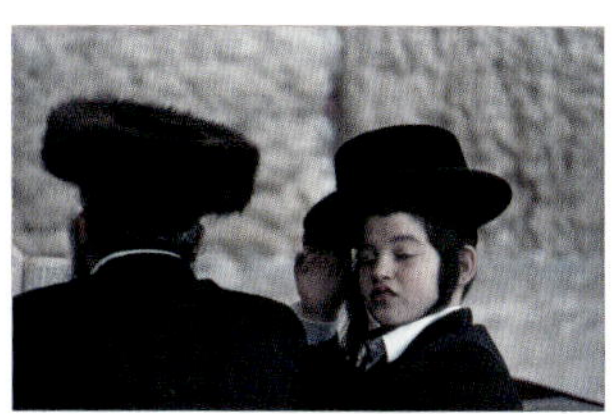

Next to **the holiest place** for the Jews – the Western Wall, Jerusalem.

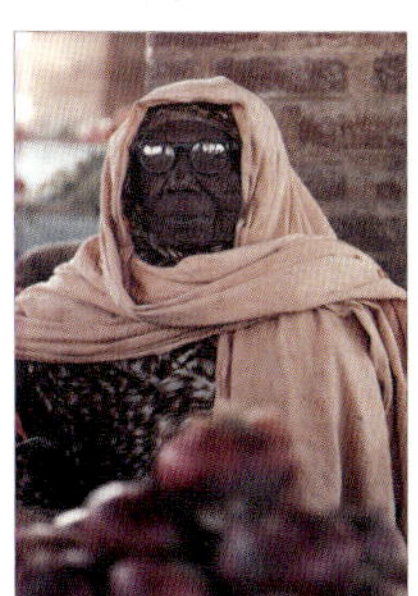

Mama Dongola. Vegetable market in Dongola, Sudan, came as a big surprise – they didn't allow people to take photos – they screamed, "No, no tasuir!" (no photos), and soon afterwards policemen came and took me to the other side of town – without any explanation, just to while away time. When they released me the market was over! For three days! Then the same story again – but the lady selling onions was cool, observing me and letting me observe her. I was back in my heart.

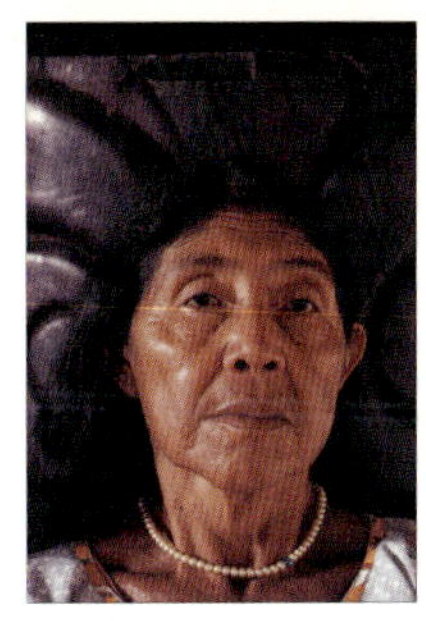

Chiquito Indian, Bolivia. Christianity has proved to be a universal message in South America since, after the total slaughter and destruction of their culture, the Indian survivors accepted it.

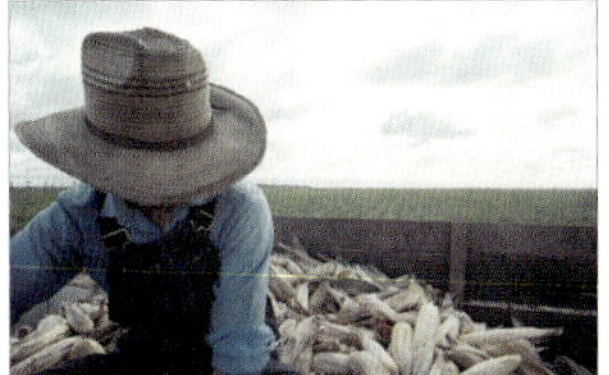

Riva Palacios and Swift Current Mennonite colonies in Bolivia, both founded in 1967, were the creation of dissenting fundamentalist groups, who previously settled in Mexico. Their origins are Prussian, they speak an archaic Plattdeutsch language and they are – of course – self-sufficient.

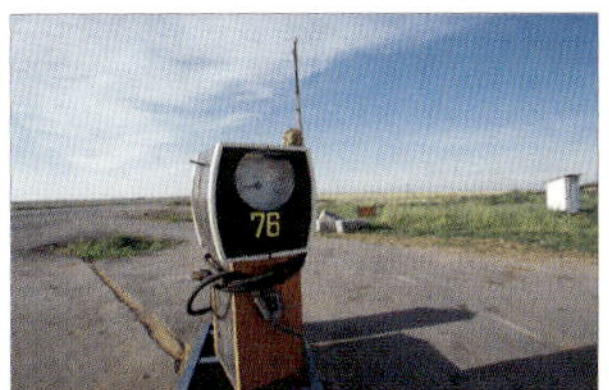

Petrol station on a highway to Saratov, Russia, 1997. Gasprom, Lukhoid and other oil companies in Russia are at the center of the new Russian economic changes. Within a few years, some people have become amongst the richest on earth. On the outside nothing has changed much since socialist times ...

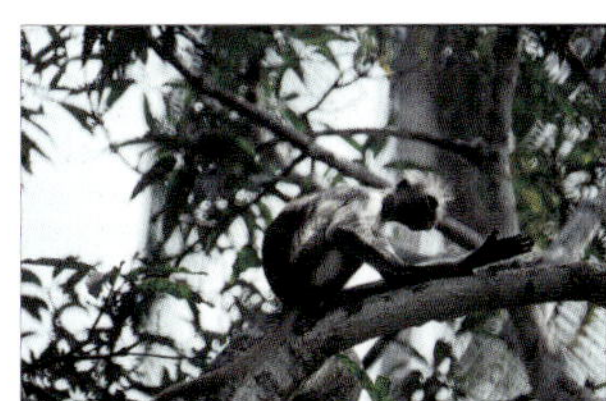

The Red Colobus monkey, called **Zanzibar Kirkiis,** an endemic species, which only lives in the Jozani Forest and can be found nowhere else on earth, Zanzibar, 1991.

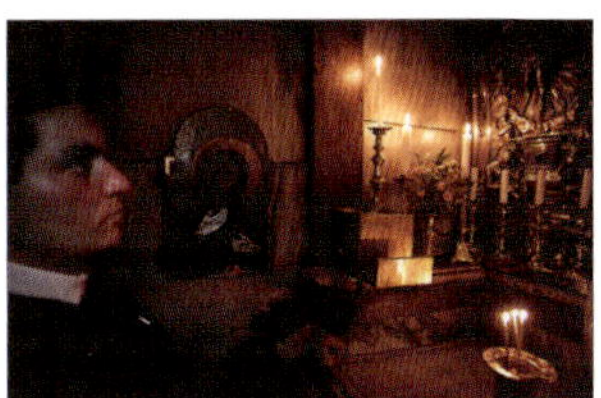

Christ's grave – Inside the Chapel of the Angels of the Holy Sepulchre, the holiest spot for Christians.

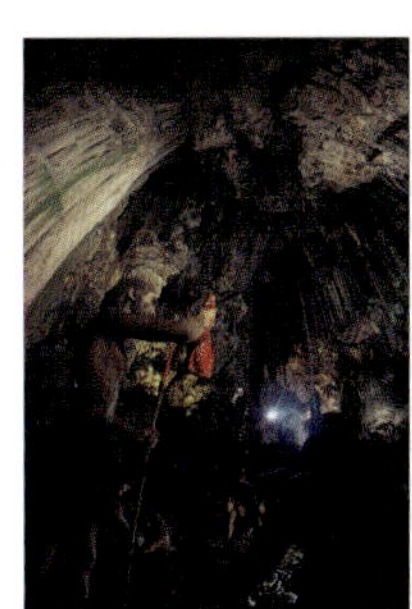

St. Michael's Cave has supposedly been inhabited since **Neolithic times**. The Cathedral Cave was long believed to be bottomless, which gave rise to a tale that there exists a subterranean passage of over 15 miles, allegedly linking Gibraltar to Africa.

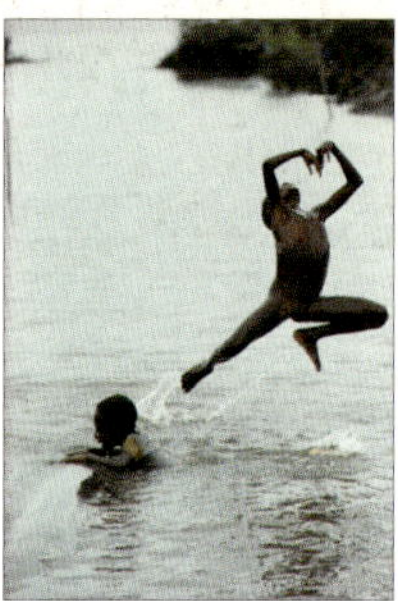

In Northern Irian Jaya, Indonesia, the village children know **nothing about schools** ...

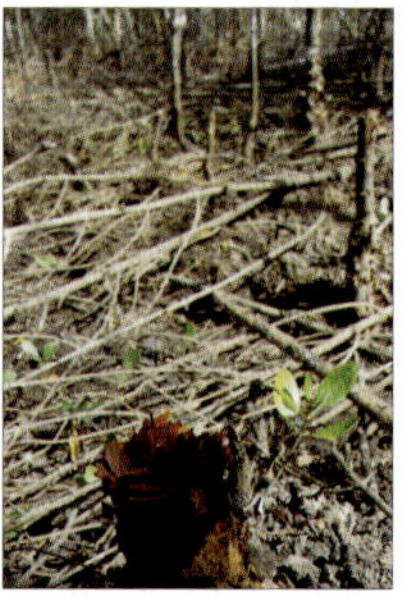

Overexploited tropical mangrove forest. Mangroves proved to be a natural barrier protecting the inner countries from the devastating consequences of the many destructive typhoons and hurricanes. The natives use root-trees, "Rhizophora," as the safest form of windshield protection. The mangroves accumulate organic mud and thus produce new soil and land. In 1292, when Marco Polo visited Palembang on Sumatra, the town was a port. Today it lies 50 km away from the coast.

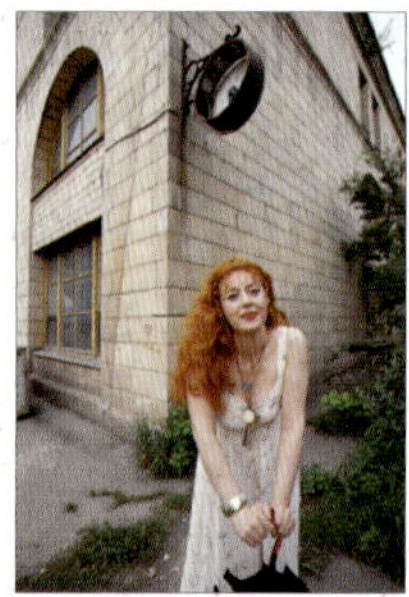

Mosfilm in Moscow, 1997 – **ex-Hollywood** of the Russian film industry. Watches stopped at Mosfilm. As part of the city of Moscow, a town for a huge movie industry is now in "the process of privatization."

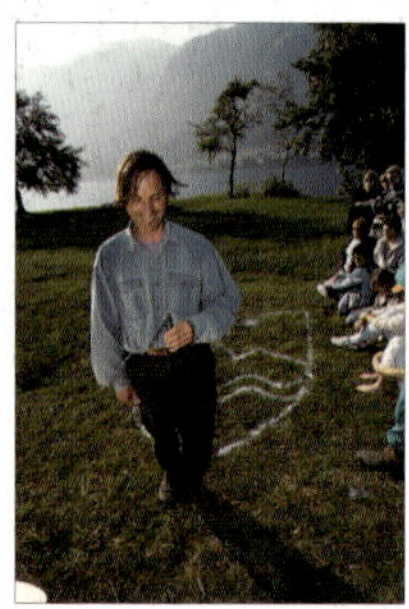

Marko Pogacnik: artist, philosopher, designer of the Slovene national coat of arms; demonstrating the energy field whilst crossing its form. When the parliament decided to accept the design, he performed the same demonstration. His message is very simple: "Everyday life offers enormous opportunities for harmonious and responsible acts. However, it all depends on whether a man is prepared to listen to his own inner microcosm or just blindly marches over the Earth."

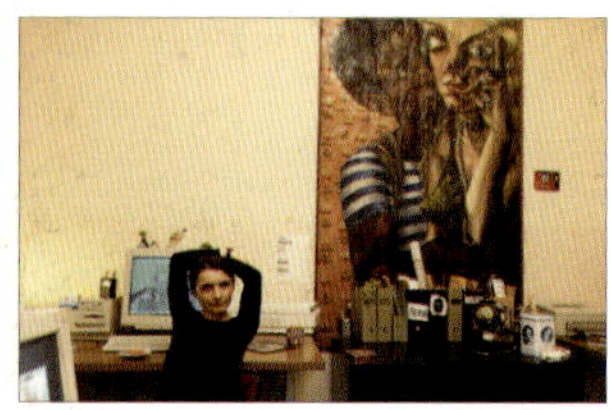

Tanja Radeš – graphic designer. Whenever I meet her in or out of her studio-it is "same-same," she always lifts my spirits ...

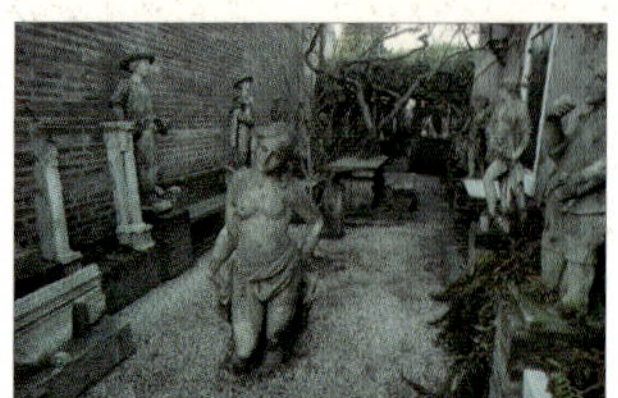

"Dry Venice" – Garden on Torcello Island, Venice.

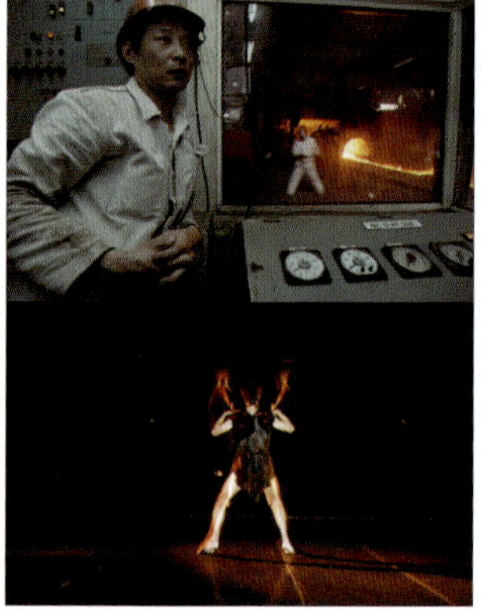

How can I defend these two photos as the last pair? "Inner and outer world, the ultimate opposites, final mirror ... the random logic of the butterfly **effect** ..."

BOJAN BRECELJ

Biografie

1953	geboren in Ljubljana, Slowenien.
1982	Anerkennung als freier Künstler und Fotograf durch den Sachverständigenrat des Ministeriums für Kultur der Republik Slowenien.
Seit 1988	hauptberuflicher, freischaffender Fotojournalist für verschiedene internationale Zeitschriften.
Seit 1990	Mitglied der International Federation of Journalists.
1991–1992	fester Mitarbeiter der Pressebildagentur Gamma Press Images, Paris.
Seit 1992	assoziiertes Mitglied von Still Pictures (Fotoagentur mit Schwerpunkt Umweltschutz), London.
1994	Gründung der unabhängigen Presseagentur I/P/A Press in Ljubljana, Slowenien.
1994–1996	Bildredakteur der Monatszeitschrift *Viva*, Slowenien.
Seit 1995	Zusammenarbeit mit Sygma Press, Paris.
1995–1996	Zusammenarbeit mit Saola Press, Paris.
Seit 1996	Zusammenarbeit mit Visum, Hamburg.
Seit 1997	Zusammenarbeit mit Grazia Neri, Mailand.
	Vertretung durch Fotoagentur Corbis UK, England.

Solo Exhibitions

1998 *Strange Friends,* Dazed & Confused Gallery, London, England
Surrender, Organizacija Gallery, Ljubljana, Slovenia
1997 *Venice Restart,* KUD France Preseren Gallery, Ljubljana, Slovenia
1996 *Raio Azul,* CD Photo Gallery, Ljubljana, Slovenia
1995 *Winter Table (Bosnian Refugees),* installation, KUD France Preseren Gallery, Ljubljana, Slovenia
1988 *Architecture of Fabiani,* Miramar Castle, Trieste, Italy
1984 *Spaces,* CD Hall, Ljubljana, Slovenia
Spaces II, Museum of Contemporary Arts, Belgrade, Yugoslavia
1983 *Mental & Spiritual Spaces/Works,* SKC Student Culture Center, Belgrade, Yugoslavia
1981 *Brick,* Gallery KC, Ljubljana, Slovenia
1980 *Healing of the Earth,* SKC Student Culture Center, Belgrade, Yugoslavia
1978/79 *Yugoslav Selection,* Trigon, Graz, Austria
1978 *4 Seasons,* Biennial Venice, presenting Yugoslavia in the Yugoslav Pavilion
In-Light, Tivoli Park, Ljubljana, Slovenia

Group Exhibitions

1998 *Cities,* Jakopic Gallery, Ljubljana, Slovenia
1997 *Prints,* KUD France Preseren Gallery, Ljubljana, Slovenia
1989 *Animan Collection,* Nikon Live Gallery, Zurich, Switzerland
1984 *Arteder '84,* Bilbao, Spain
1983 *Equrna Associates,* City Gallery, Ljubljana, Slovenia
1982 *Arteder '82,* Bilbao, Spain
Equrna Associates, Equrna Gallery, Ljubljana, Slovenia

Multivision Presentations

1988 *Mayday,* CD Photo Gallery, Ljubljana, Slovenia
1987 *A Hidden Pathway Through Venice,* Nova Gorica, Slovenia
1985 *A Hidden Pathway Through Venice,* Palazzo Grassi, Venice, Italy
Art of Man & Art of Nature, Planetarium of Arts, Venice, Italy
1984 *Four Elements of Novi Pazar/Sound Line,* Multivision, Volterra, Italy
Art of Man & Art of Nature, SKUC Gallery, Ljubljana, Slovenia
1983 *Spring Festival,* Findhorn, Scotland
Harmony & Space, CD Photo Gallery, Ljubljana, Slovenia
1981 *Healing of the Earth,* SKC Student Culture Center, Belgrade, Yugoslavia

Books

1997 Arne Hodalic/Mihael Mastaller/Bojan Brecelj. *Mangrove Forests.* Kuala Lumpur, Malaysia: Tropical Press.
Marko Pogacnik/Bojan Brecelj. *Geheimnis Venedig.* Munich, Germany: Diederichs-Verlag.
1986 Marko Pogacnik/Bojan Brecelj. *A Hidden Pathway Through Venice.* Rome: Carucci Editore.
1985 Marko Pogacnik/Bojan Brecelj. *Art in Novi Pazar.* Novi Pazar, Yugoslavia: Ministry of Culture of Serbia.

Awards

1997 Photo on the best CD cover, Zlati Petelin, Slovenia
1996 Photographer of the Year, Slovene Photography of the Year
Best Reportage, Slovene Photography of the Year
1st prize in the category "People," Slovene Photography of the Year
1984 Award for multivision, Volterra, Italy

Photographic Assignments

1998 "Egyptians are Invading the Desert" for Delo, Slovenia.
"Cefalu – the Sicilian Town that is Run by Women" for Sygma Press, Paris.
1997 "Economic Crises in Russia" for Sygma Press, Paris. In: *Mladina,* Slovenia, September.
"Paris au File de l'Eau" for *VSD*, France, June.
"Hype London" for Sygma Press, Paris. In: *Sette,* Italy, August.
1996 "Gibraltar" for Sygma Press, Paris. In: *Gente Viaggi,* Italy, October; *GEO*, Korea, no. 6.
Later publications in: *Bresil,* Brazil, August 1997; *Doobee International,* Korea, October 1997; *Altair,* Spain, October 1997.
"Slovenia – Personalities, Five Years after Independence" for Sygma Press, Paris.
"Taiwan – Same People, Different Paths" for Sygma Press, Paris. In: *VSD,* France, March; *Mladina,* Slovenia, March; *Il Venerdì di Repubblica,* Italy; *Geografica Universal,* Italy, May; *Santillana,* Spain. Later publications in: *Bresil,* Brazil, April 1997; *Sycom SA,* Colombia, 1997; *Publietas,* Italy, 1997.
1995 "Oxford – The City of Trees." Published in: *Adria Airways In – Flight Magazine*, Slovenia, no. 1, 1996.
"Jamaica's Seven Days" for *Animan*, Switzerland.
"Families of New York" for *Animan*, Switzerland. In: *Ulysse*, France. Later publication in: *Mladina,* Slovenia, January 1998.
1994 "Oman" for *Animan*, Switzerland. In: *Animan,* Switzerland, no. 68, 1995; *Mladina,* Slovenia, January 1995; *The Earth,* Taiwan, no. 117, 1997.
"Behind the Wall of Jerusalem in Prayer and Peace" for *Animan,* Switzerland. In: *Animan,* Switzerland, no. 55, 1995; *Viva,* Slovenia, September 1995; *Humanité Dimanche,* France, January 1996; *Adria Airways In – Flight Magazine,* Slovenia, no. 2, 1996; *The Earth,* Taiwan, no. 107, February 1997.
1993 "Filming the Underwater/Cave Film about Proteus, the Human Fish" for I/P/A Press, Ljubljana, Slovenia. In: *Format,* Slovenia, October 1994.
"Circuses Around the World" for *Animan,* Switzerland. In: *Animan,* Switzerland, no. 61, 1994; Mundo, Portugal, February 1997.
"Tchaikovsky – The Pathetic Life of Piotr Illich Tchaikovsky" for *Animan,* Switzerland. In: *Animan,* Switzerland, no. 59, 1993; *Adria In – Flight Magazine,* Slovenia, no. 3, 1995.
"Serbia – Living in the Shadow of War" for I/P/A Press, Ljubljana, Slovenia. In: *Mladina,* Slovenia, March.
1992 "Bosnian Muslims in Refugee Camps, Slovenia" for I/P/A Press, Ljubljana, Slovenia. In: *Mladina,* Slovenia, September.
"Moro di Venezia Shipyard – Tinkara" for Gamma Press Images, Paris. In: *Slovenian Business Report,* Slovenia, no. 8.
"Venetian Authentic Art – The Murano Glass." Published in: *Hors Ligne,* France, summer 1993; *Animan,* Switzerland, no. 63. 1994; *The Earth,* Taiwan, no. 99, 1996; *Mundo,* Portugal, April 1997.
"Shanghai City, China" for Gamma Press Images, Paris. In: *Altair,* Spain.
1991 "Sea Farming – Development Project, Tanzania." In: *Grand Air,* France.
"Zanzibar" – The Land of the Blacks" for *Animan,* Switzerland. In: *Animan,* Switzerland, no. 47, 1992; *Altair*, Spain, no. 10, 1993.
"Strangers on Earth – Mennonite (Amish) Colonies in Bolivia." In: *Marie Claire,* France, no. 475,

March; *Marie Claire,* Italy, Portugal, Netherlands, Greece; *Animan,* Switzerland, July; *Atlante,* Italy.
"Shattered Dream of Utopia – Jesuit Missions in South America" for *Animan,* Switzerland. In: *Animan,* Switzerland, no. 32; *Altair,* Spain, no 9. Later publication in: *Airone,* Italy, July 1992.

1990 "Mangroves – Forgotten Forests Between Land and Sea." In: *Physis,* Germany, March; *Natur,* Germany, July; *UWF,* Germany, no. 3; *Animan,* Switzerland, no. 39; see also list of books: *Mangrove Forests.*
"Asmat People – The Mysterious Artists in a Forgotten Land" for *Animan,* Switzerland. In: *Grands Reportages,* France, no. 157, 1995.
"Gold Rush Story – The Poor Millionaires." In: *Animan,* Switzerland, no. 40. Later publications in: *Start,* Yugoslavia, no. 576, 1991; *Newlook,* France, January 1991; *Grands Reportages,* France, March 1991.
"Sepic – The River of Spirits, New Guinea Island" for *Animan,* Switzerland. In: *Animan,* Switzerland, no. 38; *Ars Vivendi,* Slovenia. Later publication in: *Kactus*, Brazil, October 1992.

1989 "Nile – The Source of Culture, Sudan and Egypt" for *Animan,* Switzerland. In: *Airone,* Italy. Later publications in: *Animan,* Switzerland, no. 39, 1990; *The Earth,* Taiwan, no. 100, 1996.

1988 "Ganges – Old Mother Ganga." In: *Animan,* Switzerland, no. 36/portfolio 1989; *Aqua,* Italy, December; *Viaggi del Mondo,* Italy; *Qui Touring*, Italy, December.

1987 "Adriatic Islands – Island Susak, Sandy Hermit." In: *Geodes,* Italy, July/August.
"The National Park of Kornati Islands – Croatian Adriatic Sea." Published in: *The Earth,* Taiwan, no. 112, 1997.

The project was supported by the Ministry of Culture of the Republic of Slovenia

Concept by Marko Modic
Edited by Marko Modic and Bojan Brecelj
Layout by Barbara Stupica

Editorial direction by Mirjam Ghisleni-Stemmle, Andreas Ritter, Karin Schneuwly
Printed by Kündig Druck AG, Baar-Zug, Switzerland
Bound by Buchbinderei Burkhardt AG, Mönchaltorf-Zurich, Switzerland

ISBN 3-908161-40-1

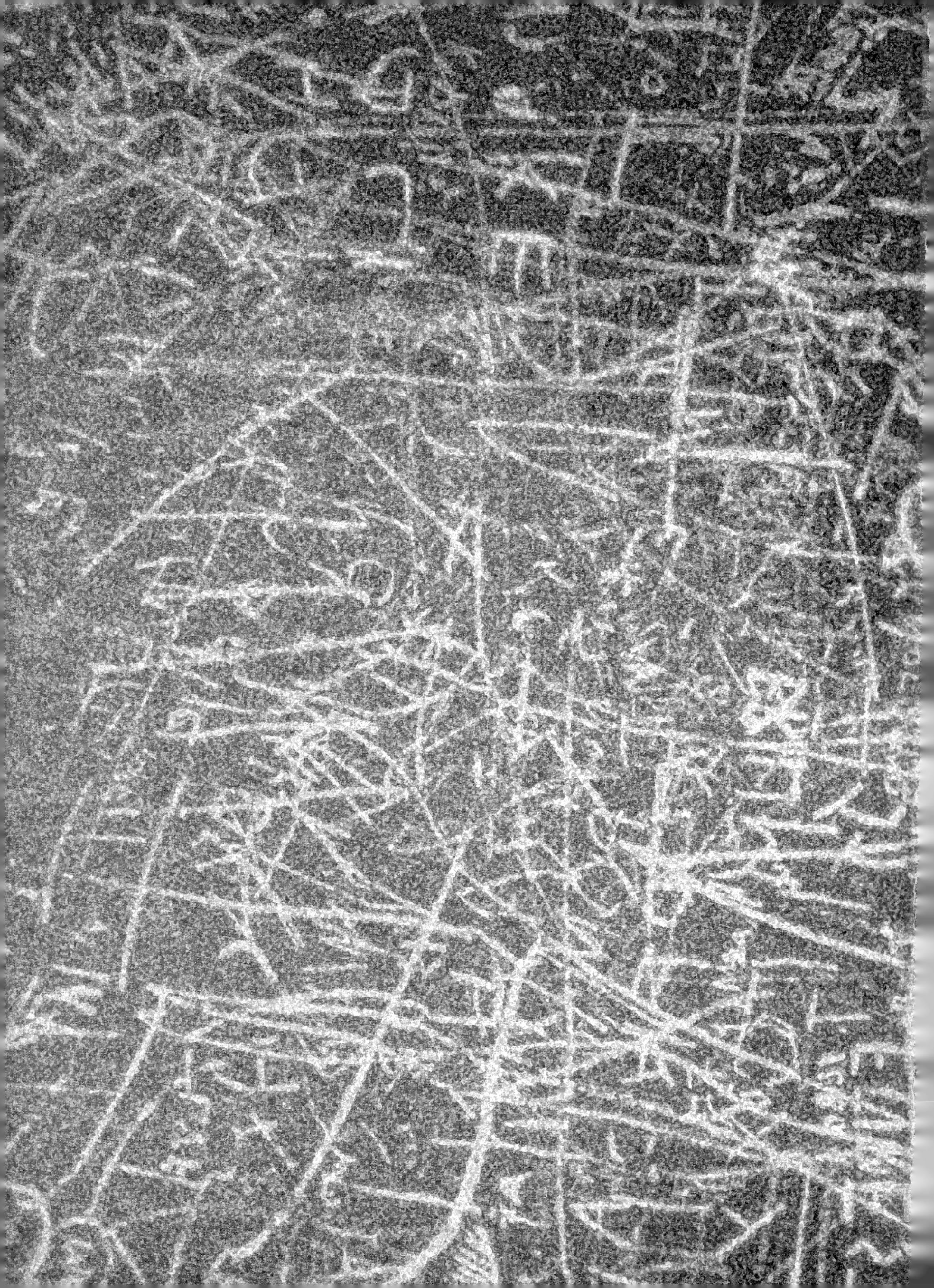